Praise for *Nottingham*

"A remarkable and comprehensive story . . . This is unique fiction that compels revision of the Robin Hood story and its place in history."

—Historical Novel Society

"What is refreshingly different is that there are no villains here. *Nottingham*'s road to hell makes use of proverbial paving materials: good intentions. . . . Robin is but one small cog in the substantial machine of Makaryk's *Nottingham* as the author presents a large cast of characters and perspectives that allow his novel to provide a fresh take on an oft-told, always-compelling story."

—*Booklist*

"This Robin Hood is so much more realistic about the politics of the time that it was like a new story greatly expanding a fragment of a myth. If you like historical fiction, then *Nottingham* may be your big summer read."

—Larry Yoder, The Bookies, Denver, Colorado

"Who doesn't like Robin Hood? The list is dangerously long, as revealed in this dark romp through Sherwood Forest."

—Elizabeth Cobbs, *New York Times* bestselling author

"*Nottingham*'s like reading *A Game of Thrones* for the first time . . . except it's a leap beyond that, a whole hundred-league leap that will hopefully drag the genre kicking and screaming along with it."

—K. A. Doore, author of *The Perfect Assassin*

"This is one of those special books. It's not one you borrow, it's one you keep on your shelf forever. . . . Clever, cutting, and just plain gorgeous."

—Sarah J. Sover, author of *Double-Crossing the Bridge*

BY NATHAN MAKARYK

Nottingham

Lionhearts

NOTTINGHAM

NATHAN MAKARYK

A TOM DOHERTY ASSOCIATES BOOK

NEW YORK

This is a work of fiction. All of the characters, organizations, and events portrayed in this novel are either products of the author's imagination or are used fictitiously.

NOTTINGHAM

A Forge Book
Published by Tom Doherty Associates
120 Broadway
New York, NY 10271

www.tor-forge.com

Forge® is a registered trademark of Macmillan Publishing Group, LLC.

The Library of Congress has cataloged the hardcover edition as follows:

Names: Makaryk, Nathan, author.
Title: Nottingham / Nathan Makaryk.
Description: First edition. | New York : Forge, 2019. | "A Tom Doherty Associates Book."
Identifiers: LCCN 2018054302| ISBN 9781250195609 (hardcover) |
ISBN 9781250195623 (ebook)
Subjects: LCSH: Robin Hood (Legendary character)—Fiction. | Great Britain—
History—Richard I, 1189–1199—Fiction. | Sherwood Forest (England)—Fiction. |
GSAFD: Historical fiction.
Classification: LCC PS3613.A3545 N68 2019 | DDC 813/.6—dc23
LC record available at https://lccn.loc.gov/2018054302

ISBN 978-1-250-19561-6 (trade paperback)

Our books may be purchased in bulk for promotional, educational, or business use. Please contact your local bookseller or the Macmillan Corporate and Premium Sales Department at 1-800-221-7945, extension 5442, or by email at MacmillanSpecialMarkets@macmillan.com.

First Edition: August 2019
First Trade Paperback Edition: September 2020

Printed in the United States of America

0 9 8 7 6 5 4 3 2 1

For Cassie and Ryland
(Ryland, you're not allowed to read past this page until 2032)

NOTTINGHAM

PROLOGUE

RICHARD OF NORMANDY

THE HOLY LAND
SATURDAY, 8TH DAY OF JUNE 1191

THIS. THIS IS A man to wear the title of King.

Sludging through the mud nearby, Richard was only a stonesthrow from the horse and the man and the crown. Of course he had seen this man before—the one the others called King—but at the right moment the spectacle was breathtaking. Atop a horse more muscle than beauty, dripping in armor, this man became an extension of the animal rather than merely its rider. The way some damned flower crawls through the cracks of a boulder. Beast and man moved as one amongst the soldiers, and the pale dawn sky cast a glow about his edges. Unstained plate, glistening mail, and at the top a beacon to everyone—across any stretch of battlefield, there would be no mistaking the spectacular warcrown that was perched at the top of *this.* This pillar.

This stupid arrogant pillar, begging to be murdered.

Only three soldiers or a desperate leap of fate away, Richard's eyes never fell entirely on the terrain. One eye on the King, even as he navigated around holes and puddles. Others, too, turned to watch as their leader passed, pausing to wonder at him. Some might want a glimpse of the power, others cursed their own inglorious births, and another might pursue that thought to its natural extension—*It could be mine, if not for luck.*

Up ahead, a wide stump and a flat rock beside it. Richard dropped his pack and rushed forward, one foot on the stump, the next on the rock, propelling him high enough to leap and plunge a knife just so, underneath the king's armor by the right breast. Up and deep, through the ribs. King and crown falls, and the war is over.

The stump and the rock and the opportunity passed by, never knowing what they could have been. A nosy soldier nearby was staring at him, so Richard looked down again and found reason to fall behind. One eye on the King.

It had only been a few maddening hours since they made shoreline, one hundred shipsworth of soldiers and steel, finally *here.* The *Holy Land.* But even that simple victory was bittered by months of delay. Each step forward now was just chasing the shadow of *what-should-have-been.* Every able-bodied man, knight, and nobleman at England's disposal had followed the king's great Crusade to the Mediterranean, only to be instantly diverted to the island country of Cyprus. A year of planning destroyed by a few shipwrecks—one of which carried the king's wife and mother. The Holy Crusade, repurposed as a domestic rescue mission. Because of propriety, because of sentiment.

But those empty distractions were thankfully over, and they had at last landed a day's march north of the foreign port-city called Acre. A month of sunsets from home, they were determined to take the city and Jerusalem beyond.

After all this work, it would be damned ironic to end with the king assassinated on the road so close to his goal.

In the narrowest part of the pass now, massive rock slabs rose three times the height of a man. Richard waited upon one as the Lionheart passed underneath, and loosed a single crossbow bolt. The shaft would catch the warcrown on its way out the other side of the king's head, arrow and crown, blood and brain, launched upward and outward to mix and mingle in the mud. Amongst the confusion, Richard could slide back into rank and file. He might even throw himself over the king's body and beat his chest in grief and sarcasm.

A pair of mounted men in bullied armor approached the king, who peeled his mount from the line to speak with them. Richard feigned disinterest, but watched. Perhaps it was nothing, any of a thousand nothings, or perhaps his game was up. A third rider called the king by name, and Richard flinched. That had been the hardest part, to forget his own name. *It's King Richard they want,* he reminded himself, *not I. I'm just a nobody.* After a short discussion, the visitors rode away, leaving their liege as unprotected as before.

If he had a horse, Richard could ride up unchallenged, throw a noose around the king's neck, and wrench him from his steed to be dragged and trampled, hooves crushing his throat and his chest and his legacy.

The same nosy soldier made a small half step over a rock, long enough to turn his head backward and glance at Richard again. Brief enough, but no accident. Their eyes met.

Richard surged forward, landed them both on the ground, and slit the man's throat as he got back to his feet. Perhaps there would be two or three seconds before the men behind noticed. Long enough for a sprint, a quick dodge around the sentinel's men. A slash to the horse's belly would bring the king down close enough for a blade at the base of his ear before Richard was dragged down himself.

Some weaker part of Richard wondered what would come of Berengaria if he died. Certainly he ought to think more achingly of never seeing his wife again. That's what other men would do, no doubt. They'd cling to the *idea* of her and remember the last time they had seen her, or carry a trinket or some petty useless remembrance as if that would help them come home alive. Whispering words into a lock of hair had, historically, never proven adequate armor against steel. He would be more than willing to accept such pedestrian superstition once he witnessed the hand of God reach down, catch an arrow, and hurl it instead at a different soldier who had never discovered true love.

No, love was no asset. Richard had watched a man grieve once over a lost lover. Really, truly grieve. Some nasty business in France where nothing had gone smoothly, the men had broken rank and rampaged through an unimportant fishing village. One of Richard's companions—whose name he couldn't place now—suddenly collapsed. The man was not injured but his eyes were wide, unmoving. They locked on a woman's body down the lane, a tangle of black hair with one rigid arm clutching some amount of pretty fabric. Bone and dark crimson stretched wide toward them from her side, split open. This man, some man, his eyes nearly dried to bark so long did he not blink. He was oblivious Richard was even there staring at him—oblivious to what a Richard might be. All the man could see was the woman's body, a trick of the mind mistaking it for his lover's. Richard was awestruck. Impossible, that the body could be so entirely shut down by emotion—a tangible reaction to *nothing.* Richard was almost jealous. *He had never felt anything that powerful.* This otherwise healthy man *broke,* simply broke.

Some confused being broken with being weak, but anything can break, no matter how strong. *The one thing you can never judge in a man,* he recited, *is what makes him break. But you can learn from him, to avoid having that same flaw.*

The King, that other Richard, had waylaid his war for his weakness. History would remember that single pathetic act, and how it sealed his fate. It gave his enemy time to prepare a defense, to strategize, to lay traps. Enabling a single assassin, embedded in the English army . . .

"I didn't mean offense," a voice belched. The suspicious soldier was now next to him.

"Grumble," Richard responded. He tried to analyze what words he meant to say, and realized with disappointment that he actually said the word *grumble* instead of anything that could be considered language. The soldier didn't seem to notice, but incorrectly took it as an invitation to continue talking.

"It's just that you look familiar, is all. Have we met?"

They hadn't. Some of the companies had been reorganized upon landfall, which was why Richard thought he might go unquestioned so close to the king. This observant soldier had insulting eyebrows and a scar across his nose, which seemed more likely to have been received by slapping his helmet on too quickly than from an enemy hoping to cleave it off. "Are you with Lincolnshire?"

"I keep to myself, and don't intend that to change," Richard lied, readjusted his pack, and broke to his left. His jaw chomped on the ugly English language, and no doubt the stranger heard his accent beneath. But it wouldn't matter. That man would never speak to Richard again.

The path leaned straight here, hugging a gentle slope littered thick with curious trees, a rarity in this terrain. If Richard were an army, which he sadly noted he was not, he would hide in that hillside and noiselessly slide down into the line's flank, taking half the king's number before anyone had thought twice. Instead, he resigned himself to behaving quite unarmylike for a while longer, pushing on along the road, doing his best to be unnoticeable, one eye on the King.

By day's end, the army stopped well north of Acre to regroup and supply. A campsite for eight thousand men was a wild animal, constantly twitching and kicking. An endless rolling noise combined complaint with cheer, lament with laughter. Richard closed his eyes and breathed it in, the hammering and arguing and power, all intertwined into a single voice, the sound of *men.* This is what made him unable to ever miss a Berengaria. The breathing of an army was unlike the breathing of a woman. His hands could feel the softness of a woman, but his heart could never be engrossed in it. A thousand men, out of their element, relying on nothing but that which they carried on their backs and the bond of the brother beside them, living for one more night of relative safety . . . this was something to be overwhelmed in. Richard wished he could get drunk on the sound and forget himself. There was simplicity here, a joyous numb stupidity that was shut off to him now, for whenever he opened his eyes he was closer to the king's tent and to his duty.

The husk of a wagon offered him its darkness, but the nearly full moon gave him a clear view as the king and his entourage approached. Each man ducked through the heavy flaps of the command tent. The king, escorted by his personal guardsman—handsome men both—and a handful of company leaders were there to talk strategy. But Richard didn't watch them enter. He had already sprinted around the back of the tent, flattened himself against the ground between two tent stakes and pulled the thick cloth over himself, rolling inside and quickly upright again. Furs hanging from ceiling to floor masked Richard's presence as the king's company rifled inside, cursing about this and that and tearing their armor off, believing themselves safe. Richard's blade, short enough to be tucked into his sleeve, was now in his palm. When the commotion was loudest he moved, two steps behind the king, his right arm reached around with the knife, his left hand grabbed the king's shoulder to push his neck through the waiting steel.

"Dead," he stated.

He said it in English, the one word he envied them, its French equivalent lacking the finality of its hard *d*. He touched the blade to the king's royal throat, and the king's royal lips smiled.

"Very good, Your Grace," answered Robin of Locksley, removing the crown from his head.

"Excepting you died first," came a second voice from behind. Richard felt a tap at his back, the edge of a sword. "We would have killed you outside, but figured you wouldn't want the commotion."

Richard laughed off the excuse, but still surrendered his knife to the man behind him. William de Wendenal took the weapon with a slight laugh, and emerged from the shadows with obvious satisfaction.

"Even so," Richard swung fully into the light, "you let me get too close."

"Well I forgot to mention that my throat is protected by God Himself," Robin said, "and He would never let you damage it." He stood to trade places on the throne with its rightful owner, which Richard accepted. The chair warmed to him, it preferred his touch over either of his two body doubles, it could recognize a true king's power over any impostor's. Richard flopped himself down, gave his crown a cursory inspection, and thanked his guardsmen for their work. There had thankfully been no surprises awaiting their arrival in this foreign land, but it was only the first day of many.

"Now then," he leveled his eyes on the others. A council of sycophant noblemen and misplaced egos, and their armies outside. The sum of Richard's plans and taxes had brought them here—not the best England could offer, but certainly the best it could afford. It would suffice, because it had to.

They awaited instruction, as every well-curbed dog does.

Richard gave it. "Let's war."

PART I

A WOLF IN LION'S CLOTHING

ONE

MARION FITZWALTER

LOCKSLEY CASTLE, NOTTINGHAMSHIRE

MARION PLACED HER HAND on Walter's shoulder and gave a meaningful squeeze. Her fingers found more bone than muscle beneath his modest doublet, and she flinched, worrying she had hurt him. But Lord Walter of Locksley simply smiled, hermit lord no longer, and wiped an embarrassed tear from his eye.

"I can't remember the number of years it's been since I've seen the dining hall so lively," he said. "Sometimes I forget to just sit and take it in, you know? Even at my age, I have to remember to enjoy the little moments."

It would have been an understatement to say it warmed Marion's heart. To see Lord Walter thriving again, and his estate flourishing, was to see some great wrong lifted from the world. "You have plenty of years ahead of you," she said, straightening his collar. "This is just the beginning."

The dining hall was brightened only partially by chandeliers, and the rest by personalities. The room heaved and swelled like the ocean, mixing together sounds of laughter, dining, and *life*. It reminded Marion of her youth, when her family would visit Locksley often, when she and her sister would play with Lord Walter's sons.

It would certainly be good to have new, happier memories of the place.

Only a year earlier, she solicited Locksley's help for a man named Baynard—an aging local gentleman with an unfortunately common story. Ever since the war tithe was implemented, the *Saladin tax*, nobles were finding creative ways to minimize their assets—such as evicting their least valuable vassals. People without masters, like Baynard and his family, were still legally subject to pay *son vassalus* for themselves. This was a typically empty threat outside of a city, but had been increasingly enforced in the last year on account of the war's thirst for coin. And poor Baynard had been naïve enough to petition Nottingham for assistance, where he might have been thrown into a debtor's cell if Marion had not intervened.

She recalled her trepidation in approaching Lord Walter on the matter, given their history, but was now so glad she'd taken that chance. Relocating Baynard to Locksley Castle had been a gamble that now paid off a hundred-fold. Despite his reputation as a recluse, Lord Walter was a charitable man with wealth to spare, and his manor was in dire need of tending. Hoarding his coin for decades at the expense of his estate had earned him the nickname of "the hermit lord." He was thought to be quite peculiar by those too young to remember, but Marion knew better. It was not greed or eccentricity that had closed Locksley Castle's doors, but heartbreak.

Fittingly, it was compassion that opened them again. Baynard's family was here now, amongst all the other souls Marion had sent in the last year. Here lived a community of refugees who found new purpose in each other. Locksley Castle had been resurrected, a dozen or more families had been rescued, and the rumors continued to spread across the county.

Lord Walter was the man to see when you couldn't pay your taxes.

"Thank you," he said, his voice tight with the sheer gravity of what it meant to say those words to her. "I don't know why you've done this for me . . ."

She hushed him. He didn't say her sister's name, but it was there on the tip of his tongue. *Vivian.* Instead, she squeezed him tighter. "Please don't."

She might have said more. She might have said *That was so long ago,* or *It wasn't your fault,* but there was no point. She had tried so many times over the years, but Lord Walter would carry what happened on his shoulders until the end of his days.

He turned his face away from the hall, his thin muscles tense with the momentary emotion he could never hide.

Vivian's death was the first to darken Locksley's door, but hardly Walter's only ghost. His wife Helen passed slowly from a wet cough a dozen years ago, which began his recession from a public life. His eldest son Edmond was lost to the world, and would hopefully never reemerge. Lastly there was Robin, gone from England to join the war. He was alive and sane, but still the sharpest of Walter's losses. Marion shared that pain—she would always have a tender spot in her heart for Robin, or rather for the eager young man he had been when they first met, before their two families had been entwined with tragedy. Lord Walter chose to bear the burden of the past with exactly the same enthusiasm that Robin used to avoid it.

"Shall we dine?" he recovered, returning to the mirth of the dining hall.

"Go on without me." Marion had far more important demands on her attention this night. Lord Walter gave a goodbye and stepped into the bustling rapture of Locksley's halls. It had become one of Marion's favorite places, which was one of the reasons she found herself visiting so often of late. It was subtle, but the mood within Locksley was unlike any other manor or castle in England. Part of it was that every single soul here knew how lucky she was to be alive, and to work for a living. The other part, Marion could not define.

"Oh my!" she blurted as she almost tripped over a young boy. She wrapped her arms around the child's shoulders, but he promptly wriggled free and ran away. *Oh my* seemed a terribly quaint thing to say, and she flushed to wonder when it had become an instinctive phrase. The boy barreled recklessly down the path between dining tables, his long golden-blond hair flowing behind him. Marion tried to recall his name but it slipped out of her mind, fluttered away, and probably had a very nice life without ever missing being a part of her vocabulary. All she could recall was the boy was an orphan, found alone by a river, and had been collectively adopted by four or five families since.

Children and families. It would be a lie to say this was the most able-bodied group in the world. There were more women than not, children, and elderly. They were, at a cold-blooded assessment, the obvious choices to be exiled from their previous masters' vassalage. But a percentage of them were men, and a percentage of those men were physically and mentally fit. And a percentage of those capable men were willing to go beyond normal, lawful work to show their gratitude.

And those men were Marion's other reason for visiting.

IF MARION HAD TIME to waste she might spend it thinking backward, prodding at her own memories like a loose tooth, to recall the first point she strayed from a truly honest life. She had been raised with a fear of the law and the Lord in equal measure, and as a little girl had been exacting in her obedience to both. But as a lady at court, the granddaughter of the esteemed Earl of Essex, she quickly discovered both the law's limitations and its failures. Policies that genuinely helped the country often neglected the poorest of its citizens. And in a world of politics ruled by men, charity had somehow become a character flaw.

It may have started off as something as simple as a dilapidated footbridge, kept in neglect by the rivalry of the noblemen on either bank. No one but Marion would ever know who eventually tended to its repair. From there she might recall the next time some accidental political slight had gone unnoticed, and unpunished. The bread crumbs would lead to increasingly daring acts of willful disobedience. She would likely remember the fitful balance of risk and reward, and of maintaining deniability. She'd recall the people who received new seed after being robbed, the problematic raiders who mysteriously disappeared, or a missing delivery of wool blankets that its baron would never miss.

More than anything, she would relive the discovery of what it meant to be female. Despite her "damnably inferior brain," her kinship to King Richard opened the doors of England's court just enough for her to learn about the cases being ignored. To be a woman was to wear an invisible cloak, but that loathsome fact was absolutely advantageous in the world of misdeeds. She had learned how easy it was to fake apologies, feign ignorance, to smile wide and let men blame her gender and forget. If she had time to waste, she'd relish it all.

But Lady Marion Fitzwalter was ever a lady without time to waste.

"How did it go?" she asked John of Hathersage, lumbering beside her as they walked away from Locksley Castle. He did an admirable job of keeping up with her overland, despite his size. A decade ago his mass would have intimidated any man, but now the muscle had been reluctantly replaced with something decidedly spongier, and the thick beard of his neck showed more grey than not. Gratefully, neither age nor stuffing could slow down John Little.

"How did it go?" he repeated her question back at her, sing-song and out of breath. "Well it didn't go . . . why don't you tell me again how it was *supposed* to go?"

"That's reassuring," Marion said flatly. "It was supposed to go simply. You were to intercept the Lord Oughtibridge's convoy between Sheffield and Locksley, drive its grain wagon into the forest and eventually back here, with nobody injured or alarmed."

"Yes, that," John replied.

"*Yes, that,* what?"

"Yes, that." He laughed. "That's exactly how it didn't go."

Marion's love for the man could survive any mistake he made, but she cringed to think what could have gone wrong with this job. "Tell me."

"Best walk. Better to see it."

It had admittedly been bold in concept, but the beauty was that its consequences should have been nonexistent. Lord Geoffrey of Oughtibridge, a middling lord of well-more-than-middling weight, had spoken openly in Marion's company about his unsavory tactics in avoiding his taxes. When confronted with an impending assessment from the county's tax collectors, he opted to temporarily transport several wagons full of rarer foodstuffs to a friendly neighboring lord rather than let them be counted against him.

Since Lord Oughtibridge had no legal recourse to complain about lost goods he claimed never to own, there should have been no risk. Marion had been the one to inform him of the tax collector's upcoming visit, and she legitimately felt a twinge of guilt that this was an absolute lie. But she simply didn't have time to linger on such trifles. That time was better spent doing more worthwhile things, and moving food from noble hoarders to people in need was, inarguably, a thing worth doing.

Yet in light of John's impending bad news, her pace quickened and her breath shortened. She tried to assure herself that John was overreacting, but her stomach seemed to know something she didn't.

They continued in silence except for a few hurried greetings to the people they chanced upon. A wide-eyed girl named Malory and her friend Maege, followed by a milk-sopped young man named Devon and his wife. While most families tended to stay close to the safety of Locksley's manor, farther from the castle were the more curious type. Lord Walter's generosity had also attracted people who sought haven from troubles more immediate than short taxes. There were men here with questionable histories, or outcasts from city gangs who claimed a new calling. As they passed a few millers on the path, hurrying along to the dining hall, Marion could feel the heat from their bodies. They gave wearied hellos that spoke to the difficulty of their day's labor. She was mortified to realize she did not know either of them by name, since they were honest workers. *Honest* and *useful* had become increasingly exclusive characteristics in her friends. If Marion had a few moments to throw away, she might have considered what that meant.

Soon enough they drew upon their destination, an uncomfortable departure from the path against a broken rockface. Their camp was below, hugging under the outcropping, safe from casual onlookers. A hundred thousand responsibilities ago, the young Robin of Locksley had shown her the way to this secluded glen, and she had fancied that it might become a secret hideaway just for the two of them. She had fortunately matured significantly since then, as had her intentions for this place.

But any hope that John's bad news was exaggerated quickly vanished at the sight of the path down. Not only had they posted a guard, they'd used a man whose very existence screamed *go away*.

"It's that bad?" she asked, trying to hide her reaction.

"Ma'am," was all the sentry said.

The White Hand. Tall and gaunt, his skull pushed through his face, so sunken were his eyes and cheeks. He was always helpful when needed, but nobody seemed to know what the ghost-man did with the rest of his time. He kept himself stolen away under a dark hood, but there was no mistaking the bleached white glove on his right hand. Marion had no doubt that half the stories about it were utter rubbish, and that the remaining half only bore a shred of truth, but even that sliver was enough to give the man his leave.

But she knew his name. Gilbert with the White Hand was one of hers.

Down the steep path, far enough to pretend deniability, a leap away from the politesse and politicking of her public life, Marion came across their camp. John Little whistled sharply as they approached, rousing a dozen of them from their makeshift dinner around a modest campfire. Marion did not need John's warning to read their body language, each of them hesitant as a child who knew she was due a scolding.

"I'll be the first to say, I don't think this was entirely our fault." Will Scarlet, as defiant as he was immature, was likely to blame for whatever had gone wrong. Where many of this group were outcasts by force, Will and his lover Elena Gamwell were here by choice. They claimed to have once led a major gang in Nottingham, and were both abominably talented at sneak-thieving. The fact that Marion did not bother to chastise his flippant welcome spoke volumes.

"Just tell me . . ." she said, " . . . *Alan*."

She turned sharply to Alan-a-Dale, a scrawny olive-skinned farmhand who would sooner be caught dead than lying to her. "It started off well," Alan stammered, wiping a flop of dark hair from his eyes. "At least I thought it did. I'm probably not the best person to ask."

"You're probably not the best person for anything," Arthur cut in playfully. Arthur a Bland's spite for the world was mostly for show, an intentional disguise against a blindingly loyal heart. "It started off terribly, and it only went worse from there."

"You said there wouldn't be any guards," Elena threw in, cocking her head intently.

"There shouldn't have been any guards," Marion responded, mostly because there definitely should not have been any guards.

"Oh, there were guards," John Little grunted beside her, in a tone that defied contradiction. "What there wasn'ting, was food."

Marion stared at him.

"He means there wasn't any food," Alan translated.

"I know what he means, Alan." Marion did not break away from John. He simply folded his wide face in half and looked importantly past the campfire, where Marion could see the faint glow of a large hulk beyond. It was no simple wagon, but a strong boxed carriage with sharp iron features and reinforced edges. It was not the sort of thing a middling lord like Oughtibridge would have access to, precisely because it was not his.

They had stolen from the wrong caravan.

"What's in it?" she whispered, afraid it might awaken.

"Nothing we can eat," John bellowed, inviting her to investigate. Its rear side boasted a thick hinged door that had been opened with what appeared to be a ludicrous amount of force. Inside lay a dark abyss of possibilities, though none of them seemed better than crawling away and pretending this wasn't happening. A barrage of questions demanded to be answered about the number of guards, and whether anyone had been harmed, what colors they had worn, and how her crew had even been successful at all.

But those questions would all wait. First she needed to figure out exactly what brand of trouble they had bedded. She eased the carriage's door open enough to let the firelight trickle therein. Whichever nightmares had been brewing in her head were not as terrible as reality.

"Oh my," she said, whether she wanted to or not.

There were crates upon crates upon crates of swords. Packed in bundles, stuffed with hay, oil still glistening from the forge. The amber light wormed through their shadows just enough for Marion to recognize their purpose. An obvious flared Crusader's cross was stamped into each hilt.

"This is not the wagon I told you to steal," she said, focusing on what was immediate and true.

"*Wagon?*" asked Will Scarlet with caution. "Singular? This is only the first one."

Marion's stomach, against all sober advice, started dabbling in acrobatics.

"What do we do with them?" John Little asked.

"We bury them," Marion answered instantly. "We bury them and pray."

TWO

ROBIN OF LOCKSLEY

ENGLISH WAR CAMP, ACRE

THAT MEASLY TWINKLE WAS the city of Acre, transformed by the distance into a faint collection of fiery pinpricks, barely visible in the night. Robin raised his hand up until the entirety of the foreign city sat on the base of his thumb. Such a small thing from here, such a tiny little parcel of planet, but somehow the center of everything. In the last few months the city had withstood assaults from a dozen armies, each of which had failed and crawled home as wretched, unlovable failures. Sadly for them, only one country could be England. The French and Austrian armies still lingered, rightfully predicting that England's arrival would change the tide and bring Acre to its knees.

"But the poor city," Robin said gravely, "never expected an attack . . . *from above.*"

And his forefinger came down to meet his thumb, quietly snuffing the city out of existence.

"I don't think that worked," William chuckled beside him. "I can still see it."

"That's always been your problem." Robin kept one eye closed, rubbing his fingers together to grind the city's walls to rubble. "Perspective."

He smashed the city's gates, he scraped the towers to the ground with his fingernail, he flicked the arrogant soldiers from the walls into the clouds above. For over a week, King Richard's army had done nothing but stare at the city while its citizens mocked them for their inaction. Robin hated the insults almost as much as he hated that they were right. The delay had driven Richard to fits of rage, sudden and unpredictable mood swings that Robin found entirely justified.

"Just wait until the morning," Robin threatened the city with a wag of his finger. "And we will annoy the shit out of you. You might even lose a bit of sleep."

William laughed, and they both glanced over at the silhouettes of the siege machinery. Two lonely trebuchets were finally complete, while dozens of others were little more than empty framework. It would probably take most of tomorrow just to wheel them within striking distance, but clearly nobody was concerned with Robin's critique. The few trees that could be found in this land had proven too flexible to be of any use, and their first trebuchet's arm had shredded itself to sinew rather than hold any weight. Most of the new timber came by sacrificing the hulls of their ships. "You don't think those two will do it?" William asked whimsically.

"We'll take the city," Robin answered, in sincerity. "But not the way Richard wants us to. And not soon."

"Which is probably good," his companion kicked at an offensive stone, "given the other problem."

Robin hated that, too. "Given the other problem. We ought to check on that next."

William's silence lingered into agreement.

"You're in the crown tomorrow," Robin added, thinking that might cheer William's mood. "You'll get to launch the first volley."

William rolled his eyes as obviously as possible. "Our men could run the trebuchet wheels nonstop for a month and the city would laugh it off. No, I think wearing the crown promises no glory any time soon."

They rotated that responsibility. Each day one of them donned the king's mantle while the other lurked nearby. They normally chose at random, or by a throw of dice, or a drinking game when William wanted to win. Richard himself preferred to go "slumming with the soldiers," or the packmen, or wherever he found curiosity each day. Some of the noblemen in his retinue thought the strategy reeked of cowardice, though they'd only admit it beneath a barrel of wine. But Robin saw it more about giving the king freedom than taking the target off his back. Richard preferred to observe, without worrying about how his every pause or hesitation might be interpreted by others. Robin and William's main task was to exude confidence, protecting the king's reputation as much as his body. It was how he came to be called Lionheart, because he never appeared to fear for himself. Though that title was ever a misnomer. Lions, so Robin was told, were solitary beasts with little cunning in their hunt. Richard and his two private guardsmen relied on mutual strength and deception. *A wolf in lion's clothing.*

They were hardly identical, and anyone close to Richard clearly saw through the ploy, but none of the common soldiers could ever tell the difference. The war-crown surrounded one's face with mail, and all three of them were of comparable height and hair. *"And handsome,"* as Richard always insisted. Robin had no doubt theirs was the finest position in the English army. While in the crown, Robin was effectively King of England, trusted to make decisions and commands. King Richard had his secret ways of directing them, or providing quick counsel, but for the most part he trusted in their competence on noncritical matters. If only Robin could write his father and describe his daily duties, then old Lord Walter of Locksley might die of fury. Robin had joined Richard's retinue four years earlier, well before his coronation, and even then Lord Walter had been livid over the affiliation.

It was probably part of the reason Robin enjoyed it so.

"I try desperately to be unlike my father as well," King Richard had once laughed when the subject was broached over a cask of ale. *"My father was King of England, and my father spoke English. Sharing one of those traits with that monster is quite enough."*

"It's pretty," William said absently, and Robin didn't recognize what he meant until he waved his hand at the foreign landscape. The ocean to their right ate up the bare moon, splitting light as wide as the horizon, black and sharp. The distant city would have seemed like a promise of comfort if this were England. But here, that prettiness came with consequences.

"Don't fall in love with her now," Robin chided. "She'll look different in the morning."

"Oh, absolutely," William answered quickly. "She'll have two tiny black marks high up on that wall. Unless we lose another arm, in which case she'll only have one."

Robin swallowed. "Maybe you'll luck out and the treb'll take your head off as it falls apart."

William's face contorted. "How is that lucking out?"

"Well you wouldn't have to worry about any of this anymore."

"If I die tomorrow," William eased off back toward the main camp, "I am absolutely blaming you."

"I'll keep that in mind," Robin followed. "But if you die tomorrow, *King William,* I'll be so upset with you I very well might kill you."

William laughed. "And I'll keep *that* in mind, *King Robin.*"

ROBIN DEMANDED A REPORT as they approached, startling the group of worried noblemen into an impossibly more baffled state. Some of these barons had never been to war before, and were ill-suited for every bit of it. There were others, particularly those who had been part of the Kings' War fourteen years ago, that were anything but keen on taking orders from Robin or William. While wearing the crown they held Richard's authority, but it was delightfully ambiguous as to how much power they held in plainclothes. Both Robin and William had learned quickly that this ambiguity played far more often to their advantage than not.

"It's not good, Robin," answered an older man, the Earl of Derby, named William de Ferrers. His bald head and goblin-thin frame put him more at home in a cave than at a warfront, but his was a patient, gentle soul. He was one of the few commanders whose wisdom seemed sincere, and never treated Robin's command with disdain. However, he stiffened when he realized Robin was not alone. "Wendenal," the earl said respectfully.

William ignored the greeting. "How is it not good?"

Ferrers shifted back to Robin. "I would venture we have not even a single regiment that is fully outfitted. I've reallocated everything we have. Yes, we have complete battalions of swordarms, but at the expense of taking the shortarms from our archers and pikemen. Hazard, a thousand men have no weapons at all, and a thousand more have nothing for close quarters."

"Thrilling," Robin said. Two full ships of weaponry had sunk into the Mediterranean off the coast of Cyprus, during the storm that had capsized King Richard's family. Ferrers and his companions had been tasked with moving their remaining weaponry around, but it seemed they were slightly more fucked than Robin had guessed. "What about legs, do we have enough legs?"

"Legs?"

"Legs, two legs, like these ones." Robin demonstrated what legs were.

The earl seemed uncertain how to respond. "Are you asking me if the men have legs?"

"I was going . . ." Robin laughed it off. "I was going to say that they may not have swords, but at least they can still run away."

"I see."

"It would have been funny."

"As you say," Ferrers responded, but a slight smirk kept it light. Their situation was less than perfect, but there was no reason to be so dour about it all. "Replacement weaponry is on its way from England, we'll simply have to wait it out."

Robin grimaced. It was only the sixteenth of June, barely six weeks had passed since those ships had met the bottom of the sea, not nearly enough time for replacements. The fastest messenger might have returned to England in three weeks, but a full cog would take longer than that to return. And that didn't even include the time to collect new weapons, if they were even available.

"Hooray," Robin said dryly. "I'm sure Richard will understand." The King was furious about the missing supplies, but would not suffer the embarrassment of acknowledging reality. He had gone to extraordinary measures to fund his Crusade, admittedly leaving quite a bit of England to disrepair, foreign hands, or the hangman while raising the capital. Given the option, Richard probably would have sold London herself rather than let the war perish from lack of support. Instead of waiting even longer for the new shipment, he would likely try to fix his problem by throwing more bodies at it. Robin looked to William, who seemed equally frustrated. "We'll have to convince him to wait."

"He's going to have us move forward with the trebuchets tomorrow," William said seriously. "He wants to throw some stones. He's waited too long for his toys, now he wants to play."

Robin wouldn't have compared the king to a child, but he had come to the same conclusion. "He'll be starting something we're not prepared to finish."

"Hopefully you're right," William sent a meaningful scowl at the awaiting trebuchets, "and we barely scratch those walls."

"But we're building more," Robin calculated. "We'll break a little hole through Acre's walls eventually, without having done much damage to the rest of the city. He'll send the army in, and if we don't have enough weapons by then. . . ." The casualties would be devastating.

William's face grew as grim as Robin's assessment. With no hint of emotion, his eyes burned a hole in the earl's scabbard. "*You* carry a weapon."

Robin was surprised by the venom in his tone. Ferrers put a hand to its hilt, he recoiled only a hair. "Of course."

"Why haven't you *reallocated* that one? Or will you be on the front line when we break a hole?"

"I shall be with the King," the earl said quickly, daring anyone to call that position coward. "This sword was my father's. I've carried it into every battle. You would not have me give it up for a common soldier . . ."

William said nothing beyond a cold staredown with the earl, who opted to silence himself. Robin was left with very little idea of what to say, but William fortunately abated the tension by wandering a few steps away.

Ferrers turned swiftly back to Robin, his voice lowered. "Talk to Richard. Gives us more time for the swords to arrive. If we break that wall too early, it'll be the last thing we do."

If there was anything in the world that Robin hated most, it was being handed a bucket full of other people's mistakes.

"*Absolument pas*," Richard grumbled in French, readjusting himself on the velvet-covered close stool. What was already a disgusting task was made all the worse by the stifling hot air that persisted even through the night. But Robin had hoped Richard might be more amenable to advice in private, and the only opportunity for privacy was while the king was shitting in a box. It was as appropriate a metaphor for their situation as Robin could imagine.

"There's no need to rush," Robin tried to explain. "Why not wait until more siege weapons are built, at least?"

"While they sit and laugh?" The king reached for a linen and Robin desperately found anything else to look at. "They already watched one trebuchet tear itself apart. They won't be afraid until we start to use them. I won't suffer to be their source of entertainment another day."

"Better they laugh for a week now, than for centuries," Robin said to the sky. "They don't know we're undersupplied. But if it comes to close combat too early, they'll quickly figure that out. If we simply wait for the weapons to arrive—"

"Then there will be some other problem!" Richard snapped. "There's never a perfect moment to attack, Robin. You never have all the weapons you want, or all the men you want, or all the time you want. You make do with what you have, and I am exceptionally good at doing that. If you think I am nothing without shiny new swords, then you have not been paying attention."

Robin took it with humility. "I don't think that. I just wanted to voice my concern. Part of my duty is to dissent."

"I know." Richard tidied himself. "But I am resolute. Tomorrow we start the trebuchets." He slammed the hinged lid of the close stool down, and Robin tried very hard to ignore the soft sloshing sounds of its contents. He followed Richard back into the command tent, and the commotion of its inhabitants made it clear that William had been equally unsuccessful in rallying reason into the king's council.

By night's end, the two of them stole away to the edges of the otherwise furious tent, exhausted. They traded a few derogatory comments at the expense of the more useless advisors in the room, hoping to forget about their predicament. "You were awfully prickly with the earl, Ferrers, earlier," Robin noted. "What was that about?"

"The Earl of Derby is my father's liege lord," William explained quietly, "and there is some dark history between his house and mine."

His tone spoke to the quality of that history. But Robin knew better than to probe farther. William did not keep much to himself, so his short answers meant he did not care to say more. "Ought to make you happy, then?" Robin asked lightly. "Giving Ferrers a hard time?"

"No," William's mouth twisted. "Ferrers has had a long and difficult life, full of wrong decisions and failures. We are all only a few desperate decisions away from ending up like him."

Robin put his hand on William's leg and shook it meaningfully. It was a rare thing to find a topic the two of them could not joke about. But it was war's eve, and that always led some to grim thoughts and regrets. Robin let his friend to his contemplation, preferring a night of levity himself. About the command room, the lords of England's favor sought to distinguish themselves in front of King Richard by inventing elaborate solutions to their unfixable problem, and Robin watched in bemusement. Many of the lords and earls who had followed their king to war were determined to be rewarded for their fealty, and thought Richard cared only about how quickly and deeply they bent their knee. The truth would have shocked them, that the man they called *the Lionheart* took their obedience with contempt. Not a single lord in the army understood that King Richard would never reward naked ambition with power.

Neither Robin nor William were interested in the glories of prestige, which was precisely why Richard trusted them. And tomorrow they would launch the first volleys of war together, incessantly throwing pebbles to bounce off the walls of Acre until the world was Holy again.

Robin laughed himself straight to sleep.

THREE

GUY OF GISBOURNE

NOTTINGHAM CASTLE
SUNDAY, 30TH DAY OF JUNE 1191

THIS SORRY LOT WAS worse than the last sorry lot, which was precisely what he had thought about each previous sorry lot. With uncomfortable effort, Guy reminded himself that the most reliable men in the Nottingham Guard had trained in similarly sorry lots. Some of the least likely recruits had proven themselves with years of unerring service, while some of their more promising classmates had turned coward or deserter within months.

That didn't make this lot any less sorry.

Guy of Gisbourne leaned against the rough sandstone parapet, overlooking the castle's training yard below, and was keenly aware that he looked spectacular. This was no vanity, but strategy. He had selected this position that the morning sun would hover behind him, that his men could see the imposing figure of their Captain reviewing their work. Nottingham Castle's tan stones always looked warmest at dawn, like a lover's blush, while the air was thick still with glowing dew. He hoped the image might impress them, that they might see this castle as something nobler and greater than themselves. Because an appearance of grandeur was the only thing he could offer them of late.

"I'm going to tell you a secret," he said to Jon Bassett. His protégé's ears perked up like the dog of his namesake, but his young face was hawkish. With angular features and shrewd, deeply set eyes—he was the very picture of scrutiny. "But first, look at these men down here, and tell me what you see."

Bassett lazed his way to the edge and glanced over. "I see the tops of their heads."

"I will throw you off the rampart," Guy threatened flatly, but in truth he enjoyed Bassett's arrogant swagger. His irreverence reminded Guy of himself when he was a fresh recruit in this very castle.

The Nottingham Guard generally attracted the dull obedient type, which was—in full selfish truth—the reason Guy avoided the recruits right now. He had already met most of them once, which was exactly one time more than necessary. Besides, the quartermaster Simon FitzSimon was busy with the men below, barking orders in his thick Scotsman's tongue. Hopefully, many would drop out before noon. Eligibility standards for the Guard's trials had dipped to include anyone capable of walking and blinking at the same time, and some of these recruits might still have to test twice.

Which, somehow, wasn't even the worst of it.

"Damnation," Guy stared at them, wishing life would occasionally surprise him by being easy. "Swear to me you won't repeat what I tell you here, not to anyone."

"I also see dirt," Bassett added, intentionally unhelpful. When he received no reaction, he straightened his doublet and gave Guy his full attention. "Captain."

The men below had not come to serve the county, they came for free room and board. Skinny lads, mangy beards, they were an insult to the proud blue tabard of the Nottingham Guard. It frustrated Guy to no end to witness the erosion of his company through his fingers. Too many of Guy's best men had left Nottingham to join the war, and not enough of his worst. The castle's complement had been halved twiceover, while their work had doubled. Opportunists and thieves were quick to find advantage in the city the war left behind, and the goodfolk suffered the worst of it. The men under Guy of Gisbourne's command were often the only defense between order and anarchy, not just in the city but across the county.

Guy inhaled sharply and looked anywhere else. Nottingham Castle perched atop its hill—Castle Rock as some called it—and offered a stunning view of the countryside in every direction. Its three tiered baileys sprawled out until the castle walls stopped at the sparkling river Trent to the south, and the bulk of the city he loved to the east. Guy had seen Nottingham through every wave of prosperity and hunger, through peace and war. He'd fought bravely under his own predecessor fifteen years ago when an army swarmed Nottingham's streets to scale the castle walls. Yet Guy had never feared for his men before, nor their ability to protect Nottingham's people.

Until now.

The source of his fear loomed ominously over Jon Bassett's shoulder. Squirreled away in the top level of the highest keep, the greatest threat to Nottingham now came from within. Guy had dutifully served three different men who sat in the High Sheriff's seat, and never needed doubt the man's orders. But yesteryear's spring had brought them the Baron Roger de Lacy—and Baron Roger de Lacy had brought ignorance and corruption of the highest level to Nottingham.

Ignorance from the top, and *them* from the bottom.

Guy couldn't identify any from his vantage, but they were there amongst the recruits, pretending to be honest men.

Gerolds.

"Captain?" Bassett asked, and Guy realized he'd drifted off into thought. Saying it all out loud would feel like an admission of failure, because that's exactly what it was.

"Damnation." Guy ground his teeth, and told the story.

Only two months ago Guy had received an order that from anyone other than Sheriff Roger de Lacy would have been a joke. Guy had immediately raged about its consequences, but the baron was predictably disinterested in logic. De Lacy only cared about quick results, and had presented an easy solution to low recruitment numbers.

Once he had regained control of his bowels, Guy swallowed his pride and obeyed. But not without support—he summoned Simon FitzSimon to accompany him down to the tunnels beneath the middle bailey. Simon and Guy had risen through the ranks of the Guard together, dating back decades when they were themselves the greenest of recruits in the same class. They had actually hated each other at first—Guy hated Simon since he was so Scottish, and Simon hated everyone else because he was so Scottish. Over the years they forged a brotherhood, regularly strengthened over a cask of ale. They did not always see eye to eye, and there had even been times when they famously, and loudly, worked against each other—but always in the name of bettering the Nottingham Guard. It would be Simon's responsibility to fulfill de Lacy's bastard new policy, so Guy refused to let him do so blindly.

"I've been instructed to recruit new Guardsmen from the prisons," Guy told him, as evenly as possible. "As a way to work off their sentence. Non-violent prisoners only, of course. Tax evaders, poachers, war deserters."

It was the most backward idea Guy had ever heard. Putting prisoners together with the men who imprisoned them was a catastrophe waiting to happen.

Simon's reaction was his own. "Interesting."

"Baron Roger de Lacy is the Sheriff now," Guy continued, sensing Simon's hesitation, "and wants you to put swords in the hands of criminals. That's his right. You have the right to complain."

The previous sheriff, Ralph Murdac, would have spat at the idea—largely because Murdac had been a good man and a good sheriff. But Murdac was dead, and de Lacy reveled in changing the ways Nottingham operated. In the time since de Lacy had been assigned the position, a month rarely went by without some new list of asinine laws or procedures. They normally just made Guy's life more difficult—restricting what types of horses could be trained, mandating daily inventories of weapons that never move—but this latest one was downright dangerous.

"No complaints," Simon said gruffly.

"Nothing? Surely you have at least an *opinion* on this, no?" They stopped at the prison's entrance, a gated tunnel that dug down beneath the earthen bailey. "This is your field. Tell me truly, which I swear to reveal to no other, how the hell you feel about prisoners turning guard duty in The Simons' Yard."

"I would expect," Simon mulled, "that some of these prisoner recruits might do perfectly fine. And that others will be terrible. Most will pro'ly desert at the first opportunity. And we'd best keep it secret, or the other Guardsmen will treat them cruelly. Or worse."

Those were only the most obvious of consequences. "Try not to overwhelm me with your deductive prowess. I'm asking how you *feel* about it."

"Are we talking our feelings now?" Simon's accent turned it into a threat. "We've known each other all this time and I'm only now to find out that you've been courting me?"

He smiled, but Guy ignored him. Simon had risen as far as he wanted and was perfectly content to train wet men to swing sticks. Simon had fostered a healthy neutrality to all things political—but he'd understand soon enough.

After speaking with the gaolers and selecting some men from a list based on their crimes alone, Guy and Simon returned topside to the Rabbit Cage. That was the local name for a solitary square iron cage that sat in the center of a small courtyard beside the southern curtain wall. Its lone door was shielded by flat planks, so that it could only be unlocked from the outside. Within its bars, a gullet opened that led back down into the catacombs of the prison. This cage was normally used to sentence prisoners without chancing their escape, but now it offered them exactly that.

Their first candidate climbed up from the Rabbit's throat, escorted by two stout Guardsmen. Ludic of Westerleak and Marshall Sutton were exactly the sort of men one imagined should be prison guards. They shaved their heads regularly and probably spent their free time moving logs for fun. Their prisoner was dirty and shaken, a sizable man with pitiful eyes.

Guy led. "The Sheriff and the Lord have decided you deserve another chance at life. Unfortunately neither of them is here. So convince us you deserve it."

"I'm a good man," the prisoner stammered.

"Is that it?" Guy laughed. "Back down with you."

"Give him a chance," Simon growled playfully.

The man swallowed, eyes darting back and forth between Simon and Guy. This prisoner was the thumb-sucking dumb type. His hands were hard and callused, and though he slumped now his back was straight. This was a useful man, physically at least. All of his attention was on Simon, whom he had perhaps correctly identified as the more lenient.

"Do you know my friend?" Guy asked.

A slow, dumb nod. "He's The Simons."

Guy had been the one to nickname him *The Simons*, originally as a joke but it stuck over the years. Now every fledgling grunt that squeezed his way through The Simons' Yard said it with respect.

"And what do you know about The Simons?"

"The Simons turns you into a man." His lower lip trembled, and his glance averted.

"And what's your name?"

"Gerold."

"Gerold of . . ."

"Gerold of . . . nowhere, m'lord."

"Tell me how you ended up in prison, Gerold of Nowhere. And tell the truth," Guy added, "or you're yet to be Gerold of the Gallows."

Gerold nodded and composed himself. His mouth moved silently, he had sense in him enough to know his life was at stake. Finally he exhaled and spoke slowly. "I've been on my own for a while, and I know I've acted poorly. I've stolen more than a few nights' sleep in places I wasn't welcome, and pinched food from those that might not have had any to spare. I have regrets, and I've prayed for them, and I know they're mine." He glanced around, hoping he had made any progress. "But whatever reason they say I'm here, it wasn't me. I was asleep in an alley, and I woke up to commotion and I don't know what, and next thing ever was me pulled away, thrown in here, saying I did things I didn't. Please believe me. I've been trying to make right of myself, I have, an' it's hard, it's so hard." He sniffed harshly, seeming to wipe some wetness from his eyes. "An' I know it's not for anyone but me to make it right, not even the Lord, and I try every day. Even down here, every day I try to make something right again."

At Guy's signal they excused themselves from the prisoner. "What do you think?"

"He's a decent candidate," Simon admitted. "He may be a bit broken, but I'd wager he'd be powerful grateful to have a bed and regular meal."

"I agree. He would be." Guy bit his lip. "You don't think he'd be a threat?"

"I think he'd be more a target than a threat. He cries like that in the Yard and The Simons will have to get all Simonsy on him."

"So you'd take him?"

Simon considered it. "I would. Do you disagree?"

"Of course." Guy laughed.

"You think he wouldn't cut it?"

"This man is a liar, and a murderer." Guy knew exactly who Gerold was, he had recognized the name in the gaoler's records. Gerold stopped crying and looked up sharply as Guy raised his voice. "I watched that man smash a young woman's head in with a rock. It took five Guardsmen to take him down. Everything he just told us was a complete fabrication. I thought the blubbering was a bit much."

"Fuck me." The man's baby-face contorted. "I knew I recognized you." His entire countenance changed, whatever innocence he had faked was now replaced with cruel lines.

Simon exhaled heavily. "For the love of . . . why are we talking to him at all? Why hasn't he hanged?"

"He'll hang soon enough. But I wanted to see—no offense now, Simon—if you'd fall for it." At that, his friend's features turned hard. "I'm sorry to use you. I knew this trash wasn't an option. But what if I hadn't? If we talked to another man who gave the same pitiful story, perhaps we'd both fall for it. Just because they're arrested for something small doesn't mean that's the worst they've done. Crime begets crime, and then we've brought a murderer into our ranks. You think Ludic or Marshall would be safe, when the men they cage eat at their table in the dining hall? Everyone we talk to is going to beg for forgiveness, tell us they're innocent, and lie and lie and lie. They might even lie. This is how we're inviting danger into the Nottingham Guard. These are the sheriff's orders, and I say they're reckless and arrogant. So. Simon. Do you still prefer to shake your head and say you have *no complaints?*"

"THAT WAS IN APRIL," Guy finished, still staring out over the Yard. "We've pulled prisoners every month since, thrown them into training. The Simons and I conceal their pasts, and they're under strict orders not to reveal anything themselves. They receive only a fraction of the normal payment, enough for the barest of necessities."

Jon Bassett's eyes were full of judgment, but not blame. "Any problems with any of them yet?"

"Not yet." But its potential was in each of their faces.

"Why'd you tell me?"

"Because at the rate you're going, you'll be captain someday," Guy answered. Upon seeing Bassett's surprise, he added, "Not *soon,* mind you. Don't get any ideas. There may be grey in my beard but I'm a long ways from dead. But it can't hurt to start thinking like a captain now."

His protégé pursed his lips, but wisely said nothing.

"Besides. I could use someone aside from The Simons and the Sheriff to complain about it with."

That earned a dry laugh, and the two of them returned their attention to the training in the Yard below. The recruits were running physical exercises, while Guy instinctively categorized each of them into tiers based entirely on how useless they would be. Between the war and Sheriff de Lacy, it was hard to guess which had been more disastrous to Nottingham's safety.

After some time, Jon Bassett clicked his tongue. "What happened to Gerold of Nowhere?"

"Hanged as scheduled," Guy answered.

FOUR

WILLIAM DE WENDENAL

ENGLISH WAR CAMP, ACRE
MONDAY, 1ST DAY OF JULY 1191

WILLIAM DE WENDENAL POINTED his index finger and retracted it, again and again.

It was, inarguably, fascinating.

He had no idea how it worked. A casual inkling in his mind commanded his muscles to stretch forward, every time, with no sensation of any interaction between cause and effect. The more he tried to study it, the more it became unknowable, like a word repeated too many times until it became gibberish. He wondered if the same was true with power. If King Richard was aware at all of the sequence of events that followed his every command, or if he simply thought things and then waited for the world to inevitably bend.

Richard was in a whimsical mood, despite another day of less-than-whimsical news. Leave it to a king to assume he can do the impossible. They had advanced their camp along with a dozen trebuchets, but they might as well have had none. With each stone thrown, the very earth worked against them—shifting the machine's trajectory so they could not concentrate on a single point. The city's walls were thicker and harder than anticipated, while the rocks they launched often shattered harmlessly to dust upon impact. For two weeks straight their strategy had failed miserably, and showed no signs of changing. The only advantage of failure was that they had yet to draw steel even once against the Saracens, which would hopefully give enough time for the replacement weapons to arrive. But the King was not infuriated by any of this, he seemed to find each day's disappointment to be another chapter in an increasingly hilarious tale that only he could read.

"Alright. You're the funny one," William nudged Robin's ribs, "why is he laughing?"

Robin raised a grim eyebrow. "How am I the funny one?"

"Solid point." William nodded. "I'll correct. You're the one who *thinks* he's funny."

Robin's head wobbled back and forth in consideration. "Thank you. And I have no idea."

They watched the King silently for a bit, as he pointed at apparently random positions on a map with his retinue of lords, his fairweather war council. William might normally impose himself into their debate, but he suspected the correct strategy was, as every other army had already discovered, to sulk back home in defeat. So he lingered at the back with Robin, sniping comments under their breath. "He knows he's not the first person to try to capture this city, yes?"

"I don't think he knows that, no," Robin answered.

"Do you suppose he could return to England and just *tell* everyone he won the war? Do you think anyone's really going to check?"

"You're right." Robin blinked. "I'm the funny one."

William watched the lords debate and strategize, each far more eager to be heard than to be right. Their ideas were as useless as the swords sitting at the bottom of the Mediterranean. William instead watched Richard, detached, no longer interested in opinions.

"You said those weapons would be here by now," William whispered.

"No I didn't. I said this was the *earliest* we could expect them."

"Well I hope they arrive soon. I'd prefer to be alive when we get them."

The night's intrigue came in the form of a foreign man with dark features, dressed in a simple but well-tailored smock. Short, flat hair speckled the messenger's round head, and his hefty beard looked recently washed. Even surrounded by English soldiers, there was no sign of fear in his eyes. *Anything unexpected is an opportunity.* It was a lesson William's father had impressed upon him, though he was ever a student in its application.

The stranger gave proper greetings behind a smug smile, and spoke half-decent French. "Saladin welcomes you to his city, and wonders why you idle your time by giving us rocks, of which we have enough already. He has been expecting you for several months. He has heard news of your exploits on Cyprus, and apologizes that your holiest of intentions must need be delayed by the frivolities of women."

The deadpan sarcasm translated across the language barrier. This was the second despot to challenge Richard's decision to delay his Crusade by rescuing his own wife. Isaac Komnenos, the violent leader of Cyprus who captured her after she shipwrecked, also saw the hypocrisy of that situation. *"Why are you even here, Richard? Take your Crusaders off my land, or has your God told you that Cyprus is now part of your holy quest? Is my tongue Jerusalem, that you are so quick to tame it? Is your woman Jerusalem, that you must so desperately occupy her?"* It had riled Richard then. He left Isaac a prisoner bound in silver chains, an insulting kindness after promising not to leave him in irons. William hoped such sarcasm would not rile him again. King Richard was ruthless to those who insulted him, a petulant selfishness that was his most difficult trait to imitate.

"Saladin hopes your visit will be pleasant," the messenger continued. "Our country is vast and beautiful, and appreciates your desire to see it. But he begs you against keeping camp longer than necessary. The winds can be cold, and the sun warmer than possibly you are accustomed. The lips, he warns, may crack, such is the heat in summer."

Thankfully, Richard laughed. "That's clever. I am pleased to learn that Saladin spends so much time thinking about the quality of my lips."

The messenger bowed. "Very good, just as you say. King Richard, the Lionheart." He emphasized the name slightly, as if it were an insult. Then, without hesitation, he made a quarter-turn and looked William in the eyes. "King Richard, the Lionheart."

William's fingers tickled the hilt of his blade. Nobody outside of this tent, especially an envoy from the enemy, should have known William was the king's body double.

The messenger rotated again, now dead set upon Robin. "King Richard, the Lionheart."

Robin simply smirked, but the coldness in his gaze might have killed. The messenger held that heavy moment before standing again to leave. Richard raised his hand lazily and his soldiers blocked the exit. *Anything unexpected is an opportunity.* So where was the opportunity in this, William wondered.

Richard cleared his throat. "Now if *I* were Saladin, which for the first time it grieves me I am *not,* what did I just gain from this?"

"Clearly a threat," William answered. "A show of force."

Richard seemed unimpressed with the answer. "What odds would he place on the success of this threat? That three nations' worth of armies and preparations and reputations would slink away from one man's veiled insults? Not likely. So why make the threat?" He asked it scholastically, as a teacher probing his students for their participation.

"Pure pride," offered Ferrers. "They know everything about you, and want to brag about it."

"Wrong." Richard was short with him, and William enjoyed it. Ferrers deserved to be silenced exactly once for every word he ever uttered. The king slowly circled the tent, gesturing when necessary at the messenger as if he were a plaything for idle consideration. "What would it gain Saladin to posture and pose for me? I know him to be strong, I know him to be fearless. He doesn't need to show me this. So why name you out, one by one? What does he gain?"

"Surprise, I suppose," William tried to work it out, though the logic seemed clunky and rusted, pieces that weren't made for each other. "Means we need to change our tactics. Perhaps he wants to flush out the real king into taking point again."

Richard's eyes darted around the room playfully. "If you're right, *which you're not,* what would he *gain* from that? If we change tactics, he abandons his advantage of knowledge. So where is the gain?"

"Are we supposed to be afraid he has a spy?" asked another baron.

"The fact that I am still gloriously alive means there is no spy. One last time, what does he *gain?*"

Robin's voice, strong and true, "Confirmation."

"*Confirmation!*" Richard nearly danced at the word. "He didn't *know* about my body doubles, but he did *suspect.* Perhaps he heard rumor of you, or had a fancy thought flirt around his skull one night. And now he has *confirmation* of it. One man, sent under the banner of peace, can see the inside of this tent to test our reaction."

William fidgeted. The answer didn't explain everything. "But he knew exactly who we were. How did he know who to single out?"

"I was going to ask him the same thing," Richard replied, "but it also struck me that I didn't necessarily care." His casual tone was matched only by the nonchalant way he opened the messenger's neck with a knife from the table.

Bile sprang into William's mouth as if it were his own throat. He threw his hands up to keep from retching. But he could not look away from the messenger and the wild-eyed horror that consumed him. He stumbled but was restrained, he made to grab at his neck but failed, blood weeping from the open meat. William had seen plenty of death, but this struck him as too cruel, too savage. King Richard didn't even stop walking, he continued his collegiate circling of the room. He was talking still, though the words were lost to William. The dying man gurgled and mercifully passed out, slumping to the ground.

But Richard was suddenly in William's face, immediate and full of intent. "Why is he dead now, Wendenal? What does it gain *me?*"

William could not hide his disgust. "Very kingly of you."

"What does it gain me?" His breath was hot and stale.

"Well he obviously won't be talking now, Richard, though it's a hell of a way to make your point." Blood seeped into the dry ground, thirsty. The handful of entourage lords had recoiled in horror. "He was a messenger. What did he learn here that was worth his life?"

Robin, ever on the right side of things, backed William's dissent. "He came under a banner of peace, bearing gifts. The only possible motive to kill him would be in reaction to his suspicions. So this doesn't help us at all. If anything, it still gives Saladin confirmation."

Richard delighted in the response. "So what *does* it gain me?" He was rolling in the joy of it now, while William was gagging.

"I'll tell you what you *lose,*" he coughed out, "you lose a position of sympathy. They'll call you a marauder, they'll say you've no respect for the rules of war, which puts us all in danger. They'll kill any man they take prisoner."

"A terrible thing I've done, then," Richard rocked back and forth. "Saladin knows me to be no fool, he knows exactly why I *shouldn't* kill the man. He knows what I lose, he knows everything you just said! So what *does* it gain me?"

"I don't know!" William shouted. On the ground he watched the man's blood turn prickly with dirt. There had been no point to it.

There was never any point to it.

"I don't know what the hell it gains you," he repeated.

"And neither does he!"

There it was, that was what Richard wanted. He caught William's gaze and held it, the muscles around his eye clenched just so. Richard always wanted them to share his morality, to see the pieces as he did, beyond any common soldier. And William understood. He didn't like it, but damned if he didn't understand it.

"There's no earthly reason you should have killed Saladin's messenger," William said it aloud, "*that he knows of.*"

Richard relaxed, the showman gone. "Exactly. I hope that empty mystery drives him mad."

THE DWINDLING HOURS BROUGHT a camp quiet but for horses and wind. A gentle hour, lit by milky white ribbons across the sky, when a man could fall asleep without fear. If he ignored the ocean, William could almost convince himself he was at home in Derby, lazily watching the stars with his brothers. The same sky he stared up upon now looked impossibly down on England, too, and William could only be envious.

The war council's members had long left to feel more important in the company of their subordinates. But William was still awake, mind racing with a thousand possibilities of what the next days had in store. The enemy knew about Richard's use of body doubles, and there was no way to calculate what that meant. Not that it mattered. All William could do was sit and wait for Richard to make another unpredictable decision.

Days such as this left a sour taste in his mouth. The king could be exceedingly kind and competent when he chose to, but he had an equal capacity for mania. Yet in each of Richard's rants, there was always a nugget of startling clarity. Whether it was all calculated or not, William could never tell.

The king threw himself at the floor, fussing with his blanket. "We should send a messenger back to the city, with the body," he said off-handedly, as if they had already been in mid-conversation. "You're in the crown tomorrow? Send that earl, Derby. He's a tiring one, no?"

Ferrers deserved many wretched things in this life, and worse in whatever came after, but he did not deserve this. Sending the earl to the city with the dead messenger was a certain death sentence. "A bit obvious, that?" William said mildly. "I thought you'd let Saladin stew and wonder for a couple days."

"Hm?" Richard seemed to have already forgotten his own order. "Oh, yes, I suppose that's fine. And on second thought, I'll stay in the crown myself tomorrow."

The king looked up, where the wisps of smoke from the tent's brazier curled through an opening to mingle with stars above. William, on the other hand, found himself staring down at the dark spot below where the messenger's blood had fed the dirt. Within moments Richard was asleep, disappearing from the world without a care.

Why William had bothered to save Ferrers's life, he couldn't say. The man was responsible for so much of the grief that defined William's past. Fifteen years ago, Ferrers had answered another call to war, to fight for Henry the Younger in his attempted rebellion against King Henry. William often wondered how different his life would be if not for that one selfish act. The rebellion had failed, Ferrers's siege of Nottingham Castle was unsuccessful, so nothing would be different for most of the world. But his brothers would be alive. William probably would have married Arable de Burel, and her family would have escaped ruin.

Selfish acts and their unknown consequences, they tugged at William's fingertips. Returning to his bedroll, he caught Robin's gaze across from him, eyes wide open, giving solemn approval of his suggestion that spared Ferrers's life. But William could only wonder what his own father would say of this tiny act of mercy, and chose better than to linger on it.

This war would have consequences, too. And William knew that if things went poorly, King Richard would not lose any sleep over them. Power was worse than any wine at dulling the senses. William knew exactly why his king had tried to casually send an annoying earl to his death, and exactly why he had taken a messenger's life for a petty mind game.

Because he can.

William could only hope that, given the same power, he would make different choices.

FIVE

ARABLE DE BUREL

NOTTINGHAM CASTLE

Of course Arable was still awake when they came through the kitchen. Their voices carried right through to the maids' chambers loud and clear, even though they thought they were whispering. And of course they found it necessary, as all young men do, to touch everything they walked by. She could tell precisely where they were by the number of times the soup lid rattled open and crashed down again in disappointment. Each one slapped the side of the wide stone archway that split the kitchen in half as he walked through it. Each one clattered his hand against the line of hanging spoons above the cutting table. Four tonight. Then the soup lid again. *Good thing you checked, your friends may have not looked hard enough.* Five.

There was no point in following them. It was past midnight and she was tired. Her hands were sore from scratching wax trails off of candleshelves and something wasn't sitting well in her stomach. She'd already visited the cold castle privies several times to relieve herself and was likely to need another, judging by the strange crackles in her belly. That was why she had left her stockings and shoes on, in case she needed to go again. Not so she could follow the errant Guardsmen when they returned tonight. Following them would be dangerous, and pointless. Better to roll back to sleep, and let them about their business.

Arable de Burel was always losing her own arguments. She slipped out of bed to follow them.

"Don't do it," tisked the younger girl from the bed below. Gunnore was probably half Arable's age, just barely old enough to be indignant about still being called a girl. She had more brat than sense in her, but even she knew the folly of prying into Guardsmen's secrets. But Gunny had never known anything beyond a servant's life, so her concept of danger was limited to that which risked her daily meal. Arable had yet to succumb to the hopelessness of this life, and prayed she would not need to. Someday she'd climb up again, when it was safe. But for now her safety depended on Roger de Lacy's generosity.

And when men gathered in the night to whisper secrets in the bottom of the castle, it usually meant trouble for someone at the top.

"Don't follow them," Gunny whispered again.

"I'm not! It's my stomach!" Arable actually felt bad about the lie.

Gunny gave her a sad pout, waving her over to brush her hair back.

"You poor thing, here," she said, tying Arable's black curls behind her head. "In case you retch. This is the second time tonight!"

Third, Arable thought. *You must have slept through one of them. Back to sleep with you now.* She tucked Gunny in and stole away, careful not to wake up the other girls, sleeping row upon row above each other. If the other maids could sleep through headmistress Roana's snoring, they'd never notice Arable leaving. But still, she made sure to walk softly, pulling up on the balls of her feet with each step, rather than plodding them down like meat the way the Guardsmen in the kitchen had.

The maids' chambers were connected to the kitchen by only a wide foyer, since the castle was built by men. A hundred years ago, William the Conqueror wanted no time to pass between the time Arable woke each morning and the time she started cooking. She was probably the only servant in Nottingham who even thought about *why* things are, rather than just reacting to *what* things are. Arable tiptoed through the kitchen without touching anything *which wasn't very hard* and came to the cut spiral steps that dug down and curled under the floor. Down the staircase to the wine cellar at the end, just like last night, but this time Arable didn't hesitate to slip into its darkness. Last night she had been too fearful to approach the door, and then drove herself mad wondering what they'd been up to. *No good,* that's what they'd been up to. Which was exactly what Roger de Lacy had asked of her, his only stipulation for keeping her surname a secret.

"Don't go out of your way now," he had insisted. *"But keep an ear out for anyone up to no good. I don't have as many friends in this castle as a sheriff should."*

Nearly two years she had been here now, almost as long as de Lacy himself. The longest she had lived in a single place for fifteen years, and the closest thing she had to a home since she had been forced to flee her real one. Arable had played the role of a forgettable face in dozens of places since, almost always in exchange for her privacy. But she had learned that *staying small* rarely meant *staying safe.* Before Nottingham, she had spent half a year outside Grantham assisting an aging cartwright with his clerical and household chores, and happily seen nary another soul in that time. But her security there was exactly as unreliable as his failing business. When Roger de Lacy was made High Sheriff, Arable dared to write him. He was an old acquaintance of her family and gave her pity enough to bring her in. But that stability, too, brought risk. A position within Nottingham Castle, so close to Derby, might mingle her with those who could have once recognized her.

Fortunately, she had found advantage in the role's anonymity. It was better than hiding, because as a servant she was invisible. Perhaps that was what gave her the courage now to breathe through the pitch black of the corridor, softfoot by softfoot, into the vegetable larder beside the wine cellar. A tiny spot of light trickled through a hole between the rooms, back against the wall and impossible to see through, but when Arable pressed her ear to the stones she could hear the muffled whispers of the Guardsmen much clearer.

She snuggled up against a sack of potatoes and let her weight down slowly, one limb at a time, into a position she could keep. It was cold down here, more a cave than a room, and her ear went quickly numb against the stone. She listened as long as she could stand it, and though she could not make out all of what was said, she heard enough to know she had to visit Sheriff de Lacy as soon as possible.

BARON ROGER DE LACY—High Sheriff of Nottinghamshire, Derbyshire, and the Royal Forests—kept his office in the highest level of the highest keep. There was a proper room at the bottom of the tower which every sheriff had used since the first Peveril, but not Roger de Lacy. He preferred the tiny confines of this bird's nest. Arable had asked him about this once, on a perfect spring morning well over a year ago, when he had invited her to stay and share in the breakfast she had brought. He answered by moving to the window and pulling it open, inviting her to push her face out with him, looking down upon the hills of purple crocuses to the southeast.

"I chose this room," he'd whispered, conspiratorially, *"for the singularly spectacular reason that it is the farthest I can possibly get away from Nottingham."*

Arable had climbed the five sets of stairs to his office a thousand times by now, probably more. Along the way she often wondered about who had first laid the stones together, and if they had been proud of their work. She always lost her breath by the top stair, but she rarely took them any slower, for the same reason de Lacy chose the room. Though he did not often have time to idle with her, she treasured their infrequent conversations and often found herself memorizing his clever retorts. Even when he tired of her, he wouldn't complain. *"I must make for terrible company,"* he'd say, *"surely there's some younger man who you'd prefer to give your attention."*

It was one of the few times he was mistaken.

On this morning, Arable climbed those stairs as soon as the sun braved the horizon. Her secret had made a poor bedfellow and she'd barely slept at all, but still she was apparently not early enough. Not only was de Lacy wide awake, he had company. The Captain of the Guard, Guy of Gisbourne, sat with the unmistakable pursed lips of someone on the losing end of a conversation.

"Arable," Roger de Lacy cleared his throat, his thin face brightening immediately upon seeing her. "Did I call for something?"

"If you did, she didn't bring it." Gisbourne squinted at Arable's obviously empty hands. "Did you call for nothing, perhaps? She has plenty of that."

"Oh, don't take it out on her," de Lacy grumbled. His face was well weathered with deep lines, forged in equal parts from smiling and scowling. Watching them fold upon themselves as he shifted between the two was like opening a wooden puzzlebox. But for Arable his eyes were always kind, the corners of his lips always turned up. "What brings you, then?"

She hesitated and glanced at the captain, who gave no indication he might offer them privacy. *No matter.* Guy of Gisbourne was a good man if a bit stern, and this news was just as important to him. "I overheard a private conversation between a group of young Guardsmen," she explained, "that I think you should know about."

Arable described everything she heard. She mentioned the five Guardsmen and their late-night meeting, she talked about the wine cellar and the larder, and their mysterious whispered plans. "I could not make out the details, but they were talking about some other Guardsman. I don't know who. They mean him harm."

"Some sort of fraternal indoctrination, I would guess," de Lacy waved it off. "Just normal roughhousing. It happens all the time when you throw men at each other."

"No," Arable insisted. "This wasn't playful, and it wasn't normal. I got the impression they meant something much more serious."

"I know precisely what this is," Gisbourne turned sour, but it was aimed at the Sheriff, "and I warned you this would happen."

De Lacy's response was careful. "You don't know anything yet."

"Shall I wait until one of my boys is dead?" The captain placed his fingertips on the table. "Thank you, Arable, this was very important. You were right to bring this to us."

"I know," she said flatly.

"Did you recognize any of these men?" Gisbourne asked. "Their names?"

Arable shook her head, suddenly feeling foolish.

"Hm. What about their faces?" he pressed.

"No." She only knew a handful of the Common Guardsmen anymore. *Thankfully.* She rarely worked in the barracks halls, where she quickly became a target for the men's drunken gropings. Early on, de Lacy had reassigned her to duties centered in the upper bailey, closer to him. She was friends with most of the Guardsmen in Gisbourne's private regiment, but not many others. Which meant she had no names to share. *What a waste of time,* she scolded herself. "Unless . . ."

Gisbourne raised an eyebrow. "Yes?"

"They've gone through the kitchen each night before they meet," she continued, before she fully thought it out. "I suppose I could hide there and spy on them as they pass through."

"Of course not," de Lacy was quick to protect her. "You've done enough already, I should think."

Gisbourne nodded. "Agreed. Besides, I have a good idea who they are. I ought to just throw them all back into the gaols where they belong."

"You *ought*?" de Lacy turned sharply on him. "You have a whisper and a rumor, and you want to condemn innocent men for that?"

"We're using a new definition of the word *innocent,* are we?"

"You want to prove me wrong?" De Lacy gave a labored smile. "Then gather evidence, not hearsay."

That challenge lingered in the air a bit, leading Gisbourne to turn reluctantly back to Arable. "I wouldn't want you to do anything with which you feel uncomfortable, but I need to know which recruits you overheard."

Arable ignored his patronizing tone. "I wouldn't have offered if I wasn't comfortable with it."

This was, apparently, an impressive thing to say. "Very well," the captain continued. "If they meet again tonight, try to get a good look at them. Focus on just one if there's not enough time. Then you can describe him to me in the morning."

"*Describe* him to you?" Arable was incredulous. It would be a dirty young man with pale skin and long brown hair. The Nottingham Guard was full of them, and not much else.

"Do you expect him to have an obvious scar of some sort?" de Lacy mused with a wicked smile, leaning back in his chair.

Gisbourne rolled his eyes. "Alright, describe him to me *if you can*. If not, then . . . here!" He quickly drank the last drop from a dented pewter tankard at the desk, and placed it in Arable's hands. "I'll recognize this cup. Tomorrow night at the dining hall, be sure to catch my eye. Serve this cup to the man you recognize, and then think no more of it." He gave her a meaningful smile and returned to his seat, throwing his leg over its back like a saddle.

De Lacy flashed his eyebrows playfully at her. "What a delightful bit of morning. Intrigue before breakfast!"

"It's not delightful, it's dangerous," the captain scowled. "Tell me I'm wrong. I'll wager anything it's one of your new recruits."

"You're so eager to assign me the blame for this. I trust you're equally prepared to give me full credit for each day we do *not* have an incident? Or is causality only important when it plays to your favor?"

Gisbourne shrugged it away. "I warned you if we pulled men from the gaols, they would turn on us."

"And I warned you," de Lacy's voice tightened, "to be *discreet*." He threw a piercing look at Arable, but did not ask her to leave. She wondered if the captain expected her to miraculously close her ears in his presence, or if he simply forgot that girls were smarter than rocks. "You were also meant to be diligent in your selection. There are plenty of men in gaol for tax evasion, yet you seem to have recruited the ones comfortable with plotting secret beatings. I fail to see how this deficit in reasoning falls on *my* shoulders. Unless," he wrapped his fingers delicately around each other, "you're purposefully trying to undermine my policy?"

Gisbourne seemed honestly taken aback. "We may disagree on a very many things, but I would never intentionally put my own men in danger. That hobby remains solely yours."

"Hm." De Lacy squinted but did not contest it. "Investigate this. And stop recruiting violent men."

"You overestimate the number of debtors in our cells."

"Then find more of them." De Lacy's eyebrows crawled up his forehead. "If you don't like your lot down below, start enforcing the tax collections, that you might have more docile options. But do not complain to me of being shorthanded and also complain about my solution. You can't throw a rock in this county without hitting someone who didn't pay their part of the war fund. This would put them to work."

"That would be much easier," Gisbourne countered, "if I had more men."

"Oh, for heaven's sake," de Lacy reeled, and turned his attention back to Arable. "Fetch me a carriage, Arable. If we're going to go round in circles all morning I might as well be comfortable."

She laughed and excused herself, lingering just long enough for him to give her a warm smile. She closed the door carefully, and it was not until she climbed down the first set of stairs before she paused, contemplating the dented pewter tankard in her hands. Spying on the men in the cellar was one thing, but doing this was a choice to get involved. *To be noticed.* For nearly half her life she had done everything she could to avoid attention, to hide her name. She had finally saved enough coin to travel south, once she knew where to go. But that depended on her staying hidden. Now she risked losing that, *and for what?*

But she understood enough of their conversation to recognize the danger. If debtors were being arrested and given Guard duty as a sentence, they might naturally start to conspire against the men who arrested them. She thought of Reginold and Bolt, the near-brothers in the Captain's Regiment who always included her in their jokes. She thought of the sweet mountain Morg, the size of a bull with a heart of kindness. Even Jon Bassett, the incorrigible flirt, did not deserve a knife in the back. She couldn't stand the thought of someone hurting them, not if she could stop it.

A flurry of footsteps came from above, and suddenly Captain Gisbourne nearly barreled into her. "Arable, thank goodness. Not a word, yes? Not a word of what you heard, to anyone. About the gaols, you understand? I spoke out of turn."

I'm not an idiot. "Of course," she said.

"You can understand why that must remain secret, yes?"

Again. "Of course."

"Good girl." He touched her shoulder with a surprising sincerity, his grim countenance replaced with a reassuring smile. "I'll watch for you tomorrow night. Thank you."

SIX

ROBIN OF LOCKSLEY

ACRE

THE SIEGE WAS OVER, the city was taken. While the losses had been fewer than Robin's prediction, they were still profound. Now they were faced with regrouping and securing an angry city, before they could continue the war forward to Jerusalem. But worse than any of that, Robin's muscles were simply *furious* with him.

He'd been in the mix of it, by William's side in the thick of the fight, but now that recent memory was almost a dream. War was like that, too impossible to believe afterward. From a purely logical point of view, it didn't make sense that such carnage could actually happen, so instead Robin focused on today's tasks. The procedural things that had to happen next. So, as ludicrous as it was in the wake of days of brutal bloodshed, climbing this staircase was the hardest thing Robin had ever done.

Some backward mason probably thought the staircase was well-crafted. The only thing that distinguished it as a staircase and not a curiosity of landscape was that it led somewhere useful. It was a cliffsedge, really, wrapping around the outer defensive wall of Acre up to a stronghold overlooking the sea. Each step angled slightly down in a way that invited a man to take a casual tumble and die in the ocean below. It was probably designed for a king's desperate escape, but Robin was using it to haul the massive bundle of swords on his back into the fortress, for a bunch of soldiers who apparently couldn't be bothered to do it themselves.

The cool relief of shade devoured him at the top of the climb, where an unnatural opening in the stone wall brought a chance to drop pack and stretch his arms. The ceiling of the storeroom was rotted and weathered by the sea air, letting in shafts of light from the wooden ramparts above. It was a welcome break from the merciless sun. Robin's pack clattered angrily to the ground, practically all steel. Swords, knives, a few of the curved Saracens blades, anything he had been able to carry. It was a drop in the bucket, a tiny bandage on the disorganized war effort.

Robin lowered himself to the ground to massage his calves. Though the hostilities in the city had ended, the aches in his body were still very much at war.

Three days earlier, a lucky trebuchet shot had shocked them all. A single weak point had cascaded into a massive collapse of a section of the city's wall, and the English army surged eagerly toward the hole. But King Richard had caught a sickness one day prior, and was in no condition to manage the assault. So even though neither of them had doubled for Richard since the day of the messenger's visit, William claimed the king's warcrown—to Robin's shock and admiration—in order to command the troops.

Fortunately, Acre's defenders had been equally surprised. The shortage of shortarms had not crippled the English battalions as much as Robin predicted, but mostly because a bulk of Saladin's army had apparently already withdrawn from Acre to Jerusalem. But even with those advantages, the invasion was hardly easy. Robin had marveled at William, who somehow flourished under the pressure of chaos. Nobles study war scholastically, or command from the back ranks, but William seemed to know it by its first name. He knew the frenzy and confusion, the sweat and blood and horror of fighting for your life and for the lives of those around you. Taking a city isn't about well-ordered soldiers in rank and file, it's all elbows and corners and nobody knowing anything. It's a blur of noise and action, more than most people can handle, which is why so many soldiers get killed by a friendly blade, and innocent people get butchered.

But that had not been this city's fate. William had earned the name of Lionheart that day, and the city was rightfully his. Robin had been at his side, protecting him, but the victory was William's.

The King had neither commented nor chastised William yet for his decision to don the warcrown, and returned to his new aversion toward their doubling, even despite his lingering sickness. But William currently lounged in the safety of the opulent tower Richard had seized for himself, which seemed like approval compared to Robin's role of carrying weapons up the staircase. There were several degrees of bullshit at play there. Protecting the king still had its benefits, but Robin had to admit he missed the weight of the crown.

Kings, after all, didn't have to haul lost weapons.

The slatted ceiling beams groaned and creaked, as the movement of men above scattered the light to dance about the cluttered room. Its musk was of grains and vegetables, a storage area for those on guard. The rest of the room was all structural, holding up the walkway above, providing plenty of nooks and shadows that concealed the boy with the knife with whom Robin casually found himself locking eyes.

Neither moved for several heartbeats.

It took Robin that long to register he wasn't alone. The boy was probably six or seven, dark tan skin, hair cut short—*the boy attacked.* Noiselessly, the child barreled out of the darkness with a knife held out in both hands. Robin instinctively pushed backward, but he was already against the rock wall and he barely managed to snap a solid kick into the child's ribs. If either the knife or the arms holding it had been longer, the tip would have punctured Robin's chest rather than skid across the floor. The boy grunted, and Robin rolled quick to pin his tiny body down. Eyes wide with terror, the boy was not fighting back so much as flailing. Robin put his hand over the boy's mouth—if the soldiers above came down to investigate, there was no telling what punishment they'd see fit to give. There'd already been plenty of dead younger than this one, and rushing a soldier with a weapon was death sentence no matter the age.

Eventually the stabhappy boy stopped struggling and went completely limp—not dead, just resigned to die, if he knew what that meant. Robin imagined this boy had already seen more death in the last week than he ever should, had likely lost much or all of his family. Stealing rations, and likely the knife, too. When it seemed safe, Robin asked, "Do you speak English?"

The response was a renewed struggle, which Robin quickly stopped with a firm slap across the boy's face.

"Stop it. Stop it." Obviously, he said it twice since the boy didn't speak English. "What's your name?"

The boy eventually went limp and stared, blankly, at something in the back of Robin's skull. This boy didn't have a clue what was happening to him, or the city, or how to react to anything.

"Alright, listen you. I'm Robin. Robin. That's my name," he pointed to himself, and then to the boy's chest. "What's your name?"

The boy seemed to understand, and answered, but whatever language he used was full of noises Robin's brain couldn't re-create. A few of the strange syllables sounded very much like English profanity.

"That's your name?" Robin gasped, stifling a laugh. He couldn't repeat back to a child the vulgarity he'd obviously misheard. "I can't call you that. How about *Stabhappy,* that seems to describe you well enough. So listen, Stabhappy, I'm not going to kill you, alright?"

He mimed stabbing the boy in the chest and then shook his hands as if this indicated his peaceful intent. The boy didn't react well.

"You're small, I'm not going to kill you. You're going to grow up, see, you'll be as big as I am someday, and strong, too." He flexed his muscles, but was only rewarded with a confused stare. "Yeah, that's you. You're gonna be this tall and this strong. Little Stabhappy's going to be Big Stabhappy. And *then. That's* when I'll kill you. But not today, alright?"

He picked up the boy by his scrawny shoulders to get him on his feet, but the boy started running toward the wooden doorway that led out to the battlements.

Robin redirected him back around. "No, not that way. They'll kill you that way. Go down the stairs, see? It's genuinely horrifying, but you're small, you'll be fine."

The boy hesitated, until Robin realized he wanted to reclaim his knife.

"Hey no, fuck you, you don't get that back." Robin picked it up. But by the look of it, it wasn't English. More a tool than a weapon. It wouldn't matter in the long run. "Never mind, take it, just don't let me see you again."

He handed it hilt first to the boy, who coughed out some more utter gibberish and disappeared down the cruel staircase, practically running, but not missing a single step. Robin had seen boys like that butchered, too recently. They see their fathers and brothers fighting in a war and they think they're supposed to join in, and most soldiers don't even flinch. A quick blow to the head with a sword hilt, or a shield, and that's one less enemy to worry about in ten years. But a little kindness might change that boy's mind, it might stay with him longer than any of the death.

That, at least, was something Robin was proud to have within him, and to know was instinctive. Not the intellectual mercy philosophers could argue endlessly about. Knowing the *theory* of mercy is easy. Anyone can tell you not to kill children. Nobody wakes up and thinks, *Today's a right day to kill some babies.* But in the moment, nine out of ten men outside this room would have skewered little Stabhappy before knowing to stop. Mercy isn't learned, it either lives in the bones or it doesn't.

Other people would have killed the boy. Robin didn't.

He repeated that to himself with pride, and tried not to think of Edmond.

THAT EVENING, ROBIN RETURNED to Richard's terraced new residence in the greatest part of the city, hoping to share his story with William. The room was filled with colorful silks and curious tapestries, but its only occupant at the moment was the Earl of Derby, William de Ferrers. Robin was predisposed against the man based on William's warning, but the earl stopped Robin before he could excuse himself.

"Locksley, might I ask a strange question of you?"

"Well I don't suppose I can say no now," Robin answered cautiously. "Though I may have strange answers."

"Does the King ever mention me?" the earl asked, with only the faintest taste of embarrassment. A loneliness swam behind his eyes. "Does he hate me?"

King Richard hates everyone, Robin almost answered. *It's why he's king.* Instead he kept it diplomatic. "I can't speak for the King."

"Can't you?" Ferrers mused with a sad smile. "That's part of your job."

"I can't speak for *Richard,*" Robin corrected, but could tell that his evasion would not satisfy. There was a naked and humble quality about the earl's face. Skinny, and unassuming. "Have you given him cause to hate you?"

Ferrers bent backward, laughing deeply and honestly. "I would think I've given most of the world cause to hate me by now. You can't rise by making people like you." His lips twisted to say more, but something wistful crawled up and seemed to choke away his focus. "I was hoping he might allow me to negotiate the surrender of the city, but when I asked him, he . . . seemed absolutely baffled at the prospect, and gave it to Goddard of Leicester instead."

"If you're asking me to . . . put in a word . . . ?" Robin stammered.

"No, no," Ferrers replied. "I'm just . . . forgive me. It has been a taxing few days. I'm a bit out of sorts."

"Think nothing of it." Robin moved to leave, but frankly had nowhere to go. A warm night air meandered through the room's open space, bringing the strange sounds of exotic instruments in from the city. He considered the earl a second time. "Why did you want to negotiate the surrender?"

"I think I'd be good at it," he answered quickly. "Kind, that is. To the other side. I've had to surrender an army before."

Robin nodded. Ferrers had sided with Henry the Younger in the Kings' War, and lost nearly everything for his failures. Now he scratched for meaningless diplomatic laurels. "I think *William* hates you," he said, as if that might be a more satisfactory answer.

"Wendenal." Ferrers tasted the name like an expensive wine. "I would think you're right. But that one, at least, I don't carry on me."

"Carry on you?"

A terse smile. "You're young. Relatively," he added after seeing Robin's raised eyebrow. "All the decisions you make when you're young, you think they're building to something. Some perfect version of *you,* that you'll eventually . . . finally get to be. But you never get there. Eventually you start looking back, rather than ahead, wondering where you missed your chances. I have a lot of regrets, Robin. But what happened with the Wendenals and the Burels isn't one of them. I would not have done it differently."

Robin felt his will soften. He did not know what compelled the earl to speak his mind, but he guessed it was alcoholic. Still, he could tell the man was in need of human connection, and Robin knew the feeling. "Regrets are hard. Avoiding them takes a lot of work. Have you ever killed anyone?"

The earl gave a small nod.

"Most men," Robin explained, "will tell you stories about the first man they ever killed, and how it sticks with them the rest of their life. They think that taking a life is a hard thing."

"Isn't it?" Ferrers kicked back, seemingly happy for the change of conversation. "I certainly remember the first man I killed. Some poor farmer defending his lands. He was there, and I was the closest one to him, and I swung my sword down and it just took his face off. Right off."

"That's the point, that it's not hard." Robin replayed some of the last few days over in his mind. *Bodies under rubble. His sword, red down to the hilt. Men, crippled, begging for mercy.* "Dying is much easier than living. Prick a man in most places and he just bleeds out. Pick the right place and he's dead on the spot. Everything he ever lived for, gone. This thing, this *you,* that you say your life is building to . . . it's the easiest thing for someone to steal that from you. Gone. Your story ends with a quick slash of someone else's sword. Thirty years of a complete waste of everybody's time."

"Or sixty." Ferrers spread his fingers wide.

"Or sixty. What's more important," Robin raised his finger, thinking of his curious little Stabhappy, "is when you *save* a life. When you restrain yourself."

"And do you remember the first person you *saved?*" Ferrers asked.

"No." But he remembered the first person he *didn't* save.

That heavy silence seeped into the air a bit, threatening to end the conversation, until an errant breeze flapped the silks against each other and broke the moment. "Some people would argue," the earl stood to search for his wineskin, "that if you commit yourself to noble acts in this life, you'll be rewarded in the next."

"*Some people* will believe anything," Robin laughed. "They only say that so we, the living, don't feel so bad when they, the dead, get all dead."

Ferrers smiled, but it was a courtesy. "You don't have any children."

Robin shook his head.

"Not married?"

"There was never anyone worth it," he lied. He was neglecting exactly one person from that assessment.

"Once you have someone to pass your life on to, then your actions are for them. And though you die, you live on in a way, through your lineage." Ferrers scratched at the wispy little hairs that had escaped from his chin, awaiting a reply. The natural response was a place Robin didn't care to go, and Ferrers seemed to guess that. "I'm familiar with your family's history, if not the details."

Robin ground his teeth. "Then there's no reason to speak of it."

"You talk like him," the earl said softly. "Your father."

"I'll consider that an insult, thank you."

"You talk of *saving people*. You don't think you got that from him?"

"I talk about *judging* people, so that you know *when* to save them. So you know who deserves it, and who doesn't. My father would let one hard worker starve so two useless skivers can each have half a meal. That doesn't save anyone. That hurts three people, rather than two." Memories of his father, memories of *her,* they were better left untouched. It was easier to talk of them when they were so far away, they had the same surreal nonexistence as the war's violence. "You have a son though, yes?"

The earl nodded.

"Let me guess, you named him after yourself."

Ferrers laughed at this, because it was true. "I had my chances in life," his smile soured, "and failed. My son has to live in that shadow. My mistakes have become his burden. I'm not here for me, I'm here for him. So that someday Ferrers will be a name to respect again."

Robin smiled and said no more. He had heard the name *Ferrers* used as an insult before, but assumed it was just a slight variation of *frère,* the French word for brother, and that it was meant to poke fun at the French. It was slang for a useless man, a fool. Sometimes even a traitor.

Names carried powerful weight to them. And the most insulting thing he could imagine would have been to ask Lady Marion Fitzwalter to bear the name of Locksley.

SEVEN

GUY OF GISBOURNE

NOTTINGHAM CASTLE

"SHE COULD BE PLAYING you," Simon FitzSimon warned, giving a demonstrative swing of a felling axe above a pile of uncut firewood. "She pro'ly rolled with some Guardsman and turned sour when he left her. Trying to get you to punish the man."

"You grant her a good deal of cunning," Guy said absently. Arable's news of the five Gerolds conspiring in the wine cellar had consumed his thoughts for the last day. "She isn't the type. She's the type that believes in good and evil and that praying for her family is going to protect them."

"Oh, and you're above all that, then?" Simon rolled his head, kicking at the dirt of the training yard. It was empty but for the two of them and a sharp morning sunlight, but soon it would be flooded with the newest class of recruits for morning routines. "These five Gerolds you won't stop going on about, you seem to think they're evil enough."

Guy stared at the double doors of the barracks, ready to vomit out its collection of wet boys. "Not *evil,* no. There's no such thing, good and evil. There's just good and . . . disappointing. Everyone starts off good, you know, until they choose to disappoint."

"Is that how you punish your enemies?" the Scotsman laughed. "Sit 'em down and tell 'em how very disappointed you are?"

"I said nothing about enemies. You're talking morality, and I'm talking politics." He reached out for the axe from Simon, and tested out its weight. "If assuming your enemies are *bad men* makes you feel better about fighting them, that's your prerogative, but it certainly doesn't make it true."

"I don't have any enemies."

"Of course not. You must have opinions first to have enemies."

Simon balked. "I have opinions!"

"You have opinions on soup. Nobody goes to war for that." Guy swung the axe down into a log, but it remained in one piece. Guy frowned at it, but still it did not split. "I bring you along to recruit from the gaols because pulling an ill opinion from you is a difficult thing. If *you* don't like a recruit, they must be a particular new brand of filth. Myself, I tend to hate everyone. Primarily based on the fact that most people I meet are human, and humans are a generally foul lot. So everyone we interrogate rubs me the wrong way, but if one rubs *you* the wrong way, that's something else. So do me a favor and judge harshly, so that our servant girls won't have to be afraid of any monsters in their beds."

Simon shook his big beefy head. "I lost track. Are humans all born good, or are they all filth? You seem to want it both ways."

Guy tried to pry the axehead free. "Just because I hate most people doesn't mean they're evil. I'm just particular." He gave up and moved away, not in the mood for being questioned. He was in the mood for yelling harsh things at people who were forced to listen to him, which was delightfully about to happen.

The armsmaster grunted as the barracks doors groaned. Guy gave the man control of his yard, and moved to its perimeter. There waited Guy's ever-subservient shadow of an attendant, William de Ferrers. Guy slung his black cloak from his shoulders and handed it to the young Ferrers, who carefully folded it over his arm and kept his eyes on the ground. The heavy ivory cape he wore himself was the only thing that distinguished him from any generic stableboy. Ferrers was, in Guy's estimation, a tangible demonstration of political failure. His father was the Earl of Derby, but none of that prestige had made it into the son. The elder William de Ferrers had lost nearly all prominence fifteen years ago when he sided with Henry the Younger in the Kings' War. The earl brought his army to Guy's city to claim it for the usurper, and failed. Quickly thereafter ended the rebellion, the earl's claim to everything except his title, and any possibility of his son making any mark on the world. Guy himself often forgot the young man was even there, so flaccid was his presence. He had taken the assistant as a favor, though privately he saw the young Ferrers as something of a trophy. In the Kings' War, Guy had helped defend his city from the elder Ferrers, and his prize now was to keep that earl's useless son as a nameless servant.

The word *ferrers* itself had become slang in Nottingham for a traitor. This young Ferrers was a cautionary tale, a warning of how easily one's life might become a joke simply by picking the wrong side.

The Simons' Yard was now filled with *ferrers* and *gerolds*.

Within an hour, the yard was thick with sweat and stink. Put a straight birch branch in a man's hand, tell him it's a sword, and he turns into an epic hero every time. They picture themselves in full plate mail etched with elaborate engravings, miraculously not slowed by the weight. The fairest of women swoon at their fantastic display.

In the real world, the fairest women Guy had ever met weren't very fair at all, and wouldn't be caught dead around the stank of The Simons' Yard.

Simon could correct their form, but it was Guy's duty—and pleasure—to bring this army of would-be knights back down to reality. He perused the crowd—there were forty or fifty hopeful recruits here, and half would probably be rejected at the end of the month. He couldn't know for certain if Arable's five conspirators were in this group, or if they were from a previous class that had already graduated to common patrol.

"What's your name?" Guy always started his speech the same way, enjoying his own impression of the armsmaster who first trained him. The world was likely full of impostors just copying their forebears, and hoping nobody noticed. The question wasn't directed to anyone in particular, but a redheaded young man nervously answered.

"Dillon Fellows," he said, only slightly faltering.

Guy knew the name. Not a gerold. "Are you ready to fight for the Nottingham Guard?"

"Yes, Captain."

"What's the Sheriff's name?"

Dillon Fellows paused. "Captain?"

"No that's *me,* you useless blodgett. What's the Sheriff's name?"

With all the certainty of an idiot and not even a touch of humility, the boy actually said, *"The Sheriff of Nottingham."*

Guy let his jaw drop. "You're ready to fight for him but you don't know his name?"

"I'll do whatever is asked of me, in his name."

"His name is Ralph Murdac."

"Ralph Murdac. Sorry, I did know that."

"No you didn't, because Ralph Murdac is dead. He died two years ago." Some chuckles rippled through the men, who were mostly standing in what they incorrectly assumed was a stance of respect. Others leaned on their sticks, while a few had already plopped to the ground in fatigue. Guy tried to pinpoint the ones who didn't laugh—the ones who weren't enjoying themselves. He catalogued every suspicious reaction. "I don't right blame Murdac for dying, I warrant that death was a preferable alternative to being guarded by the likes of you."

"I'm sorry, Captain. I'm ready to fight."

"You're ready to—" Guy laughed out loud, and let it roll into a deep, hearty roar. "Dillon Fellows, I don't even know where to start with the number of things wrong in that statement. You are many things, but *ready to fight* is not one of them. And who exactly is it that you think you're being trained to fight?"

"The enemies of Nottingham?"

"And who the fuck are they?" Guy breathed down onto Dillon's face. "You want to fight someone, we'll ship you off to the Crusade, no problem at all. I'm sure King Richard could use a few more men to die off in the front lines, since all the other *Dillon Fellows* we've sent him have probably been used up by now."

Dillon shrunk. Guy kept at it, walking amongst the men. "There's nobody to *fight* in Nottingham, lads. You're not in the king's army, and you'll never be knights. If you are here for glory, I will give you a glorious death right now and we'll both be happy. That's not what you'll be doing in the Nottingham Guard. Here, you'll man the towers, escort the sheriff, yell at gang children, and you will do a very lot of standing around with very little moving. You'll notice we're not training you how to do that, because we assume you arrived here with more talent than an average tree."

The smirks and amused eyes in the crowd faded. Most here would never rise above the Common Guard, which meant a life of monotony and discipline. Or a quick death at the hand of the damned gerold next to them. "You are being trained to swing a sword without killing yourself, in the unbelievably rare event you will need to use it before someone slightly less incompetent than yourself comes to help you. If you are lucky you will someday rise from the ranks of those who *stand* and do nothing to the elite order of those who *ride* and do nothing. You will enforce the sheriff's laws, you will collect and escort supplies, you will make lords and nobles feel more important. Perhaps you'll be lucky enough and one will pay you to join their retainer, and then you will be very happy because you won't ever have to see me or The Simons again. And we will be equally happy to never see your face as well."

"What about criminals?" Dillon Fellows asked, unaware that it was not his turn to speak.

Guy raised an eyebrow. "Criminals?"

"Won't we be fighting them?"

"Only if their crime," Guy leaned in to investigate Dillon's face for any sign of intelligence, "is that they are currently fighting you. But if The Simons has done his job and you look like you know how to swing a sword, they won't want to fight you in the first place. So I'm terribly sorry, you won't be killing any of your fellow countrymen. This is England, not Barbaria!"

This garnered a wave of laughter, though when he thought back on it later he was fairly certain that Barbaria was not a place.

"If you find yourself," he continued, again addressing the entire crowd, "in the unfortunate circumstance where some fool is trying to kill you, it will not be a graceful dance of swords. There will be no songs written of your prowess. Who here has been to a tournament and seen dueling contests, and jousts, and the such?" Hands and nods. "I cannot possibly stress how little this resembles a real fight. Those tournament men have been trained to study moves, to read each other's footwork, and are aiming to impress the lords and ladies of the court. If you have some sod villager attacking you, he is not trying to impress anyone. His attacks will be random, unfocused, and adhere to no rules of combat. And it will be over before you realize it is happening. *Your primary goal is to never let any situation escalate to this point.* If combat is inevitable, you make the first attack, and you do it correctly. Your only advantage is that they don't know how to fight. Children, you see, play with sticks and you *tap tap tap,*" he mimicked a sword gently reflecting off another, "only making clink-clink sounds. People think they can stop a sword just by letting it touch another one. A real man with an arm of sharpened steel swinging with full intent to kill, this isn't a thing you can simply stand there and take. They don't know that. You do. So Simon." He turned it to the armsmaster. "Get them to work."

The Scotsman's face lit up, and he did just that. The recruits would not spend this day sparring. They wouldn't even touch a real sword for a week. Instead they would chop firewood, move stones, run the perimeter of the bailey, back to back, again and again. The goal for now would be to build their stamina. When blades come out in the real world, it often involves a fair amount of running first. A Guardsman who is out of breath after a chase is likely to never run again.

"So is that where barbarians come from?" came a woman's sarcastic voice.

Guy turned to find a quartet watching him from the relative safety of a stall a few feet away. Jon Bassett was the only one who belonged there, and he held an uncomfortably stoic face that meant he was trying to exude authority. The redheaded guest beside him was no stranger to the castle—the Lady Marion Fitzwalter, a woman of no actual power but who felt entitled to all of it. She tended to stick her nose in the sheriff's business, lobbying for trifling matters with a religious zeal. Her presence usually meant that Guy would have to send a few men to search for some lost child who was just hiding in a tree, or something impossibly less important. Her requests were only entertained on account of her relation to King Richard, a fact that she was quick to reiterate to anyone who tried to be rid of her.

Guy smiled exactly wide enough that he could not be accused of frowning, and no more. "Barbarians can come from anywhere they wish," he answered. "That's what makes them barbarians. Jon, what can I do for the lady?"

"*The lady* can speak for herself." Marion left Jon wide-eyed, lips shut tightly. "I was told you wanted to see me, actually."

"Were you?" Guy squinted against the sun to make out the other two bodies, both attendants to Lady Marion. The tall slender figure to her left was a rare thing indeed, a knight who had not answered the call to war. To her right was a handmaid of no importance and even less beauty. "What did I want to see you about?"

"In regard to Locksley Castle, Captain," Jon Bassett answered, again trying his best to appear official.

"Ah yes." Guy snapped his fingers. He had needed to speak to *someone* in regard to Locksley Castle, but if he'd known it would be Lady Marion then he might have changed his mind. "I've received some curious reports from Locksley. Something about Lord Walter locking one of our tax collectors in a room overnight, threatening his life?"

Marion's wide mask didn't budge. "I was there, and I can guarantee you the story is exaggerated. There was some innocent fun, at his expense admittedly, but no harm was done."

"He wasn't the first tax collector we've sent to Locksley, though," Guy recalled. "I don't tend to get involved with such things personally, except when the collectors find their debtors to be . . . problematic."

"I assure you there is no problem." Marion's lips pursed. "It's the very reason I came to Nottingham today, to speak with the Sheriff and sort out any question of Lord Walter's perceived debts."

"*Perceived* debts?" Guy had not heard that inventive phrase before. "That sounds problematic in and of itself."

"It won't be. No need to worry yourself about it. I'll settle the details with the Sheriff. Is that it? I am late for my appointment with him as it is."

"Heaven forbid. We'll send a third tax collector to Locksley soon, you'll see to it that there are no more stories to exaggerate?" He did not wait for a response.

He returned his attention to the men practicing in the yard, wishing time might be merciful and pass the remaining hours of the day quickly. But the words *perceived debts* flitted about Guy's mind, seeing what damage they could do. In their latest meeting, Sheriff de Lacy had suggested Guy might conscript debtors *before* they were actually behind bars, which was admittedly a better plan than what was happening now. Not foolproof, but a leap beyond putting traitors in the uniform.

As he watched, Guy noticed a thick recruit—whose name he could not remember—bend down to claim the wooden stick another man had been using as a sword. He gave the new stick a few swings, seemed to like it better, and dropped his own thinner stick in its place.

"Lady Marion!" Guy called out, and turned to see they had not yet left earshot. They were paused at the gatehouse up to the highest bailey, where Guy shortly joined them. "One more thing. I don't suppose you've heard stories of a caravan of war supplies that recently went missing in the Sherwood?"

"I have not," she squinted. "But the Sherwood is a big place."

"Oh, indeed, plenty of places to hide within. I mean no accusation," he lied, "but it seems your friend the hermit lord, if he finds himself with these insurmountable tax problems, might be prone to . . . desperate acts?"

"Lord Walter has more than enough coin to pay what is owed," she answered curtly, "provided that number is accurate. Which is, again, the reason for my visit."

"Of course, your ladyship."

Guy smiled and let them leave. Whatever Lady Marion intended by entangling herself with the hermit lord, it was likely to nobody's gain but her own. Walter of Locksley had once been a good man, but it was not difficult to imagine how the recluse of his recent years could turn him disappointing. But if a castle full of debtors lay within half a day's ride, this week might prove productive after all.

Dinner promised more than the average night's entertainment. With any luck, Arable would identify at least one of the ungrateful gerolds by face, and it might be all the ammunition Guy needed to put an end to de Lacy's abhorrent policy.

He leaned against a worn wall at the lower ring of quarters, far enough from the dining hall to discreetly watch his men gather. This was his family, in a way. He had tried his hand at a real family earlier in life, and was better off not thinking about what could have been. That path would never be his again. He had remarried, but only as a favor to Murdac's widow. She had convinced him to take the hand of a young woman in need named Elaisse Longchamp, whom Guy had seen exactly twice in their years of marriage.

The Nottingham Guard was the only family he cared for, and somewhere amongst them tonight were five gerolds who threatened the rest.

A change in the torchlight caused him to look down the hallway, where a short, aged figure swimming in a sable-lined dressgown was striding toward him, eyes wide and a world away. The Sheriff was muttering to himself, or rambling perhaps, though his thin lips were barely moving. The skin stretched tight around his skull and neck, and the silver throughout his hair caught the light in a way that defined his every move.

He stopped abruptly, aware that he almost collided with Guy's chest. De Lacy's eyes sharpened rudely, and Guy felt instantly unwanted.

"Sheriff."

"Yes," de Lacy cleared his throat. "How *keen* of you."

The baron slid past him, waving him off wildly with one wrist, and disappeared around a corner.

Guy intended on saying "Enjoy your evening, Sheriff." For whatever reason, by the time it came out of his mouth it had turned into, "Fuck you, old man."

The men of the Nottingham Guard slowly filled the great volume of the dining hall, minus those on duty. Barely a hundred. A small army in the right hands, but it meant a great many empty benches, with some of the longtables entirely barren. Guy couldn't help but shake the feeling that even a complement such as this was but a skeleton crew.

With Arable nowhere in immediate sight, Guy let himself get distracted by dinner. The men of his elite Captain's Regiment had claimed the table closest to the raging main hearth, and he happily joined them. As he approached, the huge brute Morg stood and barked out, "The Captain on hand!"

The others stood even as Guy shot them down. "Sit your asses down unless you mean me to spank them."

"What honor have we done, that we are so richly rewarded with as prestigious a visitor as the Captain?" Reginold of Dunmow was so good with a bow it made up for his need to use every word he knew every time he spoke.

"Don't waste my time, Dunmow," Guy responded, "or I won't be able to get to your mother by sundown."

"His mother's dead," whined Bolt, the lame-legged runt of their group, so nicknamed for the crossbow he preferred.

Guy winked. "My apologies, not all women can handle me."

Bolt never laughed out loud, but he grinned wide and his neck clenched tight, as if his whole face was swallowing itself. Reginold and Bolt were implausibly good men, and would have joined the war both if not for Bolt's limp. Reginold had refused to leave his "little brother" behind.

"You all heard about Bassett's big fish this week?" Guy turned to his young protégé. Bassett had recently arrested a few members of the Red Lions, a wharfside street gang that often tried to claim control over Nottingham's fish market.

"Heard about it?" asked Eric of Felley, twisting his long hair into a tail. The once-crown ranger pounded his fist to the table. "We were there!"

Guy patted Bassett's shoulder, "It was a fine job, Jon. That's praiseworthy."

"Oh, I wish it weren't." Bassett shrugged it off. "Never cared much for praise."

It was the right answer, and Guy took pride in it. Before he had started grooming Bassett for leadership, he'd been as sharp a brat as any. "I imagine those Red Lions were just as surprised as I was to discover that beneath your bullshit, you may actually be a decent Englishman."

Bassett's eyebrows danced. "Try not to tell anyone."

"I intend on telling everyone," Guy returned. "You're coming with me to Locksley tomorrow."

"What's in Locksley?"

Recruits, but he couldn't tell the others. "Some people that need a reminder that we still punish people for little things like crimes."

Guy wasted ten minutes or so with the boys. They laughed, drank ale, and swapped stories. Their recent arrests made for legendary tales since action in the Guard was generally few and far between. Any stories more exciting than tax evasion were good for morale, and catching legitimate criminals made for legitimate heroes. Amongst these men, Guy was almost able to forget about the troubles beyond the table, the threats that lay hidden behind every false smile within the Common Guard.

He scanned the crowd again for Arable, and found her emerging from a sidewall with fists full of ale. She walked directly toward him, eyes wide, begging for attention. Guy rose from his chair to watch her, to find the gerold she had identified.

But instead she came to him, even serving his table first. The boys hooted and whistled at her, but her eyes never broke from Guy's even as she slammed the drinks onto the table in front of each man, deliberately, ending with Jon Bassett. Only then did she break her gaze down to that final cup, the dented pewter tankard.

Guy's throat clenched, a harrowing sense of betrayal claiming him. He instantly regretted telling Bassett about the recruits from the prison, if only to avoid this heartbreak.

Arable had not overheard a group of gerolds conspiring against good men. She had overheard Jon Bassett planning something against the gerolds.

EIGHT

WILLIAM DE WENDENAL

ACRE
THURSDAY, 11TH DAY OF JULY 1191

"FUCK AUSTRIA!" KING RICHARD coughed, and William hoped very much it was not a command.

Richard had been sick for over a week, and his face had aged a century. Though he had barely left the tower since the city's capture, he still refused to let either William or Robin double for him even to make the simplest of public appearances. It was possible the king resented William's decision to wear the warcrown on the day the walls broke, but it seemed unlikely. That had been a simple act of necessity, the very type of strategic thinking Richard demanded of them. In hindsight, it was barely even worth mentioning. No, William thought it more likely that the messenger from Saladin had affected Richard more than he would admit, feeding into his inherent paranoia. Others more prone toward conspiracies and ignorance thought the messenger was even responsible for Richard's illness itself.

William and Robin accompanied him by his circular bed, adorned in silks, where the king was in as much of a tirade as one could successfully throw while lying down.

"Fuck Austria!" he repeated, then rolled into a wheeze and a fit.

The entire world's population had tried unsuccessfully to siege Acre's walls before England's arrival, but the Austrians had at least waited until England and France arrived. They thought this earned them the right to be treated as equal liberators and wanted their flag raised as well, which Richard had refused. Richard's fever dreams led him to scream some additional choice obscenities about his feelings for Austrians, and the unfortunate size of their collective genitals.

Leaving him to his misery, William drew Robin a comfortable distance aside to talk about supplies. The fighting had stopped, but the city was anything but safe. *Surrender,* after all, was a fine word for kings to throw around, but in William's experience it never seemed to matter much to a city's people. *"It was their nature,"* Richard had explained, to fight back against whatever occupation they thought was upon them, even their own. The Saracen population at large was peaceful, but factions were prone to gathering in small groups that attacked wherever they saw opportunity.

And now William had heard disturbing stories of soldiers stealing from each other, for want of weaponry. Their replacement shipment had yet to arrive, and many suspected it never would. "We're losing more each day. Deserters take swords with them, or sell them. If our men aren't armed, they get scared, they make poor choices."

Robin dismissed it. "We got through the siege without them."

"Because we put the swords in the front. The skirmishes that break out now . . . they could happen anywhere."

"The men can make do." Robin shook his head. "It's war, not a county faire. If they can't adjust to shifting circumstances, they shouldn't be here in the first place."

That made William laugh. "Half this lot are here as a punishment. The other half are farmers trying to avoid paying taxes. Anyone of title is trying to show the King how faithful they are so they'll be rewarded when it's all over. Not one of them should 'be here in the first place.' But they deserve to have England protect them while they're here. They deserve to have a sword if they need a sword."

"For England to protect *them*?" Robin said with a sly smile. "Are you familiar with the concept of war? They're here to protect *England*. They're here for their king."

"Please." The open walls of the tower room afforded a breathtaking view of the city, its many tiers of rooftops cascading down to the sea walls, and the stormy seas beyond. But gorgeous as it was, it was not England. And Acre was but the first battle in the war. Nobody *wanted* to be here. "Show me a single man here who is honestly trying to save Jerusalem for Christianity."

Robin pointed his finger uselessly and let it drop. "Alright, you have a point. Call it duty then."

"Duty," William echoed. "Duty is a thing you do because you have to. An obligation."

"Duty is a choice," Robin countered. "You choose to do your duty against your own personal interests, and there's tremendous sacrifice there, because it's the right choice."

"Hm." William's father had done his duty, and it had been anything but *the right choice*. "The right choice is whatever protects the people."

"Then all the more reason, I say! If they can't do without a sword, they should have brought their own."

William stared at him. "Farmers don't usually own . . . are you familiar with the concept of farming?"

"They could buy one."

"You just don't want to climb that staircase again."

"That plays a heavy factor, yes." Robin laughed. "But if you really think a dozen swords will make a difference, I'll climb it again."

William kicked Robin's leg playfully, and they lingered to listen as Richard hacked, coughed, probably died, and coughed again.

"No. You're right, they'll have to make do. Those replacement swords . . . they're not coming." Perhaps it was Richard's health that had him on edge. They had not discussed what would happen if his ailment went south, what an unthinkable future might hold if the king perished here. William guessed he and Robin could grab the crown, roll Richard's body into a river, and rule England together in secret for the next five years.

The very thought of it made him nauseous.

Robin grunted. "We can agree that the Austrians are terrible though, right?"

"Absolutely."

"Useless bastards."

THAT AFTERNOON, THE KING's complement was to meet publicly with local leaders to finalize the city's surrender. William had finally convinced Richard that "the king" needed to be present, and then successfully tricked Robin into carrying that responsibility. After all, it wouldn't do for the king to celebrate too heavily, so William took that grave task for himself.

The details of the surrender, of course, had been worked out privately between Richard and Saladin's envoys over the previous week, but these things required public pomp and tradition. The war was still far from over, but Saladin's armies had retreated from Acre.

Robin sat high on Richard's white horse, the king's deeply tapered war helmet cropping his face to an indiscernible nose and chin. William stood on foot at his side, a freshly washed white tabard over his own mail. Traditionally, Richard himself would have been nearby as well, disguised as a squire in a deep hood, but his health prevented his attendance. The diplomacies would be carried out by Goddard of Leicester, Richard's selected envoy, which meant Robin would spend his entire day only sitting on a horse looking important. Every now and then, he stole a chance to "accidentally" kick William's helmet, and William could barely keep himself from giggling.

The location was some holy site which was supposed to guarantee their honesty, but William could see little of importance in the dirt courtyard. Its open space was tiered with low stone rings that offered ample visibility to the center. Richard's footmen stopped in fine formation at the edge of one tier, Robin the only one on horseback. The Saracens, of course, were denied any show of military strength, so a collection of dirty old men wrapped in dirtier rags assembled across the courtyard. They sent three of their number to the central area, where they were joined by Goddard and a few others.

Thereupon followed an unbearably boring account of names and acreage of land proclaimed loudly by Goddard, repeated in some ungodly non-language by the elders, followed by murmurs of both spite and agreement from afar, all of which were far short of interesting. William chose to focus on anything else. Which was how it came to be that, as all other eyes were on the proceedings, he accidentally discovered he was staring at a group of two dozen men scrambling onto a rooftop several buildings away, carrying long poles.

He blinked to be certain, and he was.

"Robin. Danger."

Robin didn't react, and William was unsure he'd been heard over Goddard's grand voice. He glanced up at Robin who, even under his helmet, was giving him a whimsical stare.

"I'm sure you mean *Your Grace*?" he corrected, deliberately.

But William couldn't care about his slip. He turned around to squint at the distant gathering again, just in time to realize they were not poles at all, but longbows. His gut twisted, and this time he used his full voice. "Archers!"

He could sense the release of the arrow volley at the edge of the world, just a whisper in the air. Richard's soldiers didn't panic, they methodically unslung their shields and knelt in defense. William slid his own shield up to Robin, maneuvered behind the horse for protection, watching the attackers the whole time. The arrows fell limply down from above, rattling and snapping harmlessly against shields, or missing entirely. But a few screams were there, too. When the volley was over, William emerged from behind the horse to see the cluster of dignitaries in the center of the courtyard stumbling to their knees, and then the ground. Goddard, too, had been pierced through the chest, and staggered down into a lump.

Behind William, the English soldiers that had been standing at attention, shields still raised to their shoulders, were now swarming down the terraces, *good men*. Battle cries, and a stampede of soldiers eager for a solid kill. But Robin, in a commanding voice that William had not heard from him before, called out, "Hold! Hold!"

He held his broadsword aloft, demanding attention. Though the violence of the moment had taken over many, some obeyed and slid to a halt. The screams of those rushing forward died down until all were staring at Robin, sword still held high.

Good for him, William thought. *There's a Lionheart.*

It was a hell of a moment—an army stopped in its tracks, seeking direction rather than revenge. The archers on the far rooftop were not preparing another attack, and there did not appear to be any other surprise groups making assaults. The citizens were as shocked as anyone. Had the army surged forward in retaliation, they would have butchered a hundred innocent civilians in a heartbeat. Instead, Robin only needed to send one contingent to seek out the archers and—

"Hold!" Robin yelled again to the men. But he was jolted by his horse, kicking and fighting at the reins. William realized she had taken a few arrows in her side . . . and one had penetrated Robin's shin, deep, through the muscle.

"Hold—" once more, but the horse hopkicked in pain and Robin lurched forward.

The movement twisted the arrow that pinned them together. Robin's face clenched but he did not scream, unlike his mount. The animal reared up, lost her footing, and stumbled, her back legs crumpling as horse and rider came down in a horrifying crash. The roar, *the roar, by God,* was tenfold what it was before. The soldiers Robin had stopped pulled their steel and flowed down the garden tiers, a wave of men, then an avalanche, crying vengeance. They crashed not into but *through* the crowd of bystanders, too dumb to run or yell in their own defense.

William grabbed Robin, kicked the arrow hard to snap its shaft, and pried his leg free of the thrashing horse. This time, Robin cried out. If not from the pain, from having lost control of the situation.

There were more men huddled around than William could count. He stood and unsheathed his bastard sword, swinging slowly over Robin's body, yelling for everyone to back away. The horse made a startling lurch in an attempt to rise, then screamed something hideous. The fall had given her a grievous injury, too severe for the horse to ever walk on. He plunged his sword deep through the poor beast's throat, a black river of blood pouring out. The horse's body spasmed and sunk, kicking as she died. William continued to push men back, and commanded two young footmen to fetch a stretcher.

"I can walk," protested Robin, unconvincingly. The clamor of riots in the surrounding streets undermined his calm. A glance at the offending rooftop showed the archers had since fled, or moved to defend against the advancing soldiers, or died. Probably some of all three.

"Where the fuck is Craton?" Robin demanded of the nearest man who could possibly know. Craton, a youngish man who was better kept away from combat, should have the king's horns.

"Yes, good," William agreed, chiding himself for not thinking the same. He grabbed at the nearest soldiers. "Hold this ground, there! You, I need five men on that terrace. Quickly, barricade that alleyway—no, not alone! In pairs!" He rattled off commands on instinct, ordering men to hold certain areas, to fetch runners, to check behind doorways. He did not care about fortifying the area so much as he simply wanted to give men specific responsibilities. The fewer people willing to join in on the wanton bloodshed, the better. Soon enough those men were barking commands of their own, and down the line. The two foot-soldiers returned with a stretcher, and the three of them lifted Robin onto it.

The relative calm might have lasted if not for a throng of civilians that ran back into the courtyard, a mob of roughly twenty men who were probably fleeing one gang of soldiers only to find themselves back where the fighting began. They had weapons, mostly improvised, and paused for only a second. Then they switched into offense, screaming unknowable curses and rushing for the quite visible crown on Robin's head.

William was closest. A handful of soldiers stood nearby but only one had a weapon, which was probably why they hadn't joined in the first swell of violence. William thought about the dozen swords that Robin swore would make no difference.

He rose to meet the oncoming line.

Breathe.

One man led, three behind him, the others behind that. William was safe at his flanks, but could not let the crowd get past him to Robin. Only thing to do was focus and react.

It's the easiest thing in the world, killing a man.

All William saw was a collection of vital points, and all he had to do was get the tip of his blade to each of them. Prick a man just about anywhere and he bleeds, slice in the right place and his life, everything he was, simply slips away. Some men study swordplay, practice their footwork, train for tournaments and sport fencing. They learn to deflect and riposte, counter and target. Not these men. They didn't know how to fight. They wouldn't thrust or lunge at the right places. They were easy.

So while the soldier next to William met his first opponent with full energy, hacking at the man's club, William had already side-stepped and *jabbed, jabbed, sliced* into the ribs of two men and across the belly of a third. He didn't pause to see if they fell, he moved on, quick movements, just the tip, into just the right place, just enough to puncture and pull that hot spray of blood that held their every moment until now. The edge of his blade shattered the teeth of a man who thought screaming would help, then his hilt collapsed the temple of another who would have been saved by a helmet. William stepped shy of a wide swing coming from a man older than his father, and pricked him just hard enough at the top of the sternum to notice his neck go limp. None of these people would fight until their dying breaths. Each would drop, shocked, hold their wound, and curl up in the hopes of surviving, then surrender to the darkness.

But of course, it didn't last long.

Bodies slammed into him, and they all tumbled down. Two against twenty were never winnable odds. But their weapons were useless in a dogpile, no room to pull back or swing, and William's mail protected him. The hairy man on top of him struggled to leverage his sword, while William dug his thumb into the man's neck, just under the jaw, hard enough to break the skin. The man rolled away into the legs of another who tumbled over and cracked his jaw against the stony ground. Then suddenly the swell of men was retreating, they turned from rage to panic. William stayed down, let them run, and watched a few catch crossbow bolts in their backs as they fled. Rolling up, he laughed out loud to see Robin, being carried away safely on the stretcher, aiming a crossbow at the fleeing men. Each successful shot brought forth a rally of cheers from his soldiers, and they held his stretcher dangerously high in salutation, breaking into an old victory song and carrying him up and out of the plaza and out of sight.

William climbed to his feet and took in the carnage. *It was a fucking mess.* Scrambling toward him was the boy Craton, though he wasn't as young as William remembered.

"Call a return."

"What?" Craton seemed to forget what the words meant.

"*Return*. Now."

Craton nodded, unslung a horn, and blew the notes, loud, that were meant to bring the soldiers back to the line. Not a retreat, a return. Retreat may have caused them to panic, but return meant it was safe.

Slowly the soldiers arrived again in the plaza, trickling in from the alleyways of its perimeter. Their white tabards streaked with blood, swords still out and shining of gore. Every one of them grinning so wide their heads could have split the fuck off.

They walked through the center of the yard, stepping over bodies with no care. A chorus of stories rose, each one of the returning men telling a tale to a soldier who had stayed behind, most of them embellished to godlike prowess. William kept silent, looked down at the collection of dead civilians around them.

He counted which ones were his.

He counted again, in case he had missed one.

Nine lives, nine souls, still dripped off his sword. These weren't soldiers. He doubled the number, that was how many parents would grieve. He tripled it, the number of siblings. And children. They suffered for no reason, caught up in a fight they didn't understand, unnecessary casualties of someone else's war.

It was the way William's brothers had died.

Some still wriggled their last throes, and he couldn't watch. He turned to catch up with Robin's stretcher.

NINE

ROBIN OF LOCKSLEY

ACRE

Consequences were stupid things.

Just as easily as the tip of a sword stripping a man of his life, the arrow through Robin's leg changed everything. It had sliced right behind the bone, through the calf muscle. Robin braced himself from the quivering pain as the doctor dressed the wound, a thick tarry salve pressed into the open skin on both sides just before the muslin wrappings went on. It would be a hell of a recovery, and it wouldn't take place here.

"Richard's sending me home," Robin told his friend.

"Thank God, I can't stand you." William cocked an eyebrow at the leg. "You can't travel like that."

"Not yet. In a few weeks. But I'll be limping for months, so I won't be much use as a body double like this." He'd be likely to change the king's moniker from *Lionheart* to *Clubfoot*.

"I think he may be done with the double-work," William said gravely.

Robin had guessed the same thing. He had only allowed Robin to wear the crown at the surrender because the king had to be present, and Richard was too sick. "Because of the messenger?"

"Because of the messenger," William confirmed. Ever since Saladin had shown his hand, Richard had grown increasingly suspicious of those around him. Perhaps that was exactly what Saladin wanted. "But the army will be here for a month, at least. Why not recover here?"

"Oh, I don't get to 'recover' at all. He wants me to investigate what happened to the missing supplies," Robin answered, echoing what Richard had told him.

"They're probably at the bottom of the sea with the last ones," William humphed.

"Probably. But Richard wants to be certain. Worried that someone at home may be trying to sabotage him." It didn't feel right. At first, the order had struck Robin as sharply as the arrow. Returning to England early felt like he was being dismissed, that he was abandoning his duties while there was still tremendous work and danger in front of them. But Richard would not be persuaded. Fear told Robin he was being used, sent off to die the way Richard had tried to send Ferrers. Or perhaps this was just another of Richard's spontaneous decisions that held little backing. Either way, there was no arguing against the king once his mind was made.

Robin was bedridden for nearly a week before he could put weight on his leg at all. Much of that time was spent in the same room as Richard, recuperating from whatever sickness had taken him. *Arnaldia* was its name according to the doctor, a haunted man who spoke his own opinion too freely. *Arnaldia—God's curse.* After Richard's recovery, Robin had made a point to ask the doctor, *"If the sickness was God's curse, does this mean Richard is stronger than God?"*

"Every man," the doctor had sighed deeply, *"is stronger than God."*

During that week of recovery, Robin and Richard spoke of many things—including the oddity of commanding a war without being able to see it. The opulence of the tower room was at odds with the poverty outside. It was hard to marry the stories of death with the luxury of their makeshift hospital. Every so often, the barons said, another pocket of insurgents would strike somewhere in the city. Richard listened to the casualties with little reaction. "They say a king is responsible for everyone in his kingdom. The care for every man, every woman, every child, should weigh on the king as if they were his kin. Have you heard this?"

"I have," Robin coughed.

"*They* say it. Who is *they*? Which great king said this? Which of the mighty Roman philosophers passed along this truth down through the centuries to me? How many generations of men have carried it on their tongues in the hope of it someday reaching my ears, that I would be made a better man and king for knowing it? And do you suppose it changed at all in that time? Perhaps women were not included until a mother added it. Has it changed languages, do you suppose? I would think it must have. Some languages have a hundred different words for family, and half of them are insults. And I am to treat all my people as my own family. My kin. What is kin? Which word was this bastardized from?"

"Does it matter?" Robin answered.

The king's eyes sharpened with alarming precision. "I'll tell you why it matters, because it was never spoken by a king. It came from men who would never rule, and never could. To be truly responsible for every last person, it would drive a man mad. It's not a possible thing. How many men died here today? In the last month? Would I send my own family to their death in such a way? Of course not."

"You'd send John," Robin smiled, knowing the caustic relationship the king had with his youngest brother.

"Yes!" Richard laughed sharply, fighting through a cough to stand. "I would send John. But only because it would do him some good."

Robin considered Richard's words, and the difference between a king's family and anyone else's. It was no wonder he took offense to the phrase. Richard and his brothers—Geoffrey, Henry, and John—had all loved their dear father so much they tried to kill him. Their father eventually died without any help at all from his children, and Geoffrey and Henry had also been killed off in one creative manner or another. In a royal family, *kin* meant *threat*. If Richard were to treat every one of his vassals as family, then . . . well, then that would actually explain quite a bit of his behavior.

But frankly, Robin agreed with Richard. He certainly didn't want to be held responsible for his own family, either. It was senseless to be bound to another person, to be obliged by their mistakes, for the mere coincidence of being related. True bonds, such as the one he shared with William, were earned.

A week after being able to walk again, Robin was well enough to travel. He had desperately hoped Richard would change his mind, but been disappointed as usual. Robin would leave the war as a cripple chasing a diplomatic waste of time. There was, however, one bright bit of news.

"I'm coming with you," William de Wendenal said with a grin, pulling his pack onto his shoulders.

"Bullshit," was all Robin could say. "Why? You're not injured."

"King's orders."

"Why send us both?" Robin couldn't understand it. "There are any of a dozen lords he'd happily be rid of, but we're valuable to him."

"Those lords would be happy to go back." William shrugged. "Perhaps he's sending us because he knows we don't want to go. Or perhaps to keep each other honest."

"Well damn," Robin said. "That means we're going to have to actually investigate the missing supplies."

William snorted. "Did you have something else in mind?"

"Ride a mile north, set up camp for a month, then ride back and say we couldn't find anything?"

"That sounds helpful."

"We're helpful *here,*" Robin said, more seriously. "But something tells me you're going to insist that we actually see this one through."

"You're right as always." William slapped his back. "Richard needs someone he can trust to fix this. Whether I care to admit it or not, you and I are the smartest people here. Which means we can make short work of it, and get back here before they march for Jerusalem."

Having his closest friend as a companion would make the journey far better, but Robin still felt uneasy at the mission. It would likely be months before they returned to Richard's side.

But those were the consequences.

The damned consequences.

Robin had few goodbyes to give, but made certain to visit the Earl of Derby, William de Ferrers. He had not seen the man at all during his recovery, and wanted to visit him before departing—if only to comment on how lucky he had actually been to not officiate the surrender. But outside the home Ferrers had claimed, Robin was greeted by a group of French men-at-arms who had made themselves quite comfortable. They had been living there, they explained, ever since the ambush. It seemed smaller riots had broken out throughout the city that day, acts of opportunity really. The Frenchmen further explained that Ferrers, whose name they hadn't even known, had been stabbed to death by a young beggar boy, whom they had subsequently cut down and thrown over the breakwall.

Robin closed his eyes and, in the interest of living with himself for the time being, was halfway successful in believing the boy in question wasn't his little Stabhappy.

PART II

WITH ASH AS HIS INK

TEN

ROBIN OF LOCKSLEY

SHERWOOD FOREST, NOTTINGHAMSHIRE
THURSDAY, 3RD DAY OF OCTOBER 1191

To Robin's dismay, it even smelled more like home.

He'd never admit it aloud, but the Sherwood in Nottinghamshire had a comfortable feeling to it. There had been other forests during Robin's time away—the steep prickly spears of Cyprus, or the massive columns in the Holy Land. But nothing like this. The Sherwood was a real forest. Its great oaks rose through the rolling flatlands, a gentle canopy of branches let the sunlight pour in, scattered into ever-changing shafts. Collections of white birch trees broke out in clumps, interspersed with hollies and looming hawthorns. The tall grass was easy to walk through and kind to bare skin. While greens were still visible here and there, the bright colors of autumn now made fiery tips to the sun's fingers. The crisp crackle of fallen leaves underhoof was a welcoming noise. These were the woods Robin had played in as a boy, where he'd learned to hunt, and let girls chase him to steal kisses or more.

"Funny how easily a smell takes you back."

"We'll have plenty of time to smell it."

Aside him on his own horse, William de Wendenal smiled. Their journey had been unnotable but for its length, and the number of times Robin thought he was dying. The wound in his leg refused to heal, at times bloating into oily red roses that dragged Robin into days of fever sleep. They'd sailed most of the way back on an empty cog, the *Haligast,* one of the many merchant vessels in Richard's fleet that made nearly continuous trips back to England. Robin and his injury were as useless as a sack of mealy potatoes, but the *Haligast*'s crew was fortunately hungry for stories of war. Wendenal recounted the ambush in Acre, omitting their participation as doubles for Richard, and the sailors spat obscenities at the rebels and praise for their slaughter. Robin's role was greatly dramatized in William's retelling—he apparently took down a dozen men before the arrow even struck him, and the crossbow bolts he loosed from the stretcher went through one man's neck and into another's. The sailors punched each other as if the glory had been their own, they sang songs, and did not complain that Robin was unable to help on deck. When the winds were idle they rowed, though Robin was too weak to help there, either. He felt a waste of a man while the others worked mercilessly, but William's help kept any scorn from coming his way.

William let his hair grow since they'd left Acre, already sporting the makings of a beard. But Robin continued to groom himself clean to best match Richard—partially out of habit, partially because he did not want to grow comfortable being away. For here he was amongst the yellow leaves of the Sherwood, his leg numb but healing, and the thought of dragging their mission out longer than necessary was no stranger to his mind. Perhaps Richard had sent William along for this very reason. Easy enough to lie to oneself and turn deserter when no one would know, but admitting as much to a brother was to own one's cowardice.

They said goodbye to the *Haligast* at Plymouth, then spent a few days hopping short rides from dock to dock speaking with harbor masters and sailors, investigating the shipments that had passed through in the recent weeks. Eventually their search took them all the way up to Grimsby, a city whose name matched its pleasantness. According to the caravan captain there, the main supplies from Derbyshire, Leicestershire, Rutland, and others were first amassed in Nottingham before traveling by the Sherwood Road to Grimsby. And so Nottingham became their destination, and Robin found himself in the forest of the life he'd left behind.

"If this investigation takes us further west, perhaps my family could be of help," William offered. His father was a distinguished lord in Derbyshire, quite close to Nottingham. The Sherwood played its role in William's past as well, and under slightly different circumstances he and Robin could have been childhood playmates. "Have you thought about dropping in on *your* father?"

"I've no need to see him," Robin answered.

Would I could strip you of your name and the titles you have gained from its use, I would not hesitate, his father had written, in his most recent letter. No, there was nothing to be gained at Locksley Castle.

"You and Richard," William chided. "Fathers aren't supposed to be your friend, you know. They're supposed to turn you into a decent person. Which, at risk of paying you a compliment, you are. Does it ever occur to you that your father might have had a hand in that?"

"I'd say I ended up who I am *in spite* of my father, not *because* of him."

"Either way," William tilted an odd smile toward him, "you might want to thank him for it."

"If you're going to judge a man by how well his children turn out . . ." Robin started, but did not finish the thought. William did not know about the violence that Edmond succumbed to, and the world could never be improved by that tale. "Let's just say if that were the case, my father should be in prison."

"Ouch," William reacted. "Now you sound just like Richard. Those are his words in your mouth there. Is that a familiar place for him to be putting things?"

Robin made to kick his friend's shin, and instantly regretted trying. A sharp pain ripped through his calf and he felt the scabs over his wound break open. William laughed himself silly, joining Robin's leg in mockery of his current life. They stopped the horses, and William helped him down to a nearby boulder where he could redress the wound. His breeches were sticky with blood, but it was a relief to have his boot off.

"I knew it would open up on me again."

"Well you got what you deserved."

"We can keep riding, I'll make do."

"Don't bother. We're right by the river here, and we're low on water. I'll go. Perhaps I'll find something that's both thirsty and tasty while I'm at it." William fastened his quiver across his back, picked up his longbow, and pulled his hood over his head, flashing his eyebrows wildly. He hopped off the path, deliberately reminding Robin of how incapable he was of hopping himself.

Robin tended to the joyous task of cleaning out his wound. A quick scouring of the dried blood caused him to invent a few colorful new curses he hoped to remember for later. He chewed out a chunk of a bitter salve he had purchased in Grimsby, and covered the raw area of his skin with it. The strappings he wrapped tighter than normal, but he wanted the wound to set. The pain was bearable, but he knew to keep off it as much as he could.

Returning the remaining tar to the saddlebags, he eyed their letters from King Richard. Sealed with his royal signet, they specified with little flexibility that Robin and William had the authority of the King himself on any matter concerning the transport of war supplies. He wondered if such a letter would buy any praise from his father. Practical omnipotence granted by the King of England—no, somehow even this would be unacceptable to Lord Walter.

A rustle to his left, and Robin's breathing slowed.

He carefully repositioned his arm to keep his bag from shifting, and twisted his head. There, not a dozen paces away, was a surprising visitor. A beautiful stag, its heavy crown of antlers rising proudly from the golden underbrush. Though it was more meat than they could possibly need, and definitely illegal, Robin savored the thought of sitting by the stag's body when William returned from his hunt empty-handed.

His own longbow and quiver were within reach, and a few seconds later he stood and quietly nocked an arrow. He had to reposition himself awkwardly to favor his good leg. The stag's head dropped to graze as the arrow flew, but Robin's aim was high regardless. The animal didn't dart away, but looked casually at Robin as if he acknowledged the attempt and disapproved.

It would seem my father's influence has extended this far, Robin thought, and moved cautiously toward his quarry.

The stag descended the slope away from the main road, down toward the river that had been their sometimes companion throughout the day's journey. Robin slid his hood over his head to keep the sunlight from his eyes, and stalked as best he could with only one boot. This was a pleasure he had not enjoyed in quite some time, and knowing his brother-in-arms William was out there hunting as well instantly brought back a competition he had forged with his real brother in these very woods.

They would steal away, the two of them, shirking responsibilities at the manor to see who could bring back the greater game. Edmond was sloppy but unusually lucky, while Robin had both patience and skill. Even then there were signs that Edmond was *touched,* as his mother described it. She'd died when Robin was only twelve. Nothing but snippets of memories remained—her cold hands, dry, clasped over his own. *"Watch over Edmond. He's touched, but he's your brother."*

He hadn't understood then. Robin would bring home two rabbits, clean kills, and Edmond would bring three—bloodied and beaten beyond recognition, guts ripped apart and useless for anything but flavoring stew.

"I ran out of arrows, so I had to use rocks!" He'd chortle, and it seemed innocent at the time.

The memory brought a pit to his stomach. He had a sudden longing to be elsewhere, back on the *Haligast,* back in Acre, rather than here, alone, in the woods and in the past.

But the forest drew him deeper.

Age had brought confidence for Edmond. He was by all accounts the more handsome of the two, once they reached an age where it mattered. Both boys and girls were drawn to Edmond, his reckless nature mistaken for charisma. He had a way of getting others into no end of mischief, mostly harmless, but occasionally going too far. Theft of a chicken one day, loosing horses the next, then shooting an arrow at Lord Stannington's dog. There was no excuse Edmond gave aside from just having fun. Lord Walter had beaten them both—Edmond for having done it and Robin for not being there to stop it.

There was only so much Robin could do, as a brother. Whenever he gave Edmond a lecture about his wilder side, his brother would apologize and occasionally cry, thanking him for caring. Days or weeks or months would pass and Edmond would be a perfect son and brother. Until something happened, and the cycle would repeat.

Until Marion and Vivian.

The stag was long gone, and Robin blinked away wetness in his eyes. A cloud had obscured the sun, the river water was black, the air cold. The Sherwood was just a collection of trees, and he had work to do. Retracing his steps was a simple thing, and they were best to be on their way as soon as possible. Upon arrival, he eased the weight off his leg and sat on the boulder again, letting his quiver and bow down by the saddlebags.

There was another noise in the woods. William re-emerged, trudging his way back down the path, at exactly the same moment Robin realized the horses were missing.

ELEVEN

WILLIAM DE WENDENAL

SHERWOOD FOREST

THE SCENE BEFORE WILLIAM looked very unlike the one he expected. Robin was there, but where once there had been two useful horses was now an emptiness that could only be described as horseless. Robin mimicked his baffled reaction, as if this sudden change in horse quantity was equally perplexing to him.

"Here's the thing . . ."

"Oh the thing!" William moved closer. "I'm dying to hear the thing."

"The thing is, those horses were wrongfully subjugated by the King."

"Oh they were, were they?"

"Most certainly." Robin presented the empty space proudly. "They hadn't paid their taxes, you see, and the King took them into servitude as payment. I couldn't bear the sight of their slavery. So I set them free, their families are quite happy about it, and I have been anointed the Horse Lord of England."

"I don't believe you. Not because it's the stupidest thing I've ever heard—which it is—but because a real Horse Lord of England would have horses. Whilst you have just lost yours."

"I didn't *lose* the horses . . ."

"Well *I* certainly didn't lose them!" William stuck his arrow in the ground, the small lizard he had skewered flopping down its shaft into the grass. He walked to the spot where, once upon a time, the horses had been. Their rope's knot must have slipped, and the well-traveled road offered no help. He would have to pick a single direction to search, as Robin was in no condition to run after them.

Robin resigned himself. "We'll get new horses in Clipstone."

"*You'll* get new horses in Clipstone."

"*I'll* get new horses in Clipstone. We could hike there in a few hours."

Or longer, William thought, eyeing Robin's leg. Locksley Castle was also only half a day's travel away by foot, and the comforts of a family estate seemed a welcome alternative to begging for help in Clipstone. But that was Robin's call to make. He'd undoubtedly prefer to avoid the embarrassment of a wounded and horseless homecoming.

"Clipstone it is."

"And then we'll get on to Nottingham."

"And then we'll get drunk."

"Agreed, King William." They bowed to each other.

"Agreed, King Robin."

"Did you hear that, Alan?" came a sharp new voice from the woods. "We're amongst royalty!"

A shape that a second ago had been a tree moved silently sideways in a decidedly untreelike manner. William's hand twitched for the sword that was not on his belt. The shape was a boy, or a man, a short boy-man dressed in browns and high black boots, with a cloud of arrogant golden hair, a thick belt, and an offensive grin. Robin's back was to the stranger, but his eyes locked onto something else behind William.

"I didn't realize we had more than one king," said the something else behind William, whose name was very likely Alan. The manboy was unarmed and all smiles, but his eyes were shrewd. It was easy to forget that dangerous men were found all the world over, and William kicked himself for letting his guard down. Undoubtedly a third man had their horses.

"Oh, didn't I mention that I'm a king?" asked the manboy, talking to Alan but slowly circling the rock Robin sat upon.

"You know, you may have, but I couldn't hear you over my own kingliness."

Alan's voice was traveling as well, balancing the blond's movements. They knew what they were doing.

William adjusted as they moved. "I would advise against sneaking up on members of the king's personal guard unannounced."

"Unless you have a reason for this interruption," Robin casually picked up his boot, "I'd suggest you move along, gentlemen."

A chortle came from Alan, still unseen. "The king's personal guard?"

"Which king?"

"Me or him?"

"King Richard the Lionheart." William's tone was all steel, but these two boys didn't seem to be intimidated by authority.

"Lionhard? Never heard of him," the manboy scoffed.

"I thought the king's name was Henry?" Could be they were simply a couple lads having fun with some travelers. Or could be they meant to take everything William and Robin had, which included letters from King Richard granting immunity to its bearer.

They had made a half circle around now, enough that William and Robin traded which one they watched. Alan had a lean, long face and darker olive skin, a young man but without his friend's boylike charm. A brown surcoat over a dirty ivory woolen smock, its hood still draped over his head, the color of the birch trees behind him. A heavy broadsword rode unsheathed in his belt, too heavy for a man of his stature.

"Henry, yes that sounds right! He's the one with his face on all those pretty little pieces of gold we've been finding, isn't it?"

Their circle had tightened, but they were still too far away to make a surprise rush.

Robin smiled and laughed. "Pretty little pieces of gold you've been finding? Why, we must have missed that part of the forest. Your luck is extraordinary!"

"It is! Thank you! You see, whenever we come across a couple of kings like yourself, which seems to happen all the time these days . . ."

"All the time," Alan agreed.

". . . we find more and more gold! Sometime on the ground, sometime in their pockets. Sometime in their hands." The manboy's voice turned grim. "Which we have to pry open."

Alan cocked his head smugly. "Which is why we prefer it to be on the ground."

"And we'd prefer this to happen quickly."

"If you don't mind."

"If you don't mind."

The two were overlapping each other, which might have kept their regular victims disoriented. William and Robin had no trouble tracking the target in front of them.

"Gentlemen," William bluffed, "we are expected at Nottingham Castle by Baron Roger de Lacy." But this name also failed to impress the strangers, who simply cooed and laughed. "This is not a fight you should be picking."

"Woah, now!" Alan stopped moving, a hand to his chest as though deeply offended. "Who said anything about a fight? Will, did you suggest a fight?"

"I never said that word."

William briefly startled to think they knew his name, then realized the manboy was also a Will.

"We were, in fact, downright civil!"

"Until the good king with his boot in his hand . . ." the new Will was on the edge of William's vision again, so once again he and Robin changed targets, ". . . started issuing threats."

"I don't want to get in a fight, maybe they're right," whined Alan.

"Frankly, I'd prefer not to fight as well." Will's circle widened and he bowed deeply. "We sincerely apologize for getting in your way, your royal highnesses."

"Highness . . . es . . ." Alan tried the word.

"Oh wait!"

"Highnessies?"

"I just remembered!" Will danced in a little spin. As he turned, William got a glimpse of his backside—two wide guardless short knives sheathed on his belt, handles protruding in opposite directions. "I actually have a friend who would downright *love* to get in a fight! He's always talking about how much he loves them, isn't he, Alan?"

"There's no need to bother him."

"Now, normally I would agree with you, but these two good gentlemen—"

"*Kings,*" Alan corrected.

"—pardon me, these two good *kings* seem to be begging for a fight! I can't stand them myself, you know. I've always thought simple people should put aside their differences with words, but these kings come from a different lot than we, Alan."

"He has a point."

"He does," Robin agreed with a bemused smirk.

"Then we are all in agreement!"

Will stepped a few paces into the forest and whistled sharply between his fingers, then cupped his hands around his mouth. "Hullo, John!"

Alan winked. "He'll just be a moment."

That was enough. The two young men were looking for coin, and a little bit of it might easily send them on their way. But William barely moved toward his bag before Alan's sword was suddenly close, its point kissing William's chest. He nearly reacted on instinct—he could have disarmed the young man in any of four ways without even thinking about it—but that was a line best not crossed. Whoever John was, he'd be on them soon, and he might have friends. *There's a peaceful way out of this,* William reminded himself, easing away from the steel.

"Maybe you ought to sit down with your friend." Alan's whine was not a suggestion. "After all, there's no need to stand for John. He's not royalty."

"As we are," reminded Will from behind the trees.

"As we are."

William eased down next to Robin, exchanging a quick but knowing glance. "That's an interesting make of blade you have there," Robin said, though it was clearly for William's ears.

William noticed it now, too. Alan held the sword too far away from his own body, he had no leverage to make a thrust if he wanted to attack. His hands were clasped over each other on the hilt, betraying his poor form as well as the signature flared cross pounded into the pommel of the weapon, a design reserved for a Crusader.

Alan smiled. "Family heirloom."

"That blade, along with many just like it, was due to be delivered to King Richard's army not so long ago."

Alan nodded smugly. "I've a large family."

His boots were new, not the beaten footwear of a thief. The white smock underneath the brown surcoat bore the red tips of a Templar cross peeking from its edges. *How bizarrely convenient.* William wondered how many shipments of missing supplies might lie just beyond the treeline.

"Here's my friend now," Will returned, flicking his tongue about needlessly. "Goes by the name of John Little. Don't let his name fool you."

There was indeed no fooling when it came to the size of the man who lumbered out of the woods. He had clearly been left for last intentionally. He stood two full heads taller than little Will, though that wasn't saying much. A pair of great trunks of legs carried him closer, and his heavy barrel of a chest heaved from side to side with each step. Grey fleeced the slope from his chest to chin. In his hands he carried a quarterstaff as impressive in size as he was, more of a small tree than a staff at all, wrapped in dark leather and studded with knobs and cracks.

"Hullo, boys." When he smiled, the prickly grey needles that littered his cheeks stood at attention. "What a beautiful morning, wouldn't you agree? Well enough with the small talk. Why don't you hand over your belongings before I break open your skulls?"

He snapped his hands tight around the quarterstaff, and William swore he heard the wood creak under the pressure. Beside him, Robin did not look nearly as confident as he had a moment ago. They both lowered themselves humbly to the ground, disrobed their belts, and very obviously unbuckled the saddlebags.

The thieves, at least, gave them a wide berth, and William rustled his bag loudly to mask his whisper. "I don't suppose you can run?"

Robin gave a terse shake of his head. "We could fight? Where do you put our chances?"

"They're just trying to scare us. These are bandits, not murderers." If these men had any interest in killing them, it would have happened already. But if they were attacked, that attitude might change.

Still, there were more important things at stake. William eyed Robin and exposed the letters from Richard. "We can't lose these." A couple of thieves with letters of immunity from the king seemed like an epic disaster.

Robin's face turned serious. "Agreed. We'll have to split up."

"I don't like it."

"Nor I, but you have to get those out of here. I'll distract them, you run."

"Hurry up with it," groaned the mighty John Little. "And be sure there aren't any surprises waiting in those bags."

William's mind reeled to think of an alternative. "I won't go far. I'll wait for you down by the river."

"No, don't stop. Go all the way to Clipstone."

"What if you get in trouble? Your leg . . ."

"I'll get there eventually. As you said, they don't mean to hurt us."

A twig bounced off Robin's cheek, and the young Will threw another at William, darting his tongue out. "What are you two whispering at?"

"Just arguing about which one of you is more handsome." William smiled.

The young thief smiled back. "John, tell us again what it was you were thinking of doing with their skulls?"

Time was up, and the mountainous man again demanded their belongings, which his two companions hustled forward to collect.

With only the slightest nod, Robin and William moved in symmetry. William slipped his body low and grappled Alan's legs, hoisting him up to flip head over heels onto his back. Beside him, Robin swung the heft of his saddlebag into the chin of the blond boy, then pulled him down.

Careful, William thought, *don't hurt them too badly.* But he did not dally. He heaved himself up and away, shouldering his saddlebag and pushing off to the south as fast as he could.

With luck he might come across the horses and return to heroically save the day, but he was just as likely to be ambushed by more of the thieves' gang. He could not risk the latter. He braved one glance backward, but had already lost sight of Robin. Alan, however, was back on his feet and giving chase.

William controlled his breath for a long run and focused on the terrain. A tiny dark doubt in his gut screamed guilt at him for abandoning Robin to the mercy of these bandits, but this was Robin's plan after all. Odds were they'd be drinking and laughing about this within hours.

Either way, it was a fitting punishment for Robin having lost the damned, damned horses.

TWELVE

ROBIN OF LOCKSLEY

SHERWOOD FOREST

STARING AT THE YOUNG brat Will, who was rolled into a ball and clutching his head, Robin decided against all reason to run away. He had not meant for Will's skull to collide with the boulder, but he was certain that an apology would not protect him from John Little's massive quarterstaff. Fortunately the brute took a moment to tend to his friend's injury, and Robin did not intend on being punished for it. Despite his shin, he knew he could navigate the forest better than the giant, so he hopped away from the road and down the slope on one leg.

The grass grew longer as he made it closer to the river, wide and shallow here. His limping made a terribly sloppy noise of it all, but he hoped the water and softer ground would hide his movement. He only needed to hide long enough for the man to outlive his anger. Robin sloshed on, though certain pockets in the ground turned out to be deep and his good boot was now soaked through, and it hurt fierce to pull his injured leg out of the mud whenever it sank in.

When the land flattened out again, the huge bear man was simply standing there waiting.

John Little barreled forward with surprising speed, and Robin's stomach lurched at the inevitable impact. But it didn't come, and instead the quarterstaff slung wide toward him, too short, and Robin slapped it as it passed and grabbed at its other end with both hands. The brute slammed his shoulder full into Robin, and he dropped into the water trying to move with the blow. He rolled, out of the mud, deeper into the river where movement was slower but the ground was even. Breaking the water between a few nearby rocks was a thick, straight birch branch, which Robin pried free and turned to defend himself.

Little was close, but not advancing. He squinted, letting Robin get his bearings, the way a man might watch a child learning to walk.

"Nice stick."

"Stick, you say?" Robin gave the branch a few practice swings, feeling its heft in his hands. It couldn't have been riverborne for long, as its core was strong rather than rot. He could flourish it well enough to look like he knew what he was—

Little's staff swung heavy and down to Robin's left. He caught it, *just barely,* with the north pole of his branch, and instinctively he swung back with the south, *too obviously,* Little was there as well. They traded two more snaps at each other, but there wasn't enough weight behind the blows to push Robin down. *He's toying with me.* His hood was loose around his neck, and he tried to swing it around his back again. *He's toying with me and he'll win that way.*

"Seems perhaps we had the same teacher, my friend."

"Same teacher, you say?"

Round the staff came again, on the opposite side, and Robin's leg screamed as he pivoted. High and low he managed to block the next flurry of blows, until Little swept broad and flat. Robin avoided one end only to have the other crack his side. The scaled plates in his leather vest kept his ribs from breaking, but only barely. He rolled away with the force of the blow, stumbling down into the water. He had to push up to his elbows just to keep his head above its surface. Cold water flooded him, refreshing and brisk, but it would weigh him down.

Little passed his weapon from hand to hand, smiling, beside himself. "This is my game!"

"Alright, alright," Robin admitted, a hand out, begging for time. *Time is all you need,* to give William a chance of escape. Robin didn't need to win this fight, he could take a little beating in exchange for William's safety. He spat mud from his mouth. *Or you could kick this oaf's ass—that would be a fine alternative.*

Robin clambered to his feet again, wheezing for breath, wondering why his opponent didn't need to do the same. Bigger lungs, he supposed.

"I think I've got a handle on you now."

Little laughed. "Do you, now?"

Robin nodded and moved forward, spinning his branch elaborately behind his back, then suddenly jabbing out. The ogre flinched away and retuned a volley of lashes on both sides that Robin struggled to keep up with.

Pay attention, Robin, he's telling you where he's striking. The man's eyes gave away his next target, and he pulled back too far each time, giving Robin the opportunity to block. Even still, the next one he stopped sent a painful shock through his forearms. The sheer power of each attack could break his wrists if he took it the wrong way. Then the butt of Little's staff clipped forward unexpectedly and smashed into Robin's sternum.

He was in the water again and the world was blurry and dark.

"That was fancy," his better was saying, trying to swing his staff behind his own back, but his arms were stubby and his body quite the obstacle. Instead he settled for waving it around childishly, entertaining himself, mocking Robin, "You a court jester?"

"You have no idea," Robin coughed, and why he was on his feet again he wasn't sure. He picked his branch up, fighting the massive pain across his chest. He breathed, then again, stretching his ribs. The pain was there but nothing felt broken.

"Alright, let's go again."

Little raised his eyebrows and laughed, so Robin laughed, and then they both laughed harder, and when Little attacked it was the same lunge he'd used before. Robin feigned hard away and slapped his branch up and quick onto John's knuckles, then fast around to bury the south end into his exposed armpit. As the massive quarterstaff fell to the water, Robin pushed the middle of his branch up, up fast and hard into Little's nose, which gave way, blood popping out each side. Little's lumbering weight toppled backward into the river with a crack and a heavy splash, and Robin was quick to follow. He raised his weapon, wanting to smash it down again, to give back some of what he'd taken.

But Little's battered face was wrought with blood and defeat, his hands out in surrender. The water rushed over his shoulders and into his mouth.

Robin's muscles tensed.

Edmond would keep swinging. Beat him bloody.

He blinked it away, and let the branch dangle loosely from his hand.

His head was buzzing, his right eye was swollen though he didn't remember taking the injury. But even with water still clearing from his ears, he realized there was another noise in the melee. Sharp steel touched his back, *just so,* between the plates in the leather, just hard enough to keep him off balance.

"Let's be perfectly clear on what's about to happen," the recovered Will breathed through his words. "I'm going to tell you to surrender, and you're going to turn and attack me, because you think you're that fellow who always outsmarts his enemies. But you're not that fellow, see? I'm that fellow. I'll sink one knife through your ribs and the other where your neck meets your shoulder, then I'll wash your blood off my blades in the river, have a very nice lunch, and forget about you and my morning entirely."

Robin couldn't see behind him, couldn't tell if the knife was in Will's left or right hand. If he picked correctly he could turn quickly enough. If he picked poorly it would go just as described.

Below, Little's hand touched Robin's leg, softly. He looked scared, his big eyes locked hard. No longer a giant, he was just an old man stuck in a river. Little gave a curt shake of his head, a warning that said, *Don't.*

Robin hadn't dropped the branch yet. "You're a cocky little thing."

"I know when I'm right."

"You do this a lot, I imagine?" Eyes still on John, who squinted at him and nodded his head harder, telling him to drop the branch. "Not a bad living if you can keep it up?"

"Stalling to catch your breath?"

"Most people don't put up too much of a fight? Aren't expecting it?"

"I'm hungry." This one was a threat. Robin looked down, hoping for a shadow or reflection to give away Will's stance, but he was just a whisper in Robin's ear and a knife in his back, nothing more.

"Unfortunately, I've actually traveled quite a distance just to find you," Robin said. "Didn't think you'd make it easier by coming out and greeting me like this."

"What does the king's personal guard want with me? Recruitment?" Will's blade wasn't the only thing that was sharp. He had remembered one of the first things they'd said, even after a painful blow to the head. *This may not end well,* Robin realized.

He decided to turn left.

"Now hold your say a moment," John interrupted, and started the labor of rising to his feet. "Seems we're at a bit of a misintroduction. What was your name?"

Robin hesitated, but was fairly certain William had already said it aloud earlier. There was no point in lying. "Robin," he said, intentionally leaving out his surname.

"You say you know King Richard?"

"Well enough," Robin answered cautiously.

Little wiped some blood from his nose and let the water take it. "You a knight?"

Definitely not. Knights are worth ransoms. "No, an archer."

Something important passed between John and Will.

From behind, Will's voice. "Your name's Robin, and you're an archer in the war." It wasn't a question. Robin had given up only two bits of information, but they knew exactly who he was. He felt very much at a disadvantage, mostly because he was.

But John just shook his head. His dark green tunic clung desperately to his skin, the fur lining his collar now matted black. "Scarlet, stow your metal."

There was hesitation. "They're not satisfied yet."

"Stow them." The edge disappeared from the small of Robin's back. A few splashes meant Will, or Scarlet, was retreating to the banks. Little tugged on Robin's branch and forced his help in rising, then chucked the branch into the middle of the river where it quietly floated downstream.

They moved out of the water, slowly. "You're a long way from the war," John said.

Scarlet's knives were sheathed again, but he kept his distance, hands on their hilts. "He's a long way from the truth, I'd say. Here . . ." he reached down and gingerly selected an arrow from Robin's quiver, which he must have brought along. *But he'd opted to approach with his knives rather than use the bow. Must be a poor shot.* "For your life, I'll bet you couldn't hit that oak from here."

The tree he pointed to wasn't an oak, and would have been an easy shot for any novice bowman. Robin made a show of thinking about the challenge, then snapped the arrow in half over his knee. He cast the pieces away into the shallows. "I'm not here to fight."

"I'll bet he's a deserter."

"I'm not a deserter, but there are plenty of men who are. The army's supplies are dwindling. Weapons, food, supplies aren't making it to the men. Specifically those coming through Nottingham. We figured it might be the Sheriff, hoarding and keeping it all—"

This seemed to touch a nerve, for Will at least. "Oh, it's definitely the Sheriff. Let's deal then. We'll let you go, and in return you can kill the Sheriff to your heart's content."

Robin almost laughed out loud. "Kind enough, excepting three things. First, I wouldn't be *killing* the Sheriff, that's not really quite sane."

"Pity."

"Second, and more importantly, is that *you're* the ones stealing the supplies, yes? Not the Sheriff at all."

Little frowned. Soggy and sopping, blood flowing pink into his grey moustache and beard, he had lost all his ferocity. "A solid point. And the third?"

"The third? Well, the third being it wouldn't be *you* letting *me* go," Robin did his best here to stand tall, and he hoped his soaked and tousled garments didn't make him look unusually foolish, "it would be *me* letting *you* go." After a moment without reaction, their mutual laughter told him he looked precisely as ridiculous as he felt.

"We're your prisoners then?" asked Little.

"That's right."

"That's right. Alright. Alright." Little turned and moved back toward the river, plodding his way through the water to dip his hands beneath its surface and wash his face off. His beard was still pink, and he motioned for Robin to follow.

"Come on, now!" Will picked up the quiver and the saddlebag, too, already hopping after his friend.

They made no effort to bind him or drag him along like a proper hostage, nor did they need to. He was wet and injured. They had his weapons, his food, *and his horses.* If they meant to ransom him to his own father, then they were at least invested in keeping him alive. That was more than he could say for the next traveler who might find advantage in his obvious vulnerabilities, were he to try to run.

So Robin limped forward, following their lead.

Besides, he told himself, *they were potentially leading him directly to the missing supplies.*

That reasoning made it feel less like a surrender, but only a little.

THIRTEEN

WILLIAM DE WENDENAL

NOTTINGHAM CASTLE

"Come inside," grumbled a voice with a grinding cough, and William was escorted through a small uneven door into a space something closer to a privy than a sheriff's office.

The room was tiny, which William did not find surprising given its location at the top of the tallest keep in the castle, but it was certainly an unexpected size for its occupant's esteem. The cramped stony walls angled oddly, as if threatening to crumple. Only one small shuttered window let in some crisp air and the setting sun's last glow, but the two walls beside it were lined with candles, dripping long tails of wax down to the floor. There were shelves built into the stones filled with scrolls and books that had no discernable order. Behind the desk, awkwardly placed and entirely too large for the wall, an unflattering portrait of the Sheriff glowered down upon the living one.

Baron Roger de Lacy had a long face and sunken cheeks, which William assumed was the cumulative look of a man who had spent his life scowling. William's first thoughts were unkind. Perhaps the sheriff was a private, squirrelish old man who enjoyed such cramped quarters, but to William this would be a prison cell.

"Baron," barked the captain, a stiff man who was skeptical of William's story. "Pardon the urgency."

"No need," de Lacy waved off the apology. He cleared his throat and rose from his table, a slab of rough wood covered in papers and small ornate boxes. His eyes sharpened harshly, as if he would prefer to deduce William's existence for himself.

"I bring word from King Richard—" William started, but the captain cut him off.

"He claims he's with the king's private guard."

"I have letters that prove as much—"

"He carries letters to that effect, but their seals are broken."

"They were damaged—"

The baron quelled the explanation with another wave of his hand, continuing to scrutinize William. Roger de Lacy's eyes were skull deep, his skin thin. He wore a heavy furred robe but no jewels or rings, and his grey-brown hair stuck clumsily to his head in an unimportant way.

"Do I recognize you?" he asked.

"William de Wendenal. We met once." Truth be told, William could hardly remember anything more than a name. He had been grieving for his brothers then, and de Lacy had been only one of several judiciars involved in his family's compensation.

A justice disinterested in justice, his father had complained.

De Lacy's eyes lit up, seeming to recall a different version of the same story. "Ah yes, I thought so. Lord Beneger's son. You've . . . grown, haven't you?"

William had no interest in small talk, no luxury of getting comfortable. Robin was still in danger, and time continued its rude march.

The captain fidgeted. "He demanded an audience, Baron. I refused him due to the late hour—"

"Yes, thank you, Gisbourne, your irritation has not gone unnoted. Go on now. I'm sure you have other people to harass."

Gisbourne bristled for a moment, then nodded obediently. His men lowered William's weapons and saddlebag to the ground, drawing a bit of attention in trying to find an available space for them.

"I'll be close," Gisbourne promised as he shut the door behind them.

"I'd like to say he means well," de Lacy stared through the door's thick planks, "but I'm a poor liar."

The Sheriff seemed instantly more at ease with the door closed, alone but for the two of them. William took the opportunity to push. "Baron, I come with an urgent matter from King Richard himself."

"How is your father?" De Lacy leaned over the desk to clasp both hands on William's shoulders, looking deeply into his face.

The question caught him off guard, because he didn't know. Writing casual letters simply wasn't a part of their relationship. "Well, when last I heard," he said. "Which was some time ago."

"Good. Good." Roger fingered a decanter on the table, and began pouring two glasses. "Sit, drink some wine. How long will you stay? Will you need lodgings?"

"I . . . may." He fought to hide his agitation. "This is somewhat urgent, Baron."

"Unless you mean to make love to me," the Baron offered, "then I doubt it. I have been alive significantly longer than you, William, and I have never known anything else to qualify as *urgent* after dinner." He paused, then added, "Except urination. That's a new one. Strange thing, the human body, it forgets how to do the simplest tasks as it ages."

"Yes." William blinked. "Baron."

"Drink."

William was admittedly ravished. He had barely stopped all day. After being certain he had outrun the young thief Alan in the Sherwood, he doubled back overland to search for Robin. The site of their encounter was deserted, and offered no signs of what had happened. Pure chance had brought him two mounted members of the Nottingham Guard, who were themselves returning home. Skeptical at first, they eventually took his cause as their own, even going so far as to ride to Clipstone first in hopes that Robin had found his way there. The loan of a third horse made their afternoon faster, though the sun was setting by the time they reached the sprawling city of Nottingham. Exhausted as he was, William was still ready to lead a search party for Robin immediately.

But if the Sheriff insisted on sharing wine first, he would have to abide. De Lacy took a long slow draw from his cup and patted his lips together, a miniature applause for a drink well done. William drank second, out of courtesy, but mid-pull, the Sheriff spoke. "So. You're here to talk about stolen supplies."

William choked to answer. "I am."

"They've been missing for months. How confident are you with your understanding of the word *urgent*?"

He took the insult, it wasn't worth fighting back. "I need your assistance. I was traveling with a friend, another member of the royal guard. We were separated, and he may be held captive by outlaws who waylaid us in the forest."

"That's unfortunate." De Lacy's concern seemed earnest, if detached. "I doubt they'll hurt him. They'll take his things and let him loose. But I'll have Gisbourne arrange scouts to go out at first light to find him."

William glanced out the window at the fading light, and realized with some disappointment there was little else he could hope for. Robin would be on his own for the night. "Thank you."

"Of course. Now then, your war supplies. Say whatever it is you've come to say. Then you can tell Richard himself you tried your best before being sent away empty-handed." De Lacy smiled and moved toward the door. "Do you mind if I step out while you talk? I hardly see the need for me to be here. Just talk at the painting if you wish, and tell Richard I listened."

This, fortunately, was familiar territory. William could win at a game of sarcasm, and he had already practiced this conversation during the ride. "Baron," he composed himself, shifting his mindset to the matter at hand, "King Richard doubts either your loyalty, or your ability. Could you tell me which one it is?"

De Lacy's jaw tightened. "Both are beyond reprisal."

"With respect, your king disagrees. If you are indeed loyal, then you are apparently incapable of securing your trade routes. Or if you *are* capable, you must be complicit in their disappearance. I don't see a third option."

"Oh, your simplicity is impressive." De Lacy wet his lips. "Very well, I'm either impertinent or incompetent. Let him appoint someone else as Sheriff. I never wanted this post in the first place. You can have it, if you think obedience is its only requirement. However, in six months' time Richard will send a replacement for you as well, because it's not *my* intelligence that starves his army."

"I'm not here to replace you—"

"The people are hurting." Roger de Lacy had a ferocity to him now, which raised the hair on the back of William's neck. "Richard raised the taxes, you know. He sold everything he could and some things he couldn't, all to fund his precious Crusade. The *Saladin tithe* he called it, to a country of hard-working people who can't even comprehend who a Saladin is. What is the result? Some of them pay, yes. They pay, starve, die, and then stop paying. Others don't pay at all. So we don't actually increase our coffers because it more or less balances itself out. To which Richard brilliantly replies, *'Well . . . raise the taxes again!'*"

William swallowed. "Baron, I respect the difficulties of your office, I do, and I did not come here to insult them. I have nothing to say as to taxes. But I crossed your county line this morning, and I already know more about Richard's missing supplies than you do. I don't know if you are aware of this, or if you even heard what I said earlier, but there is a gang of outlaws in the Sherwood Forest operating with, apparently, wanton freedom."

De Lacy emptied his cup and his countenance changed, the anger gone as if never there. All his harsh features shifted into a grandfatherly smile, sharing some secret between them. "Have you looked at my face, William?"

William tried not to sigh. "What am I looking for?"

"Do you see all the scars, all the little broken chunks of wood embedded in my flesh?" He leaned in close that William could see him better, but there was nothing but wrinkles and veins. "No? That's interesting. So William, do you know why my face remains unscarred and *unembedded* with little broken chunks of wood?"

"No."

"It is because I do not regularly make a habit of ramming my own face into this table here," he cleared away a small section of papers to show its thick, craggy surface, lowering his face so that they almost touched, "even when it otherwise sounds like an excellent idea. And do you know why I do not regularly ram my face into this table?"

"Do tell."

"*Because I'm not an idiot.*" Now he stood, curiously taller than before. "I am well aware of the brigands in the Sherwood, I know precisely what they have taken from the king, and I know that I have a foot at the end of each of my legs. I hope you did not travel this far to tell me things of which I already have intimate knowledge."

"I have not," William bit back, refusing to be patronized. "I have come because I have friends in the war who don't have a sword to fight with. And as I traveled home to fix this problem, the man who stole these very swords assaulted me in the forest! You'll forgive me if I find the solution to this problem *glaringly obvious!*"

"Glaringly obvious," de Lacy repeated the words, rolling them in his mouth as if he were tasting the wine. "My apologies, but I don't see it. You want me to . . . what, go out and . . . go out and *get them?*"

William stared back. "In as many words, yes."

"Let's explore that, shall we? We have a displaced group of peasants living in the forest, who on occasion steal some warbound supplies for their own use. What is the appropriate response?"

It was almost shocking that William had to put this into words, so he used short ones, and carefully. "You stop them."

"Ah," de Lacy seemed to love the answer, "Captain Gisbourne thinks the same thing, that we ought to kill them all. And William, would that appease the king?"

"If you stop the thieving, you restore the supply chain, and the army is fed."

"Yet it is not my duty to feed the army," de Lacy countered, "it is my duty to enforce justice. Would this be justice, to kill these outcasts?" His fingers graced a book on a shelf—a Bible, by William's guess. "*'You have heard that it was said, An eye for an eye, a tooth for a tooth.'* Lex talionis. Do you consider this to be a fair enough principle?"

Another time, with less at stake, William would have relished the discussion. Instead he aimed for simplicity. "In many circumstances, yes."

De Lacy tapped the edge of the book. "Then by what right would we take their lives? They haven't killed anyone, and I have no intention of making them feel they should! By justice, what we should do is take back what they've stolen. But by all rational means, we stole it first with these ridiculous taxes! They did not start this. We did. Or rather, King Richard did! I'd say we're lucky they haven't killed anyone yet—they would certainly be in their right mind to do so."

William wasn't sure what to say. "You make apathy sound like a virtue."

"Apathy?" One bushy eyebrow jolted upward. "You haven't been listening."

"It's easy for you to stay out of it," William continued, "because the ramifications of your inaction are currently half the world away." But William had seen it with his own eyes, he'd counted the bodies. "What of the king's army? Without supplies, our soldiers desert. Or die. Richard's army is dwindling, the war failing."

"I will not . . ." the Sheriff's finger trembled, crooked and pointing at William, ". . . *aggravate* them. Leave these outcasts to their own, and they'll soon realize there's no great opposition. They're poorly organized, they won't last through the winter. This shall pass. If a few shipments get lost traveling through the Sherwood, so be it. If your war's success is bound to that which gets lost in my forest, it had no hope to begin with."

"Perhaps I ought to join these rebels," William said glibly. "Sounds as though they're paid better than I am."

De Lacy ignored the comment. "You've come a long way, William, not because Richard needs supplies, but because he doesn't like to lose. His hubris is not worth bloodshed at home. I will not allow it."

William sighed, at a loss for words. De Lacy's attitude implied that the matter was settled, but William could wait to sway the man's politics. Robin was better at dealing with politicians, and he could fix this once he made it to Nottingham. "A matter for another time, then. I should get some rest, for tomorrow's search."

"Indeed." De Lacy dismissed him with a wave. "Gisbourne will arrange the details. Your missing companion, what was his name?"

"Robin of Locksley."

The room itself shifted, so obvious was the Sheriff's unease at the name. William's hair stood on end. It was as if he had uttered some arcane spell, which had the power to change men's minds. "Do you know him?"

"No," answered de Lacy, carefully. "But I've had dealings with his father. When we first raised the taxes, Lord Walter of Locksley was one of the first to bear complaint. He gathered quite a bit of support over time, and what followed was . . . less than desirable."

It had not occurred to William that Robin's surname might be a liability in this area. If his captors learned his identity, they might choose to exploit him. Whatever guilt William already carried for leaving his friend behind suddenly multiplied, and threatened to mutiny.

"I can lead your captain to the place I last saw him. We'll need a formidable host for a search party."

"I doubt I have so many to spare. But we'll send what we can." De Lacy was distracted, picking at papers on the table, and whispered the name *Locksley* again. Then he stood and leaned close to William, speaking softly as if someone else might be listening. "The weapons that are missing. If you're able to reclaim them, do so. Ask for a man named John Little. He should be reasonable."

"He's the reasonable one?" William coughed. "He offered to smash my skull."

"But do not hurt anyone," de Lacy added quickly. "No arrests, no fights. A peaceful solution, understood?"

William nodded slowly, unsure what had changed the man's mind.

The Sheriff opened the doorway, then looked back from the corners of his eyes. "Roger de Lacy, do you like that name?"

Baffled, William quietly agreed that it was a fine name. De Lacy held his gaze with a curious smile, judging him for something William couldn't understand. After a short groan that could have easily been acceptance or disapproval, he was gone through the doorway, closing it behind him. Only one de Lacy remained—painted, framed, and scowling on the wall—offering William exactly as many answers as its human counterpart.

FOURTEEN

ROBIN OF LOCKSLEY

SHERWOOD FOREST

THE GOING WAS SLOW, overland with no identifiable path. His two captors stayed far enough ahead to avoid conversation, leading their newly stolen horses. Will Scarlet kept disappearing into the woods while John Little plodded along firmly, but both had to stop frequently to wait for Robin and his limp to catch up. They had given him a pack to shoulder in case he wasn't already slow enough, while they carried little more than his weapons. After some time the two of them squabbled with each other, on and off for an hour, after which their route changed into something decidedly more circular. If they thought to disorient Robin with their confusing path, they had doubly wasted their time.

Eventually Robin's body grew accustomed to its pains, and they gave him plenty of chances to rest. Along the way they checked dozens of snares but found only a single rabbit, and they even spent a bit of time fishing in the river. Robin offered to help just to keep them moving, which they refused and insisted—with unkind words—that he keep his mouth shut. John Little dozed off for an hour while Scarlet kept watch over Robin, sharpening his blades in an obvious but effective attempt to appear intimidating. They even lost some time chasing after one of the horses, which Robin found endlessly ironic but was forbidden to say aloud. The sun had nearly disappeared over the horizon by the time they finally came to their destination, at which point Little left them behind and they waited even longer.

Eventually, the man returned and led Robin into a clearing that sprawled wide and flat. Long grass swayed in a breeze that found its way from the other side, between which were twenty or thirty ramshackle tents. They were dirty and flapping about, each one built shoddier than the last, as though he'd come across some great contest of incompetence. Here and there were empty fire rings, skinny dogs chasing after each other, and a gathering of people faring only slightly worse than their tents. They clustered around a great oak tree, standing alone in the middle of the clearing, its massive low branches reaching out and down, either protecting or eating the people beneath. A crowd had already begun to gather.

"If you still see yourself as having the upper hand," John said, "thought you'd want to meet the rest of your prisoners. Hope you don't mind the imprisonment of women, children, and men of the cloth amongst."

He spoke true enough. This was no gang of thieves, not the rogue band of mercenaries Robin expected. Old men, backs crooked and skin tanned bronze, women carrying bundles of canvas and straw, children who were too skinny, and men who were little better.

A young girl with inky dark hair, braided with twine and trinkets, came running and flung herself into Will's arms. A sister, Robin guessed, until she gave him a kiss that said anything but. On second look, she was not as young as he'd thought, just small, and Robin forced himself to look elsewhere when he realized they were still kissing.

"Who'd you catch, darling?" she asked loudly, though her lips were still only inches from Will's. "Someone important?"

"Apparently so."

"All on your own?"

"Well Alan ran off, and John spent some time swimming, so yes, all on my own."

"I had no doubt."

She bit his lip and tugged it, cocking an eyebrow at Robin. Dark, almond eyes, paired against smooth white skin. *Lucky boy.*

"My apologies to all!" John called out, settling the crowd. "We knew this time would come. I'm afraid we are but surrendered!"

This was met with a variety of animated reactions, none of which seemed to take it seriously. Any fear that Robin had of being held captive or ransomed had vanished at the edge of the glen, but neither were the tables reversed. He wished William was here, he was always better at dealing with people.

"Quiet now, quiet," John calmed the banter. "This here, well he's a friend of the Sheriff."

A bevy of boos and hisses followed as though they were the audience of a Passion play.

"And he's asked for our captivation. So we've had a good time, but it seems this here is the end." He turned to Robin, holding his hands out and together as if bound. "Your prisoner, John Little."

"A pleasure to meet you, John," he lied.

"Will Scarlet you've met," he gestured. "That one attached to his side is Elena. You'll be needing a double cell for the two of them. It's awfully hard to keep them separate."

Elena uncurled from Will's chest and poised herself, a limp hand extended toward Robin. "Lady Gamwell will do fine."

"Lady Gamwell." Robin bowed deeply to her, holding her hand ever so gently and giving it a brushed kiss. He could tell she hadn't expected him to play along, but the cold stare from Will was worth it.

"Please tell me you blindfolded him," Elena said, absolutely unamused. Robin had wondered the same thing during their day's travel, but saw no reason to question it.

"We . . . did not," Will answered matter-of-factly. "But the terrain, he would have fallen over every couple of seconds. We would have had to carry him."

"You could have punched him," offered a redheaded man with a sharp face. "You could have punched him until he fell asleep."

"That's not how sleep works, Arthur," Elena scolded.

"And we still would have had to carry him," Will replied. "That literally fixes nothing."

"But you had horses." Elena put her hands on both of Will's cheeks to aim his head at the horses they stole. "You could have blindfolded him and put him on a horse."

Will looked stupefied, and Elena kissed his cheek.

"Love you."

That answers that, Robin thought. They had let him see the way to their camp because *they were idiots.*

The introductions shifted to the redhead Arthur a Bland, and a lean man with long blond hair named David of Doncaster. By quick glance they were the most able-bodied of the group, and they fidgeted at Robin's sides in an effort to appear as though they were guarding him. Both had Crusader swords slung under their belts, with visible rust creeping onto the broad sides. Other men and women nodded in turn as Little named them out, and Robin smiled and looked each in the eye, all while scrutinizing their camp. A row of swords plunged into the ground a few paces apart each, a line strung across their hilts, wet laundry drying over it. Inside a tent, a bedroll was made of rolled Crusader tabards. The charred wood in the campfires wasn't the dark remnants of firewood but of straight boards, crates, and boxes.

Robin picked a random girl in the crowd and asked for her name, which was Malory. The pregnant pause that followed was the exact length in which a normal person might ask for Robin's name. But through all the introductions, he had yet to be asked for one himself. He assumed they were either terrible humans, or already knew who he was. Or both. *Probably both.* But he didn't know yet what advantage they sought.

The only thing obvious here was that this hapless group of unfortunates had no idea they had started an international crisis, or the amount of trouble they had brought upon themselves. And if William came hunting for him with any help, this entire group might find themselves in chains.

A young boy, aged seven or eight, pushed through the legs of a woman to stare up at Robin, his blue eyes big enough to fall into. Little beamed, "Here's the miller's son, Much."

Robin bent over to meet him. "That's your name? Much?"

Much shook his head proudly.

"It's more of a nickname really," John admitted.

Robin wrinkled his nose. "Not a very good name, now, is it?"

Much angled his head with purpose. "It's better than what they called me before."

"Oh, and what was that?"

"Not much!"

Robin laughed, and the child shifted and kicked him hard in his shin, right into the arrow wound. Robin let out a cry for which any grown man would forever be teased.

"That's for laughing!" Much squealed and vanished between Arthur and David, who tussled his hair as he passed. Robin was proud of himself for not muttering *little piece of shit* loud enough for anyone else to hear, particularly the small man who was in front of him next.

Again John introduced, "The curtal Friar Tuck."

Robed in browns and tans, his body seemed to be confused about hair growth. It had forsaken the top of his head entirely and smattered his neck and chin with curly scraggles that, on anyone else, would have been in an armpit. The undeniable odor that hugged almost everyone was practically tangible around the friar.

"A friend of the Sheriff?" Tuck asked.

Robin chose a non-answer. "A friend of the King."

"Funny, isn't it, how different those two answers are?"

Robin answered by way of a noncommittal grunt. With the introductions apparently over, he seized the chance to take command. "John, may I have a word with you?"

"Your servant." He gave a slight bow and signaled the crowd to go about their business. A young woman with a slight harelip smiled for Robin, while an older woman with two young boys at her side scowled ferociously. John led Robin closer to the mighty oak, walking past a well-used firepit and a lazy circle of makeshift benches. A small group of children watched nervously from afar. Still farther out at the perimeter of the field was a solitary hooded man holding a tall spear—his other hand bore a distinctive bright white glove, his attention unnervingly all on Robin, even from so far away.

Robin began harshly. "What the hell is going on here?"

The question bounced harmlessly off John's face. "How long have you been gone?"

"John. Robbery in the Sherwood is nothing new, it's long been a place for men to hide out their troubles. But women and children? This is no place for them, how are you living out here like this?"

"We make do."

"I see that. By stealing."

"I do what I can to protect them. And yes, that includes banditry."

"You lead these people?"

John moved uncomfortably. "Not quite. But they respect me."

"That's evident. They trust you. So I hope you're able to understand that living like this is a death sentence. My friend and I, his name is William de Wendenal, we have orders for the Sheriff from the King himself, to do anything necessary to keep his supplies safe. You've stolen too much, you've been too greedy. They'll be sending men to hunt you. And since you ambushed us today, William has a damned fine idea of where to start looking."

John fidgeted. "Well, *my* friend Alan is sure to outrun *your* friend William, so I won't be betting our safety quite yet."

That was certainly possible, but Robin hoped for Alan's sake it wasn't so.

William could kill Alan in a heartbeat if he was forced to. And if these people foolishly chose to fight when William brought back a host from Nottingham . . . well, it would go exactly as well as the massacre in Acre. A wall of trained soldiers, cutting through these civilians like butter. He could blink and see them all splayed over the red grass, bodies cut to ribbons. Robin shuddered to think about it.

"If they do come, you'd be wise not to be here."

"And where would we be wise to be?"

"You need protection. There are any number of lords and barons outside the forests, with land, with manors and castles. They need people to work the fields, and they'll provide your people with protection. That's how it works, that's how it's always worked."

John hesitated. "Again, how long have you been gone?"

"Two springs."

"Two springs." John's words were heavy, as if he thought that a lifetime ago. *They couldn't have been out here for that long.* "You've missed a lot, Robin. Nottinghamshire's not a safe place for those who can't afford to pay the sheriff's taxes. The lucky ones get prison. We have water here, and the forest feeds us, and we take anything else we need. We're better off in the forest, trust me. We've tried it."

Not hard enough, clearly.

Robin shook his head, watching the group of children disperse, chasing at each other. "Food will be scarce soon, and fewer supplies are going to be sent through the Sherwood Road. You have no fields to sow, and your shelter is . . . wanting. The seasons are changing, the winter will freeze you out. There are children here. You're a big man, you can bear it. The others can't."

There was concern in John's face. He had a lovable fatherly quality to him, when he wasn't bashing your ribs in with a tree. "People live off the land. They always have."

"And they die that way."

His face twisted. "People die everywhere. Nobody will take us."

The answer was right there. There was exactly one man on earth who could find more pity than poison in this group.

And he was nearby.

CHARITY WAS EVER A recurring argument between Robin and his father. As a young man he'd believed in his father, too naïve to question otherwise. They'd once been riding from a town, Robin and Edmond and Father between them. Lord Walter had given a coin to a beggar.

"What did he do to deserve it, though?"

"It's charity, Robin. The man has nothing, and needs help."

"Why must Edmond and I work all day for you to give us our coin then?"

"So that you'll appreciate what hard work is worth."

"Why can't the man do hard work like we do to earn the coin?"

"He's likely done more hard work in his life than you'll ever know, Robin."

As the years progressed, and Robin grew more comfortable challenging his father's stance, the conversation expanded.

"He offers us nothing, Father. He offers England nothing. Life is a difficult thing, and not everyone can be successful at it. He's failed, and your coin won't change that."

"Are you so quick to judge the value of a man's life, then? What is a man worth? Is it limited to that which he can do for England in his twilight years? Does a lifetime of hard work not earn him respect when he needs it most?"

"You're only guessing that he's worked hard. He could have been lazy his entire life, leeching off his family, until finally they kicked him out. If he'd earned respect his entire life, wouldn't he have people to take care of him now?"

"Shall we go back and ask him? Would you have him explain every sorrow he's been through so you can personally judge if he's earned this one coin?"

That was when Robin was still young. But as a man, only weeks before leaving home, he was not so easily silenced.

"What breeds criminals then, Father? A man who has nothing, with nothing to lose, will lie for your money. He'll steal it when he can, will kill for it if he has to. Show me the pauper who ever turned his life around through honesty and virtue."

"This is the very reason why it is our duty to help them!"

"And degrade all society! You help one man but you foster an environment that breeds thieves, and it hurts the country! You were the one that taught me not to place my own value over the greater good, you called it selfishness!"

"It is selfishness now too, Robin," his father had said furiously, *"no matter what you disguise it as! Have I raised such an ungrateful child that he cannot find the value of an action that serves another before himself? I've lost one child to madness already, Robin, and I'll be damned if I'll let you there as well."*

His father had eventually apologized, and cried when he did. Edmond was a topic they were not to discuss. Not his madness. His father could never do enough kindness to make up for Edmond. But he'd tried, and was still probably trying. It still terrified Robin, too, not understanding what had gone wrong in Edmond's mind. Not knowing if he himself carried the same desire for violence. His brother, staring vacantly, softly repeating to Robin, *"I saw red."*

"I saw red."

"I saw red."

These people in the woods, John Little's people, were a threat to others and themselves. There was no knowing who might suffer if these thieves weren't stopped now. The child Much was staring at him, reminding Robin of the mercy he had shown to Stabhappy in Acre. Letting that boy go had meant the death of the Earl of Derby. Letting this entire community stay in the forest, continuing to steal whatever they wanted . . . there was no telling how much more damage they would do. Sometimes with consequences halfway around the world.

"Damn it." Robin already regretted his decision. "Are you familiar with Locksley Castle?"

An odd pause. “More than passing.”

“My father has long been a friend to those in need. Usually to a fault.” He hissed in sharply, bracing himself for what would be an awkward reunion. The absolute last thing his father would expect would be for Robin to show up at his doorstep with a flock of refugees in need. Lord Walter would be so damned proud it made Robin want to vomit just thinking about it. His only solace was that some of this group—the men, and Will Scarlet in particular—would still pay for their crimes. “Locksley isn’t far from here. Your people can set up in the lands around the castle, earn an honest living. No prison, no torches.”

Little didn’t move. He just looked at Robin and bit his lip.

“As I said earlier, you’re all my prisoners. I’ll have to take you in immediately, I’m afraid. I can offer you the finest cells in all of England—lots of open air, no walls, that sort of thing. Your trials will be held the day after never, and your punishment is that you’ll have to work to earn your keep. In exchange you can live your lives in a way that best suits you. John. Get your families out of the woods. Stop robbing the caravans to Richard’s army. My father will help you out with the tax collectors, and I can get back to where I belong.”

It was the best offer they’d ever receive, and they would be fools not to see it. With one leg tied behind his back, Robin had just saved the war. His only regret was that William wasn’t there to marvel at his victory.

Still, it surprised him that John did not put up any resistance.

“We ought to see the place, then,” he said. “Just a handful of us, for now. Spend the night here. In the morning, we’ll follow you home.”

FIFTEEN

ARABLE DE BUREL

NOTTINGHAM CASTLE

SEVERAL BURLAP BUNDLES OF wrapped meats and hard sausages waited side by side—meals for a dozen Guardsmen and a few days' worth of travel. Arable had been instructed to deliver them to the stables, and it did not yet appear they would deliver themselves.

Gunny could do it instead, but if word got back to Mistress Roana, questions would be raised that Arable did not want to answer. The truth was she felt like a captive in the castle of late, existing only at the mercy of the secrets she had told, and yet knew so little about.

It had been three months since she informed Captain Gisbourne of Jon Bassett's unusual late-night meetings in the wine cellar. So far as Arable could tell, absolutely nothing had come of it excepting her own misery. *How foolish.* The moment she recognized Bassett's face, she should have realized he was too important to be punished. But seeing Gisbourne laugh with Bassett in the dining hall that night, she couldn't help herself. She could have held back, pretended she knew nothing. Instead she'd pounded that infernal cup by Bassett's plate, thinking someway it would matter. She thought Gisbourne would do the right thing. But Bassett was not only still in the Guard, he was still in the Captain's Regiment. And Gisbourne had not spoken to her since.

Every time she was now assigned a task involving his regiment, she froze with fear. She did everything she could to avoid them, at the expense of some of the only friendships she ever had. But she didn't know if Bassett knew she had fingered him, or what the rest of the regiment knew at all. That uncertainty was a danger all too familiar, as it had been her companion for half her life.

The only advantage of this servant's life was supposed to be anonymity, and she had foolishly thrown that away. Her honest deed had made her an enemy of some of the most powerful men in the castle. Thinking on it too much led to fits of panic, and she physically ached from being constantly on edge. She flirted with the idea of running away again, out of Nottingham entirely, but the reality of that dream was so much harder than the dream itself. Over the years she had stashed enough coin aside to travel south, but it was useless without knowing where to go. She only had a single bit of rumor, overheard years ago, that implied a Burel had made it to France. She didn't know if it was a brother, a cousin, her mother, or an absolute lie—and it didn't matter. "France" was as useful as "the moon" without better information. The world was full of hungry mouths in need, and she would just be another beggar. There was terror in taking her chances on the road, terror of the unknown. At least here, she knew the terrain.

A palpable relief overcame her as she entered the stables and realized Jon Bassett was not there. Only Reginold and Bolt sat on the ground, preparing their packs, and they greeted her warmly.

"Arable, my darling, what wonderful timing, perhaps you'll help us settle this philosophical quandary!" Reginold twisted the tips of his moustache tight and rolled up to his feet, extending one hand for her.

"Hi, *Bellara,*" Bolt grinned, looking away.

"Hi, *Tolb.*" She kicked at his good leg, causing him to snicker silently and twist. Reginold and Bolt often included her in their antics, ever since they discovered they could make her laugh. She also suspected Bolt had taken a bit of a liking to her, despite his being a few years younger. She rarely saw them anymore. *And she had only herself to blame.*

"We were discussing death," Reginold said dramatically, his eyebrows dancing. "Not the kindest subject for your ladylike lady-ears, but we'll skip the grisly parts. More specifically, we were discussing the inestimable mystery of what happens after the grisly part. What happens to the soul."

He accentuated that by sheathing a sword, and proceeded to buckle it to his horse's saddle.

"You either go to heaven or you go to hell," Arable answered cautiously, certain there would be some clever linguistic trap awaiting her.

"Nobody contests that," he continued. "Nor do we contest which one awaits us. Heroes such as we," he spread his arms wide toward his *little brother,* "already have our stations reserved."

"That's not the point." Bolt got up, some embarrassment overtaking him.

"The point is what *constitutes* heaven." Reginold raised a finger. "Heaven is supposedly an unending paradise, beyond this world, in which you are reunited with all your loved ones. Therein lies a difficult question. What if your loved ones don't love you back? Would they be forced to spend their heaven with you?"

Arable shook her head and smiled. "I'm sure I don't know." She placed a bundle of wrapped sausage in his hands.

A quick sniff apparently marked his approval. "Let me ask it another way. What if your idea of heaven is to spend all your time with someone you've long . . . admired?" He flashed a knowing smile over to Bolt, who busied himself obviously with his belongings. "The old sheriff, for instance, Murdac. Let's say Bolt wanted nothing else but to spend his eternal days chatting with Murdac, because he admires him *so* much. But Murdac, quite famously, found Bolt to be insufferable. So whose heaven wins?"

"Just to be clear . . ." Arable offered a package for Bolt, but he averted his glance. She tucked it into one of his saddle bags, patting it so he'd know where it was. "In this scenario, both Bolt and Murdac are dead, and you want to know which of them suffers more?" They both laughed for that. "Sorry, I've never been dead, so I can't really help you with your quandary."

"Oh, that's not the quandary." Reginold hastened next to her, petting the neck of Bolt's horse. "We both decided the question was ridiculous. The *quandary* is whether or not Bolt is actually insufferable, what say you?"

Bolt turned skittish and moved away. "Knock it off."

Boys were boys, but at least they were predictable. "Oh, I don't know," Arable replied, keeping her tone playful. "How long have you two known each other?"

"Since the war," Reginold calculated. "Fifteen years? Ever since I watched him jump off that curtain wall, right there," he pointed. "Just a child, scared out of his wits, trapped on the wrong side of an invading army. Last time he jumped anywhere."

He snickered, but the words *an invading army* stuck in her. Arable's father had died in that army.

"Well fifteen years is a long time," she smiled, without missing a beat, "and you've suffered every one of them. Therefore, he must be sufferable."

"Thank you," Bolt said from across the room.

"I'm not convinced that was a compliment," Reginold called back, giving a friendly wink. But Bolt was gone, swinging his lame leg proudly as he left. Arable laughed it off, while giving a nonchalant check to see if there were any other eavesdroppers nearby.

"Can I ask you something?" she asked once she was convinced they were alone.

"No, I cannot marry you," Reginold lamented, throwing an arm over his face. "My daughter would murder me." Once he realized he got no reaction, his tone softened. "Of course, what is it?"

"Jon Bassett." She tried to hide any disdain for the name. "A few months ago, was he ever . . . in any sort of trouble? Did the captain come down on him for anything?"

Reginold of Dunmow had a witty response for everything, which made it worrisome when he did not. "Why do you ask?"

"Nothing," she tried to shrug it off. "Just something I heard."

"What did you hear?"

"Nothing, forget I said anything."

Reginold studied her, his theatrical characteristics turned serious, razor-sharp. "I wouldn't exactly call it a secret, but nor is it something we'd want to be circulating as rumor. Captain had been grooming Bassett for command, but that stopped on the abrupt. Nothing scandalous there, as there wasn't anything official about it, and the captain is certainly allowed to change his mind. The salacious part is Devon of York."

Arable found herself leaning forward. "The new recruit?"

Reginold nodded. Arable had barely interacted with the newest member of Gisbourne's regiment, but he had exactly as much of an impression on her as a wet blanket. "Devon had only been in the Common Guard for a week. Odd choice to promote him to the Captain's Regiment, by anyone's judgment?"

"I would think so."

"Young fellow, and green as they come. Skittish as a stray cat, but here he is.

And it may be just my imagination, but the captain's curious protective of him. Almost as if he's grooming Devon for something more, the way he used to do with Bassett."

So Bassett *had* been punished. It was an odd relief. "That sounds very awkward for everyone."

The idea seemed surprising to Reginold. "Oh, I suppose. Been a bit odd, lately, yes. But such are the rolls of the dice, you abide. So your turn then. What do you know about it?"

She recoiled. "Oh, nothing, just rumor, as you say!" She tried her hand at a girlish giggle but it came out something more like a dying piglet. She packed up the rest of the food and handed it to him. "Do you just want the rest of this?"

"Alright, keep your secrets," he said slyly, taking the bundle from her. If he meant to say anything else, he abandoned it when he glanced at something over her shoulder. "Actually, give one to him, would you? Our visitor from the war."

He returned one package to her and shouldered the rest, leaving the stables as she turned around.

What she saw froze every nerve in her body.

The walls of the stable fell away, the ground disappeared beneath her feet, the air in her chest flew out that it might see for itself. As if walking out of her dreams, William de Wendenal stood in front of her.

My God, someone said, probably him. *Arable?*

It took every bit of her strength to believe it could be true, but when she blinked he was still there, impossibly there. His cheeks were thinner, his neck was fuller, but every nuance of his face was unchanged, and a thousand emotions reached through time to punch her distinctly in the throat.

She said his name, her voice broke and tears poured out. She covered her mouth and retreated, but he came to her in an instant, his arms surrounding her, shutting out the rest of the world.

Over the years she'd imagined a moment like this, though with far less frequency as time rolled on. In some of those fantasies she'd stomp her feet and demand an explanation, while in others she'd remain aloof and let him grovel for forgiveness. But even in the beginning, those would have been acts. All she had now were reactions, and the naked joy of seeing him had flushed every other thought from her mind.

"What are you doing here?" William asked, and she pulled him in tighter. There was no telling what would come next, but she could make this moment last just a little bit longer. He tried to release her, but laughed when she wouldn't let him, then finally pulled back long enough to look her in the face.

The years were evident, but the comfort of the young man she had once fallen in love with was still there. "What are you doing here?" he asked again.

"I'm not here. You can't tell your father."

"My father? No, of course not. I haven't seen him, I don't intend to."

"Good," she said and grabbed him again, but mostly to wipe her tears on his chest. "Thank you."

"It's been so long," he said, distracted by something outside. "You never wrote back."

"I left Derbyshire," she said quietly. "You know I had to."

He opened his mouth to answer, but closed it again. Because he knew she was right. He knew exactly how far his father had gone to remove the name of Burel from the earth. She'd grown a comfortably thick callus over the idea that William could have done anything to stop it, and wouldn't let him ruin that thought by doing something as silly as talking about it.

"I can't believe you're here," she said hurriedly. "I heard you joined the war."

"I did. I'm still part of it, really." His hand came up to wipe a tear from her cheek, and she almost let him. But she turned away instead, surprised to realize how quickly her excitement had faded. He continued, "I'm only here on an errand for King Richard. Once it's settled I'll have to be off again."

That was a second punch. "I see," she said. She did not know what else to say.

"It's nothing . . . negotiations. I don't have much time, I'm leading the captain's men out momentarily. How . . . how are you?"

How are you? As if she could answer the lifetime of struggles she'd endured since last they'd been together with a single sentence. She wondered what word could possibly describe the loss of one's whole family, to leave a comfortable life and to go into hiding with nothing. How might she describe the humiliation of asking old family friends for help and being denied? What clever turn of phrase would summarize the years of traveling from town to town, trading what few skills she had for food and shelter? Which word would tell the man who once loved her that, at her lowest point, she had nearly resorted to prostitution to survive?

"Fine," she said, gasping on the word. "I've been fine."

"But like this? You could have reached out to me."

"I'm serious, William, I'm fine." She controlled herself now. She would not allow him to pretend he could simply change her life in an instant. That would be too cruel. "I reached out to Roger de Lacy, I'm under his employ. This is just . . ." She gathered her maid's gown in her hand and shook it dismissively, ". . . it isn't perfect, but it is what it is."

He frowned, but with that young coyness he always had. "I would have thought you married."

I tried, she didn't tell him. *Nobody nearby wanted me, and nobody farther away cared who I was.* There were other things she could have said. *None of them were you.* Instead she settled for a shake of her head, and tried desperately to transition away. "There's a shortage of good men in Nottingham."

William laughed. "There's a shortage of good men everywhere in England."

"Baron de Lacy could use someone like you. Someone trustworthy."

He paused. "What makes you say that?"

"He doesn't have much support here. He was assigned this post by Richard's court, which upset a number of people. The High Sheriff of Nottinghamshire,

Derbyshire, and the Royal Forests? Your father was amongst those that could have taken the seat."

William grimaced, but wisely didn't respond. Once upon a time, Lord Beneger de Wendenal had been like a second father to her, and there were still times when she had difficulty separating her warm memories of him from what he had done later.

"Please, don't repeat anything I said," she added hastily. Within only a few minutes of seeing him, she had said too much. That was a lesson in trust she should have learned months ago. It was too easy to fall into old traps, of sharing everything with William. *Only to be disappointed,* she reminded herself.

"Arable, I promise you, anything you want to say is safe with me."

She had to laugh at this, sadly, and he could sense the weight it carried. With some difficulty, "You shouldn't make me promises, William. The last promise you made was that you'd come back." She laughed at this, too, because in retrospect it was hilarious. Hilarious that she thought it would end any other way.

"I did come back." William was quiet, almost ashamed. He reached out to touch her shoulder, but she moved away. "I'm here now."

"Yes, well . . ."

"And I have to go."

"You do."

"I'm sorry."

"There's food for you."

"I'll see you again."

"Don't say that."

William reached out and touched the back of his hand to Arable's cheek, but she didn't recoil this time. "I promise." She reached up and held her own hand on his, and his wet eyes reflected the sun's brilliance. "I can't believe you're here."

She closed her eyes and he disappeared, but she held onto that. She did not want to dare hope, for she had learned long ago how useless a hobby that was. *But just a sliver,* she thought, *just a sliver of hope might go a long way.*

For a moment, her own problems seemed a thousand years ago. But once William's mission was complete, he'd leave. *Everyone only cares about their own world, that's just the way it works.*

She wondered if she ought to take this as some sort of a sign, proof that there was nothing for her in Nottingham. If she truly had a family member living in France now, she could only hope to find them by going there. It was only fear that kept her from trying, which meant that she'd always be living in fear. Once William returned to the war, it would be her turn to leave as well.

Arable slid into the back of the stables to compose herself, but was startled by a movement behind her. *William had returned,* she wiped at her eyes.

But before she could look she was jolted sideways, a rough hand was over her mouth. She tasted the salty sweat of a man's skin, blocking her air, pushing her down.

"So you're the little spy, are you?" came Jon Bassett's all-too-familiar voice.

Reginold had told him of their conversation. She panicked and pried at the fingers over her lips, but lost all sensation as she went crashing down into the straw. She had no bearings, she kicked out, and then *something hot was dragging across her cheek,* and fear turned her vision white.

"This is what happens to nosy young ladies."

She couldn't scream. The hot sharp thing flashed against her other cheek, then the ground bit her in the face and his footsteps were disappearing outside.

But all she could see was her own blood dripping into the straw beneath her.

SIXTEEN

ELENA GAMWELL

LOCKSLEY CASTLE

THE WAGON WHEELS GROANED, because that's what wagon wheels do. Nobody comments on how miraculous a thing they are, to turn and move, move and turn. Every creak and bump leaves the impression that the wagon is a little worse for wear, a little closer to the end of its life. And still the wheel doesn't ask for recognition. It doesn't demand applause for its job.

This Robin of Locksley would do well to learn from the wagon wheel.

Elena Gamwell was perched on the seat of the wagon, foot on the rein hitch, enjoying the rumble of the Sherwood Road. Will vaulted up and balanced, teetering over the buckboard, to steal a kiss from her. Another push and he was off again, darting away. He took every opportunity to scout the road ahead, while Elena was trapped listening to their guest's version of conversation. Elena made a note to make Will pay for his escape in some delicious manner later. He was, as always, damned lucky that she loved him.

"What about me?" John Little asked beside her, pawing at the space Will had been, pursing his lips for a kiss.

"Here." She grabbed his arm with both hands and planted her lips on his big furry cheeks.

"Oh my." His eyebrows danced. "Didn't anyone ever tell you not to kiss dirty old men?"

"Oh John." Elena leaned her head against his shoulder. "You're not that dirty."

"I knew I should have driven the horses today." Alan gave a weak laugh, sulking. Elena threw him a smile out of pity.

"Now if you want to ride a *real* horse . . ."

Locksley started talking again. It seemed to be his only skill. She was more than happy to let the man earn their respect, but so far he'd missed every opportunity. Elena had not known old Lord Walter of Locksley as long as the others, but she had grown to care for him. That fondness should have extended to his family, but she was beginning to suspect that the son was a thousand miles from the father in character. Admittedly, he was at a disadvantage, and it was Elena's fault. When John gathered them around before bringing Locksley into their camp, she had been the one to suggest they keep quiet. *"Don't let on that we know who he is,"* she'd said. *"Nothing about Lord Walter."* Some of them still didn't have that instinct, to realize that every bit of knowledge is power. Not just what you know, but what others think you *don't* know.

So it was hard to see the man as anything other than a fleeting day's worth of entertainment, no different than any other mark. But John Little urged for their compassion, and he had his reasons for most things. Elena forced herself to smile as Locksley continued, thinking he was regaling some random travelers who didn't know him. He talked and talked, little memories about this spring or that cluster of woods, more frequently as they grew closer. Elena tried to find the man behind the bluster, but it was hard to hear the stories as words at all. All she heard was Locksley's wheel groaning, closer and closer to its breaking point.

Some of the others, they couldn't distinguish the son from the father. "If you're better with a bow than a sword," Alan crooned, "why did you leave the archers for the Royal Guard?"

"Well, my swordsmanship isn't exactly poor." The mare in front of Elena took the opportunity to release a hefty fistful of her shit, and Elena decided she'd call the horse Robin from now on. "But my skills as an archer would have been wasted if I'd stayed where I was. In a war, archers don't need expert marksmanship, they just need to be part of the volley. Fifty men release and a cloud of arrows goes up in the air, and come down on the enemy like rain."

"That's a lot of arrows," marveled Alan, throwing a smile toward Elena to include her in the amazement. She just stared at him. He should have been atop the cart, as he was best with the horses. Instead he lingered at Locksley's side, a little girl in love.

"Can't say we hear much about the war." Arthur scratched at his beard. "Is it . . . uh . . . going well? You doing important things?"

Locksley seemed to find that amusing. "I don't know that I'd call it *important,*" he made a mockery of the word, "but it has its moments."

Aside from herself and John, the others walked—making a long day's journey to Locksley Castle. Will had joked that John's weight would be too much for the horses, but Elena saw that his age was catching up to him. He was known to complain about his knees, and his back too. His massive quarterstaff was carried more often as a cane than a weapon. Living off the land had trimmed John's body of much of the fat he'd worn a year ago, but underneath he was thick as a log. Moving that amount of muscle couldn't be easy.

As the daylight hours rolled by, she made a game of counting the times Robin mentioned *how close he was to the King* and *the times he'd counseled the King* or when he'd *ridden with the King into battle* or *thought the word ring, which rhymes with King,* and fuck all. She lost count at thirty, but only because she'd gone from thirty to fourteen and not realized her mistake until she hit thirty again.

She reached down and touched Locksley's longsword at her feet. The longbow, too, finely made, a deep purple stain at its tips and a smooth notched grip entwined into the first. Not a fighting bow, this was a dandy's collector piece. It could buy them a parlie chest of food for the winter. Will, having wandered close again, sensed what she was thinking and pulled the bow from the cart to inspect it. He gave a self-satisfied shrug to dismiss it, then gave its string a test pull. He snapped out a little yelp and grabbed at his arm, hopping around in pain.

Elena could only laugh, but Locksley apparently saw an opportunity to dazzle them with his expertise. "You're holding the bow incorrectly, you know. You have to turn your elbow out to the side."

"I know how to shoot a bow," Will snapped back, but the large pink welt blooming on his forearm undermined his point.

"You know how to throw arrows at trees, it's not the same. I'll show you. Pick it up."

Will did, exchanging an uncomfortable pout with Elena first.

"Pull it back. There, see how your elbow is pointed down at the ground? It puts the fat part of your arm in line with the bowstring. But if you rotate your elbow around to the outside—" he slowly twisted Will's arm, "then look at the inside of your arm. See how flat it is? The bowstring can't hit you that way."

Will didn't seem impressed, but he tried again without hurting himself and humphed.

"And don't ever shoot at faeries," Locksley said with some agitation.

"Shoot at faeries?" Tuck, quiet until now, was curious.

"Sorry—imaginary target, imaginary arrow. Don't ever loose the string without a real arrow."

"Why not?"

"Think of the bow, and all the energy that you're holding in when you draw the string. When you loose an arrow, all that energy travels into your target. But if you release the string without an arrow, all that energy has nowhere to go, but back into the bow itself. Then you have a broken bow."

Elena pointed. "That bow's not broken."

"Eventually you have a broken bow."

"Eventually you'll always have a broken bow."

"Not if you treat her well."

"God's teeth," Will laughed, "is that what they teach you in the royal archery? How to talk sweetly to your bow? Do you sleep with it and rub her every night?"

Elena laughed so hard she snorted, and met Will's eyes for a moment. He was grinning wide but flashed her a hand gesture, tucked close to his chest, of his middle finger and thumb extended. It was a symbol meant to point out an arrogant mark who deserved to be robbed, but in this context—combined with a raised eyebrow—it roughly translated to, *This guy's a prick, right?*

Elena wiggled the same sign back to him and shrugged her shoulders. *Probably,* it meant, *but it doesn't matter.* They owed it to Lord Walter to give his son the benefit of the doubt. This younger Locksley simply wasn't important enough to get under her skin. He was just a poorman's dandy who couldn't suffer to not be the center of attention for even a moment. It was no surprise—son of a nobleman, right hand of the king, he'd been told his entire life that he was important, special. No wonder he believed it. Elena, on the other hand, had been told every day of her youth she was shit. Told she was a *bitch.* By men like Robin of Locksley, who thought themselves taller than the world.

She had known Robins of Locksleys her entire life. They were her marks in Red Lion Square or the parlies, and their coinpurses were always lighter for having known her. Men born with privilege, with money, with title, and thought they were humble to complain about it. Elena had left the gangs of Nottingham behind, her and Will, but the instincts were still there. That street stab in the gut that tells when a person is trustworthy, or when their every word is candied shit.

And Locksley's mouth stank of it.

When he described the king's personal guard for a third time, how they were like brothers, it was more than Elena could stand. "What about your real family, then?" she asked through a smile. "You have any actual brothers?"

"Excuse me?"

"You said your friend is like your brother, so it stands to reason you're familiar with having a brother."

"No," Locksley lied, thinking nobody could know otherwise. "No brothers."

That legitimately shocked her, and she exchanged another glance of alarm with Will. Lord Walter had spoken sadly and often of his children, while Robin had just denied Edmond's existence. Tells a thing or two about a man, though what exactly that was, Elena wasn't sure. Shame, maybe. Though shame was not a river that ran deep in this particular Locksley. Pride, more likely. His reputation with his precious King wouldn't shine so brightly next to his murderous brother's.

That agitation got the best of her. "Oh, so you were lying to us?" she asked.

"Pardon?"

"If I said there's nothing in the world that compares to waking up next to a handsome man, I'd be telling the truth. Right? Because I've experienced that. But if Alan said the same thing, it'd be a lie."

"What?" Alan startled. "How did I get involved in this?"

"Actually," Arthur broke in, "Alan might know that."

"No, I . . ."

"So if you don't have any brothers, you don't know what it's like to have one. Therefore, you're a liar. Lessin' you were lying about not having a brother. But why would somebody lie about that?" Elena repositioned to throw Locksley an obvious glare, but all she got was John Little's prickly face and an elbow in the ribs.

Wait, his face said. He would understand soon enough.

"We're almost there," Locksley chimed in shortly after, upon sight of a notable copse of hawthorns. "Another hour and you will all, delightfully, become my father's problem."

If he'd been aiming for comedy, he'd missed. Elena felt herself sour to him further. All day they had assumed his intentions, if not his words, were kind. Lord Walter had taken people in to help them, while it seemed his son was only interested in getting rid of them. He had no interest in lending a hand, he just wanted his father to wave a wand and *fix it.* He thought they were incapable of anything on their own.

For as long as people had used words as insults, they told Elena the things she could never do. They told her since she was a girl, she couldn't fight. They told her since she was poor, she would always have to follow orders. They told her since she was pretty, she would have to use her body. She'd denied all of that. She'd refused to be someone else's plaything. That wasn't the way to find freedom, not out of the streets, not out of a life. Not by someone else's charity—she'd *worked* to earn Walter's hospitality. You can't climb a ladder by clutching onto those higher and hoping they drag you a few rungs before shaking you off. Doing so would mean she would never belong where she had arrived. It was simply another form of possession.

Robin of Locksley thought they were skivers. Boot-clingers.

He'd learn.

Elena urged the horses faster.

A FADING AMBER LIGHT cut through the shafts of trees to show the burnt husk of Locksley Castle. Her stone walls still stood, mostly, though every window or doorway was scorched black. Grey dirt and weed surrounded everything, what once was tall grass. Here and there, ivy tendrils crawled their way back up into the cracks, the earth itself not satisfied that the structure still stood. Lower walls had crumbled, a few taller sections had collapsed. There was no sign of any door, shutter, or banner. Anything consumable had been taken by flame. The sun bit harshly onto what remained, giving an orange glow as if the embers still lingered.

Locksley had stopped a dozen or so paces back, hands limp at his side. Elena had her own solemn memories of this place, which she wrestled down. She wanted to focus on watching the son's reaction. If anything could slap the arrogant smirk off his face to reveal the actual human beneath, this would.

"Not quite home sweet home," John apologized.

"Yes, Locksley Castle!" Will burst in. "Thank you so much for the fine accommodations!"

Locksley closed his eyes. "What happened here?"

Eventually Tuck, with his usual blend of kindness, "Something that shouldn't have."

"I'm sorry we didn't tell you," John huffed, descending from the wagon. "Thought this would be better seen."

Locksley moved slowly, placing his steps to the entrance with care, as if he were remembering each one. Against her will, a part of Elena felt sympathy for him. A small part, a pinkie, or the useless wattle of skin at the elbow. The Robin of body parts. They all had mourned this place in their own time, and come to terms with it. They'd had to, such was the way with grief. It consumed your thoughts like a fire, but once there was nothing left to burn, all that remained were scars. Robin of Locksley was still made of kindling.

This may have been his home by birth, but it had been Elena's by choice. Whatever memories came as his hands brushed the blackened rock archway of the empty main door, they were not what rose in Elena's mind. She had found Lord Walter at this door once, propped open with a candlestick, sideways, a bitter wind whistling through. Elena had asked what he was looking for and Walter startled, then clutched Elena's shoulder.

"I know it's pointless," Walter had confessed in a weak voice, *"but some nights I keep an eye out for them."*

She'd felt dumb to say it out loud, but had nothing else to offer. *"Your sons."*

Walter had nodded, after a long pause. *"Robin. Edmond."* Both names stung, in different ways. *"And Helen."* Elena had left him to the cold and the wind, having nothing else to say, not knowing what she *could* say. Later in her own bed, she curled up against Will tighter than normal and realized she shouldn't have left at all. Instead, she should have bundled up in the whistling wind, cracked the door a little further, and said, *"I'll watch with you."*

But she hadn't. She'd left.

That night, the wind had beat the doors so hard Elena thought they might break off. The image of them gone now made it seem they had, and carried Walter away with them.

"There's so little left," Locksley commented, as if his grief were limited to furniture and tapestries. The walls wore black rectangles where once they had hung, scorch marks and stains, piles of unrecognizable debris. Locksley mourned them with the specificity of a tax collector.

It disgusted her. She'd missed one night with Walter and still regretted it. Robin had missed so many more, and apparently didn't care what his absence cost. He didn't even have a good reason. No grand cause had dragged him from home—he couldn't even bother to call the war *important*.

They kept walking.

"Any number of travelers had their pick of the place," John explained. "Even the rocks."

The dining hall was a tomb. Some tables hadn't completely burned, their brittle wooden timber lying askew, twisted chandeliers on the ground, echoes of movement scurrying underneath the rubble. Rats or rabbits. Part of the roof had collapsed. The tall broken windows here faced westward, letting in red fingers that pierced through and left an empty black between.

This was where Elena and Will had first met Lord Walter. A year after leaving the Red Lions to make their own life, a year of discovering the world beyond the reach of Nottingham. But after a year they were tired and hungry, and followed the rumors of a generous nobleman looking for talent she and Will could provide. They had never thought of themselves as poor, but arriving empty-handed made it impossible to pretend they were not beggars. Elena didn't quite know how to beg, and she'd only gotten on one knee before Walter picked her up. He asked her how she was best suited to help, then made both of them promise to never drop to a knee again.

"Not just to me," Walter had smiled, *"but to any man. You kneel to show that you are less of a man. I don't allow half men here."*

"I'm not a man at all," Elena had replied.

"Good on you." Lord Walter had smiled. *"A wise choice."*

A month later, there'd been a cripple at the castle who was missing a leg and was too weak to use crutches, pushed around in a small wheelbarrow by his wife. Walter nursed him to strength again, and found him suitable jobs that restored his dignity. In poor taste, Elena reminded Lord Walter of his own words. *"I thought you said you didn't allow half men here."*

"Luther is ten times the man of any I've ever met. You could get on my shoulders, and I on King Richard's, and we'd barely reach Luther's knees."

Before that, Elena hadn't even known the cripple's name. That night the dining hall had smelled of cheeses and wine, of heavy roasted boar, and of people. Tonight it carried sulfur on the cold wind.

Three months ago, it had carried fire.

The memory of the sheriff's men in this place was not a kind one. They had arrived unannounced, and old instincts told Elena and Will to hide. The familiar blue tabards of the Nottingham Guard had always meant trouble, and usually a night or two locked up in Sinner Mary's. The Nottingham *Gords* had a smaller presence outside the city, but there was still no avoiding them. That night in Locksley, the gords and their captain had been greeted kindly, stabled, fed. John Little had even encouraged Elena to help tend to their belongings, insisting that they were *"people too."*

Ultimately, he was right. But they were the terrible type of people.

"My father?" Locksley asked, at last.

Nobody spoke, which was all the answer he needed. A bird flew through the hole in the roof and burrowed into a nest high above, some twigs fell silently down and were absorbed by the ash.

Will said it. "They burned him."

"That's not how it happened."

Tuck's words hung gravely in the air, hoping for help, but no one else spoke. Elena wasn't interested in telling the story, but she also didn't want Tuck to water it down with any religious bullshit. "I can tell it."

Locksley turned to her. "You were here?"

"Of course," Elena said sharply. *And you weren't.*

Tuck, of course, tried to keep it calm. "Robin, your father was one of the finest men I've ever known. Foolish, to be so fine in a world such as ours."

"What happened?" was what Locksley asked, though the proper response should have been *Thank you,* or *Rest his soul,* or better yet *I'm sorry I wasn't here. I'm so very very sorry.* Some apples fall from the tree, roll down the hill, land in a cart, and are sent a world away.

"The Nottingham Guard came in search of debtors," Elena answered. "It was well known Locksley was a haven for those fleeing the beggar's debt. I suppose the gords thought it would be an easy sweep, but they had it wrong. Lord Walter had already paid every penny owed. Except his own. He was the only person here they had cause to arrest."

"And he fought back," John added, with pride. "He gave them a round chase, he had a spirit to him you wouldn't figure for a man of his age. Your father was sharing a bottle of wine with the Captain, then he broke it over the table and attacked him with it!"

"What?" Locksley seemed astonished.

Tuck bobbed his head. "He ended up in the stables. Some guard went in after him, and came out a moment later with blood pouring from his nose!"

"Your father had quite an arm for horseshoes!" Both John and the friar were now delighting in the story. It wasn't a story that should be delightful.

"Well, nobody wanted to step foot into the stables after that." Tuck smiled, all crooked teeth and scraggly beard. "The Captain tried to talk him out, but he flat refused."

John nodded, but his smile waned. "We thought maybe they'd give up and go about their business. Until someone had the good idea to . . . to smoke your father out."

Locksley closed his eyes and squatted down into the dirt. He traced his fingers through a pile of it, the ash clinging to his skin.

"You know those stables. There was naught but one entrance and one window up high. Someone lit up the end of a fresh spruce, and it gave up a thick heavy white smoke. They pushed it in through the front door with their toes, see, like this." John imitated the guards, his hands over his face to protect from flying horseshoes. "And then ran back again as little pups. The smoke poured out the window as we watched, and we thought he'd give up. He should've given up. This wasn't worth it. We yelled for him to leave."

John paused, so Elena leveled her eyes on Locksley. "The smoke turned black." It was a sight and a feeling Elena would never forget. It was like the whole world had just flipped over to let them fall into the sky.

Tuck continued. "Once the fire caught, there was nothing anyone could do. Lord knows we tried. And not just us. The guards, the captain too. Every man and woman was rushing off for water, or hacking away at the stones to make another exit for him. There was no use. The doors were a wall of fire, the stones were too thick, and the black smoke . . . it ate everything. It was morning, but the sky was pitch as night. It was an accident, Robin."

"The man who put that fire in the stables didn't do it by accident," Locksley growled.

"No, he didn't. But we let him, and that's our burden, too. It should have just been smoke. Alan swears there was nothing close enough that could have caught fire so, unlessin' the devil himself had a hand in it. Which he may have. The fire rode the air, it rode in the smoke, and we were too worried about the stables to notice when it spread. It spread so fast. It spread so fast."

"It wasn't the devil," Elena broke in, hating the friar's easy excuses. "It was men. The choices they make, the things they do. And the things they don't." Those words were for Locksley, and she let him know it. Lord Walter had been part of this family, but his son was as welcome here as the fire.

"Accident or not, they did not come here to kill your father." Tuck measured his words with care. "But that's not the story that spread. People simply heard that the Sheriff was burning down houses, even of noblemen like your father, of those who didn't pay their taxes. No arrest, no punishment, just the torch."

"That's why we can't find another home, Robin," John added gravely.

Tuck folded his hands. "We tried. No lord will take any refugees, for fear we can't pay our way. And we're certainly not the only ones out there, either."

"You were all there," Locksley's words were deliberate, "and nobody helped him until it was too late?" Silence. "He was fighting, and running, an old man, your lord, and you watched it happen."

"That's right, *Locksley,*" Elena snapped, furious at the accusation. "We were there. At the very least, we were there. I know my regrets, but I know that I tried like hell to stop what happened here." She and Will had left their hiding place as soon as the black smoke erupted. They'd gathered well water. She'd worked side by side with the gords. She was there, for every devastating beat of it. "And where the *hell* were you?"

"That's fine, Lena," John quieted her.

"*Like hell it is.* What are your regrets, Robin? What did you do to try and stop this? Your first reaction is to accuse your father's most loyal friends of neglecting him? Where's your remorse for abandoning him?"

"I said that's fine," John repeated sternly, pawing her away toward the ruined staircase.

Locksley's face betrayed no emotion, no humanity. He was interested in doling blame, nothing more. He had expressed no interest in the quality of his father's life. Or where they buried his body. Nor what had happened to their own families in the aftermath. It wasn't just Walter's stable that burned, it was a home for a hundred, maybe twice that. It was livelihoods and survival and safety and family. Robin of Locksley was away plundering riches from foreign lands *while they went hungry.*

She could have left. Will would have gone in a heartbeat. They could have moved on to the next town, wandered on, pinched their way into something new. Instead they stayed, true to their group, part of it now. This arrogant ass was Lord Walter's blood, he'd done literally nothing, and he wanted to know why *they* didn't do more.

"Lord Walter hated the king, you know," Elena spat.

John snapped at her. "That's it, you're done!"

She looked Robin in the eye. "You deserted your father to protect a man he hated." If there was any part of Robin of Locksley that had a soul, Elena was glad to have a role in crushing it.

He just stared, with those dull beady eyes, full of hate. It's easy for a man to hate. It's the easiest thing in the world. Why wouldn't Walter's laziest son be an expert at it?

SEVENTEEN

MARION FITZWALTER

LOCKSLEY CASTLE

LITERALLY ANY OTHER PLACE would have been a preferable choice for a reunion. Marion had only been back to Locksley Castle once since the fire, only once since poor Walter died. This place was as devastating to her heart as the fire had been to its stone-and-timber walls. It hollowed her out. She had not been present for the fire, and had only inconsistent accounts to piece together the truth of what happened. Captain Gisbourne had described Lord Walter as a madman, throwing wine bottles and horseshoes, while Alan-a-Dale insisted that Walter meant no harm at all.

The hardest truth was that the truth didn't matter.

The fire did not care what caused it, nor the events that followed. Walter's people scattered or fought amongst themselves for the remains. Then nomads and raiders tried to pick it clean, until the Nottingham Guard chased them out again. In Nottingham, the castle wasn't even called Locksley anymore, as there was no one to claim the land. In a mere three months it had become "Thieves Den," a mythical place where the hermit lord had launched a rebellion and been stamped out of existence.

Marion had done everything she could to find sympathetic lords to take in those who had lost their home again, but still she failed most of them. Only a handful had been safely relocated. The others had either fled or, to her utter heartbreak, refused her help. As for her most loyal pack, they had chosen to stick together and carve out a living in the Sherwood Forest.

Three times she had petitioned Sheriff de Lacy for his assistance, but he could only do so much. Three times she had ignored her father's summons from London—he thought he could lure her home with some fresh political scandal. Her grandfather, the Earl of Essex, had also written, but with different intentions. His advice was that she speak with a recently widowed lord in Clavering for help. Normally she found joy in rejecting his obvious attempts at arranging a marriage for her, but this time she was only disappointed. Her family's reaction was a sobering reminder of how easy it was for those with power to turn a blind eye to the suffering of those without. She couldn't be bothered with any of it now. Not while she was still juggling the ramifications of her failures in Nottinghamshire.

She shared the blame for Walter's death, the guilt of orchestrating it all. To return to Locksley now was to look her victim in the face.

She slowed her rouncey Medus, who stomped his hooves in protest. They stopped before the dead jaws of the castle's once proud main doors. Neither moat nor wall had ever protected Locksley's entrance, often prompting Walter to insist it was a *manor* and not a *castle,* a scholastic distinction that would never matter again. She swung her leg free of Medus's saddle and Sir Amon Swift helped her down, as diligent in his duties as he was silent in his opinion of them.

"I'd prefer to take a look first, my lady," he said, and she let him. She doubted there was any danger here, but he was the most expensive gift she'd ever received and it was best to let him feel useful. A knight in times as these was a rarity, but her father had insisted on her protection. He paid the entirety of Sir Amon's retainer after realizing he couldn't stop his daughter from "gallivanting through the woods." Sir Amon wisely bit his tongue on such matters, but had little issue in reminding her that his orders came from her father, and not her.

As Sir Amon side-stepped to the castle's front entrance, Marion helped her attendant Clarell down from her own horse. Her puckered face was bright from the long ride.

"Stay here," Marion said. "Tend to yourself, and the horses."

In little time, Amon returned. Although there was little light left in the sky, Marion had no difficulty identifying the lean man at her knight's side.

"Lady Marion." Alan-a-Dale seemed relieved, and stumbled over himself.

She did not waste any time. "Where is he?"

"Inside." Alan blew out his cheeks. "We didn't think you'd get here so quickly."

"I was in Sheffield, luckily." She rarely used the room she paid for there, but David of Doncaster had found her with no difficulty. *"We found someone you'll be interested in,"* he had said. *"We're bringing him home."*

Alan shifted. "Do you want to—"

"Lead the way. Sir Amon can stand watch."

Alan abided and hurried within, through corridors she had once known well. Its air was cruel with echoes now, its floor littered with careless debris. The orange light at the end of their path seemed like a threat. She almost wished Alan would not walk so fast, to put off seeing it a bit longer. But all too soon they were within the cadaver of Locksley's great dining hall. Once lit from above by either daylight or chandeliers, now the hearth was its only light. Lit from below, it was like walking into hell. Giant's shadows stomped across the crumbling walls, every crag and cleft was turned into an open canyon.

"Does anybody need a pretty lady?" Alan announced glibly to the room. "I found one just wandering around."

Will Scarlet perked up from where he lay beside the fire. "How pretty?"

"How pretty?" Elena, next to him, gasped and smacked him.

Marion gave them no heed, and kept surveying the room until she saw him. She had actively refused to believe it until this moment—her mind had closed itself off to what it meant for him to be here.

"Of all things. Robin."

Robin of Locksley, a little older and amusingly thicker, squinted back at her. "Marion?" They had evidently not told him she was coming. He likely didn't even know about her involvement with this place.

"I didn't believe it when I heard, but here you are."

"Here I am," he said absently, and did not move to greet her. There was a beaten quality about him. She could tell he was still in the midst of dealing with what had happened here.

"I'm so sorry," she said, feeling the utter inadequacy of those words.

Robin nodded, but he didn't thank her, and he had not said hello. Some silent bond between them made greetings and farewells unimportant. However, she did not care for the way he asked, "What are you doing here?" As if she had no right to be here, as if she had not nearly called it home as well.

"Well, it's nice to see you, too," she said.

"That's not what I meant."

"What are *you* doing here?" she asked back, aiming for sarcasm. "I hadn't heard the war was over. Did we win?"

"He's a deserter," Will Scarlet moaned lazily, lying down again by the fire.

"I'm not a deserter—"

"He's a deserter," Scarlet drowned out Robin's protest, "and our prisoner. What do you suppose we could get for him?"

"Wait," Alan startled, "he's *our* prisoner? I thought it was the other way around?"

Scarlet blinked with his entire face. "Are you serious?"

"That's what you told me."

"Alan. There are . . . six of us. There's one of him."

"Right."

"We have the weapons."

Alan laughed. "No, I know we're not *actually* his prisoners . . ."

"*Do* you?"

"Go on, I knew that."

"God's balls, you're—"

"Boys!" shouted John Little, ever the father. Only now did Marion take stock of the rest of the room, finding Arthur a Bland also hiding at its edges, and Tuck kneeling by the fire. It was a bitter homecoming for them all.

"I promised you all whatever help I could offer," Robin addressed them, "but it would seem that's not much. There's a cave against the rocks out past the south wall. Doesn't look like much, but it opens up. We used to store rations there. Hard to see if you're not looking for it, so it may have survived the raiding."

Elena rolled forward into a stand. "We'll have a look." She snapped her hand out and plucked Scarlet's ear, tugging him like a child. "Let's go, *pretty lady.*"

"There's nothing there," Arthur called out after the two lovers, but they had likely only been looking for an excuse to disappear. "There's nothing there," he repeated to Robin. "Weren't you paying attention? We lived here. We know this place."

"Worth checking, though," Little said glumly, plainly to give Marion some privacy. "There may be a cask of wine in the back."

The magic word had been spoken. "Wine, you say?" Tuck asked and was gone. Alan took the hint and left as well, but Little lingered at the door.

"Not aiming to run off, are you?"

Robin shrugged. "Would you care?"

Little's nod was grim. "Sorry about all this." It was an apology as well as a goodbye.

Marion threw a serious look up to Arthur, who had not left, and by the stone scowl on his face did not mean to. He was leaning on the balcony rail of the second floor, and made a show of getting comfortable. It was his way of protecting her, and Marion did not protest. Instead she lowered her voice and drew close to Robin.

"It's good to see you. Alive."

He gave her an unenthusiastic smile, and used his toe to punish a nearby pile of ash. "Maybe it's better this way."

Marion studied him. "What's better this way?"

He grunted and turned away. That had clearly not changed. Robin had never had an easy time discussing his feelings, and she had no idea what he meant by *"maybe it's better this way."* It was cruel to imply that Lord Walter was better dead than alive. It was naïve to say the castle was better burned than destroyed. It was horrifying to think Lord Walter deserved to die in the same place as Vivian, so many years earlier. But with Robin there was no knowing when he was trying to be funny or when he was a raw nerve. He might have meant nothing more than a pithy insult at the pile of ash he had flattened, that it was "better this way."

"I had no idea things had grown so bad," he said.

Marion blinked. "Would it have mattered?"

"What do you mean?"

"If you had known that *things* were so *bad,* would you have done anything differently? Or is that why you're back?"

Robin took some time to consider before answering. "No," maybe to both questions, then he lost his thought.

"You know, your father was something of a hero."

"A hero." He repeated the word like it was rotten.

"He housed a lot of people here. Gave refuge to those with nowhere else to turn. He paid their taxes, they tended his land. Locksley was quite the little kingdom." Her smile faded. His kingdom had been doomed, with no heir. "For a while."

"I've heard all about it. Is it true that he paid everyone else's taxes, but not his own?"

"Yes." That gave Marion a chuckle. "I suppose he thought he could prove a point. Thought he was too prominent to be evicted."

"It sounds as if he only made things worse."

"Worse?" She had to bite her lip. Robin didn't know he was insulting her as well.

"These people he helped," he pointed loosely up at Arthur, "have now been chased into the forest. Living as outlaws, stealing to survive. They have no land, they won't survive the winter. Are they better off now, dying in the cold, than if they'd simply paid their taxes?"

"Simply paid their taxes?" Marion repeated back at him. "You think they chose this?"

"I know they chose this! I spent the day with them. They came here because they knew my father would pay for them. Isn't that right?" This too he threw up to Arthur, who clenched his jaw and walked away. Robin relished his tiny victory and turned back to her. "Exactly. Why wouldn't someone choose that?"

"Nobody was here to take advantage of your father," Marion tried to explain. "Landowners started abandoning their own people so they couldn't be taxed on them. The wording of Richard's decree was sloppy and inexact. The Sheriff has done his best to make sense of it, but when armed men and tax collectors pound on your door, you run. If they hadn't run here, they would have died."

"They'll still die. Just later, and colder, and poorer. That's my father's legacy."

"Your father fought for them," Marion said sharply.

"He died hiding in a stable, throwing horseshoes at tax collectors!" Robin's voice echoed in the dining hall. The rats under the table scurried out to stare at him, and back again. "This is a great hero? What was he fighting for?"

Marion was seething, but wouldn't let him see it. "It's easy to fight for yourself. Your father chose to fight for someone else, people who couldn't fight for themselves. That's a hero."

"He should have known better."

Several emotions lunged forward, but she bit them off one by one and swallowed them down again. Robin's eyes were in the fire, the same untouchable silence that had defined their relationship for decades.

Marion could not remember the first time she met him, he was simply a permanent connection in her life, like a family member. The same was true with Locksley Castle—it was a place that had always been. As a young lady, her family split their year between Essex and Sheffield, which was only a stonesthrow away. Nobility were always excited to pair young people of comparable age together, and her parents had been no different. And so, Marion and Vivian were frequently paired off with Robin and Edmond.

Over a few years their friendship had naturally bloomed. Vivian was the prettier of the two and found that in common with Edmond, while Marion and Robin shared a love for learning. She would spend hours with Robin in the forest reading books aloud to each other and wondering about the stars at night. One night as they walked home, their hands briefly brushed together. Whether it had been an accident or the bravest thing Robin had ever done, Marion would never know. But both possibilities amused her, so she took his hand with her own. She walked closer to him and pressed her cheek against his shoulder, just before they returned to the manor and found Edmond staring at Vivian's body, bloodied and beaten with her guts spilling onto the cobblestones, like the rabbits he used to hunt.

Robin had closed off to her after that. Even now, Marion had too many things to say, and it seemed Robin had too few. She forced herself to remember he was still reacting to his father's death, and he needed time. At long last she asked him, "Why don't you come to Sheffield with me?"

He smiled, but not kindly. "That's good of you, but I don't mean to stay."

"You need to sleep somewhere."

"I'll take one of your horses, if you can spare it. I have pressing issues in Nottingham."

This time their eyes met, and the silence was long.

"Don't do that," Marion almost whispered. "Don't run away again."

"I'm not here on holiday, Marion. I have an errand for the king, your cousin, you may remember, and when it's done I mean to return to him."

"You could stay."

"There's nothing for me here."

She almost gasped, but caught it. "Nothing?"

"No, not . . . I didn't mean that."

"Oh don't get too full of yourself, Robin," she chastised him. "I wasn't asking you for my sake. Your name carries weight here. People would listen to you. You could help things."

"The way my father helped things?" Robin threw his arms out and paraded about the room, as if she were blind to its devastation. "Here's how to help things—they give me the weapons they stole, and then they never steal anything else again."

Marion was shocked. For months she had wondered if they would ever be held accountable for those war supplies, fearful that someone would one day come hunting for them. Someone finally had, and it was the one person who should be on their side. But Robin treated their lives as an annoyance from his own.

"This group needs to disperse. Move back to their villages. They pay what they can, and the Sheriff stops persecuting them. Everything ends up fine. The solution here is to do *nothing.* I'm not very good at doing nothing."

She could argue that he was, in fact, a master of it. But instead she let it slide, happy for him to retreat to the hole in which he'd been living. "Fine. You're right. There's nothing worth fighting for here."

"Marion, you know that's not—"

"Go take a fucking horse, Robin. Any one will do. Actually, no." Her eyes leveled him. "The fastest one."

Whatever his response was going to be, the moment was stolen by Will Scarlet gliding back in from outside, swiftly, noiselessly. He slid an arm intently around Marion's waist and eased her toward the rear of the hall.

He said one word. "Riders."

Alan was beside him, rushing toward the hearth. "Put out the fire."

"It's too late, they've seen it," Scarlet said, loping to a slag of fallen stone. He rounded the hall, both knives out, until he flattened by the main hallway. Arthur rejoined the room from above and started down the stairs, but Scarlet signaled for him to stay put. Marion concealed herself behind the arched curve of an empty doorway, but no further. Her mind raced to think on who could have followed her here.

Robin didn't budge, oblivious to the possibility of danger. He gazed halfinterestedly as footfalls echoed in from the entranceway. Whoever it was had already entered the building, which meant they had gotten past Sir Amon and Clarell. A single figure appeared, a man dressed in dark pleated leather armor. A thick hood slumped off the back of his head, the same outfit that Robin was wearing. A longsword was slung from his belt, and he carried another in his hand. Robin squinted at the stranger, then laughed out loud as the two embraced. "Now here's a real hero."

"Thank God, Robin."

"William."

Scarlet was there in an instant. One blade he held gingerly out, the tip touching the intruder's back. "Hullo, again!"

"Put your weapons down." Robin was all smiles. "How'd you find me?"

"This was not the first place I looked," the man named William replied. "These are . . . our friends now?"

"Friends, no," Robin said. "But we've come to an understanding."

Scarlet remained still. "I'm not so sure I'm understanding this understanding."

Marion pushed against the cold stones, hoping for a better look. Robin's friend appeared agitated but held no animosity. "I'm looking for John Little, actually. We mean to negotiate a peace between him and the Sheriff."

"A peace?" asked Alan. Marion opened her mouth to reveal herself, but felt a large hand at her shoulder easing her back again.

"Stay put," John Little whispered into her ear. "Might yet be you need to disappear."

He tugged her back behind the doorway, and she reluctantly let him. They had long taken the risk of their enterprise together, but they would be in far more danger if she were ever incriminated with them. On their own they were forgettable. But with her, they were scandal.

More noise came now, muffled and far-off at first like a storm, but then increasingly distinct. The rumble of new bodies poured into the hall, the clatter of chain mail and weaponry.

Guardsmen poured in. Six of them, side by side, the signature dark blue of their tabards robbed of all color in the orange light. Behind them were two more—a skinny squire in an ivory cape, attending a man whose presence here was near blasphemous. His signature was written on every wall, with ash as his ink.

EIGHTEEN

GUY OF GISBOURNE

THIEVES DEN

"AS CAPTAIN OF THE Sheriff's Guard, I speak for the Sheriff himself and you may consider my word his law," Guy announced.

He doubted they would cow to authority, but it was the only strategy he had. William de Wendenal had already compromised their approach by barreling ahead alone, forcing Guy to follow blindly. He counted only three combatants in the hollow dining hall, which meant there were likely more hiding in the surrounding corridors. His men were at every disadvantage, at risk of being surrounded, and in unfamiliar territory.

Not entirely unfamiliar, he corrected. Guy had been here before. These ruins were a testament to the ease of destruction. A scant few months ago he had visited this place with the hopes of recruiting debtors to the Guard's ranks, and instead discovered a rebellion in the making. The traitor lord had been quietly gathering an army of disciples who thought themselves more important than the law. Like a common cutpurse, the mad Lord Walter had fled when confronted, and chose to martyr himself before answering Guy's questions. The most loyal of the lord's crew escaped into the woods and had been causing minor disturbances since, ignorant to the damage they'd done. The true victims, Guy knew, were those desperate men and women who could have been part of a thriving community, but were led to ruin by one man's misplaced ideology.

All that remained now was char, and Guy's men had chased raiders from the ruins on three or four occasions. With no heir claimant to the land, multiple rogue groups had tried to settle it in the last three months, earning it the moniker of *Thieves Den*.

Guy continued. "This land has been seized by the Sheriff, and by staying here you are guilty of trespass."

He eyed his newest recruit at the back of their formation, wondering what effect this place had on him, but the young man's face was rightfully concealed in the shadow of his heavy hood.

Across the room, the remnants of the traitor lord's army fidgeted nervously. They had long ago made the disappointing choice that could lead only to a prison cell. Unfortunately, they were unlikely to share Guy's assessment of their fortunes—they were the type that preferred sharpened weapons over sharpened minds.

Guy surveyed the room, and focused on the man with whom Wendenal was standing. "Is this him, then?"

Wendenal confirmed with a nod. "I've got a hold of this, thank you."

Guy ignored the comment and smiled, hoping to put the stranger at ease. There was no need for hot minds when peace was an option. "Robin of Locksley, a pleasure." He approached cautiously but shook the man's hand with enthusiasm. There was not much of the man's father in Locksley's softer features, and Guy could only hope that extended to his personality. In this very room, Lord Walter had distracted Guy's men by throwing a wine bottle, which had landed with a thud on the table, unbroken, and slid to an embarrassed halt. After that, the chase. "I am so sorry as to these circumstances. This is not a homecoming I would wish upon anyone."

Robin winced, genuinely. "Captain. Thank you."

"I'm sure you have many questions, and no doubt you've been given many answers. If I were you, I would doubt their authenticity."

The fact that Locksley's hands were not bound behind his back meant the outlaws had potentially tried to radicalize him. No doubt they had played to his sympathies as a son, ignoring the truth of Lord Walter's treason. But Wendenal had spoken strongly of Robin's character, and there was always hope.

"As the arm of the Sheriff, there are some complications to deal with in regard to your father, and his land. But as a father and a son myself, please accept my regrets for your loss."

"Piss off!" shouted one of the raiders, lingering at the edges like a carrion bird.

"I also apologize for their disrespect," Guy conceded, "and for your treatment in the last day or so. Policing the Sherwood is one of our highest priorities, and your capture is a disgrace. A problem which, I'm told, you're here to help us with."

Robin relaxed, another good sign. "That's true enough."

"Lord Gisbourne," Wendenal interrupted again. "Thank you for your assistance, I shall take things from here."

"With respect, your task here is complete." Guy eyed him strongly, unsure just where he meant to *take things*. "We've successfully found your friend, healthy and alive. But this search has also brought us to a group of woodland rebels—a trifling matter, but one in which, I assure you, I hold authority."

"Roger de Lacy asked me—"

"Lay your weapons on the ground," Guy raised his voice, knowing fully well that they wouldn't obey him. They never did. Every fool criminal thought themselves a mastermind—they always thought they could outthink or outfight or outrun the Nottingham Guard, and it rarely went their way. Perhaps it was animal instinct, or perhaps just a blind rejection of reality. Guy did his best to explain, to not startle them. "It will go much better for you, I promise, if you go peacefully."

"You will take no one!" growled Wendenal. "Captain Gisbourne, the Sheriff himself told me these men were not to be harmed or arrested."

He might as well have doused Guy with a bucket of river water. *"What?"* Guy reeled at the betrayal, but had no chance to strategize.

"I have come with an offer of peace, and that peace will be respected!"

"No arrests?" shouted a short scofflaw with a young face. The young ones always thought they knew the world. "Sounds like we can do whatever we want!"

His hands drifted to his back, and Guy's men responded in turn. Morg tightened his grip on his halberd, while Reginold and Bolt looked to each other for guidance. Jon Bassett's fingers twitched, ready to pull steel. If anyone were to spring this too early, it would be Bassett.

Guy's eyes sharpened again on Devon of York, the latest addition to his regiment.

The only gerold who might prove himself worth the spit on his sleeve.

Guy squinted, hoping the young man would have any insight. Devon's head gave a quick quiet nod, an affirmative. It was Guy's only advantage here amongst the enemy, crippled by the Sheriff's short-sighted pacifism. Guy chose—and prayed he chose correctly—to trust.

Guy ordered his men to stand down.

"If you are eager to throw your own lives away, then think not of yourselves. Think of your friends, your family. Look around at this place, and consider heavily what comes next." They were quiet, and Guy reserved a small place in his mind to hope this might go well.

A deep voice bellowed from the edge of the room, "Let us hear this peace then!"

Emerging like a bear from a cave, the man carried a quarterstaff that made a heavy *thunk* with each step. Guy gave a quick glance to his men, whose eyes clearly begged for instruction.

"Weapons down, then," he commanded. "And take a seat. Let's talk of peace."

Their eyes screamed with fear, but each of Guy's men obeyed. The halberds lay down on the ground. Their hands did a remarkable impression of laziness. Guy let his own belt slip loose, sloughing its weight into one hand and lowering it onto nearby slag. The beast of a man with the staff nodded with some gravity at the gesture.

Wendenal bowed his head. "John Little?"

"Aye," spake the bear.

"I am Lord William de Wendenal, and I parlay for the Sheriff." Guy flinched at the implication. Wendenal was the son of a marcher lord in Derby, and should have no grounds to speak for the Sheriff. Guy began to compose a library of grievances to pound at de Lacy's door when he returned.

John Little smiled darkly at Wendenal. "I remember you."

"The Sheriff does not wish to aggravate you, but instead to find some common ground."

Little grunted. "The spirits in this hall may disagree."

"An unfortunate coincidence." Wendenal lowered his head in respect. "Perhaps we can give them some peace."

John seemed to accept the answer, or at least to pretend to. "What does he propose?"

"You will not be persecuted for your crimes of thievery against the King, provided that you return what you can of the weapons and supplies belonging to the King's armies, and will refrain from interfering with future shipments. He is eager to make arrangements to bring your people back to fealty, under conditions you both consider fair. It is in everyone's best interest for you to live productive and healthy lives, so long as you abide by the King's laws. Agree to these terms, and all else is forgiven."

"All else is forgiven?" shouted out one of the thieves.

"Oh, all we have to do is hand over our weapons?" mocked another. "And you promise not to arrest us? We've seen what the Sheriff's word is worth." He spat on the ground. They had no idea how insanely lenient this offer was.

"What the hell do *you* forgive *us* for, anyhow?" asked the young one. "Maybe instead, we take these very weapons you're asking for and watch you bolt for the hills again."

"There's a slight problem with your plan, Wendenal." John Little eased his staff from hand to hand. "Most of the weapons have long been sold off. Some are still ours, aye. But if they weren't, I don't think your boys would have stopped at that door. The rest bought us soup and bread. Should we open our bellies up? We could give it back to you, but you may not like what's become of it."

The gallery laughed at this.

"If you don't accept the offer, then the Sheriff's peace is off." Guy eyed Wendenal, who reluctantly confirmed. "Which means you will each return with me to Nottingham. Whether on your own two legs or not."

It was taken as a challenge. "How are your legs, boys?"

"I think I'll be walking fine," another snarled. "Arthur?"

"Let's dance."

Damnation. The thieves poised at readiness. They did not move yet, but the young one slid two knives out.

"There will be no blood spilled here today!" bellowed Robin of Locksley, with startling authority. "This is my father's land, passed on to me. These men were his servants, which by right makes them now mine. I am Lord of Locksley here. If you have need of arresting someone on my land, you will kindly bring the matter to me."

"Your servants?" the one named Arthur nearly choked on the word.

"Robin," Guy was careful not to acknowledge his newly claimed title, "legally speaking, your father failed to pay his taxes. He was posthumously evicted, his lands were seized, reclaimed for the Sheriff, in the name of the King. Your intent is commendable, but for now you have no official standing here."

"Forget the weapons," Wendenal surrendered, a master of negotiation. "But leave the forest. Find new homes. Let this pass."

Wendenal and Locksley were amateurs here, who apparently thought they could sweep merrily into town and make everyone work together. That was a dream too fanciful even for children's stories. A lifetime of working and running the Guard had taught Guy otherwise. He would give de Lacy's peace one last shot, then do things his own way.

"You should take the deal," he said, honestly. "You will never, I *promise*—" he made pointed contact with Wendenal, "—receive another like it. Decide quickly. Do you take peace, or do I take your men into custody?"

"I think I may take something of my own."

A female voice, full of venom, it came *from behind*. Guy couldn't react before the blade touched his throat. He jerked away by instinct but her hand was in his hair, yanking his head backward, *white fear his son's face falling snowfall on the castle walls,* but the blade did not cut him.

Guy gasped to be alive. He blinked furiously at the tears that had sprung to his eyes, while his heart smashed against his ribs. He forced himself to focus, he stood as still as a statue and wrestled his attention back from the brink. A riot of noise, men screaming, the girl's voice in his ear, *black water in the hole, Murdac's funeral, no*—the pain in his scalp, metal on stone. He raised his hands, slowly. "Hold then, hold!" he sputtered, his apple brushing the sharp steel.

Glimpses of his men. Eric of Felley screaming for him. Morg desperate to grab his weapon from the ground.

"Hold, then!" Guy insisted, then she pulled his head back farther, his throat stretched, *blood on his son's lips, coughing, purple crocuses blowing off the lump of his grave.* He focused on the dim charred roof of the dining hall, and the monstrous shadows. The noise settled. He could sense a hesitation in the air. *Calm,* he forced himself. His assailant had snuck up behind him, and there was no knowing how many others lay in wait.

"Do you see, Wendenal, what it is we've been up against?" His neck muscles clenched. "These men only know violence."

"Be careful who you call a man," warned the voice behind him, her sword's point tracing up to the hook of his chin.

"That is quite enough!" came a new voice, a woman's this time, and Guy could tilt his head just enough to throw an eye at its bearer. Openly mingling with criminals was a new pastime for the Lady Marion Fitzwalter. There was no secret to her involvement with the traitor lord in life, but only rumors placed her with the fallout of his followers. It seemed she had no problem confirming those rumors now. She emerged from a side gullet, a heavy cloak stirring up the ash at her feet.

"Weapons down," the girl's voice came from behind, "or I slice him open."

"You will do no such thing, Elena," Lady Marion ordered.

"My apologies, lady," Wendenal's voice, "but I'm not sure that I know you."

"My name is Lady Marion Fitzwalter. I am kin to King Richard the Lionheart, and you will hear me out."

"Under what capacity," Guy said carefully, feeling the blade follow his jaw, "do you speak here, Lady Marion? Which authority do you claim?"

"As I say, that of my relation to King Richard, and my grandfather, Earl of Essex."

That was a curious vaguery. "You stand with these outlaws?"

"I stand for what I believe to be right. And it appears you are in need of a calm voice to negotiate."

Guy would have laughed if the action wouldn't have killed him. "Just passing by, then? How coincidental."

"Lady Marion," Wendenal again, "what do you have in mind?"

"The Sheriff's offer is decent, but there are too many details to be decided upon here. *Here,* of all places," she sounded disgusted. "I will accompany you to the Sheriff along with John Little, whom you will promise safe passage." That elicited a grumble in the room, though Guy could not tell if it was from his own men or the outlaws. "The four of us will come to an agreement, and until then both sides remain at bay. Little, do you agree to this?"

"Don't do it, John," warned one of the thieves.

"All they need is an excuse to put you away."

Lady Marion's voice was slow and precise. "I won't allow that."

"Aye, lady," came the massive John's voice, "I agree."

Against Guy's every instinct, the ruined hall felt a little less dangerous. That was something new. He wasn't sure he'd ever seen words win over steel in a situation like this. Even the blade at his neck seemed like an inconvenience now rather than a dire threat. William de Wendenal laughed through the tension.

"Would you mind calling off your . . . men?" He stumbled awkwardly on the last word.

"Elena. Come on girl." John Little gave the command. "Let him be."

The sword, hesitant, slowly retreated from Guy's neck. He put his palm to his throat, alarmed at how thin his own skin seemed. She had drawn a drop of blood, no more, but he winced now to feel it. When the girl slinked around him, he was shocked to see her. Just a little wisp of a thing, and young. She had sharp pale features and a bitter stare for him. Her sword, which would have been just a dagger in a man's hands, slipped back into her belt as she retreated. She curled her lip as if she owned the world, as if she were *right.* As if she had the authority to judge anyone or anything beyond her ability to spit. In that moment, she was every self-centered whelp he'd ever arrested. She was every thief and murderer who took what they thought the world owed them, every reason to be suspicious of the dark. She was misplaced righteousness, she was every hypocrite's ignorance.

It was instinct that made him speak, be it just under his breath.

"Bitch."

The tiniest moment of weightlessness passed before it all fell.

NINETEEN

ROBIN OF LOCKSLEY

LOCKSLEY CASTLE

ELENA WAS ON THE captain within two steps, too quick for either to draw a weapon, and barreled into Gisbourne with both fists wailing. Robin spun for a flash sense of the room, too late to stop anything. It reeked of the swarm back in Acre. The guard closest to Elena caught a fistful of her hair and yanked her back hard, wrenching her off Gisbourne and thankfully into submission.

But Will Scarlet cleared half the room in a heartbeat to help her, leaping over rubble, and Robin lunged to snag his elbow, spinning him into William's chest. Elena was already in trouble, but Scarlet would likely get himself killed if he got involved. There was no chance to explain it—the riot of the room overwhelmed thought. Scarlet ducked from William's grasp, then threw himself at the nearest guard. His fist smashed the man's nose as Robin grabbed at him a second time, keeping him from striking again. Two guards converged and tackled Scarlet to the ground, then buried a fist into his stomach, then again, a third, then his face. Too much, and Robin barked at them to stop, but had to abandon them. The rest of John Little's crew was surging forward, with Robin and William the only thing between them and the rest of the Guardsmen.

Mathematics and priorities. Arthur and Alan were fastest, so they were the first ones that needed to be stopped. Robin bent his knees and took the brunt of Alan's chest in the shoulder, shoving at the man's hips to spin him off balance. William made similarly short work of Arthur, but it left an opening for John Little to lumber past the both of them.

Wide-eyed with anger, he aimed directly for the men beating Scarlet. His staff cracked against the back of one guard's head, then its end crushed the chest of the other. Robin's gut clenched—*John wasn't pulling his punches.* This was no brawl. This would lead to blood, and death, and tragedy, within seconds. Robin moved to grab Little's staff from behind and—

—his head smashed sickeningly to the side, a familiar weight of flesh and knuckles cracking against his cheek. White sparkles shot into Robin's vision and his legs turned to mud, but his body was on instinct. He had not told himself to pivot, but he already trapped Arthur's arms under his own. The man's face was unbearably close, furious with pain. Robin unclenched his fist. He had already punched Arthur in the throat, one knuckle extended, and Arthur opened his mouth uselessly and slipped down. Robin knew how it felt, he knew that Arthur's vision was fading to black, and Robin caught his arms to lower him safely to the ground. No need to crack a skull now, when enough damage was already being done. The beast of violence had been set free, there was no calming its hunger now, and Robin could only hope to give it a wide berth.

Steel drew across steel, as he knew it would, the sharp pang of weapons finally drawn and colliding. Alan-a-Dale found himself an opponent, their blades cracking the air, but Robin could instantly see that Alan was well outmatched. He might have left it alone, but Robin wondered if the Guardsmen had enough training to keep themselves from killing. Alan barely dodged a thrust that would have skewered him, and Robin had his answer. Fortunately William was there, sweeping Alan out of the way and holding his hand out to the guards. Only one of them listened, the other crashed down mistakenly toward William, who spun away. Alan tried to defend himself from another slash but the impact jostled him off-balance, sending him to the ground. William pushed at the attacker, urging him back, giving Robin the opportunity to grab Alan by the damned scruff of his neck and hoist him to safety.

A sharp cry of pain wrested their attention to Captain Gisbourne. Elena was biting into his hand, which he'd clearly been using to quiet her. He released her and smashed the back of his other hand across her face. She went tumbling, stumbling back to the hearth side of the room, leaving only Scarlet isolated between the two parties. His blades were out, level, but unmoving.

For a moment everything stilled, all eyes on Will Scarlet, silent. No one wanted to test him. Robin was behind him, and had only one chance to end this now.

"Will—" he whispered, but instantly it all burst again.

Scarlet feigned toward Robin with one blade, then hopped in the other direction, cutting through the air, a third slash followed, a tornado of steel, and the guards recoiled from the onslaught. The first man to find an opening lunged deep, but Scarlet captured his enemy's sword with both knives, then threw it back as he brought his knee into the man's ribs. Robin was on him now, terrified of being caught by an errant swing, but the guards swarmed in, too. The largest of them locked Scarlet's arms from behind and picked him up, dragging him away as his legs kicked into the empty air.

Robin spotted Gisbourne at the perimeter, nursing the bite in his hand, and made for the opportunity. With Scarlet subdued, Gisbourne might call his men down, but he needed to give the command. Robin vaulted a slab of rubble to find a path to the captain, and instantly yelped like a pup as his injured leg gave way beneath him. He winced and keeled over, furious at himself for forgetting his handicap. For a moment he could do nothing but watch.

Elena had engaged several Guardsmen, her face lit up with excitement. She was the joyous heart of a whirlwind. She slashed low, caught one guard's sword and used it to capture a second, then pushed herself back, her boots sliding purposefully in the loose dirt. A hairy guard came down high onto her, but she slipped underneath him, grabbed his beard, and yanked his face down as she smashed her knee into his teeth. She screamed as loud as he did—hers a shrill war cry and his in toothless bloody horror. She enjoyed her victory for only a split second, as William wrapped his arm around her waist from behind and picked her up like a child. She squirmed and wriggled but he threw her away from the melee as if she were nothing.

Both sides were clambering back to their feet, and one single glance with William said everything. Robin abandoned his attempt to talk to Gisbourne. In a breath he was up again and next to William in the middle of the room. They turned back to back, and in symmetry they eased their longswords from their scabbards.

These arrogant outlaws didn't know the meaning of combat, nor the rules of a sword. To draw steel was to sanction its use. Both he and William had kept their blades sheathed until now, a promise of safety. But the skirmish had escalated to riot, and if Robin needed to take a life to save others then he would. In a single graceful move he and William rolled around each other, each blade kissing out. Robin disarmed Elena with a well-practiced flick, and William but twisted his blade into the head of a Guardsman's halberd and it leapt from its owner's hands. The captain and his guards regrouped on one side of the room, while the outlaws retreated to the fire.

But Will Scarlet leaned in to make a move, and Robin swept to meet him. *Different story when you don't take me by surprise, boy.* Robin's instincts begged for revenge. He deflected the thrust and slipped his sword's tip beneath Scarlet's knives in riposte, that he might slice him across—

Marion stood behind Will, her every feature a flash of horror

A look he had only seen on her once before

Exactly once

It stayed his blade.

"Stand down, damn it!" William ordered the room, his weapon saying the same thing in a language none could misinterpret.

Robin blinked away the moment, the touch of violence he'd almost satiated. It was different than the war, against nameless foreign enemies. Here, in his home, in his father's home, in his brother's home. These thieves on his land had nearly turned the ruins of his family into a butchery. *They never should have come here.*

The damned consequences of it all.

Captain Gisbourne, sucking the blood out of the bite wound in his hand, finally called for his men to retreat. His squire led the way, his white cloak receding from the doorway. Gisbourne buried his injured hand into an armpit. "This isn't over."

"Get your men out of here!" William shouted, taking a step toward them as if to give chase.

Gisbourne, to his credit, lingered last. He seemed interested in saying some last bitter thing, but eventually, wisely, just stepped back in the shadows. Their footsteps clattered down the hallway, and nobody moved until they heard the horses start to ride off.

THE THIEVES TENDED TO their wounds, muttering derogatory slurs at the departed Guardsmen. They had no idea how lucky they were to still be alive, how much restraint and mercy they had received. In all honesty, Robin wished the captain had arrested them, as it would have neatly ended the very problem he had come to solve. Instead, their days left alive could now be counted on a single hand, and there was no guessing what damage they'd do on their way out of the world.

William de Wendenal found a moment to steal away with him, still breathing heavily from the skirmish. "This is out of control."

"We have to stay focused on why we're here. War supplies," Robin answered. "We found them. This? This is not our problem."

William laughed, but his smile quickly faded. "So you think we should just leave? What about these people?"

"What about these people?" Robin turned the question around. "These people are criminals, and the Nottingham Guard will make short work of them. I don't think they'll be a problem for much longer."

"That's a little cold, don't you think?"

"No, not cold. Look where we are, William." He gestured to the soot and ruin. "This was my home, and there's nothing left of it, because of these people. If this were anywhere else, we'd be happy for them to be handled by the law."

"I don't know." William's eyes were searching for something he could not find. "What's the point, then? What's the point in going back to a war if we can't keep the peace here in our own land? What are we fighting for, then, what are we trying to protect?"

"That's a bit grandiose." Robin smiled. "We can't cure the entirety of crime. We have responsibilities. To Richard. To fight for England."

"Then let's fight for her people! So they're not subjected to what we see in the war! My God, think of the ambush in Acre, Robin. Do you remember how the people came to fight, old men and boys, armed with sticks, and our men just ran them through? That's what's going to happen here. The Sheriff's Guard will tear through these farmers like they were nothing. That's where this road leads."

Robin didn't flinch. "They know where this path leads. They still chose it."

"Can you honestly let that kind of bloodshed happen here at home, knowing you could have stopped it? They don't know any better. There can be a peace in Nottinghamshire. They simply need someone to show them how."

Robin shook his head. "That's not why we're here."

"We're here to secure the supply route. If we don't intervene, on *both sides of this,* I think it's going to get worse. That is *precisely* why we are here."

Robin hated it, but his friend—as always—was right. If these thieves didn't get themselves killed promptly, as he predicted, then they stood to make life even worse for everyone. "So what, we split up again?"

William nodded. "I think I can make some headway with the Sheriff. What about you?"

"Oh, I have to stay here?"

"They'll respect you. They respected your father."

That was not a kind comparison. "I don't think they'll listen to me."

"Just try to keep them out of trouble. I'll keep the captain off their backs, and we'll get those peace talks."

Robin let it sink in. It wouldn't be easy. "We can't get too entangled here."

"We won't have to. There are simple solutions to all of this. I'd say a week."

"I'd say you're optimistic," Robin stared across the room at Arthur, who did not hide that he was staring back. "Worst case?"

"Worst case . . ." William clicked his tongue. "Not more than a month."

A month. It sounded like a death sentence. *Staying in the woods with these people . . . with Marion . . .* "Guh, a month." Robin conceded. "Certainly no longer."

"It won't come to that." William prepared to leave. "But if everything goes sideways, in case we can't communicate at all, let's meet right here at the next full moon. Peace or no peace, by then we'll have at least done what we can."

"And then we'll go home."

William's only answer was a quizzical stare, and Robin realized its cause. *He had called the war home.* Robin was sitting in his own castle but he didn't consider himself home. It was nothing but a gravestone for his father to him, and a poor one at that.

They embraced again and said their goodbyes, slapping each other tightly, and William de Wendenal pulled his hood over his head and rushed off. Off to a month of hall meals prepared in a kitchen, a month of beds and civilization. While Robin would be stuck in the forest with children who seemed hell-bent on suicide.

"You idiots," Robin said, to everyone. They were silent, and had probably overheard the end of his conversation. "You've brought this upon yourselves. All of it."

They each rejected the shaming in their own predictable way. Marion alone seemed to understand the truth of his words. "What would you have them do?" she asked.

"Do you honestly think you can take on the Sheriff's Guard? A dozen of you? You'll be decimated."

"We're a hundred strong and growing."

"*Women and children,* John. Unless you were hiding your strongest men, you're the best of them, right here. You barely survived against six Guardsmen. How will you fare against twenty? A hundred? Next time they'll be organized. You won't have the drop on them, and they won't have orders to stay their weapons. They're trained fighters, and none of you really know what you're doing."

"So teach us." Alan was the only one still sitting, in the same spot he'd fallen, where he might have been killed if things had gone even slightly differently. "Honestly. Teach us."

Will Scarlet, sitting on the stairs, gave a dry laugh.

"You're something special with the King's army," Alan continued. "You said so. And we all saw you. The two of you could have taken on all of us."

"We couldn't have."

"If you can teach us to fight like that . . ."

"You're not listening!" Robin kicked at a stone. "You shouldn't be fighting at all!"

"You're the one not listening now," John Little lectured. "We don't have homes to go back to. We have families to feed. And now you've brought a lot of attention onto us."

"I'm here," Robin drew his words out slowly, "because you stole from the war. I'm the *result* of the attention you've created, not the *cause* of it!"

"No gain in throwing blame," Little conceded. "Trouble's upon us. You can fight. I'd like to know a little of what you know."

Robin shook his head, something particularly painful crawled into his voice. "Violence is not the answer, John. Not ever." That was the lesson they truly needed. Yes, he could train them to defend themselves, but along the way he might be able to train their minds as well. To tame their instincts toward violence. It would be a long road, and Robin hoped he had the clarity to walk it. He had failed with Richard, when he wanted to start his war too early. He had failed with Stabhappy. And Edmond, he had failed most of all. It chilled him to think of what would happen if he was equally successful with these people.

The good news was that he had already mastered all the wrong ways to do it. Surely that meant he was homing in on the right one.

He meant to say more, but something caught his eye that arrested his thoughts. A glint in the rubble. When Robin realized what it was, he silenced their commotion.

"We have to leave."

He moved carefully, as it was his own black shadow that concealed the unconscious Guardsman, unmoving and abandoned, lying amongst the rocks.

"Ah damn it," John Little moaned. "I think I did that."

PART III

A THIEVES BARGAIN

TWENTY

GUY OF GISBOURNE

THIEVES DEN

"They think they're smart," Eric of Felley's voice was distorted by the injury that bruised the bottom half of his face. His two front teeth were gone, smashed from his mouth by the wild hunter girl Elena, and his bloody gums bled gruesome beneath swollen lips. "But there's smart, and then there's *smart.* They split up, probably hoping we'd lose their trail. I'd say four horses, all in different directions. But which one . . ." he pointed downward obviously, at two perfect lines driving away from the ruins, ". . . do you think is the right one?"

Guy stared at the tracks, their only lead. "A carriage. Or an oxcart?"

Eric snapped his fingers. "That's why you're the captain."

They were hours behind the outlaws, and Guy was responsible for every second of that gap. Each of his men blamed themselves, of course, which only added to Guy's guilt. They had been ambushed twicefold—physically by the gang of thieves, and diplomatically by the Sheriff's order to stay their blades. Guy couldn't fault his men for panicking in such circumstances, but he himself should have been above that. His duty was first to each of them, and he failed. They had ridden half an hour, nerves on fire, before letting the company regroup. It was half an hour more before they came to the heavy conclusion that Jon Bassett was not coming. No one had seen him leave the castle.

Guy had abandoned one of his men.

It was guilt compounded upon guilt, turned into something there was no word for. He already felt to blame for his once-protégé's fall from grace. Guy had raised the young man up too quickly, with too long a leash. That summer day when the servant girl Arable had revealed Jon Bassett as a conspirator against his fellow Guardsmen, Guy's heart had both broken and shifted. He had trusted Bassett with the knowledge of how they recruited men from the gaols, and Bassett had betrayed that trust by telling others. They had planned to beat one of the gerolds bloody, as a warning, even though the gerolds had done nothing. Bassett openly admitted it when Guy confronted him, as if it were an obvious answer to their problems. That opinion was Guy's shame.

He should have taught Bassett better. He should have protected him.

That guilt was the reason he kept Bassett in the Captain's Regiment, rather than demote him to the Common Guard. His prospects for leadership were over, and that should have been punishment enough. But the world, apparently, was not satisfied.

By the time they returned to Thieves Den, there was nothing but muddy trails to follow. Reginold and Bolt bickered over whether the thieves were crafty enough to mislead them with false tracks, while Eric triple-checked his findings. Eric had been a crown ranger once, rescued from a life of boredom into Guy's regiment, exactly for situations such as this. But a mouth full of blood seemed to distract his tracker's instincts.

At the edge of the group, holding one arm in the other, was Devon of York—Guy's penance for demoting Bassett. Bassett's actions had forced Guy to spend a long time with his own thoughts, to face his own prejudices against the gerolds, to wonder how much his biases had influenced Bassett's misguided thinking. Guy had met that fear face-first, by choosing to place a gerold in his private regiment. He needed Bassett—and the others, in time—to understand. Guy picked Devon of York partially because he was as physically unintimidating as a human could possibly be—his face looked like the sound a child makes when he sees a puppy. But more importantly, Devon had been an unwitting accomplice in the criminal world. He had become indebted to Locksley's insurgency, pressured into an uprising he did not agree with. Fortunately for Devon, he'd been arrested the day Locksley martyred himself. Rather than join the rest of the forest bandits, he ended up in the prisons beneath Nottingham for Guy to find. Devon had a gut of regret for his part in the rebellion, and now was his opportunity to prove himself.

"We're leaving," Guy said softly to Devon, away from the rest of the regiment. "If you have anything you can add, anything at all, now is the time. Any idea where they might go?" It was a plea, not a demand.

The young, disheveled redhead was staring up at the broken hulk of the castle, his face haunted as if he could see the ghost of Lord Walter dominating his kingdom from beyond the grave. The traitor lord's influence was still here, his heretic religion of treason had spread beyond the confines of death. Locksley had taken advantage of the poor, he paid their debts but bought their servitude. He had quietly grown an army, to which Devon had been a slave.

"I don't know, Captain," was all he said, eyes locked on the charred ruins. Everything about his face screamed innocence, from his saucer eyes to the sunspots that peppered his nose. "I can tell you about some of the men we fought tonight. I don't know it'll be helpful."

Guy nodded. "It may be. Ride in the back with me." The rest of the regiment mounted their horses, eager for the hunt. "They have Bassett. Any idea what they'll do with him?"

Devon pursed his lips, looking every bit the disappointment he must have felt.

Guy patted his shoulder, hoping to ease his nerves. Devon's temperament was even younger than his age. "Don't worry, I'm not going to throw you back. But try to think. Even a small detail might save Bassett's life. We're not a band of thickskulls like they are—well, excepting Morg." Devon chuckled at that, watching Morg fail for a second time to heave himself onto his horse. "You ride in my company now, so you'll be using your brain as often as your blade. Both require regular sharpening. Or did you think it was your formidable swagger that caught my eye?"

Devon kept his voice low. "I know why you picked me."

"Your history with these outlaws is coincidental. I picked you because you're sharp, you see things others don't. Men with mettle," he tapped his temple, "the kind up here, beat the men with metal," he tapped his sword, "every time. They've already beaten us, and they have a hostage. It won't be muscles that win this." It was only a slight shift in Devon's face, but it made a difference. "You could have ended up, but by trick of fate, on the other side of this fight. So tell me how they think. That's the only way we get Bassett back."

THEY MADE HASTE, EVEN in the dark, even as the sky blotted spit at them. They would thunder furiously down the path for a while, then break only long enough for Eric to check the tracks. He could find evidence of the oxcart's passing within seconds, while Guy only stared at meaningless terrain. He felt waves of uselessness, and tried to fight them off. He had been given good advice on the matter once from Ralph Murdac, the last real sheriff.

"You're sometimes much smarter than me, Gisbourne," he'd say into his drink, as was his style. *"But I'm the one smart enough to have you as captain. Your successes are my successes, too. But your failures, you don't get to keep those. They're mine, and mine alone."*

It didn't help. Recruiting Eric five years ago had been a success, but losing Bassett was more than a simple failure.

At the next stop Eric waited longer than normal, glancing with irritation at the mottled clouds that obscured the moonlight. The infamous Eric of Felley boasted a deep patience—claiming he had once hunted a deer by lining up a perfect shot and then waiting for a tree limb to grow out of his way. But his lips were crusted in blood and he spat globules of it out, and Guy wondered how long he could keep up such focus.

The spittle in the air turned to droplets, then to rain, and their stops became frequent. The trail was vanishing beneath them.

"They must have come this way," Bolt insisted with his usual urgency, looking to Reginold for support. "Why not keep going until we come to a fork?"

"If they went off path," Reginold explained, breathing warm air onto his hands, "we'll lose them. And if they're even halfway smart—which might be generous—that's exactly what they did. So if the tracks are still here, we go forward. If they're not, we'd be going in the entirely wrong direction. And losing more time."

Morg grunted his agreement, but it sounded much like his grunts of annoyance. The man liked to grunt.

Guy stole what opportunities he could to listen to Devon's memories of his time at Locksley, and the men they were chasing. They could only speak alone, as Guy had yet to divulge Devon's past to the rest of his regiment. The day would come when de Lacy's reckless policy became public knowledge, but that danger was best delayed as long as possible. Guy had threatened some truly terrible things to Bassett and his four co-conspirators in the Common Guard, should they ever loose their tongues on the subject. He had given them each a second chance, but none of them could ever earn back his trust.

Devon described the outlaws one by one. He had barely known the hunter girl and the knifeman and only identified them as the Scarlet Twins, though they were lovers and not siblings. He had more to say about the men, Arthur a Bland and Alan-a-Dale. Alan was apparently more of a follower than anything, but Arthur was a nasty one. More than a few times Devon had been on the receiving end of a beating from Arthur during mock sparring lessons. Then there was John Little, Lord Walter's right hand, famous for intimidating those in the community who didn't fall in line. Devon told a story of a time he botched a job skinning a hare and John snatched the knife from his hand. *"There's naught to you but skin and bone, so I don't know why it's so hard for you to pull your weight,"* Devon recalled.

"He made quick work of the hare, and could have gutted me just as quickly. Just as thoughtlessly."

"All men can be harsh," Guy said. "But are they killers? If Bassett doesn't give them a fight, would they kill him in cold blood?"

Devon gave it serious consideration. "They would."

"What makes you say that?"

"They've killed before. People who were a threat." He swallowed to prepare for a story. "Before the fire, I had taken to eating on my own in the field. Away from the big dinners Lord Walter held in the dining hall. Away from the crowd, that's where I met the skeleton man. He wasn't there tonight, but he's part of them. Never learned his real name. I didn't know who he was at first, thought might be his reasons for eating alone were the same as mine. But he wasn't like me. One night he led me out, away from the castle, farther than seemed safe in the dark, until we came to . . . a corpse, a man, face down in the dirt. The skeleton man said he'd caught the man days earlier, tied him to the tree. Said he'd been stealing food. Said he didn't know what to do with him, but in the end he let him go. And then strange things. He said . . . said he was responsible for giving the man his life back, which meant it was his to take again. So he did. I wanted to run. He took his knife out. Said Lord Walter gave me my life. Asked me if I was grateful for it. Then left me with the corpse, in the woods."

Devon shook his head, and the rest of his story seemed to slip away.

Guy didn't know how to react. His thoughts tainted black with images of Jon Bassett trapped with savages such as these. "They like leaving messages. Could be they'll use Bassett to make one."

"They didn't come this way," Eric called out, coughing blood. "We have to double back."

This earned an array of curses from Reginold and Bolt, and a grunt from Morg, but Guy just closed his eyes. Devon sank in his frame.

There weren't going to find him.

But they would push on nonetheless.

TIME WAS TOO CRUEL to let them guess the hour when they finally rediscovered the tracks. Eric chastised himself for missing it earlier, showing where the gullet of the wheels drove sharply off the road into the birkland. "None of the rest of us saw it either," Reginold defended him. "We wouldn't be on their tail at all if not for you. Don't beat yourself up on this."

Bolt winced, and nudged his friend. "You're making it worse."

"Exactly," Eric said, his shoulders slumped. "It's on me to follow them. That's what I'm supposed to be good at."

The idea that Eric thought he was not doing enough spoke volumes about Guy's own share. The discovery invigorated them, but only until the new path petered into a deer run that cut back and forth too harshly for a cart to navigate. It was a truth too dangerous to speak aloud.

One by one they broke off, hoping to catch any new glimpse of a lead, but it was gone. There were no more tracks to follow, no path, nothing. If it were daylight, or if the weather were kinder, they might have fared better. But they had ruined it now, tromping through the forest's understory, switching back and second-guessing themselves. Guy pulled Devon aside and lowered his voice.

"At this point, we just have to guess at a direction and stick to it. North, south, doesn't matter. I just need a destination. The odds are against us, but making the decision matters, it'll give the boys a goal. So give me something, Devon. Anything. Where would John Little go to hide? It doesn't have to be right, it can be an instinct. But your instinct will at least be informed, while mine will be a blind stab."

"Hathersage?" Devon tried, with little confidence. "John Little came from Hathersage. I don't know if he still has any ties there, but he would know the area."

"It's better than nothing," Guy nodded. "Thank you."

Better than nothing—at this moment, Guy was the nothing. He had lost control of the situation earlier in the evening, and now could contribute nothing but guesses. This gerold was better than him. Better than nothing.

The morning sun was three fingers over the horizon when they finally settled for rest, halfway to Hathersage. Guy's legs and back burned from riding, and his eyelids were even heavier than his arms. He bought his men a few rooms at a decent-looking waypoint called The Third Pig, even after its innkeeper offered to house them for free. They had stopped at every village and hovel along the way, waking as many people as they could, hoping for stories of a group of riders making their way in the night. They were desperate for any confirmation they were headed in the right direction, as every step they traveled was potentially putting them farther from their target. Every hour made the rescue less likely.

Guy tumbled unconscious on his way down to the straw mat, knowing he'd see Bassett shortly, in whatever fitful dreams awaited him.

Dreams of his mistakes.

Dreams of the hole . . .

Once as a young recruit, Guy had foolishly lost his company in unfamiliar woods, and then doubled-down on his idiocy by stumbling into a sunken muddy hole. It was only barely deeper than a man stood tall, but it was half-filled with a rank stale water and he rolled his ankle during the fall. Logic insisted it would be easy to climb out—but with every attempt the mud walls sloughed down on him, his ankle would hold less weight, and logic shrugged its shoulders and moved on to the next fool. Guy could neither stand with any comfort nor sit without his head submerging. Eventually panic took him, and it ruled his brain in a way he could later only marvel at. Guy might have spent hours there, always only one solid handgrip away from safety, fighting in the wet and the cold. As time slipped on, so did his mind. He watched the walls pulse and sway. He gazed into the water and felt a sympathetic urge to drown himself. Though he never admitted it to anyone, he heard voices—half whispers and non-words only he could understand.

And the worst part was that none of it seemed unusual. He hadn't known he was going mad.

His company eventually backtracked to find him, and it only took one man's hand to hoist him out. As if it were nothing. Only a few feet were all the difference it took for him to limp away and live the rest of his life. But the hole had revealed something to him—the importance of strength, of body and of mind, and the blood-turning ease with which either could be taken from a man. He had needed help then. Jon Bassett needed it now.

"Good news, Captain."

He awoke to Reginold's thick red moustache and self-satisfied smile. It took Guy a moment to recognize the room in The Third Pig, and what business it had being in Guy's life.

"You were right, they came this way." Reginold smiled with unwarranted energy. Meanwhile, Guy's muscles were silently protesting everything and petitioned to take the day off. "Got a surprise for you in the common room."

Barely a minute later Guy lurched into the inn's musty main chamber, hoping his stiff legs might be mistaken as swagger. They were all met, but the cruel morning sun told Guy he must have only slept for an hour or so. Reginold was still spry on his feet, and might not have slept at all. Guy could have managed the same, but he had used up all his youth some years ago.

A large bald man sat in wait at the largest table, wolfing down something hot the innkeeper had made for breakfast. There was a wooden bowl for each of them.

"Glad I found you," the stranger said between mouthfuls, and he kicked a stool over to Guy. The others passed around the bowls of slop, which the stranger had apparently paid for. Bolt was already tipping his bowl back to finish whatever was in it.

"I'm Guy of Gisbourne, Captain of the Nottingham Guard—"

"I know," the bald man's voice was so low it scraped the ground.

"I've filled him in," Reginold said, twisting the corners of his moustache. "Care to repeat for my friends what you already told me?"

"I think I saw who you're looking for." He was thick as a horse, and his baldness was not from age. Even sitting down eating breakfast, the man looked like he could kill any one of them just by flexing the right muscle. "I heard a mess of horses late last night, off the road near Hallam. Something more than suspicious about it. Went into town and asked around, and folks said you were hunting these boys down. I've been chasing after you for hours."

"That's unusually kind of you," Eric said, fishing for chunks of food with a knife. "Why exactly do you care?"

Reginold grinned widely at the stranger. "My apologies. Some of us have forgotten what a knight even looks like." Guy's senses sharpened, and his men all jerked into somewhat more respectful positions. "Boys, this is Sir Robert FitzOdo of Tickhill Castle. Treat him with the respect he's deserving."

"We've met," Guy recalled, with some difficulty. The name was familiar. FitzOdo had played a role in the defense of Nottingham during Ferrers's assault in the Kings' War. But Tickhill Castle sat at the border of Nottinghamshire and Yorkshire, controlled by Baron Roger de Busli—who had selfishly kept his knights rather than send them to war. "You serve Red Roger now."

"When I must," FitzOdo winked, instantly earning Guy's trust. "As I was saying, these horses last night struck my curiosity. I followed them a bit, enough to see they had a prisoner with them. They broke for the night in a set of caves, I think mostly to get out of the rain. I can't promise you they're still there, but I can tell you this much. You're going the wrong way."

Hallam. Devon had been wrong. Hallam was practically where they started, much closer to Thieves Den than Hathersage. Their long rain-soaked night had been wasted, while their quarry had been sleeping rather than traveling. Guy glanced at Devon and saw the horror of this knowledge crawl up into his asshole for some heavy frolicking. *Poor man.*

"Eat up, mount up, and let's go," Guy said.

"Forget eating up," Eric answered, pushing away his bowl with a finger. "Jon needs us. I don't want to make him wait."

"Eat," Guy demanded. "You're no use to him if you don't take care of yourself. We have a few hours' ride ahead of us. A few minutes won't make the difference."

Eric humphed, but didn't eat any more. It was possible he wasn't able to, given the state of his mouth. "If they're there," he said darkly, "the girl's mine."

"If they're there," Guy matched his intensity, "we take them in."

"Captain—"

"That's not who we are. If you want to play by their rules, if you want to take whatever you want just because you want it, then go join them. We're better than that. Justice, not vengeance. You'd all do well to keep that in mind." Guy received a nod from each, excepting the young Ferrers, who didn't seem to think it applied to him. "You heard Wendenal. The Sheriff didn't want those outlaws harmed."

"That was before they captured Jon," Eric growled.

"Eric." Guy said it carefully, refusing to raise the man's temper. "Why are you here?"

The two locked eyes, and Eric's anger subsided. There was a reason Eric wasn't a crown ranger anymore, and it wasn't a pretty story. He had chosen once to make justice personal, and it nearly cost him everything. Left alone, the man was still at the mercy of his own demons. But Guy had given him a second chance rather than a gaol cell, and he'd earned it every day since.

In some ways, Guy realized, that made Eric the first gerold. He'd never thought of it like that before.

FitzOdo reared his massive head and stood. "Let's at it then, and hope they're still there."

THEY WERE.

FitzOdo had called it a cave, but that was an exaggeration. One tussocky hill rolled over another, and left a barren overhang that provided only a meager bit of shelter from the elements. Guy lay on his belly in the heather with the others, having crawled to the top of a neighboring hill to spy down on the camp. It sat in a wide bowl of a muddy hollow, but the night's rain clouds had rolled along and left them a clear view even from a distance. Regardless, Guy could not make out any details. A slender white ribbon of smoke floated up and out of the blackened overhang, evidence of a campfire, but Guy struggled to identify any of the shapes around it.

"There's movement," Eric mumbled. "Can't tell how many, though. No sign of the horses, or the carriage."

"You're certain that's them?" Reginold asked, squinting his eyes in rapid succession to prove how little it was helping.

"Could be a different pack of thieves with a different Guardsman as a prisoner." FitzOdo rolled his head obviously, as if daring them to question his story. Bolt choked a little, his version of a laugh.

"We have a few options, then," Guy said, sliding back away from the ridge. It was probably ridiculous to stay prone at this distance, but nobody was willing to risk messing this up. "No horses and no carriage could mean a few things. Could mean they abandoned them earlier, to throw us off. Or could mean that's only half of them down there, and the rest are out doing whatever unsavory things thieves like to do in the morning."

"Raping, I'd think," Reginold said, though no one even gave him a courtesy laugh. "If I were a thief, I'd think you'd start your day off with a good rape or two, then maybe some ham."

FitzOdo stared at Guy dully. "He's always like this?"

"Unfortunately," Bolt answered, earning himself a smack in the chest.

"If they're not all there," Guy continued, "we risk losing Bassett again. Might be wiser to wait and see if the others return. At the same time, if that *is* all of them, waiting only prolongs the danger he's already in. I'm open to suggestions."

There was a short amount of face-making at this, and FitzOdo answered quickly upon seeing their reaction. "We should go now," he barked, rising as if the decision had been made. "While we still have the advantage."

It seemed to be exactly what everyone wanted. It had been a long ride back to Hallam, and there was nothing they wanted so much as to put this behind them.

But Devon didn't move. Guy caught his eye, saw his urge to say something. He gave him a tight nod, permission. Devon's lips parted and his voice was weak. "What advantage?"

"What?" FitzOdo said, barely noticing the distraction.

"You said we have every advantage, but I don't . . . I don't see that."

"Are you serious? Is he serious?" FitzOdo chortled. "They don't have any horses with them. We do. You want to wait for more of them to show up, with fresh supplies and horses? Or you want to ride down there and take care of them while they're sleeping?" He sneered and turned to the others for a laugh. "Or perchance the word *advantage* is just a little too big for you?"

For a moment, Devon shrank. But Guy saw the look in Reginold's face, and the way Bolt shifted his eyes while pretending to smile. They weren't comfortable with the way the knight had just insulted Devon, and frankly Guy wasn't keen on it, either. Against all odds, Devon shook off his worry and spoke, quickly, his eyes buried in the heath.

"You're right. Or you would be, if all we wanted to do was storm down there and kill them. But like the Captain said—that's not what we do. We're here to end this peacefully, and to get Jon Bassett back alive. If we ride down from where we are now, they'll see us coming. They'll have a chance to prepare, they'll be ready for us, and they might even kill Jon before we get there. Or they'll put a sword to his throat and make us all strip down to our privies before stealing our horses and running off. Your plan only works if we don't care about Jon's life."

"It doesn't matter, boy—" the knight bellowed.

"On the other hand, we can take an hour and reposition to another side. We approach from on top of that hill where they can't see us, and slip down the sides of the overhang. We'll be inside their camp before they have any clue. A few of us can stay here with the horses, so that we can storm down on them just as you described. But that's not the real attack, that's just the diversion."

Reginold and Bolt nodded to him, there was a pride in their approval. Guy gave him a wink.

FitzOdo alone hated it. "That is a waste of time."

"It's better than a waste of life," Guy said, with finality. "Let's make it happen."

TWENTY-ONE

MARION FITZWALTER

SHERWOOD FOREST

"I THOUGHT THE SWORDS were bad, John," Marion said, her eyes strained and aching. They had volunteered to watch over the wounded Guardsman in shifts, though Marion stayed nearby even when it was not her turn. He had not yet awoken in nearly a day, which seemed a bad sign, but at times he would stir in befuddled agony long enough for them to force some water into his mouth. If he ever woke, Marion wanted to be the first to speak with him, to try to convince him he was safe.

"How's that, then?" John Little asked.

"The swords," she repeated. "I thought that was as bad as it would get. I was wrong."

"Ah," he said, his mouth closing quickly. He bore the burden of this awfully, and she had not meant to shame him. John insisted he only struck the Guardsman once in the chest, but the force of his quarterstaff had clearly broken something important. "I've made some mistakes lately, there is that."

"You're just out of practice," Marion tried to lighten his mood. "It's been some time since you've brought a lady gifts. We're not fond of swords, John, and we're not fond of dying Guardsmen, either. Try flowers."

"I'll keep that in mind," he said solemnly, but broke a small smirk. "I gather you won't be giving me the same advice on how to handle this one?"

Marion laughed. "Bury him and pray? No, that would be the worst thing we could do. If we bury this man, we might as well dig our own graves beside him."

They had debated about bringing him to a city to find a doctor, but it seemed risky to transport him any farther. They had found a relatively safe spot to camp beside a glade of silver birches, and they had fortunately brought enough supplies for a few days. Marion sent Clarell home for her own safety, and the hope that her horse's tracks might mislead their pursuers. She had asked the same of Sir Amon, who predictably refused to leave her. Instead Arthur had taken Amon's horse, to bring word of their predicament back to the Oak Camp.

Friar Tuck tended to the wounded Guardsman's comfort as best he could by keeping him cool and washing his soiled clothes in a nearby stream. There was little else to do besides pray for his recovery, upon which so much depended. Before the skirmish, they had been on the verge of peace talks. Robin swore his friend Wendenal was still trying to keep that promise, but Sheriff de Lacy could not honor any such agreement if they accidentally became murderers. Poor John Little knew it, and carried the guilt of that precipice. The only thing he didn't seem to know was his own strength.

Will Scarlet and Elena naturally protested the entire endeavor. Both had argued heavily to leave the fallen Guardsman behind, and despite their impetuousness Marion wondered if they might have been right. When Captain Gisbourne inevitably returned to search for his lost man, he could provide far better medical assistance. His resources in Nottingham would be greater than anything to be found in the Sherwood. The simpler side of Marion's conscience insisted the moral choice was to help the man, as they had done, and that leaving him behind would have only compounded their error. Yet beneath that excuse was something a bit darker she did not wish to dwell upon. Trying to help the guard now meant she could later argue they'd done their best to save him, even though he stood a better chance at surviving if they left him for Gisbourne to find.

Marion had gambled the man's life for her own reputation.

She needed him to live, that she would not have to regret that choice.

"You can see why they need you," Marion said softly, sometime later, when Robin found himself idling behind her. He had remained stubbornly quiet since their departure from Locksley. He would offer determined bits of succinct advice, on how to move the man safely, on how to hide their trail, on terse facts. His opinions were few, which was a rarity for him. It was more than obvious he regretted his decision to stay. If the Guardsman's unconscious body had been discovered even a few minutes earlier, Robin would undoubtedly have left with Wendenal, and been all the happier for it. Every inch of his skulking linger spoke to that truth.

"They need to disappear," Robin said, not taking any care to hide his callous tone. "Before they do more damage."

"You know they don't have that option," she replied. The Guardsman's chest gave a short stutter as if to emphasize her point. "This is what happens when they're left to their instincts. They steal the wrong wagon, they nearly kill someone when they don't have to. They mean well, you can see that, whether or not you believe it. They just need training."

"Training in how *not* to kill someone?"

"Not that." She didn't have the right words to piece it together. It was another facet of what she'd seen building at Locksley Castle, a glimpse of what was possible. "They need training in just . . . in just how to *be*. Does that make sense? Without a master, they have no rules, like a child without a parent. They don't have any experience living outside of direction, outside of . . . the law."

"Congratulations," came his dry response. "You've figured out why they're called *outlaws*."

"Shut it." She could feel that fake smile on his face even behind her head. "But yes, they also need to learn how to control themselves. How to avoid a fight. How to steal without getting into trouble, before something truly terrible . . ."

Her sentence drifted away to horrors of the past. Robin was silent behind her, for likely the same reason. That soft part of her told her to let it lie, but it was an open wound in him that she could sting. He had proven himself unconscionably prickly so far, and she was feeling something shy of charitable at the moment.

"You need to do this for me," she finished simply. "You have to try."

A quiet eternity passed before he responded. "Alright. On one condition. You stay, too. That captain knows who you are, and I can't protect you if I'm in the woods."

Marion didn't have the energy to explain how misplaced his heroism was, but she'd already come to the same conclusion. Nottingham wouldn't be a safe place for her until this had blown over.

"Well then," Robin continued. "First thing, they have to stop stealing war supplies."

"Obviously."

"They steal from the army, the Sheriff has to respond. If they want to steal from someone, they should steal from a stealer. There are plenty of men who have grown fat off the war who shouldn't have. They get robbed, and who can they complain to?"

Marion nodded.

"It's just a suggestion. Only take from those that can afford to lose it, and don't take more than they're able to do without. Keep the violence to an absolute minimum. That makes it harder for the Sheriff to justify hunting them down."

There was a finality to his sentence, as if it were that easy. "That's not enough."

"It's a start."

"Laying low isn't enough," she repeated. "Not with winter on the horizon. You've seen their camp, they can't survive there."

"That's true," he said softly. "I'm surprised they've lasted this long."

"They need real shelter, they need to stockpile, they need to be able to protect themselves from others who would see them as easy targets, too."

She felt a puff of warm air on her neck, Robin's laugh. "You want me to build houses for them? I appreciate your confidence in me, but . . ."

"They'll need help for all that. They'll need to pay for that help."

"Which means even more coin."

"They'll also need to pay for that help to keep quiet."

"Which means . . . a stupid lot more coin."

"It means more than coin, Robin. They need allies."

"Alright," Robin rolled with the idea. "Then they need to be a force for good. There are others out there who need help as well. If they're going to be stealing a stupid lot more coin, we might as well shoot for the sky. Enough that they can *endear* themselves to the people. They'll need friends in the villages, in the towns . . ." He trailed off, thinking it through.

"And stop being such a wart about it." She brought her hand up to her shoulder, reaching for him. A few moments later, his hand slid into hers. "You're here with us, you might as well enjoy it. Try to pretend you're not an ass."

"That may be asking too much," he said, but she could hear his smile this time, and he squeezed her fingers.

"I'm serious," she followed. "If you're going to be here for a month, I need you to believe in this. This is not some casual distraction from the war. It's not enough to just avoid the next disaster, we need to work *toward* something. Do not idle your time with us. I need this to work. And it's going to work."

She could feel him hesitate. His breath abated, even the constant sway of his feet stopped. But his hand was still in hers.

"They're here because of me. I convinced your father to open his doors, I convinced these people Locksley was a safe place for them." She had been trying to help. It was her sister's death that first led her to the comfort of helping others in need. It drew her from her melancholy, it brought purpose to the life she rudely still had. Over the years, her family's status shined a light on the things she touched, bringing attention to her causes. At court she had become well known as a voice of dissent, so much so that she sometimes felt her involvement in a situation actually hurt it. If she was its champion, some assumed, then it must be another unfixable charity case.

She liked to think she changed minds. Even when she was overruled or ignored, she hoped to have a cumulative effect, over time. She was a river, slowly eroding centuries of selfishness. As a woman, she was not so crippled as the other lords that acted only for their own betterment. It was, in fact, one of the reasons they suffered to listen to her. Unmarried, she had dangled a potential betrothal into her family's influence during many a negotiation, just to open the door a little.

Even at that, she had found no victories. Some mockingly compared her to Saint Jude, the patron saint of lost causes. The terrible truth was she enjoyed the reputation. She liked being the troublemaker, the underdog, anything that upset the way things were. It reminded her of Vivian.

"All the coin in the world won't matter if they don't believe they have a future, Robin. They need to believe they can win. And I need you to believe it, too."

"Alright," Robin whispered, adding no jokes or bitterness. He didn't need to say any more than that.

These people were on her. She needed a victory.

WHEN THE GUARDSMAN AWOKE it was accompanied by a gasp of pain and vomit, followed by a wheezing sound that bubbled in his throat. They rushed to clean his face and offer water. Tuck brought a cup of stew that had been simmering, but failed to find a chance to give it to him. Over half an hour he roused, wild-eyed and jumpy, though Marion did her best to speak calmly and explain what had happened. Twice he lunged and tried to run, only to stumble and hurt himself in the process. Despite its connotations, Marion allowed Will and Arthur to bind his legs and feet together, for his protection. They enjoyed the task a bit more obviously than she would have preferred.

Eventually he could talk, though his voice was a rusted rasp. His lungs could barely manage more than a few words at a time. He had taken neither water nor food in over a day, and needed deeper rest to recuperate. His name was Jon Bassett, and what labored breaths he made were spent swearing the Nottingham

Guard would find them shortly, and they should release him immediately. Marion did her best to explain he was no prisoner, and they meant to help. She hoped her presence alone would be enough to prove their peaceful intentions, but Bassett did not seem keen to trust her. She could hardly blame him.

"We don't liken to have you any more than you liken to be here, which is little," John grumbled at the man, doing his best to match the Guardsman's salt. "But we couldn't leave you behind. I did you a number, that's plain. But you were putting one on my friend, too, which wasn't a kindness. You wouldn't have gotten far on your own, and we don't see how letting you die would help any. But do us all a favor and speak up the moment you're able to fend for yourself so we can be rid of you."

Jon Bassett snorted, expelling clumps of dried blood from his nose. He tugged at his newly earned restraints as if to imply he was ready to leave now.

Little knelt down. "You're not well yet. Don't be lying to us. Haven't you heard? I eat liars."

As the day grew longer it became obvious they would keep camp another night, but Jon Bassett did show signs of improvement. Once he was properly fed his energy returned to him, and they took shifts walking him around the campsite to ease his muscles. He moved impossibly slowly, like a man passing a kidney stone, but it was progress. Marion's promise that he was no prisoner was made somewhat flatter by the stretch of rope they used to leash him on his walks. He could not breathe deeply without significant pain, but the rest of his body, and his spirits, seemed quick to recover.

"You don't remember me," his voice creaked, as Marion took her turn to limp him about. She did not hold the rope herself, as the others insisted he might be feigning weakness. So Sir Amon walked beside her, the tether wrapped twice around his arm. "I've seen you at Nottingham."

Marion was embarrassed to admit his face was unfamiliar.

"I escorted you . . . a few months back. To see the Sheriff. We talked with the captain . . . in the training yard."

She remembered it now, though he had made no impression on her.

"Everyone knows you collude with them now," he said. "And you'll get yours, no matter what you do to me."

The threat caught her off guard. "You don't know anything," she scoffed. "Maybe I'm only with them right now to make sure they treat you well. I could be in danger myself, too, for all you know."

His lips pursed in disbelief. "You parlayed for them at Thieves Den."

"I've parlayed for lots of people," she answered sharply. "If you knew me better you'd know that. I once defended a tanner's daughter who accidentally burned a dozen hides. Do you think that makes me the one who dropped the torch?"

Of all the battered muscles in Bassett's body, the one that apparently worked best was used for raising a skeptical eyebrow. "Do you think I'm blind? I know you run with these thieves. I can see they do your bidding."

Marion wished that was as true as it sounded. A great deal of trouble might have been spared so far if it were. But she matched his steely tone. "As I say, my involvement here is entirely benign. So I would suggest you reconsider what you think you know. Because *I* know that they didn't *need* to take care of you. But they did. And at the moment they intend to return you to Nottingham once you're healthy."

The Guardsman's shoulders shook in a quiet laughter, though his face remained stoic. "I see. In exchange for my life, you demand I vouch for your . . . *benign involvement?*"

"I've made no demands." She met his eyes. "The manner of your gratitude is up to you."

"Ah yes, very thankful. Look at all my good fortune." He tried to splay his hands wide, but his restraints stopped him quickly. "That's the difference between us and you, you know. Selfishness."

Marion felt a pang of offense at being labeled the outsider. But she let him continue.

"You want me to make a deal to save my own skin. They call that a *thieves bargain*. It has that name for a reason—no decent person would ever take it. I'd be selling short my friends to help myself. The next time I see you in Nottingham—yes, I could keep my mouth shut . . . about what you do here in the forest. And I wonder who would be hurt by that? I wonder which of my friends might suffer the next time your group here play their games of terror? Whose life am I trading for my own?"

"I'd say you're being a bit overdramatic. We're not hurting anyone."

He just held her stare and coughed with a targeted irony.

"They're good people," she insisted.

"Sometimes, might be. Everyone is good people when they're good. But you're a fool if you think that's all they are. You'll see. They'll turn on you. They'll turn on each other, and they certainly won't let you set me free at the end of this."

"They will." She stopped walking to make a point of it. For the first time she truly took in his face, the forced clench of his jaw, the slight twitch to his eye. There was the young boy he once was, and the potential for friendliness in his dour lines. It was so easy to label him as *Guardsman*. Here was a decent man named Jon Bassett who was tied up in the woods by those he thought meant to kill him. Of course he was terrified, and of course he would antagonize her. "You'll go home safely. You have my promise on that."

Jon Bassett shook his head. "I've already seen your promises. They only last until the first thief pulls steel."

Marion had no response.

"Why not turn them in?" he added, his eyes darting toward the others. "Get us to the horses. The three of us leave right now, and you can still land on the right side of this. And *you* . . ." he shifted his attention to Amon, ". . . you might even keep your knighthood."

Amon wouldn't betray her in a thousand years, but the point was real enough. Their safety was only as strong as the weakest of them.

Worse, she felt the prod of that weakness within herself. She would be lying to say she did not see the reason in his offer. Marion risked losing too much by all these complications, and not just for herself. If she were disgraced or labeled a criminal, it would be blamed on her "woman's folly." And woe unto the next ambitious woman who braved her head amongst the men of court, if Marion set such a precedent. Her responsibilities extended so much farther than herself.

Far off across the glen, a flurry of birds took to the air.

"You know I'm right," Jon Bassett urged.

She shook it off. "You realize what you're offering me, don't you?" she asked. "I believe they call it a *thieves bargain*. I'm told that no decent person would ever take one."

TWENTY-TWO

GUY OF GISBOURNE

THIEVES' CAMP

EVERY SECOND THAT PASSED was merciless. The extremes of exhaustion and excitement battled over Guy's nerves. He stayed at the top of the ridge with Devon and Ferrers, waiting for the others to signal their readiness. Morg and Bolt went their own way, setting up in a concealed position close enough to the thieves' camp for Bolt to use his crossbow once the trap was sprung. Sir Robert FitzOdo originally insisted on leading the horseback charge, but changed his mind when he realized Devon would be a part of that as well. Guy's new recruit had certainly gotten under the knight's skin, which was an impressive thing to do. So FitzOdo opted to join Reginold and Eric in their long run around the valley to circle behind the enemy camp. Once they were in position, they'd be hidden from the outlaws below, but plainly visible from Guy's vantage.

That meant there was nothing to do but wait, and Guy found it hard to fight off the pull that wanted to smother him into sleep. He had barely closed his eyes at the inn that morning, and felt far crispier than he would prefer for a maneuver like this. Fortunately, every errant noise in the distance startled him alert. He was endlessly afraid the thieves would spot them and make a run for it, and Devon's plan would spell their disaster.

"What you said earlier took bravery," Guy said to the young Devon, as Ferrers slipped away to relieve himself in the bracken. "You haven't interacted with a lot of knights, I'll guess."

"That was the first one," Devon admitted.

"Hopefully not your last." He smiled, hoping to give the boy some confidence. "Brave or naïve—they're cousins, after all. Best be sure your expectations for this next part are tempered then. The odds we get Jon Bassett back alive are narrow. It's good to have hope, but the reality is he's probably dead already."

Devon seemed confused. "Then why are we trying?"

"Don't ask me that." Guy turned to look at him plainly. "Ask yourself. You're trying, aren't you? You spoke up against FitzOdo when you didn't have to. You could just take orders, happy to be outside of a prison cell. But seems like you actually care. Why? Why are you here?"

The question might as well have been a woman, as Devon had no idea what to do with it. Guy certainly couldn't expect the young man to have distinguished a keen sense of morality so quickly. He had likely only accepted this position in the Guard to save his own skin. But Guy hoped to guide the young man, in all the ways he had failed to do with Jon Bassett.

When Devon answered, it was with little conviction. "Responsibility?"

It sounded less like a real answer than a guess at what Guy wanted to hear.

"Responsibility." Guy raised an eyebrow. "That's a fake thing, we made it up. Us humans. We created the word so we wouldn't sound so selfish all the time. Honor, piety, responsibility. They sound wonderful and we tell our children about them so they'll behave. I'm no different. I told *my* children about them, as well. I'm a damned proud hypocrite. Yours is still too young, yes?"

"Very much so."

"He'll grow up to respect them, thanks to you, and he should. As should your other children."

"We only have the one daughter."

"For now. You'll have more. Trust me, have many more." Guy pictured his two sons, Henry and John, young and happy as they'd once been, and tried not to think about how old Henry would have been now. He bit it off and continued. "It's good for them to respect those words when they're children, but later in life they'll realize they're all brands of the same selfishness."

"Selfishness?"

"Absolutely. Don't make a face. Selfishness is what keeps every man alive. It's why we don't sit still and starve. It's why we're here, right now. Am I wrong?"

Devon appeared to be at a loss. "But I'm tired, and I hurt. Wouldn't it be selfish of me to give up and go to sleep?"

"It would be. So why are we still trying?"

This time he answered quickly, and it rang of honesty. "Because it's the right thing to do."

It was an improvement, if unimaginative. Guy had to teach the boy better. His men were the future of the Nottingham Guard, and it was his job to make that future a bright one.

"Right and wrong are arbitrary. They're just words we use to describe actions that either help us or hurt us. In the Sheriff's Guard, we try to maintain order, so we say interfering with us is wrong. We decide capturing one of our members is wrong, to protect ourselves. We believe England is safer and better off when its people are protected, when its laws are absolute and not open to reinterpretation by every fool lord with an inflated sense of importance. Because such a country protects us, which makes our endgame selfish, no?"

Devon chewed on that answer, but did not accept it. "I don't see how wanting the country to be safer is selfish. It helps ourselves, yes, but it also helps so many others. Selfishness serves only one person. Order and laws, these benefit us all. Why call them selfish?"

Guy smiled, and dared to hope that the damned little gerold might actually be worth his own weight.

WHEN IT HAPPENED, IT happened fast. Three black shapes moved across the distant hillock, wiggling just enough in what Guy assumed was a wild waving of their arms. He gave the word and backed down from the ridge, with Devon and Ferrers following suit. They each selected one of the unwieldy halberds they had brought with them, planting the base of the long shaft in their saddle's stirrup. Neither had any training in such a weapon, but they only needed to ride with it, to give the impression of a mounted assault. It would look awfully threatening from a distance, and panic the thieves as FitzOdo and the others attacked from behind.

Guy heaved himself to his own mount, a black palfrey named Merciful. She awaited his command, happy to ease up over the ridgeline to begin their descent. It was a long slope of pitted heather down to the camp, which made a gallop impossible. Guy's thighs were already bruised from the amount of riding they'd done in the last day, so he could barely feel whatever more damage he was doing to them now. It wouldn't matter once this was over.

He screamed from the bottom of his lungs, and was rewarded with the sight of four black shapes darting out from under the overhang. He was too far away to identify their faces, but the smallest one at the edge with long hair must have been the girl, Elena. Two others were men, but none of their shapes seemed to match the massive John Little, or the young knifeman.

The fourth shape was taller—Robin of Locksley. Guy had given Locksley every opportunity to position himself on the right side of the law, and he'd thrown it away to follow in his father's traitorous steps. What came next was anyone's guess.

The bodies scattered, stumbling, two of them diving back into their camp, but Eric and Reginold were there to meet them. Every hoofbeat brought Guy closer, able to see more details. Reginold put an arrow through one man's thigh and then tackled him, pinning him to the ground by sitting on his chest. Eric caught the other, spinning him around in his tracks and smashing the hilt of his sword into the man's face.

Guy didn't even flinch at the violence. Baron de Lacy's asinine command had been to leave them unharmed, an instruction so meritless he had not even given it to Guy in person. He lent his voice to William de Wendenal, the king's stooge, rather than let Guy fulfill the duties of his position. That command had nearly cost them lives at Thieves Den, and Guy would not suffer to let it hinder them again. If the Baron reprimanded him for anyone harmed here, Guy wouldn't care. His men's lives were not worth taking chances.

The two remaining thieves—the girl and Locksley—ran from the assault, but headed directly toward the approaching Sir Robert FitzOdo. Guy watched Locksley throw himself between the knight and the girl, drawing a sword as she fled out into the muddy field. At Guy's command, Devon and Ferrers peeled off to the left to intercept her, while Guy continued forward to help FitzOdo against Locksley.

The shrill clash of their swords split the air, and Guy watched the silhouettes of the two men hack at each other. He leaned into Merciful, urging her harder as the ground leveled out, to close the final distance to the camp. Even though FitzOdo was bald, it was difficult to differentiate the two men as they rotated and swung wildly—but there was no mistaking the moment one man's sword smashed through the other's head, embedding itself as the victim toppled uselessly over. The sword stayed in its victim's skull, wrenched from the attacker's hands as the body dropped. It was eerie to see such violence from a distance. Guy hoped it was Locksley who had been felled. He did not want any of his men to face off against a man who could take down a knight like FitzOdo.

A sharp cry came from the left where the girl, who had not made it far, was wavering in place. A crossbow bolt was in her stomach. She looked down at it, her shoulders shaking. Elena took a few more steps and another quarrel punched through the middle of her chest, sprung from Bolt's hiding spot. The woman dropped to a knee, wobbled, then went face first into the slop.

At last, Merciful arrived at the camp, and he reined her into a walk. Reginold was yelling at his prisoner, flicking the arrow in his leg to keep him from wiggling. But it was Eric of Felley's voice that cut through everything else.

"What the hell is this?"

"I'm sorry," came FitzOdo's voice, and Guy was relieved to see the man stumble out of the shadow into the daylight, his head intact though splattered in blood. "This was the only way."

"Who the hell are these people?" Eric asked furiously.

Guy realized he was missing something. His gut twisted. He slid down from Merciful, strode purposefully over to Reginold to see the faces of his two captives—and both were strangers. Guy did not recognize either of them from the fight at Thieves Den.

"Where's Bassett?" he asked the prisoners, but he had the terrible empty feeling that he knew the answer.

"I don't feel proud about using you like this," FitzOdo was saying. "You've still done a good thing today, you know."

Damnation.

"Who are they?" Eric spat again.

"Thieves, outlaws," FitzOdo said happily, wiping the blood from his face. "Just not yours. Fugitives from York. I've been tracking them ever since they crossed the border. They holed up here for the last few nights, but I knew I couldn't take them on my own."

Guy reeled. He marched toward the body that should have been Robin of Locksley, and saw immediately how mistaken he was. The distance, the shadow of the hill—his own expectations had tricked him. Glancing out to where Elena had fallen in the mud, he no longer saw the young girl but a short thin man with black hair. White-hot anger ripped through Guy's muscles, which instantly surrendered to exhaustion. He dropped to the ground and sat, too furious to even react.

"You said they had a prisoner with them," he said, staring at FitzOdo.

"I did lie about that." The knight shrugged. "I heard you had come through Hallam, asking about a group of riders that had a Guardsman as a prisoner. I figured you might help me on principle, but . . . well you know how it is." FitzOdo laughed, as if it were just a joke.

"You son of a bitch."

"I ain't never claimed otherwise," FitzOdo sneered at him. "Still, you got a couple less murderers running loose, you can take that to heart. Mind if I take these two back to Tickhill, or are you so ass hurt about this you want to claim them for yourselves?"

"I want you to get out of here," Guy said with an unnatural calm he did not feel. "Take them with you, and make haste."

"As you say," the knight balked. "Let me take some souvenirs first. Red Roger'll want proof the other two are dead. And hey. I owe you one." He flashed a vaguely apologetic look to each of them, and took no discouragement from the lack of response. "By and by, your friend is dead. No reason for a pack of thieves to keep a regular Guardsman as a prisoner. No offense. You can get a ransom for a knight, at least."

FitzOdo cut off the heads of the two dead men, and made each of his captives carry one as he led them away. Guy and his regiment were left with nothing but a cold trail and the sickening sense they ought to start mourning the life of Jon Bassett.

THERE WAS LITTLE DISCUSSION as to whether or not they would continue their search.

"There's no picking up the trail now," Guy said. "If they still have him, they know we want him back. We'll have to wait for them to contact us."

But despite his own words, Guy insisted he was going to stay out looking, going from town to town, to hunt for any last leads. He had a few old acquaintances whose ears were still on the ground, and they were worth visiting. His men offered to go with him, but he ordered them to return to the castle.

"I know it's pointless, and I won't have any of you wasting your time. This is just for me. I'll see you in a day or so."

They begrudgingly obeyed. Devon of York lingered last, thanking Guy for trusting his instincts, fruitless though they were. Guy felt for the young man. This victory would have bolstered his confidence, and his sense of belonging. The others were sure to accept his strange addition to their ranks if he could prove himself useful, but Robert FitzOdo had stolen that opportunity. Devon's plan had worked flawlessly, but still felt like a complete defeat.

"I think maybe you were right, earlier. About right and wrong," Guy said, just before Devon climbed onto his horse. "Maybe they do exist. I'll ask ahead of time that you don't repeat this to the others. I need to be ironclad—it wouldn't do to be too passionate about this. But they're coming, even now, even thinking about it."

Guy turned away from Devon's confused reaction to blink away whatever tears were rising. He had been where Jon Bassett was before. Alone, trapped, relying solely on his companions to save him. He had touched something within himself, down in that hole, something he never wanted to feel again.

"Some things, you tell yourself they're right, so you feel better doing them. And they stack up. You're too young for that now, but over the years you'll carry them. They'll hurt. The choices will, and the grey is a heavy thing.

"But what they've done to Jon Bassett, that's pure wrong. That's why I'm still here. Because when I think of the alternative, my stomach shrinks and my skin goes cold. Jon's out there. He's a prisoner, and he's alone, and he needs us. Every step we've taken since yesterday, every bite, every laugh we've had when we've forgotten ourselves, every breath, every blink, even while we sleep, we've done it while Jon's been *in a hole*. He's in a hole, and there are people that put him there who will beat him and starve him, and it's all he knows. There isn't a word in our language for these people. We never made one. We didn't think we'd have to."

Uncomfortable and fatigued as he was, Guy had a meal in his belly, a sword at his side, and companions. Jon Bassett had none of that.

"Do you think that bastard knight was right?" Devon asked. "You think he's already dead?"

"I hope he is. I do," Guy said without hesitation. "It's better than the hole."

TWENTY-THREE

ARABLE DE BUREL

NOTTINGHAM CASTLE

Only a handful of mirrors existed in the castle, making it difficult for Arable to use one with any sort of privacy. So she stole into the widow Murdac's old bedroom, a cozy chamber on the third floor of the high keep that remained relatively untouched since the previous sheriff's death. Arable had not lived in Nottingham then, but she understood Ralph Murdac kept it solely for his wife's infrequent visits. So long as Roger de Lacy was sheriff, there was little threat of his family ever using the room. Only dusted and refreshed once a month, Arable was usually happy to claim the duty. Its décor had a forced feminine flair—a man's attempt at a woman's touch—but she found it a comfortable place to disappear now and again. A single shuttered window could see all the way down across both the lower baileys to the castle gates, though she refrained from enjoying the view for fear of being spotted from below.

A quick rummage through the widow's vanity yielded a small squarish piece of polished silver. She took it and curled up beneath the window's sill to let the last of the day's sunlight on her face, and squinted at the rippled reflection scowling back at her. Across each of her cheeks, the long straight knife wounds had grown bright red and puffy, though their edges had begun to harden and scab over. She teased her hair forward, letting it dangle on either side of her face in thick bunches to see how well they concealed her cheeks. *There was no hiding the gashes.* Arable had done her best for days to stay hidden, to obscure her face, to wear oversized bonnets that kept her cheeks shadowed. Her reflection made a mockery of her attempts at secrecy.

That knowledge burned black inside her. Aside from William and Gunny, no other soul had given her face a moment's notice. Either nobody cared about what happened to her, or they simply considered her attack too normal to bother with. Both were suffocating in their ramifications. She was faced with the crippling reality that she was exactly as weak and ignorable as she pretended to be.

There was something darkly poetic that it happened just minutes after William had left her in the stables. The very moment William came back into her life, he had not been there when she needed help. *It didn't matter.* When next he saw her, William swore obscenities and would have marched directly to Jon Bassett and cleaved his head off if he could. But the entirety of the Captain's Regiment had yet to return from their journey, and there was no word as to what delayed them. William was left to fume with no target, and to swear empty horrors upon the man once he was finally back.

Arable might have appreciated his chivalry if she had not already spent two days coping with the attack entirely alone. At first she had been in shock, clutching her face in horror for hours until a horsehand found her. Then, nearly as painful as the attack itself, it took the majority of her savings to tend to the wound. She paid handsomely for a decent physicker in the Parliament Ward, who promised he could stitch her with ant heads and catgut without leading to any greenrot. He was kind and had a calming voice, and he likely did not realize how terrible his words were to her.

"You're lucky," he actually said without laughing. *"Whoever did this used a sharp blade, and very thin. Might have been far worse."*

There was no world in which this made Arable lucky. Luck was not involved with what had happened to her.

"I won't inquire as to the particulars," he continued, *"but you were wise not to struggle. Smart girl, could have made a botch of your face otherwise."*

If her face had allowed it, she might have told him exactly what she thought of this determination. The idea that it was someway her responsibility to react appropriately when an attack like this happens was nauseating. But she could not so much as scowl without agony lancing through her cheeks, so she had said nothing. She paid the physicker once for his work and twice for his silence and returned to the castle with almost nothing in her coinpurse.

Reflected in the silver, she saw France. Her lost chance to escape was carved into her cheeks. She had wasted so much time worrying about an exact destination, and now she could not afford to have one at all.

The few times she had seen William since, his smile turned into a sympathetic frown with a thousand connotations. She instinctively took its worst meaning—that when he saw her, he saw only her wounds. As if that was all she was now, a thing to be pitied. She was no longer herself, but a victim. Bassett's victim. His signature was on her face. Surely William did not think that, but it was all she could see.

Rage filled her, and left again. For a time she even believed she deserved it, that it was her own fault for spying on the Guardsmen in the wine cellar. In the end, that didn't matter, either. It was a thing that happened, and the world wasn't fair. When she closed her eyes she could still hear Jon Bassett's voice.

"This is what happens to nosy young ladies."

He meant it as a threat, to scare her. And yes, Arable was scared of him now, but his words had taken another meaning. It was simply a lesson to be learned, an inarguable truth about the damned world she lived in.

This is what happens to nosy young ladies.

After composing herself, Arable hurried down the hallway to the keep's master solar, which was now only used for housing prominent guests. Roger de Lacy preferred more modest quarters himself, which availed the sheriff's traditional bedroom for notable visitors. She was already late for her afternoon's task, which was to wait upon the Earl of Warwick and his wife, who had arrived unexpectedly.

Though the hallway never changed, it seemed to slant up today. Her every footstep took effort—she retracted from herself as she climbed it. Her servant's mantle no longer felt like a disguise, it was now her actual life. She tugged her hair farther forward to crop out her cheeks. Not because she didn't want anyone to ask, but so she wouldn't have to feel it when they didn't.

The unmistakable rumbling of an argument carried all the way down the hall, and Arable opened the door of the solar to an absolute frenzy. She barely found room to curtsy to the two guests between the bustling of personal assistants busying themselves at ignoring the spat between the earl and his wife. The earl himself, Waleran de Beaumont, was a wild-eyed man with spotted skin and white wisps of hair that seemed eager to escape their captivity. His wife, Lady Margery d'Oily, might have been his polar opposite. She remained stoic and composed in the middle of the room, her every blink executed with precision.

"Ah, be a dear girl," the Lady Margery said upon seeing Arable, "and point me in the direction of a jewelry box, would you?" Arable only had time to open her mouth and glance about before Lady Margery waved her hand in glib dismissal. "Oh, never mind, I forgot that I have no jewelry left to put in it."

"You're going to take this out on this poor girl?" the earl asked with some derision. "Is that where we are now?"

"I would never presume to tell you where we are." Her face shrugged off any blame. "I trust entirely in your leadership. I can't recall the last time you steered us poorly."

"I apologize for my wife's flat-handed sarcasm," the earl said to Arable. "She has decided it is entirely my fault we were victim of robbery on our way to Nottingham earlier this day."

Arable made a concerted effort to have no reaction. A minute ago she had been staring at her own disfigured face trying to drum up the will to stand, and now she was expected to care about this lady's jewelry.

"I would not call us *victim*." Lady Margery turned elaborately away from her husband. "All in all, it was a rather pleasant experience. I found him charming." She toyed with her fingers, as if to highlight precisely where her jewelry had once been. "You ought to try being charming now and then."

She was pleased with herself, which she showed by lilting her head back and forth like a top.

"Try not to smile, love," the earl moaned at her. "You haven't used those muscles in decades. If you ask them to work now, they're like to quit entirely and slough off your skull."

At this the Lady Margery narrowed her eyes to slivers, her lips pursed in preparation of her next words. Arable, who was at the moment categorically incapable of any interest in their minor troubles, was still forced to participate in their meaningless banter. "A robbery, you say?"

"Yes indeed." Waleran de Beaumont snatched the chance to tell the story, his wild eyebrows burning white from the window's glow. "Not as you may expect it, though. We made haste from York, as it were, until our carriage came to an unexpected stop in the middle of the Sherwood Road. There lay a gathering of men, all quite friendly, who apologized for the delay. One of them shook my hand and slipped my father's signet ring from my finger, explaining himself thusly—*'Don't worry about this, I promise to take care of it,'* and *'You're lucky to have come across us.'*"

"Pay him no mind, girl," Lady Margery commanded. "He cannot comprehend how little you care about this."

Arable startled at the lady's accuracy. The passing inconvenience of a lost ring was meaningless to them, but a single piece of jewelry like that was worth everything she had just spent. The lady's trivial losses could send Arable to France half a dozen times over.

She would never abuse Roger de Lacy's trust, but it was impossible not to fantasize. *How easily she might return to the room later, when it was empty . . .*

But the other half of the equation was also there. No matter how gentlemanly, thieves on the forest roads were far more dangerous for a woman on her own than for a carriage full of notable dignitaries. She doubted she could survive an encounter with the same glib lack of consequence.

"As I was saying," Waleran continued, "then he slipped into our carriage and relieved my wife of her jewelry as well. It was all done very kindly and quickly. It was over before I even realized that being robbed had quite been the highlight of my day."

"I don't even have words for you." Lady Margery rolled her eyes and turned to the window.

"Did I mention what he said when he left me?"

"Who?" Arable asked.

"The gentleman thief. He said, *'Now I'm going to smell of lilacs all day.'* My wife drowns herself in lilac oil, you see, I'm sure you can smell it already."

Arable gave a quick sniff of the room, and had to admit it had a pleasant fragrance.

"I have no idea how she survives it, personally. When the thief opened the door to our carriage I would have given him half my coinpurse just for the welcome breath of air. My wife no longer needs air to breathe, you see, her body is fueled solely on my misfortune."

"What was that, dear?" Lady Margery asked idly from the window. "I'm sorry, I was distracted by something more interesting, perhaps a hangnail or some dry skin. Do talk at me again, would you?"

Arable forgot herself for a moment and laughed at this, which she immediately regretted. She felt the skin tug at her cheeks, the sharp quick scratch that meant she had torn one of her wounds open. Reaching up quickly, she found a spot of blood on her fingertips. She held her face tightly, pushing her skin back together as if it were clay that might heal itself again.

You can't laugh, she told herself, but the words dug far deeper. *That's what Jon Bassett took from you. Your very ability to enjoy things.*

The earl and his wife seemed oblivious to her pain. "Is the Sheriff ready to see me?" Waleran asked, fretting at his own clothes. "I sent word ahead of my arrival, and have urgent news. Is he indisposed?"

"He regrets he cannot see you until the morning," Arable stammered, keen on disappearing. The earl reacted as if she were personally denying him, but then settled himself into a polite smile.

"It is urgent," he said. "But I understand the day has grown late. Thank you."

She forgot to curtsy a goodbye as she grabbed at the door to leave. One glance backward, accidental, brought her a startling glimpse of Lady Margery watching her departure, her face full of exacting scrutiny.

MISTRESS ROANA ASSIGNED HER only a single task for the remainder of the evening, accompanied by the ugliest face she was capable of making. Whatever Arable had done to offend her, she did not know, but she doubted it would be a mystery for long. The task was to tend to a stateroom in the southwest corner of the Great Hall, one of the respectable bedrooms kept for the type of lesser dignitaries that rarely ever visited. The fact that it was her only task meant the room must be in serious disrepair, but several hours working alone seemed like a blessing.

The door opened to a room that needed no tidying. The rushes were clean and the bed linens already changed, a fire warmed the brazier, and Arable froze to think she had been misinformed. But curiosity stayed her, and a second sweep of the room revealed an obviously placed note pinned beneath a single candleholder, paired with an apple blossom.

She crossed the room timidly, almost certain this was some cruel trap, but recognized William's indelicate penmanship on the outside of the note.

The stable loft. I'll be there. I promise.

She stared at the parchment in shock. She was alone in a massive crowd, only to suddenly find someone looking directly at her. It took her breath away, she trembled in fear. She wanted to believe it, she wanted to fall into those words and float away, but the world had trained her otherwise. *It had to be a trick.* It would vanish later, she knew, but for one perfect moment she watched the ink blot as the parchment soaked up her tears, as her feet left the stones.

ONCE UPON A TIME, Arable was a young girl in Derbyshire and there was little in her life to call wretched. The Burels and the Wendenals were close families with neighboring estates, and Arable met William by accidentally throwing a rock at his head as he bathed in the river. They met frequently as children, but never spent any real time together until that golden age when all they could think of was to disappear and explore each other's bodies. And so they invented reasons to visit, slinking off to dark rooms or the river on a summer night, enraptured.

He invented names for every single mother's mark on her arms. She'd bite at his shoulder as they lay beside each other, and he always pretended it didn't hurt. They made promises, they spoke of love, they wondered at the stars and gave them ridiculous stories that she somehow still remembered. They thought their relationship was unique and precious, like a million people before them. Looking back she could recognize how silly it was. Still, their ending had been a bit more dramatic than most.

War, as she would discover, had a particular grudge against the happy. Then, fifteen years ago, it was King Henry the Young against King Henry the Old. At the time, she knew nothing of either of them. Both the Burels and the Wendenals owed fealty to the Earl of Derbyshire, William de Ferrers, who called upon his lords to raise an army and march to Nottingham. He had chosen for the young Henry.

Arable's father, Lord Raymond de Burel, obeyed the call.

William's father, Lord Beneger de Wendenal, did not.

It was a simple difference in opinion, but nobody could properly explain to Arable why their families were suddenly made enemies. She begged William to convince his father to change his mind, that he was being selfish, but he would not budge.

The Earl couldn't stand to be disobeyed, so demanded punishment for those that did not rally to his call. His order was for Lord Raymond to take prisoner the sons of any lord that did not ride to war. This included William and his older brothers, George and Hugo.

Arable could still remember her father's sleepless fits in the nights before he carried out the sentence. She curled by the door to his chambers at night while he was restless, whispering under the doorway for him to have strength. She never knew if he heard her. Her father swore he would take care of Lord Beneger's sons, and treat them as though they were his own children. That they would not be harmed.

As far as Arable was concerned, it was hardly a punishment at all. An onlooker in her estate would have thought the Wendenal brothers were guests rather than captives. They lived in private rooms that were not prison cells, and were given free roam of the manor so long as they were escorted. And it delightfully brought William even closer to her. For a week or so they invented delicious tricks to slip away from William's escort and hide in her room, or the stable loft. When they couldn't meet, she'd throw messages into his window from outside and wait for an hour, falling in love with the sound of his inkwell, until he tossed one out again. They made more plans, only half of which were fantasy. They dreamed of reuniting their houses once the war was over with their marriage. They decided to hold the ceremony on a bridge they'd build over the river, where she'd first thrown the rock that hit his head.

But George and Hugo were not as docile captives as William.

They were insulted by the constant escorts, and they festered an anger that Lord Raymond had obeyed the call to war. Neither Arable nor William saw it, but everyone's account was that it happened so quickly. While she was innocently giggling in William's arms in the stable loft, William's clueless escort went searching for them and stumbled upon George and Hugo instead, attempting an escape.

Apparently there was shouting, and pleading, and apologies. And most of all, confusion. Nobody could tell who made the first move. But by the end of it, George and Hugo were dead.

Arable had never seen William cry before, and she would never see him happy again.

The news from the war trickled in. The Earl's siege of Nottingham ended in failure, as did King Henry the Young's war against his father. Lord Ferrers remained the Earl of Derby but was ripped of his lands and other titles.

The boy who brought news of her father's death had a crooked nose and a dirty woolen cap.

Every night for a week she fell asleep crying, curled up at the crack of her father's door, whispering for him to change his mind, to come back.

A panel of justiciars awarded the Burel estate to Lord Beneger de Wendenal as recompense for the loss of his sons. Roger de Lacy was on that panel, though he dissented. Lord Beneger had Arable's family manor destroyed, every brick of it. Then every brick down to every pebble, then every pebble to dust.

Unsatisfied, he gave her family one day of warning that they would be hunted and tried for the deaths of his children. Her family disappeared overnight. Her mother and brothers begged her to leave with them, while she begged them to stay. Back then, she believed in the impossible. She was still so certain, so very very certain, that everything would be better once she and William married. It had become the only truth she knew, she couldn't understand how her family couldn't see it as clearly as she.

They would not tell her where they were headed, for fear she had turned traitor to side with the Wendenals.

Arable spent that night with William, in the loft of the stable they had spent so many nights in before. He swore he would speak with his father, and make him understand that she was innocent. She had once been close to Lord Beneger, and he would understand. William promised Arable he'd return the next night with an answer.

He didn't.

On the second night, he still didn't.

When Lord Beneger's men came for her, she ran.

IT WAS YEARS BEFORE she even heard news of William again. She never reached out to him, for fear of being discovered. But now when they spoke it was like nothing had happened.

The stable loft. I'll be there. I promise.

She wiped her eyes and tried to remember what it was like to believe in the impossible.

TWENTY-FOUR

WILLIAM DE WENDENAL

NOTTINGHAM CASTLE

FOR A WHILE HE thought she wouldn't come. What began as a grand romantic gesture quickly became an hour of William curled in a ball, freezing in the stables loft, regretting not bringing a heavier cloak or some blankets. Of course he could have left to find something warmer, at the risk of missing Arable or bumping into her in a corridor and spoiling the entire thing. So instead he sat, second-guessing every inch of it, as well as his reasons for being in Nottingham at all.

He had hoped to make short work of the business with the outlaws. It should have been no more difficult than organizing the peace talks already suggested by the Lady Marion Fitzwalter, and then he and Robin could finish their business by working to secure the existing supply routes. But Roger de Lacy had stopped him cold as soon as he made the first suggestion.

"Peace talks? What are you talking about?"

"Peace talks," William had explained, thinking he had slurred his words. *"They were willing to come to an agreement. If your captain had a better temper, they would have come to the castle and already—"*

"Who authorized this? Gisbourne wanted peace talks?"

"You . . . you authorized this."

"I did no such thing." De Lacy massaged his temples with his forefingers, then pushed the skin back in a crazed stare. *"I asked you for a peaceful resolution, and you mistook that for a peace treaty?"*

William had simply stared and started over, as if explaining it to a child. *"A peace treaty would be a peaceful resolution."*

"Ever a soldier, aren't you? Peace is defined by more than an absence of violence. A peace is also something private, something personal. You had an opportunity to make amends quietly, but you squandered it."

"What is the difference whether it's here or—"

"I thought you were your father's son," the Sheriff reeked of disappointment, *"but you don't understand at all, do you? I wanted you to make this problem go away, not invite it to the dinner table."*

Their conversation went no farther than that. The only concession William had won was a temporary advisory seat by de Lacy's side, although the Sheriff clearly thought this was more likely to change William's mind than his own. William even tried to leverage the authority of King Richard's letters, which earned him nothing more than a grave laugh.

"Ah, precisely what Nottingham needs. Instruction from someone who doesn't live here."

William planned to return to the topic in a few days, after it had cooled. In the meanwhile he could massage a relationship with de Lacy, but that only took a few hours of each day. A few more were spent familiarizing himself with the castle, the city, and the major issues of each. The remainder of his time—to his own surprise—was consumed by thinking about Arable, searching for her, then pretending he wasn't. He wondered how heavy a role her presence played in his decision to stay. The invitation he'd written for her to join him in the stables had started off as a fantastical seed too silly to even think on, until he found himself throwing caution to the wind and making the preparations.

How much worse for Robin, he thought, *stuck in the woods with the refugees.* William had a warm bed and civilization, while he had—

—the ladder creaked beside him, and suddenly Arable's dark curls filled the space right next to his head.

"William," she said, pausing her ascent.

"Hi," he returned.

He tried not to glance at the scars on her cheeks. The only light came from the waning moon and the open space above, which made the world safe and soft. Unbelievably cold, but safe and soft.

"You know we have three stables in the castle." She cocked an eyebrow.

"I did not know that." *Well that was a miscalculation.* "Huh."

"Yeah." Her lips were tight, her face cold. "You're lucky I found you."

"I am." He gave the words every bit of importance they deserved, pleased with how easily she had set him up for it. He let it linger, and for just a moment her façade cracked into a smile. She scrunched her face, those adorable wrinkles on her nose, but instantly hissed in pain and pressed one wounded cheek to her shoulder.

He instinctively reached out to her. "Oh God, I'm sorry!"

"It's not your fault."

"Don't smile," he said, unsure how to make it any better. "Don't react, to anything I say. Just stare at me, blankly, I won't be offended."

She tried to do this, but her wide-eyed attempt at a stare made him laugh, which forced her to look away. "Stop it!" she said, suppressing another smile.

He watched her, taking in her face, so easily transported back over the years. It was embarrassing how young he felt, how unsure of himself, how childish for him to invite her here in the first place. She might have taken it the wrong way, or been offended. He had not seen much of her in his few days back at the castle, and certainly not enough to know what burdens she still carried from their lifetime ago. But his gut told him this was right. It was as if they could pick up from precisely where they left off, erasing the empty years that separated them.

The last time they had been in a stable loft together, lying on their backs and asking questions to the stars, was the last time he would see her for fifteen years. He had promised he'd return to her, once he convinced his father to take pity. But William's father was cold to the world. Lord Beneger swore and cursed that if William brought Arable home, she would wear shackles. He was blinded with grief, unable to bear the sight of a Burel—even the sound of the name drove him to hysteria. He threatened to have his men follow William, with orders to apprehend her if the two should meet at all. And so William did not return to the stables that night, nor send word. He had broken his promise. To protect her.

Now he had the opportunity to make amends.

"That room I was sent to clean . . . that's yours, then?" she asked.

"I'll be staying for a bit. Maybe as long as a month," he explained. "I asked the Sheriff for whatever accommodations he could afford me in that time, so that's . . . my room."

She nodded. "It's a nice room."

"It's a nice room. I also asked if he could spare me an attendant, since I don't know my way around the castle, and am otherwise unattended." His words felt sloppy—he had all the grace of adolescence again.

"That's good," she said, emotionless. "Do you know who it'll be?"

He blinked, not realizing it was possible she could misinterpret what he had done.

"Oh," her eyes widened when she figured it out. "*Oh.*"

"Only for a few hours a day. I couldn't really justify any more than that."

"Ah." She seemed confused, or perhaps she was just avoiding making any face large enough to hurt herself. "So I'm to . . . serve you?"

"No!" He had messed it up, exactly like he feared. "Sorry, I didn't explain that well. I don't *need* an attendant at all. The hours you're assigned to me, they're yours. To do whatever you want. Rest, or read, or go out to the city, whatever you like. I thought . . . I thought you could use a break. There's a servant's quarters attached to the state room, it's yours, for as long as I'm here, at least. When you're not tending to your other duties, of course."

He didn't need anything brighter than the moon to see the effect it had on her. It was as if she'd never been given a gift before.

"Arable, I don't know what your life has been, I don't know how you ended up here, and I don't know what else I can do to help you. But while I'm here . . . well, I'm here to help. I'm also going to chop Jon Bassett's hand off and feed it to him, but I can only do that twice and you deserve more than two gifts."

She bit her lip, at last her tension melted. "Thank you, William." And then, after several emotions fought across her face for victory, "I've missed you."

He kissed her.

It was as thrilling as their first kiss, new and heart-stopping, and yet simultaneously comfortable, familiar. But it cut too short when she winced, pulled back, and brought a hand to her wounds.

"I'm sorry!" he said again, covering her hands with his, hoping to protect her face from any more pain.

"It's alright," she whispered, a perfect private smile that made everything alright. "Do it again. *Gentle.*"

They both smiled through it, longer this time, and every problem in the world faded away. There was just her and this moment. He tried to remind himself to memorize it, to hold onto the details. She touched her nose to his, then her eyes flicked down. "You understand I'm still standing on a ladder."

"I do understand that. Do you want to climb up here?"

"I do not," she said smugly. "It's cold up there, and you are an insane person. We could have done this in that very nice room you were just telling me about."

"Well I thought that would be presumptive, asking you to my room."

"It would have been warm, which is better than presumptive. This is all very cute, but it was summer when we used to do this at home, and also we're adults now."

William ran flush with joy. She was still very much the girl he had fallen in love with, but also so much more. There were new layers to her, hidden within the ones he knew, and it was captivating. They would only have a few weeks together at most, but at the moment it didn't matter, because time had stopped for as long as they needed.

THE NEXT MORNING, THE world and its troubles rudely insisted upon existing again.

William was summoned to the Long Room, where a skinny banquet table only barely fit between the surrounding walls. The odd dimensions begged disbelief, as if the space were intended to be a hallway instead of a dining room, if not an architect's joke. There was scarcely enough room behind each of the tall-back chairs to slip a body behind, but Roger de Lacy enjoyed the awkward space and its tall ceiling, which let light pour in from gutted windows above.

De Lacy was there already, mid-conversation with his castellan, Hamon Glover. Glover looked like a wine barrel that had decided to stand up one day and exercise a bit. After William's night reuniting with Arable, it took a serious bit of work to remind himself why he was supposed to care about other things.

"Bring them," the Sheriff ordered, and the castellan wobbled from the room.

"Company?" William asked. *Robin had done it,* he dared to hope. He'd convinced John Little to—

"Have a morning bite with us." De Lacy gestured loosely to an assortment of fruits and bread at the table. "I have guests that may interest you. The Earl of Warwick, an old friend of mine, arrived yesterday with what he claims is urgent news. He's a sharp fellow, but he's the sort that is like to believe the moon is conspiring to kill the sun each day."

"Oh dear." William made a face. "The sun is always getting itself into trouble."

The sheriff answered with a stern glare, and William chastised himself for making a joke. Within a minute they were joined by the Earl of Warwick, a fidgety gentleman with greying hair that seemed mostly concentrated within his ears. *Anything unexpected is an opportunity,* William recited, scrutinizing the visitor.

"Walerian," de Lacy said warmly. He exchanged a meaningful embrace with the earl and cleared his throat. "William de Wendenal, I'd like you to meet an old friend of mine, Walerian de Newburg."

The earl smiled. "Nobody calls me that anymore but you."

"Or Waleran, Earl of Warwick, if you insist," de Lacy rolled along, "I'm not going to ask you why you're here, because it will undoubtedly spoil my happiness in seeing you. Please take a seat, we are just about to eat."

"I have news that cannot wait," the earl said, clearly eyeing William. His hesitation lasted only a second before giving him his full consideration. "Wendenal, you say? The son of Lord Beneger de Wendenal, from Derbyshire?"

"Indeed." De Lacy tilted his head. "William is here on behalf of King Richard himself. He has come a long way to hear old men such as ourselves discuss problems that have no solution."

William fought down the urge to respond, and instead took the man's hand. "The pleasure is mine."

"Don't listen to him," Waleran chided. "I'm not nearly as old as he."

"You foolishly continue to determine your age," de Lacy sipped from a wine glass, "by the number of years you've lived. By all other means you're as old as I. And William here would be old enough to have fathered us both."

He had not expected such a compliment. "I wouldn't say that, Baron."

"Oh no? Dispose of your humility, it's a cousin of shame. I say any man who has bled on the war's edge has knowledge that I never will."

"You would not say that if you'd been in a war," William answered. "There aren't any great lessons to be learned there. Those that survive rarely do so because of their skill."

"And you do not consider that knowledge valuable?" Roger raised an eyebrow and cleared his throat again. He peered into his empty glass and then over to a nearby girl who was currently failing to refill it.

"How is Warwick?" de Lacy asked.

"The pride of England, when I left her," Waleran boasted. "But I came from York."

De Lacy's eyes opened wide, then disappeared behind bushy eyebrows. "Interesting. We'd best rush through the pleasantries, then?"

"Please." Waleran nodded.

"Your health?"

"Consistent."

"Your children?"

"Unremarkable."

"And wife?"

"Still living. And here, actually."

"How unfortunate. I'm surprised she's not here now, then."

Waleran shuddered at the thought. "I do what I can to contain her. Women and politics are like two very opposite concepts that would make for a witty analogy if only I had the time to craft one."

De Lacy smiled. "I'm going to steal that. But it's cruel."

"Not at all. If I were prone to cruelty, I would wad her dress up in my hand and shovel it down her mouth until she suffocated."

"You wouldn't dare."

"Of course not. The union of our two families is very slightly more valuable than the fleeting joy of throttling her to death."

De Lacy pointed a finger. "There. You've just described the precarious balance that keeps the entirety of England alive. Are you taking notes, William?" Before he could answer, the Sheriff turned back to his visitor. "Alright then, that was delightful. You'd best explain whatever brought you here."

"As I say, I bring troubling news from York. John Marshal has been deposed."

De Lacy frowned, but did not seem to take it as a surprise. William, meanwhile, had no clear idea how to react. He was still struggling with the local politics.

"The High Sheriff of Yorkshire," de Lacy explained. "An insatiably just man, one of the few sheriffs whom I would argue was fit for his post, myself excluded. Hardly unexpected, after that business with the Jews last year."

"What incident?" William asked.

"You don't know? All the time you spent with King Richard and you never talked of such things?" De Lacy puckered his lips and grumbled heavily. "Surely you're familiar with the rumor that your friend, our king, ordered the seizure of all Jewish property and land to fund his war?"

William was absolutely familiar with last year's heinous rumor. "Which was an utter lie."

"Yes, I know. As did John Marshal in York. But not the *people*. It's the people, William, that matter. Laws and lords both can be trampled by a mob. John Marshal opened the gates of his castle to protect as many Jews as he could. He gathered them in a wooden keep, two-hundred some. But the mob was scaling his walls. No escape. Yours is the military mind, William. What do you suppose the Jews did?"

His answer was not immediate. "Barricaded the keep?"

"Ah." De Lacy seemed to think about it. "Well they chose to kill themselves."

"They set their own keep on fire," Waleran explained. "Though I imagine some fell on a sword first. I certainly would have."

De Lacy smiled at Waleran. "You lack the body weight. The blade would have simply propped you up."

"I had not heard about that," William said, trying not to picture it in his mind. "I don't know if Richard knew, either."

"Of course he did," de Lacy snapped. "He seized the property of the deceased."

William pushed the thought away. Richard had been ravenous in raising his war capital, and a cold-blooded act like this was unfortunately not surprising. Not from a man who would slit a messenger's throat in the name of being mysterious.

"It was a wretched tragedy," Waleran finished the story, "and anyone with an opinion on either side blamed John Marshal. Realistically, the seat for the High Sheriff of York opened up that day."

"Agreed. But why now? Why did it take a year?"

"Ah," the earl tapped the table, "that's just it. It is not the fallout of yesteryear's fire that brings me here today."

"Hm?" de Lacy murmured. "Go on."

"There were many who wanted to see him fall, as you say, but what do you suppose was the reason for his removal? The official proclamation mentioned *negligence of service*. Specifically, for lack of revenue sent to King Richard."

"Lack of revenue?" De Lacy's echo was heavy. For once he had no response. His jaw clamped shut tightly and his eyes searched for answers he seemed unwilling to say aloud.

William said it. "You think you're next."

Roger grunted in agreement. "Wouldn't you? If the word travels—as it will—that even the great John Marshal must be accountable to collect every shilling of taxes . . ." But he didn't finish the thought. Instead he gestured to William. "If word has reached the king that Nottinghamshire has been found wanting, everyone else knows it as well. Who is John Marshal's successor?"

"That's the worst part," the earl answered. "Osbert de Longchamp."

De Lacy closed his eyes in disgust. "Brother to the Chancellor, William Longchamp. Unquestionable loyalty. No political experience." He rapped his knuckles on his wine glass. "And a complete madman."

"I don't understand," William said, because he didn't.

"My political allies will vanish if they think I am to be replaced by someone as insane as Longchamp. Nobody wants to be associated with the man whose head is next on the block, not with a man like that in charge."

William's gut twisted. A different sheriff might be more willing to entertain peace talks with the outlaws, or he could be a thousand times worse. It was not until this moment William even realized how lucky he was that a man like Roger de Lacy was currently in charge at all. He might have found a vengeful and cold sheriff, or a coward, or corruption. Roger de Lacy, stubborn though he was, was at least interested in other people's opinions before he rejected them.

Losing him would make William's job tenfold more difficult.

"Baron, I am here to represent the king," he said gently. "If you want to secure your worth as sheriff, then help me secure the supply lines. Why not wrap things up with those outlaws, that we might focus on one problem at a time?"

De Lacy withered him with a stare, but his lips were a smile. "Found a vulnerability, did you?" He shook his head. "Forget about your peace talks. I gave you a seat here so that you might learn a little, not so you could parrot the same worthless idea whenever you find the smallest advantage."

William clamped his mouth shut. He would get nowhere if he gave offense. *Another day.*

"It's not Richard's taxes England should blame for its troubles," the Earl of Warwick was saying, "but Richard's absence. We've been left with Chancellor Longchamp, who has all of Richard's authority and none of his decency. Longchamp came from nothing, he purchased his office with three thousand pounds of war funds. Status and pedigree are meaningless before the great god of coin."

A low grumble came from de Lacy, whose face was stricken with worry. A guilty lump rose in William's throat. His first reaction had been to think of himself and his mission, while de Lacy's entire life had just been potentially upheaved. Even still, his mind could only spare so much thought for the baron, as it still raced down empty possibilities for his own options.

Suddenly Robin's half of their mission did not seem so bad. He only had to tame a handful of discontents, while William had to bring stability to an entire county that was in danger of losing its last sane leader.

Whatever discussion would have followed was interrupted by a swell of hurried footsteps from the corridor, earning all of their attention. The noise belonged to Hamon Glover, caroming down the hallway, red-faced and eyes bulging.

"Excuse me, Sheriff, but I bring important news."

"That would be the theme of the day, apparently," de Lacy moaned. "What is it?"

"Captain Gisbourne is back, your lordship."

"He's *back?*" de Lacy attacked the word. "I did not know he was missing."

"He's been searching for one of his men, Jon Bassett," Hamon answered, "who was left behind after the altercation at Locksley Castle. His regiment returned two days ago, but he apparently continued the search alone. Did you not know?"

De Lacy's face spoke to his shock. "You'll have to forgive my lack of omniscience. I only know things that people tell me."

"Did he find him?" William asked, eager to punish the man.

"No." Hamon pivoted, as if he were about to be chastised for whatever ill news he had brought. "Gisbourne searches in the city now, it seems. And he has just issued some very alarming orders."

TWENTY-FIVE

ELENA GAMWELL

THE GREAT OAK

Elena was perfectly torn. On one hand, she wanted to refuse to participate in Locksley's patronizing attempt at an education. On the other hand, she didn't want the rest of the group to see how much he'd crawled under her skin. There was a victory in being above it all, no matter how much she wasn't.

The entire camp was gathered around a collection of tree stumps, where she and Will sat alone. Robin of Locksley had climbed down from his mighty golden tower to share his knowledge with the ignorant poorfolk, and that expertise amounted to nothing but a couple of stumps.

"You should bounce!" came a chirp from the audience, and Elena flashed a smile at young Much.

"Oh look," she managed a forced giggle for him, "what a lovely carriage ride!"

She bobbed up and down on her stump, happy to amuse him, and extended her foot forward to nudge Will's back.

"I'm not bouncing," he muttered without turning.

At some distance away, Locksley led Alan in a wide circle, exaggerating his movements to show how stealthy they were supposed to be. It was pure façade here in the bare field under the Great Oak, but that was the point.

"You're not doing it right!" Much yelled again, this time at Will.

"Oh my," Will droned out a monotone response. "An excellent day for a ride. I certainly hope we don't get mauled by a bear or stopped by anyone who means to take all our gold, oh no."

Will pulled back on some imaginary reins to halt their imaginary horses in response to a non-imaginary Friar Tuck who stood before them, waving his arms in the air.

"Halt! Oh please, halt! Oh thank you for stopping, kind sirs or madams. The Lord has sent you to me in my moment of need, and for this I am thankful!"

Will dropped his head. "This is so stupid."

Of course it was stupid. They were practicing thievery using stumps and make-believe. Elena and Will had grown up with these skills, honing them in the streets of Nottingham for survival, not by playing at pretend. The group was eating more food than they could steal, and their supplies were running low, but this was the wrong answer. Most of the men and women in this camp only had talent that lay in the land, and empty exercises such as this weren't like to teach them anything. Arthur and David, for instance, had already vastly improved their skillsets by following Will along in the real world, not an imaginary one.

"I appreciate your assistance," Tuck continued. He had stopped the fake carriage in the middle of the fake road, looking as pitiful and unimposing as possible. "You are very kind, my obviously wealthy friends with no apparent military affiliation."

Alan approached Elena from the side, jumping in place as if appearing from behind a tree. The lack of actual trees made it laughable.

"I can clearly see you," she said with a smirk, which he seemed to take as a compliment.

Locksley joined them, too, from equally fictitious cover. A non-existent arrow was nocked in his bow and half-drawn, aimed at Will. Alan countered his movements and hopped up on the driver's stump, his sword at Will's chest. But this caused Locksley to call for a hold, scolding Alan for getting too close. "Remember when you two came after me in the woods? You came too close, which was when we got the upper hand on you. Remember how easily I disarmed Will?"

"I do remember that," Alan cackled.

"Shut it."

Elena nudged Will with her foot again. "I don't think I heard about that, actually."

"That's because it never happened, that's why we didn't tell you." Will grabbed Alan, who looked eager to tell the story. "Oh look, Robin has more to say! Let's all listen to Robin."

"The point is," Locksley continued, "never give them the chance to attack. If you're taking something from them, have them place it on the ground and step away from it. Don't let them hand it to you."

"You've got a bow on him," Alan protested. "He can't do anything to me. You'd shoot him first."

Locksley puffed his cheeks and shrugged. "Here, let me."

He tagged Will on the shoulder, and the two of them exchanged places. "Nice carriage," he commented as he sat.

Will sneered. "Thanks, I built it just for you."

Alan stayed where he was, placing the tip of his sword against Locksley's chest exactly as he had done with Will. Locksley looked at it calmly, then slowly raised his right hand close to Alan's face, between it and the blade. Alan looked at it dumbly for a second, and then a small movement of his left hand let Locksley flick the sword tip up and away from Alan, stealing it and reversing its point against Alan's neck. If Elena had blinked she would have missed it. It was so smooth Alan didn't even register it had happened before it was over. Despite herself, she was impressed.

"Dead." Locksley mock jabbed the blade into Alan's throat. "Too close."

"Yes, but you know what sort of men drive carriages for the wealthy?" Will asked. "The kind that don't move like lightning. The kind that are fat and slow and scared of men with swords."

He went on, but Locksley leaned back toward Elena's stump. "Did you hear that? He said I moved like lightning!"

Elena shoved him away.

"The point is, don't take a chance. Step back, Alan." He did, and Robin resumed his original position outside their pretend carriage. "Now, Will, why don't you try to disarm him from that distance?"

Will sighed but took the challenge. He brought up his right hand, flopping it about to mock Locksley. "Ooh, look at the hand! You're so distracted by the hand! Whatever are you going to do by the—" Then he lunged to snatch the sword from Alan, just as Locksley had. But the gap between them was too much, all he grabbed was air.

"So sorry my friend snuck up on you there," Locksley was back in character, bow up, "he didn't realize how twitchy you were. I'm the same way, really, so I'd prefer you have no more sudden movements unless I accidentally let fly this arrow. I'd appreciate it."

"If I kill you," Alan snarled, "it won't be accidental."

"Woah!" Locksley laughed. "Settle down, Alan! Keep it friendly! Nobody wants to be robbed, but if you make the experience as pleasant as possible, they're less likely to complain about it to the Sheriff. Remember," he winked, "we're gentlemen."

Locksley swung himself inside the carriage, landing with something he thought was grace on the stump next to Elena, oozing fake charm. "Good evening, ladies."

Elena promptly pounded the flat of her fist into his chest three times. "Stab stab stab. Dead."

The crowd whistled and hollered for her, as they should.

"And risk getting blood all over your lovely dress?" Locksley smiled. "I think not."

"Hey, she can kill you if she wants!" Will twisted to watch what was happening, but Alan grabbed his shoulder and spun him back.

"You can't see any of this," he whispered. "You're outside the carriage."

Locksley ignored him and took Elena's hand in his own, touching it with his lips. "Good evening, Lady Gamwell." She let him woo her, partially to play her part, and partially to give Will a little bit of jealousy she could use later. She wiggled in mock happiness, and brushed her twined braid back over her shoulder.

"Ooh, a ruffian!" she cooed. "Whatever shall I do?"

"It pains me to frighten you so. Lips such as yours should not be made to tremble. Please accept my humblest apologies."

"Oh, if only I were stronger and braver, but as it is I am helpless!" She kicked back and swooned.

"Are those diamonds?" Locksley gasped, "I hardly noticed, compared to your beautiful face. Does it really need such jewelry to compete with? I think not!" Locksley reached behind Elena's neck to undo diamonds that weren't there. She saw Will twitch slightly at his closeness.

"You think I'm beautiful?" she played along. "Well I don't mind being robbed at all now. Take it all! Take me, too!" She thrust herself at Locksley. Another wave of reaction from the crowd, divided evenly by sex. The men hooted as she draped backward across the stump, while the women moaned in annoyance.

Locksley didn't take the crowd's bait. "Maybe another time," he smiled, and swung out of the fake carriage. "On your way, my dear, and remember, this is our secret!"

He blew a kiss to her and she melted even further, letting her head nearly touch the ground as her body went limp. She knew what effect she had on men. Locksley, too, must be imagining her in a dozen other positions by now. *Let him wonder.*

"Here's something for your troubles," Locksley said, tossing nothing at Will, who stood blankly.

"What was that?"

"That was an invisible coin you failed to catch. Always give a little something back to the carriage driver."

"What?" Will threw his hands up. "We give it right back?"

"The driver's not rich. And we want him to keep driving through the forest, don't we? His passengers won't know we're giving it back to him. Keeps him from deciding on taking different paths, or asking his big strong friends to ride along for protection. And always leave to the back of the carriage," he said, pushing Alan off with him, "even if that's the wrong way for us. That way they think they're safe by moving forward."

Arthur shouted a question from the crowd that stilled the merriment. "What are we supposed to do with diamonds?" Nobody had an answer. "Who are we going to sell them to? Hell if I know anyone. You can't eat it. You can't sleep under it. It won't warm you at night. It'll go with you to your grave, and only help you get there sooner."

"I'm sure there are some who may be able to use it." Locksley's eyes looked out to the crowd and found Marion. She stood wrapped in her green cloak, watching from a distance, only rarely joining in on their mirth. She raised an eyebrow in silent agreement. But it wasn't the answer they needed.

"So what's the point?" Will asked.

"What's the point?" Locksley repeated, tapping the tip of his bow on the stump next to him. He nodded vigorously, his eyes moved about the crowd. He chose one person in particular and asked the question back. "What do *you* suppose the point is?"

Along with the others, Elena craned her neck to see who had been singled out. She had not even realized he was there to watch. Jon Bassett, the injured gord they had nursed back to health, sat at the back with his hands tied together and a face closed tight as a fist. He was rightfully bewildered to be the target of the question, but then again his tiny gord brain was likely to be bewildered by the sun's disappearance each night.

Locksley repeated his question, with undeserved kindness. "You're our guest here, and I'd like your opinion, too. Do you suppose any of this will work?"

The gord squinted, chewing it over. That was an instant liar's tell, and it meant the next string of words that fell out of his mouth would be utter horseshit.

It was inexcusable that they had brought him all the way back to their camp, and few of the others seemed to understand what that meant. They thought they were in trouble for the fight at Locksley Castle, but that wasn't it at all. The Red Lions scrapped with the Guard all the time in Nottingham, it was part of the game. But *targeting* a gord, making it personal, that was a line that every gang runt knew to never cross. By taking Jon Bassett prisoner, they'd gone too far.

The moment they set him free, they'd have to abandon this camp. The only alternative was to make sure he never made it back to Nottingham. But Elena wasn't sure any of them had the stones for that, even herself. Not in cold blood. Not without a fight.

Not unless the gords crossed that line first.

"It will work," Jon Bassett said.

Elena watched the crowd warm to him. They had already forgotten what he represented, and why he was here. She regretted playing along now, if it made even one of them feel somehow safer. Those that weren't at the attack at Locksley Castle, the families here in the Oak Camp, just saw an injured man. They ate up his words as if he were promising them new peace and freedom. He told them Locksley's plan would work, the Nottingham Guard would turn a blind eye to their new tactics. That they would no longer be worthy of the Sheriff's attention. They ate his lies like candy, but the only thing he truly promised them was danger.

"Don't make yourselves a problem for us," he lied and he lied and he lied, "and we'll never know you were there."

"THEY BELIEVE HIM, BECAUSE he says what they want to hear," Will complained, later that night in their tent. He was agitated, on his back, but slowly tracing the length of her shin with his finger. She sat beside him, busying herself with his hair, roughing it up and smoothing it out, over and over. "They don't *think*. They don't *ask questions*."

"We know better than to trust a gord," she answered him. Anyone who had lived under the Nottingham Guard's boot would know better. They had lost friends to such empty promises. Over-zealous guards trying to make a name for themselves, offering leniency to little fish in exchange for bigger ones. The lure of an easy life was attractive to young boys and girls in the streets. The Guard preyed on that vulnerability, their desperation. Close friends in the Red Lions had been betrayed, closer friends had been the ones doing the betraying. None of them received what they were promised. They all ended in irons.

"God's fucking teeth, how can they think he'll keep his word?"

"Because they don't know," she said, wishing that saying it could fix it. "They're not us."

"This'd be a lot simpler if he'd just died like a good boy."

She stared down into him until he noticed her pause. "Would it?"

After a quiet breath, he shook it off. "You're right, that'd be worse. But it's still a shithole, what we're in."

"What you're saying," she resumed stroking her fingers through his hair, "is that we're at a disadvantage."

He closed his eyes and grunted.

"So do what you do. How do we turn this disadvantage into an advantage instead?"

It was a puzzle, really, a game they'd often played with each other on the road. One would concoct an unsalvageable scenario, and the other would invent an ingenious escape. The riddles always eventually devolved into flying away on dragons, which was probably not an option for them now.

"He's not going to die on his own, and we're not going to kill him," he raised a finger for each fact they knew, "and he's going to tell his gord chums all about us."

"But we can decide," she closed a fist around his third finger, "what he tells them."

He considered it, then drew her hand down and kissed her knuckles. "Who cares if they know about us?"

"Who cares if they know about us?" she echoed, the truth of it hitting her at the same time. They never hid their existence as Red Lions back in Nottingham, they never thought that *being discovered* meant the end of it all. "Everyone's worried that if a gord so much as looks our way, we'll all instantly hang for it."

"That's just because they don't know better," Will continued the thought. "This is their first time breaking the law."

"Exactly. The Guard never chased us out of Red Lion Square, even though they knew we were there. So why not?"

"We weren't a big enough problem to them, not worth the hassle."

"That's only half of it." Elena tugged his hair back. "We were also too dangerous for them to try. That's the balance. Too small to be worth it, but too big to squash for fun. We could make it work out here, same as it worked in the city. Never being more trouble than we're worth, we find a few corrupt gords and keep them fat and fucked . . . it can work. Same rules, bigger playground."

"Well the first part is handled." He scratched at his chin. "That Bassett fellow surely sees we're not much trouble anymore, what with Robin's plan."

"But there's nothing to stop him from marching his friends back here and arresting everyone." Elena finished it. "So we handle the second part—we make sure he knows we're dangerous, too."

Will's hand paused on her leg, thinking it through. "Robin wants us to *make friends.* Can't remember the last time a gang got any stronger by giving all their coin out."

"I know."

He snorted softly. "What are we even doing, Lena?"

"I know."

"Stealing from rich old ladies, and politicians? Only taking enough that the Sheriff *doesn't* fight back? What's the point of all this?"

"I know."

"You know what, I *want* the Sheriff to know about us." He sat up, moving his hands down to massage her foot. "I want him to fear us. We've been driven off our own lands for no reason, and Robin wants us to go out of our way to *not* make him angry now?" Will shook his head.

"Robin's only here through the end of the month. After this settles down, we run things our own way. We need to show Bassett what that means."

"I don't see what everyone likes about him," he whispered.

"Bassett?"

"Robin."

She placed both her hands on his cheeks and looked him square. "He'll be gone before we know it. And who's been fighting from the beginning? You're a thousand Robins."

He breathed in, all the way, and out again. Twice.

"What if we just scare the shit out of him?" he asked with a boyish chuckle. "The gord."

"What are you thinking?"

"Gilbert," he said.

She loved it. *"Gilbert."*

He leaned over to kiss her shoulder, and a shiver shot up her spine. "In a clean fight, by the way, Robin wouldn't stand a chance," he said, moving to her neck, and he never lied to her.

THE GORD ATE WITH them the next night, around a large fire. He drank their hot apple cider, he joked with Friar Tuck about mishearing his name as Friar Tug. Some of the young boys in the camp spent the rest of the evening rushing up and grabbing at his tunic, yelling "Tug!" Elena watched Much run up to the gord with a mouth full of food and show it to him, as if he were some brother to play with. It was like watching a child play with a sharp knife, and it put Elena's nerves on edge. But she had plans now to deal with him, which blunted the edge a fair shade.

She was just waiting for the moment to play her hand.

"We'll escort you out of the Sherwood," Marion was saying. "I think we've proven that we don't mean you any harm."

Bassett nodded, staring into his cup. "You've been kind. My chest still hurts like a fucking . . ." He trailed off and looked at John Little, who winced in apology. "But I get it," he finished. "I do. I get it."

"You'll talk to William de Wendenal, then?" Locksley patted the man's shoulders. "Let him know we're ready to talk?"

"I will."

"Gilbert's prepping the horses," Elena said, as nonchalantly as possible.

But Marion immediately pricked an eyebrow at her. "Gilbert? No, Amon can take him back."

Elena did her best to pretend that was surprising. "Why?"

Marion had no response, she just shrugged and waffled. "This is important, and I trust Amon."

"And you don't trust Gilbert?"

"It's not that."

"Because he's *weird*?" Elena put as much accusation into the word as she could.

Locksley had no problem saying it. "Well he is weird."

"We're all weird," Elena splayed her hands out at the group around them. "Everyone thinks Gilbert is some sort of ghost story or something, just because he sticks to himself. Not everyone needs the world to like them, you know?"

Locksley gave a half laugh but stopped himself, because he always laughed, and it was exactly what she was describing.

"I've known Gilbert for years, and he's more than a glove, he's more than a spear lurking out at the edge of camp. Just because he doesn't talk to anyone, you all assume he's some sort of madman who can't be trusted. You trust this man," she pointed her finger as Bassett, "because he has a handsome face with a big friendly smile, even though he was trying to kill us five days ago. But not Gilbert. Gilbert has a creepy hand and an ugly face, so he must be some sort of monster."

Marion looked genuinely hurt. "Elena, I didn't . . . I'm sorry. Gilbert can take him, it doesn't matter."

Elena shook it off.

Perfect.

AT THE FIRST SIGN of the half-moon in the black night, they took Jon Bassett to the edge of the glen. The fading murmurs of the camp clung to the edge of hearing, the fires eclipsed by the thickening trees.

"Put this on." She handed a roughspun tunic to their guest. "We can't be seen escorting a Guardsman as a prisoner, now can we? And you'll wear a hood until you make it to the road."

Shortly thereafter Gilbert joined them, holding the reins to his horse gingerly with his gloved hand. Elena helped the gord up, but then climbed behind him and pulled the hood over his head.

"Answer him honestly," she whispered in his ear, "or I can't protect you."

"What?" Bassett asked, jerking fruitlessly, but she slipped down and motioned for Gilbert to do his part.

"What are you going to tell your captain?" Gilbert asked. He rarely spoke, and when he did it was not with the gravel one expected from a man of his curiosity. His voice was clean and smooth, like a songbird, or wind through the reeds.

"What do you mean?" Bassett asked in a panicked breath.

"About us," Gilbert drew close on his horse. "What will you tell them about what you've seen?"

"I'll tell them the truth," came the voice under the hood, hurried and uncertain. "I'll tell them you're not a threat, that it's a waste of our time to worry about you. I'll tell them you're just trying to take care of your own. That you're just like us." His voice petered out, empty.

Gilbert's tone was indifferent. "I'm not like them. I'm something different, aren't I? So I need you to know something. If you're lying to me, I will find you again. I will cut off your eyelids and let your eyes dry in their sockets. I'll slice your cock in half, down its length, and let it heal, only to do it again. I won't kill you, but your life will be over, as it were. I kept a man like that for six months once. He ate his own tongue, and most of his left arm, and he thanked me for serving it to him. This is your future if you lie to me. I keep a place in the city, I have Guardsmen who owe me far more than your little life. I promise you there's no place you're safe from me, should I choose to want you. As it were. If you intend on bringing your captain and his men back to hunt these people down, that's fine. I don't care at all. I really don't. The only thing I care about, right now, is the truth, isn't it? Do you understand what I have said to you, yes or no?"

Bassett's breath was dry, he turned hoarse. "Yes. Yes I do."

"So what are you going to say about us?"

"The same as I told you before. That's God's truth."

Gilbert looked down at Elena for approval, and she shrugged. There was no knowing if it would work, but one thing was certain. Bassett would tell the story to his friends.

Every gang needed a reputation.

TWENTY-SIX

GUY OF GISBOURNE

NOTTINGHAM

THE FIFTH RUNNER WAS a skinny lad in the Common Guard named George Sutton. The fifth summons in two hours, and the fifth distraction. It wasn't George's fault he had been sent, and he nearly tripped over his own words trying to speak. "The Sheriff demands your presence, imm-m-m-ediately," he mumbled, fearing retribution. Guy simply thanked him. He didn't punish people for following orders. But he had little interest at the moment in doing so himself.

The streets in Nottingham were grim and empty, and he did not like the haunted quality it gave his city. But grim and empty was what the situation called for. Nor was the city quite as barren as it seemed—Guy could feel eyes behind him. Window shutters twitched as he turned, and silhouettes in the shadows melted into walls. It was silent enough that he could hear bird calls above, but half of them seemed positively human.

Perhaps there were some in the city that feared him, and rightfully so. If they were afraid of the Nottingham Guard, then all the better they lock themselves away. The rest of the city, the goodfolk, deserved to have the streets to themselves for a while. They deserved to feel protected again.

It had been a merciless few days since he had returned to Nottingham, despondent and empty-handed. But he had learned one useful bit of information in his extra time away. He had called upon some of his old informants from the city in the desperate hope they might know anything about the woodland rebels. Instead he learned something about the girl who had put a sword to his throat, Elena Gamwell, and her lover, Will Scarlet. Something even Devon of York hadn't been able to tell him.

They were Red Lions.

Guy followed the wharfside alleys rather than the Long Stair. He wanted the grime of it. His feet led him to Red Lion Square, the fishmarket by the river Trent that had been long plagued by the worst of the city's gang activity. The market was deserted now, the fish pool had been drained, the stalls dismantled. His men had erased it from the city, and would not allow any reminder of its presence.

Instead they would feel its absence. They would realize they had lost something. They would feel the consequences of what it truly meant to steal. If the Red Lions were involved with the criminals in the Sherwood, then they were responsible for anything that happened to Jon Bassett as well. This message would get back to them. *If you take something of ours, we can take something of yours.* If the forest outlaws were supplied by their counterparts in the city, they'd feel this right in their bellies. For two straight days the Guard had swept up every last trace of the river gangs and doled out justice.

Yet so far, there were no leads. Nobody offered even the tiniest knowledge of what had happened to Jon Bassett.

It would come. It had to come.

Guy knelt and said a prayer at the base of the stone ring. Any other day this would be a bustling market, where a prayer would seem comically misplaced. But this day it was a promise that the Nottingham Guard was untouchable. There could be no mercy for the filth of the city who would target a Guardsman. The rest of his boys were busy with the gaols, sorting the people they'd arrested, but Guy wanted a short time to himself, in his streets. In a city at peace.

The baron had decreed that no one was to be harmed, and no one arrested. Guy had chosen something that was the opposite of that. Not blindly, though. He would accept the punishment—he just wanted a little bit longer.

The sixth runner was not a single man, but his entire regiment.

Reginold and Bolt, Eric, Morg, even Devon of York arrived with solemn faces. The symbolism was ham-handed, that the baron could turn Guy's own men against him if he so wanted. They apologized, of course, but said nothing else. Their missing member was too obvious.

Guy thanked them and conceded to return to the castle in their company. He asked them about their families, and tried to give minor memorable bits of advice. He had every reason to expect it would be the last time he would interact with them as their captain.

Baron Roger de Lacy was dining in the high keep, because of course he was. While the Nottingham Guard had orchestrated one of the strongest raids against crime in their city's history, the man who sat in the sheriff's seat ate honeyed bread. The hypocrisy was too obvious for mockery.

The baron was speaking with the visiting Earl of Warwick and the kingsman William de Wendenal, who had apparently become a regular participant at the sheriff's table. Guy cared little for those who would whisper private advice into the baron's ears, especially those who did not call Nottingham home. Wendenal's presence in particular was mystifying—rather than return to the war, he was offering de Lacy counsel on matters he should not even be privy to. It was the sort of closeness Guy had shared with Ralph Murdac, the tightness that should be natural between a sheriff and his captain.

Roger de Lacy lifted a finger to silence their conversation upon seeing Guy. "You'll excuse me, but discipline, by its very nature, cannot be suffered to wait."

Guy held his chin high. "Baron, I'm told you summoned me."

"By numerous men, and frequently. Sit."

Guy hesitated, then threw his leg over a chair and lowered himself into it.

"Not you," de Lacy growled, looking sharply at Morg—who had claimed a chair as well. The man flinched and stood upright, very likely shitting every inch of his considerably sized pants.

Guy dismissed his men and waited to speak until they were gone. "Baron, have you not received my reports from the field?"

"*From the field?* Did you make it all the way to Jerusalem? Yes, I received many men who reported your circumstances, and I asked the same question to each one. Why was I speaking with him instead of you?" De Lacy aggrandized with his hands and lilted through his sentences the way a bad storyteller tells a joke. "Each one had the same answer, that they were only doing as they were told. Obedience. A curious trend amongst your men, from the lowest guard and up, but mysteriously stops just shy of captain."

If the baron meant to take his station from him, Guy would much prefer it happen without a performance. He had no problem admitting his faults, but disloyalty was not one of them. "If they reported properly," he said, "then you understand the reason for my absence."

"Indeed, you misplaced one of your men," de Lacy answered coldly. "You must have left him next to your common sense. I understand you spent a week searching the Sherwood for both of them."

"I have reason to believe," Guy paced his words, "that one of my best men is being held captive by the outlaws in the forest."

William de Wendenal spoke up. "My friend Robin is still with those outlaws. He would not allow that to happen. I could have told you as much."

"And as you say, he is *one* of your men," de Lacy added. "One. There are many more of them that needed your leadership here. And you are one of *my* men. Your duty is to me. If I decide to waste my captain's time searching for a lost dog, you will permit me to make that decision for myself."

The Earl of Warwick seemed concerned. "Your man," he asked, "has he been found?"

Guy answered reluctantly. "No."

"If Warwick can be of any assistance, you have our support."

"Take that offer back," de Lacy interrupted. "Tell me Gisbourne, do you have any evidence that these outlaws took him prisoner?"

"He was left behind with them—"

"It was a yes or no question. Did you have *evidence?*"

Guy fumed, but swallowed his pride. "No."

"No?" De Lacy feigned surprise. "But we sent our captain and his best men out to the Sherwood to look for them. Surely there was some proof? No evidence to justify using our best resources?"

Only common sense, and the lies of the coward knight FitzOdo. "No."

"No. There has been no body, no ransom, no demand. So instead you return to the city and take your failures out on the river gangs, I am told. You've conducted these mass arrests. Were they productive? Did you find your man held captive in a shack by the Trent?"

"No." Guy's lips moved, but his teeth did not. "But I have rea—"

"That's the third 'no' you've told me today. I trust it is the last of its kind."

"Yes, Baron."

"'Yes, Baron,'" de Lacy mocked his tone. "Always 'Sheriff' when you agree with me, but 'Baron' when you do not."

"The city has been in an uproar," the earl muttered. "I cannot imagine the difficulty of containing it. What was the Guardsman's name?"

"Jon Bassett," Guy answered with precision, only to the earl. "He was also a friend."

"I can't listen to this," Wendenal scoffed. "Your *friend,* one of your *best men*? Jon Bassett is a monster. Do you know about what he did? Have you even seen Arable since you've returned?"

"Arable?" That name took Guy by surprise. The handmaiden who had alerted him about Bassett's abuse of power months ago. He had no idea how she was involved.

"He cut her up," Wendenal spat it out. "He dragged a knife across both sides of her face and you have the audacity to defend him."

Guy was speechless. He did not think he could feel more betrayed than he already did, but he had no doubt it was true. If Bassett had deduced that Arable had identified him, and connected that to Guy's loss of faith in him—it was not unthinkable at all. The poor girl.

"I consider Miss Arable a personal friend," the baron continued, stone-faced. "If you are successful in finding your man, I can assure you he will face dire consequences for this. So if you need any reason at all to question his disappearance, I would think you need no more than that."

"There you have it." The Earl of Warwick slapped his hands together. "I've seen this tale a dozen times. A Guardsman thinks he's above the law, snaps one day and goes too far, then flees. If he's with those outlaws of yours, it's probably because he's joined them!"

Guy refused to believe it. If Bassett were going to desert the Guard, he wouldn't do it in the middle of a mission. *Would he?*

Given their history, there was no knowing what else Bassett was capable of. He had planned to beat a gerold, he had apparently assaulted Arable, and he was bitter about losing his status. If Guy had missed all the warning signs, he could easily have misinterpreted the man's loyalty as well. And all of this, every last bit of it, fell on Guy's head. If he had not told Bassett about the gerolds in the first place . . .

If de Lacy had not issued that infernal policy . . .

The Sheriff, against all odds, seemed to take a cue from Guy's silence. "It's not easy when one of your own turns against you, I know. Let him go. And try not to blame yourself."

Beneath the baron's words was an impossibly self-righteous snark. It said, *It was your man, not a gerold, that betrayed you.* It said, *You never get to question me again.*

Guy was too afire to fight back. "As you say."

"Very well." De Lacy pivoted in his chair. "As for this river gang, would you care to make a proper report? I've heard of your exploits in the city, but not from your own lips. We have a lot of damage to undo."

Guy blinked, unsure he had heard the command properly. He had expected this conversation to end his career, but the baron seemed content to let it lie. He should have been relieved, but it was somehow even more insulting.

"Yes, Sheriff," he stammered to collect his thoughts. It would take an hour to describe the events of the past few days, and the details would be wasted on de Lacy. He didn't know the city, not in the intimate way Guy did. Guy could list a dozen places they had raided and de Lacy wouldn't understand the difference between any of them, he wouldn't know the history of the gangs who claimed those areas, nor their subtleties. The last three days had been a marathon of peacekeeping, which involved more than just sending Guardsmen into buildings and yelling at whomsoever they found. But de Lacy's understanding of the real work it took to keep a city safe was amateur at best, so that's what Guy gave him.

"We've raided every alley between Red Lion Street and Leenside. Sixty men arrested the first day alone. The gangs know they're not allowed to target Guardsmen. There has been some resistance, but no casualties on our side."

"What about their side?" William de Wendenal asked.

"What *about* their side?" Guy shot back. "Even if Bassett turned deserter, as you say, the rumor holds that the forest outlaws have him. These gangs have ties with them, which means they share responsibility for capturing a Guardsman. What do you suppose the people think when they hear something like that?"

Someone like Wendenal couldn't understand why Guy had used such strength. It was not petty vengeance. If the citizens of Nottingham thought the Guard couldn't protect its own men, they would not feel safe themselves. The people would instead turn to the gangs for protection, who would have run of the city within days. Even the slightest dent in the Guard's reputation could have disastrous effects. Men like Wendenal simply saw this as vanity.

"So instead, we're the ones to fill the streets with violence." De Lacy's eyes drifted lazily to the tall vaulted ceiling. "And what do we lose while the city lives in fear? When you scare everyone out of the markets, how are they to make their living? When there is no one brave enough to step outside, who suffers most? You cannot arrest everyone unfortunate enough to live in the alleys. We cannot declare a civil war within our own city, we cannot have its inhabitants terrified to live here—"

"We cannot have our men taken prisoner—"

"*—I cannot have you interrupting me again.*" The Sheriff's nostrils flared and his skin shivered. "Your impatience has wrought terror on this town. I want this resolved peacefully, immediately, and with as much favor toward the poorest of our city as possible."

Guy bristled, but there was no point in arguing. Regardless of who de Lacy blamed for their current situation, the chaos of their effort was already over. The baron seemed to think the city was at its own heels over this, but Guy's men had already wrestled it back to civility, and a calm it had not known for some time. He didn't need any praise for that.

"Yes, Sheriff," he said, as humbly as possible. "Very clear."

"I didn't ask if I made myself clear!" De Lacy's eyes were red, he raced through his sentences with ferocity, just barely able to chomp out each word before the next came on its heels. "I am not interested in your assessment of my clarity. I know I made myself clear by speaking clearly to begin with."

In a flash he was done, returning to his meal as if there were no argument at all. Guy waited, to see what further instruction or insult de Lacy felt like delivering. But his cares seemed to withdraw to a size no larger than the plate in front of him.

"If I may," Wendenal broke the silence. "It seems this has gotten out of hand. You say that you want this resolved peacefully? I could arrange to bring the leader of the outlaws here to talk. You may recall that John Little was willing to meet—"

"You and your damned peace talks!" de Lacy burst again with no warning. "I've already said no to that idea, why do you keep bringing it up? No, we will not meet with them. No, we will not invite them to the castle and *talk it out*."

Wendenal shoved his plate away with both hands. "Why not? You say you want a peace and it's right in front of you, why won't you reach your hand out?"

"Do you honestly not understand this?" De Lacy's jowls shook. "You're right, we could have a peace with them, today. Today is not a timeline I care about. My duty is to care for Nottingham's future, William, which means making decisions that protect her beyond the horizon. These thieves, these brigands, they have stolen from the king and attacked our men. What sort of message does it send if we invite them to a table? The next group sees us bending over and knows they can make us bend farther. They learn they can get what they want by hurting us, because we're willing to compromise. They take that vulnerability and exploit it. No, William, no! We cannot publicly acknowledge them as anything but monsters, not now, not ever. And it's not because they're actually monsters, it's because it would invite the real monsters to come to the feast."

Guy was dumbfounded. For once, he was in absolute, perfect agreement with Roger de Lacy.

William stammered to respond. "They're just people, Baron. They're not asking for much."

"They're not *asking* for anything, they're *demanding* it." De Lacy smashed a roll of bread to pieces and grabbed at its remains. "If a man came in here right now and demanded a single crumb from this table, I wouldn't give it to him. No matter what he threatened. Not if he held a hundred of my men prisoner, not if my very life was in the balance. You would sit there and judge me, call me a mule for refusing to budge, letting my men be slaughtered while 'they're not asking for much.' Not a damned crumb, no. Because the next man demands the whole basket. And after that, the castle. We. Do. Not. Negotiate. Not with men who use fear as a weapon."

William's only response was to swallow, and shrink into himself.

"Are these people terrible?" de Lacy continued. "No. I sympathize with them, I do. I want what's best for them, but not at the expense of what is good for us. Right now, their only power is to terrorize us. If we allow ourselves to feel threatened, their power grows. We have already made this situation worse than it should be. We fueled their need for an enemy, and they rallied at it. The only proper response against fear is to laugh at it. To ignore it. That is why I did not want to meet with them, and it's why I did not want to hunt them down, either." He turned sharply upon Guy at this. "Yes, they have wronged us, but we can choose not to react. We can let it slide, let them disappear, let it go. We don't need to *win*. We can stop this cycle of taking an eye for an eye, before every one of us is left blind."

Guy felt genuinely humbled. He had not seen such raw emotion from the Sheriff before. It was like hearing a man's final confession on his death bed. His desire for forgiveness, it was commendable. He could see now, it was why de Lacy asked him to forget about Bassett. It was the reason Guy still held the title of Captain. It was an enviable fantasy, but whether it could ever work in the real world . . .

From the side of the room, one of the servant girls was quietly crying. She apologized and dismissed herself, and they continued their meal in silence. All around the table, the others focused on their food. The earl softened his bread with some peppered oil and strawberries. Behind Guy, the slightest shift reminded him that his assistant Ferrers was still there, glued to the wall as though he were furnishing. A new girl refilled their wine, the sound of men practicing at swordplay clattered in from the windows, and the breathing of the table eventually relaxed.

After some time, the Sheriff met Guy's eyes, no sign of ferocity left in them. "Is there anything else? I should let you to your work."

Guy nearly stood but stalled. There was indeed something else that had been brewing, a byproduct of their massive arrests in the previous few days—a bitter business with no proper solution. He had been dreading its resolution, but it was the sort of decision that would be best made with the Sheriff's consent. No part of him wanted to make the choice alone.

"Sheriff, if you will. Another matter requires your counsel."

"I hope the matter is more tender than this pig," de Lacy poked at his meal.

"Most of the people we arrested will be released, of course. Perhaps a day or two in gaol will loosen someone's memory, but then we'll throw them back in the pond. However," Guy continued delicately, "some of them fought against my men. These agitators, we should be certain that they . . . serve their full sentence."

De Lacy grumbled longer than necessary, eyeing the earl. "What my captain is indelicately referring to is an edict I gave earlier this year that recruits Guardsmen from the prisons. King Richard's taxes have provided us a surplus of healthy useful men wasting away in our prisons. I've given them a second chance, and *it's not up for discussion*."

The earl nodded, though his doubt was obvious. Any halfway competent man would be quick to question the logic of the policy. But Guy continued, "We can't offer this second chance to any of these new prisoners."

"So we won't."

"I'd like to ensure that. But there are so many of them, and I don't trust our records well enough to track them all. If even one slips through the cracks, he could easily lie his way into the Guard."

De Lacy dipped his bread into a bowl of honey, and rolled it around mindlessly. "You have an idea. Go on and say it, then."

"It's not just the ones staying. Everyone we arrested, they'll never be trustworthy. If we catch one hunting in the forest a month from now, we need to know where he came from. If they land back in my gaol in a year as a debtor, we need to know. We need a way to track them. Something reliable." He felt the stir of the room hold its breath. "Something they could neither hide nor remove."

"You can't be serious," Wendenal said aloud. It was Guy's experience that anyone who uttered those words knew fully well that the person in question was entirely serious.

"There are a few options," Guy continued, hoping to keep it unemotional. "A knuckle off the small finger. A hot brand to the shoulder. If you have a better idea, I am open to it."

Wendenal waggled his jaw in a predictably naïve protest. "You can't mutilate your prisoners," he balked, "not if you want to keep the people on your side."

"Do you have a better suggestion?" de Lacy asked, his eyes closed.

"Improve your record-keeping."

"That cannot be done within the week."

"Then isolate them, immediately."

"They're already in the only place we can hold them," Guy said softly, with genuine regret. There was no pretending the gaols were prepared for this sort of crowding. They were already overflowing, and they'd have to start releasing men soon. There simply wasn't enough time. "I wouldn't bring it up if I had an obvious option. Unless you want to end that policy?"

The Sheriff closed his eyes. Guy knew what it meant. He had made this decision, which meant he had to be willing to live with its consequences if he wanted to see it through. Eventually he nodded, quite small, and looked to each of them, hoping for other solutions. His eyes, sunken and wrinkled, focused on the Earl of Warwick. "You're the outsider here, Walerian. What do you say?"

"Do not use the brand," the earl suggested, too quickly, and with a strange finality. "I would think the knife is better than the fire. Take the bottom of their left earlobe. Just the tip. Just this, what you can grab."

He tugged on the floppy end of his own ear between his thumb and forefinger, yanking it around. All around the table did the same, consciously or not. Guy squeezed his own hard, but it barely hurt. Perhaps it wouldn't be so bad.

Somewhere in the world, Jon Bassett was still in a hole.

Or he had deserted the Guard.

De Lacy alone did not move. "Is there anyone at the table who has a problem with this?"

"I have *every* problem with this," Wendenal sputtered. "You've already turned this city upside down, terrified everyone, now you're going to start cutting the ears off of innocent people? Do you honestly think this is a step in the right direction?"

Guy wanted to bite back, but the baron beat him to it. "You offer condemnation, Wendenal, but not alternatives."

Wendenal breathed heavily, but did not say more. There was no other logical option. Everyone present looked at each other, a resigned camaraderie forged in those silent moments. How strange, Guy thought, that this would bring them some sort of unity. None of them liked it, but justice wasn't meant to be liked. It was meant to serve the better good—and at this moment, the better good required a necessary cruelty.

"Very well. Have it done, Gisbourne."

"Yes, Sheriff."

They resumed their meal in silence. Roger plucked the bread from the honey and it slopped onto his plate. "It's too sweet to eat now," he growled.

INTERLUDE

WILL STUTELY

THORNEY VILLAGE
FRIDAY, 18TH DAY OF OCTOBER 1191

"STUTELY!"

Stutely announced himself as he arrived so that they wouldn't need to interrupt themselves to greet him. He unleashed a great roar of laughter from his barrel belly, so loud he couldn't even hear them join in. The fire was low, because Munday didn't know how to build good fires, even though Stutely had told him to do it better a dozen times last week. Munday was a little thick. He'd always been jealous of Stutely, and wished he was as big and as strong, being just a skinny wafer of a man himself. And with only a joke of a beard. The short red catfur on Munday's chin was nothing next to the fistfuls of manflow pouring gloriously from the peak that was Stutely Mountain.

Stutely greeted them by reciting each of their names, one by one, with only two mistakes. Most simply mumbled their response, intimidated by his personality. But Stutely had learned long ago to not waste his time pitying weak people. Munday made room for Stutely to sit on the log, across the flames from the two Billinsgate brothers, Hanry and Rog. Both were field-workers who were jealous of Stutely's strength. They'd never be able to push a 'barrow the way he could. Pushing the 'barrow meant Stutely could move around the fields from worker to worker each day, taking in the sights, telling stories. Pushing the 'barrow was the best job of them all, so Stutely always made sure to give a grand show of how great it was, so the others would have something to dream about.

"We ate without you, we got sick of waiting." Hanry flicked the ladle in the cooking pot. Hanry's beard was thin and patchy, and it made him look stupid. Stutely pretended to think and used both hands to stroke his own beard, just to remind Hanry of his place. Stutely didn't say anything out loud about beards, though, because he didn't want to make it too obvious. He was crafty like that.

"Perfect, you left me the best part!"

They didn't even realize that a lot of the chunks in soup would end up at the bottom of the pot, so Stutely could scrape out the bowl and eat a better meal than any of them. Which he deserved. Hanry was always angry when Stutely was late, but mostly he was jealous that Stutely had other important things to do. There were a lot of folk in Thorney that didn't know what to do when they had free time, but Stutely was always busy. Sometimes he'd move big stones around in the creek to try to redirect the water, or other times he'd practice sneaking up on the goats.

Next to him was Rog's family, his scrawny wife Sarra and their stickly little stick boy Hugh. Hugh had arms like sticks, and legs that looked like sticks. Hugh was only ten years old, but he looked up to Stutely. Probably because his father

Rog had a beard that was only a few inches long. Rog was also jealous of all the words that Stutely knew. Some days Stutely would give little Hugh a new word to learn, and the boy would use it all day long until his parents got so jealous they'd tell him to stop using it.

"Anyhow," Sarra said to little Hugh, "if you see anyone you don't know, you just stay away from him. This fellow sounds rather dangerous if you ask me."

"Who's dangerous?" Stutely laughed. This person they were talking about, whoever he was, didn't sound so dangerous to him. But, of course, Stutely was much braver than most. If there were some sort of dangerous man looking to steal their goats, Stutely would chase him back to whatever pathetic mother had borne him. Beside, this goat-thief they were talking about probably wasn't even good at catching goats, because sneaking up on them was very difficult, and nobody had more practice at it than Stutely.

"No one," Sarra answered. "There's some band of pillagers out there is all, and they're just looking to steal more and more from people like us, so we'd all best keep our eyes and ears open for a few days."

"No they 'ouldn't!" little Hugh answered. "They're not taking anything from anyone, they're giving it out! They 'ouldn't takes from us. If Robin brought his men to Thorney, Robin 'ould give *us* gold, too!"

"*Robin Hood*?" Stutely coughed on a burnt piece of the meat he was trying to chew on. "Who's that?"

"You haven't heard about it yet?" Munday slapped Stutely in the arm hard, but obviously not hard enough to hurt. "It was just a few days ago in Godling. You know how it is there, too many people and not enough food. Until one morning they wake up to some strangers sitting on a wagon with barrels of food and a pot like this one here full to the brim with coin! Overflowing, they say! And they hand it out to everyone, and people would take so much they wouldn't even want any more, that's what they said."

"That never happened," old Wrinkles cackled, one of the older men. "That's some fool story."

"It did happen, it did," Munday came back at him. "I heard it from a fellow who says his brother went through Godling and heard it himself. They say this Robin is a knight who went off to war and came back again, not being able to stand being away from home and all. He walked up to King Richard himself and says, *'I have to go back to Nottingham and take care of the people,'* so King Richard put him in irons. But he escaped and stole all the Sheriff's money and he's come back to give it out to anyone who needs it. That's why they're after him."

"That doesn't even make sense," Wrinkles groaned. "You're a right brick you are, Munday."

Stutely laughed at this loudly, and spat the inedible piece of fat back into the pot. He'd never even wanted it in the first place. "He's right, you're a brick, Munday," he said, wiping his fingers in the pot to wash off the black burn. "This Robin Hood wadn't never no knight. Beside, anyone can steal. You want a real story, you should talk about me. I'm an outlaw, too, you know."

Hanry grabbed the pot. "Hang off it, Will, you're not an outlaw."

"I am so!" Stutely barked, and Hanry flinched. Of course he flinched. All he was was a coward and that's all he ever would be. "I had half the guards in Nottingham after me once upon a while, and they ain't never found me."

"They ain't *looking* for you since, since they ain't *caring* about you."

Rog laughed with his brother. "Every time he tells it there's more guards in it. Last time there was a hunred guards. Now you've got half of Nottingham after you. I'll bet there was only two guards and both of them was drunk."

Since Rog had clearly forgotten the details, Stutely started to tell the story of his famous escape. "For your entertainment, ladies and . . . well we only have ladies here, don't we?"

He rounded the fire ring and plucked a bowl of stew from one of the older men who had fallen asleep. There was still plenty of food in it, the old fool.

Sarra stood up and walked away, probably to fetch the rest of the village before they missed too much of the story. She tried to drag little Hugh along with her, but he broke off and huddled under a cloak with Munday.

"It was a night just like this one." Stutely claimed a stick from the fire and waved it through the air magically, creating a trail of smoke that floated upward and away like a trail of smoke. "I was deep in the King's Wood. I hadn't eaten in three days and my belly made a sound like a bear."

He growled out into the night, and it sounded so realistic some of the men and women who had already gone off to sleep nearby shouted out for someone to kill the bear, being afraid for their lives.

"That's when I saw her. A great big stag, bigger than any stag you'd ever seen before, and she—"

Something suddenly clattered above him, a pinecone or a rock or a boulder that sailed through the lower limbs of a tree and skittered across the dirt.

"Who threw that?" Stutely yelled, dropping the stick. Whoever had thrown the something was a coward and was already hiding. "Where was I? The stag. She was a beauty. Staring at me. I didn't move a muscle and neither did she, and I could feel some sort of connection between us. So I stared at her and thought as hard as I could, *don't move,* reaching out with my mind. I was in control of both of us."

Little Hugh was amazed by the way he described it, probably because he had been sure to use a lot of fancy words that made it seem like it was happening right now. Stutely had always been really good at telling stories.

"Here, I'll try it on you," Stutely kneeled in front of little Hugh and opened his eyes extra wide. For a second it felt as if it was working. Then little Hugh laughed and flopped his arms around and stuck out his tongue. But Stutely hadn't really been trying very hard. He only meant to have fun, because he was a fun person and people liked him.

"And that's when it happened. The stag suddenly dropped dead. Just like that. But when I walked up to her to claim my prize, I saw she was stuck with two arrows, sure as day. See I didn't kill her with my mind like I thought. Nobody can do that. No, all I had done was frozen her there, making her an easy target for these two other fellows out hunting as well. But I wasn't going to let them take my stag, no I wasn't. So I took my knife out of my belt and I went screaming at them, waving and yelling. But they weren't no huntsmen, they were two archers with the Sheriff's Guard."

"No . . ." moaned Munday, even though he'd heard the story before. Or maybe he'd forgotten that part. Little Hugh smiled big and chewed on something in his mouth.

"Well it's against the king's law to go hunting in the King's Wood you know. And soon enough I could see torches all around me, as far as you can see, and people yelling and screaming and dogs barking. Well, anyone else would have probably gotten down on the ground and started crying, but not old Stutely. I'm too smart for all that. I knew they was looking for a big giant man, so they wouldn't pay any attention to an animal. I broke some branches off a tree, and held them up like this."

He put his fists on his head where he had placed his fake horns, and in his imagination he could still feel how big and heavy they were.

"I headed back the way I came, and they never found me none. Some of them came close, but all they saw was a stag and not me."

Munday laughed. "I always love that part. I like the idea of you running through a forest with your fists on your head, pretending you're a deer."

"I was a stag," Stutely corrected, "and they was horns not fists." Munday had ruined the end of the story with his own stupidity. Stutely huffed. He had wasted his time on them. "The point is, I'm an outlaw more than this Robin Hood person is, so I don't know why he's got everyone so excited."

"I don't think that's his name," Munday muttered.

"Yes it is, I heard about him. His name's Robin Hood and he's a goat thief and a big ol' liar, and if he shows up in Thorney trying to hand out stolen gold and food I'll knock him on his ass and let him know what Stutely thinks of big ol' liars, is what I'll do."

STUTELY WAS DREAMING OF beautiful women riding white bears when Robin Hood showed up in Thorney. Almost the whole village gathered around a strange wagon filled with crates and barrels. A great big giant man sat atop, calling them out to gather. Five or six others he didn't recognize walked around the crowd, talking and laughing, pulling crates off the wagon and sharing its contents. More and more stories had come through Thorney lately, about Robin Hood and Will Scarlet and Little John, and now here they were.

"I don't believe it," Stutely said, pushing his way through the crowd to get closer to the cart, where a bald troll man greeted him. His teeth were crooked and his beard was pathetic, like the hair that grew on the tops of Stutely's feet.

"Good afternoon, friends!" said the little troll, even though they'd never met.

Munday elbowed Stutely in the ribs, not enough to hurt. "I told you it was true!"

"These are trying times, are they not?" asked the troll. "Well, the Lord helps those who help themselves . . ." he continued, very seriously, and then pulled open a small soft sack and laughed, "so help yourselves!"

The bag was filled with gold shillings, so many it looked like it might rip and pour gold out onto the road at any moment. Munday's hand darted into the sack and pulled one out, and others around did the same. Stutely slapped the tops of some of their hands for being too greedy. He didn't trust the troll man. He picked a coin and looked at it closely, and smelled it and tasted it. It didn't much smell or taste like anything, and he was pretty sure real gold coins would smell and taste like something pretty amazing.

"Are you the one?" Munday asked.

"Am I the one?" the troll asked back, because trolls were full of puzzles and riddles.

"He means Robin Hood," Stutely answered. "Are you Robin Hood?"

The troll looked confused. He was probably not used to being outwitted so quickly.

"You must mean Robin over there." The troll indicated a man with short hair, and a hood hanging from the back of his neck. He didn't look anything like the stories had made him out to be. He wasn't nearly skinny enough to go running silently on tree branches, and Stutely laughed out loud when he saw that Robin Hood didn't even have a beard at all. His pudgy beardless face smiled dopily, and the troll man introduced him.

"Ah yes, this is Robin Hood!" he said, loud, and then he and Robin Hood whispered to each other quietly and laughed.

"Yes, that's me," the unimpressive dope said when he got close enough.

"The things they say about you aren't true, are they?" Stutely asked, but then Munday shoved him angrily.

"Of course they're true, don't be rude!"

"What do they say about me?" Robin Hood asked, pretending not to know. They must have heard about Stutely's storytelling skills, since the others gathered to listen as well.

"Munday here says you walk around in the branches of the forest and jump down on rich folk and steal their jewelry. They say you snuck into Nottingham Castle and stole out of the Sheriff's pocket itself."

Munday giggled and clutched his fake gold coin. "This is the Sheriff's personal money! And I've got it!" He laughed and doubled over, turning the coin around and around in his hand as if it were real.

The giant man leaned closer and asked, "Where'd you hear those stories?"

"All over, sir." Munday bowed. "A lot of people come through this road, and every one of them has heard about you. Everyone knows Robin Hood and his men are stealing from the rich and giving back to the people!"

"*His* men?" asked a small blond whelp with his arm around a bony girl.

The girl echoed with "His *men*?"

Stutely knew the stories were lies. "Who in their right mind would just throw away good coin, eh? What sort of trick is this?"

The troll and Robin Hood tried to say the gold was real, which was as sure a sign as any that it wasn't, since that would be exactly what a bunch of liars would say.

"Is Robin Hood the only name you've heard of?" asked the blond.

"No, no," Munday laughed, "there are stories about all his men, too!"

"Oh good! Have you heard of Will Scarlet?"

"Yes! Yes," Munday scratched his head again as he tried to remember the stories. "Yes! They say Will Scarlet wanted to join up with Robin and his men, and he found them in the middle of the Sherwood Forest. Scarlet challenged Robin Hood to an archery contest in order to join the group. He handed one arrow to Robin and said, *'I'll bet you can't hit that tree down yonder.'* So Scarlet shot an arrow first and hit the tree right in the middle. Then Robin pulled his arrow back, let it fly, and it *split Scarlet's arrow in half,* feather to head, right down the middle!"

The blond's face went red and he started yelling things, even as Munday finished. "They say he's the best archer in all the lands!"

"That's not what happened!"

"That's exactly what happened, my friends!" yelled the big man from the cart, climbing down and laughing. He was big, bigger even than Stutely, which meant he was fat and probably slow, too. "You want to know about Robin Hood? The real story? Robin Hood was fighting with King Richard himself, you know. He's the son of a rich land owner . . ."

"Did he call me a son of a bitch? What are you telling him about me?" Robin asked, but the giant shoved him off, walking away with Munday and a crowd of people interested in hearing more lies. Robin Hood looked at Stutely as they left.

"None of those stories are true, you know. Robin *Hood*? Where'd I get that name from?"

His friend the troll laughed and flicked at the hood he was wearing. "You wear a hood," he pointed out. Stutely laughed. This Robin was as thick as Munday if he didn't even remember what he was wearing.

"That's the stupidest thing I've ever heard. Listen now," he looked Stutely square in the eye, "don't you go running around telling those stories anymore. I don't need my name out there attached to all this. If you hear someone tell a story about this Robin Hood, you just tell them it's a complete lie, and the real Robin is nothing like what they say."

"I knew it wasn't real!" Stutely gloated, looking around, but there was nobody close enough to hear. It was just the troll, Robin, and a short lady with dark strawberry hair. She had strong child-bearing hips and no man with an arm around her. "I knew he wasn't nothing. What makes him so different 'en me? That's what I'd like to know."

"Nothing," Robin answered curtly. "That's the point. I'm just like you."

"Well, you're not *just* like me, now are you?" Stutely asked, flashing a smile to the strawberry woman, whose eyes widened. She knew it, too. Stutely was ten times the man of any Robin Hood. "There ain't much to you, now is there, and not even a little boy's beard!"

"That's not quite what I meant," Robin said, but the woman who was slowly falling for Stutely found it amusing. "I mean about being a hero. I'm the same as anyone."

"The same as me? Did you put antlers on your head when you heard the Sheriff?"

Robin blinked. "I don't know what that means. You're missing the point, friend."

That's right, Stutely winked at his new lady. *I'm a fancy talker, with lots of words, even the great Robin Hood can't keep up with me.* He resolved to start telling everyone Robin was a wanted poacher, too. That ought to make them believe his story about the stag.

They walked for a bit together, and Stutely meant to aim them to a place where he could give the woman an opportunity to sit down and take her clothes off. But he noticed her arm slip under Robin's, and Stutely knew she wasn't for him. What a woman like her could see in a lying coward like Robin Hood, he didn't know. She had probably never even been with a man, and liked Robin because he reminded her of her girlish playmates.

They continued talking about themselves, and Stutely tricked them into walking ahead so he could fall behind and leave without them noticing. They'd be so puzzled when they realized he was missing, and would wish they had asked him more about himself when they'd had the chance. But they didn't really deserve to hear any stories about Stutely's bravery. They liked to talk haughtily about feelings and ideas, and there wasn't anything Stutely hated more than people who were full of themselves, and so out of touch with the real world.

Eventually the visitors all returned to their cart and said their goodbyes. Near everyone was out to give thanks to the "hero" that Stutely alone had actually met. He'd be sure to correct their opinions once the cart left. The troll pulled a leaf-shaped lute from the wagon and strummed a chord, to the delight of all those around. Stutely could have played it better, but most instruments were built so poorly they broke when he played them. The troll sang a verse,

Stop and listen, gentlemen,
That be of freeborn blood,
And I shall tell of a goodly man,
His name is Robin Hood.
Robin was a prude outlaw,
And against the law he fought,
So courteous a leader as he was one . . .
Whether he wants to be or not!

They laughed, and the villagers laughed, and everyone laughed because not one of them knew anything about the truth. Stutely took the chance to grab the blond's elbow as he moved to catch up with the wagon.

"The stories aren't true about him, you know. He's nobody. That's all he is."

"I know." The boy scowled. "He's a joke."

"Thanks." His girl scrunched her face, then grinned at the boy. "So you mean Robin Hood didn't split your arrow in half?"

"He broke it over his knee!" he yelled out angrily as they both leaned into a run to catch up. The singing and laughter drifted away down the road, and the people of Thorney watched them leave and then started talking amongst themselves about their good luck and what they were going to do with the coin they'd received or how well they'd eat tonight.

Except for Stutely. He wouldn't eat a single apple they'd brought, if they'd brought apples, or anything else that had been given by Robin the Liar. He'd said it himself, he was nothing special, just a coward with important friends. And now that they'd gone, there was nobody in Thorney better for having met them.

They'd eat fine tonight, but come tomorrow they'd rely on old Stutely again to push the 'barrow, and then they'd see what a real hero was. Not a smooth-faced boyman who sings his way into town and gives out stolen food, but a big strong man with a big strong beard, who provides for them day in and out, with never a care for himself in the world. They'd see, and they'd thank him one day, and they'd sing songs about him, too, and wouldn't wrinkle their nose so much when he walked by, or laugh at him behind his back, which he always heard.

PART IV

A NECESSARY CRUELTY

TWENTY-SEVEN

ARABLE DE BUREL

NOTTINGHAM, MARKET SQUARE

"The craftsmanship is mediocre, the design uninspired and asymmetrical," complained the Lady Margery d'Oily, casually listing the flaws of the rolled carpet that settled heavily over Arable's shoulders. "Whoever made it clearly thought its value was proportional to the amount of time she wasted upon it."

"Then whyever did you purchase it?" asked the Wilford sister.

To break my spine, Arable might have answered.

"For normalcy's sake, dear." Lady Margery's lips gave a smile that her eyes did not share. "The Market Square is a tangible metaphor for the health of the city. We must do what we can to nurse her back."

Who's going to nurse my back?

She groaned. Humility struck one of the Guardsmen in their entourage, who offered to take the carpet from Arable's shoulders in exchange for a silk-lined box of beeswax candles. Arable whispered a *thank you* to him, and massaged her shoulders as she regained her bearings.

The Market Square indeed seemed sickly to Arable, as it had been for nearly two weeks. Ever since the Nottingham Guard raided the Red Lion Fishmarket, the city streets were practically graveyards. The Guard had clamped down the city like a judicious parent, needing little reason to arrest anyone they saw. Arable had mixed feelings about it all. The Guard was still searching for Jon Bassett, and while she hoped they never found him, the city would suffer until their manhunt was over. Apparently they had yet to identify even a single person linked to Bassett's disappearance. The anonymity of that was somewhat rewarding—as if the entire world had collectively agreed it was better without him. But by punishing no one, the Guard was punishing everyone. It someway gave legitimacy to Bassett as a human, when his absence should have gone as unrecognized as the swatting of a fly.

In the end, the Guard blankly blamed "the gangs," which led to this imposing new policing of the streets. Many of those arrested had since been released, and now the Guard was focused on keeping the city safe from retaliation. Even still, the city markets remained desolate. A few older vendors had recently braved the opportunity to return to the Market Square, and Lady Margery had insisted on spending her coin.

Her *husband's* coin, actually, as she had been quick to correct. *"And I am eager to trade it for anything that will infuriate him."*

Lady Margery had admittedly grown on Arable. Her husband, the Earl of Warwick, had departed Nottingham the previous night without his wife, which

Lady Margery found little mercy in mocking. "Serves him right for keeping me in the dark. Always wrapped in ham-handed conspiracy and political scheming. He would have you believe there is an incalculable machination that guides all events, from the assignments of new earls to the schedule of their bowel movements."

"My goodness, Lady d'Oily," balked Lady Delaney Oughtibridge. "Whatever must they think of you?"

Lady Delaney was a furious weaving of self-indulgence and self-pity, and Arable took a moment to consider how much more pleasant she would be were she falling down a well. The woman was exactly as useful as the carpet Lady Margery had purchased. Most of the ladies in their throng were equally intolerable. The sisters from Bridgeford and Wilford—Alison and Avery—were the terribly important daughters of a terribly important lord who arranged a terribly important set of marriages in exchange for something long lost and forgotten. Now the sisters found little joy in life aside from traveling to Nottingham to glimpse the notoriety their lives would never have.

Not that Arable could complain. She, too, was the daughter of a once-prestigious family, notable now only for how efficiently it had been removed from existence. She wondered with a grim nostalgia if she might have ended up just like them, had she not been thrust from that life before it was too late.

Their group was rounded out by a few younger ladies, a throng of attendants such as Arable, and an uncomfortable complement of Guardsmen. Whatever hope Lady Margery held of inspiring confidence in the city's market dashed against the perimeter of those Guardsmen. Their presence assured each merchant no other customer would visit so long as the ladies lingered, which led to Lady Margery's decision to use them as beasts of burden. The Guardsmen bore the bulk of her purchases, including five baskets of white grapes, a series of bronze hammered jewelry boxes, and two bolts of widow-lace satin. The man who had shouldered the rolled carpet for Arable already appeared to regret his chivalry.

"None of it will do," Lady Delaney lamented melodramatically, turning away from the vendor stalls. "I need earrings, or a necklace, but only of the highest quality." She sighed deeply, as if she had expected to find such craftsmanship in the aftermath streets.

Lady Margery said nothing, earning more of Arable's admiration.

"I don't know if I mentioned it," Lady Delaney repeated herself to the younger girls who were kind enough to pretend she had not, "but on the twelfth of October we were robbed on our way here from Oughtibridge. It was Robin Hood himself, you know, and he climbed into my carriage and took my brooch from me with both hands. I was as close to him then as I am to you now. He kissed my wrist, you know, this one here. He said if he had a spare horse he would have stolen me as well, for I was far prettier than the brooch."

Gossip had quickly turned it into the latest social contest. The Lady Miranda of Thurgarton had been the first to boast of her misfortune in the Sherwood, so the rumors went, and her account of the thief with a knight's physique and a gentleman's tongue had titillated the envy of many. The handsome outlaw plucked only a collection of thin silver bracelets from Thurgarton, but when he stole both the earrings and a kiss on the neck from the daughter of Lord Maunsfeld, the challenge was met countywide. In the previous week, restless ladies fabricated any number of reasons to visit Nottingham by way of the Sherwood Road, taking their joyrides and picnicking needlessly into the forest. Lady Delaney had fashioned bells to every rein of her eight-horsed carriage to make herself a more obvious target. "He only needs an excuse to find me," she said, tracing her neck with her fingertips, "although if I have nothing for him to steal, I fear he may take something else entirely."

The ladies blushed and pretended to encourage her while they all schemed to be the first to bed the outlaw.

Arable had to bite her lip to bear through their chatter. William had explained how his friend Robin of Locksley was embedded with the thieves, attempting to domesticate them. Frivolous escapades with the county's ladylings seemed domesticated enough, but Arable worried something more was growing.

"Geoffrey insisted we take more men to protect us," Delaney was laughing, "but I was able to convince him otherwise. And he never asked why I needed to wear so much jewelry!"

"Perchance I'll visit you in Oughtibridge," a vacant-eyed ladyling mewed to Delaney. She held a few wispy shawls up to her face. "Which color do you suppose Robin Hood prefers?"

They giggled and each purchased one, threatening to ride into the forest before the others with increasingly few servants. By the time they would be done, their offers would involve walking into the forest alone, entirely nude but for a single diamond necklace. Only Lady Margery seemed to share Arable's disdain for their twattling banter, but she was much better at hiding it.

Arable sighed and counted the hours before she would be free. She coveted the time she'd been assigned to William each day, and had grown very fond of having a room to herself. They usually spent those hours together if William was not otherwise indisposed, despite his original promise that they were a gift for her to enjoy on her own. She enjoyed spending them with him, and a flattering suspicion told her he had hoped as much when he made the arrangement.

A commotion was brewing between a Guardsman carrying grapes and a stranger in a loose brown tunic. "What's the matter, you deaf?" the Guardsman barked, blocking the man's path. "Move along or we'll move you along."

"Oh, you'll arrest me again, will you?" the man wailed, his bulgy young face peeking at the ladies. "What'll you do to me this time, trim my nose?"

His head was closely shaven, making the grotesque red stump of his left ear more obvious. Soft tissue scarred halfway down his jawbone. Arable instinctively reached up to touch the scars on her own cheeks.

The Guardsman stretched his neck. "You want to make me tell you again?"

"Or what, you'll throw grapes at me?"

The basket hit the ground with little regard for the poor grapes, but another Guardsman ordered the first to back down. Arable didn't know either of their names. At the far end of the Market Square, the once empty space was slowly filling with unlikely customers. Boys and young men, lingering and leaning, casually appearing from avenues and doorways. Arable could feel her heartbeat quicken. Most had short hair, some cut as close as the agitator here, while others kept longer hair only on their right side.

The Guardsman turned to Lady Margery. "If it please you, Lady d'Oily, we could return to the castle now."

With barely a word spoken, the Guardsmen formed a channel for the ladies to travel safely, leading away from the Market Square to the south, as the crowd was blocking the direct route to the castle. Even Lady Delaney was silent as they walked. They kept their heads down and pretended to be unnotable.

All talk. There was no secret thrill in these street thugs. The ladies would not be vying to be their first target. Arable chanced a glance behind, hoping the seamstress they had just visited would not be punished for some perverted sense of class betrayal. More of the boys appeared ahead, sidling either side of the street, and Arable held her breath in fear. She wondered if they might accept the candles she carried in exchange for safe passage, even as she knew how ridiculous an idea that was.

But the young men stepped aside, abiding the Guardsmen's orders with smug disinterest, staring back with wicked smiles. Another young man snapped his teeth at them, notably missing the lower lobe of his left ear.

Despite her fears, they passed out of the market with no altercation. The Guardsmen continued their quicker pace through the smaller streets while their commander took to describing the city casually, to calm the ladies' nerves. "They call this street Wheeler's Gate, as it was the main causeway for carriages to St. Peter's Square, there ahead of you," and so on.

By the time they passed the spear of St. Peter's Church and were on the long wide lane that wove back to Nottingham Castle, the other ladies were laughing nervously and chatting of frivolous things again. Arable felt a curious pang of relief that the Guardsmen had been there, despite her usual anxiety in their presence. She said a silent prayer that whatever grudges they held for her had vanished along with Jon Bassett. Or at the very least, that she had become the least of their worries in a city gnashing at its own tail.

THAT NIGHT, SHE DRAGGED William out to the castle's barbican at the eastern edge of the lowest bailey. They often walked out into the city if they had enough time, but the odd encounter at the market left her craving the safety of the castle. So they climbed up one of the squat, round towers to stand above the main gate, with nothing but a cloudless starry sky above them and the movement of people walking below. She recounted the day's misadventure with the mewing ladies, and William laughed.

"At least *someone* is enjoying this." His arms surrounded her from behind and she leaned into his warmth.

"I don't know that Lady Oughtibridge *enjoys* it," Arable considered, "she just wants people to talk about her. Which I am, so I suppose it worked."

"Oh, I was talking about Robin." William chuckled. "Sounds like he's having a delightful time out there. To think, I was worried he had the harder task of the two of us."

There was complaint in his voice. "Still struggling with Roger?"

"Mhm." He brushed her hair aside to place a small kiss at the base of her neck. "He won't *talk* with the outlaws because it would be too nice, and he won't *stop* them because it would be too mean. So instead I've been focusing on ways to secure just the supply caravans, but he won't assign any manpower to it. The city's still recovering from Gisbourne's shutdown of the fishmarket, and every single Guardsman is apparently required here. He won't take my advice on anything, though he wants me present for every meeting he holds. I don't know . . ."

He went quiet, and she squeezed his elbow. "What?"

"The strange thing is, he might be right. These last two weeks, things have been getting better. No fighting, no arrests, and these stories of Robin Hood seem to be entertaining most people."

She smiled and pushed into him. "Are you jealous?"

"No, I'm *useless,*" he scoffed. "I think Robin's fixed it all on his own, while I have been completely ineffective."

"Well, you gave yourself an impossible task, of course you were going to fail. Nobody changes Roger's mind but Roger. But if what he's doing is working, as you say it is, then what's wrong with that?"

"That's just it." His voice lowered. "It only works so long as . . ."

Behind her, William's rhythm changed, he held a breath for too long and she knew exactly what it meant.

"You know something."

"I . . . no, it's just a rumor."

She twisted around to look him in the face. There was no moon out tonight, only the fires at the gatehouse below gave his features any definition of worry. "What is it?"

"You obviously cannot tell anyone, Arable. But de Lacy suspects Chancellor Longchamp will soon replace him, with someone more . . . loyal. Or corrupt, I suppose, depending on how you look at it. Once that happens, this little equilibrium will be over."

Someway, he thought he should smile about that. He thought it was something worth making a little joke about. Arable had no words to speak so she simply shoved him away.

"What? What's wrong?"

"*What's wrong?* How long have you known about this?"

William stammered for an answer. "It was . . . it was when the Earl of Warwick first arrived. The day after the stables," he added, as if that ought to make anything better.

She could scarcely believe it. "That was two weeks ago! Why didn't you tell me about this?"

"What?" His face implied it had never crossed his mind.

"You didn't think that was something I should know about?"

"It wasn't really my secret to tell."

"Do you understand what this means?" She backed up against the battlements, trying to find something more stable than him to support her. "I am here, I am *only* here, William, at Roger's hospitality. He knew my father. He knows who I am. If he were to leave . . ." Her words failed her—she could only begin to grasp the fear of having to run again.

"What is there to be afraid of?" he asked.

"Are you serious?" She was shocked he could be so ignorant. She had spent half her life running from her family's name. It wasn't just William's father, it was anyone who sought to earn favor with him. Even so many years later, Lord Beneger was known to reward those that brought him any news of a Burel, or of their misfortune. They had not talked of it for seemingly mutual reasons, but Arable suddenly wondered if William was even remotely aware of the suffering she had endured over the years in the shadow of his father.

"I'm sorry," he said, and at least it seemed genuine. "I didn't think about that."

She shook her head, stupefied. "I don't know how that's supposed to make me feel better. You've known this for two weeks. *Two weeks,* and you didn't think about what this would mean to me."

"I'm going to fix this." He stooped his head and leaned into her, an easy answer that she did not want to grant him. "Besides, it's only a guess. It's been two weeks and nothing has happened. De Lacy could be sheriff for years still. But either way, I will fix something for you."

"How?" she asked.

"I don't know. I'll figure it out. But you don't have to live in fear, never, not again."

A moment ago he was complaining how ineffectual he was, and now he thought he could solve her entire life with a wave of his hand. The disappointment was a familiar feeling. She had learned how to live on her own, and she didn't need him to protect her. She would find a way to fix her own problems, *as she always had.* He would be gone in another two weeks, and there was nothing he could do to keep his promises from a thousand miles away.

But while he was still here, all she wanted was for him to pretend she was as important to him as he was to her.

"Promise me you won't keep these things from me," she said, tugging at his sleeves. "No secrets, not between us."

"I promise." His voice was resolute. "And I'm sorry."

"Alright," she said, though it wasn't. She moved away from the edge, having lost her interest in watching the city. But she let him walk with her. Their time together was already so short, there was no point in holding a grudge against him.

And she suddenly had far more pressing matters to concern herself with.

TWENTY-EIGHT

ELENA GAMWELL

THE GREAT OAK

"Good, Elena."

No, it wasn't. She glared at Locksley. She had missed the mark by an arm, and it was barely twenty feet away. Locksley's archery lessons were amateur, giving even terrible bowmen like Alan the false impression they had a knack for it. Elena had missed because she shifted all her weight onto a single foot, hovering the other just above the ground. Not because it was good form. To train herself to shoot under the worst circumstances. If she ever needed to shoot an enemy less than twenty feet away, she wouldn't have the luxury to square her feet and steady her shot.

But Locksley complimented her. "Good, Elena."

No, she wasn't.

Locksley's view of their world was limited to flippant encounters with nobles traveling the Sherwood Road. Yes, they had made easy coin with little trouble, and yes, they built a helpful reputation amongst the villages. But they had traded their freedom for dependency. Dependent on the right marks coming within their grasp. Dependent on Marion selling their loot to her anonymous friends. Stealing from the rich and selling to the rich was just another kind of slavery.

She and Will had left Nottingham hoping to find something different, something permanent. *Important.* She thought they had found it at Locksley Castle, in the family there that was tighter than any gang. But the world was far bigger than they had realized, and it cared very little about their intentions within it.

But that was also their advantage. Away from the city, nobody was watching them.

Back in Nottingham they had grown to become the largest fish in the market, which meant every fool gord had his eye on them. But maintaining their secrecy out in the Sherwood was offensively easy. There was no city guard to march through their camp every day, no patrols to outsmart. And if the gord Jon Bassett had been frightened properly, the Nottingham Guard wasn't like to come ambling about to make trouble any time soon. It was time to take everything they'd mastered with the Red Lions, and scale it up. Gambling, forced protections, organizations of slickpickers, there was no reason they couldn't make it all work outside of a city.

But first the others would need to train at more than just archery. And Locksley's easy answers had quickly made some of their group alarmingly docile. It was already more like running a troupe of actors than a gang. There were—admittedly—pieces of it that were fun, that she'd steal after Locksley left them. But cheap theatrics and charity could not keep them afloat for long. The real work was there for them to take—black market trades, smuggling, the like. Less fun and not as profitable, but it would sustain them in the long run. After their jovial little carriage heists petered out. After Locksley left.

It would be her turn, hers and Will's, soon enough.

"Make way!" Will shouted and Elena turned to see that Much had been provided a bow and arrow, and a log to stand on. The log was critical, as the bottom of the bow reached lower than his toes.

"Whose idea was this?" she asked, slipping in to bite softly at Will's neck.

He gasped. "It was his!"

Her hand wrapped around his waist and pulled him close. His breath sharpened. He couldn't lie to her like this, she knew his every weakness.

"I swear, he begged me to use the longbow."

"You shouldn't let him embarrass himself," she warned, her hand on his chest.

"He won't embarrass himself," he insisted. "I only gave him the bow. *Yes!*"

He clapped his hands hard, twisting away from her as Much started to line up his shot. He meant well, but Will was too eager to see Much grow into the same boy he had been himself. That was no surprise, of course. Much had thirty fathers and thirty mothers in this group, and each sought to remake him in their own image.

The bow gave a *huff* rather than a *twang*, and Elena's heart sank as Much's limp arrow leapt to the right, only a few feet away. Much threw the bow down, hopped off the log in frustration, and stormed off.

"I told you," she said.

"Where's he going?" Will's face twisted. "Much, you have to practice, you can't just . . ."

The other men called out their empty condolences but laughed it off and returned to their own efforts.

"You have to be careful with him," she scolded Will, gave his forearm a knowing squeeze, and loped off into the forest after Much.

He had not gone far. She found him sitting on a fallen tree a dozen paces into the woods. Picking at the bark with his fingers. She stomped loudly to announce her arrival.

"Don't you worry about it," she said when she caught up to him, messing her fingers through his blond mane. "Nobody gets it right their first time."

"You do," he mumbled.

"It's not my first time," she corrected him. "I've been shooting arrows since I was your age, and I started off terrible." He made a face, but she was quick to follow. "You held too long, and it tired your arm out. And the bow was too big for you. That's all."

"I wanted to make sure I hit it," he grumbled.

"Here, fix this." She sat beside him and flipped her long braid onto his shoulder. She felt him tug at it, untangling the twine she kept weaved within. "It doesn't work that way with arrows. You have to trust your instincts and let the bow do the work."

A *whip-thunk* followed by cheering made her look back at the men. David had made his shot and everyone celebrated. A flash of jealousy covered Much's face.

"I'm not strong enough," he complained.

"Of course not, that bow is huge! I can't use it, either." She shrugged. "But I'll lend you mine next time. And not everyone is good with a bow, you know."

"You are."

"I am." She tilted her head back dramatically to accept the compliment. "But I could never fight with a quarterstaff the way John does, now could I? And he's not very good with swords. You're probably better at that than he is."

"I don't know." He tugged at her hair, then moved away. "I'm not good at anything."

"Hey, stop that," she said, turning to look him square. "Why do you say that?"

"I'm too small."

"I'm pretty small, too." She sprang to her feet, dragging him with her. She was barely a head taller than him. "I'd rather be small than strong any day. We can move faster, and we can squeeze places they can't, and we can walk a lot quieter, too. Didn't you hear about how I snuck up on the Captain of the Sheriff's Guard himself?"

Much nodded.

"That's what you'll be good at. You'll be a little sneak. Nobody will ever see you coming."

At last his face brightened, and she reached out to mess at his hair again, but he ducked away and ran into the woods.

"Your feet can't touch the ground!" he commanded, and jumped onto a log and ran its length, then jumped to an exposed root, then a rock. Elena ran after him, following his steps exactly. She turned to see Will watching after her, blew him a quick kiss, then gave chase.

They played for half an hour, and Elena was embarrassingly outmatched in energy. She eventually changed the game to a hide-and-seek just to catch her breath. The bed of the woods was covered in crisp, freshly fallen leaves eager to be trampled, and the sun streamed through in wide bands that were almost enough to make her forget how rotten life had become. There was something to be said for the fresh air here, and the wide open spaces, so very different from the cramped alleyways of Nottingham.

If nothing else, Much was lucky to grow up playing chase and make-believe. Elena's youth was full of cutting purses and slipping marks, mingling and sparring with the gangs of Nottingham's slums. The Ten Bell Boys of Nottingham had to teach themselves everything. Back then, brawling and thieving didn't have any consequences beyond going a day without food. Or gaining a new scar to show off. Every now and then it was big news when someone got thrown into Sinner Mary's, but they were always let loose soon enough, no worse for wear. A life without repercussions had weaned them bolder than most, and more hotheaded and reckless as they grew older. Pickpocketing turned to horse thieving, simple lies developed into repeatable cons. They organized as their numbers grew. Then came leaders, reputations, and jealousy, infighting and ferrers. Rivalry. Brawls with guards turned into planned attacks, then ambushes, and boys that got arrested didn't come back again. The Ten Bell Boys eventually took over the fishmarket in Red Lion Square from another gang, and renamed themselves to suit. Each took a *red* name—Bloody Rudder, Rob o'the Fire, Crimson Tommy, and Ten Bell Will became Will Scarlet.

Elena was the only one who hadn't taken on a red name.

If it hadn't been for Will, she'd be there still. Helping the Red Lions all try to get themselves hanged, if she hadn't earned herself a knife in the back yet. Such was the life they'd been bred into. The Red Lions were full of suspicion and betrayal, which they had appropriately left behind. Now, they had built a loyal crew.

Or rather, Walter of Locksley had built it. She and Will, they just inherited it.

Lord Walter had started something. A life in which each person is only accountable to herself, and not to the arbitrary rules of some parlie sheriff or king. A world where it was acceptable to throw a wine bottle at a captain when he tries to take what's yours. Or put a sword to his throat when he calls you a bitch.

When we scale up, she wondered, *would the trouble scale, too?*

She panicked for a moment to realize she couldn't find Much, and put away her thoughts on the future. She closed her eyes and waited for noise until she caught the faint patter of his breath to the west.

Good on you, boy, she thought, hoping he had strategized to put the sun in her eyes. But when she sprang on him from around an oak, he gave no reaction. He stood still, staring upward, eyes unblinking, barely there.

He wasn't looking at anything, and she didn't even bother to check. She'd seen him disappear like this before, his cheeks puckered as his breath quickened, and she knelt down to take his hand. "Breathe," she said. "Breathe. Shake it off."

His fingers were cold and limp in her palm, and she bit back a knot in her chest that would have turned to tears. She whispered Much's name in his ear and held his head close to her breast. She squeezed, and eventually felt his body sag, his head roll, and he looked her in the eyes.

"Sorry."

"Don't be sorry," she said, finding her own voice too tight. "It's not your fault."

He didn't answer.

It was impossible to know exactly what triggered these episodes, but they all knew the cause. He had been with the group well before Will and Elena, and sometimes he felt like the child they might have had in some other, easier life. John Little called him the miller's son, on account of finding him by a river outside a mill in Bernesdale. Not one of them knew what had become of his parents, but whatever it was—*Much had witnessed it.* He'd never spoken of it. And the few times they ever asked, he was like to disappear as he had now.

"How are your dreams?" she asked gently.

A shrug.

"Good and bad, yes?" She squeezed again. "Either they're good dreams that are bad when they end, or they're bad dreams that are good when they end, yes?"

"I guess."

"Everyone has dreams," she whispered. "They're always good and bad."

"Gilbert doesn't dream."

That gave Elena pause. "You talk to Gilbert about your dreams?"

He nodded. Gilbert wasn't exactly known for his sensitivity. *"I'll cut your cock in half, the long way,"* he'd threatened the lost gord. Most people preferred to keep a heavy distance from the White Hand, which was how he preferred it. He was the only one of their group Will and Elena had known from their old life—not a Red Lion himself, Gilbert had been more of an associate. Too old to be in the street gangs, but known to work with all of them. He traded things, things that couldn't be procured within the city. A curious and closed man, but trustworthy—he took even the simplest task with solemn responsibility.

He'd be damned useful as they moved forward, but not exactly the best role model for Much.

"He taught me to count," the boy continued.

"To count?"

"When I can't think straight," he added. "He taught me to count. I can count to thirty sometimes, without even blinking. He says the trick is to think about something else. If you think about blinking then you blink, but if you think about something else then it doesn't hurt at all. He says you can make your mind blank."

Elena didn't know what to say. "And that's why he doesn't dream?"

He bobbed his head. "He says it's like snuffing out a candle."

Somewhere off in the woods, a tree limb snapped and fell to the ground.

"You know, if you ever can't sleep, you can come and find me," Elena said. "Doesn't matter if I'm out on watch, doesn't matter if I'm with Will, doesn't matter if I'm asleep. You can find me, alright?"

Much nodded yes.

"Aahhh," she added in a panic, "lessin' you hear Will and I . . . wrestling. If you hear anything like that, maybe call my name first, right?"

The knowing look he gave was far too mature.

"Alright then. Let's get back to the group. It's sword practice next, and I think you were promised a turn today."

Elena paired up with David of Doncaster, to challenge herself against his longer reach. They divided into pairs, spread out in a long line beneath the Great Oak. Each of them held a long stick, tree limbs with the twigs broken off, bark smoothed down at the ends. Fake swords. There were plenty of stolen real swords about to use, but Locksley insisted they needed to work on the basics. It was more than a little insulting.

"One! Two! Three! Four!" Locksley yelled, and all the attackers swung high on the left, then on the right, then low on both sides, all at the same time. It was more dance than swordplay. Still, Elena followed his commands, readjusting her stance to compensate for David's height. She swung hard, and David winced every now and then as he defended.

"Advancing! Three! One! Two! Four!" Locksley yelled and the attackers took a step forward with each attack, their partner backing up and blocking them away.

Locksley would pass by and inspect each of them. Elena purposefully shifted her weight as he approached. She brought her feet too close together, and swung for a spot well shy of David's body. David blocked it, though he had no need to, their sticks *click-clacked* in the empty space between them where neither could get hurt. There was a pause in Locksley's gait. He was considering fixing her stance, her aim.

Instead, "Good, Elena."

No, it wasn't.

Because he wasn't training them to be good. He was only training them to be good *enough*.

Still, good enough was a high goal for some of them, so Elena did not object. Locksley put his hands on David's shoulders, rotating him.

"Turn to the side, make yourself a smaller target."

"Go on, John," Will snickered nearby, paired up with John Little. "Make yourself a smaller target!"

John smiled and turned sideways, laughing at his own giant belly. "It doesn't appear to be working!"

Will swung his stick to attack, but was blocked, and again. But next he smashed the stick in half over his knee and swung at both of John's sides at once, tapping him for a killing blow.

John just swatted it off. "Be careful there, people will say that Robin split your sword in twain!"

Even Will found the humor in that, though he didn't seem eager to show it in front of Locksley. As the laughter died out, one little voice came springing from the rest.

"It's my turn now!"

"Not today, Much," Locksley said, more patronizing than ever. "Why don't we keep working on your archery instead?"

"No!" Much wouldn't let him get away with that. "Yesterday you said tomorrow, and that's today. I'm going to tell everyone that Robin Hood is a big liar."

Elena made a point of it by breaking their formation, and quickly enough everyone was grateful for the break. Much likely wouldn't get a chance like this again—it was the sort of thing Lady Marion would put an instant stop to. But Marion was gone at the moment, having traveled south with her heirloom knight to magically transform stolen jewelry into usable coin. Which meant nobody was like to stop a friendly sword match between Locksley and a child.

Much stood his ground, both hands wrapped around a stick that was only slightly too large for him, a grim determination in his eyes. He was, from head to toe, adorable. Locksley was left standing alone, curiously more uncomfortable than he had any right to be. He shifted his own stick around in his hands, but did not adopt any fighting stance.

"Why don't we use *real* swords?" Much challenged.

"Real swords are real dangerous," Locksley said sternly, a tone that was too condescending for Elena's taste. "We don't want anybody to accidentally get stabbed now."

"You can't hurt anyone with a stick."

"Oh, you certainly can!" John blurted out.

"I've got a couple of ribs that would agree with that," Locksley admitted, patting his sides. "Do you want me to go over the numbers with you?"

Much proudly recited each of the numbers, swinging his stick in succession, though his two highest numbers were closer to Locksley's navel than his head. But the display was impressive, and the others started chanting Much's name, along with "*Get him!*" and "*Duel to the death!*"

Don't humiliate him, Elena hoped. Much needed a win.

"Watch your stance now," Locksley pointed at Much's feet, "and remember to keep your foot back."

"I've been in a fight before!" Much yelled. But still he shifted his feet.

"And I'm sure you were ferocious," Locksley answered, and bent his posture into reluctant readiness. "One!" he yelled, and swung his stick slowly at Much's right shoulder. The boy was ready to block it long before it got there. Locksley went at the other side just as slowly.

"Not like that!" Much complained. "You're going too slow!"

Locksley raised his eyebrows to the crowd, but received little support. John Little egged him on, and they started calling Locksley a coward, too afraid to fight the mighty Much. Elena couldn't help but smile from ear to ear.

"Alright then," Locksley said. "I'm coming two, four, one, three. Got it?"

He moved immediately, and Much flinched in the wrong direction and only barely blocked the first attack, and then had to jump backward away from the remaining blows, but it didn't shake his resolve. As soon as the four slashes were over, Much pushed forward on one foot and stabbed up at Locksley's gut. But Locksley stepped away casually, he flicked the tip of Much's stick up and slid his own to lay full across Much's stomach and held it there. "Dead."

Elena, and the rest of the crowd, booed.

"You cheated!" Much protested, trying in vain to pull away. "You didn't say a number!"

"Neither did you," Locksley held onto Much's back with one hand as he pretended to saw him open with the sword at his belly. "And neither will they. So, brave Sir Much, how did I kill you?"

"You're bigger than me," Much complained, finally escaping Locksley's grasp.

"It doesn't matter who's bigger. Look at Will Scarlet, he's not very big."

"What?" Will asked.

"You gave up your advantage," Locksley continued. "You attacked me, and you opened yourself up. An unskilled attacker is always at the disadvantage. You should focus on defense."

"That's boring."

"Staying alive isn't boring," Locksley said, in that same tone he'd used before. He knelt down and looked Much in the eyes. "I'm only teaching you this so you can protect yourself, do you understand? Most people aren't going to swing a sword at someone your age, but if they do, you need to know what to do. You block it, and then you run away as fast as you can, do you hear me?"

Much glanced at the crowd, but nobody would argue otherwise. Elena gave him a tiny nod, and he turned back to grumble, "I hear you."

"Good, now try that. Parry and run. Watch, I want you to deflect me as I come in, alright?"

Locksley stood up, leaned back, and slowly pushed his stick straight at Much's stomach. Much hopped to the side as instructed, pushed his stick away with his own, then slapped the tip onto Locksley's forearm and ran away. The crowd rewarded his victory with a wave of encouragement, and Locksley bowed to Much. "You see, that was better."

He was finally smiling, but it didn't last long. "You don't run away from fights."

"Yes, well," Locksley muttered, "I'm bigger than you."

"Don't worry, Much." Elena sprang to her feet to escort him away from the field. "You'll be bigger than John Little someday, and you'll be the most feared fighter in all England! And remember what we talked about. Defending yourself is good, but don't forget about the element of surprise!"

She knelt quickly, squinted her face at him, and pointed back at Robin. Then she whispered in Much's ear and shoved him.

"Death to the Sheriff!" Much screamed, and ran directly at Locksley, who turned around too late. Much smashed into him and the two went tumbling down to the ground. Both of their screams turned to laughter. Locksley grabbed Much and rolled over and over, then lifted him up in the air again and threw him over his shoulder. They spun around in a circle, with Much screaming and laughing until Locksley finally set him down on his feet, too dizzy to stay standing.

It was, odds on, the most fun Elena had ever seen Much have.

Despite the play, Locksley glared at her, *"Death to the Sheriff?"*

"I don't know where he got that," she lied with her widest smile.

Good, Elena.

TWENTY-NINE

GUY OF GISBOURNE

NOTTINGHAM CASTLE

AT SUNRISE EVERY SUNDAY morning, before the church bells called their masses, the castle gates were opened with hot meals prepared for as many people as were interested. Few people were as old as Guy to remember how the tradition started. Sheriff Osbert Sylvanus, who was also a bishop, wanted to give an incentive to the people to get their asses out of bed and into a church. One's immortal salvation was usually not reward enough, but a hot bowl of stew and potatoes could get anyone to their feet. A shambling crowd would enter through the castle gates and take their food, and then had little excuse to avoid St. Peter's on their way back through the city.

Sylvanus had not lasted even a year in his role, but forty years later the Sunday Temperance Lines were still a tradition. Along the way it collected some additional religious slog, something about walking the savior's footsteps by caring for the poor. This dubious description meant it was an "honor" to work the line, which for Guy meant it was easier to assign the duty to a Guardsman who would otherwise hate it. It wasn't exactly near the top of Guy's favorite tasks, either, but still he made sure to stand the Temperance once every other month or so, if his responsibilities allowed.

"You're welcome," Devon said, beside him, extra careful as he poured a ladle of the morning's barley porridge into a bowl. Guy never ordered any of the men in his private regiment to stand the food line, but Devon was here of his own accord.

"That girl didn't say thank you," Guy noted dully.

"Doesn't matter, she's still welcome." It was no surprise that Devon would delight in such things. The man had escaped the hell of captivity twice—first from the traitor lord, and second from a gaol cell. Now he was in a position to help those in need, and he reveled in it. Guy wondered how long it would take for Devon to become a sour old grump like himself.

"You're welcome." Guy gave a smile to the next person in line.

"Thank you for doing this," came the woman's reply, in earnest. Her muscles were pulled back in a reflexive wince, the sign of a life lived constantly at wit's end. One knobby hand clutched two young girls who held out their bowls without emotion. "It's good to know that someone's looking out us."

"Of course." Guy put a husk of bread in each of their bowls, staring intently at each. Neither child moved a muscle.

"Thank goodness," she repeated. "We don't get any Robin Hood here in the city, so this'll have to do."

Guy bit his lip and said nothing.

"Don't be fooled by those stories," Devon chirped. "They're just stories, after all. Believe in what you see, and what you can *taste.*" He winked, and gave the woman an extra scoop of the day's sludge. Her eyes widened as she tugged her daughters away.

"Neither of those girls are touching their food," Guy said, leaning back to spy on them as they left.

Devon shrugged. "What of it?"

"Probably not her children. She's using them for the extra rations, I'd wager. Beats them, too. And you gave her an extra helping."

Devon's reply came in the form of another smile, for another stranger. "I'd rather trust and be disappointed later, than to just assume everyone's awful. They're not, you know."

"Sure they are," Guy responded. "You just have to meet them first."

The Temperance Line kept on.

"Ho now!" Guy barked at the sight of an impressive brute, a tall man that was clearly built for pulling a field plow. "What are you, a mason?"

"Docks," the stranger grumbled, tilting his head back. With even a single word Guy could hear his northern accent. Most of those that came to the food line were desperate—it was rare to see someone in good health.

"Docks are full of runts and skivers. You ever think about putting those muscles to better use? The Guard could use a man like you."

"Yeah, maybe," the man grunted, but did not pause as he moved along. Behind him, a skinnier fellow snickered, trying to keep in the former's shadow. He wore a loose padded arming cap, a trend that Guy loathed. It practically screamed that the wearer had no intention of ever putting a proper helmet on top of it.

"Good Sunday to ye." Devon offered out his ladle. Guy reached out and pulled it back to the pot.

"Mind taking that cap off?" Guy asked.

"What for?" returned the skulking man.

"I said, mind taking that cap off?"

He scoffed a non-answer and held his bowl out to Devon. The cap's ties dangled loosely down to his chest, which made them quite easy for Guy to snatch and whisk from the man's head with almost no movement at all. The man was slow to react, first at the offense of having his cap stolen, and second to hide the puffy red scars of his left earlobe.

"Outside," Guy demanded, thrusting the cap back into the man's chest. "Temperance is for honest folk. Get back to the wharfs."

"Fuck on you." The man sent his empty bowl flying, twitching as he broke out of the line to head directly to the gates.

"Sorry," Devon apologized once it was clear the man would make no further incident. "I didn't know."

Guy brushed it off. "Don't apologize."

"That would never have occurred to me, but it's the first thing you noticed."

"I have a significant head start on you in being cynical."

"I'll do better." Devon straightened himself, eyes flicking about the crowd as if he hoped to identify an assassin amongst them. "I want to learn."

"Not too quickly, I hope." He tried to make it seem casual. But he had pushed Jon Bassett into responsibility too quickly, and did not want to make the same mistakes again. He hoped Devon would hold onto his youthful optimism for years, rather than go too fast. And frankly, Guy hoped that some of that learning might come back his way as well.

A few tables down the line, a basket of fresh bread was being delivered by none other than the servant girl Arable, who kept her face down and a bonnet to mask the scars Jon Bassett had given her.

Not too quickly, Devon.

"Unbelievable!" came a deep-hearted roar, and Guy snapped his attention to a throng of men pouring through the front gates. Not a crowd of miscontents, this was the entourage of the visiting Lord Geoffrey of Oughtibridge. Every movement seemed to take effort from the huge man, and his face was bright red and bursting just at the slight incline from the gatehouse. "This is the top of it all, that's what this is!"

"Your lordship." Guy slipped from behind the table to meet the dignitary. "Is anything the matter?"

"Everything is the fucking matter!" he belched, and did not stop as he barreled to the front of the line to inspect the day's offerings. "What is this?"

The crowd retracted from him, watching in alarm as he snatched a lump of bread and squeezed it to pulp. Guy wondered if this was supposed to be a demonstration of strength. It was tempting to answer the man's question of *What is this?* with the obvious word *bread,* but decided to keep quiet until he learned what had prompted the lord's rage.

"I came to see the Sheriff," Oughtibridge continued, sending a look of disgust to everything within arm's reach. "He keeps sending tax collectors at me, so I decided to finally pay."

A loose gesture indicated two of the men in his entourage, who each held one end of a sizable wooden chest they appeared eager to be rid of. They jostled its weight to the ground and took a step back.

"But this, this just proves my point." Oughtibridge stuck his nose into a nearby bowl held by an old man who did not know enough to retreat. "This is what he's doing with my taxes, then? This is why he's so desperate to count every last coin I have, so he can give out food for free?"

"I don't think the two are related," Guy answered, fully aware it was only for himself.

"Limp-wristed fop, where is he?" Oughtibridge drove every inch of his significant body closer to Guy. His moustache was thick and wrapped all the way down and up to his ears again, giving the remarkable impression that his hair itself was trying to reach around and suffocate him.

"The Sheriff is unavailable," Guy lied. "I will convey your displeasure if you like. My men can see to your taxes."

"You'd best *convey* it well," the lord snarled, but his lips pulled back into something that gave all other smiles a bad name. "You see to it that he gets these taxes, directly, you understand?"

"Of course."

"Open it then," he stepped back.

Guy was immediately suspicious, but there was no reason to find danger in a coinchest. Guy signaled two of his men from the edge of the tables to claim the thing, while Guy knelt down to unlock its clasp. He could smell something foul as his face moved closer, but did not expect what he found when its lid flipped open.

"What is this?" Guy asked, recoiling, though he knew the answer.

"*Horseshit,*" the Lord Oughtibridge announced proudly. The chest was full to the brim with it, a mix of dry and wet clumps smashed into each other, seeping from the corners. Guy realized some of it was on his fingers from the clasp itself. He flicked it off and a chill ripped through his spine.

"Horseshit, because that's what these taxes are," the lord continued. "If I'm going to pay something, I'm supposed to get something in return. I told the tax collectors he sent, but the Sheriff clearly hasn't gotten the message. I can't travel anywhere without being harassed by these damned thieves in the forest, and de Lacy refuses to do anything about it. Until he can secure his own goddamned roads, I'm not paying a single fucking shilling."

Guy watched the man strut back to the Temperance Line and grab an empty bowl from beside the pot of porridge, startling Devon down to his nethers.

"And this is the topper," Oughtibridge cackled. "This is how he's spending it. Here. If he wants to take my taxes and give it to the people . . ." he scraped the bowl into the chest to scoop out a slop of the excrement, then marched back to the line. ". . . then eat up!"

The bells from St. Peter called out a deep slow call to mass, and on the third strike Lord Oughtibridge dropped the entire bowl, shit and all, into the porridge.

THIRTY

WILLIAM DE WENDENAL

NOTTINGHAM CASTLE

Over the course of a thousand years, William explained, erosion could carve a gullet through a smooth field and cut it in two. He had watched the same principles lay waste to Nottinghamshire in a mere three weeks.

"I will not say I regret coming to Nottingham," he added, catching a tease of protest in Arable's eye, "but I think Robin was right. Neither of us are helping anything. I doubt he has any idea how significant the ramifications of his actions are, and meanwhile I'm stuck here unable to . . . ramificate anything."

Arable threw him a coy squint. "Ramificate isn't a word."

"I know," he pouted. "I started that sentence before I knew how it ended."

It was an appropriate analogy for his every effort in the city.

She led him through the tall grass with care, forward, holding one of his hands with two of her own freezing fingers. Tall stone walls protected them from the rest of the city, which even the sun had yet to brave this morning. The burying ground was overgrown and poorly tended, dawn dew turning each blade of grass into sparkling ice. Simple, unadorned headstones haphazardly littered the courtyard under the modest spire of St. Nicholas. It was the nearest church to the castle besides the abbey in the middle bailey, and Arable had insisted they visit it this morning.

She turned back to him, her cheeks flushing red from the cold. "You know, things might easily be much worse, if you weren't here."

He had to laugh. "I think the castle would have to be on fire for that to be true." William glanced up, just to double-check that Nottingham Castle was still there, peeking over the tips of the walls. "I honestly thought it would be simple. Talk things out peacefully, re-establish the supply lines, and mercy wins the day."

She moved slowly, tugging him along. "But . . ." she prompted.

"But everything," he answered.

The city had yet to recover from Gisbourne's shutdown of the markets, and it was obvious now that it couldn't. "There simply isn't enough coming *in* to Nottingham anymore, be it coin or goods. Between the rumors of de Lacy's impending replacement and Robin's robberies, nobody trusts the city. And now, neighboring lords are withholding their county dues until an effective sheriff can properly secure the roads."

"I know," Arable said. "I was there."

"You were? Is it true that Lord Oughtibridge shat right in the stew?"

"Not quite," she laughed.

William wished he could laugh about it. The more familiar he became with the city's fragile mechanics, the more helpless he felt. Every day, more lords took on Oughtibridge's stance and refused to pay their share. Even traveling merchants were avoiding Nottingham until they knew it was more stable. This might have normally created the perfect opportunity for local trade to thrive, but there was more coin to be earned in the Sherwood than the city. "Instead of coming together, everyone is retreating into themselves. They're all standing in the same pit, watching the flood water rise, refusing to work together."

"What does Roger say?"

"Not much. But he's getting riled."

William had sat with de Lacy throughout numerous negotiations, and grown a heartfelt respect for the man's patience and competence. The balancing act he played to keep his county operational was impressive, but with Oughtibridge's demands the whole thing was now tipping dangerously away from him.

"The city suffers when the markets suffer, the markets suffer when the trade routes suffer, and the trade routes suffer because Robin is far more influential than I am. And now he's accidentally rallied the county lords to a near mutiny."

"Mhm."

"It's not *all* Robin's fault," William made the distinction, dragging his finger across the rough surface of a nearby headstone.

It was a perfect storm, each issue amplifying the next. Robin was the only variable that could actually be managed, but there was no way to communicate with him. That had probably been their biggest mistake. "He's doing exactly what we said we'd do. I can't blame him."

"Mhm."

"I think de Lacy can keep the strings together for a while," he considered. "But if he indeed gets replaced, this is all going to explode."

"Mhm."

He startled to realize, again, that he'd been ignoring her. He didn't mean to, but it was too easy to get caught up in the thick of it all. He quickly apologized, and went to her. She was kneeling in the wet grass in front of a small cracked cobblestone, uniquely colored but pounded unimportantly into the earth. There was nothing to imply that it was a grave marker and not a mistake.

"This is my father," she said.

A cold fist clenched around William's heart, instantly shamed and horrified at how distracted he had been. But then she continued, "Well, not really. I don't know where he was buried, if he was even buried at all. So I found this little stone here about a year ago, with no name, and I'd like to think maybe it could be for him."

William had never put much thought into Lord Raymond de Burel's fate. He had been a prickly man in life, albeit with a curious charm for those he deemed worthy. He had died nearby, fifteen years ago, during the failed assault on Nottingham led by William de Ferrers. In all likelihood, he might have been killed in an ambush by the citizens of Nottingham, defending their city. It was impossible to know. If there had been anything on Lord Burel's person to identify him as the head of a household, it wouldn't have helped him here. Those that participated in the assault were seen as traitors to this city, and would have not received any formal processions.

"Maybe one of his men protected his body," Arable suggested, matter-of-factly, "and found a place for him. Maybe this marker was left blank for a reason, as something that couldn't be said."

William could not imagine how difficult it must be for her to live in the city. Her family name was a danger to her in Derby because of his own father, but here it bore an insulting history as well. *Ferrers* had become synonymous with *treason* in Nottingham, and the names of those that aided the earl in his revolt fared little better. Nottingham had a long memory, and a cruel one, but Arable endured that prejudice for the protection de Lacy alone offered her.

A protection which would not last. And William had yet to offer any real alternative, despite his promise to her. She had mentioned the hope of searching for her family in France, but had nothing to follow but rumors. Only a single idea had come to William's mind, but it was risky. His father was the world's expert on the location of Burels in the world. He could write home in the hopes of getting such information, but if his father suspected William's motives, it would put her in greater danger.

Arable touched the stone gently. The marker bore no actual significance, but the emotional poverty of that action chilled William to his core. He had no words to help her. He wished her grief could stand and scream at him, could pull steel that he could fight it like a real enemy. He had no idea how to kill something that refused to be touched. It was the same impotence he felt by de Lacy's side unable to do anything besides comment. Nothing that amounted to progress.

"I'm sorry," he said, because they were the words he was supposed to say.

"Don't be sorry." Her eyes pierced him, begging him to be more than he was. "Our sorries are long over. I didn't bring you here to make you feel guilty. This boring rock in the ground is the only thing I have left of my family, William, and it's not even real. And why? Because my father did as he was expected. He knew it was wrong to march on Nottingham, but he didn't know how to say no. Your father was right to refuse the call. Don't learn the wrong lessons from the past, promise me that. You'll be gone a week from Sunday."

There was a small accusation there, as if it were his choice to return to the war. But he and Robin had made their plans, and failed.

"You know I don't want to leave you."

"That's not my point. You're leaving, so you have nothing to lose. Use that. Don't sit by and let the wrong things happen if you have the ability to change them. I've seen this growing, from every side, and it's not going to balance out on its own. There are a lot of things that Roger can't do, because he has to represent the city. You don't have that problem. You don't have to get his permission for everything."

He reached down for her hand, their fingers interlocked. The pieces started to take shape in his mind. "He won't take action against the outlaws, because he doesn't want to legitimize them. But if they were to disappear on their own . . ."

She was watching him, a private smile ready to bloom, ready to push him to the natural conclusion of his own thoughts. *De Lacy could claim that victory. And in so doing, maybe even hold on to his sheriffcy.*

"Arable," he rubbed her fingers to warm them. "Do you suppose de Lacy would let me have you for the entire day, tomorrow?"

THIRTY-ONE

ROBIN OF LOCKSLEY

SHERWOOD ROAD

THEY DIDN'T EVEN MAKE bets anymore, is how bad it was.

At first every carriage heist was a gamble, not knowing if there would be an armed escort or some heroically spirited driver who might challenge them. Some of their targets surrendered easily, some made agitated displays, and only a few tried to escape, which of course Robin allowed. Eventually patterns emerged, based on the number of travelers, their speed, the breed of the horses, or any number of other details. So the thieves would make bets on how each encounter would play out, and then surreptitiously attempt to influence that outcome. There was never real danger. They never stole anything large enough to get in trouble, and Robin generally thought he ought to pat himself on the back for a job well done.

The stranger evolution came when some of their victims began to enjoy it.

There were horses with bells, there were colorful banners, there were *audience members* riding atop certain carriages who would hoot in ecstasy upon seeing Robin's crew. It was the pinnacle of surreal theater. When Robin waltzed out from behind a tree with an arrow nocked loosely in his bow, he received—of all the unfathomable things—*applause.*

And now it was so predictable, they didn't even make bets.

"Do we look like a bear?" asked John Little.

This was a real question, an actual and honest inquiry made from a living breathing human being, who very much wanted the answer to be yes. *"Do we look like a bear?"* was not the sort of thing one ever expects to be asked in life. If Robin hadn't been shot in the leg by some damned archer half the world away, he would be currently answering questions about troop placement and siege weaponry. Instead he was left staring at the curious combination of John Little's massive body and young Much's tiny one, sitting atop John's shoulders, with his arms reaching upward and his fingers curled into what were likely supposed to be claws. A brown sheep's hide was draped over Much's head, and rather than stating that the entire thing was ridiculous Robin was forced to admit that they did, regrettably, look like a bear.

"I told you!" John triumphed, squeezing Much's legs, and lumbered off to his position making sounds that were not bearlike at all, as they were in fact just the words *stomp stomp stomp* repeated with each step.

And worse than the eager robbery victims, worse than the growing monotony of making easy coin, and worse than the two-headed non-bear, was the fact that Robin was actually enjoying himself.

"I will admit this," he cocked his head to Marion, "they are not who I expected."

She raised an eyebrow that spoke volumes, and he even knew how she'd phrase it before she asked. "Not the gang of brazen scofflaws you thought they'd be?"

"No, they're exactly the gang of brazen scofflaws I thought they'd be," he returned with a straight face. "But everyone else. The villagers, for instance. Did you see yesterday, outside Keeton, I gave a man a shilling and he asked if I could break it into a dozen pence instead? That he could give out to his friends."

"I did see that." She tilted her head back at him, every inch of her smug smile saying *I told you so*. "You want them to be greedy, don't you? You want them to be mean and greedy and lazy, so you can say you were right."

"I do like being right," he considered. "I am usually very good at it."

"Well I'm sorry they disappointed you by not disappointing you. They just can't win, can they?"

She turned to give a playful swirl of her cloak, its heavy furred edges making havoc of a bed of broken leaves. Two weeks ago Robin never would have allowed Marion to accompany them on a robbery, but now there were spectators from their camp on every adventure. There was an aging woman named Amelia who always brought one of her three children for the day's entertainment, and a young brunette named Malory who was constantly trying to catch Alan's eye. The fact that Much was allowed to participate in today's robbery was a testament to the ease of their task. Friar Tuck had long given up on using believable excuses to stop the travelers, instead concocting increasingly preposterous tales of woe.

"It's the travelers, too," Robin added after some thought. "Not what I expected."

Marion scrutinized him. "How so?"

"Well, don't forget who my father was," Robin said, knowing she would understand. "Growing up with the unfortunate circumstances of being Lord Walter's son, I developed a slightly skewed impression of landowners."

Her lips pursed into a smile. "Did you think all noblemen were as kindhearted as Walter?"

"No," he scoffed. "And yes. My father would have fed hay to a dead horse. So my impression of anyone who fell outside of that generosity was appropriately wretched. If a lord kicked some poor sod out," he fumbled for words, "he must have really, truly deserved it, yes?"

"For your father, yes." Marion pulled a single arrow from his quiver and absently inspected its fletching. "But many lords were not so discerning. When it comes to hoarding their coin, one fewer head to count was all they cared about."

"But that's just it." Robin cocked his head meaningfully. "The people we stop, they attribute no weight to the coin we steal. They don't feel its absence."

"Because they're spending it," she said. "On entertainment. They'd rather pay for the fleeting thrill of an adventure in the forest than give it to the county as a tax."

"Or to someone in need."

"And you didn't expect that."

He shrugged it off. "There are still plenty of honest lords, and plenty of greedy villagers. But it's not . . . it's not the *ratio* I would have expected."

She slid the arrow back into his quiver, and her hand found the nape of his neck. Her hands were cold. He remembered that about her, how they'd laugh about her irrationally cold fingers. "Don't worry, Robin. It's not the first time you've been wrong about things. You should be getting better at it any time now."

He smiled, and watched the others giggle with delight in preparation for an approaching carriage. Robin tried to remind himself it was perspective, and perspective only. He had spent three weeks with the thieves in the Oak Camp, and it was natural to find common ground with them. Even the Guardsman Jon Bassett had softened his stance during his stay. Once Robin returned to the war, he knew he would once again recognize this miniature world for what it was.

But a part of him was sad that he might lose this sense of connection.

"Help me, a bear has eaten my arm!" came a cry from the road, entirely too intelligible if it was meant to be believed. "Oh please, kind sirs, please, would you tell me if you have spied any bears about, perchance one with an arm in its mouth?"

"One carriage, two drivers," Arthur a Bland whispered, suddenly beside Robin. "City horses, bells. No onlookers. I'd say one woman inside, and I'd bet anything that she'll make suggestion about you 'stealing a kiss' instead of her jewelry."

"I'd warrant you're right," Robin sighed, making out the faded colors of the carriage through the trees. "Why don't you take this one, then?"

"Ah, no," Arthur huffed. "I think they want Robin Hood."

It went exactly as Arthur predicted. The two men atop the carriage's bench were alarmed, but not surprised, and were quick to throw down their weapons at the sight of Elena and Alan's bows. There was only a small purse between the two of them, which was tossed to Much once John Little ambled close enough. Robin bowed to the two drivers, noted both of their names, thanked them for their time and patronage, and convinced them to calm their passenger within into compliance. Then he poured every drop of grace he had into a swing that brought him inside the carriage's belly, finding himself sitting across from a somewhat mousey but pretty woman with dark curled locks nearly obscuring her face.

"My apologies," he swooned.

"You're Robin?" she asked, all business.

"I am *enchanted,*" Robin answered, diving into the character that had somehow taken a life of its own. "But you may call me Robin if you prefer to save your lips the extra syllable."

"I bring a message from William."

It was the last thing he had expected her to say.

"William de Wendenal," she added. "Or *King William,* he said you might understand that."

Robin's mouth talked without him. "Who, what, you?"

"My name is Arable." She glanced through the curtains of the window. "I'd ask that you keep your voice low, as my drivers do not know I've come to speak with you. They think we are delivering a gift of rare wine to the Lord of Oxton, which you will kindly steal from me so we can immediately return to Nottingham."

She pivoted her legs to the side to reveal a small swollen cask, stained red at its mouth.

"You bring a message from William," Robin repeated, unmoving, his voice low. It was still another ten days until November's full moon, when he and William had planned on regrouping at Locksley to make their way back to the war. "I'll take it."

"He did not write it, for fear of the other thieves finding it and turning on you. He trusts me with the message, and begs you to trust me with your response as well."

Robin scrutinized the woman. Her jaw was taut, her teeth clenched. Her hands lay at a comfortable position on her lap but her fingers gripped each other with intensity.

"Are you alright?"

"I don't do this sort of thing often and I'm hoping not to vomit on you."

That put Robin remarkably at ease. "Alright. What's the message?"

"Two words. *Back down.*"

Of all the words in the world, Robin had none of them.

"William says that, as usual, you're too good at what you do. He says there are ramifications to your actions you can't possibly know about, and he needs you to ease off on everything. He says your half is done, but he can't finish his half until you stop it."

"This was his idea!" Robin gaped. "William was the one who wanted me to stay and teach them all a little discretion."

"And now he's asking you, as a friend, to stop it." She curled half her face into an uncomfortable fist. A quick glance out the window revealed Tuck chasing after John Little, putting on a show of trying to reclaim his arm from a giggling Much. "And if you don't mind my saying so, is this really your definition of discretion?"

There was simply no way of watching the display outside and answering, *Yes.*

"You must have stolen enough by now," she continued, "to let you lay low. The Sheriff needs a symbolic victory over your Robin Hood, or else he faces an all-out revolt. William asked me to remind you that you came to fix things peacefully, not this. He says it's his turn to be in the crown now."

That was all Robin needed to know. William had the advantage of seeing the entire battlefield, so Robin trusted him to make the right call.

"You may have started with the right intentions, but the jewelry, the ladies, the . . . showmanship of it all?"

Robin laughed. There was something distinctly humbling about a pretty woman detailing exactly how unimpressive he was.

"That isn't part of William's message, by the way, this is me saying that."

"I know."

She threw a dismissive smile and then brushed the hair from one side of her face, an instinct she immediately tried to stop. Robin caught sight of a puffy pink line that slanted down across her cheek. He had stared at the hole in his own calf every day for months. He knew the difference between a rash and a wound.

"Are you alright?" he asked, craning his head for a better look.

She ignored him and tipped the edge of the wine cask for him to grapple. "We should be off. Unless you normally spend longer than this in a carriage, as I don't want your cohorts to become suspicious."

There was something offensive about the word *cohorts,* but Robin let it pass. He took the weight of the cask into his arms, and made to open the carriage door again.

"Arable, was it?" She nodded. "Thank you for not vomiting on me."

She made a bashful smile and readjusted her hair. "Thank you for listening. William has a lot of faith in you, and I have a lot of faith in him. Do you have anything you'd like me to say to him, from you?"

"I have so many things," Robin admitted, "so very many things I'd like you to tell him, but they would all be quite vulgar and I would feel bad if I made you repeat them."

"I understand." She bobbed her head. "I'll just make up some of my own vulgarities then, and tell him they're from you."

"Brilliant." He laughed. "Tell him I'll see him soon."

A few minutes later it was over, the carriage made an awkward circle to return from whence it came, and the lot of them was left complaining about the single coinpurse and the wine cask.

"Hardly worth it," Arthur grumbled, popping the wine open to smell at its mouth. "This is supposed to be rare?" He dipped a finger and tasted it, his face explaining exactly what he thought of it. David found a cup to pour into, which they all passed around to lend their expertise in wine tasting.

Robin found the opportunity to draw Marion away, trying to calculate how he could convince her of what needed to happen. "I think it would be best if we back off a bit."

"What do you mean?"

"We've made our mark. We've collected more coin than we know what to do with . . . what say we put a pin in it for now, before we get too greedy?"

"We're helping a lot of people, Robin," she chewed on the idea, "and we can help a lot more. I don't see any reason to stop while it's still going so well."

"It only takes one mistake, you know." He tried to sound worried. "And besides, maybe it's time they tend to themselves. Rather than give all this coin out. Prepare the Oak Camp for winter. There's a lot of work still to be done in that regard."

"That's true." Marion turned to the rest of the group, who were debating whether Much should be allowed a swig of the wine. "But there's still plenty of time."

"Do what you want." Robin put his hands out, trying to play it off as innocently as possible. He didn't like manipulating her, but he was also fairly certain he knew how to do so. "But you asked me to stay so I could advise them. This is my advice. I know it's hard to stop while things are going well, but the alternative is to wait until things are bad and then regret it."

Her mouth closed, a silent admission that she had no rebuttal.

It probably wouldn't matter. If Robin could divert their energy for even another week, it would give William whatever victory he needed to finish his work in the city. Once he left, he had no doubt Will Scarlet and John Little would get straight back to making poor choices, and the consequences would be entirely on them.

There was no reason in the world Robin ought to feel guilty about that.

Not a single one.

Apparently against his will, Much took a sip of the wine.

THIRTY-TWO

WILLIAM DE WENDENAL

NOTTINGHAM CASTLE

ROGER DE LACY GRUMBLED without purpose, his fingers clasped over his eyes. "Let them in," he ordered, and Hamon Glover wobbled off to see it done.

Today they were at the long table rather than de Lacy's tiny office in the high keep, his bony frame dwarfed by the tall narrow walls. In his office he could be a giant, and perhaps it made decisions easier when the world seemed small. From where he stood by a glazed window, William could see the gathering of lords and their retinue in the training yard outside. Five of them, though they represented dozens now, all protesting their monthly assessments. From this distance, the only one identifiable was the elephant Oughtibridge. Soon enough Hamon would join them and invite them up, so that de Lacy could answer their demands in person.

William could tell how much the Sheriff wished to be elsewhere, his fingers parted just wide enough for the light of his eyes to shine through and beg for mercy.

"I don't suppose," his words coughed out, "you have enough of your father in you to know what he would do, would you?" He smiled sadly, his white knuckles rapped absently onto the table. "I always thought it was greedy men that made the world so unlivable. I thought it was the temptation of power, the addiction of wealth, that turns our leaders into animals. After all, what are uprisings and rebellions if not the products of injustice? I thought a bit of understanding could fix this. I thought I could avoid the escalation of events by *allowing* that which was *forgivable*. Why can't people accept that which they have, rather than take that which they do not?"

William wished he could succinctly explain this perpetual problem of humanity. "My father would say the key to true justice is to think as your adversary," he said. "To see yourself as their enemy. In their position, how have they been wronged, and what would they want in return?"

"Lord Beneger is a wise man, but I disagree. I should think the world only grows worse by considering yourself an enemy to others."

It was a noble thought, and rare in a leader. William hoped he had played this correctly. Not quite a week had passed since he'd sent secret word to Robin to stop his escapades, hopefully enough time to make the difference he needed.

There was noise down the hall and below, of people approaching. De Lacy looked down into his hands as the footsteps amplified. "You see, it isn't greedy men at all who make the world so unlivable. It's men like me. I thought I could give people a longer leash, and that they'd stop pulling at it so. I erroneously convinced myself that *nothing* was an acceptable reaction to *something*."

The door creaked open and the room was suddenly full. Oughtibridge led them, followed by the lords of Papplewick, Norwell, the barons of Maunsfeld and Lowdham. Each carried their smug righteousness in the air with them, suffocating the room. The sheriff's assortment of counsellors was also invited, including those that regularly disagreed with him. William was familiar with most of them by now—the easily startled old coinmaster Arnold de Nottoir, the conservative trademaster Gerome Artaud—a dozen or so in total. Hamon Glover and Guy of Gisbourne were paired with a few others, trusted voices such as William who held no authority in Nottingham but whose opinion was valued. The Lady Margery d'Oily was one of them, though she was no doubt only a substitute for her absent husband the Earl of Warwick. A handful of Guardsmen filled in the gaps of the room, along with servant girls to wine them. William craned his head to search if Arable was amongst them, but could not find her.

Their "guest of honor," Lord Geoffrey of Oughtibridge, subtly tried to find an armless chair to accommodate his girth, and instead hovered at the head of the table as awkwardly as possible.

Introductions went around. As the unpleasant pleasantries concluded, de Lacy turned flamboyantly to William to start. "Well. Let's talk about our friends in the woods."

A dry voice interrupted, "Have they killed someone?"

William was shocked to see this had come from the Ferrers whelp, standing behind Gisbourne. His presence in Nottingham annoyed William, only partially because of what his existence meant to Arable. William tried not to blame the son for his father's mistakes, but that was a difficult bias to shake. Gisbourne instantly reprimanded his page for speaking and nearly sent him out of the room, but de Lacy stopped it.

"No it's fine. It's fine." He stood, meeting the young man's eyes. "Here's your first lesson in real politics, boy."

De Lacy popped open the lid to an ornate gold keepsafe and pawed out a handful of coins, then climbed onto his chair and, rather surprisingly, onto the table itself.

"The world beyond these walls is made of dukes and farmers. Duke . . ." he singled out Lord Oughtibridge from afar, and nimbly danced over the tabletop of plates and glasses to pour gold into the man's hands. He then turned back at Gisbourne, halfway down the table.

". . . and farmer," he finished, flicking one last coin through the air to his captain, who barely flinched to catch it.

"The farmer farms, which is useful, and the duke . . . dukes. Which is not." De Lacy's hand flapped about, equating precisely what he thought of the daily activities of dukes. "However, the duke pays taxes, which is quite useful, and he pays quite a bit."

De Lacy swung around again, picking up the keepsafe and opening it for Oughtibridge to deposit a portion of his coins back into.

William was surprised by the performance. Roger de Lacy was a man of extremes—there were times he preferred to cut savagely to the point with no frills, and there were others such as now when he relished in the storytelling of it all. He was literally dancing on the tabletop as if their worries were trivial, even though his career hung in the balance. His every reaction, William marveled, was a calculated part of his balancing act.

"The farmer is weak, but he makes food. The farmer gives the duke food, and the duke gives the farmer safety. This has worked for centuries. Are we all caught up?"

His advisors gave their compulsory agreement, though few seemed to enjoy it as much as William. De Lacy clapped his hands once and continued.

"Enter Richard's taxes, the Saladin tithe. Taxes on everyone, and everything, except for those who march off to war. But meanwhile, here at home, the duke pays more taxes, and he *hates it.*"

De Lacy again presented Oughtibridge with the keepsafe, into which he deposited another portion of his coins, along with a forced *garrumph* that drew laughter from the room.

"The farmer, on the other hand," de Lacy trip-stepped his way back across the table, "is still making food, and he pays more as well, and he *hates it.*"

Gisbourne, without performance, placed his single coin into de Lacy's hand.

"Or he doesn't pay it, and he still *hates it.* Or he goes to prison, and he *hates it.* Or he hides in the forest, and he *hates it.* It doesn't really matter, because look at how much he can pay." De Lacy showcased the one coin about. "I couldn't care less if he pays or he doesn't, because caring about it would cost more than what he's paying."

He flicked a finger and the coin lobbed high through the air, a smooth arc that ended at the staircase where its pathetic tiny *tink* tumbled down to a lower level where it was already forgotten.

"The farmers still farm, the dukes still duke, and everything is the same except that everyone generally *hates it* a little bit more."

More chuckles for this.

"Until," he raised his voice and a finger, and let it hang while he stepped slowly back to the center of the table. He set the keepsafe down gingerly, and made a silent and steady show of removing two handfuls of coin from its stomach. The coins dripped from his fingers and he drew his words out painfully slow.

"Until a band of supposed heroes comes by and steals from the duke, and just gives it to the farmer." Ever so softly, he stepped and leaned out to Gisbourne, dropping the coins in front of him.

"Now the farmer has it all. He has money *and* food. And he realizes that he's been hungry, and that he'd rather eat his vegetables than give them to the duke. Meanwhile, the duke has neither money *nor* vegetables, so what does he do? He *stops paying his taxes.* And now, now my friends, now I suddenly care again. Because without the duke's taxes, there's no money at all coming in, so there's no money going out, not to the King and not to the Chancellor and not to anyone at all, and I *hate it* as much as everyone else."

He snapped his foot through the keepsafe to an explosion of coin and noise, and though it rained money nobody dared to move. When the last of the clatter had clicked and rolled and tinkled to a stop, de Lacy descended from the table and sank into his chair to conclude viciously, "It doesn't matter who the sheriff is, Nottingham is crumbling. So we're here to discuss practical solutions. I think you'll find it's more difficult than digging your feet in the ground."

Gisbourne took the reins quickly. "So let us resolve the situation. Eliminate the outlaws."

"How, Gisbourne?" De Lacy snapped his teeth. "You and fifty men go marching randomly into the Sherwood hoping to *get lucky*? You tried that already."

"We have dealt with situations like this before. Sheriff Murdac had no problem—"

"A fight is the last thing they'll give you." De Lacy shook his head in exasperation, his temper high. "They'll hide, they'll wait for you to pass, and you'll never find them. Even if you did, what would we do with them? It would take more money to search them out than they're even stealing! Hell, I should give them bloody subsidies!"

William cleared his throat, seeing the opportunity he needed. "If I may, I think this meeting is entirely unnecessary. The robberies have all but stopped in the last week."

"Only because merchants won't travel the roads anymore," the Lord of Papplewick announced with a nasal sneer. "I wish the same were true for my wife."

The other lords groaned in agreement, but William put his hand up to silence them.

"Have any of them been stopped in the last week?" A few raised eyebrows, but none answered. "As I say, these thieves had already been routed, thanks in particular to the leadership of Sheriff de Lacy. He and Captain Gisbourne focused their attention on the gangs here in Nottingham, which were supporting the thieves in the Sherwood. It took a few weeks, but those efforts have paid off. I think you've seen the last of them. But this business about not paying your taxes, frankly it's exactly what they wanted. Rebellion, uncertainty. You've let them play you, even after they're no longer a threat. The baron has played this properly, and I think we owe him our thanks."

There was a quiet in the room, and more than a few raised eyebrows. De Lacy's eyes pierced him, demanding answers for the unlikely compliments. William dared to hope it would work.

"Even if this were true," Gisbourne said, "it wouldn't matter to the people. These songs going around, the stories of Robin Hood, those will continue. Until we make an arrest, until we can put a *public* end to this, the people are going to live in fear."

"Besides, laying low for a week doesn't mean they're gone," Lord Oughtibridge thundered as he shifted his weight from one unfortunate position to another. "They have the money to turn every town and village in the county against us."

William glanced at de Lacy for help, but the man shook his head. *It was a good try,* his eyes said. *But it's beyond that now.* He felt the threads slip out of his hand, like the tether to a boat taken by the current without him.

"Yes, but who is buying?" Hamon Glover was asking. "Diamond necklaces and earrings don't do them any good."

"Perchance they have more friends than we think," came the trademaster, rising. "Perchance there are some lords in Nottinghamshire who are financing this terrorism, for their own reasons." *Blame,* William realized. He had offered solutions, but they wanted punishments. It wasn't that he'd missed his mark, it was simply that nobody cared.

"We know who to talk to." Gisbourne drew close to de Lacy now, though he could hardly hide his voice from the rest of the table. "We know she's helping them. She could be the public ending we're looking for."

De Lacy's face twitched as he measured the suggestion, then responded with all gravity. "I trust I don't have to remind you who her family is."

Gisbourne snorted. "Her family."

Marion. She'd made a strong impression upon William at Locksley Castle, before all hell broke loose. But as highly as Robin spoke of her, she was treading in dangerous waters. If she was indeed responsible for turning Robin's stolen jewelry into actual coin, then she might be the key to stopping it all. William cursed himself for not pursuing that thought earlier.

"If she were here, I would speak with her," de Lacy admitted. "But nobody has heard from her for weeks. She keeps a room in Sheffield, which we are watching. But we cannot idle ourselves until she resurfaces. We have the more pressing task of getting our own house in order. We've failed so far. *I've* failed so far. I want options on how to proceed."

"You don't know how it is out there," Papplewick whined. "Half of my people are gone. I already lost half to the war. How am I supposed to live on what's left? How are any of us? If the Sheriff of Nottingham cannot take care of a problem like this, I don't know why I came here to ask for help."

"Let's be honest, at least," Roger replied. "You did not come here to ask for help. You came to ransom it."

"Why should we pay," Oughtibridge huffed, "if we get nothing in return? You're the High Sheriff. We'll pay your taxes when you prove you can protect us from this sort of treason!"

He sloshed his wine about and cursed it when it spilled, along with a few other things about the room he found worthy of his expletives.

William tried to salvage something from it all. "We need to encourage merchants to use the Sherwood Road again. Gisbourne, couldn't you assign men as escorts through the forest?"

Gisbourne scoffed. "Escort duty? We're the Sheriff's Guard, not mercenaries for hire."

"Your dignity aside," William licked his lips, "could it be done?"

"I worry that would do more harm than good," de Lacy countered. "It gives the outlaws legitimacy. We're practically telling everyone else we know they're in there and we can't find them."

"Then let them stay hidden," William suggested, desperate to find some leverage. "As I said, the robberies are decreasing . . ."

"If we can't find them," dry and low, Ferrers spoke again, his arms clasped behind his back, "why not draw them out?"

"Ferrers!" Gisbourne barked, but de Lacy put his hand up.

"Go on."

Ferrers. William focused everything on the young man, his pock-marked weasel face. He rolled his eyes from one person to another at the table, touched his lips with his tongue, and then spoke smooth as silk.

"The stories they tell about this Robin Hood are quite detailed. They describe him as an expert bowman, and prideful of his skill. This, then, is his weakness. We shall announce a public archery contest, open for any to compete. His pride alone will draw him out. To be certain, we shall offer a large prize he should think to win, and hand out as he does. We won't let him win, of course. We'll have our own best archers there as a guaranteed victory. We know what he looks like. When he steps up to compete, we simply capture him—publicly, as you say—along with any of his men foolish enough to come along."

Each occupant of the room, perhaps even the room itself, let the idea sink in. As each did, they locked eyes on Roger de Lacy to gauge his reaction, letting him respond first. He drew a long steady breath in through his nose and smiled, clasping his hands. Then he leaned back to Ferrers.

"I'm sorry. The adults are speaking. Surely you're missed, at your mother's teat."

William bit his lip to keep from laughing. Ferrers did not so much as bat an eye, even when Gisbourne turned gravely to him and whispered, "You're an embarrassment, Ferrers. Wait outside."

While the doorway was only ten paces away, it was the longest and slowest walk that William had ever witnessed. His footsteps descended into the same forgettable elsewhere the coin had fallen earlier.

"What an ingenious plan," Lady d'Oily mocked. "An archery contest."

"He is an idiot," Gisbourne apologized.

That explained what an earl's son was doing as a glorified squire. He had no ambition in him like his father, no political machinations. He had not gone to war, he was not even serving in Derby. He'd been shipped as a ward to Nottingham to serve in a position that, even in its simplicity, was too much for him. There was no mystery or conspiracy to his presence, William had overlooked the easy answer. Namely that he was incompetent.

This was what William was truly combating. This was the quality of character left to rule in the England that the war left behind. This is what Arable had meant when she begged him to stay. Intelligence had become a commodity rarer than coin.

"Forgive me," Lady d'Oily spoke again. "I feel I may have become distracted earlier, and missed part of the conversation. When you gave that babe his lesson in politics, you spoke of the farmer and the duke. You said the farmer used to trade his food for security. He no longer has security. That is something only a duke can give." She looked importantly over at the Lord Oughtibridge, who seemed to like it very much. "Might that not be something of which you could . . . remind them?"

The same pregnant pause hovered over the room. But with Ferrers's idiocy preceding her, it had been a perfect opportunity for her to speak. William noted the calculated manner of her speech, how she had put forth her own idea without implying she knew better than the men in the room. That had been quite a gamble, but it seemed to work.

"It's a fine point," said the Baron of Maunsfeld. "These miscreants give out one coin for every two they steal. If we can't stop the thief, we can certainly stop those that profit from him."

"And that ought to be a public enough demonstration," Oughtibridge belched. "That says to fuck off."

William was mortified. It was the opposite of a good idea. They weren't interested in actual results, they only wanted the illusion of action. He had just discovered he was trying to play chess in a game of checkers, and had no idea how to reorient himself.

"Indeed," Roger de Lacy cleared his throat. "Let's be pragmatic then. Lord Gisbourne, put together your men. Break into groups. Visit the smaller villages, the communes, the forest dwellers. Make them pay. Supplies, foodstuffs, anything of value."

William couldn't believe what he heard. "You're going to take food directly from the people?"

"They've already been paid for it, William. Your boy Robin has given them the money. Our money. And if the thieves are indeed gone, as you say, this will keep them from coming back again."

William stammered to respond. This was not what he intended at all. This wasn't justice, this wasn't logical. De Lacy was simply placating his feuding lords. *Because he knew how to play the game.*

"This is wrong," was all he got out, feeling like a child. And they had already kicked one from the room.

"Just take payment. Keep it civil. Lady d'Oily is right," de Lacy said, almost proudly. "Robin Hood can't provide them security. That's something only we can provide. Let them see what sort of security comes with Robin's brand of justice, and I'm willing to bet they'll return to their old ways. Winter is close. They won't bargain their lives over it."

"That'll be a lot of supplies," Gisbourne noted. "We'll need a place to store it all."

"Pick someplace friendly, somewhere a bit outside the Sherwood of course, and gather it all there. Then transport it all to the city when you're done."

"I'll need a lot of men."

"Take them all." De Lacy's words were perfectly clear, but Gisbourne still seemed uncertain. "You can do this in one day. One strike, that's what you wanted, yes? All your men on this tomorrow, and the day after you can go back to the fisherman gangs."

Gisbourne nodded absently. He was already calculating how to put the plan in motion.

Arable's plea rang in William's ears, to *do something,* to stop this. But he had nothing. The room had consented, they thought this would make everything even. William had done everything he could to influence them toward reason, and they had chosen the alternative.

De Lacy clapped his hands once. "No bother waiting then. Lord Oughtibridge?"

The heavy man bowed his head in agreement, and in as many words the meeting was over. William thought to linger long enough that he might speak with de Lacy once the others had left. But the Sheriff was a statue, grim and unmoving, his eyes burning into a spot on the table where nothing lay. William repositioned obviously within the edge of his vision but still he stared, and William knew his would be an unwelcome company now. The decision had been made, and William could do nothing but wonder what he could have done differently.

THIRTY-THREE

ARABLE DE BUREL

NOTTINGHAM CASTLE

"Nottingham is crumbling," Roger had said.

And later, *"Someone else will have to clean it up."*

The castle was a frenzy, there were a hundred tasks to accomplish to prepare for the morrow's raids. William's plans for peace had failed, and it seemed likely that within a week both he and Roger de Lacy would be gone. Arable couldn't care about packing meals for Guardsmen now, her only thoughts were in the dark abyss of what her life might be a week from now.

Amongst the other pressing matters, a request came in from Lady d'Oily's room, which Arable quickly claimed. She climbed the stairs, passing the ghosts of its faceless builders, to the master solar where Lady d'Oily now resided alone. There was nothing else she could think of. William had promised he'd find a way to secure her safety after he was gone, but had yet to define what that meant. And he had not so much as noticed her during the Sheriff's council. Sadly, she had gotten used to being ignored—but usually not by him.

She shifted her hold of the quill and inkwell—a gift to the Sheriff from a Spanish dignitary—and knocked on Lady d'Oily's door. It cracked open with no invitation, and Arable moved into the room as quietly as she could. Lady d'Oily, draped in a dark sleeping gown, gave only her back and a vague gesture toward a small writing desk at the side of the room.

Say something.

Arable placed the writing instruments down gingerly, as if she were afraid the desk itself might collapse under their weight. She did not want to leave, but nor did she know how to begin a conversation. She realized she was trembling when Lady d'Oily dismissed her without a glance. *Foolish girl,* Arable cursed herself, and moved to exit as quickly as her feet could carry her.

You're running again.

Whatever morsel of bravery stopped Arable at the doorway was not hers. She turned to realize Lady d'Oily was staring at her, open mouthed at her insubordination. But she had made up her mind.

"Excuse me, Lady d'Oily," Arable barely said, "I was wondering if I may have a word with you."

"You've stolen quite a few words from me already, girl. Should I let your headmistress know she has a thief, or shall you be on your way?"

Arable's lungs seized, but she did not move. Still, she was humbled enough to bury her face downward. "I just wanted to say that I admired what you did earlier. The way you were able to . . . be heard."

Lady d'Oily moved to respond, and bitterly by the look on her face, but the insult seemed to catch in her throat. She bit it back and her demeanor softened, if only a shade. "Being heard is important, and uncommon. For women it is easiest to be heard when you choose not to yell." She gave Arable a withering look. "You did not come here to compliment me. What is your name, girl?"

All Arable's plans unraveled and slipped away. "I'm sorry to disturb you."

"Out with it." Lady d'Oily moved to prevent her departure, the weathered lines of her face turned into chasms by the harsh light. "You've already called me by my name rather than *m'lady,* so there's no point in hiding."

Arable dropped her eyes. "Arable, your ladyship."

"And you're not actually a servant here, are you?"

"I am." *It hurt to say.* "But I was not born to . . . such a life."

"The details of which are, I have no doubt, fascinating," Lady d'Oily said coldly, making it clear how boring she would find Arable's pitiful history. But her eyes sharpened in curiosity. "I recognize you. You've been escapading with Lord Wendenal, haven't you? It's quite obvious, and a little embarrassing. My husband says he stumbled upon you two in a hallway."

"William is . . . we knew each other. Some time ago." It wasn't an apology.

"Why then are you knocking on my door this evening rather than his? I cannot imagine this is nearly as exciting for you."

Arable summoned up her bravery. "I was wondering if you may have need of another servant in Warwick. I have many useful skills." She steeled herself against the well of tears that built behind those words.

"You want to leave Nottingham?" Lady d'Oily studied her. "What about this William de Wendenal, you want to leave him as well?"

"He'll be leaving first. He's only here for another few days, then he returns to the war. If you'll have me, I promise I won't disappoint you." She felt like she was begging for her life, like she was nothing.

Lady d'Oily made a sour face. "I suppose I could ask the Sheriff for this favor, but I don't see—"

"No need," Arable interrupted her. "I am not sworn to him. I'm here . . . by choice."

That clearly pricked the lady's attention. "Arable, you are a terrible servant. You speak and engage yourself with those you should not, and you have neither humility nor obedience. I don't know what on earth I would do with you, aside from break you."

"Even still." Arable swallowed. "I would go with you."

"Where is your family?"

"I'm the only one." It was her practiced answer. She didn't even know if it was true.

"What of this Wendenal? His father Lord Beneger is not insignificant. Couldn't you go play servant in Derby and await your beau's return?"

Arable bit her lip. "I'm not welcome there."

The thin blue skin at the edges of Lady d'Oily's eyes widened in shock. "Arable, what is your family name?"

She should have known better. No longer able to hide her fear, "I have no family."

"Don't answer questions I didn't ask. You have no family, as you say . . . *anymore.* But you were a Burel once."

Arable felt an icy grip at her heart. She could see Lady d'Oily putting together the pieces. *A Burel, a Wendenal, and a Ferrers, all in the same place.*

"You're not following me, you're running from something else. I will only consider your offer if you answer me fully and truthfully, starting with your next breath. Why are you running?"

"I don't think I'll be safe here," Arable's words came with a wash of relief she had not expected. "I came here two years ago because I knew Baron de Lacy was a good man, who would take care of me, but I don't think he'll be here much longer."

"You're referring to rumors, which I have heard, and already discounted."

"Not rumors," Arable returned. "Roger is prepared to leave."

"Why do you say that? Speak now."

"He told me so." She shrugged. "He said something about his grandmother's lands, and that he *'wouldn't miss Nottingham one bit.'*"

"This happened recently?"

"This happened ten minutes ago."

The lady's eyes widened again. A shrill whistle escaped her cracked lips. Then she stood straighter, which appeared to take some effort, to scrutinize Arable.

"You're not without some cunning. Your desire to attach yourself to me and my family is wise. My father is the Earl of Hereford. He married me to the Earl of Warwickshire, he married my sister Maud to the Earl of Oxfordshire, he married my sister Magdalena to the Earl of Huntingdonshire. My family is strong, and you would certainly be safe with us. But you're only asking for my help because your current protector has found himself in a momentary decline. Firstly, I would never bet against Roger. And secondly, you've shown me your loyalty only lasts so long as it suits you, which is not loyalty at all."

Arable didn't know what to say. This had been anything but easy for her.

"But Roger needs friends, and it sounds like you're one of them. So if he is forced to leave, then yes, you may join me."

Arable hadn't realized she was holding her breath until it burst forth from her in a tearful fit. "Thank you, my lady," she squeaked.

"You can call me Margery." She softened. "But only in private, of course. I think you'll learn a thing or two from me. Roger made an unfortunate decision this evening—these raids—because he thought he had no other options."

"I thought—" Arable sputtered, unsure if she had interrupted the lady's thought. "Weren't you the one to suggest these raids?"

"They were the only solution that would let him save face," she said with some gravity, "but I wish there had been another. Roger put himself in a box, I just pointed the way out. Men are difficult things, you know. A decade of marriage to Waleran has taught me how to challenge a man without insulting him, how to lure out his desire to explain himself without making him think his words are wasted upon a woman. This world is tenfold more difficult for us women than for men, but neither are we prone to absolutism the way they are."

"Absolutism?"

"They prefer to find enemies," she explained. "They blame their troubles on wicked men and cruel gods rather than their own shortcomings. They'd sooner believe that some arcane black magic has been aimed against them than to realize they have their own faults. They think their successes are proof that God smiles upon them, or that they have magic of their own. But there's no magic in the real world, Arable. *Magic is cheating.* Reality demands that we defeat our enemies by being craftier than them, to battle our dragons with policy and prose. Roger has been trying to do this alone, for too long."

"What can we do?"

"We can remind him he's not alone. We can push him when he needs to be pushed. And look for the opportunities he doesn't see. These raids are no kindness, but they are worth it to keep Roger in power for a bit longer. As you are very well aware, barons and earls can be contemptuous, selfish things. Nottinghamshire has no idea how lucky it is to have Roger de Lacy at its head. His grandmother's lands will simply have to wait."

Her cheeks hurt when she smiled, but Arable couldn't stop herself.

"Both you and Roger, Arable, have been losing for years. Not because the world is set against you or because your enemies have divine power, but simply because you have not been crafty enough to outwit them."

Margery tapped the table with the quill.

"We're going to change that."

THIRTY-FOUR

MARION FITZWALTER

THE OAK CAMP

THE QUALITY OF DINNER had vastly improved. What once was meager rabbit stew for every meal had been upgraded to fresh venison, salted potatoes with garlic, and flasks of wine that could compare favorably to any nobleman's cellar. There were stores to spare, though not yet enough to make the winter seem less daunting. For the moment, however, Marion let herself enjoy their accomplishments. Life was not so comfortable as it was when Locksley Castle thrived, but only because they now had a bounty on their head. Otherwise, the company was joyful. For a week they had focused on themselves, building up their campsite, raising real structures that could survive the winter. They ate a well-tended meal around a healthy fire, and enjoyed conversation and frivolity again. It was a luxury, Marion recognized, for life to be comfortable enough that laughter was an option.

Some way or another, tonight's dinner turned into a competition of macabre theatrics, as they shared dark stories about Gilbert with the White Hand.

"I see him talking to himself at night sometimes." Arthur layered his voice thick with dread, ripping the meat off a bone with his hands and sucking on his fingers. "Talking to his dead family. You haven't heard his story? He was a tanner in Nottingham, spent all his money on whores. When the tax collectors came, he just barely had enough to pay for himself. But not for his sister, or his wife, or his son, or his daughter, and especially not for his horse."

With every name Arthur grew quieter, and the crowd leaned in to enjoy the tale. It certainly wasn't Marion's preferred subject, but there was no point in spoiling their fun. Elena tried to put her hands over Much's ears, but he wiggled free.

Arthur continued. "So rather than let himself be arrested, he killed every one of them. He strangled his children each with one hand as his wife watched, then he tied his wife and sister to a table and set his shop on fire."

"Arthur!" Marion scolded him. "In front of Much?"

"It's just a story," the boy scolded her back.

"His shop burned down," Arthur continued, "which meant he didn't have to pay his piece of ten on it, so the tax collectors let him keep his horse. He rode out of Nottingham . . . but the souls of his family wouldn't let him go. They grabbed his hand and tried to pull him into death, and their touch withered it down to naught but bone. That's why he keeps the glove on, so nobody knows that he's half-dead already."

Some of the crowd laughed, others pretended not to be disturbed. Marion simply rolled her eyes. Gilbert was a haunted man, no doubt, but by no supernatural means. His nature probably hid little more than unlucky choices and a lonely soul. But as much as she hated to admit it, there was value in turning him into a ghost story. The caricature of a spectral assassin might scare off their enemies, just as the myth of a benevolent Robin Hood had brought them allies.

Marion eyed Robin, who seemed to sense her thoughts and winked back. What Lord Walter might think, if he heard his son had become the very figure of charity. Yet there was an undeniable change in Robin of late. He had eased out of his recalcitrance and enjoyed himself, at times behaving much like his new namesake. The thing that Lord Walter had started, whatever it was, was still alive here. It was taking a shape Marion had not expected.

Part of it unfolded before her. They could only delight in scary stories now because their days were no longer defined by fear. Life was still difficult, and they had ample concerns to worry about, but there was safety behind it all. It was the same at Locksley Castle. They did not live in fear of their lord, and Walter did not use fear to keep them in line. Their relationships were described in degrees of gratitude.

It was a better way to live, Marion knew it. Robin's tactics had simply found another path to it.

He winked at her again, larger and more obvious, and she had to laugh.

"We all have our reasons for coming here," John Little said with some weight, still talking about Gilbert. "And they're not all pretty."

"He's not like that," Much said matter-of-factly, plunging a small potato in his mouth.

Marion grabbed his chin and made him look up at her. "Have you been talking with Gilbert again, Much?" He hesitated and shook his head no, then opened his mouth for her to see the mush of his potato.

"So he does talk, then?" Robin asked, half-joking. "I think Gilbert's only stared at me so far."

"John," asked David, "I thought you said Gilbert never had no family?"

"I did say that," John nodded, "but that's just instinct. He has the look of a man who never had none. I don't believe Arthur's story for a moment. Even still, Lord Walter told me once that Gilbert had a notch or two on his belt, so to say. Didn't incline who they were, or how many."

"I heard it was many," Will Scarlet said in a dramatically raspy voice. "I heard he only takes his glove off when he kills someone. You ever notice how he don't use it when he eats? He saves that hand for death. It's stained deep with the blood of his victims, and he never washes it. Killin' is sacred to him, and he won't let his hand do anything else, to keep his act pure. Nobody's ever seen him take the glove off . . ." Will snarled, ". . . except for those that are about to *die!*"

He jumped out and grabbed Elena, who shrieked and slapped him on the chest. The story upset Much, who stood and ran from the fire in a pout, forcing Will and Elena to chase after him with apologies.

"It's just a story," Arthur complained, as if Much had no reason to leave.

Marion eyed the fire. "Stories have power." She was counting on it. There was more at play than survival now, a goal greater than simply weathering the storm. She had seen hope become as infectious as fear. They had started a ripple that was building in strength, though she knew not what they were destined to crash into. "Haven't you heard the story about the Robin Hood?"

Robin laughed. "I'm willing to bet that one will come back to bite me."

"How so?" asked the friar. "Robin Hood's become something for the people to believe in. Good for the people, good for the heart. Those are the best types of stories."

"Even if they're false?" Robin asked glibly.

"*Especially* if they're false," Tuck hit back, a smug charm in his eye. "I know that better than most people."

"Ah," Robin rolled the sound around his mouth. "That's been something I've meant to ask you. What exactly does the Church think of what you're doing here?"

"The Church?" Friar Tuck threw his hands up in disgust. "Honestly, I haven't the faintest. I'm sure they'd say any number of things about it, and some would be true, and some wouldn't, and all of it would mean we hadn't given them enough tithe last week. If I cared what the Church said about the things we do, I wouldn't be out here doing them." He chuckled, massaging the snags of his beard. "I suppose the Church would have us stay true to the laws of the land, but *the Lord* would have us stay true to our hearts. In better times, aye, those would be the same. Our job is to do our best to keep the two in harmony."

"Try to find a middle ground?" Marion suggested.

"Not quite. A harmony is two voices, both singing their own part. They support each other, dance around each other, and neither sounds good without the other. So we use our heart to weigh how we follow the law, and hopefully we make the laws to weigh how we follow our heart. That's harmony."

Again, Marion marveled at the optimism that had become their group. The fact that nobody laughed at Tuck's notion that they could "make the laws" spoke to it. This is what was possible when people were no longer afraid for their lives all the time—instead of looking behind their backs, they could look to the future.

"What if you're completely breaking the law?" Robin asked. "I only ask because it happens to be that you are completely breaking the law."

"Well, as every choir boy knows," the friar smiled, "if you cannot harmonize, then just hope nobody hears you singing."

Marion sipped from the hot cider Tuck had made for them. Again, Robin caught her eye. She'd be a liar to say she had not enjoyed his company, though she could certainly do without the antics the others used to give her and Robin privacy together. Men always seemed to think every relationship with a woman, even a friendship, was defined entirely in terms of sexual congress. Nothing of the sort would be taking place between her and Robin. He would be gone in a few more days, and Marion intended on keeping him productive for every second of it.

It was an easy and obvious reaction to grow fond for someone under these circumstances. They had a common goal, shared a romantic past, and for the most part they were isolated from the rest of the world. Only twice in the last month had she left the Oak Camp to sell their contraband in Huntingdon. The rest of the time was filled with moonlit skies and the camaraderie that came with simple adventures. Finding herself drawn to Robin again wasn't a magical intimacy so much as an obvious prediction. She refused to succumb to such uncreative prophecy.

When he gave an exaggerated wink for the third time, she had to actively grapple all her excuses back into place.

"So you're worried you'll get in trouble?" Arthur asked after a bit.

Robin shrugged. "No. William would vouch for me if it comes down to it."

"You mean," Arthur wavered, "if it came down to . . . us all being arrested?"

Robin hissed in some air and held it. "Well, if I fail and get you all arrested, you're not exactly going to want me around. Besides, you're all much better outlaws than I am. When we see the Sheriff's Guard, you all instinctively hide. Whereas I think, *Oh good, they're here to help.* You all have legitimate reasons to hate them. I can only pretend. It won't be the first time I've pretended to be something I wasn't."

"That's true for everyone, I imagine," Tuck mused.

"Well, I made a career out of it."

Another pause passed, but Tuck cleared his throat. "I'm been thinking of asking *you* about that. You say that you would dress up as the king, and give orders as the king, so that if an enemy were to attack they would kill the wrong man, yes?"

Robin nodded.

"You know what I find interesting about that?" Tuck asked. "It's a clever ruse, designed to trick your enemy. But I'm willing to bet it worked on your friends as well. Well, not *friends,* I suppose, but the men he commanded."

Robin bobbed his head. "It did. In the armor, there was no way to tell I wasn't the king."

"Ah, but weren't you? What's the difference between being *dressed* as the king, if you *are* the king in the ways that matter? People don't know the face, they simply know what he represents. You tell someone, *Look there, do you see that crown? That's the King,* and they'll believe you. It's not the man who's important, it's the crown, and the illusion of power. The armor and bodyguards, they help tell a story, you see? The story that the man is important."

Robin took his time to think on that. "King Robin."

"Robin Hood," Marion added importantly, but he didn't respond. The fire lit his face softly, his features transformed into the young, hopeful man he'd once been.

THEY WERE NOT QUITE finished with dinner when a bell rang at the edge of camp, and a collective pause followed as they listened for a response. When the second bell came, indicating an outsider, they flew into commotion. Some shoveled the last bits of food into their mouths, while others scrambled to arm themselves. Marion watched Elena pounce down to look Much in the face.

"What do we do when there are strangers?" she whispered, prompting Much to run with determination.

As Marion moved away from the fire, reaching out to grab Robin's arm, she realized how cold the night air had become.

It was Alan-a-Dale's voice that called out to them. Once he was visible, approaching the camp's glow, Marion could see he was accompanied by a stout figure lumbering at his side. Their momentary panic subsided as Alan called for them to gather, aiming straight for the campfire. The stranger boasted a giant beard and an ugly patch of fur thrown over his shoulders. Marion noticed he carried no weapons, and thought she recognized him though she could not say from where.

"He was wandering through the forest all on his own," Alan explained, reaching out for the fire's warmth. "Screaming for Robin Hood."

"Robin Hood, thank you!" came the stranger, his voice thick but desperate. "Thank you! I've been looking for hours."

"And you brought him here?" Will Scarlet gasped. His hands remained at his back, fingering the handles of the two idiotic knives he always kept strapped there. *The twins*, as he called them, never left his belt even when there was absolutely no call to be armed. The others simply amassed around the visitor in a normal display of curiosity.

"He insisted on talking to us," Alan continued, finding Robin. "I couldn't turn him back, who knows who may have found him yelling like that?"

"We shouldn't let just anyone know where our camp is," Robin said.

"I know. But just listen to him. He's got something you should all hear."

"Do you remember me?" the visitor asked eagerly, though John Little's massive arm kept the man from getting too close to Robin. "It's me, it's Stutely."

Marion at last recognized the man, more by his smell than name, from one of their visits to the villages.

"Will Stutely from Thorney, we talked about—"

"Just tell him what you told me." Alan guided the man to a stump to sit, and he obeyed.

"It's the Sheriff," Will Stutely said to his hands. "He raided our village. A dozen guards, maybe twenty, they rode into town and just started taking everything. Stealing right out of our homes, everything you gave us and then some."

Marion gasped audibly. "What? He wouldn't—!"

It was unthinkable. Roger de Lacy was a pacifist to the bone, and this simply wasn't in his nature. Either this man was misinformed or there was something new at play, something that had forced the Sheriff's hand. Marion's stomach heaved and a sudden stab of guilt shot through her body as rigid as an arrow. She should not have stayed in the forest so long. If she had visited Nottingham even once in the last month, surely she would have seen the signs of something like this, and could have prevented it.

"They just barged right into my home," Stutely reported. "They threw whatever they could into my barrow, and then they took the barrow, too."

"He has no right." Friar Tuck shook his head. Marion noticed how the crowd started to cling to each other, mothers holding their children closer. It wasn't for warmth.

"And not just Thorney." Stutely reached for a half-eaten dough-cake on the rocks by the fire. "It's everywhere. We went to Godling and it was the same there, and Lowdham and Lanley Marsh. We didn't have nowhere to go after that, we were too tired. We have children, you know? What were we supposed to do?"

Will Scarlet at last removed his hands from his blades, and instead patted Stutely on the shoulders. "I knew this would happen! We *lay low* and we stay out of the Sheriff's way, and what happens? The Sheriff thinks he can do whatever he wants!"

Stutely chewed on the cake, but it didn't stop him from talking. "It's worse in Bernesdale, I hear. They took over the city, booted everyone out of their homes, every last one. They say they're bringing wagons and wagons there, stockpiling. That's when I knew I had to come find you, no matter what it took."

"Wait." Tuck put his hands out. "This is out of the realm of our capabilities."

Stutely's eyebrows smashed together. "Out of the . . . realm . . . of your . . . capabilities?"

"It's beyond our help."

"Beyond your help?" His confusion led him to look around, for the first time connecting with the remainder of the crowd. He choked for a moment and then spat his food into the fire. "You're going to fight for us, aren't you?"

"*Fight* for you?" Robin asked. "Has there been fighting?"

"No, no. I don't think so," Stutely stammered to understand. "We thought you would do that for us."

Marion took the full weight of that expectation like an axe. Beside her, Robin too reeled with the ramification. "So you just abandoned your homes," he laughed, half-heartedly, "expecting me to come and rescue you?"

"Robin." She reached out to him, but he shook her off. A log popped in the fire and a cloud of embers floated up and away.

Stutely didn't answer. He studied the faces of each person watching him, and apparently found disappointment.

"I knew it. I knew you were full of shit." He snatched an unattended wooden cup and drank everything in it, its liquid pouring out the sides of his mouth and into his beard. "I told my friend Munday you were a liar. But I came anyways. I knew it."

Scarlet, naturally, took first offense. "Hold on a moment—"

"Fuck on all of you," Stutely added. "I'll just take my coin and go."

Robin spun his head around. "Excuse me?"

"Coin," Stutely said slowly, deliberately. "I need some more of it. When you came through last week, that fool Munday got two or three times as much as I did. He doesn't even need it. He's so skinny he doesn't eat much anyhow. He's doing fine, but he got more than me. Didn't think that was very fair at all."

Marion reached out to Robin before he said a word, but it was still too late. Whatever improvements she had witnessed in his character sloughed off like mud in the rain. He barged past John and the fire, grabbed the stranger's fur with his fists, and launched him away from the group.

"Get out!" he screamed. "Get the hell out of here right now or I swear . . ."

Arthur and David forced themselves into the midst, pulling Robin off. Friar Tuck hastened to escort Stutely away. "Come along, friend, now's not a good time, perhaps in the morning."

"Out of the camp!" Robin bellowed. "He doesn't stay here. This isn't charity!"

"Robin, it's dark," Marion tried, but he only glared at her. It was a chilling empty stare, as if she were a stranger.

"Didn't think that was very fair at all?" he repeated. "We're supposed to be helping these people, not putting their pants on for them."

John Little joined them. "Settle down."

"I should have let you all be arrested," Robin hissed back.

Scarlet dug in. "You think this is our fault? Really? We've done everything you said, *Robin Hood*. We started robbing the roads because you told us to, then we stopped because you told us to. All this was your idea, remember? But we were doing perfectly well before you came along."

"Perfectly well? Living in the woods and stealing from the King?"

"Oh, the King! The King!" Will threw his hands in the air in ridicule. "Yes, we mustn't do anything to upset the King! We've heard all about how you're best friends with the King, and how much he does for us. Well I say piss on your King, Robin. I've got a best friend, too, and he's right here." He threw his hands onto Alan's shoulders. "He's *right here*. In England. He was born here and he speaks English and he does more for the people every day than your King has done in his entire life."

"You can't fight the Sheriff—"

"Whose side are you even on?" Will laughed. "All you do is defend the King and defend the Sheriff, and you give away everything we make. What about *us*, Robin? Why aren't *we* worth fighting for?"

"Stop it, you two!" Marion blurted out. She couldn't suffer to see such bickering after all their progress. She would not watch it all fall apart for no reason. Their world had burned down before, and was poised to do so again. "This is not the time. There are people hurting out there."

Arthur grunted in agreement. "What are we going to do about these raids?"

"What *to do* about them?" Robin shouted. "You don't know the first thing about what's happening, but you already think it has to be stopped, and you're the ones to do it? You're nothing compared to the Sheriff's Guard. There's a dozen of you and hundreds of them. And that's aside from the fact that you shouldn't do anything at all!"

"There it is," Will snarled. "There's your great plan again. Sit back and do nothing. Back down, tend to ourselves. That's what he said last week. We move backward, they move forward, that's how it works. You told us this would all blow over, Robin, but we've got a storm bearing down on us. How long should we wait it out? Oh I know, how about another three or four days? That's when you're leaving, isn't it?"

He spat in the fire. Elena's hands dropped down to stroke Much's head. "The Sheriff didn't just take our money and our homes," she said.

"That's right." Will snapped his fingers. "He took our way of life. He took our dignity. It's awful easy for you to tell us to wait for things to get better, because you have a life to get on back to. But we're here. Our life is here. This is it. We're sick of waiting. Things aren't going to get better lessin' we *make them better.*"

John Little tapped the dirt with his staff, seizing the attention. "Robin. You've had the best of intentions, but Will's right. This isn't your fight, and never was none. Your heart isn't in it like your father's was. Like ours are."

"My heart's not in it?" Robin said dryly. "I lost a father."

"That you did," John said. "But that was years before he died."

The truth of that sentence was staggering, but Robin ignored it. "John. Don't do this. You're going to get these people killed."

"Not me that's doin' it." He frowned. "A call this important . . . Marion, this one's for you."

Her attention was fully in the fire. She saw Locksley Castle there, and the shattering difference between good intentions and reality. But while Lord Walter's fate was by any account an accident, these raids were a deliberate act. Marion could not take back her mistakes any more than she could convince Roger de Lacy to undo something that had already—

"What is he talking about?" Robin interrupted.

"Quiet," she snapped at him.

But his jaw was dropped. "You've been directing them this whole time?"

"Of course," she answered, shocked he had to ask.

"I thought you were here because I asked you to stay, not because . . ."

"Well, I can't help the things you think, Robin." She didn't mean to offend him, but there were more immediate concerns. "I probably shouldn't be here at all. I'm normally able to protect them through my connections, stay abreast of any information. I didn't know about these raids, though. I could have known, could have done something."

"Marion, it's too dangerous." Robin took her by the elbow and brought her away from the fire, as if she were some doll that might get burned. "If anyone were ever to find out about this . . ."

"Everyone knows about this."

"Everyone?"

"My house was openly against the new taxes," she said flatly. "Your father stood at our side. It's no secret which side of things we're on."

"What if the Sheriff were to come after you?" he whispered.

"Why? And how? He can't. King Richard is my cousin. As long as he's king,

I am well protected. If Sheriff de Lacy tried to arrest me, the political ramifications would decimate him."

Robin just gaped, with nothing substantive to say. "Why didn't you tell me?"

At another time she might have laughed at his ignorance, but now it struck her as an insult. "I thought it was obvious. It *is* obvious. But you . . . you just don't see me that way, I suppose."

"How have you not heard?" John asked, loud enough to remind Robin they were all still listening. "All the villagers talk about Robin Hood and Marion's Men."

"*Marion's* Men? I did hear that," he mumbled. "But I thought . . . I must have heard them wrong, I thought they called you *Merry* Men."

Little coughed. "Merry Men?"

Will burst out red. "Do I look fucking merry to you?"

"This is unbelievable." Robin shivered. The matter should have been over, but before Marion could return to her previous thought he exploded. "So why am I here at all, Marion?"

"Don't be like that."

"What am I *doing here*? You're just using me for my family's name, for my father's name? What did you want from me? You needed my father's son for them to rally behind? You needed a Robin Hood? Well, I'm not Robin Hood. I don't even know what the hell it means. Here." He pulled the leather cowl off his head and shoved it angrily into Alan's chest. "You. You're Robin Hood now. Me? *I'm done*."

"You're more than that, Robin." Marion moved after him. "We need you."

"Do we?" Robin threw his arms out, staring at the others.

"I need you," she said again, quieter. It was harder to say, and she honestly did not know if that was because it was a total lie, or the total truth.

He reacted to that hesitation, and for a tender moment he was hers, desperate to impress her and make up for the shortcomings of their past. But that potential shifted away, imperceptibly, when neither of them said anything more. The silence that had so long connected them was—finally—damning.

"I've spent my time," Robin closed his eyes, "leading battles, pretending to be a leader I'm not. If I'm going to run around as a figurehead for people to shoot at, I'd much rather be a king than an outlaw."

He turned and left.

She didn't move. "You're just going to walk away?"

It stopped him, but only long enough for him to sling a few final insults. "I have a few days left before I go back to your cousin, who, by the way, is a better man than I'll ever be. Until then, I'm sure I can find better company than that of thieves . . ." he targeted the men with that name, then aimed his final words directly at her, ". . . and liars."

Perhaps the worst part was that he was right.

"I think I'll take you up on your previous offer," he added, marching toward the horses. "The fastest fucking one."

From behind, Will hollered "Good riddance!"

A movement by her legs alerted Marion to Much, who pressed his body into her hip. "Where's he going?"

"He's going away," she said, wiping her eyes. "It's what he does."

Marion took Much's hand and pulled him back to the fire with the others. The sky was pitch black, and she had things far more important than regret. Will remained by the fire, the others huddled around him. They awaited her command.

The answer had already formed itself. She couldn't let them slide backward, to a place of fear. If they allowed themselves to be victims again, then the sense of progress, the rise of agency that had been building, it would be taken back tenfold.

"We can't sit back on these raids," she said, as much as she hated it. "We have to stop it."

They collectively exhaled.

Elena spoke first, walking behind the circle the others had formed. "She's right. We don't need Robin, we never did. And this was never his fight." Arthur nodded, and John breathed in deeply. "These are *our* people. *Our* friends that need us. If Robin is willing to turn his back on people in need, then so be it. That's his choice. We have to make our own."

She finished her circle at Will, and slipped her arms around him from behind. She whispered in his ear, but it was loud enough for everyone. "But there are some of us here with the strength to stand up and do what's right."

Will squeezed her hand, and spoke slowly, "We're not going to do nothing anymore. And we're not going to wait, either."

Arthur and David gave a *hear hear,* which Alan joined in upon.

"Right now, Gisbourne's men are spread out all across Nottinghamshire, raiding villages. If we wait until they're done, they'll take it all back to Castle Rock. But right now, *right now,* they're divided. In small groups. They wouldn't know we're coming."

"We have the element of surprise," Elena said, and winked to Much.

"So we've got to move fast," John smiled.

Will licked his lips. "It's time to fight back. Marion?"

She nodded.

INTERLUDE

JOHN LACKLAND

TICKHILL CASTLE
WEDNESDAY, OCTOBER 30TH, 1191

RED ROGER'S BEST WINE was terrible, and his prettiest daughter was delicious. John Lackland intended to spend the day in bed with both.

The round tower-castle was a tangible expression of the fat baron's pride. Its highest level was open to the world, ringed by pillars supporting a stone canopy. On an inclement day the wind might rip mercilessly through the open space, but on a day such as this John had no trouble keeping warm between the wine and the girl's naked body.

He suspected the traditional use for the "room" would be for surveying troop sizes, or to hold prominent weddings that those below might stare up upon. But John wanted to use it for debauchery. He had demanded, by asking politely of course, that the baron move his largest bed to this rooftop gallery. Baron Roger de Busli, or *Red Roger* as he notoriously branded himself, had been as accommodating as steel thicket.

"With respect to you," he had growled (a phrase that had never been followed by anything resembling respect), *"the castle of Tickhill is expressly exempt of your charge."*

"Which is why you shall accommodate me," John had said, even then giving a squeeze to the daughter of his choice. *"Out of generosity, rather than obedience. A much more trusting relationship that way."*

He'd taken the daughter's hand, whose name he would later learn was Myla, and spun her about to get a full look at her. She'd giggled and blushed when he gave her a light smack, which was all John needed.

"It occurs to me that while Tickhill's castle is indeed not mine to command, the same cannot be said for every inch that surrounds it. I wonder how long it would take to build a wall in front of your gates?"

So they'd moved a bed for him, and kept the wine flowing for him, every cask worse than its predecessor, but it made his head swim wonderfully and he'd ravaged Myla for half an hour before he could finish. She had been timid at first, but later she moaned so loudly that her voice carried on the air and down the hill to the baron's manor house, where John could only hope her father was forced to listen in rage.

Tickhill Castle, tall as it was, was made ever taller for sitting on such a perfectly round hill. Myla was lying on her back next to him, recovering, and John twisted her nipple.

"This is us . . ." he said, and traced his finger around her breast, ". . . this is the hill . . ." and down to her navel, ". . . that's your father."

She laughed and batted his hands away, fretting that he was tickling her. "I am. Tickling you. In Tickhill. I'm Tickhilling you. There's a joke there, I'm sure, I just don't know what it is." He was wittier sober, but a better lover drunk. He had the day to meander between the two, and try at both incessantly.

"Show me the rest." He vaulted to his feet, which had not been consulted on the idea and rejected it entirely. He opted to crawl. "I want to see what I can see. I am here to survey my lands. Show survey them to me."

That didn't sound correct.

Myla, still entirely naked, climbed onto his back and rode him to the edge of the room, a balcony that dropped sharply down to the green grass far below. Crawling had been a wise choice, as he would not have wanted to attempt standing so close to the lip.

She wrapped her fingers through his hair and tugged his head about. "I like your hair."

Most girls did. Its red was so dark it was almost brown, but was all fire in the open air and sunlight up here. Hers grew down to the small of her back, unbraided. He could have spent a lifetime in the soft curve of her waist. Not his own lifetime, of course. Some lesser man's lifetime. With every year that passed, his own future grew closer. So many hands pushing him closer and closer to the edge of responsibility. Rather like the edge of this tower, over the lip dizzying downward.

"That's Sheffield," Myla cooed, and pointed his head to the west.

"Which one?" He squinted at tiny specklings of towns, their colors faded to the same pale nothing of the rest of the land.

"It's too far to see," she laughed. "But it's that direction."

"Well that's mine, then," John said. "I own it. I can do whatever I want with it. Would you like to own a town?"

He breathed in deeply, and tried to estimate all the land between here and there. That was all his, too. Every tree and rock and deer shitting in between was his to cherish, or whatever it is one was supposed to do with land.

Myla tightened her legs around his waist and pointed him north. "We are halfway between the castles of York and Nottingham. Yorkshire's that way," she twisted his head to the right, "and the rest is Nottinghamshire."

"I didn't know you were a map."

"I didn't know you were a horse."

She slapped his ass and wrenched his hair again, until he twisted and grappled her onto the floor. "The majority of the things there are to know about me," he said as he kissed her neck, that soft spot at her collarbone, "are probably things you didn't know. What would you like to know about me next?"

"What would you like to tell me next?"

John rewarded her answer by moving up to her ear. "Did you know that I'm the King of Ireland?"

She pursed her lips and raised her eyebrows. "I did not know that."

"No? Then you must be Irish." He rolled over in search of another bottle of wine. "I was there for the first time some five years ago. I was eighteen. *Eighteen.* I had been King of Ireland for eight years, and they treated me horribly. They had no respect, they have no idea how to govern themselves, they're a terrible people. Terrible. You're not really Irish, are you?"

"No," she giggled, tugging at his feet.

"I thought you said you were."

"*You* said I was."

"Yes, that sounds like something I'd say. They're terrible people, and hairy. A man should never have a beard longer than his cock." He rubbed his chin, clean and smooth. "So fuck the Irish, is what I say. What do you say, *Waleran?*"

Waleran, a pompous old name for a pompous old man. This old man still sat, unmoving, at the maw of the staircase. For hours he had sat there, desperately unhappy but too proud to leave.

"He's someone important," John had explained to Myla, *"and insisted he speak with me. But your tongue can do far better things for me than his ever could, so why would I choose his? But he insisted, so I made him a deal. I would allow him one sentence for every time we make love. Provided, of course, that he sit patiently."*

The man had wasted his first sentence by introducing himself, well before John had taken Myla the first time. She had been shy at first, undressing in front of the earl, but as the wine flowed she found the joke in it all and soon they were both oblivious to Waleran's unfortunate presence. When they were done, the earl had asked if he was allowed to speak, which John counted as a sentence. The third had been their longest, slower and sweeter, and they rolled so close to their guest once that he scooted backward. For the long interim between three and four, John had baited his guest with innocent questions, but he never responded, just stared and chewed his lips.

He must have to piss fiercely, John thought, having relieved himself over the edge of the balcony twice, *and be a eunuch as well, to have not been roused by watching.*

Unfortunately, the drink was not enough to fade away the man's name.

"Speaking of maps," John extended a finger at the Earl of Warwick, "Waleran is my neighbor, so to speak. Warwickshire and Gloucestershire share a border, yes? Well the Duchess of Gloucestershire and I share a marriage."

"You brat! You're married?" Myla teased him, tugging on his earlobe with her teeth.

"Don't worry, she's not a threat to you. Isabelle's my cousin." Myla feigned disgust and stomped about the room, trailing her arms in the hanging silks. "Of all the innumerable slights that are my life, my marriage is my favorite. John Lackland, they called me, youngest son of the king, with no lands to own nor to inherit, and four elder brothers to eat the world up before I would ever get a crumb. The best that my father could do for me was to betroth me, as a young boy, to the notably brotherless Isabelle of Gloucester."

Myla snickered, but John put a finger to his lips. "That's not the good part. My brothers had their rebellion, as you know, and started dying one by one. Three of my brothers have made their last kick at the world. Only Richard is left, and every day that he wastes at war leaves me with the terror that one day a messenger will come to me. *King Richard has been killed,* he'll say, and even in my imagination I vomit, cut out the messenger's throat, and sail as far away as a ship can take me."

She laughed again, so he put his finger in her mouth. Her tongue played with its tip. "I've told Richard a thousand times that I want him to rule, and rule long, but he doesn't trust me. He did nothing to earn or purchase my loyalty, so he doesn't believe it. So he bought it, retroactively. He showered me in property and power, in both England and France. I have so many titles now I can't recognize them. But even though I suddenly had all the land I could need, I was still betrothed to Isabelle and one simply doesn't break those things. So I'm told. It was a punishment, really, for not being any of my ambitious dead brothers."

Myla moved from finger to finger now, and John felt an urge as he fought to focus. "The best part was days later, when a *papal* envoy informed us that our marriage had been annulled by the pope himself. After some investigation, it had been discovered that Isabelle and I are related through a mutual great-grandfather. Richard fought it, and eventually the marriage was condoned by the Church, under the strictest—and most pleasantly ridiculous—doctrine that we refrain from sexual intercourse.

"Which was fine," he added, drawing Myla to the floor, bidding her to lie on her stomach. "I haven't seen her since."

He carefully poured a small amount of wine onto the gentle curve of Myla's back, pooling into the subtle cup just above her cheeks. He lapped it up with his tongue, even as she squirmed and long red streaks escaped, which he chased around to her navel, turning her over. This is how he had spent his time, *surveying his lands* from the southwest finger of England up to Tickhill, his northernmost city. From here he frankly had no plans on where to go.

He was ready for another go. He poured himself a cup of wine and dipped his prince in it that she might taste it.

"The good news," he sighed as he felt her tongue, "is that I'll never be king. Richard's appointed that curse to my dead brother's son Arthur. Of course, he's only four or five, so he wouldn't make the *best* king. So the real fear is that Richard gets himself killed at his little war, and they ask me to take over until little Arthur gets his first bleeding."

He raised the cup and drank from it. "So long live the King."

Myla paused just long enough to ask, "Why wouldn't you want to be king?"

"King? Good God, I cannot think of anything I want less. If they put a crown on my head, I would put it on my horse. I would carve a hole in the throne and use it to shit. My father was king. My brother is king. Do you know what I've noticed? *Nobody likes the king.* Everybody wants to *be* the king, but as soon as you become the king all you do is spend your time dealing with the people who used to love you and now want you dead. Do you know how often kings die? Every time. I don't think I've heard of a single king who has lived gloriously and ascended to heaven as a divine ruler, but I know of an awful lot of them that have muddled their way through ruling and died in one awful way or another. You can trust me, it's something of a family tradition.

"Prince is fine with me. People *love* princes. Princes get gifts, I've noticed, and promises. As long as I am not the king, my life is spectacularly better. There is no chance that this would be happening right now, any of this, you, *Waleran* watching us, if I were not prince. Keep me prince. God keep me prince. And you know the real truth of it? I'd be terrible. I wouldn't have a fucking clue what I'm doing. I tried in Ireland, I tried in France, I'm no good at it. I don't want to be good at it. Richard's good at it. If only he'd come back and just be a king, it's all he ever wanted. He's fucking it all up, being so far away, he should just come back and be happy. Fuck. Fuck."

And the world disappeared. And when he was done, his body went limp, and he closed his eyes and let the breeze tickle his skin.

To hell with being a king, when being a prince is so much more entertaining.

Time was slower now, his limbs were heavy. All the muted colors of the world faded together. There was nothing but the beautiful grey that swallowed his thoughts. Few were the ways to quiet his mind. But it didn't last as long this time as it had the last, and already his eyes focused on the land outside the tower. He wondered who would want control of it, what they would offer him for it, and what he could extract from that person's enemies in exchange for doing the opposite. John's flock of troubles came to land on his branches again.

"Alright, *Waleran,*" he drawled out the name, "make your sentence good."

The earl breathed in heavily, licked his lips and stood, a sharp movement John had difficulty following. After a heavy pause, Waleran spoke directly and with purpose.

What followed would be one of the greatest things John had ever ignored. That was something of a pastime for him—ignoring responsibility. His favorite trophies were his memories of avoiding things. Going to a tavern instead of an important function, for instance, or making jokes about Waleran's eyebrows while the man spoke, for nearly five minutes, without actually ending his sentence.

When a period finally came, John blinked. Myla had burrowed into the bed and watched in amazement. "That was a fine sentence," John said. "You may say thank you."

"Thank you."

"I nodded off in the middle," he teased, but unfortunately he had retained more of the sentence than he would have liked. "The castellan here, the castellan of Tickhill, his name is Baron Roger de Busli, did you know that? Baron Roger de Busli. But you talked about the Sheriff of Nottingham, Baron Roger *de Lacy.* You're telling me that there are *two* Baron Roger de-somethings in charge of castles in Nottingham? That seems one too many Baron Roger de-something for me to keep track of. So I missed part of what you were saying while I was thinking about that."

Waleran twitched, as though he had just prevented a violent sneeze.

"Don't worry, I think I tasted the general flavor of your soup." John tried to rise, but the world wobbled in three directions at once, which was two more than seemed advisable. The earl had the singular luck of being the only thing that John was currently capable of focusing upon. To Waleran's benefit he had been impressive, but he had also put a definitive halt to John's enjoyment of the day.

"So," John continued, "I don't know the Sheriff of Nottingham, so I don't care if he goes away. You seem to think I hate the Chancellor enough to appoint someone else as the sheriff just to beat him to it."

He probably should have expected that. He'd run into Chancellor Longchamp in London a month or so ago, and pulled a prank on him. The prank involved trapping the man in the Tower of London and convincing him he'd be killed if he left . . . and it may have gotten a bit out of hand after that.

"But see, I don't care who is your next sheriff. So . . . I'm willing to let you *purchase* my decision." The last few words he slurred, maybe on purpose, and he hoped it would sound unsettling.

Waleran appeared unsettled.

"Why don't you tell me what you can do for me, and I'll tell you if it's good enough?"

The uncomfortable earl bristled.

"Oh, you can talk as much as you want. Myla, be a dear and count his sentences. I'll pay you the debt."

She made a delighted chirping noise and rolled off the bed, hiccupped something that was more than air, and rushed over to the edge to spit it over.

Waleran ignored her. "I have rallied many supporters for you, with many ears. We are already allies."

"Boring," John said, since it was. "Never trust a stranger who tells you he's your friend. Myla, do you suppose your father would like to be the Sheriff of Nottingham?"

But she was busy sending a second wave of purple over the lip.

"I also know the Chancellor's supporters," the earl suggested, "and their weaknesses, and their crimes. I have been diligent in cataloguing them, with evidence and witnesses."

"That's better," John said, though he was sure to say it in a way that still implied *boring.* "But it's nothing I couldn't do on my own. What can *you* offer me? Do you have children? Do you have daughters? Don't worry, I don't mean to fuck every daughter in England. I need marriages. The best way to build alliances is through marriage. It's also one of the best ways to block other people's ambitions." He had been exiled from England for three years, and denied ownership of any castles, lest he foolishly decide to wage war against his brother. That exile was finally over, ended a bit early even, and he was eager to find other things to own.

Waleran fidgeted. "My son and heir is married. I have a second son, with my namesake. My only daughter is at Pinley Abbey."

"Oh wonderful. A nun and another *Waleran*."

John felt suddenly cruel for toying with the old man, when he honestly meant him no ill will. In fact, if John had not meant to spend the day avoiding responsibility, he would have actually liked old *Waleran* and his plans. But that didn't mean he wouldn't take advantage of the situation. "Very well. Any name you want, I'll agree to it, since frankly I don't much care."

"I have already drafted an edict for you. All that remains is for you to fill in a name and sign it."

"Leave it and I'll send it off by morning. My price is this . . ." He let the man sweat. "*Something.* I don't know what it will be. Some favor. Maybe something small. Maybe something unforgivable. But something. I'll only ask it once. It may not be for many years. But you'll owe it to me, and you'll do it. Tell your sons that you owe this. I don't want you to die before I use my favor. Agreed?"

If he thought he was gaining an ally, or swearing himself to the devil, all Waleran did was swallow once. "Any name?"

"As I said," John burped. The man may be a complete idiot if he needed to ask the question. Or perhaps he was brilliant.

"Agreed." Waleran retrieved a small parchment from his bags and placed it on the floor beside him, weighing it down with a cup. He stood and descended the stairs, pausing only when his head alone was still visible. "The name is Waleran de Beaumont. My second son."

Then his head vanished and the sound of his footsteps drifted away, leaving only Myla's retching into the wind.

"Clever fellow, that. Do you think he outplayed me?" John asked, but the girl was long gone from conversation. "His son. He never would have given that name if I hadn't pushed him. I don't care one shit who sits as Nottingham's sheriff. He has no idea how small his world is, and how large mine is."

John wished Myla was able to recognize how profound he was being. "Brave fellow, then. He sold his dignity in favor of his family. I'm sure there's a lesson there we should all be learning if we weren't so fucking sick right now."

AFTER WALERAN LEFT, JOHN passed out and eventually awoke again, naked, freezing in the early night air with nothing to protect him. Myla was gone, and John chanced an eyeball over the edge to look for her body. Only colorless grass below. She might have rolled off a different edge, but he decided against caring.

He descended, entirely nude, into the barrel of Tickhill Castle. He brushed against Gay Wally, who had fallen asleep but pretended he had not. Only thirteen or fourteen, the lad had a knack for memorizing everything he heard. He also had a knack for leaning forward when he spoke and blinking too much. He'd been assigned to John to catch him up on every name, affiliation, and history of the lands he now owned. His real name was Walter de Gray, but John had decided such a name should only belong to an ancient advisor and not a milksop like this one. Gay Wally was a better name.

The boy sprang to keep up. "I need food," John said, and Gay Wally made a few different faces in reaction, none of which brought any food. Wally was good at information, but not at fetching.

In the lower levels he found servants of the more useful variety, who had water warmed and brought to his chambers. After washing himself and redressing, his head was clear enough to consider the drunken promises he'd made atop the tower. He threw a wet cloth at Gay Wally.

"Tell me about Waleran de Beaumont. And take me to wherever it is the Baron de Busli eats."

This involved leaving the castle tower and marching down to the main manor at the bottom of the round hill. By the time they intruded on Red Roger's private dinner, John was fully versed on the old Earl of Warwick. He seemed a detestably loyal man, and ferociously protective of his family. Gay Wally said that Waleran had once fed a man to a bear simply for doing an unfavorable impersonation of his brother. John didn't mind a man having a cruel streak, but a loyal one was unnerving. John wasn't so sure he wanted to climb into bed with anything that valued honor over intelligence.

Baron de Busli made the same face he had made when John took his daughter off to the tower. It was possible that he was only capable of making one face, which he used for every emotion. Food and gravy coated his moustache, which had not required any help to look ridiculous.

"What are you doing in here?" the baron nearly choked, spewing uneaten chunks of disgusting.

"I'm doing quite well, thank you," John answered, "as I assume that's what you meant to ask."

The baron ate alone, though there were many men present. Three or four servants bustled about, filling the baron's wine or bringing new plates, while in the corner a boy who would never enjoy a woman was abusing a harp.

"I'm fat and have too much food in my mouth," was not what Red Roger said, but it was the best translation John could think of. He followed it with, "Oh, I'll bet I can cram that in here, too," as he shoveled something greasy from his paws past his lips.

"I have one matter to tend to before I leave," John called out. "An opinion. Baron Roger de Lacy, the Sheriff of Nottingham, is not long for his office. I'm to decide on his successor."

"High Sheriff of Nottinghamshire, Derbyshire, and the Royal Forests," Gay Wally quickly corrected, blinking, but John gave him the tiniest of nods not to speak, and it almost seemed that he understood why.

Red Roger took another bite before he spoke. "If I may," the words gurgled out, and all waited as he picked a thing from his teeth. "Sheriff de Lacy is a waste of shit. He's tried to coddle Nottinghamshire like a baby. But it isn't a baby, it's a wolf, and still he tries to let it suckle him, teeth and all."

He grinned and laughed, and those that served him laughed as well.

"This county needs a man who isn't afraid to get bloody."

A thick bald guard behind the baron bellowed out *"Red Roger!"* which was picked up and repeated a few times by the others. The bellower was congratulated by the other men near him.

"Sir Robert FitzOdo," the baron introduced the guard, not because he was important but because he was a rather expensive piece of jewelry. A knight in his private retainer. "Why should Richard get all the knights? You don't train a hound and then lend it to someone else."

Actually many people do, John thought, but didn't say so. FitzOdo answered by thrusting his fist again to chant the baron's name.

John pretended to be impressed. "Red Roger, indeed. I've heard quite a bit about that moniker of yours," *thanks to Gay Wally,* "and if the stories are true, then you are a man who isn't afraid to get bloody."

Red Roger pounded his fist a few times on the table to prove indisputably that he was capable both of making fists and pounding things with them.

"We know how to deal with forest thieves here in Tickhill," he boasted. "The problem with these sheriffs is they don't stick around long enough to learn anything. Every ten years or so, some group of thieves crawls into the forest and shits on everyone. But Sheriff de Lacy wouldn't know that, because five years ago it was Murdac who hunted them down. Ten years before that it was FitzRanulph. They never know what the fuck to do with themselves. But the thieves don't come to Tickhill anymore, and do you know why?"

FitzOdo shouted out "Red Roger!" again, and John had to hide his face as he considered that *Red Roger* could be a euphemism for a man's cock. The knight barked it a few more times, pumping his hand each time, and John could have died happy.

"This is why," the baron continued, holding his fist out, tapping a ring on his middle finger. It had a thick talon sprouting forward. "I bled the last man who decided he was a prince of thieves. It's only a little prick, but it does the job."

John almost snorted. *Now he's making it too easy.*

"I tied him up against a wall in town, and give him a little tap. Every tap opens him up, and he bleeds. Not deep enough to kill. Shallow, see, but I give him a little tap all over his body. When they heal, I tap them again. And he bleeds out. Slow and terrible. For everyone to see. That's what you'll get when I'm Sheriff of Nottingham. None of this fucking around. I'll bleed this Robin Hood like I bled the last one. Red Roger!"

The name was repeated around the room again, one too many times by the awkward harp-boy, who then hid his face.

"Those cages outside of town, those were thieves then?" John asked. There had been two rotten bodies in iron cages hanging by the road to the town, each of which had another head impaled on a spike at the top.

"Courtesy of Red Roger!" the baron boasted, and he raised his glass to his trophy knight. This led to another round of cheering.

John waited for the commotion to die. "Would you really want to leave Tickhill for Nottingham?"

"Fuck Nottingham. I'd rule from here."

From this table, quite likely, as Red Roger had yet to move from it.

"Bold." John played coy. "Do you have enough men? Or would you ask Nottingham's captain to move his entire force here to Tickhill?"

Everything Red Roger had eaten attempted to escape his body. After coughing it back down, he hacked out some expletives about Nottingham's captain. "Guy of Gisbourne? He's a joke. A fucking joke. Ten times worse than de Lacy. First thing I'd do as Sheriff is replace him. That fucking idiot had Robin Hood in his grasp and then ran away. He lost one of his little boys, and ran all around the county looking for him like a fucking dog. He even begged my FitzOdo to help. Heard he went mad, arrested every man, woman, and child he could find in Nottingham, and still couldn't even find his own cock. Gisbourne's the most incompetent piece of shit to ever wear the uniform, and that says a fucking lot. He couldn't find his men if he checked his own asshole."

His crowd laughed again, even though the joke made no sense. But that didn't bother John nearly as much as the second mention of a name that he did not recognize.

"I'll take what you've said under consideration." John excused himself, and gave the requisite number of farewells. The boy with the harp started singing a song that glorified Red Roger and much of the hall joined in, its drunken muffled chorus filling the hallway as John led his entourage away. He noticed a girl that may have been Myla, and was surprisingly pleased to think she hadn't fallen to her death.

Once there were fewer ears around, he asked Gay Wally, "Alright, who's Robin Hood?"

The boy leaned forward and blinked, but for once his lips didn't move. John asked him the question again, and he blinked a few more times.

"I cannot say with certainty. There are more than a few speculations going around. Some say he's a nobleman masquerading in the night, others say he's a simple yeoman who made a name for himself. I've even heard that he's a knight, deserted from the war, with only hatred for King Richard."

"That was fascinating," John lied, "now would you mind telling me what in the hell we're talking about?"

"He's just some bandit," came a rougher voice, a curt swordarm named Hadrian. John had promoted the man to the head of his contingent after dismissing the French knights that had been assigned to him, which he was expected to pay for. Hadrian was paid, too, but without all the bullshittery that came with being a knight. "Some group of men stealing from those that travel through the Sherwood. Nobles mostly. The ladies seem to find a sport in letting themselves be robbed."

John couldn't have been less impressed. "Why do I care, again?"

"Apparently," Hadrian continued, "he's very good. And he doesn't keep what he steals. He gives it out. The peasants here in Nottinghamshire are having a better time of it than the nobles lately. That's what I hear at least." He gave a sneer to Wally.

This was tasty. Not the thief, of course, but his effect on others. Move a little money in the wrong hands, and suddenly even a fat sloth like Red Roger could be stirred to fury.

"He sounds delightful," John said after heavy consideration. "Why the hell would I want anybody to kill him?"

Social upheaval was precisely the sort of thing that delighted John. His world confined him to the biggest pieces on the board, but there was no arguing that the smallest ones could sometimes do the most damage. The more John thought about it, the more he was lured by the idea of hiding in the forest, making tiny amounts of hell for tiny amounts of people. He could play both ends toward the other.

"I'd very much like to meet this Robin Hood."

Hadrian scoffed. "Nobody knows where to find him. That's the problem, my lord."

"I'm not your lord." John rounded the corner and they were outside again, a smattering of rain greeting their walk back up the hill to the tower. "Of course *somebody* knows where to find him, we just don't know how to find that *somebody*. I shouldn't spend my precious time correcting your gaps of logic."

"Of course."

"You say the ladies make sport of being robbed by him? Perhaps we can become very attractive ladies."

Hadrian clicked his jaw. "Your entourage is too large. No thief would attack a garrison armed such as we."

"Then we'll travel light. Only a few of us."

"It would be too dangerous."

"Then we'll have to double-check, before we leave . . ." John turned in the doorway to the tower and let the rain collect on Hadrian's head, ". . . that none of us are giant pussies."

He closed the door dramatically on Hadrian, who of course opened it again a moment later. But John enjoyed himself nonetheless. He sprinted up the circular stairs that spiraled up the inner wall of the tower to his official guest room. Hadrian would probably worry all night that John would dress him in women's clothes the next day with a wig on his head.

Poor Red Roger, John thought, *you could have been an entertaining sheriff.*

Needing ink and well, he called for Gay Wally, who hid his resentment of being used for such clerical tasks. John also asked for the edict that Waleran de Beaumont had left for him to sign.

"I should appoint *Robin Hood* as the next sheriff. Wouldn't that be a thing."

"Did you not promise the Earl of Warwick the title to his son?" Wally asked it in that polite way that was not actually a question.

"Look at you," John applauded. "Did you listen in on everything today?"

Wally didn't respond, but he might have blushed.

"My apologies, boy, but I've been a terrible role model. Some lucky day when you get a girl naked yourself, you shouldn't expect it to last as long as what you overheard today. That only comes with nearly perpetual practice."

"I've been with a woman," Wally said, stumbling only slightly on the word *woman.*

"How terrible for her. I wonder who is crueler with their little pricks, you or Red Roger?"

There was wine in the room, so he poured a glass for himself and, feeling reckless, one for the boy, too. "Yes, I *did* tell Waleran that his son would have the sheriff's seat. But all I got in return was a blank promise. He had nothing else to offer. Red Roger offers to kill Robin Hood for me, but I don't want him to do that at all. Thieves are fun, they make the world unpredictable. *Waleran* wants to make Nottingham a better place, he wants to rid it of corruption and disease. It's all very noble. Sickeningly noble. Red Roger wants to make Nottingham a better place, too, in his own way. They want to make it better because their worlds are only as big as they can reach."

John leaned in close now, as the boy brought a candle and wax without even being prompted. "Listen to me, now. This is important. Their worlds are so small, but mine is so big, don't you see? They can't make Nottingham healthy as long as England is diseased. They're trying to put bandages on a finger, without realizing that the forearm is rotten. It needs to be cut off. If Nottingham were a better place . . ."

John shook his head. *Tiny men have tiny goals.*

"This Waleran wants me to go after the Chancellor, and he wants me to *win.* But I don't intend on winning. I told him. I don't want to be king. England needs a good king, not me, it needs my brother. Not ever me. If we start making England a better place, then Richard has no reason to come back.

"But if England burns," John continued, taking the quill, "then he has to come back. He simply has to."

The edict was complete but for a signature at the bottom and an emptiness in the middle where he was to appoint a name as the new sheriff. John signed his own name at the bottom, then wrote *Lord Guy of Gisbourne* in the empty space. *Ten times worse than de Lacy,* Red Roger had said, and John was counting on it.

The candle burned his finger when he dripped its wax onto the paper, but John didn't mind the pain.

PART V

LEX TALIONIS

THIRTY-FIVE

ELENA GAMWELL

BERNESDALE

ELENA GAVE WILL'S LIP a soft bite, and for a moment there was nothing but him. She tried to pull him closer but he pushed her off, the brat, softstepping away into the dark, turning just in time to flash that irresistible smirk. His warmth was still there, on her chest and in her arms, and she held onto it until the chill took over. Only then did she turn back to see John Little's patronizing smile, which turned into a silent pucker and a flash of his bushy greying eyebrows.

"Get your own," Elena teased him, and looked back at Bernesdale's market.

Removed from the rest of the village, a wide shoulder-high stone ring circled a dozen or so long low storehouses, all made from the same heavy misshapen stones and straw thatching. For an hour or two, that wall and the night had given them plenty of cover to watch the comings and goings of the raided plunder. A steady fire was kept raging at the center of the ring, where there would normally be a motley of merchants and roving traders. But there were no colorful wares or tradesmen now, just the blue and steel of the Nottingham fucking Guard.

Fortunately, as they predicted, only a handful of gords actually stayed with the supplies. Most were out collecting it. Every now and then a wagon would roll in, sometimes two or three, with men huffing to keep pace beside. There was always some sort of confusion as to what they were supposed to do with their loot, until eventually it was organized and distributed to different storehouses. Then they'd leave again, back on the road, or to find shelter over in the village. Elena watched one empty wagon driven by men in plainclothes, who actually *loaded* supplies and left again toward Nottingham. That had given Will the inspiration for their plan.

"You expect them to simply up and give it all to us?" John Little had asked.

"Actually, yes." Will had winked. *"That's precisely what I expect them to do. Look at them—they're just doing their jobs. So let's help them out."*

"They're probably the bottom of the barrel anyhow." Arthur grinned. *"They've got dozens of regiments out there, stealing from as many places as they can at once. That's where the best men will be, where they think people might fight back. These here are just a bunch of gord rejects."*

"I wonder if that Jon Bassett is here," Alan whispered.

"I hope he is," Arthur spat back. *"I told you we shouldn't have let him go. Promises to tell them all how wonderful we are, and now they're raiding every village on the map. I'd love to ask him, face to face, whether he had a hand in this."*

"You can scratch your balls later, boys," John said, causing everyone to hush him.

Even when he whispered, his low voice carried further than he thought. *"Dawn's getting close, and whatever we do, it should be done before daybreak."*

"It's not even going to feel like stealing," Will snickered to Elena. *"It'll just feel like . . . work."*

That was just as exciting, as far as she was concerned. *"That's the best sort of stealing, when they never even know you were there. Even better, they'll never even know they lost anything. It's brilliant."*

She'd said those last words directly to him. *You're brilliant.* He needed strength, he needed confidence, and she knew exactly how to give that to him. Will needed to know she was right about all of this.

She'd been right about Robin of Locksley, after all. Of course he had abandoned them the moment real action was needed. The only thing Elena had been wrong about was the idea that using Gilbert to scare Jon Bassett would make the Guard afraid of them. But this would be a far more effective way to say the same thing. With Locksley gone they could finally start growing beyond their merry little band, and into a proper gang worth reckoning.

The Sheriff seemed to think he was unopposed, but this morning he would learn otherwise.

"What do you want *me* to do?" little Much asked.

"I want you to go home," John Little whispered at him, "but I don't get everything I want."

They had been halfway to Bernesdale when the boy popped out of a barrel, scaring them all halfway to shit and back. John Little had plucked Much and hurled him out of the cart, but Much insisted that he'd be coming along whether they liked it or not.

"It's too late to turn back," Arthur had warned, *"and we won't get an opportunity like this again none, neither."*

"Maybe he'll be useful," Elena had persuaded them. *"I can think of a few things a little boy can get away with that none of us could."*

Now, she smiled and gave Much a wink.

Bernesdale. It's where he had grown up, and it was the source of whatever terrible thing from his past gave him waking nightmares still.

"You're going to climb that tree," Elena explained, pointing to a gnarled oak to the east of the market ring. "Keep an eye out for any unwelcome visitors. You see anything you don't like, you make a call like we promised, right? Nobody will think twice of a boy climbing a tree."

That was something Elena had played up for a long time. Even years after she was old enough to resent it, her young face and small size had often let her avoid suspicion.

"What sort of 'unwelcome visitors'?" Much asked, fumbling over the phrase.

"Gords," she said. She could have said *monsters.* They'd already seen too many. Two of them had guarded the Sherwood Road just outside the town. Eventually one left to piss in the woods. John Little had taken care of him with a lovetap

from his quarterstaff. They'd used Much to distract the other, a skinny lad with a limp, then Will had surprised him with the heavy butts of his twin blades.

As Much trudged away toward the tree with his mission, Arthur exhaled. "Are we ready to do this?"

Alan clicked his tongue and was away, along with Arthur and Tuck, to crouch by the ringwall with Will. "Alright," John Little whispered next to her on the wagon. "Let's steal some shit."

SHE RUBBED HER HANDS between her legs for warmth. She and John would drive the cart into the ring of storehouses, under the assumption they were the least dangerous-looking of their group. The others would approach from behind the ringwall, using the oxcart's dust cloud as cover, to meet at the back of one of the supply buildings. Tuck had suggested they focus on the one housing ale, but they'd settled on the one with farming supplies and smithing tools. Those items were irreplaceable, and invaluable to those with the right skills.

"What do we do if they catch us?" John whispered. "Robin never taught us that none."

Elena had to smile. "It doesn't work that way. We're only guilty if we act guilty."

"How do we act . . . not . . . guilty?"

"Listen. Real thieving isn't about sneaking around in the shadows. If a guard sees you do that, they know you're up to no good. The trick is to let everybody see you, but give them reasons not to care about you. It's the easiest thing. Once they've decided you're not worth worrying about—poof. You're gone. They'll never look at you again."

John nodded and smiled, then nodded, and smiled again. "How do we do that?"

"These fellows here are following orders. They like following orders. We say, *Well Captain Somebody told us these supplies needed to be moved right away,* and now they're more worried about going against Captain Somebody than they are about us. It's about pretending you're right, and making them doubt you're wrong."

John still didn't seem to understand.

"I once snuck into some jeweler's house on Greenhound Road in Nottingham. I thought I had the place to myself, but I walk in and find he has some sort of manservant, stiff and prickly and twelve ways of suspicious. He yells at me, but I say, *'I'm supposed to be picking something up here, I'm sorry I'm late, could I get it?'* This prickled bastard lost everything he had going for him, and asked me what it was I needed. Soon enough he's helping me fill my pockets and wishing me a good day."

"Bollocks," John said.

"Swear it." Elena laughed. She'd eaten for a month that day.

Of course, the next time she'd tried the trick she'd been cracked on the back of the head before she'd gotten away. But there was no need to tell John that.

John tugged the reins and they were off. Up ahead, the silhouettes of the others huddled by the ringwall, waiting for them to rumble on by. Their cart clattered past into the great circular market area, pushing up a soft cloud of dirt. John drove their horses in a full wide round circle, easily seen by the gords that lingered at the fire. Not a one seemed to care. A cow-eyed farmer and his wispy daughter must have seemed about as threatening as pea soup.

After dismounting and securing the wagon, they moved with purpose, daring any gord to question them. They pushed through the main door of their selected storehouse as the others snuck in through the rear. Two through the front, four through the back, they wove their way through dark tables. Hammers and pitchforks, sickles and hooks, baskets and whips, harnesses, plows pushed against the side wall, sacks of seed, and wire thimbles. The six of them met in the middle, giggling like children. Alan couldn't even close his mouth.

"Look at all this! This is the biggest take we'll ever get! How much do we get to keep for ourselves?"

John Little cocked his head at Alan oddly. "What do you suppose is fair? Half? One in four?"

"Half'd be great!" Alan laughed. "But even a quarter'd be everything we ever need!"

"Every stitch of this," John grumbled sharply, "is taken from another man's hand. Every piece of this bounty of yours was someone else's yesterday. They needed it. You think you ought to have it instead of them?"

Elena kept her mouth closed. She had felt excitement, too, but John had a heavy point.

"We've got to keep some of it at least," Alan pouted. "What's the difference? They were never going to get any of it back without us."

"What's the difference indeed," John responded, but it answered a different question. If some poor villager had his tools stolen, what was the difference to him if they ended up in the Guard's hands or Elena's? When she looked around the room again, it seemed less like a treasure trove and more like a graveyard. Every item had a price tag written in guilt.

"We keep nothing of what we get here. Now get to work." John sighed. "We'll barely scratch the amount of wrong that's been done today. We'll take what we can, but this doesn't mean we won none. It only means we lost a little bit less."

Alan's smile faded to a guilty frown, but once John turned away he slunk close to Elena. "If we can at least find a sack of onion seed," he whispered, "I'll never complain about rabbit stew again."

John disappeared out the front to begin the slow display of unloading the empty crates and barrels they'd brought along. They had positioned the wagon at the side of the storehouse, that they could unload it from the front and load it up again from the back unseen. Arthur and Alan started dragging sacks of seed and crates of trowels.

"Take anything large and flat first," Arthur said when he saw Alan pointing in wonder at a plow yoke. "We can stack them high, and throw anything else on top."

They moved quickly and quietly. In seven or eight passes, John sat down the last empty barrel they had brought for show.

"That's it for the front. Still nobody giving as much as two looks this way."

The friar twisted his beard in his hands. "You know, I think the building to the right is where they were storing the wine . . ."

"Don't get greedy," John said, with a paw on Tuck's shoulder.

Will smiled. "Pretty sure there's a quote or two about that somewhere in that book of yours."

"Greed?" Tuck played dumb. "Can't say it rings any bells, actually."

John cleared his throat. *"A greedy man brings trouble to his family."*

"Oh, I see the confusion." Tuck grinned as he lingered at the front door. "Trouble's in the building on the *left*. I'm going to the building on the *right*. A greedy man brings *wine* to his family. Wine, you see?"

He opened the door, in love with himself, and only once he was gone did John crack a smile.

Elena helped Alan drag a particularly large sack. "I'm already tired," he complained. "I can't believe I used to pull grain all day. We should walk up to the guards and ask them to help."

They heaved the sack onto the wagon. It was almost full, groaning with each new crate. Elena wondered whether they should heave off while they could. If they broke the axle on the way back to the Sherwood . . .

The tiniest squeak from far away.

Elena froze. "Did you hear that?"

"Hear what?"

The sky was warming, and in the quiet it came again, just a morning lark chirping its first song as the stars slowly disappeared.

"Nothing. Just keep an ear out for the signal from Much."

He would have given a long, trilling whistle, not a quick chirp, if he'd seen any signs of trouble. But they'd been inside half the time, or talking. Might not have heard him.

"Don't worry." John plopped down an armful of horse blankets. "He can see everything from the treeline. Just keep moving."

The minutes slipped by as they carried and rolled and dragged the last goods they could. Every now and then, John would crack the door and peek out. The gords at the fire were only talking amongst themselves or sleeping. Whenever possible, Elena snuck a kiss from Will as their paths crossed, to the point where they almost laughed and dropped their bounty. Tuck waddled back in with a devil's grin, a small cask under each arm and a red stain down his beard.

"Was there ale in there?" John asked, and Tuck answered with a flourish of his eyebrows. John elbowed him eagerly, and the friar hurried back for more. The wagon complained terribly about its weight, and Elena eyed it with each added strain, thinking about how much more they would add to it with their bodies, particularly John.

"Will's a lucky man," John Little said importantly to her, while they both took a moment to catch their breath at a table full of leather harnesses.

"Why's that?" she asked.

"Don't ever let him take you for granted, Lena. What I wouldn't have given for a girl like you." John winked, his wide face smiling deeply. "Don't mistake me now. You know I loved Marley with all my heart, God rest her soul. But she was ever a *wife,* and that's what she cared about. It's better she's gone. She wouldn't have fared too well with what we're doing here. But to have a woman like you, who's willing to go on robberies and fight with you back to back, a girl who'll put a sword to the throat of the man who insults you . . . now that's love."

For the second time, Elena's heart skipped at a noise from outside.

Voices and horses.

And a scramble of other noise, and John was already peeking out the door. "Another delivery," he grumbled. "Livestock. Chickens and goats. Bastards."

"They're delivering bastards?" Elena whispered.

The sound of the wheels and the chickens grew louder, creaking to a stop too close outside, so close that John retreated from the front door and shooed the boys away. Will hurried the others out through the back, and then Elena heard a trilling little whistle at the edge of the world.

Much.

She whirled around to grab John, too late. The door opened and the growing light outside made a square around his massive frame, with the shapes of two men standing at the open doorway.

"What's this here?" one voice with a northern accent barked, and the other, "What's that back there?"

Get out of here, she thought to Will.

John answered with a dry sarcasm, readying for the fight. "Tools, mostly. Farming. Can I get you something?" He leaned over and picked up a pitchfork from the table.

Let me get there first, John, don't take them on alone. But there was too much distance between them—

"We have knives," the first man warned, and John was rounding a table with his pitchfork. Elena grabbed at a trowel on the table. If she could throw it *just right*—"Do they go in here, or is there another place for weapons?"

The air went out of Elena's lungs. "We'll take them, we'll take them!" she shouted, as casually as a shout could sound. "We'll organize them, don't worry."

"Thanks, girl," the man at the door said. "Go grab that box o' knives, would you?"

The second man hustled back to the chicken cart. John looked at Elena gravely, and placed the pitchfork down on another table, slow and dumb, too relieved to think. The men weren't Guardsmen, they wore simple tunics and plodders. Just wagon drivers.

"Chickens mostly, we'll be glad to get rid of that," the one said, kicking the mud off his boot.

"I hear you. We just sort the shit," Elena said, affecting her voice to match the stranger's northern lilt.

"We have a small chest or two of coin, too, where do we drop that off?"

"Oh, we'll take that," Elena shrugged nonchalantly. *God's shit.* "And if it gets a little lighter between there and here, won't no one be looking for it."

She winked. That was another trick, one she should remember to tell John. Give a smaller secret, and they won't suspect the bigger one. If you can get them in on it, then you've turned an enemy into an ally.

"You sure?" the man asked, eyeing John Little.

John took his cue. "Just don't take anything they'll miss."

The driver nodded and clicked his tongue. He had heavy bags under his eyes, every inch of him looked exhausted. When the second fellow returned, Elena took the box from him. It was full of short picks for horse hooves and fruit paring. These pathetic little tools and the words *we have knives* almost got them all killed.

Then Elena was out the back door, to find the others in case they still thought there was danger. The last thing they needed now were swords drawn. She found them by the wagon, Alan sitting on its lip, mouth agape and trying not to laugh.

"*'Excuse me, where should we drop off all this coin?'* You two are the luckiest sons of bitches I've ever known."

He grabbed Elena by the neck and shook her playfully, so hard she almost dropped the knives on their feet. John joined them a moment later, walking out the back door and shaking his head numbly.

"God's knees," Elena said, "you should have seen John almost spear them with a pitchfork."

"I hope we stole a box of breeks somewhere," John planted his finger on Will's chest, "because I think I shit myself back there."

"I'd say we have enough." Arthur smiled. "Time to get out of here?"

Will giggled. "Don't forget the chest or two of coin."

"It's all yours," Elena said. She'd had her brush with danger for the day. Will slipped back inside to fetch it, while John untied the horses from the sidepost.

"You think we'll get it moving?"

"She'll move." John nodded, patting the horses on their haunches. "If they can carry me all the way here, they won't even notice the rest of it."

Elena gave a quick look over the wagon, trying to count what they'd taken, and what it meant to those that would receive it. She couldn't help but wonder. If they kept even a fraction of the haul for themselves, they could start to turn their camp in the woods into a real village. They could live off the land rather than what they stole, they could govern and defend themselves. It was what they were growing toward, stability. A central point where they could live freely, from which they could branch out in time.

For only a moment, her mind touched on John's sermon. That everything they were taking had been taken from others already. This promise of prosperity relied on someone else, somewhere else, going without. It was only a split second, but the dream was sour now. She chose not to think of it.

Arthur was on top of the wagon with the reins in hand. John was behind ready to give it a push. Elena ducked back inside to hurry Will, who was standing in the middle of the room with one small chest in his arms, unmoving, just staring.

"Trying to figure out how to pick up two at once?" she joked, and jogged between tables and barrels to help him.

Will didn't respond, but instead he grew larger, sideways, a shadow growing from behind him, cloaked in black—its arm was wrapped around to the front and held a knife to Will's throat.

"Silently she gets on her knees," the voice said, and Elena's blood went cold. "Silently, or she watches her lover die."

But Elena was already on her knees. She hadn't even thought about it.

"Silently she unbuckles her belt, silently," it said again, "and drops her weapons on the ground."

Elena's fingers fumbled on the buckle, even though she had no weapons on it, and she tried so hard, *so hard,* to place it down without making a noise.

"Silently, she moves back, silently."

Elena crawled back on all fours, sliding each limb without a breath.

"Not as much fun on that end, no?" said the voice. "As Captain of the Sheriff's Guard, I should let you know that I speak for the Sheriff himself and you may consider my word his law."

Elena closed her eyes and there was a sharp noise, *the sound of Will's throat opening,* but no, it was the back door slamming open.

"Come on, you two!" John shouted, and was five paces into the room before he registered what was happening.

"Put your weapon down and get on your knees," Gisbourne said softly.

"Damn it, that's fine, that's fine." John leaned his quarterstaff against the wall. "Just don't hurt him."

"On your knees."

John put a hand on a table, but his legs wobbled when he tried to lower himself. "They're not so good these days."

"My apologies then, why don't I fetch you a divan to rest on, or you could get on your fucking knees."

John winced as he did.

However long the next moment lasted, it was an eternity. But it ended with a quiet hoot from outside. "That's it, Captain."

"Very good, come and grab their weapons, will you?"

The front door opened and men poured in, more than had ever been at the fire ring, clattering through the room, taking their weapons. Elena's eyes darted for anything left behind, a smithing hammer or a small blade, anything. A long thin hook lay on a table to her right, maybe small enough for her to pocket, if she could get to it. Gisbourne shoved Will forward and the chest spilled coins like blood on the ground. "I don't know why I didn't think of this earlier," he gloated to a skinny man beside him in a light cloak. "Why bother wasting time trying to find a bunch of rebels in the woods when you could get them to come to you instead?"

John still had some fire in him. "What you're doing here is wrong."

Gisbourne looked insulted. "You're *literally* stealing. We just caught you, in my supply house, taking things that are not yours. Please don't tell me what I'm doing is wrong. Stealing is wrong. That's something your king and your God agree on. Or do you think yourself smarter than them?"

A beefy guard with a thick beard tapped his foot in front of Elena. "A lot of sharp things in this room, eh? You think that's the best choice you could make with your life, given recent turn of events?"

Elena had only shifted an inch or two toward the hook, but it had been noticed.

At Gisbourne's command, the Guardsmen started to drag them outside. The beefy one crouched down to look Elena square. "You know there are two ways we can do this," he said.

This, at least, Elena had been through before. So she nodded, and then there were hands on her arms, lifting her up and moving her outside. She was surprised to see the tip of the sun piercing the horizon. The wagon with its chickens had moved to the side. By the central firepit, Arthur was on his knees surrounded by three or four guards. Elena managed a look back down the alley between the buildings, and already there were guards unloading their wagon, and disappearing to the back door to return the crates.

"Don't worry, we'll count everything you took," Gisbourne said as Elena was shoved to the ground. "It's important that we know exactly how much you stole from us, as the punishment may depend on it."

"You stole it first." Will spat out dirt. "Maybe we'll share a cell."

"This is property of the Sheriff, boy." Gisbourne scowled. *He could be riled.* Elena wondered if that could be useful. "What you see around you, these are taxes, nothing more. Paid a little late, but finally paid. Ah, here's another one."

From the adjacent building, poor Friar Tuck was being led to join the rest of them. There was more red in his beard now, and it wasn't wine.

Gisbourne scrutinized the six of them. "Is that it?" he asked, and a smattering of men affirmed. "What about Robin of Locksley? Where's he?"

For once, Elena wished that arrogant piece of shit hadn't left them, simply so he could suffer as well. "He's not one of us," she said.

The captain raised an eyebrow. "Not one of you? Hm." He walked a few paces around them in a wide circle. "You can keep your secrets if you'd like. He'll be here soon, I imagine. I have men searching the treeline as we speak." It was everything Elena could do to keep herself from looking at the tree where Much was hidden. If she did, they'd rout him out in a minute.

John spoke up. "It's true, he left us. Seems he didn't have the stomaching for this life. This is all of us, there'd be no point in us lying about it."

He's trying too hard, Elena thought, but John's heart was in the right place. Every moment they delayed gave Much time to run. *What would I do, in Much's place?* If she'd held watch instead, she wouldn't run. Something terrible told her that Much might try to do something, thinking to prove himself. But he wouldn't be foolish enough to attack on his own . . . something in town, maybe. *Or the town itself.* Over the fields, there were still people living in the rest of Bernesdale, people who wouldn't care for the captain's occupation of their village. People who could be provoked to riot by a young boy screaming for help.

She could only dare to hope that Much would think the same thing.

"Well if Robin isn't with you, then he may actually be smarter than I thought. But there is one person still missing, which you cannot deny." Gisbourne looked them each in the eye. "His name is Jon Bassett."

"Bassett?" Elena was confused. "The gord? We let him go weeks ago."

"You let him go." His scrutiny focused on her. "So you did have him."

"We nursed him to health, aye," John Little said. "Which was something we did not have to do. What did he tell you?"

The captain stared, and gave a pitiful single laugh. "That's your story? That you *helped* him, and that you *set him free.*"

"It's no story," Arthur tried.

"Let me try this, then. If Bassett is dead, all of you will hang. Except for whomsoever admits the truth to me, right now."

A gaping shock rolled through them, but no one spoke. Gilbert had returned Jon Bassett to Nottingham, he said it went smoothly. Elena stared at the captain, unsure what play he was making. She had never had a real look at the man. Older than she had thought, there was white in his beard and at the edges of his brow, and the crow's lines around his eyes were deep. His blue doublet was frayed and worn threadbare at its seams, and hung on his frame loosely. It breathed with him. *He was not wearing mail beneath it.*

Of course not, she realized, they had dressed light to set this trap. If Much was able to rally even a small group in time . . . Elena played it out in her head. *The guards turning, unsure what was happening, Will and the others swarming, the six of them taking three or four men on one side of the circle, enough to make an opening and run. Steal one blade and sink it in Gisbourne's gut.*

It was possible. Meanwhile, the captain shifted his jaw about, a hard jaw. "Alright, let's try it another way. Morg, break one of their arms."

There was no time, they needed more time. A guard moved in, a mountain more meat than man, and snatched Friar Tuck from them.

"No, take me," John protested, but the huge gord just smiled and swung Tuck like a doll, twisting his arm harshly and awaiting Gisbourne's command.

"Let's try again, now. I wouldn't recommend you lie more than . . . twice." Gisbourne counted Tuck's arms obviously with his fingers. "Where are the rest of your men, and where is Jon Bassett? Easy questions. It is in your best interest to help us, brother. I'm looking out for my people. You can look out for yours. So tell me truly, where are they?"

Elena tried to peek out of the corner of her eyes for any sign of commotion from the village.

The friar looked up, as well as he could, his cheeks hanging low. But his eyes were wet and bright. "As God is my witness, this is everyone. And we sent your man home. If you won't believe me, then do what you will."

He closed his eyes.

The captain turned to the skinny man in the light cloak. "What do you think?"

This man was tall and gaunt, and when he spoke it was without inflection, slow and bored. "I can't think of a single reason why we should believe a word any of them say."

"You're learning quickly," Gisbourne said lightly. And then, to the brute, "Go on then, break it."

"No!" Will shouted, along with Alan.

"If you won't believe us anyways then what's the point?" Arthur roared, but midsentence Tuck's arm snapped back, impossibly too far, the sickening crack drowned by his gasping scream.

Rage.

"He still has another arm!" Gisbourne bit at them instantly, "So who would like to tell me another lie?"

Elena couldn't think, she was watching Tuck, dangling from the arm still held by the guard. He had passed out from the pain.

Gisbourne pulled a long thin knife from his boot, "What should we take after his arms?"

Elena was yelling something, but she wasn't sure what, and she couldn't even hear herself over the noise the others were making, all anger and regret.

"*Where's Jon Bassett? Where's Robin of Locksley?*" Gisbourne shouted over them as the guard grabbed Tuck's other arm.

"There's one more! There's only one!" John bellowed.

No, not Much.

Gisbourne smiled. "You see how easy the truth is? You could have said as much ten seconds ago and the good friar would be much happier. That's on you, not me. Very well, where is he?"

John swallowed, and stood up. Some guards took a step forward, others one back.

"It's Robin Hood," he announced, and the name whispered through the air as the guards repeated it. "He's watching us from the trees right now." John threw a fist high in the air. "This is the signal. When I drop my arm, he'll rain arrows down upon you all."

Gisbourne wasn't impressed. "Put your arm down."

"No, don't!" one guard shouted, twisting around to look at the trees, but the trees were everywhere.

"He could put an arrow through two of your necks in the blink of an eye," Alan said.

"Could be any of you," Arthur joined.

"Call him off!" one guard yelled, backing up beneath the overhanging roof of the storehouse. The guards all squirmed, craning their heads. Panicking.

"They're lying, you fools!" Gisbourne yelled, even as he retreated to the relative cover of the alley between two buildings. "They're just trying to catch you off your guard!"

Now, this is the moment. This is the distraction. Go!

But Elena hesitated.

"Death to the Sheriff!" the shout came from behind Gisbourne, from the alley.

The captain heard it and sprang sideways, wheeling around to meet the attack. His dagger thrust out where an assailant's stomach would have been, but there was no mob of villagers there, no surprise rescue. There was just the tip of Gisbourne's knife as it pierced the apple of Much's neck.

The world stopped.

The force of the blow lifted Much's feet off the ground, his legs kicking limply forward, his body suspended on the blade. His eyes were so wide and blue in the half moment before his blond hair flung forward, obscuring his face. A small sword fell from his hands, twirling as his fingers lost their grip. There was nothing else to be seen. Everything else was white, and there was no noise. Much and Gisbourne moved to the ground, one over the other. When Gisbourne pulled the knife out, with it came a thick dark ribbon, just flowing out, just like that. The white moved in on them, fuzzy and numbing, until all Elena could see was the pinpoint of Much's face, and then nothing, just the white, but it was fading grey.

She was pummeling a guard's face with her fist, over and over, her knuckles broken and bloody. Then there was a shoulder in her gut and the ground slipped away. She was airborne and tumbling backward. Something struck her face hard and she was down, but her legs scrambled beneath her, then someone else's hands wrapped around her head and grabbed her hair, throwing her down. A knee crushed into her jaw. There was copper in her mouth and her face couldn't feel.

But the image was still there, of Much frozen in midair, Gisbourne's knife through his neck like a potato.

Maybe Much would be fine. Maybe the friar could bandage him. If they got to him quickly, they could bandage it tight enough, but not so tight as to choke him. It would heal except for an impressive scar stretching from his clavicle to his chin, and later the girls would all ask him about it. Much would tell them how he'd been lanced through, and played dead, only to rise and strike down the man who'd tried to murder him, and all the girls would want to kiss his neck.

Elena's hands clasped into a single fist and swung through a guard's face, then her leg swung hard and snapped across the man's chin when he tried to roll up. She tried to bring her boot down into the man's teeth, but she was yanked backward and around. By a fool's roll, she watched a fist miss her by an inch and she flung her own elbow in, finding the soft of the guard's neck. Then there was steel, the screech of swords, even though there was no noise.

Time rolled backward. A minute ago, Much was hiding in the alley between the buildings. He must have swiped the sword from another storehouse, and was building up his bravery to make an attack. He made it softly and carefully, and the captain had his back to him, with no one between them. Much ran forward, screaming, and he plunged his sword into the captain's back. Gisbourne fell, and the guards dropped everything and scattered for the trees, where a hundred hidden archers dropped them one by one, and Elena and John hoisted Much above their shoulders and shouted his name.

Elena was ducking under the reach of a long sword, and as she came up her knee found the belly of its wielder. There was a rock in her hand, and it smashed the man's temple. Nearby, Will had found a sword, but was being beaten backward. Elena threw herself on his assailant's arm, only to find herself leaping to the side as the thrusts came her way now. Something smashed against her face hard, too hard. Her vision blanked out, and it was only the pain that let her know she had not died. She was sliding back in the dirt and dust, her feet giving way, but when she could see again it was Will in front of her, standing over her, wielding John's massive quarterstaff. Gisbourne was there, still over Much's body, pointing at Will and yelling. Then the two of them flew at each other.

She was on the ground again, in the ring, and the guards were worrying about Robin Hood: She had seen the chance, the same opportunity Much had taken, but she had hesitated. This time she didn't. She rose and took the legs out from under a guard, and that was all it took to make a distraction. Much cut the captain in two and retreated. The rest of them rose, while a mob of villagers took to the courtyard, flooding it. Will vaulted off a quarterstaff and bludgeoned Gisbourne's teeth in . . .

Gisbourne swung slowly, and Will easily met him with the center of the staff, again and again, driving forward *or was he being driven back?* until he snapped the staff around to the side of the captain's head, then hooked the murderer around the neck, pulling him forward. Elena tried to rise, to help him, but her body would not obey. If Will had his twins he could have ended his fight, but another guard came at him and he had to abandon Gisbourne. He threw the staff at the new guard with both hands. The man caught it in front of him and Will smashed his nose in with a fist. Grabbing the staff again, Will spun and whipped the man to the ground where he punched his face a second and third time until the man went limp and released his hold.

Much popped out of the barrel on the cart, a few hours ago, smiling and laughing, and John took him in his giant arms and held him, and John was so big and Much was so small that you couldn't even see him in there, and John could protect him from anything. Much asked, "What do you want me to do?" and John told him, "I want you to go home," and this time he did.

There were four guards around Will, and one slashed in high and found only splinters in the staff, but another came from the side, and Will blocked it too late. The sword slapped against his forearm, and he couldn't avoid another. Then a boot was in Will's back and he went down, the staff rolling away from him. Elena screamed for him, only to find she was already screaming.

It was hours ago now, when she told Much they were leaving, when she mentioned the name of Bernesdale, when he drifted off into his own thoughts. "You should come," she said, "hide in a barrel until it's too late to turn back." She had hoped he would confront his past, she had hoped to give him a victory.

"Don't go!" she screamed this time, but the memory wouldn't change.

It was over. John Little was on his back with his hands in the air, Alan and Arthur on their knees with their heads down, Tuck was curled in a ball clutching his arm. Much's lifeless pile was still where it had fallen. A dozen guards surrounded them. Four, then five stood over Will, their swords leveled low, and Will had nothing. There was a hole in their circle. She could run now if she wanted to, but she'd be leaving Will to the mercy of what came next.

Elena closed her eyes and tried to think of the first time she'd seen him but the memory was black.

She ran.

THIRTY-SIX

GUY OF GISBOURNE

BERNESDALE

It was wrong that the sun could rise. It was wrong that light should shine on this. It should be kept in the dark, the world should swallow it up rather than let anyone see what happened here. Guy's forearm was just a muscle, a chunk of meat stretched over his skeleton, and he despised it. It quivered, and every twitch reminded him of his grip on the knife, how easily it held the blade and the entirety of the boy's body. He did not need to look to know exactly where the boy lay. He could feel it in his soul. It was a tiny hole that had opened up and broken everything.

God damn you, Guy breathed, because they were the only true words left. *God damn all of you.*

He heard his own voice say the words. There was blood on his lips, still warm, but he would not wipe it away. He didn't know if the blood was his or the boy's. A chill rippled through his spine that he hoped would never end. He never wanted to be over this. He never wanted to be better.

What do we do, Captain? someone asked, and Guy's mouth answered on its own. He did not know what he said. He did not know how he was still standing, he did not know how a man could be expected to do anything now. *They had brought a child.* The horror was too much to bear. *They had trained a child to kill.*

"You brought this on yourselves." Those words were his, his eyes were focused on the group of thieves in front of him. "There's not hell enough for you."

Their sudden attack had accomplished nothing. Guy's men had routed them back, recaptured them precisely where they were before, gathered in the dirt. Nothing had changed save for the body of the boy. No reason for blood, no reason for death. Guy tried to count his own men, praying that none had been seriously injured. Reginold and Bolt were both still absent, though they had been positioned at the north road. Morg clutched the biceps of his right arm, blood seeping through his fingers and dripping down to his elbow. Some of the Common boys had split lips and bloody noses. For no reason. For these outlaws to kick at the world one last time. That was all they wanted, and it sickened him. Their only goal was to hurt.

Devon of York stood, pale as a statue, eyes locked on the child. Whatever innocence had once defined his features was gone now, replaced with this new gruesome reality. Guy wondered if Devon had known the boy, back before he had escaped their company. It was too terrible to think upon.

His mind raced to wonder if he could have done anything differently. It had happened before he even knew it. He never even saw the child. He only felt his weight on the blade, and had felt nothing since.

The years crawled up from his gut, old tracks in his heart he had long closed off. His first wife Loren, the one he'd loved. Their children. Henry, his wide toothy grin, his smile that burst from nowhere and lit up the world. His sickness. His body. The empty weight of it in Guy's hands.

He heaved and vomited—his throat burned as fiercely as his eyes. It tore him back to the present, to the sounds of shouting, of curses.

What do we do, Guy? Eric of Felley's face, bringing him back. His beard was matted with blood, his missing teeth bled fresh.

"The girl got away," he was saying. "She might be going for reinforcements. We'd best handle this group now."

The ground bobbed, which meant Guy was nodding.

"How do you want them, Captain?"

They'd trained a child to kill. They'd used him as a distraction. A quick death wasn't good enough. But it wasn't always about what they deserved, Guy managed to remember. There was a fairer world once, where these things didn't happen, where Murdac was still sheriff. He had to find his way back there. There was more at stake now than dealing justice to a handful of criminals. If he killed them here without any witnesses, there was no telling how their sympathizers would twist the story. There would have to be a trial, and a public display, or the truth would never get out.

"Bind them," he ordered. "We need them alive."

"All of them?"

"Most of them," Guy snorted, daring them to try another escape.

"Aye, Captain." Eric was drenched in sweat, but did not hesitate in getting to work. Morg lurched to join him, wincing at his arm that was clearly shaking now.

The calm barely lasted a second. Eric ordered them to lie on their stomachs, and most of them did. But they were screaming, yelling. One of them pushed off the ground and Guy's men swarmed him. Guy would not have so much as blinked if they'd cut him to pieces, but instead the thief backed down, retreating, back to the ground with the others.

He heard a panicked breath and realized it wasn't his own. Devon stood over the thieves, his whole body trembling, he was pointing his sword's tip out over them loosely. His eyes wide, his muscles shaking, he looked utterly lost but certain he was supposed to do something.

"Hold!" Guy yelled. Devon was too spooked to know how to control his reactions, he did not have enough training for this. He held his weapon as if it were a snake, and he was more likely to hurt himself than anyone else. "Hold, Devon!"

He turned and relaxed, his eyes softened and focused on Guy, just as an arrow pierced him square in the heart.

Guy had to look twice to be sure it was real. Devon's mouth opened wide in confusion, but no noise came, then his shoulders keeled inward and he fell backward. Guy closed his eyes against the rest of it.

There was a scream, primal, a noise beyond what any animal could make. Guy opened his eyes to see his men in a panic, bolting for the relative safety of the nearby supply houses. Guy spun around in search of the archer, momentarily blinded by the sun above the supply house behind him. A figure stood there—silhouetted, only a few feet away—bow in hand, drawn taut, aimed directly at Guy's chest.

"Robin Hood," his men gasped.

"Let them go," belted a voice, but it was not Robin of Locksley's. "Or you'll be dead before you speak."

It was the girl, the wild forest girl, Elena. She knelt on the slanted thatched roof, arrow nocked, trained on Guy. At this distance, she would be sure to hit.

Guy's hands moved out to his side, wide, hoping to stay her shot. When last she had held his life in her hands, visions of his past had flooded him. Nothing came to him now, no fear or regret, just a cold calm. He made a slow signal down, away, for his men to lower their weapons to the earth. With his right hand he found the tie on his belt, letting his baldric slip off his waist. He didn't care if she loosed the arrow, he would welcome the relief. But he would not lose another man. Not another Jon Bassett. Not another Devon of York.

Reginold and Bolt, he prayed. They were still out there. At any moment Elena could be plucked from the roof by Bolt's crossbow, by Reginold's arrow. They needed time.

"We're leaving," the girl cried, her voice born of fury. "And you are not going to follow us. John, get Much." Slowly, just as slowly as Guy himself had moved, the thieves rose. John Little lumbered over to the body of the boy. *Much* was his name. Little knelt and peeled the boy from the ground, sticky with blood, and carried him like a baby.

Time passed. Reginold and Bolt did not attack.

The thieves claimed their wagons, Reginold and Bolt did not attack.

They stole additional horses, they prepared to leave. Reginold and Bolt did not attack.

The girl didn't move, the tip of her arrow trained on Guy's chest. Her arm should have given out by now.

"You'll hang for this, you know," Guy said softly to her, as it seemed increasingly likely they would actually escape. "I'll see to it myself. That's a promise."

"You want a promise?" she cried back. "We promise you this. Anyone. *Anyone* responsible for hurting one of our own will pay with his life. That's a promise we'll take to our graves."

She vanished, replaced by blistering sunlight, which Guy stared into. Even as she ran backward along the roof, even as she slid down to join the others and the awaiting horses. Guy's men hurried to Devon's body, but the man was long dead. They asked if they should pursue, they asked for a plan, they needed leadership, they needed justice. Guy couldn't give it. He was imagining telling Devon's wife, Hannah, about what had happened. He was thinking of Devon's baby daughter, now fatherless.

They found Bolt at the north road, unconscious, but alive. Reginold was not as lucky. His body was off the side of the path, his pants were down, he was sitting in a pile of his own shit, his forehead was caved in. His legs twitched still. Guy pushed his sword through Reginold's heart and wept.

THIRTY-SEVEN

ROGER DE LACY

NOTTINGHAM CASTLE

Lord Guy of Gisbourne.

The words hadn't changed, despite refolding and unfolding the message again twice. So predictable of the parchment, to display the same words every time simply because they were written there. How much more interesting the message would be if it offered a different name each time Roger opened it. How much he would have enjoyed the surprise! What a delight, he could cycle through every name he knew, searching for one even more insulting than Gisbourne's. It would be quite the promotion for Morg.

Roger had guessed his replacement would be someone dangerous or reckless, and he was insufferably bored of being right. There was no joy there anymore, just a disappointment in the world for having long lost its creativity. *Unquestionable loyalty, no political experience, and a complete madman.* Words he had used to describe the new sheriff in York, and increasingly fitting to Guy of Gisbourne. In the last month the captain had abandoned his post to search the forest for hunches, and crippled the city's trade by shutting down the dockside markets. His ineptitude had forced Roger to authorize the barbaric act of disfiguring every suspected criminal, and his diplomatic skills inspired a lord to publicly defecate into a charity meal. These were the rabid actions of a man in decline. But the captain had always been ambitious, and it seemed he had set other machinations at play behind Roger's back.

"It's my own fault, I've been worshipping the wrong gods." Roger peered over the lip of his wine glass, letting it obscure most of Margery's face excepting her eyes. He hoped the gesture was as mysterious as it felt. "I've prayed at the altar of reason. As it turns out, that's rather like betting on chickens in a dog fight."

"Perhaps you should have tried Catholicism," Margery offered, pouring herself another glass. "It is a somewhat more standard selection."

Roger had asked for the oldest bottle in the cellar, which had proven undrinkable, but settled on another rare vintage that was appropriately inappropriate for the occasion.

"It's blood, that's the real power," Roger lamented. "Logic is nothing to blood. You know I don't like praise, but I'll tell you with little regard to humility that everything I've done here as sheriff has been nothing short of brilliant. I've restructured everything about the office, changed countless policies in favor of new ones that merit results. But all in ways nobody notices, and certainly doesn't talk about. No one comments on my clever redistribution of textile trades last year because it's boring, even to me. But a few thieves rattle some branches, and suddenly I'm seen as incompetent."

The worst part was that he had foolishly fought against it. He thought if he could wrangle Lord Oughtibridge and his allies back into obedience, that it might be victory enough to keep his title. He'd retreated into a corner rather than hold his ground. Gisbourne was still out "reclaiming" taxes from innocent people now, and Roger had authorized it. It was wrong, and it made him sick. And for what? For one last futile grasp to stay in power.

While the damned document in his hands had already been signed.

Somewhere in the world, an old woman named Marie de Clere was growing even older. She'd made Roger two promises the day he asked for her hand in marriage. *"I'll be as true to you as you are to me,"* was the first, which Roger had mistaken for a pledge rather than a threat. The second, *"I'll never leave France for you,"* he mistook for a joke. Two mistaken promises that defined their life since. She had been attractive then, therefore he was attracted to her. He had mistaken that for love. And once upon a time he was unimportant enough that he could marry someone on such irrational grounds as love.

What he had endured in the many years since was a real love, the kind no poet would ever write about. There were no pretty whispers or flowery words that could describe the love that is forged over a lifetime. Real love is all crag and crevice. It looks different from every angle, each mood casting a different shadow.

It had been two years since Roger had seen his Marie, since his unusual appointment to this abominable sheriffcy. Marie had been many things, and half of them were infuriating, but the better parts of her had fit well with his own shortcomings. When he struggled with the pettiness and selfishness of mankind, she had a way of bringing him back. Over the last two years without her, those grudges had dragged him down. Had she been here, perhaps he could have found a way to placate his rebellious lords other than by giving in to their demands. Perhaps her absence was the reason he had failed, and so completely at that.

"You were speaking of blood," Lady Margery whispered, looking over the lip of her own glass.

"I was speaking of blood," he rose, to peer out the sliver window. It was an early evening outside, the sun setting, the Trent sparkling below. In spring there would have been a field of purple crocuses sprawling away to the west, but not now. Still he preferred the view from this room for its singular remarkable quality—that it contained not a single stone or citizen of Nottingham. "It doesn't matter what I've done, all that matters is what is in my veins. Or, more applicably, that which is *not.* I am the third son of the third daughter in an unnotable family made no richer by its marriages. You'll notice that none of the words I just said sounded anything like *Richard.*"

"Except for *richer,*" Margery said, and all of Roger's thoughts scattered and hid in tiny black cracks. He chose to blink. She clarified, "*Richer* sounds like *Richard.*"

"Why would you stop me when I was being clever?"

"You weren't being clever." She shrugged. "If you'd been clever, I wouldn't have found such an obvious flaw in your cleverness."

"My point," he grumbled, "is that there is nobody important in my family."

"I know what your point is," she spoke over him. "You presume that if you had a deep cousin who married one of Richard's deep cousins, you wouldn't have been deposed today. You think that would have protected you from the Chancellor?"

There was a question behind her question. He hadn't let her actually read the message. She was prying, trying to find out who was pulling this particular string. He grunted a half affirmation, letting her think the Chancellor had issued the order. It didn't matter. He had expected this exact letter from the Chancellor, but Prince John had sent one *first*. They both had the authority. He collapsed the paper again onto the table and placed the wine bottle on top of it.

"Look at you, Roger, whining about your lot. It's true, your family is unimportant, but that was the hand you were dealt. You've had sixty years to come to terms with it. Sixty years to overcome it, and you failed. The blame is on you."

Somewhere, there was a perfect combination of words to counter Margery's insult. It was there in his mind but the pieces wouldn't fit together.

"You and my husband, you're two sides of the same coin, as they say. He shakes his fist at the world, believing blood and family should dictate who has power, hating any man who finds another way to achieve it. Here you are, a man who rose to be sheriff through talent alone, hating a world that prefers blood and family. Do you play chess?"

Roger assented with a grumble.

"Do you ever curse the gods of chess that your bishops only move diagonally? No? You and Waleran both, whenever you lose at politics, you blame the rules of the game." She stood, lazily, but there was a sharpness to her teeth. "Perhaps you should simply *play it better*."

She meant to exit, and dramatically, but he wouldn't let her. He locked his eyes upon her as she retreated, and she couldn't break the gaze.

"If I were a younger man," he ground his throat, "I would clear this table and do the most wonderful things to you."

"Oh, Roger." She rolled her eyes. "You forget that I knew you when you were a younger man. And you never did."

A breeze whispered in, cooling the sweat on the back of Roger's neck. "I suppose the rules were unfair then as well." He thought of Marie, but she was so far away, and there was no point in being good anymore. "But my body still works."

Whatever Margery d'Oily's reaction was, she didn't leave. "I suppose this is the part where I remind you that we're both married."

"Have you seen a mirror lately? You're anything but a young girl. Don't be boring by speaking like one."

"My, don't you know how to make a woman feel beautiful."

"You aren't beautiful. You have had many years to come to terms with that. Would you respect me if I pretended otherwise?"

"Respect? A deposed sheriff, a victim of his own inaction, whining away his last few hours in office? Respect was never exactly on the table."

But still she didn't leave, nor had either looked away. Roger's heart was pounding. Beneath the chill, he was on fire.

"What would you propose?"

"If you need me to tell you, then don't bother." Margery tilted her head. "But for now, I'm the only person who knows about this letter, yes? How long do you think that will last?"

"Only until tomorrow, no doubt."

"Tomorrow." She relished the word, she held it in her mouth the same way she had held the wine. "I may only be an ignorant woman, but I'm fairly certain there are still a few hours between now and then. Do you know that tonight is All Saints' Eve? Tomorrow is for saints. Tonight . . ." she let it linger, and cracked the door to leave.

He glanced at the window, darkness devouring the sky.

"Someone once told me that Sheriff Roger de Lacy was nothing short of brilliant. I wonder how much he could accomplish if he didn't have to worry about keeping his office?" She closed the door behind her, pausing just a breath. "That would be a man I could . . . respect."

Damn it all.

Roger looked up at the pompous painting of himself, of the man he had been when he came to this office. A man who believed in reason, and its ability to promote peace. Some sort of damned idealist, who would slowly watch his standards slip away like a rider in the fog. Soon the same flamboyant painter who had made this atrocity would be creating the portrait of *Sheriff Guy of Gisbourne.* He would be effective, certainly, with his lies and alliances. His passion for justice was a fanaticism, and he would exercise it at the expense of every common man that Gisbourne didn't find personally useful. He held no care for the people, nor the rules that kept them safe.

Ironically, that care was why Roger had failed. He had spent the last two years slowly trying to change the rules for the better. But Margery was right. There were still a few hours left to outright break them instead.

ARNOLD DE NOTTOIR WAS asleep at his table, which gave Roger a few moments to consider the weight of what he was about to do. The senior tax collector had inherited the maintenance of the records in this room, and was likely the only person who knew how to navigate their numbers. Roger selected a pile of papers that would look most dramatic when scattered off the table, and set them on their way.

"What is it?" The old man drew out of slumber, wiping a chain of saliva from the corner of his mouth to his shirt. The muscles about his eyes strained to focus on Roger, but he worried at the papers in the air. "What is it?"

"A most curious thing happened to me," Roger said, purposefully selecting papers at random from the table and replacing them elsewhere, "as the reports came in today from Lord Gisbourne's raids. Perhaps you remember them? Surely you caught a word or two in between naps at our council meeting the other day?"

"I don't, I never! I was not asleep! What is the problem? What day did you say it was?"

"You gave Gisbourne a list of parties with significant tax debts, did you not?"

The tax collector's face exploded with recognition. "I did! Yes, I did. I have it here."

To Roger's surprise, Arnold's fingers darted into a mound of papers on the table and promptly removed a leather tome, which he placed open amongst the rabble and rifled through with unusual dexterity. Roger was reminded that there were many versions of talent, and found in the unlikeliest of places.

"Let me see it," Roger said, rounding behind Arnold and dragging his fingers across the ledger.

"It's quite extensive," Arnold said proudly.

"*Quite* extensive, is it? Do tell how that differs from *normally* extensive." Roger mumbled through a few names which were legible enough, then took the offensive again. "You idiot. This list is an exact duplicate of another. One that I gave your predecessor last year. A list of men who are away at the Crusade *and are thus exempt* from paying taxes."

Arnold's mouth dropped, and he pored himself over the document. "It cannot be, I've been over these names, we went over them twice. It cannot be!"

"Not only can it be, but far worse, it *is*. I don't know what blind picnicking you substitute for work down here, but you have evidently been copying from the wrong list for months."

What Roger was saying probably didn't make sense. He knew little about how the records were kept, but was hoping to be vague enough that Arnold would fill in the gaps for himself. To his satisfaction, the man started muttering any number of possible explanations, calculating potential mistakes, listing exemptions and loopholes they might use to right the error.

"Terrible, yes," Arnold concluded, "but we can fix this."

"We?" Roger lifted an eyebrow. "You are under the mistaken impression that you and I are in the same boat."

Arnold swallowed. "My apologies. That is . . . *I* can fix this."

"Not before you die."

Arnold started making noises, some of them quite entertaining.

"Oh settle down, I'm not threatening you," Roger said. "I'm simply predicting the future. I will have to return everything that Gisbourne has collected. Every coin, every straw. The Sheriff's Guard will be a mockery, the people will be outraged, and I doubt you have the stamina to survive the ensuing riots."

"Riots?" Arnold's head was probably filling with better nightmares than Roger could possibly describe.

"This is a mistake of catastrophic proportions. The moment anybody else hears about this, we're all done. All of us. Those that aren't stabbed in the streets will die there nonetheless, alone, once the Chancellor has his way. You and your damned numbers, Arnold. They've destroyed us. *You've* destroyed us."

He tried to leave an opening for Arnold to suggest the obvious, but the old man wasn't there yet. Roger flirted with giving it away. "I certainly don't have much choice in the matter, I have to take this to Gisbourne immediately before the raids are over."

Still nothing. Roger stooped to feeding him his line. "Unless . . ."

Arnold was, at this point, exactly as useful as a parrot. "Unless what?"

"You can't be serious?" Roger recoiled theatrically. "We could never hide something this important! Why, you're holding the evidence in your hands! It only takes one person to look inside that book, and see the same thing I saw."

The old man's eyes were moving now. Finally, self-preservation sparked to life somewhere in his brain and throttled his propriety into submission. "Then nobody must ever see this book."

Voila.

Fifteen minutes later, they burned tome after tome together. Arnold believed it was his idea. Every record of debt owed in Nottinghamshire, every name and number cracked and blackened in a metal pot.

"Hide it," Roger whispered as the embers fluttered in the air. "Move your numbers around, Arnold. Use your magic. The list may be gone, but it's up to you to balance the rest of it. Get creative. I'll do everything I can to protect you. I'll even take the fall if I must. But for God's sake, if anything happens to me, you must take this secret to your grave."

One fell swoop, and Nottinghamshire's villages were free from the fear of being evicted and arrested. Everyone could start anew. He could not undo the damage he'd done already by letting Gisbourne's raids go forward, but this would put a stop to them going any farther.

One down, three to go.

SIMON FITZSIMON WAS NEARLY alone in the massive dining gallery, since the majority of Nottingham's Guardsmen were out on the tax raids. The giant Scotsman appeared smaller in that great emptiness, huddled over a bowl making the disgusting sorts of noises that larger men make when they eat. A few guards lingered at the outskirts of the hall, short skinny things, no doubt the freshest of recruits. The hall gave Roger's footsteps an epic quality as he descended the wide stairs, and Simon begrudgingly stood at the sight of him.

"Master-at-arms!" Roger called out, liking the way his voice echoed. "Which part of you is the most incompetent? Tell me, that I may remove it from your body and feed it to your children."

Simon simply chewed, slowly, giving the effort his full attention. "What can I do for you, Sheriff?"

"I should say you could fall on your blade, but that end is generally reserved for more honorable men." Roger toppled an empty tankard over with a single finger, still half the room away from FitzSimon. The guards at the edges pretended not to listen. "The least you could do is leave Nottingham tonight, and never be seen again."

"Are you going to tell me what's going on," Simon ground his jaw, "or do you just insult me until I guess?" Roger rarely interacted with the arms trainer, as there was little overlap in their worlds. But FitzSimon was well respected in the Guard, and worked closely with Gisbourne. So Roger was betting they shared the same opinion on a certain *policy*.

"There is only one real type of secret in the world," Roger curled his lips on each word, "the kind shared by the dead. You thought that your pet boys would never say anything? You put swords in the hands of criminals and ale in their bellies and trust that they'd behave? You're an even bigger idiot than your size would suggest."

They weren't actually Roger's words. Gisbourne had fought Roger at every step when enacting the plan to recruit nonviolent tax offenders into the Nottingham Guard. Some men would always consider the word *prisoner* to be synonymous with *evil*. No doubt it would be the first policy Gisbourne would destroy upon taking the sheriff's seat tomorrow.

Simon squinted. "What the hell am I supposed to do? They know not to say anything."

"So you admit it, then."

"Admit what?"

"This obscenity. This utter corruption of justice!" Roger chose to wave his arms in increasingly large circles, fearing he'd laugh at himself if he tried to continue seriously. "Your use of men from the prisons as fodder for Guardsmen! Putting wanted men side by side with those loyal to Nottingham? Inviting betrayal into the ranks! Are you even vaguely familiar with the concept of a criminal?"

Simon put his hands out, his stubby fingers spread wide. "I. Agree."

"What do you mean, *you agree*?"

"I mean just that." Simon scratched the red at his chin, and Roger imitated him. An old trick, to gesture like a person makes them think you're on the same side. "I never would have trained those men to fight if I hadn't been ordered to. Men come to the Guard for a lot of reasons, but those that only do it to save their own skin . . . I don't trust them one bit."

"'If you hadn't been ordered to?'" Roger feigned confusion. "Gisbourne told me this was your idea."

"My idea?" Simon's face turned the color of his beard. "He told me it was your idea!"

"My idea?" Roger spat and gaped, turned and harrumphed, everything that Simon was doing, mirrored back at him.

"That son of a bitch," Roger offered, and Simon bit it.

"I—son of a bitch!"

"Well," Roger coughed, "now I understand how my wives felt when they met each other." Obviously a lie. "It would seem we have something in common. We've both been lied to. *Gisbourne.*" He seethed the word, and it poisoned the air.

"He played us both against each other," Simon said. "Damn it all, he's got one of those gerolds in his personal regiment. After everything foul he said about them and you, he took one amongst his closest men."

Roger didn't know who Gerold was, but he loved watching the lie solve other mysteries in Simon's head.

"He must be up to something," he continued. "Something big."

"The man has ambitions," Roger nodded importantly. "Best not let him know we're on to him."

Tomorrow, when Gisbourne ascended to sheriff, Simon would see the wheels at work. Without the support of his own master-at-arms, Gisbourne would have a much more difficult time accomplishing his own agenda. It wouldn't stop him, no, but it might slow him down, and keep healthy opposition and dissent alive. It would keep Gisbourne from ruling as a tyrant.

Two down, two to go.

He'd saved the people from their debt, and hurt Gisbourne's authority. His next step was to miraculously find a great deal of wealth to send to King Richard. A wicked plan had been uncurling in his mind all night. It involved an outrageous lie, the unwitting participation of the good Lord Oughtibridge, and a very particular coinchest full of shit.

Which, it occurred to him, he could not possibly carry on his own.

"I need two of your men," he told Simon.

Simon barked out, only to scare those at the periphery of the room. There were few Guardsmen left at the castle, and the two young guards who stepped forward—engulfed in their blue cowls—were hardly intimidating. For a moment Roger doubted himself. Young new recruits such as these two . . . might Gisbourne retaliate against them for their part of this?

Somewhere in the world, Marie told him to trust his instinct. Then he was moving again, with two of the future of the Sheriff's Guard keeping time behind him.

A REMARKABLE TEMPTATION OCCURRED to Roger at the top of the four flights of stairs that led to his office. Aside from the joy of knowing he would never climb them again, he realized what he might do after he was no longer sheriff. He hadn't spared a single thought to what came *after,* and doing so brought a renewed sense of drive.

He'd take his name back.

He'd been Roger de Lisours for most of his life, but every other de Lisours he'd ever met made him despise the name. There had been but one notable de Lisours, his grandmother Albreda. When she died the rest of the family fell on itself to divide and claim her considerable lands. Roger wanted none of it, and that unthinkable lack of greed made the rest of his family untrusting of him. They demanded he take the barony of Pontefract, a county away in Yorkshire, and in exchange he abandoned his name. But legally he still had every claim to it. And the night had whetted his appetite for taking things.

Marie could suffer to wait for him in France a while longer. Perhaps he could stay a player in this game, if Roger de Lisours reclaimed his land and kept a neighborly eye on Gisbourne. *Being deposed may even be the greatest thing that could happen here.*

Roger pushed open the door to his office to find William de Wendenal inside, startled. Between his fingers was a parchment with which Roger was quite familiar, famous for refusing to change the name written upon it. Wendenal started to apologize, but Roger waved him off.

"It doesn't matter. I see you've read it."

In a world full of Gisbournes and Oughtibridges, Roger had found a rewarding friendship in Wendenal. He had provided clarity of thought and well-needed *conversation*. Actual conversation, where people develop and strengthen their ideas, rather than blindly throw their own at the other with increasing volume.

Another step into the room and Roger realized Wendenal was not alone. The haste with which Arable was adjusting her dress said more than enough as to what they had been doing.

"I'm sorry," she said, and she was the sort that meant it.

"There's no offense." Roger smirked. "After all, it's not even my office anymore."

"That's not what I meant." She reached out and touched the letter.

"Is there nothing to be done?" Wendenal asked. He seemed freshly shaken. Perhaps he had only just read it before Roger walked in.

"It's my fault, all of it." Roger stiffened and straightened his hair, looking at the other version of himself hanging on the wall, which looked back with derision. "I've made many mistakes, you know. Anything that has happened, I am solely to blame."

"Has anybody seen this?" Wendenal asked, and then, noticing the two guards behind Roger, "Wait outside." They closed the door, and he repeated the question.

"Nobody else has read it."

"Not Gisbourne?"

"Gisbourne's still in Bernesdale, as far as I know."

Arable's face was pale. "That man is a monster. He can't be given so much power."

"He will be," Roger confirmed. "He has."

"He'll spend the entire coffers searching for those outlaws," Wendenal thought aloud. "The county will be bankrupt and your people will be living in fear."

"I'm working on that. I've done a poor job of managing all this, I see that now. I should have been more decisive. But I have a few final acts I've set in motion today, and one or two more before this night is over. I may be able to salvage something from this . . . debacle." He hesitated before the final word, realizing that he was describing his own career.

"One night? That's not enough time."

"It's all I have."

Wendenal snatched the parchment and held it over a candle.

"What will that accomplish, William? Another would come in a week, along with the men to enforce it. Do I want to be remembered as the sheriff they had to drag out of his office by force?"

"A week is all we need." Wendenal's eyes were bright now. "Do you want to be remembered as the sheriff who gave up, or the sheriff who brought peace to Nottingham? You know as well as I that Gisbourne's raids will do nothing to change the outlaws in the Sherwood. If anything it will embolden them further."

"Oh I know," Roger felt the anger in his veins, "but I could think of nothing else. Oughtibridge wanted the appearance of action, and this at least did not involve violence."

"But it gives you the public display you wanted," Wendenal shifted, "so why not come to a truce with them at the same time, secretly? If we simply meet with the outlaws—"

"You and your peace talks again." Roger turned away. "I told you. We cannot bring them here, we cannot—"

"We don't bring them here. We bring you. To them."

He stopped. It was a left turn he had not expected. The idea bounced about his skull for a bit, searching for a jagged line. "If you're about to tell me that you've known how to find them this entire time . . ."

"I don't." Wendenal raised his hands. "I swear. But Robin of Locksley and I planned to meet, no matter what, in three days' time. If you come with me, into the Sherwood . . . he'll take you to meet them. And you can end this, peacefully, with nobody knowing about it."

Surely with an hour to think upon it, Roger would find some flaw in the plan. At the moment, it admittedly seemed like a decent option. But it would only work if he was still the sheriff in three days, or else he could not honor any agreement made. *Which meant burning the prince's order.*

"Do you think you can still trust him?" Roger asked. "It did not take long for your friend Robin of Locksley to transform into this renegade Robin Hood."

"Trust me," Wendenal smiled, "we can trust him. Think of it. A lasting peace. The last act of Sheriff Roger de Lacy. Or hell," Wendenal smiled now ear to ear, "maybe you'll get to stay."

He had already chased that mirage. Roger squinted, letting the candlelight turn into perfect white pins. *But a peace would go a long way.*

"Does anyone else know of this letter?" Arable asked.

"Lady d'Oily," Roger thought aloud. "But only that I've been deposed. She doesn't know who is to replace me. Hell, she doesn't even know who wrote the damned thing."

Wendenal sucked in air. "Can you trust her?"

"Probably not." The truth tasted sour.

"But she trusts me," Arable squeaked. "I could tell her whatever you need me to, if it will buy you a little time."

"Arable, you shouldn't risk yourself—"

"It's nothing. I can do it. Anything is better than *Sheriff Gisbourne*."

The pieces fell together, then crumbled.

"No," Roger grumbled. "We are not the only ones who know. Gisbourne would undoubtedly have received a letter as well."

"But Gisbourne's out on his raids," Arable said. "If a letter came for him, he hasn't seen it yet. We just have to find it first."

Wendenal nodded, smiling. "We'd better go. Quickly."

But he didn't move, he waited for Roger to agree. And Roger was not yet certain.

"I know it's a lot," Wendenal pressed, "but imagine the good it can do. You say you've made mistakes. Now's your chance to fix them. You know this world better than I. If you tell me it's too dangerous, then I'll believe you. But imagine the gain."

Wendenal didn't know what he was asking. To go against this edict, it could have dire ramifications. Roger could obey it and still have a future, a future he had just barely begun to think about. Or he could do as Wendenal asked, fight for a week's worth of work, and potentially lose everything. Somewhere in the world, Marie was there, reminding him that the easy choice was never the right one.

"Well, fuck me," Roger said. "But I feel rather a bit like Robin Hood."

"Thank you, Roger." Wendenal hadn't called him by his given name before. Arable found her way under Wendenal's arm, and he touched his nose to hers. "Important people are depending on you." With a heavy look they left, closing the door behind them.

"Ah, the young and ambitious," Roger told the portrait of himself on the wall. "They just stole your happy retirement."

The portrait, rather predictably, scowled back, unamused. He still had two visits to make this night.

He wondered if Margery would be asleep by the time he was done with Lord Oughtibridge, and sat to craft the letter that was pivotal in his ruse. The lord and his wife, quartered two floors below, intended on leaving in the morning. Roger would see that they did so under quite different circumstances than they expected.

Halfway through the letter, the door opened behind him. Roger turned to see the two Guardsmen who had been waiting outside enter cautiously.

"My apologies! I need you to fetch something for me." He felt poorly asking them to carry the fetid chest, which had been taken to the stables but never emptied. But before he could direct them, they closed the door and slid the heavy iron barrel through its breach hinges.

Something was happening outside.

"What is it?" he asked. In his head, a thousand scenarios played out too quickly. *Gisbourne's raids had gone horribly wrong, and there was rioting outside the walls. Or perhaps one of the Guardsmen recruited from the prisons had indeed snapped and was on a murdering rampage through the castle.*

Or worse, he had overlooked something. *Someone else knew* . . . and Gisbourne was marching to take his throne. Whatever it was, Roger was suddenly thankful for the two guards he had with him, no matter how small or untrained they were.

They pulled their hoods back from their faces. The first was so young, and he looked downright terrified.

The second was a girl.

"Baron Roger de Lacy," the first could barely speak.

"The Sheriff of Nottingham," the girl finished.

"What is it?" Roger asked again.

"That was an interesting thing you said earlier," the girl's voice wavered, "about being to blame for everything that has happened lately."

"What is going on outside?" Roger insisted, but it was the wrong question. *There's nothing going on outside.* "Who are you?"

The boy's face turned to steel. "You wouldn't know if we told you."

"You're from the prisons, aren't you?" Roger looked them over, but neither responded. "I don't know what you think you know, but at this moment I am—"

"What we know," the boy said, as his face was fighting tears, "is that a child was murdered by your actions today."

"What?"

"And I promised that the man responsible," the girl took a step closer, "would pay with his life."

With one hand she brushed a long braid from her face, and with the other she pulled a short knife from her belt.

"Slow down," Roger barked. "Who was killed? I don't have the first clue what you're talking about."

"You can lie to us all you want," came the boy, "you're going to pay all the same."

He had a knife, too. Roger had rounded to the back of the table. The room was too small.

"Wait. Just wait." He cleared his throat. "Listen to me. I need you to tell me what you're talking about. What you're thinking of doing here, it would accomplish nothing. I understand you want to blame someone, but killing me, really? Think this through. If you were to kill me, there's simply going to be another sheriff, and he—"

"Then we'll kill him, too."

The boy moved, quickly, he was too close, and then Roger's vision went white. He smashed the palm of his hand at the boy, who reeled backward.

What the hell is wrong with them? Roger wanted to scream, but his throat was tight and his clothes were drenched with sweat. The boy took a step back, and the knife in his hand was dark. *He had been too close, did he hurt himself?*

But no, Roger's clothes were sopping, and he looked down and saw the blood soaking his robes by his own stomach, dripping on the floor between his feet. *No,* he thought, he needed this week. A wound like this, he could be bedridden for a month. He didn't have that time, he had too many things to do.

The girl must have been behind him. He felt her blade slip between his ribs.

His arms went numb, they were cold, *my God they were so cold,* and he was on the table, his limbs smashed its contents across the room. Except for a letter under his face that read *Lord Guy of Gisbourne.*

Lord Guy of Gisbourne.

He hadn't had a chance to burn it.

He had to burn it now. No. *He had to leave,* he had to get over the table and to the door. No, he had to talk to them. They had to understand. This wasn't an option, it simply wasn't. His fingers weren't working, he was staring at them, but they wouldn't move. With his elbow he shoved himself upright, stumbling back into the wall. He couldn't believe how cold he was, it came from within him, like nothing he had ever felt before.

The boy was breathing heavily, the girl had to hold her knife with both hands. These two weren't killers. They were only playing at it.

"You're children," he said, only realizing how much that meant as he said it.

Every color burned brighter than it had ever been. The boy was there again, the girl, too, and Roger told his arms to stop them, but they just hung at his sides as the knives bit into his chest again, once, twice, three times each, and the wall behind him disappeared.

He had so much to do, he would be late to talk to Lord Oughtibridge. For some reason he remembered Arable telling him he was a good man, and her poor face. Someone had hurt her and he'd never asked more, he had neglected to take care of her. Something slipped out of him, and then he drifted into dark.

THIRTY-EIGHT

WILLIAM DE WENDENAL

LOCKSLEY CASTLE

WILLIAM HAD ONLY BEEN here once, and briefly at that. Though the sun was yet to set, the full moon hovered over Locksley Castle, waiting. *"Peace or no peace,"* William had told Robin as they parted, *"by then we'll have done what we can."* Simple words then, that carried so much weight now.

Locksley Castle looked beaten. If stones could look soft, this castle was a wet rag flung against a craggy hill. A month ago he had only seen it after darkfall, but this time there was light enough for him to take it in. This barren stone corpse. It must have been a terrible homecoming, and his heart hurt for Robin. As much as his old friend claimed to have left his father behind, William could tell there was a softer truth there, one too tender to probe.

William clicked his tongue and pulled the horses back, sliding from the saddle to the road. He memorized a clump of trees and the crook of the path, leading the horses into the thick to the west. He'd brought one for Robin, too. William rewarded each horse with one of the apples Arable had packed.

"Peace or no peace." It almost made him laugh, that they had thought peace was an option. *We wanted to send a peace offer, and they sent assassins.* He'd been as blind as Roger to believe that, given the option, all people wanted peace. That was a dream that had died with de Lacy.

IT COULDN'T HAVE BEEN more than ten minutes after he and Arable left the baron in his office when Nottingham Castle tore itself apart. Shouts are different than screams, and these were screams that ripped through its halls. They had just broken into Gisbourne's private quarters, desperately searching for a letter that wasn't there, and they thought they had been caught. In the helpless depth of one minute, they made promises to each other, wistful wishes in what they feared were their final moments together.

But even as they whispered those hopes, Roger was already dead. Their fears simply had to catch up with reality. He lay gutted in his own blood, two stories above, murdered by two petty thieves whose vision extended as far as *I want this, so give it to me.*

The castle had been nearly deserted for the supply runs. Still, there were a dozen or so leftover Guardsmen swarming the dining hall, incensed in bloodlust—in the middle of their mob were the two murderers. But William didn't know who they were or what had happened, and he called on the men to *stop,* of all awful things. If he'd known then *whose blood* soaked their shirts, he might have killed them both on the spot himself. He might have let the crowd take them and rip their limbs from their bodies and throw their heads from the battlements.

But he hadn't. He'd raised his blade and demanded explanation, and the men obeyed. He recognized the thieves. The boy was the same arrogant cutpurse who came upon him and Robin in the Sherwood a month ago, and the girl had started the skirmish at Locksley Castle. She'd been all iron then, but now she was crying, *wailing*, from the bottom of her soul. The Guardsmen were calling them murderers, and William defended them, *by God, he defended them*. Because he still believed in peace then, back when the world made sense.

It was FitzSimon, the big furry quartermaster, who eased his way through the crowd and gently pushed William's sword down.

"It's de Lacy," the Scot whispered, his whiskers prickling William's face. "They killed de Lacy."

THERE WAS NOISE IN the woods to his left, stirring William from his heavy thoughts. He lowered to the ground. Two deer broke and skipped away, but William waited another minute to be certain he was the one that spooked them. Once he was convinced, he moved again, cautiously, low and quickly, toward the rubble that once was Robin's life.

Thieves Den. The grisly possibilities of what awaited him clouded William's mind. Either Robin was waiting for him here, or his body would be hanging over its entrance. The outlaws could be watching him even now, ready to shower William with arrows before remembering to threaten him first. Thanks to Lady Marion Fitzwalter, he knew that Robin had fortunately left the outlaws before the assassination. But they could have easily tracked him here, and there seemed to be no level of violence they were unwilling to cross.

Lady Marion. She had arrived in Nottingham yesterday, seemingly oblivious to the capital shitstorm. Had Gisbourne learned of her arrival, he would have thrown her in a dungeon and interrogated her as an accomplice to de Lacy's murder. But she had only come to Nottingham for Robin's sake, to let them know he was no longer part of the outlaws, that *Robin Hood* was gone. It was their mutual fondness for Robin, and a curious instinct that she still had much to offer, that prompted William to protect her. William convinced her to leave—hopefully to the safety of Sheffield, for if she foolishly rejoined the outlaws she would share their fate.

There was a low greystone wall enclosing the courtyard that had once been the manor's main entrance, now just an open black wound in the crumbling façade. The remaining light was at his back, and still no sign of life. William moved closer, finding patterns in the dirt, but he could not tell how old they were. Then the slightest *tink* of metal on stone came from above, and he pressed himself against the wall.

After a few pregnant seconds the noise repeated, and at the edge of sound there was movement. William crept low and away until he could spy at the openings of the manor's second story, and was immediately rewarded with a flicker of light. Faint, perhaps a lantern or candle, and another *tink* that came from a window on the west side. Could be a scavenger, could be Robin. Or could be a trap.

He discreetly slipped the knife from his boot out and buried the blade into the dirt. An old habit, in case they disarmed him within. Its handle mingled with the long strands of grass, and he alone would know it was there if he needed it. He pursed his lips and let out a low warbling whistle, a bird call they used in Richard's private guard as identification.

No answer came.

A massive hole yawned above the entranceway, a second-story room exposed from floor to ceiling, and the collapsed stonework offered an easy climb up. He shifted his baldric to keep his sword from tapping stone as he scaled the wall, tested out his footholds, and clutched at charred holes barren of their timber. Within a few seconds, William hoisted his legs up into a bedroom, recognizable only by the rotten remnants of a bed askew in its middle, crushed under the slag and debris of the ceiling.

He waited, staring into the darkest corner, letting his eyes adjust. He half expected to hear enemies inside trying to compensate for his unexpected climb. Instead there was the noise again, lazy and brief, a scraping sound, closer. He pulled his sword with one hand and side-stepped out of the bedroom into a black hall. A lone pool of light revealed a door down and to the left.

For some reason, as he crept closer, he wondered if this is what Will Scarlet had felt, sneaking down the hallway toward Roger de Lacy's office.

Step by step the sounds grew. More shuffling, the creak of wood, a brushing noise. When they came to an abrupt end, William froze, one foot in midstep, hovering over his next footfall. He opened his mouth to breathe out, and cursed the imperceptible stretching sound of his leather belt.

Then, low and warbling, a whistle came from the room.

William answered with the same call.

"William?"

The door opened drastically, shattering the pause, and Robin was there with a small metal lantern and that smile.

"Robin. Thank God you're here." William grabbed him, pounding his back with his fists, laughing. Just like that, and suddenly the large dark castle was safety. "Are you alone?"

"What? Yes," Robin answered. "I've been here a few days. I was starting to think you wouldn't show. Last night's moon looked full to me."

"A few days? How many? Two days? Three?"

"Last night was my fourth night here. *I . . .*" he raised his finger, moving back inside, ". . . am ready to leave. Glad I didn't have to go and rescue you."

William laughed, having just climbed the outside of the castle to perform a rescue of his own.

"Come here, take a look at this."

There were more candles lit inside the room, which seemed unremarkable. More rubble, burnt leftovers of furniture, an open and scorched chest on the floor, all the makings of the rather ordinary.

"This was all mine," Robin said, tapping his fingers on various bits. "Obviously I kept it in better condition, but this was my room."

"It's a good thing you weren't here when this happened," William offered, not sure what else to say.

"No, that's not what I mean. This was my room, from the day I left. It hasn't changed. He kept my room the same as when I left it." He dragged his fingers through the ash in the chest and let it trail off. Then he turned and grabbed something from the corner. "Look at this."

At first William couldn't tell what it was, a twisted mess of corners. It was a wreath, made entirely of metal, with delicate craftsmanship. A circlet of metal leaves that wove around each other, and underneath the age and soot were golds and reds and browns.

"I found it in a pile of ash, practically buried in the corner," Robin said. "He had this made for me when I was young. He told me it was about making mistakes. Or something."

"Mistakes?" William asked, inspecting it. "Looks quite well-made to me."

"No, it was more about it being a circle. About each point being decisions we make, or mistakes we make, I forget. He said that we travel in a circle, endlessly, thinking it's a straight line, but all we ever do is make the same choices again and again, in different places. I forget what the point of it was. I never really thought much about it." He put it down again, but his fingers traced its tips. "But he kept it. He kept it up."

On the door, a faint light silhouette of the wreath was barely perceptible in the wood, the area its metal had protected from flame. All William could do was nod in agreement.

"Sorry, William," Robin said, "you caught me in mid-thought. It's good to see you."

"It's good to see *you*. Four nights, you say?"

"Yes," Robin dragged out the word, and left the room to start down the hall. "I received your message, wrapped in a pretty package. But they weren't exactly interested in listening to me. So I left them a bit early, I thought that might slow them down."

William could only shake his head. "Do you want to tell me about Robin Hood?"

"That wasn't my idea," Robin chuckled, "and it turned out they were really only interested in using me for my name. They practically worshipped my father, and they wanted another Locksley to rally behind." He rapped his knuckles on another door. "They should find my brother."

William let a solemn moment pass. "You were supposed to be making things better, Robin."

"I tried. I taught them discretion. And you know I actually thought it was working, too. We were helping out the poorer communities, making a difference." Robin continued forward, down a large set of stairs at the side of the dining hall. William had been here before, when Gisbourne was held hostage at the edge of a sword. He suddenly felt terrible for having left Robin with these people at all. "But some of them wanted more. They wanted blood. I don't think I could have bred that out of them. I almost don't want to know, but . . . when I left them, they seemed eager to go get themselves killed. Have you heard anything?"

William eyed Robin for a moment. "So you didn't know? Just promise me you had nothing to do with planning what happened."

"Excuse me?" Robin smiled.

"With what happened three nights ago."

"Three nights ago I was here, I told you. What . . . what happened three nights ago?"

"Robin. They assassinated the Sheriff."

Robin's jaw dropped, and he turned away. Eventually he lowered himself and sat on the stairs halfway down, and covered his face with his hands.

"I wasn't as successful as I would have wished, either," William admitted. "But I was close. Roger de Lacy was finally willing to find a peace. That's not exactly an option anymore."

Robin spoke through his fingers. "Are you sure? Do you know who did it?"

"Will Scarlet. At least, that's the name he gave. The same one that attacked us in the forest, fiery little thing with blond hair?"

Robin nodded. "That's him."

"And his girl, too."

"Elena? Are you sure?"

"Absolutely. We caught them trying to escape."

Robin's voice caught in his throat. "They're dead?"

"No," William said, and Robin seemed oddly relieved. "They're in the prison. They killed two Guardsmen on watch and took their uniforms. The castle was nearly empty, the entire contingent was out collecting taxes. They must have walked right in. We made it damned easy for them, but that's our fault."

That's Gisbourne's fault, really. Those would be the sort of tunnel-vision mistakes a Sheriff Gisbourne would make on a daily basis.

"Those idiots," Robin whispered to himself.

"It's best you're not with them anymore. Your name is nearly synonymous with their movement at this point. I don't think I could have protected you." The best thing for Robin now was to get out of the country as quickly as possible, before he accidentally became an actual outlaw. "Do you remember how to get to their camp? It would save the Guard quite a bit of time, and probably a lot of lives."

"Yes, of course, I'll draw it out on a map. They have markings all through the Sherwood, if you know what you're looking for." He stood up, then stopped. "How will you get this to them? Is there someone with you?"

William clenched his jaw. "You'll have to go on without me."

“Don’t be silly,” Robin laughed, “I can wait here another day. Until you come back.”

“I can’t.” It was all William could say. “I still have work to do. You’ll have to go back to King Richard and inform him what’s happening here.”

“What? No . . . William,” Robin climbed back up the staircase, “we said we can’t get entangled here. I know it seems important, I know. But we’re not even supposed to be here. Richard needs us. Peace or no peace, remember?”

“I remember.”

It was so tempting. They could just get on their horses and leave, just as they’d promised, back to the beautiful simplicity of the war. Richard would thank them with promises of lands and riches he would never actually give. Already, away from the city for just a few hours, the events of the last month felt less immediate. More like a story or a dream.

“They killed the Sheriff.” Robin shook his head, eyes wide with curiosity. “Huh.”

His reaction was impersonal, William had to remember, because he had not met Roger de Lacy. To him it was indeed just a story, and he couldn’t fault that. William would have the same reaction if it was just news coming in from somewhere else. If they had never come home, neither of them would care at all.

“Do you suppose we botched this one? You think this is our fault?” Robin asked, still detached. “No way to know, I suppose. Fuck, what a month we’ve had!”

Robin grabbed his arm and pulled him down the stairs, and William surprised himself by laughing. There was a comfortable camaraderie with Robin, and it was so easy to slip into it. The two of them, back to back, against any odds. Untouchable.

“Are you thirsty? Hungry? I’m a terrible host in my own home, what can I get you?”

William was, indeed, starving. Eating had seemed a savage insult in the wake of the murder. And the apples were for the horses. Robin led him down to a smaller chamber adjacent to the dining hall, a private dining room that no longer had enough walls to be called a room. Part of the once-wall lay in the middle of the space, piling to an appropriate table height where Robin had evidently been making his meals. There was ample meat and vegetables, wrapped in cloth, for William to share.

“I’m sure it’s nothing compared to what you’ve been eating,” Robin apologized.

“It’s perfect.” William licked his fingers, thankful for every bite.

They ate. William let himself relax, though he was partially unnerved that he was able to. But there was no practical distinction between leaving now or in an hour, and there was no knowing when he’d see Robin again. They traded stories of their adventures since they’d split a month ago, and tried to top each other with tales of increasingly stupid things they’d seen. William won that competition, with the young Ferrers's proposed strategy of organizing an archery tournament.

"Wow." Robin laughed heartily. "Yeah, that would not have worked."

William let the smile linger on his face, grateful to feel such a thing again. "Oh just so you know," he realized, "I saw Marion yesterday."

Robin breathed in and sighed. "What did she say about me?"

"She said you'd be here."

He nodded. "How did she seem?"

"She was pretty angry, about the Sheriff. And at herself."

Robin continued to bob his head, chewing at his lip.

"It ended badly, then?"

"Ended?" Robin was going to make a joke, it seemed, but got lost in his thoughts instead.

"Sorry, brother," and he meant it. But he couldn't resist tagging on, "Not everyone can be as successful with the ladies as I am, you know."

"You asshole." Robin kicked him playfully in the ribs. "You've spent the last month in a castle surrounded by women, telling them stories about riding with the King, and I get stuck with the vagrant forest folk. Please tell me you're joking."

William couldn't help but laugh. "Not at all."

"How many?"

"How many girls, or how many times?"

"You asshole," he repeated, and this time William spat out food.

"Just one, just one!" he coughed as he defended himself. When Robin relented, he finished with, "but easily three or four times a day—" and then Robin was snatching all the food that was left and throwing it in a sack.

"You don't get my food anymore!"

With that, Robin and William went tripping backward and out of the room, slapping at each other and shouting insults, taking turns guarding and dashing back into the room to grab another bite of food and devour it loudly, or to pull from the wine before the other gave chase again.

When they had both resigned themselves to the floor, catching their breath, the large dining hall was a deep indigo, the full moon and clear sky pouring in through the empty gaps in the ceiling. Robin was on his back, still heaving.

"Did you bring horses? I never got ours back."

"That would be the second time on this trip," William calculated, "that you have lost the horses. But yes," he added, before Robin could retort, "I brought one for you."

"Good. We'll leave in the morning, then." Robin's laugh lingered and died.

William hoped this wouldn't be difficult. He had promised Richard he would settle this no matter the cost. And he'd made another promise, more recently. When he left Arable, when she gave him the apples, he promised he'd be back. He wouldn't break that one again.

"I was serious, Robin. I won't be going with you tomorrow. I have to deal with this."

"You *don't* have to deal with this. You *want* to deal with this. I know you do." He propped himself on an elbow. Of course he was taking it all so lightly, he was eager to leave the company of those he had spent his time with. "But things have only gotten worse in the last month. Which is exactly what I predicted."

"Did you predict they would assassinate the Sheriff?" William asked dryly. "You spent a month with them, you had no idea they were organizing something like that?"

Robin flinched. "No, they never talked about anything like that." He looked William dead in the eyes, genuinely offended. "You know I wouldn't have let that happen if I had known about it."

William chose his words carefully. "You know I believe you. But you have to admit, you've been up to some unusual things. You can't blame me for worrying about . . . about whether your priorities may have . . . shifted. Even Marion had her doubts about you."

That seemed to strike a nerve.

"What does that mean?" Robin asked. "What did she say about me?"

"Nothing." William replayed the conversation back in his mind, the *what-ifs* they couldn't ignore. "She thought perhaps you had gone back, and were responsible for it. She was worried maybe you were . . . trying to prove yourself to her."

"She actually said that?"

"Actually, she wanted me to give you a message. She said she truly hoped you had nothing to do with it, for the sake of her sister." Marion hadn't explained the message, but insisted it would mean something to Robin. And it did. His mouth gaped without an answer, he sat down and tried to shake it off, but he was rattled.

"Well I didn't," he said at last. "I didn't see it coming. Honestly William, I don't know why on earth they would do such a thing. I really don't."

This part, though, William knew. He had visited the killers in their cells yesterday morning, hoping he would lose control and strangle them. "They said there was a . . . a child that was killed."

"What? They killed a child, too?"

"No, no. One of theirs. They claimed it was revenge, for an incident in Bernesdale, they said. Some boy, some orphan boy."

Robin sat up, instantly alert. "Much?"

"Much, yes, that was the name."

Robin stood, clearly agitated by the news. "I never should have left them."

William hadn't guessed Robin would have known the child. Surely he could recognize he wasn't responsible for what happened. Robin was no more to blame than Roger de Lacy. "I'm sure you did what you could."

"No," Robin jerked, "I didn't. I was supposed to train them. I knew they had violent instincts, and I . . ." He trailed away, and his face flushed red.

William had no idea what to say. He swore there were tears forming in Robin's eyes. But Robin bit it off, he breathed in deeply and came back down.

"My brother," he said, staring elsewhere, "killed Marion's sister. Edmond was my responsibility. I was supposed to train him, I was supposed to teach him how to control himself . . . and I didn't."

"Robin," William's heart broke for his friend, "you can't put this on yourself. Whatever your brother did . . . whatever these outlaws have done . . . it's not on you. Don't do that to yourself."

But Robin grimaced. "I could have tried harder. I dismissed them as hopeless, but they didn't know what they were doing. I, of all people, should have recognized that. They have no idea . . ."

"It doesn't matter now." William stopped him from going down that route. "It's done. The best thing for them now is to go quietly, and quickly. Get a map and show me where they are, they'll be rounded up before they make it even worse for themselves."

Robin didn't move. "What will happen to them?"

Something nagged at William that he should lie, but he couldn't, not to Robin. "Scarlet and Elena will be hanged at de Lacy's funeral."

Robin shook his head. "And the others?"

"I'll do everything I can, but I don't know. Don't think about that. They've made their choices."

"Is there no possibility of keeping the peace?"

"They assassinated the Sheriff!" William hadn't meant to come off as angry, but hell if he wasn't. If King Richard had been killed in the night, Robin wouldn't be thinking of how to treat his murderers kindly. "They're not stealing jewelry anymore. They snuck into the castle with one purpose—with the intent to murder. Roger de Lacy did everything he could to give them their space, to let them their freedom. To forgive that which is forgivable. *This is not.* They'll be hunted down, imprisoned, and hanged. And they'll deserve it, Robin. You couldn't have stopped this. They're murderers and thieves, deserters and traitors. The new sheriff will not be able to turn a blind eye to them the way de Lacy did. No."

Robin's eyes narrowed, but he didn't disagree. He nodded, breathed out, and accepted it, because he had to. He chuckled, that was his way. "Who's the new sheriff?"

William didn't know why he had been avoiding this.

"I am."

FINGERS OF BLOOD, SPIDERWEBBING away from de Lacy's body. Arable entered the room behind him.

"Oh God, William," she moaned, then her face was unrecognizable, destroyed with grief.

"What the hell are you doing here?" he shouted at her, but he closed the door and barred it—*there were bloody handprints on the bar.* William's stomach lurched. He tasted copper in his mouth, it was in the air, it was in the goddamned air.

"I didn't know what was happening!" she cried, moving to the window and trying to breathe. "I thought Roger should know we couldn't find anything—"

But he didn't have time to deal with her. At any moment someone might enter the room. William thanked God he had the presence of mind to understand what had to happen. He might have minutes, or he might have seconds.

Arable's eyes couldn't leave de Lacy. "Oh God, was it Gisbourne?"

"No," William barked. He rifled through the papers on the table. Some were still sticky with blood, he had to peel them apart. "Where the hell is it?"

"Please don't yell, William."

"I'm not yelling at you," he yelled at her, and she shrieked. "Don't scream!"

He ran to her and put his hand over her mouth. He couldn't risk anyone coming until he was done. She squirmed under his palm, but then melted into him and he cradled her head into his chest.

"I'm sorry, I'm sorry, Arable, I need you to be strong, I need you to help me here. I need to find the letter I brought with me, the letter from King Richard—"

She moved before he finished saying it, plucking it from one of the cluttered shelves sunk into the stone wall, where he never would have found it. "Why, what do you need it for? What's going on?" she asked, but he was back at the table. Roger's feet were there next to him.

"We're not losing like this. Not to this."

"What do you mean?"

"To this! To this . . . insanity! It's not too late, it can't be too late."

"William slow down, you're scaring me."

"I need ink. And a quill. I'm sorry. I don't mean to scare you." Her eyes were huge, and wet, her mouth nothing but a tiny trembling dot. He wanted to comfort her, and he would. Later. "Ink."

She found it, and he had to close his eyes to focus. He had to write calmly, confidently. It was tricky to find a place on the table that was free of blood. Arable seemed to back down from her fear. "What are you writing?"

"King Richard's letters gave us royal authority on the matter of securing the supply line."

He dictated as he wrote, slowly, it helped to calm him. "I, Roger de Lacy, in respect and loyalty to the crown, of my own wit and will, allow an extension of that authority, and hereby appoint the High Sheriffcy of Nottinghamshire to Lord William de Wendenal."

He signed a name at the bottom, *Baron Roger de Lacy.*

"William."

"Wax, and his seal."

She shook her head no, only slightly.

"Arable."

"You can't do this. It's too dangerous."

"It's the same risk I asked him to take."

"And look what happened!"

"I only need a week. We can still do it." He folded the parchment and slammed his fists into the table. "His wax and seal!"

But she had them already, she was holding the wax over a candle.

Not in vain, Roger. He savored a long final look down at de Lacy's body, his face obscured, his hands twisted. William wished he could have seen his face one more time. Above, the painting on the wall scowled downward, looking at something on the table.

Shit. Almost forgot.

He peeled the letter from Prince John off the table, the despicable command that had started everything this night. When they were finally safely away, he put it in Arable's hands.

"Burn it."

"ROGER DE LACY WAS leaving anyway. He was tired, tired of everything. But he was surrounded by lackeys. When he met me, he wanted to groom me for the position. I refused, of course, but apparently he made it official. They found the assignment in his office the night he died. Signed and sealed. His last official act was to name me his successor."

The lie came out easily, he had already told it so many times in the last two days. But it tasted sour when he told it to Robin.

"That's insane," Robin cut in. "You'll have to turn it down. We can't stay. You can't take over as sheriff. We have our orders."

"That's just it, Robin, we have our orders. And, whether I asked for this or not, I have the opportunity here to really . . ." he searched for the word, but he was too afraid Robin hadn't believed him, ". . . to really *do* them. I could fix a lot of things that led to this supply problem in the first place."

"You can't be the sheriff." Robin laughed at him, but his eyes were serious. "We're glorified bodyguards. You think they'll let you run the county? This isn't like putting on the crown for a day."

Actually, the similarities were haunting. In Acre, William had taken on the warcrown when Richard couldn't, and that leadership had saved countless lives. Here he could do the same. "Don't sell us short, Robin. My father is well known in Derbyshire, of no small title, and we are personal advisors to the King himself."

Robin was clearly jealous, in light of his time with the rebels. Going from soldier to sheriff was a hell of a leap. If their roles had been reversed, William would have argued against it as well. But jealousy was just an emotional pettiness, and Robin was better than that.

"As I said," William continued, "I can't leave. I brought you a horse, I only came to say goodbye, I'm afraid. I didn't want you to wait around for me. And I needed your help."

He tapped the map, the one that Robin still had not marked. He was being unusually evasive on that point. William knew this wasn't what Robin wanted to hear. He wouldn't want to travel alone, or to return to Richard as a failure.

"What are you going to do with that?" Robin jabbed his finger at the map.

"As I said, we'll round them up. For their own good, Robin."

"You'll throw them in a dungeon. For their own good?"

"Are we talking about the same people? If they hadn't killed the Sheriff, there would have been a peace. I was working on a peace. But as it is, I'll have to play this through."

"Play this through? By hunting down women and children?"

"Thieves and murderers."

"Who are fighting for their own survival—"

"By killing the Sheriff?" William cut him off. Robin was grabbing at straws, he had to realize that.

"They're good people, William," he pleaded, but half-heartedly. "Most of them are families, chased off their land, or have lost too much. You can't punish all of them for the acts of a few. Their situation is not their fault—it goes back a year ago, when the Sheriff raised taxes."

"I know where this goes back. It goes back to when your father incited a rebellion." William instantly regretted it. But the name *Walter of Locksley* had been said too many times in the last month. The great instigator. Robin's father had built his own private nation in the middle of England. Walter of Locksley taught the common people that they were allowed to ignore their country's rules. Robin should consider himself lucky he was not branded a traitor's son.

"What did they tell you about him?" Robin asked.

"Your father started this war, Robin. These outlaws, your father's outlaws . . . this was his plan all along."

"You didn't know him." Robin paced the room now, back and forth in front of the crumbled walls and the moonlight. He shook his head—he almost wasn't even speaking to William anymore.

William had to find the words to go back, to let Robin see. He could explain this all perfectly well, if he only had the right words, but it had gotten too complicated. Too personal. "Forget it. It's not important. Let's just remember what we're here for, alright? You're going to ride for the shore. You're going back to Richard."

Robin's lips bulged forward, as if they would not let him utter his next words. At length he swallowed and looked William in the eye with a newfound certainty. "I'm not."

"You can't wait for me forever."

"I'm not waiting." Robin's eyes were strained, he closed them slowly. "You're going to see this through? Fine. So will I. I can help. I can still effect a peace on my end."

"Peace is not possible anymore!" William blurted, and it echoed through the hall. "Nottinghamshire cannot have a peace until your outlaws are gone! All of them! There's no way around this, I'm sorry. Are you going to tell me where their camp is, or not?"

Robin shut his lips tight.

"I thought you would be happy to help," William said. "I could have gotten this information from Marion, but I didn't want to put her through that."

"Don't you dare," Robin said. "Don't you *dare threaten her–*"

"I'm not threatening her! Listen to me, Robin! You can't help these people!"

"I can, damn it! I have to."

They stared at each other. The sun had gone down. Their breath turned to steam, alternating clouds that pulsed through the room like a heartbeat. William couldn't believe what he was forced to say.

"Robin, if you choose to join them, I can't . . . I won't be able to protect you."

Robin stood still, and William was terrified of what his answer would mean. He could hear his own blood pounding in his ears. He squinted to keep his eyes dry.

Please don't do this.

"What's the price of your peace, William?" Robin's voice was tiny and hurt. "Would you kill me for it?"

How the hell did it get this far? What had happened to him in the last month? Good God. William's heart could have dropped out of his chest. *Am I in danger?*

The question hung heavy in the air. *"Would you kill me for it?"*

William was chilled by his own response. "Would you make me?"

Robin shook his head. His body was in shadow. "Give me more time."

"I can't. Your charge is to return to King Richard."

"I disagree."

Such a simple phrase, but it was insubordination on the light side, treason on the heavy. Just like his father. "Are you leaving your post?" William had to speak fiercer to keep his voice from trembling. *"Are you deserting your king?"*

Robin met him in fury. *"Are you?"*

And then there was nothing left to say. He couldn't convince Robin. He couldn't force him to leave, not without violence. William's mind was drawn to remember the knife he concealed in the dirt outside.

"Out of respect," William forced himself to say, "I'll let you go. But if I ever see you again . . ."

"Don't be silly." Robin backed up, into pitch black. "You won't see me coming."

Then, elaborately and deeply, he bowed to William, his face glancing a streak of moonlight as he dipped. "King William, Sheriff of Nottingham."

"King Robin," William choked.

But Robin clicked his teeth as shadows devoured his features.

"Robin Hood."

And then he was gone.

PART VI

THE DAMNED CONSEQUENCES

THIRTY-NINE

MARION FITZWALTER

THE OAK CAMP

THE TUNE WAS SLOW and sad. Slow, because Tuck could barely pluck out the notes with his swollen, broken arm. Sad, because that's all they knew.

> Now is the knight gone on his way,
> The game he thought, full good.
> And when he looked on Bernesdale,
> He walked on, Robin Hood.
> And when he thought on Bernesdale,
> On Scarlet, Much, and John,
> He blessed them for the best company
> That e'er he had come.
> "Take thy bow in hand," sang Robin,
> "Late Much shall be with thee,
> And so shall William Scarlet,
> Let no man die for me."

The fire was dying but nobody could be bothered to add a log, or to stoke its embers. It left a low smolder that changed directions at its own whim and burned the eyes, so each of them kept their face turned away.

Marion almost had not come to the Oak Camp at all. She had doubted her ability to control herself, certain she would burst into tears or fury upon seeing them. In the end she was glad to visit one last time, even if just to say goodbye. They had planned a short service for Much in the morning, which would be more terrible to miss than to endure. But she could not help them anymore. It didn't matter that Will and Elena had acted on their own, disappearing after Bernesdale. Everyone associated with this group was a traitor now in the eyes of Nottingham.

That judgment included Marion. She had traveled to the castle, ignorant of everything, and luck alone had put her in the company of William de Wendenal. He ushered her safely away again, warning that the Captain would likely arrest her on sight. Whatever fleeting power she once held was gone, and she had no idea how deep was the hole into which she had fallen.

"Why are you singing about Robin still?" grumbled John Little, looking up into the sky.

"The people like him," Tuck explained.

It was true that the commoners liked the stories of Robin Hood. But that, too, would have to end now. It was one thing to spread scandalous stories of barely gentlemanly conduct with traveling ladies—it was quite another to idolize an assassin. The public already attributed Roger de Lacy's murder to their fictitious Robin Hood, not knowing Robin had abandoned them. Marion wondered if Tuck could insert Robin's departure into the lyrics. He'd have to find an elegant rhyme for "your fastest fucking horse."

John coughed. "You should be singing about Much." It wasn't a suggestion, and there was no point in arguing with him. For some, grief was a boulder cascading down the side of a mountain. There is no stopping it, no slowing it, and no telling how much damage it would do along the way. All one can do is stand aside and help pick up the pieces when things begin to settle. "There's some generosity, I think, in that his parents weren't alive to see this happen."

Tuck let his fingertips brush the lute's strings. "Did you know his parents, John?"

"I did not."

"Nor I," Tuck admitted. "I think the only person who knew them was Much, and he never spoke of them. Which means they're gone now, too. So yes, I'll be singing a song about Much. So that people don't forget."

"You mentioned Will twice," Alan's voice cracked. The young man had spent much of the last few days on his own, vanishing into the woods for hours on end. Every time he returned, it was as if there were somehow less of him. "But what about Elena? Why don't you sing about her?"

Tuck nodded. "The song's not done yet. Perhaps you could help me with some of it?"

But Alan just shook his head and swatted at the smoke.

Marion did what she could to visit each campfire, to give heartfelt apologies, to explain that they would need to disband. Some of the women treated the news like a death sentence. Mothers like Amelia and Fionne had long sacrificed everything for their children, and had nothing left to give. Marion did what she could to help, but a handful politely declined her company. That, perhaps, stung the greatest. For all her best intentions, she had let them down. Lord Walter's death was indeed for nothing.

Before she found a bedroll for the night, she visited with Friar Tuck in his tent, sharing the glow of the last wedge of a fat candle. She had leaned on the man for sound wisdom over the years, but rarely for advice on faith.

"Funerals and weddings make everyone devout." Tuck warmed his fingertips over the waning flame. "Something about lives coming together or being pulled apart makes most people pray harder, to seek guidance."

"They'll come to you," Marion said, "but what can you do? How can you ease this pain?"

"I listen," he smiled. "Grief is the only thing I've ever known that grows smaller by being added upon."

She reached out to him. It couldn't be easy, to put aside his own mourning, to ignore his broken arm to heal others.

Upon being touched his eyes sprang up to hers, the wrinkles in his face all sharpened. "Funerals and weddings, I see them as uniquely human milestones. The Lord can nurture love in a man's heart, but it takes two people pledging themselves to another to make a wedding. The Lord can put reason in a man's mind, but it is always the *man* who abandons it when he takes a life in wrath. Funerals and weddings aren't holy moments. The Lord is only a bystander to these. They are proof we can do things, great or horrible things, completely without Him. Those aren't the days to praise Him, they're the days we should fear Him, and the gifts He's given us."

He blew out the candle.

TUCK KEPT THE FUNERAL service short and humble. He read from Romans and called for silent prayer three times—once for each soul that had not returned. The longest, of course, for Much. There was some less-than-silent shuffling during the silences for Will and Elena. There were those who blamed them for what would come next. Marion had few arguments why they were wrong, but that did not lessen the blame on her own shoulders.

Some were already gone. The widow Fionne and her daughter Maege had been seamstresses for Walter of Locksley, and had mended every torn shirt and cooked many meals without complaint. They slipped away at the end of the funeral with the rest of their family, without even giving farewells. Marion wondered if they were afraid someone would try to stop them. Gilbert with the White Hand had vanished like a ghost. Perhaps he was never even there at all.

Others wavered, half-packed, unsure what to do or where to go. The kindly Amelia feared for her children. "Whatever it is that started in Bernesdale, we all know it won't end there. We can't fight. What do we do?" Her husband Baynard had been Lord Walter's chamberlain, but was arrested on the day of the fire and never heard from since. Her oldest boy Norman was Much's age, and the comparison terrified Amelia. Her little girl El was too young to understand any of it. Marion asked her to have faith, to pray, but her words tasted hollow.

A flurry of ravens tormented the group with their ceaseless cawing, as if even the Sherwood would no longer tolerate their lingering.

"WHO DO I PRAY for?" Marion asked Tuck, watching another family disappear past the treeline. "I want to pray for Will and Elena, to give them whatever peace is left. But Roger de Lacy had a wife, he had family. Do you suppose they pray for Will to suffer? Whose prayer speaks loudest?"

Tuck shook his head. "That's not how prayer works. At Bernesdale, when they broke my arm, I prayed for myself. *For myself.* My face was in the dirt, praying I would get out of there alive, and I didn't even see what happened to Much. Do you suppose what happened to Much was my fault, because the Lord was taking care of me instead of him?"

"Of course not."

"Of course not," Tuck said firmly. "You're asking the same questions every man and woman has ever asked. But prayer is not for asking things from God. Not as I see it. Prayer is for giving. It's for offering yourself to God, for devoting yourself to whatever it is He wants of you. And whatever that is, all we can do is accept it. Through prayer we are closer with Him, which gives us strength. But that's only half of it. We give God strength as well, when we give of ourselves, unselfishly. Why ask Him for His help, when you can give Him yours instead?"

They were fine words, but for another time. A panic swelled in her, born of exhaustion, at the idea of giving any more. For once, she would have preferred one of Tuck's empty, pretty stories. She would have liked to simply hear it was going to be alright, even knowing that it wouldn't be.

"I WANTED TO SAY goodbye," Alan said softly, standing with his pack slung over a shoulder. It was a fine day, with clear skies that bathed their field in even light, marred only by a small lump in the ground with a crude cross. "I wanted to say thank you."

Marion would have thanked him in return, but she was too weary. "You're not going off on your own, are you? You're valuable, Alan. Find a group, go with them. They could use you."

Alan just balled his face up and shrugged his shoulders, over and over until he had decided that was his answer.

"Alan?"

"I'm no good at it," he scoffed. "Not without Will. I'm just playing at it. I never really knew what I was doing."

There was indeed little about Alan that could be called brave. But he had lived at Locksley. He'd been part of the group since before the fire. He had heart in him, perhaps too much. Perhaps that was what called him away now.

"I'm sorry about them," Marion said. "I know what they meant to you."

"I could have left earlier, you know. I wanted to, I was going to. When we had that Guardsman here, Jon Bassett? He said I could go with him, he said it would be safe for any of us. It would have been safe."

That seemed like a lifetime ago now. "Why didn't you leave?"

Alan's eyes were wet. "Will. Elena. They were here." Marion's heart ached for him. "Now they're gone, and now it's not safe anymore."

She met his eyes. Alan seemed so young at times, so unsure of his place in the world. He had never found his own strength. "What will you do?"

Alan watched a bird fly from one end of the field to the other, then he just shrugged. "I'll work. I was good at that." His arms opened for an embrace, and Marion stood and gave it to him. "It was silly of us, thinking this would last? That we'd get away with it?"

But he didn't wait for a reply, he turned sharply and started away, glancing sheepishly over his shoulder after a few paces to see if anyone else was watching him leave.

"AND WHAT ABOUT YOU?" John Little asked, his face stone and serious. It was no surprise he would stay the longest, doing his best to see everyone off safely, including her.

"I don't know," Marion answered, searching for anything to inspire some small cheer within him. The muscles in her cheeks strained to remember how to smile properly. "I could go to Sheffield and wait, but I wonder if there's any point. I worry that they're waiting for me. I think the safest thing would be to go home, back to Essex, and hope that none of this follows me there."

"But you won't do that," John predicted, "until you know you've tried your last here."

That time may have already come and gone. A crippling fear suggested she still had every opportunity to make things even worse. If every one of her choices so far had brought them to this point, she should have the wherewithal to realize her choices weren't helping anyone.

"Where will you go?" she asked him back.

"Don't worry about me." His answer was quick, and it brought tears to her eyes. Because she knew he had no other answer. He would stay until everyone else was gone, and then it would just be John Little alone in the woods, with nowhere to go, until the snows buried him.

FORTY

WILLIAM DE WENDENAL

NOTTINGHAM CASTLE

WORDS WERE IMPORTANT.

William always preferred to think he was fairly good with words, better at least than average. He selected his words with care and tried to stay away from vagueness or exaggeration. He was no wordsmith, of course. Meeting an expert like Roger de Lacy reminded him of how pedestrian he must sound, and he was never able to craft a sentence together to make it sound like art. Still, he was careful not to *mis*speak, at least.

So when he said, "I am surrounded by enemies," it was not a clever turn of phrase. Coming from a man who had literally stood in the center of a foreign city and held his blade against a swarming mob, he knew precisely what those words meant.

And frankly, he would trade Nottingham for Acre.

"This was suicide," he said, taking a rare chance to breathe, his face pressed to the fresh air slipping through the crenel in the cold stone walls of the keep's staircase. He felt Arable's hands on his back, patting him, rubbing back and forth as if she could abate his woes the way one pets a dog. "I should have left with Robin. Once I realized he wouldn't help me . . . I didn't think this through."

"You're doing the right thing," she whispered, petting him again.

"It would have been the right thing if Robin had helped me." He slapped the stones. "If I had apprehended his group, I might have had a shot at this. I couldn't imagine he would choose not to help."

"You can still do this."

"I don't know that I can." William glanced down the staircase, but he had not heard anything. He just wanted to twist away, so that she'd stop petting him. "Nobody believes de Lacy appointed me his successor, and why should they? A sudden reappointment the same night he's murdered? It was stupid. I didn't think it through. I look like a damned collaborator! Nobody believes it, they're dying to challenge me on it."

"They're shaken," she said, her voice soft. "Nobody knows what to do. You rose up and took control. They'll listen to you. People just need to be told what to do. They're scared."

"They know I'm a fraud," William whispered. "And what's the point? Why am I even trying to be the sheriff, with what has happened? I wanted to bring Robin's people in for peace talks, and that's not an option anymore. I should just leave this to Gisbourne. He'll—"

"Don't say that." Her voice turned to ice. She turned him around briskly.

Arable's face was red and puffy, which made the scars stand out all the more. "He's why you have to do this. You're the only competent person in Nottingham right now. Of course that's going to frustrate you. But it's the reason we need you."

William was humbled by his own selfishness. "I'm sorry. I know. It's just . . . it's just so much."

He hadn't even explained the depths of the situation to her. The sheriffcy was in absolute chaos. William had hoped to reshape the tax laws in ways that would feel just to the landholders as well as prevent them from abusing their vassals. But neighboring lords like Lord Oughtibridge were already in a state of revolt, and the city's master tax assessor Arnold de Nottoir apparently had no records at all of their individual debts. It was absolute anarchy, and it would take William months to set it straight. And that was only if he were allowed to focus on such problems.

At the moment everyone wanted to secure themselves from the threat of *Robin Hood,* and de Lacy's funeral had to be arranged. William found no help from anyone regarding either problem. The majority of people saw him as a usurper, potentially complicit in de Lacy's death, and took little effort to hide their animosity. Some were already actively working against him. Others swung the other way, feeding him fake smiles and compliments to reap benefits from his sheriffcy as quickly as possible. None of them, including William himself, expected him to last a week. In light of the assassination, the appointment of a legitimate sheriff would undoubtedly come from someone above. *And they were right.* Prince John would send men to enforce his previous edict, and then Sheriff Guy of Gisbourne would become a reality.

"I can't believe Robin could think I wanted this," he groaned, forcing himself to breathe. He had to focus on one problem at a time.

"Just tell me what I can do," Arable said.

"Keep doing what you're doing," he replied. "Get Lady d'Oily on my side. Convince her that de Lacy appointed me legally. If I can win her, I can win her husband. One at a time, I can start gaining some support."

Arable responded with only a small hum.

"I'm sorry," he said again, turning and taking her head in his hands, pulling her to his chest. Her arms wrapped around him and she squeezed tightly. "I don't mean to ask you to do anything you're not comfortable with. But if you could keep me informed, with whatever you hear, it would help."

She released him. "Right. I'll keep you informed."

"Thank you."

He returned his gaze out the sliver window, out to the city of Nottingham beyond the castle walls. He thought of his father. William had always assumed he might take his father's place in Derby someday. Ironically, his father now owed him fealty.

His father, he startled to remember. He had been considering mining his father for any news of Arable's family, for her sake. But he'd never done it. And if he were to write now, he'd have to explain everything else that was happening, and then his father would come to Nottingham. He would be a guaranteed ally, which William desperately needed.

But William would have to hide Arable from him.

No, even his own father could not aid him.

"I need to get Robin's outlaws," he said solemnly. "That will gain me all the political purchase I need."

"What about Robin?" Arable asked.

"I think I can protect him," he said. "Once his group is arrested, he won't have any excuses to stay. I'll be able to get him back to the war."

But there was no way to communicate with Robin now, even if William had the words to persuade him. Sending Arable out in a carriage hoping to get robbed would not work a second time, and if Robin meant not to be found he was going to be successful at it.

But there were exactly two people in the castle who knew where to look.

THEY CALLED IT THE Rabbit Hole, apparently, a square cell in the center of a small courtyard in the middle bailey, whose only door could not possibly open from within. Inside that cage was a gullet staircase leading down into the caves below Nottingham Castle's sandstone base, into the catacomb of underground prisons. It held a single occupant at the moment. A beast of a Guardsman named Marshall had deposited her before withdrawing down into the tunnels again.

William had to ready himself at the sight of her. Such a small thing, so thin, but she had driven a knife into Roger de Lacy's chest a dozen times.

"Good morning, Elena."

"A good morning? Did you die?" she asked him, out of the corner of her eye, as if she could not be bothered by his presence.

"No."

"Then not good enough."

Of course she was impertinent. She had decided she was the victim.

"And what do you suppose would happen if I died this morning?" William aimed for an indifferent tone, the one that all inquisitors adopted. He wasn't sure he was successful at it. "You've started a career in killing sheriffs, so am I next? I presume you thought this out. Baron de Lacy is dead. You were successful. Congratulations. But you don't strike me, at this exact moment, as much of a winner."

"You're welcome." She smiled at him.

"So what were you hoping would happen? Am I to stop all taxes in the entire county and start giving out coin for free? As you and Robin do? If I die this morning, will the next sheriff do just that?"

"This is a nice castle." Elena glanced up at the keep towering above her. "It must have nice beds."

As much as he wanted to reach through the bars and strangle her, he needed the information she had. "Is that why you killed Roger de Lacy? For his bed?"

She scoffed, and it drove a piercing iron nail into William's patience. Her scoff said she thought Roger's life was hers to take, for whatever minor trifles she'd suffered. She had not known the man. He'd just been a symbol to her of the world she saw as an enemy. Bitter little souls like Elena Gamwell were born every day, while a Roger de Lacy came along once in a century.

"I'm not going to play your game." She smirked. "You and Robin of Locksley, working together. Doing damage on opposite ends, fighting your way into the middle. Sorry for disrupting your little war."

"War, now?" William actually laughed. "Girl, don't pretend you know a thing about war. You imagine yourself on one side, and the Nottingham Guard on the other, and that's all it takes to constitute a war? This is no war, Elena. This here . . . this is a holiday. What a luxury when paying your taxes is your greatest concern. I've spent my time at the brink of humanity, at the war's edge, where civilization ends. Real war. You probably can't even dream of it." He thought of the dumbfounded citizens of Acre, rioting on a whim, getting cut down in their own streets, in their own homes. That was where Elena's tactics would lead. "I promise you, killing people never solves anything."

She didn't answer. She was staring at a leaf on the ground. Eventually, "I agree, more death won't help anything. I can save you two dead bodies. Let us go."

That's what he needed, her plea for survival. "I can't do *two,*" William said casually, in a way he hoped might catch her attention. He lowered his voice, conspiratorially, such that even Marshall might not be able to hear him at the base of the staircase. "But I may be able to help *you.* Perhaps you're willing to bargain."

Frankly, escaping the gallows to spend the rest of her life in a cell was a poor trade, but she might be young enough to think otherwise.

"Willing to bargain?" she asked with feigned innocence, a mocking *I'm just a girl and I don't understand* tone.

She didn't want to be patronized, so William tried at the truth. "You killed the wrong man. Sheriff de Lacy did more to help the people of Nottingham than you could possibly understand, but you killed him before he could finish what he started. The man you should hate, the man who killed that boy of yours, Much? His name is Lord Guy of Gisbourne. You put a sword to his throat. Taking it away may have been the biggest mistake of your life. He's a ruthless one, that, with more support here than I. He has the desire to take this role of sheriff from me, and he may have the ability, too. He will storm into the Sherwood, he will hunt your people and kill them like dogs, he'll parade their corpses through the towns. Our rich friends will hail him as succeeding where Roger de Lacy and I failed. His family is far more influential than mine. This is inevitable. Which means my only option is to beat him to it."

"You want me to help you kill my friends?" she asked dumbly, but he could tell she had wavered. She was impulsive, but not without some intelligence. "What sort of an offer is that?"

"Not kill. Arrest. They'll stand trial, and only the men. The women and children will be left alone, I can promise that. It is a far better option than what

Gisbourne will do with them. With a little time, most of your people will receive leniency. Some time in the prisons, yes, but nobody dies."

"Except Will."

"Scarlet?" William scowled. "Do yourself a favor and forget about him. He'd already be dead if we didn't need to make a show of killing him. A lot of important people will come to watch the Sheriff's murderer die. But nobody outside these walls knows there were two killers. And besides, a woman on the rope is a hard sight."

Elena rolled her head. "Will's is the only life I'm 'willing to bargain' for."

William brushed himself off and stood taller, that she would have to look up at him. He dropped any pretense of civility. "Let's not mistake this situation for something it isn't. There is no scenario in which Will walks away, not one. You two snuck into this castle and assassinated the Sheriff. Will isn't in prison because *I'm* a terrible person, he's in prison because *he* is. Death is exactly what he deserves. Hell, it may be what you deserve as well, but at least do me the favor of pretending it was all Will's idea. There's no bargain that gets him out of that cell until he goes straight to the gallows. That's not how real life works. If he doesn't hang, I would be seen as the most incompetent sheriff in England."

"Then your competence is the price of peace." She stepped up to the bars, her breasts pushed against them, just barely. William tried not to look. "You're asking me to sacrifice my friends, and you're unwilling to sacrifice your reputation?"

"*I'm asking you to save your friends!*" he spat. He shouldn't have. She shouldn't have been able to rile him, but he could feel the potential for success slipping deeper into the earth than the cells below. "Goddamn it, we can help each other here. I am trying to strengthen my position, to keep Gisbourne away from you, don't you see that? I've got everyone after me, I don't have enough men, and if I lose this position, you lose your life. My reputation is the only thing that keeps you alive. So yes, it is paramount. I wouldn't expect you to understand."

"What *would* you sacrifice for your peace, then?" she asked, raising an eyebrow. Her fingertips gently traced the bars. "Would you sacrifice a friend? A lover?"

Robin. Arable. "Only if I had no other choice. And you have no—"

"Then I pity you." She leaned back, fingers curled around the iron. "I, too, want peace. But I want peace *for* my friends, and *for* my lover. I would sacrifice anything for them, but *not them.* Without them, there's no reason to fight at all. I wouldn't expect *you* to understand."

There was no point in talking to her anymore. She was ruled by her scorn. William could try with Will Scarlet, but he would have even less to bargain with. No, this strategy was a dead end, and he did not have the time to entertain it further. Catching the thieves was the surest method of solidifying his position, but there were other avenues at his disposal. Different enemies to corner, different allies to embrace.

He turned to leave, pausing only to offer one final threat, just for the empty fun of it. "If I catch your friends without your help, I will hang them all."

She let go of the bars and dropped to the floor, crossing her legs. “I killed the Sheriff, alone. Will is an innocent man. Hang me, and let him go.”

“You give up your life for a dead man. Tell me, where is the great sacrifice in that?”

She smiled, cruelly. “We may still surprise you.”

FORTY-ONE

MARION FITZWALTER

THE OAK CAMP

"ANSWER ME THIS," MARION asked Tuck, warming her fingertips at the nearly depleted tallow candle within his tent. "Do you hold that God is all-knowing?"

"He must be," Tuck answered, "for He is God."

"And do you hold that God is all-powerful?"

"Again, He must be. If He were not all-powerful, He would not be God."

"And all-caring? Does He love us all, every one of us?"

"He does, despite our mistakes and our sins, for all of us can be redeemed."

"I can't believe you," Marion sighed, wishing that the stories from her childhood could actually be true. "I could believe any two of the three, but not all of them. He may be all-powerful and all-caring, but perhaps He cannot see everything that happens. Or He may be all-caring and all-knowing, but lacks the power to intervene. Or if He is all-knowing and all-powerful, then He clearly doesn't care. What happened to Much . . . how can you explain that? It wouldn't happen if God knew about it, cared about it, and was able to stop it."

Tuck nodded, as always, but his smile was personal and painful. "I sought those sorts of answers myself once. In a lot of places. In my travels I've spent time with Jews, pagans, Muslims, and stranger types, and a colorful variety of sects within each one. The White Monks at Fountains Abbey claim the key to revelation is in isolation. I shared the road with a Carmelite Friar named Pantaleo for some time, preaching the power of building communities. None of them had all the answers, of course. They can't. If the answers were to be had, then we wouldn't have to call it faith. There will always be doubt, and that's good! It's what keeps us open to other people, to other ideas. The moment someone thinks their beliefs are facts, they become dangerous. It is uncertainty itself that makes true devotion possible. The divine is strongest within its mysteries."

Marion watched the lone flame flicker against the weight of their breath. "That's not much of an answer."

"Well it's not much of a question, really." He smirked. "You make your case for His three qualities, but you assume that He cares for things we care about, knows things the way we know things, and is powerful in the way we describe power. But we cannot know any of this. We cannot, and we should not. You want to describe Him with these three aspects, to make Him more human, but He is not. If we do not understand why terrible things happen, that is our failing, not His. That is the time to stay true to Him. It's the only time it really matters."

Marion breathed in, and reached out for his good hand, finding it as cold and stiff as her own. He was right about at least one thing, that there were no solid answers to be had. *"Powerful in the way we describe power"*—if there was some other version of power out there, she did not know what it was. She had used every power available to her, and half the power that wasn't, and still come out wanting. "I admire your optimism. But you want to tell me that the best answer is that there is *no* answer. How is that supposed to make someone feel better at a time such as this?"

"Honestly," Tuck's eyes twinkled, "how could it *not?*"

IT WOULD BE THEIR final dinner together around the campfire. Across the flames, John Little closed his eyes. Next to him, the memory of Will and Elena bowed their heads as well. Alan would have been next, grasping his knuckles together, his eyes closed too tightly. Much would have lowered his head but peeked around with one eye open.

Marion had exhausted her last bits of time trying to group people together, hoping to aim them in safe directions. Most were gone already, including the families that kept to themselves. Those who had not yet left would depart by morning.

Arthur and David, bless their hearts, had stuck it out to the last. They kept the fire hot, they helped the others pack, without judgment. Even now, Arthur brought her an extra blanket for her legs, for which she quietly thanked him. He ground his jaw and breathed in heavily, stepping back as if he knew it was the last task he'd ever do for her. Those two would pick their own way tomorrow, as they'd done before Locksley.

In some morbid way, she'd been successful. She had wanted to build a community of people who had a say in their own governing, who could choose their own futures. As they scattered now into the wind, their decisions were at least their own. No master to protect them meant no one to save them, either.

Whatever it was she and Lord Walter had tried to do, this was the cruelest version of it.

Marion closed her eyes and surrendered to her limitations. Her muscles went limp, and she could feel neither the warmth of the fire nor the bite of the cold night. She gave everything she could. She tried to hold onto the small morsels of advice Tuck had given her, despite her own constant shortcomings.

She didn't want an answer, or a sign, and she prayed for nobody's safety or health. All she did was offer herself.

She prayed there was some greater plan, some greater power, that she simply hadn't seen yet.

And she prayed she'd be wise enough to recognize it when it came.

Perhaps the wind stilled just a bit, or perhaps the fire glowed brighter for a moment, or perhaps the sighs of the woods all found the slightest peace at the same time, but Marion felt that there could still be some hope. Beneath it all, there had to be hope.

"Hullo, boys! You'll never believe who I found!"

The voice was Alan-a-Dale's, returning from deep within the woods. Stomping loudly. He was not alone.

When he was close enough to the fire to be seen, he dropped his pack to the ground and winked. Behind him were a handful of those who had left in the last few days, led by none other than Robin of Locksley.

Marion's stomach leapt, though she couldn't tell if it was furious or excited. Thankfully she refrained from any outward reaction. Robin didn't deserve that.

His face was simple, earnest. Humility was not a face she'd seen on him before. "I heard about Bernesdale," he said.

A grim silence met him. "You'd be headstrong turning around then," Little grumbled, head still down. "Along with everyone else. Those that are still here, we're out of options."

"You're probably right. But with your permission, I'd like to stay and help."

"There's nothing to help, did you hear me?" Little pulled himself to his feet with his staff and breathed deeply. "You've an opportunity to see yourself right with the King. No man or woman here would pass on that. Nobody judges you for it. Not one of us would stay, not one, if we could walk away and put on a crown. You'd be first fool to give that up."

Robin had this way about him, this disarming charm that couldn't be taught. If Marion had smiled the way Robin smiled and spoken as confidently, she still wouldn't have half of it. It was how Robin had earned their trust in only a month's time. It was probably how the son of a forgotten lord in Nottingham had come to be the right hand of the King. When Robin smiled it was as if he was letting you in on a personal secret, and it made anyone feel special and wanted, and *important.* Robin made people feel they could be something more than they were. Not by telling them as much, but by making them feel they had *earned* it.

"I know, John," he said through that smile. "But given the company, I'd rather be an outlaw than a king."

John melted. He'd wanted to, he just needed an excuse. "There it is, then. Welcome back."

They grabbed at each other, pounded their fists on each other's backs, but held a little longer in quiet recognition of what had passed. Others stepped up individually to welcome Robin as well. David of Doncaster smacked Robin's face and swore he knew he'd return. Arthur complained he'd lost a bet, but admitted to be glad of it. All the while Robin eyed Marion, but she did not rise. She folded her hands over her chest and watched, to let him know that it would not be so easy this time.

"Catch me up," Robin sat, and suddenly there was order. The firepit was a council, and they spoke in turns and with purpose. Marion marveled at the change. They skipped what happened at Bernesdale, being still too tender, but John described in detail their flight back to the camp and the days that followed.

"What Will and Elena did was dangerous." Robin paced around the fire. "Not just for themselves, but for everyone here. The problem with being invisible is that we'll all be held accountable for each other's actions. Every one of us could be hanged for the death of the Sheriff, no matter how uninvolved we were. But don't forget, that door swings both ways. Every act of kindness, every victory, is distributed to all of us as well. So. We need a plan."

"A plan?" Tuck's voice was incredulous, and mirrored Marion's own silent reaction. "The plan is we hide, and hope for the best."

"With all respect, Friar, that's simply not an option now."

"It's the only option," Arthur protested. "There's barely any of us left."

Robin flashed a whimsical smile. "You haven't left the camp for days then, I'm guessing?" All around, he was greeted with blank stares. "You couldn't be more wrong, Arthur. There's more of you than ever now."

"What do you mean?"

"Word traveled fast about the Sheriff. He wasn't exactly a popular man. Every village I've been to, there's a crowd ready to rise up. Ready to join. What Will and Elena did was rash . . . but it tipped the scales. The people of Nottingham are ready to fight."

While a rush of excitement breathed into the crowd, Marion cursed herself. This encouraging news was most welcome, but it was the sort of information she should have already known. Once again, the time she spent in the Oak Camp had cost her. She should have known about this swelling of support in the villages, but she'd spent all her time licking her wounds. She vowed not to be blindsided again.

"How do you think Robin found me?" Alan was saying, with a rare glow of confidence. "I was some sort of hero out there, everyone I met wanted to know more!"

"We've got the momentum, and we have to seize it," Robin said. "Now more than ever. There's a new sheriff, William de Wendenal, and he's coming for us."

Arthur snorted. "That's nothing new."

"You may remember him. He's a friend of mine. Or *was,* that is." He looked to the side, rolled his tongue in his lower lip. Marion knew the tic, he was pushing his emotions down. "I know him, I know how he thinks. De Lacy was nothing compared to what Wendenal could become. He's sharp, he's ambitious. He's damned *good,* is what he is, good at everything. Better than you all, better than me, too. Our only advantage is that he's new to the seat, he won't know how things work. It will take him some time to get on his feet, but if we let him . . . then that's it." Robin seemed short with his words. "So we have to strike quickly."

Marion finally chose to speak. "I thought you were in favor of doing nothing, Robin. You were the one that wanted us keeping to ourselves."

His eyes accepted the blame. "Things have changed. We're at war now. And that's my specialty."

"War?" He had treated the word as casually as a friend's name, rather than a line Marion had never wanted to cross.

"First thing's first," Robin continued. "We're getting Scarlet and Elena back."

Marion's eyebrow cocked itself, while John gave a low whistle. "*Back,* now? You say they're locked up in Nottingham Castle."

"Castle Rock is impenetrable," Arthur said.

"They did it," Robin shot back. "They got inside to kill the Sheriff, didn't they? Two of them, without a plan. I'm willing to bet we can do better."

But John disagreed. "The castle was empty that night, Robin. All the guards were out on raids. They must have taken advantage of that. But now, after what they've done, I'd bet it's locked down tighter than ever. Don't mistake me now, I love them both, I'd do anything to have them back here, if for no other reason than to smash their heads together. But we can't save them. We lost."

"That may be how it feels," Robin laughed, "but it's not how it looks from the outside. People are flocking to you. They want to join Marion's Men. And why?" he asked, his voice alive and surging. "It's certainly not for the stew. It's not for safety. It's because of what *we* represent, and what *they* represent. The Sheriff, the Captain, the Guard, they're the men who come into your home and take what's yours. They're the men who kill children in the streets. And who are we? We're the ones who said no to that injustice. We're the ones who rob from the rich and give to the poor. We're the ones who killed the Sheriff when he became too greedy. We're the ones who are *winning*."

Something swam in Marion's mind as he continued. He made it sound so easy, a world in which every man and woman controlled her own destiny, rather than simply found ways of surviving each new woe. She had practically abandoned that idea barely ten minutes ago, and now he made it sound like a tangible thing, which they simply had to reach out and take. The forest blurred away behind him.

"The people see us as the champions, and they're coming to help. Something big has started here. But you know what happens if Wendenal hangs Will and Elena? He takes it all back. He re-establishes himself as the power, and nobody wants to join us anymore for fear of swinging on a rope. But think, *just think,* about how far the story will spread, how much good we'll be able to accomplish, if we get away with it. The people would think we're invincible. And with them on our side, we very well may be."

"There's so much we don't know," Tuck spoke. "None of us know that castle."

"I know the castle," Marion said instantly, surprising even herself. "Well enough, that is."

"But we have no idea where Will and Elena will be."

"That's not true, Friar." Another of Robin's winning smiles. "We know precisely where they'll be during the funeral." A murmur swelled, a secret rally, and it grew. "Any of you interested in paying the late Sheriff de Lacy some final respects?"

They cheered.

Out of the most solemn and dour days Marion had seen, there was suddenly a purpose, and a drive, a bond had bridged these men who an hour ago had been gathering their things to dissolve and disappear. Robin had done more for their sense of hope in the last ten minutes than Marion had ever done.

And for it, she was thankful.

All she said was his name, and Robin left his place without hesitation to wrap his arms around her. It would have been a precious moment if the boys hadn't hooted and whistled at them, leading her to swat her cloak at their childishness. They were all little brothers for her reproach.

"Come on, boys!" John rallied them. "There's an awful lot for us to do . . . just over there. Any number of important . . . you know. Things."

He winked at Marion and the stream of men flowed past. Alan pounded something importantly onto Robin's chest, something dark. Marion recognized it as the archer's cowl Robin had torn from his head when he'd left them. The two men exchanged a quiet moment, then Alan joined the others.

Once the rumble of men passed, Marion spoke quietly through her smile. "I knew you'd come back."

He scrutinized her face, and shook his head. "No you didn't."

She had to laugh. "You're right. I thought you were gone forever this time. I'm glad to be wrong. Turns out you may be more like your father than you think."

Their heads flirted closer to each other. She enjoyed the familiarity of his arms, of his face. More importantly, the drive behind his eyes, and how he seemed to flourish with purpose. It was like seeing the man he'd always meant to be, before he'd run away from the world.

"Everything that happened," Robin was saying, "it was my fault. I shouldn't have left before, and I didn't mean the things I said."

"Yes you did," she laughed again, "but you figured out you were wrong. That's better than most can say."

"Too late."

"It's never too late to do what's right."

His cheeks dropped, his features gave way to reveal something rare and real beneath. "I wasn't sure I'd be welcome back."

Frankly, she agreed. There were plenty of grudges she could hold over him, but they all seemed so childish compared to the day's need for basic humanity. Nothing was more important than the invisible something beneath it all, that nameless connection they had always felt.

"Tragedy has a way of washing the past clean," she said softly, and Robin agreed.

"I really am sorry for leaving."

"As you said."

"Not just now, but all those years ago."

He had never apologized for that before. After Vivian's death, after Edmond disappeared, after their families had been shattered by violence, Robin had vanished. Marion had been left to deal with the grief of it all. She had become the daughter that Walter of Locksley needed to keep his sanity. She never complained about it, but it should never have been her burden to bear. The gravity of those years felt remarkably lighter with that one simple admission, that Robin knew he should have stayed.

"What you've done here," he continued, "how you've helped these people, what you and my father accomplished, it's really quite remarkable."

"Remarkable?" she joked. She wouldn't let him get away with that understatement. "It's 'able to be remarked upon'? Oh, thank you."

"It's amazing," Robin corrected himself, and drew in close to her. Her hands found their way around his waist. "I want to help in any way I can."

"Well, I'm glad you're back," she whispered as he leaned into her.

"I'm not going anywhere this time."

And the fiercest woman alive would have gone teary as they kissed. It wasn't their first kiss, they had played this game for decades. But in the past, it had always been in regret, in frustration, in a futile *what-could-have-been* that they knew couldn't last. This was the first time they seemed to be on the same page, where they were headed in the same direction. Two arrows with the same target, if she could allow herself the ham-handed symbolism. Robin held her head with both hands, they pushed their foreheads together and laughed.

Eventually she tugged at his doublet. "Do you really think William's such a threat?"

"I know he is," Robin's voice dropped. "He means to hunt us down, every one of us, straight to the gallows."

"You know him better than I do," she admitted, "but he was kind to me. He kept me safe, got me out of the city."

"Well he's not *cruel*." Robin bit his lip and looked to the side again. "But once he's made his mind, that's it. I don't know what he's been through in the last month, but he's obviously been blinded by the power. He was always more strategic than me, so I would guess he has his own reasons for keeping you away. Much more likely for his own safety than yours."

Marion considered it. If it were true, then the world outside the Sherwood may not be as dangerous to her as she feared. If her contacts in the city were still loyal, there was a lot she could still accomplish. The sorts of things she had been neglecting for the past month.

"I want to hear all your ideas," she said firmly. "In the morning, I'll leave."

"Leave?" he startled. "Where are you going?"

"I can't linger too long here. If I hadn't spent so much time away from Nottingham, I may have been able to stop what happened . . . I can't risk that again."

"You won't be safe," he postured. "William will find you."

"I won't go to Nottingham—I know that's not safe yet. I'll stay in Sheffield for now. I have plenty of friends, Robin, who owe my family many favors. They'll be my eyes and ears in the castle. I can still make a difference. Here, I'm just another mouth to feed." She laughed at his frown. "Don't worry, I'll make regular visits."

Even though they would be splitting up, it didn't feel like a separation this time. They would be working together, from opposite sides of the problem.

Robin fidgeted, but he wouldn't disagree with her. "You should take someone with you for protection. A bodyguard," he chirped. "I'll do it myself."

"Stop it. You're needed here. Amon's always taken care of me." Robin made another face, and she squeezed him a little tighter. "Don't worry, I don't think he . . . likes . . . women. So much." Robin was relieved and confused, but took it gladly. "You can guard me while I'm still here, if you like."

"Gladly, m'lady," and he kissed her again, a long kiss. He slowly rotated her in his arms before calling out grandly, "Is that better, John? Can you see us better from this angle?"

"Much better!" came John Little's bellow, and Marion twisted to see John, Alan, and Tuck all stumble to the ground from their hiding spot behind the Great Oak, laughing like little children caught misbehaving.

That night, for the first time in four or five days, there was joy in the camp. The wind was cold, but they huddled together, sharing stories of long-lost loves and childhood romances. John Little told a touching story about how he'd first met his late wife Marley. Instead of mourning Much they shared memories about him, of the trouble he'd get into and the curious things he'd say. Tuck made a few simple changes to his song's notes and tempo, turning it into an inspiring march. When Marion finally rubbed her legs and hoisted herself off to catch some sleep, she could hear the group singing together.

"Take thy bow in hand," said Robin,
"For Much will ride with thee,
And all can be together,
If no man die for me."

FORTY-TWO

GUY OF GISBOURNE

NOTTINGHAM CASTLE

FOUR GUARDSMEN LAY ON the funeral pyre. Its flames lit the highest bailey in a surreal orange bath, giving his castle's sandstone a raw, naked character Guy had never seen before, and prayed he never would again. A generation had passed since a group funeral like this. Then, it had been the brave Guardsmen who died in the Kings' War, valiant deaths of the city's first defenders. Now it was four men murdered by Locksley's outlaws, not one of them even given the chance to fight.

Reginold of Dunmow, ambushed outside Bernesdale and left for dead. Poor Devon of York, shot in the heart by people who had once called him friend. Brian Fellows and George Sutton, two young recruits to the Common Guard. Guy had not been close with either of them, but knew them well enough. Brian Fellows had a fondness for bitter ale and songs about bear-baiting. George Sutton was a skinny young man who took pride in his fletching, and scrubbed the dirt from his doublet daily—the doublet he had died for. The uniforms the assassins wore while they stabbed de Lacy a dozen times in his own office.

Roger de Lacy's funeral would not be until the first day of December—nearly a month away, which afforded the neighboring nobility enough time to arrange their visits. But the humble Guardsmen, who had no notable visitors to mourn them, burned on their pyre as soon as possible. The battlements around the high bailey were filled shoulder-to-shoulder, nearly every Guardsman in the city come to watch. Guy took a haunting record of their faces. They did not mourn the dead, but simply watched in a stupor, in fear that this was but a sign of what was to come. Reginold's sister and daughter had been invited, but refused to attend. The Simons said some kind words and lifted a tankard for each of his fallen boys, though he walked away when it was Guy's turn to speak. Bolt was there, but only in body. He spent the funeral picking at his fingernails and whispering things to the wind. He left the castle immediately afterward, and Guy knew better than to let anyone follow him. Bolt had seen Reginold as a brother. He was, effectively, a fifth casualty.

Guy's private regiment had been decimated. The ongoing mystery of Jon Bassett's disappearance had been terrible on its own, but it was nothing compared to this. Eric and Morg were all that was left, and Guy met them in his private quarters to share a flagon of ale. Eric was distant and distracted, which was entirely out of character. The man had served dutiful years as a crown ranger before Guy recruited him, and his patience was the makings of legends.

Now he scratched at the table, crossed and uncrossed his arms just to cross them again, tapped the ground with his feet, and pried at splinters.

"Eric." Guy had to calm him. "Do you need a minute?"

The ranger laughed hollow, exposing the purple hole in his gums and the teeth he'd lost in the skirmish at Thieves Den. "Sorry, Captain," he mumbled, his tongue lisping. "Having trouble thinking straight."

"I need you clear, Eric," Guy said kindly. "You two are all that's left of this regiment." Morg's small eyes were wet, his heart of gold had cracked open beneath his massive bulk.

"We are no regiment," Eric grumbled. "We're pathetic."

"No," Guy said firmly. "It has been my deepest honor to stand by you, each of you." He eyed Eric long enough to solidify it. "Not one of you can be made pathetic by someone else. You can only do that to yourselves."

"Well then that's just one more thing you can blame on me—"

"*Stop it.*" Guy punched the table, just once—it shivered through the candles that stuck at its center. "We cannot let this break us, or they win. We have a rare opportunity here, a chance to use this tragedy as a force for good." A feverish intensity pushed through him, the need to make things better. It was the only way for him to channel his grief. "There is tremendous goodwill coming our way, and it is our responsibility to the dead to take advantage of it. Anything less is injustice. *Anything.*"

The *goodwill* he referred to came in the form of men-at-arms, from all the neighboring counties. Yorkshire to the north, Lincolnshire to the east, Leicestershire to the south, and Derbyshire to the west. All had sent men in a display of sympathy and alliance. Squads of varying sizes and banners, they came to fortify the castle and the roads for the Sheriff's funeral. The middle bailey already overflowed with loyal swordarms, eager to help, eager for work. Guy intended to forge a new company out of this talent pool.

The Black Guard.

A new group with a singular purpose—to eliminate the Sherwood outlaws. For five weeks, his private regiment had been crippled by policing Nottingham, managing the wharf gangs, leashed by de Lacy's refusal to let him hunt down anything other than taxes. But a fresh crew, unhindered by any responsibilities to the city, could ferret the outlaws out of the trees in no time. Rather than scrape the gaols for a handful of gerolds, he suddenly had a bounty of dedicated men to choose from.

"But only if it happens now," Guy calculated. "Every noble coming to de Lacy's funeral has one desire—to see these traitors at the end of a rope. Which is, I'm sure, exactly what William de Wendenal is counting on."

He had not yet taken to calling him *Sheriff* de Wendenal. That promotion had almost been more shocking than de Lacy's murder. Guy may have disagreed with Roger de Lacy's policies, but there was always a combative joy in their arguments. De Lacy's opinions on nearly everything were maddeningly wrong, but he was no monster. He had respect for conversation, and there was dignity in being outmatched by him. Wendenal had none of that. His appointment proved that being friends with the King overruled all manner of logic. A week had already passed with him in charge, and every day it felt increasingly wrong.

"It does not take a brilliant man to see the strings at play here," Guy continued. "Wendenal and Locksley, both agents of King Richard. Wendenal imbeds himself with de Lacy, while Locksley trains a bunch of common thieves into a gang of assassins. Locksley killed de Lacy on the same night he signs an edict to appoint Wendenal as sheriff."

"That seems a little suspect, no?" Morg asked, always a little too slow to grasp the profanely obvious.

"It's the very signature of foul play. A brick could be more clever. Wendenal alone stayed in the castle while the entire Guard left for the tax raids, and we're supposed to think this is coincidence? Wendenal's claim to the seat is as flimsy as the paper it's written on. But he won't need that paper if he wins the support of every nobleman within twenty leagues. Which he'll do by bringing in Robin's gang."

Eric squinted. "So if we go after the outlaws, we're only helping him out."

"Not if we keep our eyes open. Their plan seems simple—Locksley starts a rebellion to create turmoil, which Wendenal smothers to solidify his power. But to smother it, he has to capture Locksley and his men. I have no doubt he means for Locksley to mysteriously escape justice—so that's our leverage. If we capture Locksley ourselves, we can use him. Get him to divulge this whole corrupt plan to us, then he and Wendenal hang side by side."

"Do you mean . . ." Morg huffed. "Do you mean work *against* the Sheriff? Won't we get in trouble?"

Guy's breath stuttered. He honestly didn't know the answer. "That's a bridge for later. For now, at least, we all want the same thing. Publicly, at least."

"Alright, well just tell me what to do," Morg said, his thick beard quivering along with his lip. "I can't follow all of this. Just give me something to do."

Guy leaned back and breathed in proudly. "You're already doing it. Welcome to the Black Guard."

Eric and Morg exchanged a look of anticipation, hungry for whatever their new titles meant.

"We need to bolster our forces," Guy said. "Not with Common Guardsmen. We have the best swordarms in five counties visiting right now, but we need to be careful. We need to only recruit men who are of common mind with us, who have no loyalty to Wendenal."

"I could help," the voice came from behind Guy, and he realized he had completely forgotten Ferrers was even in the room. He sat against the wall, as was his station, and did not drink with them. He had learned his lesson about speaking unprompted, but Guy gave him a mild acknowledgement.

"If you approach anyone from Derbyshire, consult me first," Ferrers said. "My father is earl there, but some may consider themselves friends to Wendenal's father, Lord Beneger. I could help determine a Derbyman's loyalty."

Guy bowed his head. "Thank you."

"Have you interrogated the murderers yet?" Eric asked, sucking the spit between his empty teeth. "They know how to find Locksley."

"I have," Guy answered. That had been his first hope as well. "They weren't helpful."

"Let me try, then? Put me in a room with that girl. Maybe she gets feisty and tries something . . ." Eric's sentence petered out into heavy implications.

"You can't." Guy stood. "You can't, Eric. I know how you feel. But it wouldn't serve anyone."

"It'd serve me," Eric growled.

"And no one else. They need to hang, publicly, so that the people know they're safe. There's more at stake than revenge, Eric. It wouldn't be right."

"She took my teeth!" he snapped. "And she killed Devon! Wouldn't be right?"

"She'll get what she's earned. At de Lacy's funeral."

"That's a month from now." His fingers returned to the table, scratching. "Wouldn't be right is waiting. Who knows what could happen in a month, Captain, and you know it."

Guy met his eyes, but said nothing. The rancid truth was that Eric was probably correct. Elena Gamwell and Will Scarlet sat in separate cells beneath the castle, waiting to die. If the Guard had taken care of her when she first put a blade to Guy's throat at Thieves Den, it would have served Jon and Devon and Brian and Reginold and Bolt and George and Roger. The list might still keep growing. So who else might they lose, by letting her live a little longer? Who else was even left to lose?

"We have to be better than that," Guy said at last. "I understand the desire to take matters into our own hands, to do what feels right. But that's the easy path, and the easy path is easy for a reason. There's no lasting victory there. What would make us different than them, Eric?"

But the words rang hollow. By the word of the law, Guy was duty-bound to obey the usurper Wendenal, regardless of how he claimed the sheriffcy. But Guy was already contemplating a path to undo that injustice—which required him to bend from his duty.

"Help me find men, understood?" He pounded the table to dismiss them. "Good men, who are able to step away from their responsibilities for a bit to hunt down these traitors. Bring them to me, the sooner the better."

"And what about this?" Eric asked as he stood. "The Black Guard? We allowed to do this?"

"There's precedent." Guy knew it was not much of an answer. Even years ago, when there was men and coin to spare, he would have to get approval directly from the Sheriff to build a team like this. But William de Wendenal didn't know the first thing of Nottingham's procedures, so he wouldn't even think to question it.

It was foreign territory for Guy. The selfishness of doing the right thing over doing the lawful thing. The hypocrisy of telling Eric he could not do the same. The first step on a slope he had seen too many others slide down, and it led directly to a cell in the prisons, or a blade in the back.

THERE WAS NO SLEEP for Guy that night, the air was too hot, and his skin was on fire. Eric's words had wormed within him. Guy had always been a champion of the law, but that law had failed him. There was no pride in pursuit of duty to a false leader. If Guy had seen through Wendenal's lies earlier, his men would not be dead. But Wendenal was only as powerful as those who executed his commands, which meant he was only responsible for half of the funeral pyre—Guy's adherence to discipline had built the other half. It was the law that gnawed at him, and he was the only damned person left in Nottingham who cared about it.

He couldn't breathe, his heart was too fast, there was too much to do now. Guy's leg was twitching and his knuckles hurt where he had punched the table earlier. He picked at the scabs on them and sucked on the blood. The swirling fitfulness of sleep pulled at his thoughts, down dark rivers. What might he be able to accomplish were he not so bound by the law? What might he accomplish were he as unscrupulous as a Robin Hood?

Guy opened his eyes to the darkness of his room, cold sweat on his chest, and no time had passed at all. It was too hot, and he could swear there was a taste of blood in his mouth.

He dressed and left the stone keep, up the walkway about the middle bailey, hoping the crisp night air would clear his head. The castle was disarmingly still. Even the scrape of his boots against the stone seemed unwelcome. A cat-eye half-moon gave its blanket over a clear night. The great ribbon in the sky was clear, and the constellation of the archer aimed upward. Eric had taught him those constellations.

He felt it in the air before he heard it. A ripple in silence he didn't take to, a rhythm in the city that wasn't right. He knew the castle too well. There was a pause, not audible at first, but eventually it rose—a cluster of hesitations that formed a warning. Then, an eruption of screaming, from below, and a burst of men vomited upward from the tunnel that led down into the prisons. Their words, *"Make way! Hurry! Get him out of here! Oh God, oh God!"*

It became piercing, an alarum that woke the castle itself. Guy threw himself to full pace, dashing down a set of stone steps to meet the crowd. They were Guardsmen mostly, though not all from Nottingham, fighting against one in their center. Closer, Guy realized they were *carrying* someone that was fighting back, kicking and contorting against the four men who handled him, one at each limb.

Not fighting back. Dying. A Guardsman who was covered in blood.

"Get him to the keep! Get the doctor!" one man yelled.

Screams in the middle of the night—it was a nightmare they'd awoken to last week as well.

"Guardsman injured—clear a table!" Guy ordered, bodies obeyed, pushing into the keep toward the dining hall. The wounded guard was brought to a table, thrashing, his hands desperate to be released. A mist of blood burst from his neck with each spasm.

"What happened?" Guy demanded of anyone. "What in God's name happened?"

"What do you think happened?" growled a stranger who was struggling to cover the wounded guard's neck. Girls were there now, bringing basins of water and bandage, one spilled a bowl in horror when she realized what she was looking at.

What do you think happened?

Prison break.

The bailey flew past Guy's feet. He had never moved faster. If Scarlet and Elena were already out of the prisons, there was no telling where they might be, or who would die next. But if they were still down there—there were only two ways down into the prison, and the Rabbit Cage was always locked from the outside.

He took the stairs in three long strides and ducked into the tunnel. The deep inside was inky black, and the iron gate was ajar.

"Through me," he breathed, "they'll have to get through me."

He had not brought his weapon, nor would he find any down here. Still, he couldn't wait. They could be anywhere, lurking in the dark, waiting to take him by surprise. But the sound of commotion burrowed its way up from below, and Guy chased into it. Down several passages, every turn it grew louder. Sprinting now, he came to a small hub of cells, lit by a swinging lantern throwing shadows around a huddle of men—all gathered around someone in the middle. Guy plunged himself into their throng.

His gut tightened and he stopped. In the middle of the group was Morg, sweating profusely, eyes red. His blue tabard was soaked in blood, as were his hands, with thin streaks of it across his face and beard, but he didn't appear injured. And the only riot in the room was that which Guy had brought with him.

"Is he alive?" another Guardsman asked. This was Marshall Sutton, one of the prison watch, an ox in human form. Guy was too late. The thieves had killed and moved on.

He turned, to leave the caves, to fly, to break the castle in half. But he was staring at Will Scarlet.

Inside one of the cells.

Scarlet's fingers clutched the bars. His cell door was closed and locked. His face, still swollen and purple from the night they'd arrested him, was watching with surprise. The world tightened around him and Guy stared, disbelieving.

"Is Hawkins alive?" Marshall asked again.

Guy blinked. He tried to clear his head and reassess what was happening. "Where's the girl?"

"What?"

"The girl!" He pointed at Scarlet, names temporarily beyond his grasp.

"In her cell," Marshall said, clearly confused.

The blood pumping in Guy's ears was louder than his own thoughts, and his limbs dragged downward. A pool of blood was on the ground, fresh enough that the dirt had not yet drunk it. Morg and Marshall were waiting on his answer. The other two Guardsmen were strangers in rust tabards. Yorkshire colors, he recalled now. They were Guardsmen from York.

Guy tried to calm his hands. "What the hell is going on here?"

"You didn't see him?" Morg asked.

"I saw him," Guy said. "Who was he?"

"Dale Hawkins."

"He's a horse thief, and a murderer," one of the Yorkies answered.

He was a gerold, Guy knew. He recognized the name.

"That little maggot got himself into The Simons' Yard." Marshall wiped his bald head but just smeared the blood that was there. "He's been living with us for months, just waiting for a chance to kill us all."

"I recognized him," the Yorkie said calmly. "We had him in irons in York a couple years ago. Stole a horse from some baron and botched it, killed a stable-boy trying to get away. He and a few others broke out round a year back. Caught most of them, but not Hawkins. When I saw him here, I couldn't shake why I knew his face."

Guy put his hand out. "Who are you?"

"Silas, from Yorkshire Guard."

"And this is Captain Gisbourne," Marshall introduced him.

Silas bowed his head slightly. He had a deep beak of a nose that split his stoic face in two. "An honor. As I was saying, once I placed Dale Hawkins's name, I had to be certain. I'd met this one the night before," sticking his thumb at Morg, "so I asked him."

Morg's shoulders continued to shake. His face was redder than the blood that spattered it, and he twisted at his blue tabard as if the blood would slide off.

"And Morg asked me," Marshall took up the story. "I remembered Hawkins, too, he was a prisoner here. But for *tax evasion.*" He met Guy's eyes, saying everything that needed to be said. Guy shouldn't have been surprised that Marshall would figure out what all those prisoner interrogations were about. And just as he had feared, they had recruited someone who had a more colorful history than they knew.

"Horse thief, and a murderer," the Yorkie had said. *And then a Guardsman.*

Morg blubbered his way to a voice. "We've already had our share of murderers in Guard uniform this last week. I didn't want anyone else getting killed."

"So what happened, Morg?" Guy placed his hand on the giant's shoulder. "You killed him?"

"Might be." Morg's puffy eyes blinked. "Wasn't trying to. Just trying to shave his ear is all."

Marshall explained to Silas, "We've taken to nippin' the eartips off those that come in on violent account. So we can always recognize them."

"I came up behind Hawkins," Morg tried to demonstrate, but his arms were weak, "meaning to cut his tip off. But he caught wind and turned, tried to fight back. Pricked himself right in the neck, idiot."

"Of course he was going to fight back," the other Yorkie finally spoke. "What did you expect him to do?"

"I expected he was going to kill someone," Morg snapped, "and I wasn't interested on waiting for it to happen!"

Marshall defended him. "You want him to simply ask, *Pardon me, aren't you a murderer? Would you mind letting me clip your ears now?* No."

"Seems he's gotten out of two gaols already," Morg said, finding his resolve. "He needed to be branded before he did it again."

Poor Morg thought Dale Hawkins was an assassin in disguise. If Guy had told his men about the gerolds in the first place, this wouldn't have happened. Every bit of every damned thing that was going wrong was on him. He never should have accepted de Lacy's policy on this.

He should have done what was right, instead of his duty.

The jostling of mail heralded a new flood of bodies into the room, and not one of them was a face Guy knew. There were too many strangers in Nottingham and they all wore Guard tabards.

"Which one's Morg?" the stranger's voice was kind. "Sheriff's asking for you."

"Shit." Something about the way Morg pronounced it made the word even more offensive. "Is he dead?"

"Doesn't look good. Come on now. He wants everyone."

Morg stood and straightened himself out, ignoring the blood on his tabard. He went first, the others filing out behind him.

THE BLOOD ON THE floor of the barracks' dining hall streaked away, sticky bootprints leading in various directions. The longtable Dale Hawkins had been led to was empty again but for the dark pool congealing beneath it. It alone was deserted. Every other table was filled with men and women, every soul in the castle might have been there. The air was hot with human breath.

In the center, Wendenal, the man who called himself Sheriff, was raising hell.

"Is this true, Guardsman?" He unloaded his fury on Morg as their party entered the hall. "You slit your brother's throat?"

"That is not true." Morg stood his ground. "That man was not my brother."

Every muscle in Wendenal's face found a way to turn smug. "Try to imagine how little I care for what you call him. He was a member of the Sheriff's Guard, as are you, and you put your knife to his throat. Do you contest that?"

Guy positioned himself near Wendenal, but the man had no interest in him. Instead, Guy searched the crowd. He found Eric of Felley and gave him a stern stare. There was nothing they could do to make any of this better.

"I would think we've learned lately," Morg tried to address the crowd, desperately looking for sympathetic faces in the familiar hall, "that not everyone who puts on the tabard is a member of the Guard."

"You want to talk about recent history?" Wendenal bit into it before the crowd could react. "You mean to say we should treat every man in the Guard as an enemy? You're right that wearing the blue doesn't prove a man to be deserving of the title of Guardsman, as I can see by the man who stands in front of me!"

Morg swallowed. "That boy was a murderer."

"And he became a Guardsman. You are living proof it's easy enough to change from one to the other."

"If I may, Sheriff," Silas of York took a half step forward, "I knew the man in question, from the prisons in York. I was the one that recognized him."

"And I thank York for its concern," Wendenal said, but his full force was still aimed at Morg. "So what did you do with this information, Guardsman? Take it to your captain? Or to me? Perhaps a servant girl, or a rock, anything at all that may have been more discerning than yourself?"

Morg's cow eyes opened wide, and he shrank a bit. "I didn't think there would be enough time. In light of what happened to the Sheriff, I thought—"

"In light of what happened to the Sheriff," Wendenal tasted every word and spat them out again, "you should know better than to take justice into your own hands. De Lacy's assassins decided to take his life because they thought they were right. They weren't. We're supposed to be better than them."

"I only meant to trim his ear is all, but he fought back—"

"You held a knife to his face and you think he's at fault that it cut him?"

Morg breathed heavily, his body sagged. "Is he dead?"

Wendenal looked to his right, but the men there gave uncertain responses. "You opened his throat. I've never seen a man survive that." He looked down now, just a moment of hesitation, then stood tall again to deliver the punishment. "What's your name?"

"Morg."

"Your full name."

He shifted. "Kyle Morgan."

"Kyle Morgan, you are to be imprisoned for assaulting a fellow Guardsman. If Hawkins dies, you may likely face the hangman as a traitor."

That word was repeated many times by a shocked crowd, and ever more harshly by Morg himself, whose face went red. Guy closed his eyes, unable to see the man blubber.

"We are not outlaws!" Wendenal bellowed, silencing the room again. "Not one of us, not you or I or the King himself, holds the reins to justice. If you think you should be able to kill whomsoever you please, go join Robin Hood. But if you claim to be true men of the Guard, you commit yourself to something better. To behaving as men rather than beasts. That is your choice. Kyle Morgan, I do not discount your years of honorable service. But you made your own choices today, and you must live by them."

Nothing was left where Morg stood, just meat. "I didn't mean to kill him."

Wendenal sighed. "That may rank as the most useless thing I've ever heard a man say. Take him to a cell."

But nobody moved, and Guy felt a curious wave of pride. Morg was one of their own, the beloved bear of the Nottingham Guard. They knew his heart had been in the right place, that he was trying to defend them all. And, perhaps more importantly, Guy could now count the exact number of his men who felt the same as he did, who refused to jump at Wendenal's every command. He committed to memory those who watched the new sheriff's priorities with disbelief. If he was lucky, he was looking at the future members of the Black Guard.

Wendenal eyed the room, perhaps realizing his lack of support. But there was a humanity in his face Guy hadn't expected, and his tone softened. "I don't take any pleasure in this. But we must hold ourselves to the highest of standards. Are there men here from Derbyshire?"

A small cluster of men near the back of the room stood, dark green sashes across their chests. "We are, your lordship."

Wendenal gave a terse nod, his eyes flickering back and forth before speaking. "I submit this man to your custody, please take him to our prisons, which I also now place entirely in your control."

Derbymen. Wendenal now had his own loyal regiment, giving him control of a part of Nottingham Castle. There was nothing right about this.

Guy took a step closer and Wendenal threw him a wild-eyed warning, but he could not let this go unsaid. He approached cautiously to whisper in Wendenal's ear. "It will be dangerous for him down there, Sheriff." The title tasted like bile, but Morg's life was worth it. "He'll be a target for the other prisoners."

Wendenal nodded. "Be sure he gets his own cell," he called out, "and keep him isolated from the others. Remove his tabard."

"Lord Wendenal," the lead man from Derby bowed, "we've served your father before. You can count on us."

They didn't need to claim his uniform. Morg pulled his tabard over his head and threw it to the ground. He went willingly. If he had chosen to fight, the barracks could have ripped itself to pieces. Guy noticed more than a few hands moving to their hilts, uneasy glances shared amongst those that did not know if they should act. But Morg was escorted out of the hall without incident, over the blood on the stone, out into the blackness where he would return to the prisons in a very different manner.

Marshall Sutton made a show of his anger, staring wildly at anyone nearby, perhaps daring everyone into a fight. He was joined by Silas from the Yorkshire Guard, and a few others who seemed eager to object. Guy noted their faces.

He would offer each of them positions in the Black Guard by sunrise.

As the hall emptied, a young woman in a blood-soaked white tunic hustled in from the east wing and approached Wendenal. Neither said a word. The visitor simply shook her head sadly and retreated. Dale Hawkins was dead.

FORTY-THREE

ROBIN OF LOCKSLEY

THE OAK CAMP

"A SWORD ISN'T A club," Robin bellowed, repositioning Alan-a-Dale's arms so that he did not look quite so clueless. "It's supposed to be an extension of your arm."

"You mean a hand?" Alan's joke turned glum as he grimaced against the new muscles involved in holding a sword properly.

They gathered in the field under the central oak tree, as before. They paired off against each other in pairs, as before. They breathed air, as before. Everything else was different.

When last Robin had trained them at swordplay, he cared more about keeping them from hurting themselves than about hurting someone else. They had been children in the woods staring down coachmen, and needed to know little more than which end of the sword was which. Now, they would almost certainly draw steel against the Nottingham Guard. If they could not do so confidently, they would only ever do so once.

There used to be only ten of them sparring, now there were three times as many. Motivated help had poured in from the surrounding villages, especially from those closest to Bernesdale. Robin had them change partners constantly, forcing them to adapt to new sizes and styles. Alan was currently paired up against Nick Delaney, a painfully handsome man with an equally handsome twin brother Peter. They had come to the camp along with their father Henry after Gisbourne ousted them from their home in Bernesdale for his own men's comfort. They were exactly the type of help Robin needed—even-tempered, eager to learn, and decent beyond reason. They had quickly become beloved around the camp for their assistance in all things from cooking to building shelter. They'd already earned nicknames—"Nicks" and "Peeteys"—to help explain how they could be in so many places at once. When young women fantasized about what princes and kings must be like, they imagined men like Nicks and Peeteys. Pairing one of them against the skinny hapless Alan-a-Dale was almost cruel.

"Can we use sticks again?" Alan whined. "These swords are slower and heavier."

"Not unless you want to go into battle with one," Robin returned.

"But I could fight forever with those." He stretched out his arms. "These fights don't last more than one or two attacks."

"Neither will a real one." Robin kept a stern voice against Alan's levity. "This isn't tournament fighting. A real fight is over before you even realize it's begun. Show me your stance."

Alan held his sword out and away from him like it was a sack of vomit.

"Where are your hands?" Robin asked. Alan wiggled his fingers but fortunately didn't answer, *"They're right here,"* again, because nobody had laughed the previous time he said it. Somehow he always ended up with his hands overlapped on top of each other no matter how many times Robin reminded him one should be halfway on the pommel.

Nicks seemed to take pity, and swung his sword in a slow and obvious sweep toward Alan's side. Even with the forecast, Alan only held his sword limply up to defend, and the resulting momentum knocked him off his feet to a bed of dead leaves. The others laughed, because they'd never seen a body cleaved in half before. Robin knew what the hole in Alan's side would look like, how his shattered ribs would pierce his flesh. He knew what sound Alan would make as he cried away the last of his life.

"You can't just stand there and take the blow," Robin scolded, grappling Alan back to his feet, momentarily surprised by how thin his shoulders were. Nicks's shoulders alone could have crawled off his body and beaten the life out of Alan. "Their sword won't magically stop just because yours is in the way. That energy is still headed toward you, and if you absorb it, you end up with a broken arm, at the very least. And how much fun is a broken arm, Friar?"

At the edge of the group, Tuck was drinking a large mug of beer, grinning wildly.

"Don't answer that," Robin finished. "What you really want, remember now, is not to fight against that energy, but to redirect it." He demonstrated with Nicks, signaling for the man to attack. Robin stepped back just out of range, deflecting Nicks's blade down as it passed between them and redirecting it up and away, leaving Nicks's belly wide and exposed. "Transfer the attack."

"Can I transfer the attack into something that's not an attack?" Alan asked. "Maybe a pillow? I'd be alright with that."

"The Sheriff's Guard," Robin lectured the group, "will be trained in simple moves that are designed to work against unskilled opponents. Once you recognize these attacks, you should be able to avoid them simply enough, and transfer them away from you." Most of the students were nodding, while poor Alan just shook his head in abject frustration. Not every man was built to swing a sword, Robin knew, but most could at least learn the basics. "Watch your hands, watch your feet, watch your angles."

Alan raised his hand.

"Yes, Alan?"

"I don't know what that last one means."

Robin smiled, but only because he had nothing else to offer.

"What if they're not dead yet?" came a question from Gamble Gold. A hairy man from a hairy village, Gamble was more of a brawler than a swordsman, and probably from experience. "What's the best way to kill those fuckers?"

There was a rage in his question that Robin had been hoping to avoid. There were heavy differences in the reasons behind each volunteer's arrival. Men like

Gamble Gold seemed interested in punishing any Guardsman who got in their way.

Robin frowned at him. "Remember, these men aren't so different from us. They have lives, and families. I guarantee you that if you injure them or prove you're the better fighter, they will run."

It was such an easy thing, to see the enemy as faceless nobodies. It's what they did in the war, it was the only way to justify any of it. Uniforms made it even easier, and a wash of nameless *Guardsmen* sounded like a thing that nobody could ever miss. Anonymity turned violence into a tool, a necessity which Robin refused to succumb to here. Every man who pulled steel against them would be an Englishman, and that was a crucial thing to remember. It kept that hungry beast at bay.

"So we're not supposed to kill them?" someone croaked in the back. It was another new recruit, a short sort of frog man named Charley Dancer.

Robin shook his head. "Only if you have to."

"I swear, if they hang Will and Elena," Alan tried to sound braver than he was, "I'll kill them all myself."

A few men nodded in grim approval.

"That was Elena's promise," John Little added, "and I stick to it. Whoever's responsible for one of our deaths, has got it coming back." Robin noted that more people rallied at this than when Alan had said the exact same thing a second earlier. "Any problems amongst?"

Robin had another lecture prepared, but nobody could tell John Little no. His burden in all of this made him unchallengeable. "None, none," answered Charley, folding his frog face. "That's a promise I can live by. Just wondering if they might feel the same."

"If who might feel the same?" Arthur asked.

"The Sheriff's Guard. What if they don't take to having their men killed none neither?"

"That's a good point, Charley," Robin jumped in, happy for the opportunity. "Just remember, anyone you attack might be a Scarlet, or an Elena, or a Much, to somebody else." *Or a William.* "No need to make any more enemies than we already have."

"Excepting we haven't killed any children." Little's voice was harsh. "That's not the finest of lines."

Again, there was no way to disagree. Robin proceeded cautiously. "Even still, we cannot act as the wanton criminals they make us out to be. Once we get Will and Elena back, they'll still need to answer for what they did. Without the support of the people, we cannot accomplish anything." He had returned to prevent any more senseless death, not to add to it. "Alright everyone, once around!"

Robin twirled his fingers in the air and the body of men groaned and leaned into a run. He had trained them to do sprints around the field at random times, to get used to unexpected bursts of excitement. "Where's your sword?" he yelled at David of Doncaster, who sighed and ran back to retrieve it. John Little walked at an obvious leisure, so he tapped John's flanks playfully with the flat of his sword. "Best get used to running, John."

Somehow John moved even slower, each step deliberately hanging in the air. "Best get used to disappointment, Robin." He winked.

No human being wanted to run in circles in the woods, not with winter on its way, not with so uncertain a future, no one. But they did it at his command, and he could only hope he was doing the right thing. After getting everything wrong with them in his first month, the change was as frightening as it was invigorating. There was a future to be built here, something started by his father and Marion that deserved a chance to work. Robin was still fumbling to figure it out, but he liked the shape it was taking.

Alan hadn't run with the others, so Robin just gave him an understanding nod. He needed a rest, and forcing him to run now might make him feel like a deeper failure. "What about you, Friar?" Robin turned to the man, seated on a log with the jug of small beer between his feet. "Want to learn how to swing a sword?"

Tuck looked down at his arm, strapped across his chest, in more or less the same way he would look at a wild boar sleeping on his lap.

Robin chuckled. "Right. Well, how about a knife?"

"Stealing supplies is one thing," Tuck wiped his moustache, "killing is quite another. Don't worry, I don't begrudge it you. You've done what you've seen fit. But I've chosen a path that abhors violence."

Robin instantly took offense, and had to remind himself Tuck couldn't know how invasive his statement was. "You make it sound as if I enjoy violence. I don't. I'm teaching these things to keep everyone safe."

"But we'll have to kill people to be safe," Alan said sadly, into his own sword. "Won't we? If we're going to sneak into the castle and save Elena and Will . . . there's no way we can do that without it getting bloody."

"You may be right, Alan." Robin met his eyes. "Or maybe not. We should be hearing back from Marion any day now, with all the information she's been able to gather about the upcoming funeral." He wished she was here now, but she insisted on taking frequent visits to Sheffield with Sir Amon to trade information with her contacts. "If we're lucky, we can sneak in and out without ever having to pull steel."

"It's not much of a plan yet," Alan grumbled. "The entirety of our plan is to make a plan."

That was not far from the truth. "The plan is to prepare," Robin tried to alleviate the man's fears, hoping he did not sound as desperate as they were. "That's what we're doing. Don't forget, this doesn't end with getting our friends back. That's where it *starts*. You can already see how many people are rallying to our cause, especially in the wake of the Sheriff's raids. If we pull this off . . . *when* we pull this off . . . it's going to be the start of something momentous. We're getting people to stand up for change, a real change. A *peaceful* change."

Their less-than-enthusiastic agreement was a little unnerving.

The only sounds that followed came from a clutter of birds somewhere in the central oak. Robin envied them, being largely certain the birds were not currently planning a rebellious assault on an impregnable castle. Not even *one* of them.

Eventually Tuck cleared his raspy throat. "Be careful about becoming a hero, Robin."

Your father was something of a hero, Marion had told him.

"Don't take offense now, but this isn't your fight." The friar tangled his fingers into the wild mess of his beard, but his eyes were piercing. "You never seemed to see eye to eye with your father's ideas, but now you've walked away from your king to stay and tend to Walter's dream. That sounds like a man who wants to be a hero."

Of course he had considered it. It was impossible not to enjoy the attention. But it was not what brought him back.

Tuck stood and massaged his injured elbow. "I wouldn't blame you. Where you came from, they praise the King for everything you do. But then you come here, and people are singing songs about *you*."

"You wrote those songs, Tuck." Robin pointed his finger. "Which I never asked for."

"That's true. But you came back. And I can't tell if people are interested in this peaceful change you talk about . . . or if they're interested in Robin Hood. Could be we've made you into something we shouldn't have. So be careful. There's no place for heroes in heaven."

Robin laughed. Heaven had even less to do with his motivations than heroism. "Is that in the Bible?"

"There's no heroes in the Bible, either." Tuck was sharper now, he didn't seem interested in Robin's non-answer. "Just ordinary people, doing what they could. Even in extraordinary circumstances."

Almost finished with their run, a group of ordinary people in their own extraordinary circumstances rounded their final corner, breathless and pushing themselves for a final sprint. Robin had not come back for their worship. But the fact they idolized him was proof that they needed help. Marion—and his father—had tried to build a world for them that they could shape for themselves. The opportunity was there, but none of them knew how to do it.

For too long, Robin had thrown his hands out in the air when people refused his help, as if to say, *Well, I tried. But the world is too hard.*

This time, instead of throwing his hands up, he was digging his heels in.

"Well, what about you?" Robin turned the question around. "Why are you here, Friar?"

Tuck grinned and picked up his cup. "Beer!"

"Excuse me?"

"John Little stole a ransom worth of beer from my village. I asked him where he was going and whether they needed a friar. He accepted." Tuck waited for

Robin to laugh, then threw his good arm around Robin's shoulder. "I'm no hero, either, I'm afraid. Heroes die gloriously. But drunkards always survive."

THEY SPENT LESS TIME thieving lately, as their inflow of new blood often brought supplies of their own. Besides, every encounter on the road brought an increasing element of danger now. Alan had brought back troubling news from his scouting shifts. In the two weeks since Bernesdale, the Sherwood Road had seen heavy use by contingents of guards from Yorkshire and Lincolnshire, headed toward the city. By Alan's description, a veritable army was being amassed in Nottingham. Robin accompanied him this day in the hopes of seeing some for himself, in case Alan didn't understand what he had seen. If Alan was right, he had to wonder if going to the Sheriff's funeral would indeed be suicide.

Stalking through the Sherwood again. It was a recurring hunt with a rotating cast. Robin wondered what William was doing now, what he was preparing. Again and again he replayed their conversation at Locksley, wondering what he could have said differently. *William had tried so hard to send him home,* before he had even explained what he'd done. That meant there was hope. William couldn't face Robin with his actions, because he knew he was in the wrong. After they rescued Will and Elena, once they stole William's victory, he would see reason.

He'd return to the war.

He'd have to.

The air was damp and the sky a light grey. The slightest of rain always had a way of muting the sounds of the forest. If it had been colder it might even have turned to snow, but instead water floated in the air and soaked their faces. Robin traveled through the trees with Alan, impressed with his ability to move without making noise. He thought about commenting on it, but was certain the young man would take it the wrong way. *You're very good at being unnoticed,* wasn't the type of thing Alan wanted to hear.

"I know why you came back," Alan said out of nowhere. "And it's not about being a hero."

"Oh?" Robin was, rarely, caught off guard.

"It's obvious." Alan slipped through a dense cluster of birches. "Marion. I recognize the way you look at her, even when you first showed up. She's . . . she's your *everything.* She's behind every word you speak."

"I don't know about *everything,*" Robin replied, somewhat embarrassed. After a lifetime of never talking of the *thing* between them, it was strange for it to suddenly be a reality. Their younger selves would have thought they were destined to be together like this, but life had intervened for so long. Somehow, against all odds, they had fought their way back. "I can do you one better, Alan. I know why you were able to recognize it."

Alan just squinted his face.

"I spent a lot of years pining after Marion, so I can recognize it in you. It's Elena, isn't it?"

Alan was suddenly a frightened child, caught misbehaving. “It’s not like that.”

“What’s it like, then?”

He hesitated. “I know she doesn’t want me.” He wouldn’t look at Robin, no longer careful about the noise he was making. “And that’s okay, it really is. Will is my best friend, I wouldn’t . . . I just wouldn’t, you know? Will’s a better man than me, he’s stronger and faster and smarter. Certainly funnier. She’s better off with him, I know it. I just . . .”

The leaves crunched underfoot. He kicked a bed of them into a beautiful violent plume.

“Have you ever had a perfect moment?” Alan asked, his face brightening. “A perfect little memory, that’s just yours? I had one a few months ago. We all had too much to drink. Will wasn’t there, I forget why. Elena was bumping shoulders with me, laughing at something I said, and then she leaned over and kissed my neck! Or, at least, I *think* she did. I can’t really remember. I was too drunk when it happened to know what to do, and a few seconds later it was too late to react anyway. So I just pretended it wasn’t a big deal. It was perfect, you know? It’s mine, I can hold onto that. And if it happens again, I’ll know what to do. I’ll react faster. I just need the right circumstances again, right?”

Robin might have let it lie, but he knew the recklessness such a thing could turn into. “She doesn’t love you,” he said.

“I don’t need her to. I just want some of those perfect moments. Now and then. I’m fine with that, I swear.” Robin was well familiar with the bargain Alan had made with himself. There was nothing so cruel as unrequited love. It was a thing too cruel to even call love at all—it was obsession, and Alan would cling to those little nuggets of hope. Those beautiful-terrible moments that made life livable-unbearable.

But it was *something* to live for, at least. There was still that.

A distant nothing noise distracted them. Robin looked up, noting that the thin colored ribbons they hid in the trees had become more obvious in autumn’s depths, even though no random wanderer could decipher their purpose. Still, Robin’s heart froze cold when he saw, in the distance, the shape of a thin man in a blue cloak, head cocked upward at one of the ribbons tied to a bough above him.

Instinct kept Robin calm, his muscles limp rather than rigid. For a few heavy moments he didn’t move, then he concealed himself silently behind a nearby low thicket. The stranger shifted rather precisely in various directions, the third of which left him staring directly at Alan. To Robin’s horror, it appeared Alan’s instincts in this situation were to put his hands out to his sides in the hopes of looking like a tree.

The cloaked man, shockingly, saw through Alan’s disguise. “Excuse me, friend!” The man’s voice was articulate, his clothes were far finer than an average traveler’s. Though he appeared to be alone, Robin still eased his sword from its scabbard, careful not to reveal himself yet. The strange man had a song in his voice for Alan. “Please, I beg your assistance, oh scurrilous forest bandit. I am so terribly overladen with jewelry and gold, or whatever other incentive may specifically interest you. If you have any wits at all about you, please serve me in as criminal a manner as you see fit. I should warn you that my guard is half-blind, in both eyes, so fully blind rather, it's a wretched condition. I don't suppose you could be so bothered as to fucking rob me, would you kindly?"

A dozen mysterious possibilities unraveled in Robin's mind, and he hoped this might be an innocent joyrider rather than an obvious trap. The stranger gestured for Alan to follow him, which he did. Robin trailed at a healthy distance, and Alan found a discreet moment to look back for instruction. Robin could offer him nothing.

Within a minute the trees thinned and they were upon the Sherwood Road, where there waited an unmistakable gaudy carriage outfitted with colorful streaming banners. Alan stepped onto the road ahead, nocked an arrow and aimed it limply at the stranger.

"Ah yes, perfect, thank you! I feel adequately threatened now. You have most overwhelmed me, and I humbly surrender. Take what you will!"

"Who are you?" Alan asked.

"I am a defenseless traveler with just so much gold. And I've had the hardest time finding somebody to take it from me. Have you been on holiday, perchance?"

The stranger lingered at the edge of the road. At least one more body sat atop the carriage, maybe one more inside. The stranger seemed to be around Robin's age, with dark and curly ruddy hair.

Alan was plainly clueless how to react, and simply said, "What?"

"Please," the stranger's tone dropped a bit, "for the love of anything you find holy, tell me you are not Robin Hood."

"No," Alan called out, to the stranger's obvious relief. Alan again glanced nervously back toward Robin's hiding spot, forcing him to duck down.

"But you know Robin Hood?"

"I might."

"There's no need to be a prude, now," the man said. "Have you any *acquaintance* with Robin Hood? He doesn't have to be your best friend for you to say yes."

"Aye, I know him," Alan said slowly.

"Excellent," the visitor clapped. "He's still in the thievery business, then?"

"I suppose."

"I only ask because I've been coming here for several days and haven't been thieved upon even once. Each time I bring fewer men and more wealth, but nobody seems interested in any of it. I'm feeling quite snubbed, actually. Do you like all my decorations? I don't know how we could make ourselves any more obvious."

Robin's trepidations melted as he gave the carriage a closer look. Two horses were harnessed at its lead, with bells lining their reins. Tied to the frame and dragging on the ground behind were several destroyed instruments—the bridge of a harp and the handle of a lute. A young man inside the carriage pushed his large head out to watch with mild interest. The gruffer man atop flopped his hands about to show how weaponless they were. It was another pack of tourists, who clearly had missed the news that Robin Hood's merry men had turned to assassins.

Alan's mouth waggled about. "Sorry, we've been busy this week."

The man just waved his hands and laughed. "I'm so sorry to interrupt. But I am eager to meet him, so if you would kindly lead us, we can all be on our way."

"Hurry on, then," the driver grumbled. "It's fucking cold out here."

"I can't just bring you to our camp," Alan said. "I have no idea who you are."

"Yes you do," the man sighed. "If you're the type of person who needs titles, you probably know me as Prince John."

Robin nearly gasped aloud. He had only met the prince once before, but now he could instantly recognize some of the man's features. What he was doing in the middle of the forest with only the slimmest of an entourage, begging to be robbed, was a question that would undoubtedly consume the rest of Robin's day.

"I'd ask for your name," the Prince explained, "but since we've already established it isn't Robin Hood, I frankly don't care at all. All I care about is that you take me and my immeasurable wealth to your leader, and that you do so before I strangle you out of boredom."

"Here," Robin said, moving out of hiding. Prince John turned sharply and exhaled, clapped his hands, and moved to greet Robin properly.

"Stay back," Alan ordered, once again raising his bow. "You're not allowed to get close to him."

"Yes I am, you witless sod," Prince John said back at Alan, but his eyes stayed on Robin, with seemingly no fear. "Because I'm here to fucking help you."

FORTY-FOUR

ELENA GAMWELL

PRISONS OF NOTTINGHAM CASTLE

THIS ISN'T HOW IT ends.

This prison cell, it was just a place. They'd been many places, and each was theirs to leave. Simply a matter of waiting for the right moment, and not hesitating to choose. Together, she and Will, they'd climbed out of much worse places than this.

That was a lie. This was the worst.

Elena had been in and out of gaol before, growing up in the maze of alleys on the south end of Nottingham. She'd chosen to leave that life. Catty-corner to St. Mary's Church was a gaol that earned the name Sinner Mary's. It offered more protection than the streets could, and on one occasion she'd been arrested on purpose since she knew Will was in for a stint. That was before he was hers. Rather, before he knew he was hers. She'd chosen that as well.

But Sinner Mary's had still been a normal building, a tall stone square. This prison in the castle was something else entirely. It was a cave, clawed out of the earth beneath the courtyards. On the other side of her iron gate was more cave, only lit when the guards came. Otherwise, the dark. A small hole had been dug a handswidth deep beneath the bars where she was to relieve herself. Every so often, a man with a shovel would come by and remove its contents, not caring if it spilled over the floor in the process. She didn't mind. The stink would protect her from any errant guard with an itch between his legs.

Time didn't work down here. There was no telling when it was day or night, or how many of either had passed.

It was just a place. One more story to tell later. Beads on a string. That was life—simply a series of events. It was just a matter of choosing to move from one to the next, her and Will. Too many people complained about their lot, their life, their rotten luck. Elena chose to be better than that. That's all it took, the act of choosing, and all that was left was to walk it. Out of the Alleys. Out of Ten Bell Yard. Sinner Mary's. Red Lion Square. *Anywhere.* Redford. Locksley Castle. The Oak Camp. Bernesdale. Nottingham Prison. Somewhere Else. Somewhere Better. Somewhere Safe.

This is the last bead, her fear laughed at her. *This is where you'll die.*

She pushed the thought down. There would be a chance to leave this place. She chose to be sharp enough to find it. Half of luck was simply having the courage to act when the moment was right. Killing the Sheriff, for instance, had been a perfect chance with a tiny window of opportunity. If she and Will had debated it with the others, it would have passed them by. Instead they'd jumped on instinct, and everything she suffered now was worth it. It would be over, soon enough. She just had to keep her eyes open for that next window.

Still, it was harder without Will. He was somewhere down here, too, *"down the north tunnel,"* she had overheard. Every now and then, after waiting too long and then even longer, she'd give a trill little whistle from her cell to let Will know she was still there. Every now and then, after dying of fear and pinching herself to keep from crying, and then longer, she'd hear the response, just barely from down the tunnel. Or maybe she didn't. Or maybe she thought she did. Or maybe some other prisoner was just copying her.

She wouldn't let this place get the better of her. That's what they wanted, it's why they built it. It was cold and damp because they *wanted* her to be uncomfortable. If she let that bother her, they got what they wanted. When she missed Will so much it hurt, when she wanted to scratch her own hair out, that was their plan, too. It wouldn't work, not on her. She wouldn't be staying here. This was just a place. It was just a place.

Her mind flirted with a thought. Like scratching a bug bite, she'd realize she was doing it before remembering not to.

William de Wendenal's offer.

No, that wasn't the way they'd get out of this. Not by someone else's hand. No, they would get through it together, her and Will. That was her choice.

You'll have to make another choice, her fear whispered. *The choice to leave him behind.*

Will. She didn't see his face when she thought of him, but rather a collection of expressions, just an instant long each. A flash of his eyebrows. A wrinkling of his nose. A guilty smile he couldn't hide. That stupid way he'd flick his tongue out when he thought he was being intimidating. The way he'd brush a floppy wave of blondfire off his forehead just to have it tumble forward again. His little half utterances that weren't words when he was trying to think. The stubble on his cheek, it felt differently on her hand than it did on her lips, than it did on her thighs.

For years she had skirted at the outsides of the Ten Bells, taking grief for being a girl but growing up to give as much as she took. Once they were old enough for such things, half the Bells boasted of having spent a night with her, but at least half of them were liars. Will never paid her no mind, and gave his attention instead to girls he knew he could play with and throw away.

"Why me?" he'd asked one night, lying naked in her arms in someone's bed, someone who would later come home in time to see them climbing out the window.

"You're better than them," she said, with crystal certainty. *"Everyone important started somewhere. The other boys will grow up and die here. But this is just where you start. I can see it."*

That had been all he needed. Will wasn't interested in petty gang territories anymore. They had left Nottingham that night. Will even got on a knee to ask her to join him. She only whispered one word into his ear.

"Anywhere."

THE ONLY LIGHT CAME with the gords, and left with them, too. That meant the darkness was safest, the shadows became security. The moment she was capable of seeing something, the future became dangerous.

They told her she'd hang, and she had no idea how long ago that had been. In all that time, she had not been harmed. Only once had she worried, when a gord came alone, scratching between his legs and sucking in his breath, eyeing her. That blank stare men get when they can only see one thing. *"Go ahead,"* she had said, *"if you like warts on your cock. I might even enjoy it, since no one else will touch me."*

But something told her that empty threats weren't the reason she hadn't been touched. Someone wanted her healthy, which meant she was valuable.

They could take anything they wanted from her, except her collection of facts.

The only time she'd left the cage was for that talk with William de Wendenal. But he had said, *"Good morning,"* so she had watched the shadows move, slowly. So slowly, but it had been enough. Now she knew which direction was east, so she also knew which direction was north. She had memorized the number of footsteps down each tunnelway as they traveled. She kept a map in her mind. She'd get a chance to use it. Will was somewhere down the north tunnel.

Every bit of information was a weapon in her hands. There'd be an opportunity. She just had to be ready.

When next she awoke, it was noise and light, and she kept herself curled on the ground, pretending to be asleep. An iron gate opened and closed, and for a fierce moment her blood stopped, her skin prickled into ice.

It's time, the dark gripped her. *Up to the gallows with Elena Gamwell. They'll make Will watch.*

But the door wasn't hers. It was the cell beside her, which had always been empty. So far as she could tell, there were only the two cells in this finger of the tunnels, probably reserved for exclusive guests like sheriff-killers. "Wait here," came a man's voice. "We'll get it sorted."

She peeked through her eyelids as the gord closed the door again, and rumbled off down the tunnelway.

"Excuse me," a ragged voice came from beside her. Before the light vanished, two bony fingers wrapped around the bars between them, then two more. "Are you new?"

Part of Elena wanted to respond coldly. She knew better than to befriend another prisoner down here. That was a trick the gords had used in Sinner Mary's. They'd put one of their own in the cells, to play the victim and make friends. Captivity had a way of blinding people to danger. *Us versus them* tastes good. But she could hear the man's knuckles rattle against the iron. She reached out and touched them, paperthin skin stretched over hard bone. Her heart went out to the old man, and there was no harm in civility.

"I am new," she said. "How long have you been here?"

"Have you seen my children?"

Her throat was dry now, and it was harder to answer. Maybe there was less air to breathe. She had to move away from him, for some reason she had to. "No, I'm sorry."

"Oh," he creaked. It didn't seem to be the answer he was looking for. She knew it was a terrible thought, but all that rang through her head as she turned away was *don't let that be me.*

You'll have to make that choice.

A minute later, an hour later, a day later, she felt her neighbor shift, startle, and grab at the bars again. "Are you new?" he asked a second time. Curiosity got the better of her, she leaned over again, against the bars, she felt his quivering finger, the crispy callus at its tip brushed her cheek. "Have you seen my children?"

His breath was warm but stank of rot—they were mere inches from each other. She squinted, and could make out the faintest of details. He was bald, his pupils so wide there was no knowing the color of his eyes. White and red milk mixed at their corners, and his skin was wrinkled and spotted.

"They love you," she whispered for some reason, "and they're safe."

When he blinked, his eyes were wetter. "Oh, little El. Tell Norman and Stephen to watch over their mother. Tell Amelia I'll be a little late."

Elena's heart stopped. *Little El*... she'd been one of Much's playmates, the daughter of Amelia and Baynard. Baynard had been Lord Walter of Locksley's chamberlain. Elena, along with the rest of their group, had long assumed he had died in the fire or afterward, despite Amelia's belief that her husband was still alive.

Baynard shook his head numbly back and forth. "Are you new?" he asked. "Have you seen my children?"

Not like him, the fear clawed at her skull. *You have to get out.*

THE NEXT DAY BAYNARD was gone, replaced by a new prisoner, a massive man with beady eyes amidst a mane of hair. The now familiar darkness was traded away for a regular lantern that kept the newcomer's cell bright. The gords treated him with respect, brought him a chair, gave him plenty of opportunities to stretch out of his cage. His name was Morg, apparently, and he was a Guardsman, apparently, who had done something wrong, apparently. She didn't care for the stink of gord, but his presence made a change of pace for the better.

He wasn't talkative. *"You don't speak,"* he'd order when she tried to ask him a question. Sometimes he'd respond with only a violent grunt that sounded very much like his own name. Even still, this beastman's snorting was better than nothing.

"What will you do to me if I *do* speak?" she asked him. "It's not quite as threatening when you're behind bars as well."

"You don't speak."

"I guess you're wrong about that," she snarled. "So what did you do? Innocent, I'm sure. But I killed a sheriff. Did you do anything as bad as all that? If not, it's not really fair for you to end up the same place I did, is it? I think that's sort of funny. Don't you think that's sort of funny?"

"You don't speak."

"I do speak. I just did. I'm still speaking. You're the one that doesn't speak. Except to say, *'You don't speak.'* That's sort of funny, too, isn't it?"

He didn't speak.

The gords that tended to her new friend were kinder to her as well. *They were new.* Not the same faces she'd seen in the first part of her captivity, not even the same uniform. These ones wore a fresh forest green over their tunics, which was enough to tell Elena something troubling was brewing up above.

At Sinner Mary's, the best opportunities were in the middle of guard rotations.

This was something more than that—it was a complete changeover.

This was the opportunity. If she waited a day, an hour, even a breath to learn more, it would be gone.

The last time she had hesitated, for a solitary moment, the cost was Much's life.

"Tell the Sheriff I'm willing to make a bargain," she told one of them, who raised an eyebrow but agreed. Once he was gone she stretched her arms, her legs, her back, reawakening every muscle that had found new pains since she had been thrown into the cell. She'd need them soon.

The next time footsteps approached her end of the tunnel, it wasn't for Morg. A new guard who smelled of pork and feet kicked dirt through the bars of Elena's cell and unlocked it. She'd been at the mercy of men most of her life, men who thought their brute strength made them strong. Sometimes she'd let them threaten her, she'd play meek, she'd choose to let them believe what they wanted. Other times she would correct them. A fellow like this pigfoot wasn't worth correcting. Still, her heart pumped and her face flushed cold as she was flung out of her cell.

But she could control that fear. When men spoke of bravery they thought that talking about it made it theirs. Thinking when the time would come they could simply decide to be brave. Fear was the same way. *You can't prepare to be afraid, you can only get better at it over time.* Elena had been afraid too many times in her life, so she knew what to expect. It was a shocking sensation, fear, how it simultaneously numbs and enhances the world.

She had memorized the pathways. She closed her eyes now as they walked, just to confirm she knew where she was. There would be a set of empty cages at the base of the tunnel upward, locked with a heavy gate. There were sounds, not many, mostly groans and whispers, coming down other tunnelways. She wondered about the others here, imprisoned for too long, what they thought when they saw her.

You'll end up just like them, the fear scratched. *You'll miss your chance, thinking you can save Will, too. You can't.*

Eventually the pigfoot guard grunted something only pigfeet would understand. With the same amount of respect as earlier, she was thrown to the ground outside the gate that led up to the surface cage, while pigfoot fumbled with his keys. She glanced at the holding cages beside the door, one empty with its door open, the other held a withered bald figure whose piteous fingers she recognized. Baynard.

There was no time for second thoughts. She heaved her chest into a sob, as best she could, and let her body go limp so that he'd have to pick her up. She made the pigfoot stoop to carry her, grabbing her by the armpit, and she whimpered, a wavering sob sound. His hand retracted just a hair, thinking he'd hurt her. She sobbed harder, he pushed the gate open, then nudged her through.

His head made a thick crack when she twirled and slammed the gate onto it. She pulled him back in place and slung the iron mass into his temples a second time, a dull reverberating noise loping down the hallway. She jabbed her fingers at his throat to keep him from making any sound. A third slam and his big body shivered and sloughed onto the floor. She twisted and pulled the keys from the gate, locking him on the other side, and slid into the holding cage beside the door. There she was effectively invisible, and she needed a moment to clear her mind.

A slow march of infinite time passed. Her heart was racing, but she forced herself to focus on stillness, to listen to the environment. After they'd killed the Sheriff they had run through the castle in panic, forgetting to pay attention. She wouldn't make that mistake again. She kept one eyelid closed still—there was lantern light here she didn't want to acclimate to, she would switch eyes as she moved in and out of darkness. In the deep inky wretch of waiting, she heard other slams of gates, other noises and shouts, but nothing worrying. No danger yet.

The wide tunnel to the east led up and out. But she didn't have Will.

Go now, it said. *This is your only chance.*

She breathed once, twice, calmed herself, and ran away from the exit and down the north tunnel. When she came to the first fork, she hugged a wall and pursed her lips. A short little trill, it echoed down the length, colder and hollow. Something swelled inside of her, a lazing dizziness. The skin on her arms pimpled and her feet curled into little balls, until finally the return whistle came. And it was close.

She raced down an unknown branch in the tunnels, fingers patting against the ever-constricting walls, alternating dry and wet. The cave curled into a hub of cells like her own. No lights, no lanterns. Lanterns meant guards. But the eye she'd protected could just barely distinguish the shapes around her. She peeled her body around the entrance and clicked her tongue twice, quietly. To her right came the answer, and a moment later her arms reached through the bars around him. Her lips kissed his hair, his arm wrapped around her waist and pulled her hard.

His was barely a whisper, "God's balls, I fucking love you."

She kissed his head again and again. "Keys?" she asked, and Will pointed. Off the hook they came. Carefully, to keep them from rattling, she tried each in Will's gate until it gave way, lurching outward with far more noise than she would have preferred. Will took a moment to stretch, then he placed the keys delicately inside his neighbor's cell. Elena tugged at him. *They shouldn't risk bringing anyone else.* But his neighbor oddly didn't move, just stared at the keyring, and Elena pulled Will out and away.

She held his hand as they ran, though they didn't say a word. His fingers felt thinner than normal. Lantern light grew at an intersection ahead of them, and she pulled to the side. He squeezed her incredulously, but she knew what she was doing. She put her finger to his lips, which he kissed, and the light grew until its owner could be seen, walking across the hallway, and disappeared down the other side again. Elena waited until its glow was almost imperceptible, then they were off again, keeping to the walls, eventually back to the holding cages, and the slope up.

Will tugged her toward the exit, but mercy compelled her to pause for a moment at Baynard's cage. She pushed the first key into the lock but it stuck oddly, she hastened to pull it out *and the key snapped.* With horror she knelt down and saw the broken chunk of iron, sheared off, now wedged into the keyhole's recess. She grappled at its bars and looked for any weakness, to no effect. Baynard, inside, gasped and crawled away from her. She plied the tip of her finger into the keyhole to try to scratch out the broken key, until Will's arms engulfed her from behind, holding her still, holding her tight.

"We have to go," he whispered, and Elena let the tears come, hot on her cheeks. Will cradled her head and wiped her face. She nodded and started to leave. "I'm sorry," Will said to the man he didn't recognize in the cage. "God, I'm so sorry. I'm sorry."

That was it, then. There was no rethinking it. Up the slope, the tunnel curved to the left until daylight crept in, faint at first and then sudden, blinding. It was a long even tunnel that led into the white, and no silhouettes of bodies blocked the way. Will's breath escaped him in a quiet laugh and he entwined his fingers with hers. They kept running even after the white glow became soft enough to reveal the tall even bars at the exit.

It wouldn't matter, she thought. One of her keys would open it. Or it would be nearby, as the last one had been.

But there was nothing else nearby. Just tunnel wall and the iron, a square gate in its middle, locked. None of their keys were even the right size. The air moved here, it felt glorious against her skin, but it could pass through the bars that she could not.

"Hallo, then."

There was a black shape on the other side, light all behind him. Neither Elena nor Will made to conceal themselves, there was nowhere to hide.

"Need a little help, then?"

The shape stopped too far away from the bars, too far for them to reach through and grab him. "No need to be cross then, you can talk to me. What are your names?"

"Go to hell," Will mumbled, turning away.

"I'm so sorry," he replied, "I am, that's an awful name. Must have been difficult on you. And then this, on top of it all, what a rotten day for you. Only gets worse, too. Have you seen one of these?"

The man drifted to the side, and came back hefting the silhouette of a crossbow. "Nasty business, this one. Goes through these bars more than a bit easier than you could."

"So what?" Will asked, pitiful and desperate. Elena's heart could have broken. "You're going to hang us. Why not die today rather than wait?"

The figure crouched down, a little closer. Still not close enough. His eyes were set wide, large, they pushed forward. "Boy, I don't mean to be mean. But trust me, this isn't the way to go. Hanging is clean, and before God. You don't want to die where you can't see the sky. And I don't want to kill you. Please don't make me. Go back to your cells, and pray. I'll pray for you, too, I swear it."

Will slammed his body against the bars and slumped down, letting out something between a scream and a laugh. Elena reached down and twisted her fingers into his hair, tracing the back of his neck. His other hand came up to meet hers, wrapping around her finger.

"I'll give you a minute," the gord said. "Don't be here when I come back."

"You don't escape," Morg said, once they were alone again. "You could have asked me."

It was dark, her cell seemed smaller now. "You don't speak," Elena mocked him, and he actually gave a gentle laugh.

"Let me tell you how it works. There's no way out. It takes two keys, one from the inside, and one from the outside. Every last prisoner could get out of their cell and still never get nowhere. No weapons down here, nothing to fight with, nothing to threaten us with. Do you see, girl? Besides, even if you got out that main gate, you'd be dead. You'd come out right in the middle bailey, and the full force of the Guard would come down on you with steel. You die, you simply die. You mean to kill yourself? Dash your head against the rocks and be done with."

"That's fine advice, coming from a gord."

"Girl, I'm looking at a noose, same as you. I know these prisons. If there were a way out, I'd take it myself." There were some scraping sounds then, nothing she could understand. "There isn't."

Elena closed her eyes and focused on the last moments she'd had with Will before they separated. But already the details slipped away. She didn't remember how long his hair was, or what he had been wearing, or where the bruises on his face lay. She hadn't looked at him long enough to watch him smile, or memorize the lines on his forehead. She couldn't picture his nose quite well enough. She put her hands to her own face, feeling her every curve, imagining it was his.

At some point later, maybe an hour, maybe a minute, she remembered. "The staircase up, that leads to the cage in the courtyard . . ."

"The Rabbit Hole," Morg answered quickly. "Takes two keys, same as the front."

"Never mind that. There are cages at its entrance. There's an old man named Baynard in the second one. The key is broken in the lock, the door can't open."

Morg's head nodded. "I'll tell them Derby boys about it. They'll see to it."

Elena held herself tighter. "Thank you."

It was the last thing she could think of to do. Now there was nothing but the wait. It was there, of course, that unspoken nag at the back of her mind, but she put it away.

There's no escape from this prison. That's not how real life works.

He would come and meet her again. He'd make the offer again, hoping she would be more desperate. She could still make a choice, the choice to say no. She couldn't give up the camp, not even if Wendenal swore to let the women and children leave safely. She couldn't be responsible for bringing them here. Not Arthur and David, who'd kept her safe more times than she could remember. Not Alan and his silly crush on her he thought nobody knew about. And certainly not John Little, who had been a father to her, the kindest soul she had ever known. She could protect them, by saying no.

You brought Much to Bernesdale, it laughed.

That wasn't on her.

You couldn't save him.

It was on the Captain, for trapping them. It was on the Sheriff, for ordering it. It was on Robin, for lying to them.

You can't save Will, it bled.

She pushed it down.

But you can still save yourself.

She pushed it down, down.

FORTY-FIVE

ROBIN OF LOCKSLEY

THE OAK CAMP

PRINCE JOHN'S FACE HARDENED around a lunatic's smile, as if he could not fathom the concept of being denied that which he wanted. "I wonder if you misheard everything I said. You need help. I want to give you help. And as far as help goes, I'm about as spectacular a friend as you could possibly hope for."

"Oh, I heard it all," Robin laughed, stepping down from the carriage's sideboard as the prince closed the door on himself. A moment later his head popped out its window, begging for a different answer. Robin leaned closer. "I'll consider your offer, but I'm sure you can understand I need to speak with the group before I can make any promises."

"I *can* understand that, but I willfully choose not to." John lilted his head dramatically against the window's intricately whittled frame. "That's why I became a prince. You'll find you get your way more often if you ignore everyone else's feelings. You should try it. I've already heard someone refer to you as the prince of thieves."

Robin didn't care for that moniker at all. "Who said that?"

"A very fat man who hates princes. Of all kinds."

A clatter of tortured wood and metal distracted them, as Hadrian's blade freed the carriage of its tail of broken instruments. So too went the colorful banners and sleigh bells that had draped along the sides.

"Nobody's going to believe us," Alan exclaimed, hopping at the side of the road in excitement. "I wish you would have come back to meet everyone!"

"Were you counting?" the prince asked him, staring at his own fingers.

"I'm sorry?"

"Were you counting?"

Alan paused to look down to the ground. "No, sorry, I wasn't."

Prince John slapped the wooden frame and cackled. "No, no, you're supposed to ask *what*?"

"What?" Alan asked, because he was so perfectly lost.

"Yes, just so! I ask, *Were you counting*? Then you say, *What*? And I say, *The number of times I asked you about your friends and family*. Then you would, with some difficulty probably, come to the correct answer of *Zero*. Because I have a staggering lack of interest in meeting your friends and family. Meeting *everyone* sounds like the least pleasant way I could possibly spend an afternoon."

Robin chuckled, hearing a familiar canter in John's voice. "You remind me of your brother."

"One of the dead ones? Or Richard?"

"Richard."

"Ah. Well that's odd." The prince smirked. "I was going to say that *you* remind *me* of him. I'll see you soon, I think."

At John's signal, the carriage eased to motion with no further fanfare. Its last remaining ribbon caught in its spokes until Robin stomped his foot down upon it, snapping the tether.

It was, by and far, the last way he could have possibly expected to spend his afternoon. The sky might have turned red, showered beets and carrots from the clouds, and still Robin would find it less strange than the time he chatted with the prince in the middle of the woods about starting rebellions.

"So what do we do?" Alan asked.

"I wasn't lying. I'll bring this up with the group." Robin readjusted his belongings for the hike back to the Oak Camp. "But I'm not interested in his offer."

"What's wrong with it? Gold, powerful friends on our side . . ."

"Prince John has his own interests in mind, Alan. Not ours." John didn't simply want to help them, he wanted to redirect them. He wanted to finance and franchise them. John wanted to provide his own targets for them to hit, both to burglar and to kill. He wanted Robin to train new groups in neighboring counties, all at John's discretion. In essence, he wanted to build his own secret army.

"He's not allowed any military strength of his own," Robin explained. "No castles, no armies, such were the stipulations of him being allowed back into England. Richard's always been a bit paranoid of those closest to him."

"Is that why he sent you away?" Alan asked.

Robin paused, having no answer.

Alan blew out his lips. "Well, it sounded like a good deal to me."

Which was precisely why Robin had been skeptical of it. An unusually good deal was always more suspicious than an unusually bad one. "It's a question of what we want, Alan, and why we want it. If we just want to give the Nottingham Guard hell for the sake of it, we could sign on with Prince John. But if we want to make our own difference, our own way, then do we really want to be beholden to him? What happens when he asks us to do something we don't agree with?"

"I don't know," Alan admitted. "Just seems like a lot to turn down."

"It is." If Prince John was telling the truth, his help could have changed everything. But the odds of that were staggeringly thin. Robin looked up, searching for the nearest colored ribbon in the trees that marked the way home.

"He said he was going to Nottingham. What if he could help us with the Sheriff's funeral?"

"What if he doesn't want us involved at all?" Robin asked back. "If we told him our plans to rescue Will and Elena, he might have put a stop to it." He had been careful to avoid giving up any details the prince did not already have, especially in regard to their intentions with Nottingham.

Marion could get them all the information that John claimed to have and more, and she was a good ways prettier, too.

"We don't have the luxury of trusting anyone we don't know, not until we get this done."

Alan shrugged, clearly unconvinced. But Alan was just a farmhand who had been swept into this world, and thought the distinction between friends and enemies was absolute. Robin wondered if he had been teaching them the wrong things. Training to fight was a functional skill, but it reinforced the idea that swordplay was the solution to their problems. Instead, he needed to teach them how to *think*. He had taken for granted the ease of working with someone like William, who instinctively looked for the deeper motivations behind every opportunity. Robin needed to teach someone as simple as Alan how to anticipate not the next move, but the one that came five moves after that.

He didn't have the damnedest idea how to do that.

And worse, William was on the opposite side looking five moves into Robin's future, which was four more than Robin knew himself. He had barely figured out his current step, which was a long shot on its own.

It took them half an hour to return to the camp, moving briskly, saying little. Despite the wet air the forest was dry, there was more brown than orange on the ground and the trees had begun to transform into naked spears that offered little protection. He could spy the Oak Camp from a noticeably farther distance than even a week earlier, which meant that others could, too. He thought on Prince John, staring up at an exposed ribbon in the trees, positioning himself as if he knew precisely what he was looking at.

"We'll have to break down the camp," Robin said, just as he realized it. Alan reacted with appropriate shock. "We can't stay here. We can't take any more risks. Prince John found us."

Alan struggled with it. "But he was just waiting on the road for us—"

"But he knew *where* to wait. Some of our people who left after Much . . . I'll bet some of them have been talking."

Alan gasped. "Who do you think it was?"

"Doesn't matter," Robin said. "If we can be found once, we can be found again."

That's what Robin would do, if he were trying to catch himself. And in so many ways, that's exactly what was happening.

When they entered the clearing, Robin intended on gathering the group as quickly as possible, to explain the need for a hasty breakdown. He had no inclinations as to where they would go, but elsewhere was safer than here. If Marion had not returned by the morning, he wouldn't be able to wait for her. A cold wind moved through him, as he wondered what exceptions he might allow himself in order to send her word of their movement.

The crowd was already gathered beneath the oak's boughs, but Robin was too preoccupied to guess as to its cause. "Did you see Amon?" asked John Little.

"Amon? No," Robin answered, then startled to look around the camp. If Sir Amon were here, then Marion was already back as well.

"Fack," cursed David, nudged forward by the others. "Alright, Robin. I drew the short straw, as to who was going to break the news to you."

A chill clamped over him. There was no way those words heralded anything good. "Break what news?"

Arthur swallowed. "Amon was here," he said. "Came from Sheffield. Said that the Sheriff's men . . . said they came for Marion last night."

Robin's muscles froze. Everyone in the world became a stone for him to shatter.

"He says they took her to Nottingham. Says we shouldn't go after her."

"They arrested her?"

"Worse. From what Amon described, sounds like the new sheriff aims to marry her."

In the end, it was a raging calm that consumed him. Functionally, there was nothing at the moment he could do, and his body sought to hold every slight movement in reserve, to unleash when he needed it. John Little warned the group not to bother him, and they didn't. Robin found himself at the edge of camp, his feet luring him away from them, trying to trick his body into leaving now. But Robin tempered himself. He slowly made wide large circles around the camp, keeping the clearing just within eyesight. On the edge of the treeline, on the edge of reason, dipping in and out like a man falling asleep. If forced to, he would guess an hour had passed. The air was wetter now, just enough to call rain, and it was dark within and without. Robin was cold and like to get sick from it, and didn't care in the least.

When his emotions cooled enough to form sentences, it hurt anew. Every level of it was more painful than the last. Marion being abducted, threatened. William's decision to use her to get to Robin. The escalation, the attempt to draw Robin out of the woods, to show his hand too early. The coldness of William's strategy.

The fact that it would work.

Someone, of course, eventually came for him. They must have drawn straws again since it was Alan, and he was ever so good at losing. With two steaming cups in his hands, probably the last batch of awful cider Tuck would make for some time, he came aimlessly searching. The cups were decorative, ornamental things taken from someone or other they'd stopped on the road. Back when pretty trinkets were things worth getting excited about. Alan stomped his way through the trees, lost, missing Robin entirely, his head ducked down as if the rain would ignore him that way.

Robin spoke Alan's name out of some long-lost pity, before the man wandered too far away and hurt himself. But Robin did not move to retrieve him, keeping his seat on what once was a dry stump. His own hood was over his head to protect him from the wetness, a strategy that had clearly eluded Alan.

"I brought one for you." Alan held the cup out.

Robin didn't take it. "No thank you. I won't sleep well."

"Two for me, then." He looked around for something to sit on, but it was all too wet, so he just kept standing.

"You'd best get some sleep for tomorrow," Robin said quietly.

"What's tomorrow?"

He almost couldn't believe the man had forgotten. "We're packing."

"Right."

Alan took a long sip from the cup, then another, having nothing else to do or say.

The idea of lingering in awkward silence with Alan was actually worse than the idea of talking to him long enough for him to leave. "I wish we had known about this before our visit with the prince today," Robin said.

"About Marion you mean?"

Of fucking course about Marion. "The damned timing of it all. With Marion captured, we're on our own, in the dark. We need information on the Sheriff's funeral to rescue Will and Elena, and Marion can't help us anymore. Prince John offered us exactly what we needed, but I didn't know we needed it."

He wanted to keep the conversation on tactics. If Alan opened his mouth to talk about how Marion was his *everything* again, Robin was likely to break the man's teeth.

But Alan just nodded in agreement. "Well, he did tell us how to communicate with him in Nottingham. Guess he was right when he said, *'See you soon.'*"

Robin tipped his head back to let the rain touch his face. "It was risky enough before. A public funeral, a public hanging. They're practically inviting us inside."

"So the only way to make this work is to trust Prince John's help?"

Robin made a long full bow of his head, yes.

Alan's morale seemed as soggy as his tunic. The rain went colder, a shudder cracked through Robin's spine. Little imagination was required to see how the day might unfold against them. Rescuing Will and Elena was one thing. As long as they plotted out an escape route, they could use the advantage of a sympathetic mob, the cover of confusion, theatrics. It was possible. But with Marion as a hostage William could use as leverage, the idea of simultaneously saving her made everything else a thousand times less possible. It was a perfect move for William, and Robin could only blame himself for not anticipating it. It was a trap so clever the only way to avoid it was to let Will and Elena die.

"You need to consider the reality that you will likely see your two friends with ropes around their necks," Robin said, no longer interested in tiptoeing around Alan's softness. "Hell, you might even be standing next to them."

"Maybe we don't need Prince John," Alan tried. "I'll bet I could cut both their nooses off the gallows with a single arrow."

At this, Robin laughed. It might have been the first funny thing Alan had said all day. Well after the sensation of smiling was gone, Robin finally looked up at Alan, a little surprised that he was a human, and that they were both there.

"I don't know what to do."

The poor man's face twisted into something painful. "We have to go, Robin. You're right, we don't know what will happen if we go. But we know exactly what will happen if we don't. If we don't go, they'll die."

"I can't promise we'll get them back."

"I know."

"I can't even promise we'll get close."

"I know." Alan's mouth tried very hard to leave his face. "But at least we'll die trying."

It was the sort of thing Robin had heard before, from young soldiers in the war, convinced that a glorious death in the face of overwhelming odds was somehow enviable. Robin leaned back into the tree to give Alan his full attention. "Do you mean that?"

"No," he admitted, sheepishly. "Maybe if I were Will, I could say yes. Or Sir Amon, or even Arthur, I bet they'd fight to the death. But I . . . as I am reminded far too often . . . am just Alan." There was something terrible and honest about it, and it took Robin by surprise. "I don't want to die. I don't know what the hell Will was thinking. First of all, he shouldn't have taken Elena with him. He should have taken me. And second of all, I would have told him not to do it in the first of all. I don't know how he let himself get so carried away. We all loved Much, but you didn't see the rest of us running off to kill the Sheriff."

Robin nodded.

"It was never like this before," Alan continued. "We never got into any real trouble, is what I mean. There was a scare or two, more than that maybe. But even then, it wasn't like this. Nobody ever got killed, that's for certain." Robin didn't react, but Alan quickly corrected himself. "Sorry. Excepting your father."

There was no offense given.

"I ever tell you I knew him? I'm sure you figured. Terrible thing, what happened. I'd been pulling grain for him for about a year beforehand, worked the stables some, too. How I met Will. Your father was nice, you know, he never treated anyone like they were workers. Often times he'd even lend a hand. No, he was nice, but he had a strong head about *the king*-this, and *the government*-that, said it took his boy away. I guess he meant you. He had a fire in him when it came to that sort of thing. If I were him, I would have just paid the taxes."

Robin had made the same complaint to Marion.

"Well, he believed in something," Alan's voice grew tighter, "and he got dead. Will Scarlet, I suppose he believes in something, too, and now he's about to get dead. He's gonna get Elena dead, too, for it. But even Little John, these Delaney brothers, they're all fighting for their land or the people or something. Or something. You know why I'm here?" The wetness in Alan's eyes was no longer coming from the rain. "It's *fun.* It is, you know? The stealing and the fighting, sneaking around and getting away with it all . . . you know how exciting pulling grain is? This . . . this is fun." He looked up again, where the silhouettes of the branches were darker than the cloudy sky above. "At least it was until people started dying."

Robin gazed upward at the heavy mottled clouds, drifting along so high above, not even noticing the two of them as they rumbled on elsewhere. When he looked down again, Alan's face was more real than it had ever been. Something tender had taken over.

"Have you ever seen red?" Robin asked.

Alan didn't seem to understand the question.

"Some say it's just a phrase, others say it's real. When you snap, you find out. You find out what sort of violence you really have in you." Robin paused, even the rain paused. He wasn't sure why he started saying it, he hadn't even realized it was on his mind. "I had a brother, you know. He . . . he succumbed to that. That thing, inside us."

"I know," Alan said, gently.

While Alan could only imagine the horrors of seeing his friends hang, Robin's mind had gone somewhere else. He knew what would happen to anyone who got in between him and Marion. William had picked Marion for a reason, to draw Robin out. It was a personal attack, and an absolute violation of their history together. In every dark fantasy of what happened next, it ended with Robin and William in the same room, swords against each other. It ended with Robin seeing red.

"That violence," he said at last, "I don't want to find out if I have it, too."

Alan's mouth opened to respond, but rethought it. Eventually he asked, "Is that why you always seem against us killing anyone?"

Robin shrugged. He didn't want to think on it any longer.

"If you don't mind my saying so, for someone who is so against violence, you're very good at it."

A lump stopped in Robin's throat. "You have to study your enemy."

"Robin," Alan's voice had startling clarity, "you are not your brother."

Those words hit Robin with a relief he had not realized he needed.

"Whatever you decide, we'll follow you," Alan urged him. "Just don't decide out of fear. Fear just keeps you from doing the things you know you should. It holds you back. None of us are here because we're afraid, we're here because we want to do what's right."

The rain fell on them both, harder, until it was impossible to ignore. Finally Robin smiled and pointed at the second glass, now overflowing. "You heard why Friar Tuck is here, didn't you?" he asked. "Beer. He wanted to be where the beer was."

"Tuck's a humble man." Alan shook his head. "Nobody does this for beer."

Robin stood and put a hand on Alan's shoulder. *"Nobody does this for fun, either."*

A brave young man named Alan-a-Dale raised his face to the sky to trade his tears for rain. "Then let's get Elena back," he said. "Let's get them both back."

"Let's get them *all* back," Robin agreed, because it was their only choice. And if they had to pull this off, then they would. There was nothing else to decide.

They walked back to camp together.

INTERLUDE

GILBERT WITH THE WHITE HAND

WELL, THESE GUARDS WERE an entirely different sort of who, weren't they?

Driven, as it were. Not different in their composite stuff, all blood and bone still, gristle. Men never came different as such, always two arms and legs unlessing they'd been cleaven off. Some men are greedy that way, take more than their fair. But these Guards—these whos—they leaned forward into their future, making of it what they would. Not like Marion's men, who would only ever push if they were first shoved backward, always losing ground. Driving forward never meant much if you end farther away, did it?

But that wasn't why Gilbert had left them, them being weak. Nor was it a pity or strategy that made him leave. He'd thought on it, thought harder than he'd wanted to. No, that hadn't been it. Besides, they weren't all slave to that weakness. Will Scarlet had killed the Sheriff, but boyo if he hadn't gone about it the wrong way.

Gilbert touched the pale tan stones with his ungloved hand, didn't he, because he *could.* Nothing about the stone was appealing, its craggy porous surface wouldn't make any singular thing about Gilbert's life better for having touched it. But Will Scarlet *couldn't* touch it as it were, being locked away somewhere beneath where Gilbert stood now.

The middle bailey, Nottingham Castle.

Gilbert opened his mouth and ordered a lesser Guardsman to move, if only to witness the perfection of a thing thought, a thing spoken, and a thing done. The faceless thing hustled off, his blood pumping apologies. A nothing man.

Too much stone, this place, if Gilbert had a preference. The inside of the castle was a new where for him. Not a good or a bad where, just a new one. The city of Nottingham, down by the wharfside, that had been a where, too, Red Lion Square. Gilbert knew the men there well once, and they were a different sort of who, too, not better or worse, either, just different. Less stone there, down by the river.

Some would call this place his home, then, those that needed that thing. That, with little doubt, was also not the reason Gilbert had left them. But he *had* left them, as he'd left a dozen places before, snatching that fluttering bit of thought and turning it to action. Was there a reason to decide that an action deserved a cause? He'd never been base enough to question himself before, but it nagged at him, didn't it? They might have assumed he disappeared on account of being so close to Much, but that didn't feel right. It didn't feel reason enough. Deciding upon reasons left a maddening sense of obligation. But deciding only on actions brings the satisfying sense of movement.

But that, too, didn't feel reason enough. As it were.

Approaching the castle stables, another nothing man stepped forward to question him. Everyone was new in Nottingham, Gilbert included. Nobody knew nobody. This nothing man didn't know Gilbert, wanted to stop him with a hand outstretched, which he was just as like to lose. It didn't matter what words the man would sling. Gilbert had already been given the proper ones to disarm him.

Stand down. Captain's Black Guard.

And the nothing man saluted and stepped aside, a well-practiced maneuver he would only further perfect during the rest of his nothing life.

GETTING HIS FEET INSIDE the castle had been the hardest part, but all it took was a lie. Seemed the death of the Sheriff had led every earl in five counties to pledge protection to Nottingham. Gilbert simply waited for the correct amount of confusion. That had been the hard part, hadn't it? Being asked to join the captain's private company had taken nothing other than being useful.

Frost on the ground, biting into the dirt, his boot biting in the frost, breaking flakes until they were mud again.

He was almost sad to say he liked the captain, Guy of Gisbourne, if he had a preference. Gilbert was less than pleased with what the man had done to Much, but there would be time to marry that discrepancy later. Or not. It could have gone either way, couldn't it, Gilbert might have plucked an eyeball from the captain's skull if the thought had struck him. Instead he'd listened, which offered its own sort of entertainment at first, and then interest. Captain Gisbourne spoke of deeper things than a man of his ilk ought to. The captain respected the sanctity of action, and the cowardice of regret, and Gilbert couldn't fault a man with such beautiful taste.

And so now there was this thing, what Gisbourne called his Black Guard, wasn't there, full of men—and that other one—who had been culled from the ranks of their castle's visitors. A better breed of hunters, as it were, who could build as quick as destroy. Capturing Locksley seemed to be of paramount importance, and Gilbert had yet to mention he could personally do so whenever he chose to. He wondered whether a somewhat more nothing person would have felt sour, being party to hunting down those he could have called friends, if he had a preference. Were the thought to settle itself, he could tell the Captain where the old Oak Camp was now. They could bring Marion's men to the castle in irons by sundown. Or perhaps he'd keep quiet and let them meander about the Sherwood blindly. Loyalty was a joke, a perfectly useless reason nothing men gave to commit suicide. So maybe he'd find the opportunity to plunge his knife into the hearts of these new men, one by one, when the chance presented. He hadn't much decided, and wasn't like to until the moment came, was he?

But the buzzing had been growing, and that would tip the scales, as it were. He had stayed with Marion's men a surprising long time, never worrying about what was next, and the buzz had kept itself away. But this was next now, and the now was all that was ever worth bowing to.

IN THIS PARTICULAR NOW, a stable boy was preparing a few horses, three, for the morning's task. Gisbourne's orders were to round up eyes outside of Nottingham. They split into trios to go from town to village, looking for people willing to keep wary of their Robin Hood, and bring news to the Guard when they did. Not the easiest task, given current relations. Villagefolk were fearful of the Sheriff's Guard of late, on account of the raids, and Locksley's offer of rampant charity was an attractive thing to those in need.

Today's trio included a man named Silas of York, who was too honest to be interesting, and the fop Quillen Peveril. There were others on the same hunt, and of distinctive worry was a trio led by one Sir Robert FitzOdo. This bulky knight was flanked by his two attendants—brothers whose names Gilbert hadn't learned. FitzOdo was paid by the Baron of Tickhill Castle, Roger de Busli, and had joined the Black Guard in Nottingham by his own demand. FitzOdo regularly proclaimed Baron de Busli as the man who would kill Robin Hood. Captain Gisbourne feared FitzOdo would drag Locksley to Tickhill before Nottingham, but the captain didn't appear to be in a position to refuse such ambitious help. Still, Gilbert kept his mouth shut about the Oak Camp, didn't he? He chose the myriad of possibilities over the finite. He saw no reason to intervene as long as the consequences were so captivating.

At each stop, Silas and Quillen would approach the town directly, while Gilbert rounded about on the outskirt, one of the few places he had a preference in being. Finding men loyal to Nottingham would take more honey than vinegar, and he held no delusions as to which side of the line he fell. So Gilbert slunk off to watch for those that didn't know they were being watched. On a few occasions he netted them a friend that way. In a crotch of a village named Thorney, Gilbert found a beastly sort of fellow living on the outskirts by the name of Will Stutely. Gilbert fueled the oaf's sense of importance, and the man promised to report the first thing he heard about Locksley.

In other places, the story was different, wasn't it? In a rotted hunting hollow named Godling, Gilbert came across a pair of farmers who were too healthy for their impoverished lifestyle. They hid while the others lied to Silas, so Gilbert came at them from behind and sliced a ribbon of blood from their calves as they stood. He took turns shaving tiny pieces off of them until they chose to stop fighting.

Lie to me, and you'll wake up choking on your own cock.

Gilbert always enjoyed making threats that involved a fellow's manhood, didn't he, ever since a similar promise of violence had been made to him back when he was trading with the Red Lions. Some bony cutpurse who fancied himself a slickshit, he cornered Gilbert in Dutch Alley. The bony boy had demanded Gilbert's white glove, threatening to saw off Gilbert's cock. Gilbert was forced to explain this plan involved purposefully untying another man's britches and manhandling his cock, probably with both hands. While the boy tried to defend his sexuality, Gilbert calmly delivered six inches of sharp steel up into the boy's own crotch, all while keeping his own hands pleasantly cock-free. As it were.

The gate swings both ways, he told the men whose calves he'd slashed. *My friends will reward you if you tell us about Robin Hood. But if I find he's visited you and nobody told us, then I'll take increasingly large pieces of you until the majority of your body is mine. I'll let you decide for each other which part I take next. Do we understand one another?*

They did. Gilbert thought about sliding his knife through one of their throats, he would have enjoyed it, wouldn't he? It would have satisfied the buzzing. It had been over a year since he'd scratched it, since he'd needed to. But for a breathless nagging reason he didn't. Something about the idea that Much had gone the same way.

That had been new. He didn't want to call it grief, but it rang of the ugly thing.

He didn't tell Silas or Quillen about that little incident. It was well understood, wasn't it, that cutting calves was considered rude amongst strangers. Until he spent more time with his new companions, he would have to keep certain sides of himself hidden, as he had with Marion's men. A few of them understood there was wonderful depth to darkness. But for those who believed that God was made of light, Gilbert would always have to only pretend to live in their world.

THEY KEPT QUARTERS IN the barracks of the middle bailey, four to a room. Gilbert housed with Silas, Marshall, and Peveril. But he spent much of his nights out, studying the castle, memorizing distances between doors, finding the darkest nooks where one could conceal oneself, or a body. Whether he would ever need this information he couldn't say, but he wouldn't be in want of its knowledge. As the honorary ghost story of whichever group he found himself, it was his duty to play the part. There were not many private indulgences he allowed himself, but playing to this caricature was one of them.

He'd already heard the usual bevy of theories on his glove go around the castle and back again. That he was saving his hand until it could take Robin Hood's life. That he only had two fingers and that he killed anyone who ever saw him take the glove off. One was that he only wore the glove to make people talk of it.

In the lower, largest bailey, nothing men went about raising a gallows. They were at work as soon as there was light enough to do so, hauling massive timbers and hoisting them to position. It was expected to be quite the spectacle. The public was invited, with every hope that Robin and his men would be amongst. And they would be, Gilbert had no doubt of it. The thought gave him pause, though he could not quite say why. It would not be Scarlet on the gallows, just some prisoner from down below. If Marion's men sprang to stop the execution, they would be most surprised. Scarlet and Elena would have had their throats unceremoniously opened earlier that morning, and their bodies would then be flung from the middle bailey walls for all to see. Assassins did not deserve the respect of an execution, such was the message, and the capture of Robin would be the final punchline. Gilbert was undecided if he enjoyed the joke yet, wasn't he?

The construction noticeably lulled as Gilbert strode beneath the skeleton of the half-finished gallows, the workers eyeing him, wondering which figure was more revered by death. He made a show of trailing his gloved fingers against its timbers, even paused and whispered a few nonsensical words into one of them. On the other side was the door to the cramped abbey where de Lacy's body currently lived—or rather didn't.

It reeked of incense in the cubbyhole abbey. Men were afraid of the stink a body gave off, thinking obscuring its smell would make a corpse more palatable. De Lacy's body wore death well. His face sank low and grey into his skull, his fingers were more bone than tissue, but he was handsome. All around him candles burned, sage smoked heavy in a bronze bowl, the ash lifting up and out of a grate in the ceiling. Over de Lacy's body were two more, not dead yet. Not yet, were they? Holding a rag to his mouth was a man whose purported esteem was only matched by his age and girth. This Bishop of Hereford, here to preside the funeral, if he survived long enough himself.

The other body was the *other one,* that most curious addition to the Black Guard. No hand over the mouth for this one, hovering over the sheriff's body closer than most could stomach, staring. The half of her face Gilbert could see wasn't anything to be called pretty, but most would consider it her better half. She shifted slightly to look at him. The other half of her sloughed, as it were, her eye fixed forever forward and dead. Her eyes, even the one that could see, were the first eyes that never nervously glanced down at Gilbert's glove.

"Did you ever know him?" she asked, and the Bishop of Hereford answered as if anybody cared for him to speak. Not even God listened to him. Gilbert nudged his head sideways in answer, *no,* and she shifted herself back down at her uncle.

Jacelyn de Lacy, the only member of the late Sheriff's family who would attend his funeral.

"His death was a relief to my mother. I've never seen her happier."

Jacelyn spoke at her full breath, discomforting the bishop's whispers. He made some combination of agreement and protestation to her statement, enough to diplomatically appease her without insulting the dead.

"I think he was likely the only interesting person in our entire family. Everyone else was afraid of him, afraid he'd take his lands back, afraid he gave a shit. I'd trade any of them to have him back. Or all of them. And I never even met him in person. Only in letters."

Once again, the Bishop responded, unnecessarily. She'd been talking to Gilbert.

Gilbert placed a hand on the Bishop's elbow to lead him from the room. *The Sheriff de Wendenal desires a moment of your time.* The man was only too eager to oblige, to get himself out of the stink, it wouldn't matter that Gilbert had concocted the excuse. Jacelyn wanted time with the deceased, and Gilbert had chosen to allow her that moment. She may have seen it as a kindness, which was her prerogative, but it was just a decision. He was equally likely to push de Lacy's body off the dais so that he might delight in however she would respond. This time he'd exhibited what some would call sympathy, those that were wrong about such things. The muscles about her good eye constricted slightly, didn't they, an acknowledgement of what he had done for her, but a far cry from a thank-you.

The captain had naturally thought twice of her when she insisted on joining the Black Guard. *"Afraid they'll take my womanhood?"* she had asked, only half of her face smirking. Still the captain resisted, uneasy that his new outfit was turning quickly into a pack of bounty hunters. Her interest, by her own admission, went only as deep as avenging her uncle's murder. But she proved she could fend for herself, and Gisbourne introduced her to the group as Jacelyn de Lisours. She was quick to correct. *"Jacelyn de Lacy. I have no interest in being a Lisours."*

The Bishop's mouth and body made excuses as Gilbert led him outside, under the gallows again where Gilbert traced his fingers over the same invisible sign he made earlier. Again the noise settled, but for different reasons. Ahead, a small crowd pooled at the foot of the gallows. Four Guardsmen, one at each of her compass corners, made a tight perimeter around Lady Marion.

Two full heads shorter than any of the men around her, but she still dwarfed them, didn't she? Her eyes locked upward at the highest beams, and Gilbert was glad she did not notice him beneath. She would see his presence here as a betrayal. She couldn't understand why it wasn't, which was her shortcoming, not his. Still, that disparity scratched at him, a single fingernail. Since she had arrived, she was seldom out of her room, always guarded. Her face was pale, emptier. She looked the way Locksley Castle looked now, in woman's form.

At a guard's prompting she moved again, escorted away. Into the staircase upward, and the bishop as well, and Gilbert decided he'd go out to the city, didn't he? Not a soul had the grit to stop him, if they even had wit enough to think they should. Aside from the great main gate, one postern door wound itself through the outside walls, buried amongst unimportant storage. Impossible to open from without, but perfect for slipping away.

He felt it again, scratching at his bones, the restless buzz. It had been building in the wrinkles of his mind ever since Much went. That nameless faceless threat, the only thing he truly feared. It crept down his throat into his chest where it burned and squeezed, that *need.* He felt it yesterday before he slit the farmers' calves, and the blood had calmed it, but not enough.

Much had been a calming presence for Gilbert. There had been something uneasy within that boy, something that scratched at his bones, too. Not *this,* not likely, but something prayer could never touch. Gilbert had found some solace in helping him. But that was a then, and thens are poisons to nows.

If he had stayed, it would have been one of Marion's men, wouldn't it? When he couldn't keep the buzzing at bay anymore, he would have killed one of them. Gilbert stopped midstep, curious. Perhaps that was why he had left them. But that would mean terrible things, it would mean he wanted to protect them, it would mean . . .

Gilbert shook it off. It didn't matter. Out to the city, as he had once done so often, to relieve the world of one more nothing man.

Slipping onto the streets of Nottingham felt like sliding back to sleep after being roused. He fit into them perfectly, an intoxicating sort of comfort. He remembered every step from a few lifetimes ago, taking Walnut Tree Lane toward the wharfs. It was narrow, with a thick gullet in its center beaten with the leaking slop and filth from surrounding windows. Another day might have tempted him east to the Alleys, to catch up with some of the Red Lions that hadn't gone to ground. Though they might not have the easiest time understanding why he came dressed in Guard blues, like some cock-hungry ferrers. The irony, of course, was that a real-life Ferrers was actually in the Guard with him, but he doubted the Lions would appreciate the distinction. So no, today, the Raff Yard would do, wouldn't it?

The last grasp of town before rock pushed up into castle, or crashed down into the river. Here were the poor souls who lived off the scraps of the wharfs, in every way. A muddy pit of poverty. He stowed himself behind a netted array of barrels just after Canal Street to remove his tabard and doublet, stripping all the way down to his britches and boots. The cold air was tight on his skin, but refreshing for the alertness it forced on him. He rolled his uniform into a ball and tucked it under the ropes that lashed the barrels together, and smeared himself with whatever black slurry he could find on the ground.

The Raff Yard was the same as it had ever been. He took a quick glance around, then closed his eyes to remember what he had seen. A man with a furious mane of hair and vacant eyes. A tall gaunt worker beating the ground with a thick club. A skinny mother prying open her naked child's hand. A dozen others like these, the desperate. But, fortunately for them, memorable. He gave another look, and then a third, keeping track of anyone who stood out. Finally, on his fourth pass, he looked specifically for anyone whose face he had not noticed, for those that were the most forgettable of the forgotten.

Gilbert settled on a man who sat curled up against the rockside, absently brushing dirt off his cheek. These were all nothing men down here, but Gilbert had made a deal with himself once upon a time, to never make it easy. That which he *chose* to do had no limitations, but this . . . this was something he did not choose. And for it, for being a slave to this drive, he had made rules to abide by. When his heart sang for blood, he would only take that which would never be missed. There was no joy in sitting in filth, to wait amongst this human herd. It was a punishment, which he put upon himself, which he deserved, didn't he?

Time rolled on, the cold burned his open back, he hooked the tips of his fingers between his thighs and calves to keep them from going numb. The nothing man continued contributing nothing to the world around him, until at length he pushed himself to his feet and ambled off toward the river. Gilbert followed in as inexact a manner as was prudent, pausing to do nothing several times and blend in. He followed the other down toward the water and the rocks, and privacy. He swarmed up and plunged his good fingers into the man's throat from behind, high up where the neck met the jaw, and then wrenched the man's head sideways, flinging him off his feet. A moment later, atop him, his good hand clenched tight around the man's apple so that he could make no noise. The man's eyes were wide and black and red and bulged as Gilbert squeezed.

The familiar rush warmed him, a thousand pinpricks across his flesh. *Not too fast, now, let it last.* He released his grip, enough that the man could gasp quick broken gulps of air. Gilbert placed the tip of his knife just under the man's nipple. The nobody's hands flailed at Gilbert, so he plucked one from the air and slid his knife through it, high near the wrist, between the bones, all the way through. The man would have screamed but Gilbert covered its mouth again, and watched as the blood came, beautiful and dark, out of the wound and down the skin, coating it, staining it. Black at first, and crimson when it thinned, and hot over Gilbert's fingers. He let it flow down onto his palm, dripping beautiful down his own arm. Its eyes were tight and wet now. Gilbert breathed in deeply, then exhaled and pushed the knife down into the soft of the neck, down toward the heart, and was welcomed by a red spring that leapt at his command, cascading down both sides of the body with godlike orchestration. It pooled in the pores of the skin and the rock, and disappeared into the earth. Gilbert shuddered, lightly at first and then uncontrollably, his body heaving, his extremities going numb and then limp, and finally his mind dripped empty, so wonderfully blank, into milk.

In the endless amount of time before he would need to move again, Gilbert was small and safe and warm. His bones couldn't itch because he didn't have any bones. Even the constant torture of his left hand disappeared into the red milky nothing.

But even in that white painless perfection, one small black pebble nudged him. An almost nothing, but it was there, and his soul blinked, and the world and its pettiness slowly drew back to life. That black pebble had cut it short, it had been so much shorter than before, but that made no matter now, did it? There was a body underneath him that he would need to dispose of. He was too cold, and the Guard would be looking for him soon. None of these worried him, for they were simply tasks for him to check off a list. Pebble or not, there was nothing he couldn't accomplish now that the buzzing was gone, and to prove it he sprang to his feet and heaved the body over his shoulder.

A short run down the rocks and into the shallows of the river brought him to a cutaway in the northern slope, just large enough to conceal the body until he had time to come back later with a horse and take it out of the city. It was light as air as he flung its limbs over itself, and Gilbert cut off a cluster of nearby bramble to cover the face. He washed clean in the water and left.

In the Raff, he noticed an old woman standing in place, turning slowly as though one foot were stuck, squinting, looking, searching. His satisfaction of doing the thing wavered, and for a moment the black pebble burrowed through his brain again. He couldn't avoid wondering if the old woman was looking for a man who would never come back.

Gilbert slapped his own face. He was better than regret, he couldn't be bothered with such a pedestrian attitude. It made no sense, why it would come now, why it had come in the white, for such a trivial act. He'd done far better things, things that would brand him a traitor to many, and never felt that pebble's touch. Not an inch of him regretted delivering Jon Bassett to the Red Lions. The boy had screamed and squealed as the Lions spit him and strung him. He'd begged and cursed Gilbert in the same breath as they teased his life away in the tunnels beneath Nottingham.

Retrieving his clothes from the netted barrels, his thoughts flirted back toward Locksley Castle, imagining Lord Walter's face churning and charring black in the fire. Gilbert rewatched himself light the torch he had used, walking through its halls, setting anything he could find ablaze. Every living soul had run out to the stables, trying so desperately to put out the flame that the Guards had started, and Gilbert had chosen the opposite. One thing burning wasn't nearly as interesting as everything burning. It was as much wood as stone in that place, and roof and timber both begged for flame. He had split the oil casks and thrown them against the walls of the dining hall, watching the fire writhe forward, burning hotter and deeper, brighter. That had been the longest his mind had ever disappeared, a wondrous unending mute, nothing but the warmth of the blaze on his face, and the more he fed the flames the longer his solace lasted. At one point he had thought himself wincing from the heat, only to realize he was smiling, wide and childish, uncontrollably.

They had blamed the wind. They thought the fire jumped from the stables and took a miraculous turn on the breeze to find itself inside the castle, because it was the only explanation they had. And he'd never thought twice on it, never suffered the same sickening sense of consequence he felt now over a nothing man.

What it meant, he couldn't fathom, he didn't want to, he walked faster. He looked down to discover he was clawing at his glove with the other hand, fresh blood staining it from within. White and red. It didn't matter, he had more gloves, didn't he?

When he made it back to the castle gates, he had but to gesture and the Guards opened the side gate for him. They were nothing men, too, safe until Gilbert's bones started itching again. Not five seconds after he passed, the gate screamed open again, and he turned to see Jacelyn de Lacy walking briskly behind him.

She had followed him. Her good eye bored a palpable hole into Gilbert's own. She overtook him but did not stop staring, twisting her face around. Perhaps she had only now seen him. Or perhaps she had witnessed everything. Perhaps she was doing something guilty herself and was worried he had seen her.

Not guilty, never guilty. He dug the nail of his good hand into his forearm as punishment for thinking the word. When he pulled it away he left a dark purple dent. He wondered whether he would choose to do something about Jacelyn de Lacy, but no thought came to him.

In the long room off the side of the barracks' dining hall, Captain Gisbourne asked where Gilbert had been, of course, but only because he had to. The man's mind was elsewhere. Jacelyn's half face answered before Gilbert could.

"He was with me. We heard about a man in town who claimed to have information on the outlaws, but he was only selling lies. We made an example of him."

She never looked at Gilbert, even after the captain thanked and dismissed them. Whatever she meant by it, it was for her own sake. Gilbert's interest in owing her anything was nonexistent. Favors and thank-yous are only a polite version of slavery.

THE REST OF THE day slid by in an unmemorable blur, soft and smooth like river water over rocks. By nightfall he could have forgotten about the body by the river. If he closed his eyes, who was to say that the body would even be there anymore? A thing thought, a thing said, and a thing done could go the other way—a thing unsaid, a thing forgotten, a thing that never was. All that remained was that damned pebble, that thing he could not name.

He ignored it, it was past, and Gilbert needed to tend to the now. Which led him to invite Jacelyn to take a walk with him late that night. It was unlikely she would describe it as an invitation, being woken with a knife at her lips and all, but those were the silly sort of differences that weren't worth grieving over, were they?

The deepest wine cellar had but one way in or out, which was a long journey for any noise to get back to the world. Gilbert had already left himself a candle burning on the table.

You watched me today, don't pretend that you didn't.

It was cold down here and Jacelyn's hot breath came out in thick fat clouds. Gilbert breathed his own air down through his nose, and drew close to the flame. He placed the tip of his knife one finger above the candle's pulse, slowly twisting its point to heat it evenly.

It doesn't matter to me one way or the other whether you ever walk out of this wine cellar. There honestly isn't a single part of me that gives the first shit about your life. I'd wager you feel differently. So you have from now until my blade is hot to make me trust you.

It was disappointing, wasn't it, that she didn't even look at the knife. She didn't gulp or gasp or pucker like a person ought to.

"You're going to kill me?" She smirked halfway into a laugh. "Look at me. I've been half dead my whole life. That's not killing, that's mopping up." Gilbert tested the tip of his knife against the tabletop and watched the burn it made, wondering how to deal with her unexpected apathy. "So you kill transients by the river. You think that's the worst secret I've kept?"

When the tip was hot, Gilbert placed the blade down long enough to peel off his glove. In the candlelight the hand looked worse than ever, swollen and slimy, massive cracks winding through the twisted scar tissue. Alternating soft and stone patches, a history of pain. Without breaking eye contact with Jacelyn, Gilbert placed his own wrist over the fire, the very base at the palm, the sting was an old friend, an old enemy. He had saved this spot in his wrist for a long time. The smell of burning flesh was one that compared to nothing else. When he felt his skin churn into char he pulled his wrist away and plunged only the tip of the dagger into the wound, and his vision went white and every nerve in his body ripped open, cleansing him, erasing what he had done that morning. Reborn out of the pain, and the white faded to black and his head was on the table.

"Here's what I want to know," her voice was the only thing in the world. "If you're going to kill, why not kill someone who deserves to die? They're everywhere, you know."

The words struck him as clearly as the pain. The pebble, *the guilt,* wasn't about killing the nothing man. It was about *wasting his time* on the nothing man. He had left Marion's men because he was done wasting time, which was their chiefest of skills. His rules had protected him, true enough, but they'd also hampered him. His bones would itch again, and soon, and here in the Black Guard he could put its relief to better use than nothing men.

Though whether he'd do so *alongside* the Guard, or *upon* them, was the curiosity.

Gilbert wrapped up his wrist, he caught his breath and held it, counting. Slowly. He wiped the blood from his arm, which was stiff up to the elbow. He stood from the table and leaned down to Jacelyn.

Thank you, he whispered, and kissed her on the dead side of her face, and stood and left, didn't he?

PART VII

ARNALDIA

FORTY-SIX

GUY OF GISBOURNE

NOTTINGHAM CASTLE

The punchline came, and the endless parade of Guy's misfortune was complete. All he could do now was laugh.

What a welcome relief it was, this turning point. Up until that moment, when the dramatics crashed into hysterics, Guy had been clenching his fingers into fists, and his toes, too. Little footfists. But this final proverbial straw let Guy break down into laughter, a slap-happy ticklish sort of mania that brought tears to his eyes. The others at the longtable gaped at him as if he had gone mad, and they were exactly incorrect. In reality, Guy had finally gone *sane.* Trying to keep common sense in Nottingham—*that* had been insanity.

William de Wendenal had been droning on, sitting in the sheriff's seat and wearing the sheriff's power but whining like a third child. Wendenal was trying to play the role of Roger de Lacy with only a quarter the wit. He had mastered all the strategy of an infant.

But the sycophants had come to Nottingham, both to mourn de Lacy and to make alliances with his successor. Wendenal's suspicious rise was ignored in favor of their own advancement. The collusion between Wendenal and the outlaws was undeniable even before his ridiculous betrothal to their benefactor Marion Fitzwalter. But William's tenuous position would be solidified the moment he captured Locksley's men, and despite Guy's every effort he had yet to find any leads that might bring him there first.

Now that he saw the endgame, there was no point in fighting anymore—the finale had already been orchestrated. Wendenal stared at him. "I suppose you'll tell me what's so funny about my suggestion?"

Guy smiled, deeply. "Why, if you found nothing funny about it, I must have been entirely mistaken. The Sheriff's law is the county's law, and so must his sense of humor be ours as well. Henceforth shall I wait for the Sheriff to chuckle 'ere I e'er dare smile."

Wendenal rifled through his catalog of obvious facial tics that indicated he was displeased. "Shall I repeat myself, or do you think you can manage your task seriously?"

"Why not just repeat yourself, for clarity's sake?"

Wendenal's previous display of subtlety was now topped with an old-fashioned eye roll, and then he said it again. The punchline. By itself, the punchline is never funny, as it requires the setup of the joke. And this particular joke had been several days in the making.

THOSE FEW DAYS AGO, Guy paid a visit to Simon FitzSimon. Ever since de Lacy's murder, Simon had been uncharacteristically affected, aloof even. Guy attributed this behavior to a misplaced sense of guilt—it was natural to be shaken by the terrorism that had taken place within the walls of the castle. But Guy needed all his allies at their peak right now, and it looked like Simon needed help. So Guy brought several fistfuls of ale to his armsmaster's quarters, there being nothing so successful at lifting one's spirits than one's lifting of spirits.

But the unkempt man who flung open his door was full of bitter and spite rather than remorse. Huffing and posturing, Simon denied his unusual behavior until Guy threatened to drink all the ale himself. When Simon finally let loose, he revealed a most curious story. The good Sheriff Roger de Lacy, apparently, had visited Simon on his final living night with a preposterous claim. He denounced his own insufferable idea of culling prisoners into the Guard, and swore it had been Guy's idea instead. And unbelievably, Simon had fallen for it.

"What fathomable long game do you suppose I would have been playing at?" Guy laughed. As they talked it out, reason prevailed—as it was always prone to do amongst reasonable men. And by the end of the night they both apologized and drank themselves silly, raised their tankards to the fallen, and practiced the eulogies they could only dream of delivering for the Sheriff.

"To the Sheriff," Guy slurred, "may the Lord be as wise in judging him as the Sheriff was himself."

"To the Sheriff," Simon drank deeply, dark gold leaking out into his beard, "to honor you, we hope to send a few of your favorite gerolds to keep watch over your soul."

When morning came, with its usual unwanted gifts of pain and noise, Guy thought harder on what had prompted de Lacy to tell such a specific lie. Only the slightest tug on the thread, and a piece of the puzzle revealed itself that he hadn't even realized was missing—Guy was the target.

"What if the plan wasn't just to put Wendenal in power?" he asked Simon, who was dousing his head in a horse's water trough. "What if it was to get rid of *me*?"

Simon spat water out. "You're the captain, and a damned fine one. The fact that de Lacy made up lies about you proves they have nothing to use against you. The people love you, your men love you, no lie can undo that. Why the hell would they get rid of you?"

"Because they think I'm a threat."

"Who's *they*?" Simon asked, and Guy spelled it out. He had unfortunately made his enemies the day he married Elaisse Longchamp, who happened to be cousins with the man who had now risen to Chancellor. Theirs had been an entirely arranged marriage—his once youthful interest in marriage had died along with his first wife, Loren. Elaisse meant nothing to him. But the Chancellor had, by necessity, many enemies. Chiefest amongst those was Prince John, who had already clashed with Longchamp in only the brief time he had been back in England.

And Prince John was in Nottinghamshire, according to reports, and intended on attending de Lacy's funeral.

"Damn it, I should have seen it earlier," Guy cursed. "I thought I was simply collateral damage, when I've been part of their plan the whole time. It explains so much. Wendenal was antagonistic from the moment of his arrival, even though we should have been natural allies. We both wanted to stop the Sherwood gangs. Think on it—if his goal was only to take the sheriff's seat, then befriending me as the captain should have been his first move. But instead he squeezed in, distancing me from de Lacy, and I didn't realize it was *intentional*."

Guy was long accustomed to knighted men sneering down upon Guardsmen, thinking their extravagant employ made them nobler than those who sacrificed to keep the daily peace. Wendenal was no knight, but he had that familiar haughtiness. Guy had mistaken it for a more innocent disdain.

Simon pulled wet streaks of his own moustache out of his mouth. "I'm not as smart as you, so don't be stingy. Just tell me. How can they get rid of you?"

Behind him, the main castle gate swung open, letting in a cluster of horses and men and banners, and trouble. And answers.

"By taking away my support," Guy realized. "By turning you against me, turning my men against me. De Lacy's lie is the proof, and it's just the beginning." He watched the arriving men parade into view. "There's something bigger to come."

Strangers marching into the castle was no curiosity anymore. Every corner of the lower bailey had been claimed for another contingent of men sent to help at the funeral, as if the Nottingham Guard were a limbless, blind baby. Guy would have been insulted if he'd cared about such prideful things. He'd already lost command of the prisons to the Derbyshire men, thanks to Wendenal.

But this new group's arrival had a more arrogant flair than most, each man drenched in importance and entitlement. Ten of them in total, six men in obsessively shined armor, three servants, and in their middle was the man unquestionably in charge. An insultingly virile man who caped himself in a bear fur, poised perfectly upon his blood black destrier, scrutinizing the bailey not as a visitor but as a man summing up an acquisition. His emblem was that of the bear and the ragged staff—men from Warwickshire.

Ordinarily, Guy should have been alerted of any important visitors. Instead he watched from afar the appearance of Hamon Glover—the ale barrel that someone had accidentally assigned as castellan—who clearly expected this Warwick host. Guy watched Glover greet them quickly and then escort them toward the bridge to the middle bailey.

It was only an hour before Guy's men reported the details back to him. The man in the bear cloak was the Earl of Warwick's son, Waleran the Younger, Captain of the Warwick Guard. And every snippet of whisper breathed the same warning. "He was summoned by his father," a reliable stableman confided, "and expects to stay. Seems he expects to be put in charge, actually."

The man being set up to replace Guy as captain.

That was yesterday.

Today, Guy was summoned to the Sheriff's council a full hour after it had begun.

"I see you've decided to join us," Wendenal announced, to quiet the others. Waleran the Younger was there, in all his youthful ferocity, amongst a motley crew of other important faces.

"I was unaware I was late," Guy replied, since he had arrived immediately upon being summoned. But this was an hour ago, before the punchline.

"And I was unaware that you had captured the Sherwood outlaws," Wendenal continued his poor impersonation of de Lacy. "Or is it common practice for the Captain of the Guard to drink his nights away during a countywide manhunt? I'm just curious, really, being new here."

The table chuckled for him, at his heavy-handed boring sort of humor.

"On the contrary, I commend Captain Gisbourne," added the bear man, Waleran the Younger, "for his ingenuity. He swore he would search everywhere for this Robin Hood. He was only being diligent by looking for him at the bottom of a bottle."

Wendenal spoke again before Guy could counter. "Had you been here when I asked for you, we would be pleasantly free of your company by now. Instead, you will have to wait until we have the opportunity to backtrack."

"I do not have the time to waste, Sheriff," Guy argued. "As you say, I am in the midst of a manhunt—"

"But you have time to drink all night with the master-at-arms? Perhaps if you sit and wait, you'll be sober enough to participate by the time we need you."

Then he pivoted and changed the subject. There was nothing for Guy to do but fume, a sport he had recently mastered. In the infuriating slog of time that passed, Guy curled his fingers and toes into fists, and an hour passed before Wendenal spelled out the plan for de Lacy's funeral. "I want your men in the city on Sunday. Not in the castle. There are more than enough swords here already, and your men know the streets better than any of them."

The punchline, delivered appropriately by a clown.

Guy put it all together and laughed like a madman, then eventually apologized like the fine little servant they wanted him to be. Wendenal repeated the command.

"Ah, see, that's not funny at all," Guy apologized. "Thank you for clarifying, I apparently thought you had said something hilarious. Sometimes I mishear my betters, do forgive me."

He had heard the command crystal clear. His Nottingham Guard was commanded to spread out through the city while de Lacy's funeral took place within the castle walls. When Locksley's men attacked the funeral, Guy would be blamed for letting them slip through the city. In fact, Wendenal would blame it on the traitorous gerolds, and it would be the drunkard Guy of Gisbourne who put the criminals in a place to do such damage. There was the reason for de Lacy's lie.

It would destroy his credibility. And damnation, but it would work.

The Young Bear finished the plot. "With your permission, I would that my men and I be in charge of the executions. Baron de Lacy was a good friend of my father's, and Warwick has a keen interest in seeing his assassins put to justice."

Wendenal made a poor pretense of thinking about the proposal before agreeing, and so it was set. Waleran the Younger would capture Locksley's men when they tried to save Will Scarlet at the executions, and thusly promote himself to Captain of Nottingham's Guard. Guy would be damningly absent. Locksley would be discreetly shipped back to the war, his mission here complete. Both Sheriff and Captain replaced with the Chancellor's enemies, and the people tricked into supporting them both. Nottingham was effectively under assault by a hostile power, attacking from within. What Prince John meant to do with his victory, Guy did not know. But Guy himself was presumably to slink off in defeat and accept how miserably he had been outsmarted.

There wasn't a single inch of his body that was interested in that plan.

It might have been tempting—to let it happen, to stop this endless fighting against men and politics. The farther Guy rose in life, the farther he was from the simplicity of right versus wrong, from the justice that had first drawn him to join the Guard. He could simply surrender to these schemes and fall back into the beautiful ignorance of an unempowered life. If not for those it would hurt. If not for the common people, who would suffer at the rule of increasingly corrupt men. If not for Jon Bassett, still missing. Devon of York. Reginold of Dunmow. Brian Fellows. George Sutton. Bolt, lost to the world. Morg, sitting in prison. Men who had suffered or died for no reason but the plots of more powerful men.

And the boy. That tiny limp frame in Guy's arms.

These were the voices that urged Guy to keep fighting, and they were considerably louder than the siren call of laziness.

"GROUPS OF TWO TODAY," Guy called to those who had not yet left, scattered about the stables. "And leave your blues behind."

"We finally getting blacks?" Eric of Felley answered, starting to tug off his uniform. "Been confusing people, wearing blues and calling ourselves the Black Guard."

"Later," Guy responded. "What I mean is, no uniforms. Dress down." It wouldn't be a popular order. Ludic and Marshall nodded and tugged their tabards over their heads. They had been Guy's first recruits to the Black Guard—long loyal men suddenly deposed of duty when Wendenal gave his Derbymen control of the prisons. Guy unbuckled his own doublet, pulling its hoops until they gave, and handed its weight to Ferrers. "We have less than a week to find them, and our current strategy is not working."

"Well my current strategy," Eric bellowed, as an answer for the group, "is to follow your lead. No blues."

Guy appreciated the rally. "Your nose looks good in brown."

"I don't have blues," coughed Silas, still wearing the rust colors of Yorkshire. Uniforming Guy's new members had scarcely been a priority.

"Lose what you have," Guy answered, unclasping his longsword's baldric from his belt. His eyes lingered on the pruned ivy cross on his sword's hilt, pounded by Nottingham smiths into Toledo steel. He stowed the blade away, high on a shelf above Merciful's saddle sling. "Leave anything that identifies you as a peace officer."

Silas scowled but obeyed. Behind him, Quillen Peveril inclined his head slightly in a polite refusal. A calm patience defined the man, whose hair and clothing were ever sharp and exact. The Peveril name reached back over a century to the first High Sheriff of Nottinghamshire. When the family had arrived to show their respect at the funeral, Quill personally volunteered for Guy's new company. It was no surprise he would find it insulting to remove his uniform—it was said that a Peveril's blood ran blue instead of red.

"There are a lot of desperate people out there," Quill complained, "who wouldn't think twice of doing harm to a few unknown travelers. Don't you think we'd be safer in uniform?"

"Undoubtedly," Guy answered quickly. "And if anyone here is uncomfortable with the order, you are not obliged to follow it. But consider this—the people who have been willing to help us so far, they're good people. How much information will good people have on these criminals? No, we need those desperate people you speak of, who might normally hide when they see the Sheriff's Guard. They've heard lies about us, or been bribed by the outlaws."

Nods all around, even Peveril, though he did not move to disrobe.

"Robin of Locksley changed the rules on us, and he's winning. You can't beat a cheater by playing even fairer. It's time for us to cheat a little, too. Where are the others?"

Eric answered. "Jacelyn and the White Hand left this morning. And FitzOdo is precisely wherever the fuck FitzOdo wants to be."

"That was a truly perfect use of vulgarity," Guy said. FitzOdo was just one more variable that complicated everything. He had wrecked their search for Jon Bassett a month ago, and now had returned to presumably help hunt Robin Hood. Guy trusted the coward knight as far as he could spit. He'd dealt with FitzOdo's master, the Baron de Busli at Tickhill Castle, on multiple miserable occasions. Red Roger thought himself a king within his own walls, and if FitzOdo captured Robin of Locksley first, there was no telling what would come of it. Rumor held that Prince John was spending his time at Tickhill lately, too, so it was no leap of logic to think FitzOdo was here on their behalf, to prevent Guy from finding Locksley at all. But by bringing them into the fold of the Black Guard, Guy could at least keep small tabs on FitzOdo's movement.

"I'm not sure I know how to talk like an outlaw," Silas mused. "Any suggestions?"

"Oh it's not so hard," Marshall jabbed at him. "It's a lot of *mine mine mine*."

“Just open your mouth,” Eric knelt and started rubbing dirt into his face, “and start lying. You’ll fit right in. Hey, Captain,” he turned, almost making himself laugh, “you want I should kick your ass a bit? That would certainly help you blend in.”

“You’re welcome to try,” Guy crooned back. “I hear you’re quite the fighter. Tell me again how you lost those teeth? How tall was the man you were fighting?” The boys laughed and hissed.

“Let him alone,” Ludic spoke up, a thing he only occasionally did, and it quieted them quickly. Until he followed with, “That’s the closest Eric’s been to a woman in years.”

They went about that way, slapping and poking fun at each other for a bit, and Guy was glad for it. Their spirits were still high, despite everything. Or perhaps they did not realize how much was at stake. What a wonderful, beautiful sort of ignorance. Guy occasionally wished he could know it—but he had risen to his position by his ability to see what others couldn’t, at the price of a fool’s joy.

A new voice bellowed from the entrance to the stables. “Look at this pack of limp-wristed assholes!” Guy did not have to turn to recognize Simon FitzSimon’s growl. “Make room. You’re going to need all the help you can get.”

“What are you doing here?” Guy asked his friend.

“Put me on a horse. I’m coming with you.”

Guy drew close and lowered his voice. “Simon, no. We each have our place, yours is here. You’re too valuable.”

“Fuck you muchly,” Simon spat, and wiped the spittle from his red beard. “More of my boys have been killed in the last month than in the last two years. I aim to help out with the balancing. And I guarantee you’re not interested in crossin’ me on this.”

Guy knew which battles weren’t worth fighting. “Quillen Peveril, this is our master-at-arms, The Simons. He’ll ride with you.”

“Peveril?” Simon raised an eyebrow at the name. “Well, fuck me.”

Quill didn’t even smirk. “I assure you that I will not.”

“Oh, you won’t have a choice.” Eric grinned. “Every true blue in Nottingham knows that if The Simons sets his eye on you, then you, sir, are going to get fucked.”

“Alright, that’s enough,” Guy pre-empted any more laughter. There was something fitting about Simon’s presence, now that he thought on it. He brought an appropriate sense of history and pride to round out the Black Guard. “Go throw a saddle on a bear for Simon and get out there.”

The company rallied and mounted up. “I’m with you today, Captain,” Marshall said, pulling close on a horse that looked quite surprised to be carrying an ox on her back. “You look good.”

“I look like shit,” Guy responded. He had dirtied his tunic, tied a burlap sash around his waist, sponged his cheeks with mud. They would be riding into the unknown dregs of the county, leaving all semblance of civilization behind.

"Should we get moving, or do you want to go ask his highness de Wendenal if he approves of this plan?"

"I'd rather skin myself with my own fingernails than waste any breath talking to that man."

"God's balls," Marshall scrunched his wide face as well as he could, "that's disgusting. Now I won't be able to get that idea out of my head for the rest of the day."

"You think that's bad?" Guy asked. "I have to deal with contemplating the enormity of God's balls, thank you very much."

He dug his heels hard into Merciful's side and pushed out and away from the castle, out through the city. Every hoofbeat took him further away from the disease that had taken over Nottingham, and closer to its cure.

But the disease, he was a part of it now, whether he liked it or not. They were hiding themselves, dabbling in deception, that they might steal information from those who would never deal with them honestly.

Lying, hiding, stealing.

The Nottingham Guard had fallen so low, and he had to pray that they would still have the strength to pick themselves back up again.

Once it was over.

FORTY-SEVEN

WILLIAM DE WENDENAL

NOTTINGHAM CASTLE

"You can find allies, or you can find enemies." It was no masterpiece of a sentence. Surely someone important had said something like it before William. His newfound authority, he had discovered, hinged entirely on his ability to project confidence and wisdom doled out in mysterious and spontaneous packages. He wondered how much of Roger de Lacy's profundity had been a performance, a disguise for a terrified old man who could only barely grasp the strings that bound the city together.

"You can also sleep," Arable mumbled, smoothing the heavy covers of the bed beside him. She lay face down in its warmth, her dark curls melting into the furs.

She was wrong, of course. There would be a time when William could choose to sleep again, but for now exhaustion alone could put an end to each night. He would regularly work until his mind caved in, awaking again at his desk or the floor hours later, only to immediately resume whatever he had been working on.

Arable worked just as tirelessly, as he'd taken to use her as his personal assistant. Which, unfortunately for her, meant endless hours secluded in a room copying letters and writing responses. She complained about her eyes, her back, her wrist, and he no longer had the time to ease her pains.

Sadly, her isolation was also a guilty strategy, because some of his secrets now had to be kept even from her. She did not yet know that he intended on marrying the Lady Marion Fitzwalter.

She'd take it poorly when she inevitably learned of it. The world would learn when he announced it at de Lacy's funeral, but he swore to find time to discuss it with Arable before then. That looming moment filled him with more dread than anything else he'd done yet. He had promised never to lie to her, never to hurt her, but reality was forcing his hand. *But she was sharp,* he reminded himself, and knew better than most what compromises were necessary for survival. She'd understand the political necessity of the situation, and not mistake it for anything emotional. They'd be able to continue on as they had, it would change nothing. *It was practically trivial,* from an objective standpoint. But when he thought of her face beside his in the hayloft, her nose wrinkling as she smiled, standing on a ladder . . . his gut wrenched with guilt.

"I have to go," he said, and leaned down to kiss her bare back. There was no time to spend with her anymore, and even the small guilty pleasures of sharing a bed were a costly distraction now. Every baron and lord in five counties had written Nottingham offering condolences and asking for favors. Some had come to visit personally, still others were on their way. The upcoming funeral would be no solemn commemoration of de Lacy's life, but a feeding frenzy for those that wished to profit from his death. A thousand bites to pick the sheriffcy to pieces, and William was struggling to track which predators needed to be appeased and which could be tamed.

You can find allies, or you can find enemies.

Some were easy. The men who kept the castle running were important to win over. He'd granted the castellan Hamon Glover appeasements toward construction improvements de Lacy had apparently long denied him. William had given the quartermaster Simon FitzSimon authority to recruit men however he saw fit, reversing de Lacy's experimental policies. Thanks to Arable's relationship with Lady Margery d'Oily, the Earl of Warwick now supported William as well—though he had begun to hint for a notable appointment for their visiting son. Lord Oughtibridge had swung his favor, too, though that was likely based on the sole fact that William was *not* Roger de Lacy. Other lords he had effectively bribed, using the dividends brought in by Gisbourne's tax raids. In the city, there were merchants who asked for exclusivity, trademasters who cited rules that William could never understand, and an unrelenting list of lords demanding reprieve from taxes that could not even be proven. It was a balancing act full of practiced smiles and rancid flatteries, all in the hopes that William could survive long enough to make a single damned decision on his own, someday long in the future.

He had originally thought he only needed to hold the position for a mere week, just to effect the change he was looking for. But with each new complication, the timeline he needed in Nottingham grew longer and longer.

William had to find his allies, because his enemies were out there, too. Those that sought his seat for themselves, or who questioned his unlikely appointment. Every day William worried that Prince John would send a repeat of his original command to assign the role to Guy of Gisbourne, which was half the reason he was in a hurry to secure his position. He'd even tried to appease Gisbourne—giving him extended leniency to hunt for Robin's outlaws, and trusting his men with the entirety of the city's security during the funeral. But Gisbourne's behavior had become erratic. The time may come soon for a new captain.

William blinked and he was in the dining hall. He did not remember walking there, nor sitting down. *Had he slept? Had he said goodbye to Arable at all?* His doublet was fastened, but he had no memory of dressing. There was mutton and a horn of ale in front of him that appeared to be his. His monsters were all-consuming. They'd invaded his every waking moment, he could barely even track his own movements now. It would be better after the funeral, he repeated to himself.

It would be better after the wedding.

Allies and enemies.

The hair on William's arm suddenly stood on edge, alerting him to something else he had been too preoccupied to notice. The hour was late, but there should have been at least a few young Guardsmen cleaning up. But even the uneven firelight of the room's sconces could not hide its emptiness, nor the curious lack of sounds that might normally creep in from the surrounding hallways. A more hopeful man might assume he was dreaming, but the dread that seized William's bones was too real, and too familiar.

Near the south entrance, two silhouettes rested comfortably at one of the long tables. One played idly with a longsword, its point buried in the table's surface, tall enough that its hilt was above the man's head. Instinct drew William's hand to his own belt, but he no longer carried his blade. His purple-stained doublet had embroidery rather than plating, and his soft new shoes couldn't conceal a knife like his old boots could. He was a politician now, and politicians were compelled to dress in a manner that made them easiest to murder.

"I'm told you're the Sheriff," came a voice from the unarmed man, soft and disinterested.

"I'm told the same thing," William returned. "Do I ask who you are now?"

"I'm told I'm the prince," was the reply, and then William died.

He wasn't certain how he died, but it was undoubtedly spiteful, bloody, and hopefully creative. He would be disappointed if, after everything he'd been through, he was killed in some unimaginative stabbing. Once his exhausted mind caught up with his brutalized body he'd learn more about his death, but for now it was still watching Prince John lounge his way closer through the tables.

"They could be lying to me," said the prince, still in some unthinkable world where William had not yet been murdered. "If I really were the prince, I feel like you ought to be bowing to me, which you're not."

William squinted to make out the man's face. He looked young, carried himself well. His head was a bloom of dark black rimmed in a crisp red fire. William only knew Prince John through Richard's descriptions of him—the insolent little brother whose only successes were in the magnitude of his failures.

Since William was already dead, he saw no point in hiding the antagonism he felt. "Would that make you feel better, if I bowed?" he asked, feeling proud of his final words.

Prince John's only response was a large affected frown, and another few advancing steps. As he hop-stepped closer, navigating the open spaces between wooden benches, he pointed one accusatory finger forward.

"You're not Guy of Gisbourne," he said at last.

"You know, my entire life," William cocked his head, "I've always noticed that."

"Is he alive?"

"Gisbourne? Probably. The world is yet to surprise me with good news, so he's probably healthier than ever."

The prince pursed his lips into a farcical pout. "It's just strange, because I appointed Gisbourne to Sheriff, and instead *you're* the Sheriff. Did you think maybe I'm insane? Were you hoping I wouldn't notice? Let's see . . ." he stretched his arms out and twirled back to his companion, ". . . whether or not I'm insane. Hadrian."

At this, the swordsman loped forward and relinquished his weapon to the prince, who strained to pick it up, mocking its weight. "Oh my. This is . . . this is grueling. How do you carry this?"

He gave it an exploratory lift into the air, then let its heft fall down with ferocity into the nearest table, smashing a wooden bowl into splinters. "Where's Gisbourne?"

"Gisbourne isn't here," William said, eyeing the weapon.

"We're going to play a game. I haven't decided what the rules are yet. The game is this . . . I'm going to swing this sword, until you die. It's not much of a game, for you, I suppose. I'm really bad with these things."

He pulled the sword up behind his head and made a massive slash in William's general direction, the tip cleaving down and glancing over the top of a table to splash its contents in every direction. "Oh look, I'm just terrible at this! But I'm a quick student, so I think you'd best explain yourself quicker."

"Gisbourne left the castle. He's searching for Robin Hood."

"Robin Hood." The prince lowered the sword just long enough to snap his fingers at the man named Hadrian. "Everyone loves that Robin Hood. I do, too, actually. Charming fellow, and good at what he does. Killing sheriffs, that is. I was thinking of giving it a try myself. And my, you're a sheriff, aren't you?"

Another feigned attack, the sword went sweeping wide and obvious, but close enough this time that William stepped backward.

"I'm so sorry, did I get too close to you? You really don't need to be afraid, you can see I don't know what I'm doing with this thing." Prince John accentuated his sentence with a final practiced flourish that left the blade frozen in readiness.

William wet his lips, embarrassed that he needed to. "Robin didn't kill de Lacy. We were both trying to stop something like that from happening."

"Then you were both spectacularly unsuccessful."

Prince John heaved the weapon again, spinning it on one side then another, then lunged the tip out maniacally, reaching over the tabletop that separated them. William again lurched to the side, watching the sword pierce the place he had been standing. But the prince had abandoned the opportunity for a follow-up, instead collapsing onto the table, his head supported lazily by one of his hands. "Robin Hood. You know him, then?"

"We were in the war together," William answered quickly, instincts urging him to sidestep away. He could run, and easily. There were four exits to the room. But there was no real escape, not if Prince John wanted him dead. Something told William his false bravado moments earlier was precisely the sort of thing Prince John might respect. "Robin and I were at your brother's side, actually. We're both here on his orders. We were friends."

He hadn't meant to use *were* until it left his lips. He might have used it to distance himself from Robin in front of the prince. Or he might have used it because it was true.

The prince moved more gracefully now, peeling himself off the table and shifting the sword's weight from side to side, baiting William's urge to dodge. "You're friends with Robin Hood. Now that is interesting. Precisely what sort of shit have I just stepped into?"

"We traveled here together, we were even working together for a while."

"You worked with the man who murdered your predecessor. Keep talking, this is delightfully incriminating."

"As I said, he didn't do that. We have those assassins in prison."

"And that doesn't explain why you're here."

Slowly now, and with obvious intent, John eased his blade forward. William countered with his hands, guiding the flat of the blade away, once, then again on his opposite side, the tip flicking expertly down to slip up into another line of attack, then a third slow lunge pushed John forward as William retreated. It was more of a dance now; their bodies were close as lovers. John laughed, but only cosmetically.

"My brother did not appoint you Sheriff."

William swallowed. "Yes, he did."

"Ooooh." The sword's tip dropped down and John hunched his shoulders, inspecting William's skull. "Well, now I know the other things you said were true, because that was a very obvious lie."

There was no point in hiding that, then. "He gave me the authority to settle the problems in Nottingham. I would say de Lacy's death was a problem. So I took control."

"He was killed by the men your friend Robin organized. You know I've thrown coups before, right? I know what they look like."

"Not successful ones."

The prince's eyes widened in utter shock. William would have felt like a god amongst men for having the balls to say it, if he had not also slightly wet himself in fear. He dared to push farther. "I'm to marry your cousin, you know. I guarantee your interests are my own. But Gisbourne? He's married to a Longchamp. I don't know what he's promised you, but I would doubt every letter of it."

Prince John's countenance shifted into something far more skeptical, a bird that did not know if its prey was yet dead. "Interesting. I did not know that. Huh. That would indeed have been a terrible choice." He blinked a few times. "I can't believe Gay Wally didn't tell me that."

"I don't know who Gay Wally is."

"You're better for it."

They stared at each other for a moment's silence.

William continued. "I'm not so terrible a choice as Sheriff. My father is influential in Derby, with long loyal ties to your family. It's fitting to have a Wendenal in power here, we lost so much in the defense of this city. And my father is somewhat famous in the revenge business. You wouldn't want him to turn against you."

John whistled. "Was that a threat?"

"No, a political reality. You need to find allies, not enemies." It sounded good this time around. He tried to channel de Lacy's spirit into a knowing glare.

With no warning or fanfare, the prince shrugged and passed the weapon back to his attendant. "Do you frolic?"

William had no idea how to answer.

"I didn't know that about Gisbourne. You may have accidentally saved me quite a bit of trouble, or embarrassment at least. Thank you for that. You've convinced me to let you live, and keep the little Sheriff's seat you apparently care for so much. For now, at least."

"Do I frolic?" William repeated the odd question.

"Well, William de Wendenal, you're my newest friend. Friends ought to do friendly things together. We could frolic, you and I."

William couldn't even begin to guess what reaction was expected of him. "Are you serious?"

"No."

The prince turned and walked away, signaling his man to follow. "I'll be staying here, through the funeral at least. See to it that I have an entire floor in the high keep. Please be warned, that if you are up to anything sinister, your punishment will be very creative. Think of something truly heinous, let me know what it is, and then I'll make it worse."

William was not at all sure if he had made an ally or an enemy, but he knew he was not yet dead, which seemed an improvement over his most recent expectations. Still, he reminded himself to start wearing his boots again.

"Wait," William called out. "If you didn't even know Gisbourne well enough to know he had wedded a Longchamp, why did you appoint him as sheriff?"

"I just wanted somebody who would be terrible," Prince John called back, brushing some dirt from his trousers. "I think you'll do fine."

FORTY-EIGHT

ARABLE DE BUREL

NOTTINGHAM CASTLE

ARABLE COULDN'T HELP BUT laugh at what Lady Margery said. They lounged on a small balcony in the middle bailey's wall, looking out over a cold clouded morning, having just finished a brief conversation and a bowl of dates. Arable picked up her dress and excused herself, eager to find William and share the joke with him.

"Perhaps it's only a rumor," Margery shrugged, waving her fingers in dismissal. "After all, you of anyone in the castle would know such a thing, wouldn't you?"

Her meetings with the lady of Warwick were less frequent than she had first hoped, but her need for the relationship had similarly dwindled. Arable no longer sought escape from Nottingham, thanks to William's new position. She had removed herself from the girls' quarters entirely, leaving Mistress Roana scratching her head, and lived now in the chambers attached to William's room. Her "lessons" with Lady Margery had transformed into tea-side chats and philosophical musings. They were a welcome relief from her days closeted away, helping William deal with his mountains of administrative distractions. As for Lady Margery, she had no one to call friend amongst her husband's entourage, and loathed the other visiting ladies. Arable's status as something-more-than-servant was apparently enough for her to be treated with a morsel of decency, so long as nobody witnessed it. Margery seemed eager to share her life's worth of experiences with anyone willing to learn.

Which made it all the more queer that she would voice such a preposterous bit of gossip.

"The Lady Marion Fitzwalter is no common prisoner, I'm told. Is it true that Wendenal intends on a marriage with her?"

And Arable had laughed, because it was just so ridiculous, and she was off to tell William about it now.

Not *so* ridiculous—she hated using the word *so.* That had been a lesson Roger de Lacy had taught her once, rest his soul. It hurt to think of him. She missed his delight in stories and conversation. How he'd hold his elbow out for her hand, treating her like a true lady. Never like his servant, at least not privately. She used to find him in odd nooks of the castle, enraptured in thought or lost inside a book. And not epic tomes of laws and policy as she would have expected, but old ballads and fantasies, the kinds with gods and giants.

"I read whatever I choose to read, girl," he defended himself.

"Why read stories such as those? You aren't a child, why waste your time?"

"My dear," he cleared his throat, tapping her nose with his forefinger, "reading is the opposite of wasting time. There is no finer way to enjoy a sliver of one's life than by enjoying the entirety of another's."

She never knew what to say to him. "You're so interesting."

"Never use the word 'so,'" he announced, clapping his book closed to escort her down the hall. "It's the worst word in the English language. If you modify any word at all with the word 'so', then it should become another word. If I were 'so interesting,' well then I would become 'intriguing.' And if I were 'so intriguing,' I would become 'fascinating.' If I were 'so fascinating,' well then I must be 'mesmerizing.'"

"And what if you were 'so mesmerizing'?"

"I'm not." He laughed, squinting until his skin all wrinkled up around his eyes. "Go the other direction, pass 'boring,' and you'll find me at the end."

So no, she thought, pushing outside the barracks hall. Lady Margery's comment was not *so* ridiculous, it was . . . unthinkable. *But then again, it wasn't really unthinkable,* as Lady Margery had clearly thought it. There were a great number of lords and ladies in the castle of late, come to pay their respects to poor Roger, but not one of them had come to marry William. Wherever Lady Margery had heard such a thing, she must have misheard it.

Outside, Arable bunched up her dress and pushed up to the great keep in the upper bailey, hesitating for a moment at the sight of the double-lion banners. The bailey teemed with strangers, as Prince John's attendants had practically claimed the entire thing for themselves. Arable could come and go as she wished of course, but the prince's presence was more than alarming.

She rushed through the yard with her head down, relieved to slip into the tall stone keep. But the moment she was inside, she felt a punch in her heart, as she always did. The stairs led to Roger's office. *The room where he had been killed.* It was William's office now, but she hated meeting him there. She couldn't overcome the memory of Roger's body on the ground, and the way his blood crawled across the stone floor. For a moment she forgot why she was heading there. Why she would ever want to be in that room again.

She suddenly doubted whether she ought to disturb William at all. He could become so irritated at times when he was interrupted, and had little time for anything besides critical business. Sharing a laugh over the day's gossip hardly counted as important.

Her foot trembled as she started up the staircase. If she closed her eyes, she could just as easily be climbing the stairs in the stables again, fifteen years ago. The stables she and William had always run off to, where there was nothing but the two of them and the stars through the hole in the roof. But the last time she climbed those stairs at her family's estate, it was to wait for him. He never came. Not the first night, nor the second, or the third. On the fourth, men loyal to William's father Lord Beneger found her there, and told her their orders, and gave her one chance to flee.

She took it.

As she started the second set of stairs up to Roger's office, she saw herself fleeing down in the other direction, as she had back then. She and William had been so young and so naïve to think their love was a match for that amount of hate. No, not *so* young, not *so* naïve. They had been *ignorant.*

No, not *they*. Because William had figured it out.

She was the one who waited in a stable loft for three days, concocting increasingly elaborate tales for his delay. It was a girlish sort of hope—the same one she felt all this week. That same young and stupid *ignorant* feeling that had blinded her years before.

At the top of the third stair, she glanced down the hallway. Two Guardsmen now always stood outside the room halfway down, what was once an empty salon for the widow Murdac. If they'd let her pass, Arable could knock on that door and get whatever answers she needed from its sole inhabitant.

Lady Margery passed this room every day. The Earl of Warwick was still housed in the solar at the end of the hall.

Arable knew exactly where Margery had heard the rumor.

She didn't want to climb further. But her legs kept moving. At the top of the fourth stair she felt as if tears might come, but they didn't. And by the top of the fifth stair, she realized why. She had cried it all out already. The months of feeling worthless that had turned into years, years of hating the sound of her own name. Years of seeing his face when she closed her eyes and wanting to drown herself to stop it. Until eventually it died. William could still make her happy, yes, but she had cut out that part of herself long ago that allowed him to hurt her.

And by the time she opened the crooked little door that led to Roger's office, the rumor had ceased to be funny. After all, William had proven to Arable fifteen years ago exactly where she lay in his priorities.

William was at Roger's desk, his back was to her, and something closed inside of her.

"It's true, isn't it?"

He heard her, but he didn't turn to smile at her, and he didn't stand and take her in his arms. He didn't brush her hair or put his fingers on the back of her neck. Instead he sat motionless.

"I heard about it from Lady d'Oily, and I laughed. It was so ridiculous an idea I actually laughed out loud. I came here to tell you about it, so you could laugh, too." She caught herself and laughed now, a different laugh. The only thing that was funny was that she had fallen for it. "Not *so* ridiculous, actually. *So* ridiculous that it was real."

Still he didn't move. If he stood up now and told her it was a lie, she would believe him. If he just smiled and brushed it off, it would be that easy. Even if he was angry and didn't have the time for her, it would be fine, it really would be.

Instead, the back of his head.

"It's not a joke, is it?"

The back of his head didn't have a mouth but still it said, "It's not."

"You're getting married."

"Yes." Nobody else was in the room, but he didn't say it to her.

"What did I do?" she asked. She should have asked, *What more could I have done?*

"This has nothing to do with you." That punch should have hurt, but instead she laughed again. His shoulders clenched, as if this were some torture to have to deal with her.

Again, to nobody, "This is for strictly political reasons."

"Why didn't I know?" she screamed it, because it needed to be screamed. "When did this happen? Where is this even coming from?"

"Lady Marion is cousin to King Richard—"

She cut him off. "Don't you even say her name to me."

But he kept talking, he kept saying things that didn't matter. "Her family is above reproach."

"*Her family?* I didn't realize that was what you cared about. I'm sorry my family isn't good enough for you, but your father chased them out of England. You remember that, don't you?"

"That's not what I meant."

And finally he turned around. His face was wrought with grief and his eyes were red. Even furious as she was, it was hard to see. "Arable, I love you, you don't understand. My position here . . ." *no,* he was trying to explain it again, when that was the only thing she didn't want to hear, ". . . it's resting on a knife's edge. Prince John is watching me like a hawk. Convincing him to keep me as sheriff was probably the most dangerous thing I've ever done."

She shook her head, she didn't want to hear this, she didn't care at all about the politics of it, she just wanted him to tell her he was going to fix it. "Allying myself with Lady Marion secures my position. Her family is his family, it was the only way. You remember the alternative right? Sheriff Gisbourne?" He just kept talking, talking *at* her, not *to* her. "Do you want to see him in power?"

"William!"

"Do you?"

"No, of course not!"

"We made this choice, Arable. We cannot back down from it now, not when our very lives may hinge on its success. Not when there's so much at stake. We knew we would have to make sacrifices."

He had thought it all out, it seemed. He had been practicing his excuses. He knew it was going to come to this.

"We did make a choice," she kept her voice cold and even, "together. But you made this one on your own. You know it's wrong. The fact that you didn't tell me about it is all the proof I need."

"I didn't know how!" He slammed into the table as he stood. "I haven't slept! I haven't eaten! I didn't want to hurt you . . . I haven't had the time, I've been sick. I've been sick to my stomach, I thought I would vomit. I'm trying to fix things here, but I can't do it alone, and I have mutiny in the prisons and Gisbourne breathing down my neck and suddenly I'm in charge of protecting everyone."

"So of course," Arable almost lost control of her voice, she had to grind it to a crawl, "of course you would get rid of the one person on your side. That makes a lot of sense."

William shook his head, brushing her off. As if her concerns were meaningless. It lit her skin on fire. "It's not like that. I promise you, I'll find a way—"

"Your *promises,*" it was probably the only word he shouldn't be allowed to use, "break to your politics."

Those words seemed to hurt him.

"You promised to look after me. Did you ever write to your father, to find out if any of my family is alive in France? I've been writing all your letters, and I don't recall that one in my list."

His hand raised and dropped. "It was too dangerous . . ."

"So you've done nothing, then."

He took a step forward and whispered her name, and she could feel the warmth of his body, his smell, and part of her could still forget it all and melt into him. When he reached out, she had to choose to stop him. Not just like that. He wanted the side of his hand to brush against her hair, and she found herself pushing him away.

Not until he answered the important question. "What about *us,* William?"

He tried to touch her again, and this time she stopped him more forcefully. He thought he was apologizing, but he wasn't. "You don't need to go to France. We can still . . ." and he waved his hand ambiguously about. *That. That* was the entirety of their relationship to him, a vague sexual gesture he couldn't even put into words.

"We can still . . . *what*? No, we can't still . . ." she repeated his little hand flail back at him, "I can't still . . . with a man whose wife has the ear of the King. Are you insane?"

"I'm so sorry," he said, stepping away from her. *So* sorry.

"Don't be *so* sorry. Be something better than sorry. By proving it. Put a stop to this now."

His shoulders slumped, his face sagged. He wasn't handsome anymore. He looked old, and defeated, unwilling to fight for himself, much less fight for her.

"I am so sorry," he repeated, the same empty words, and he sat back in his chair, in Roger's chair. With his back to her. Roger was there, on the wall, judging him, too. Whatever was left of William said, "But I stand by my decision."

She wouldn't be waiting three days this time. There was no point in wasting even another minute on him. She had nowhere to go, but nowhere alone was better than anywhere with him.

"You're worthless," she told the back of his head. "You could marry the King himself, and you'd still be worthless."

FORTY-NINE

GUY OF GISBOURNE

SHERWOOD FOREST

"Don't know that anyone here can help you," a craven husk of a man whined, in some little armpit farm near Carleton. "Where did you say you was from now?"

They had started in the smaller villages, and instantly noticed the stark difference in how they were treated. Without their colors they were disguised as nobodies, entering a world in which they were only as valuable as their valuables. At least within a city, there was always the mutual agreement that civilization had merit. Even the filth at the bottom still loved that city as much as anyone. Rabble such as the Red Lions and the other wharfside gangs had fought side by side with the Nottingham blue when war came to their streets fifteen years ago, because there was recognition, within a city, that all their fates were irreparably bound together. But as Guy and the men of the Black Guard strayed away from that safety, they entered the great perilous experiment of lawlessness.

"We have information we need to get to Robin Hood." Guy drawled out his words to hide his education. "It's a matter of grave importance."

They were greeted with suspicion, and a group of derelict men nearby were sizing up their chances to attack. Not one of them had the build or the tan of a proper farmer, and they fanned out to protect their storehouse in a manner that suggested they had stolen it themselves. Without his uniform, Guy was only too aware he must seem an easy target, the salt and pepper of his beard betraying his age. He was thankful Marshall Sutton was an imposing thick wall no matter what he wore, since the needling Ferrers at his other side was as intimidating as warm porridge.

"I appreciate your discretion, friend," Guy soothed the skeptic stranger, "but Robin himself told me he'd been to this village. I just need to get him a message is all. All I need is to be pointed in the right direction."

"Can't help you," was the solemn reply, but the stranger tilted his head to the east. "But I hear they may have seen him in Godling night before last."

"Thank you," Guy winked, "I'll let Robin know he has a friend here."

"See that you do."

Guy tried to hide his discomfort. If they projected weakness, they would be eaten alive. Being pointed toward Godling was better information than they had received in weeks as honest Guardsmen, and it gave Guy the bittersweet hope this would work.

It had to work. For Guy, it was the only option. If Wendenal successfully deposed him and humiliated him, the only natural conclusion would be to quietly kill him as well. After a month or so, once the drama of his departure was settled, Guy predicted he would undoubtedly meet his end by an anonymous blade in the night. If left alive, he would put all his efforts into revealing this corruption, and Wendenal knew it. His men would likely be safe, suffering on under the orders of the young new captain from Warwick, but Guy's only alternative would be to flee. And frankly, he would probably prefer the blade than to leave Nottingham.

Everything he had, his very breath, rested on his ability to be the man who captured Robin Hood. It was the only claim that would make him invulnerable, and he was at every disadvantage of achieving it.

A bulky man with an unadvisable amount of chin idled in front of Guy as they tried to leave. His eyes bulged, revealing his every thought. This was the kind that could never be reasoned with, who thought only with his gut. The creature revealed a heavy sword tucked at his side, which slowly found its way out of his belt.

"There's an awful lot of Sheriff's Guard out there." His voice had a pesky scratch to it. "More than usual."

"So there is," Marshall grunted and tried to lead his horse around the brute, but found himself blocked again. Guy cursed himself for bringing the horses into the farm. He could dress himself down as much as he wanted, but any decent horsehand would recognize Merciful as healthy and well-stabled.

But the bulk turned his blade around and offered its hilt up to Guy. "You'd best arm yourselves. Just in case."

The sword's pommel boasted a flared cross under several layers of caked dirt, or excrement. Meant for the Crusade, one of those from the first lost shipment. Guy curled his fingers around it, afraid it might turn around and cut him in half.

"What about you?" he asked, trying to match the man's tone.

"We have plenty."

Guy nodded his head slightly. He wondered where the sword had been already, whose blood it might have spilt. One reclaimed sword wasn't much, but it might save a life.

Even after the birklands consumed the last hints of Carleton, they rode in silence. The roads here were narrow and broke awkwardly into rolling ribbons of browning heath, othertimes splitting into switchbacks dense with overgrown thicket. There was black slurry always at the edge of the road, grown into slick traps by the season's first overnight frost.

"It's worse than I thought," Marshall said, since it had to be said.

"This is only the beginning of it, I'm afraid." Guy glanced nervously back. "The closer we get, the more zealous they'll become."

Marshall rubbed the stubble on his head and slapped the sweat off. "How do we handle something like this? Every man we meet is an enemy."

"No, they're not," Guy corrected him. Marshall had finally glimpsed the magnitude of their mission, and was rightfully rattled. "These are the people we're supposed to protect. They're victims of a great many things. Of the hardships of life. Of the king's taxes, certainly, but more than that they're victims of Robin Hood. He's capitalized on their gullibility, purchasing their souls for a little coin. Why *wouldn't* they follow him?"

Marshall shook his head.

"The few things they do have," Guy continued, "they don't realize they're not free. They can trade and have the opportunity to feed themselves thanks to the county. They're protected from invaders by the King. But they don't see this. It's not tangible. They don't know how much worse life would be in the anarchy they think they want. Then Robin Hood puts a coin in their hand, and it's something they can hold onto. He takes their vulnerabilities, and trades it right back to them for their loyalty. Convinces them a few coins will make their lives better. Hard work and integrity? Gone. What man tries to improve himself when he's offered a quicker path? Robin Hood is taking advantage of them at their weakest."

Marshall nodded, but he was not at ease. "Sounds like the Devil."

"Robin of Locksley is just a man, don't glorify him. But it doesn't have to be the actual Devil," Guy sighed, "for it to be his work."

THE NEXT MORNING, JUST outside of Godling, an old woman ran at them from the darkness at the side of the road, collapsing in the dirt before their horses. Her arms were mostly bone, her fingers twisted and pulled at each other as she lowered to her knees. What clothes she had were so rotten that a withered breast hung out in the open. Guy motioned for Marshall and Ferrers to halt, but kept his eyes open to the sides of the road. This was how the outlaws were known to steal from travelers, by distracting them with piteous displays and then springing their trap.

But the crone was too far gone in poverty to be a thief. "Thank God, thank God," she screeched, to no God that deserved her thanks. She unbent her fingers with some difficulty and tried to raise a palm up to them. "There's a toll here, you remember? You remember, yes, just a little bit more, just a little bit more."

"Get out of the way, woman," Marshall barked, pulling his mount almost on top of her, but Guy ordered him to stand back. Guy spied an equally emaciated boy—hidden within the overgrown bramble at the side of the road—crouching beside what could only be a dead hog, half opened and gutted.

"Just a little more, we only need a little more," she moaned on.

"Did the last man who came through here give you a toll?" Guy asked her.

"You did, it was you!" she cried out.

It was an unsettling comparison. "When last you saw me, which direction did I go?"

She squeezed her face into an even more wrinkled mess and shook her head vigorously. "Neither way, you went through," and she pointed into the dense wall of bare rowan behind her. The trees here extended their limbs low like claws, barren wild branches that made any passage impossible. Beyond them in the distance, columns of straight black trees gave the haunting image of an army at the ready. "*Thorney,* you said, you were going to Thorney next."

Guy inhaled slowly. "I did at that, didn't I?"

He tossed her a coin out of mercy. It bounced into the mud and only seemed to confuse her. There was no helping this one, nor her child. Whatever had scratched out her mind chilled Guy down to his bones.

Madness. Of all God's punishments, it was the most terrifying. Guy's father had succumbed to it in his later life, and it was said to run common within a family. There could be no worse fate, to lose oneself. To have a lifetime of memories and reason fade away. Guy had experienced a touch of it once, when he had fallen into that muddy hole as a young recruit, and been unable to scramble out. He remembered what it was like to feel sanity slip away, to think about suicide in a way that honestly felt like a logical answer. No disease, no violence, was worse than losing one's mind.

It was not only mankind's sickness to bear. A place could have it, too.

"We're coming close to the tipping point, I think," Guy said, their horses picking their way off-trail through the unrelenting bracken. It was not noon yet, and the sun pierced through the forest's sparse canopy to scatter pillars of shadow in every direction. Surrounded at all times by a thousand hiding spots, but always unnervingly exposed themselves.

"What's the tipping point?" Marshall asked.

"Let me ask you this. Which is more effective, ambition or intelligence?"

Marshall snorted. "That's easy. Intelligence. Ambitious young men do some awfully stupid things, that's when they come to me in gaol."

"Certainly," Guy considered, "but men with intelligence tend to keep to themselves. It's usually wise to play it safe, but playing it safe doesn't accomplish much. The ambitious risk more, and often fail, but to those that succeed goes the power."

"By such an argument," Ferrers brushed off a twig that had landed on his shoulder, "there would never be men of intelligence in power. But that is not the case."

"Not at all," Guy answered. "There comes a tipping point when wise men must act, when it finally becomes the wiser move. Look at our history of sheriffs. FitzRanulph was a smart man and he led for fifteen years. After him was Murdac, a good man but a bit impulsive, sheriff for six years. Next, de Lacy, a strategic imbecile, more worried about creating some legacy for himself than understanding what Nottingham needed. Two years. Now this Wendenal, with all ambition and no experience. This is the way of the world. The just are replaced by the ambitious, because the ambitious seize opportunity. Eventually, only the most ruthless claim power through bloodright. That is the tipping point history shows us, when men of intellect must step back into the arena, to put a stop to the downward slope of greed."

Somewhere unknowably ahead, a heavy branch cracked and tumbled down, snapping the air until silence again filled the void.

"I hope it doesn't get worse than this," Marshall sighed. "The world is insane enough. The Sheriff being killed in his own office, Derbymen running my prisons . . . no offense," he added, to Ferrers, who shook it off. "Captain, I don't know if you're the man who can step up and put a stop to it all, but I'll do what I can to help you."

"I don't know if I am, either. But God willing, I'm going to try."

They moved through the skeletons of trees in silence, as Guy let it all filter through his head. The burden was obviously his to bear. There was nobody else who had seen the plot unfold as Guy had, no others who were close enough to the sheriff's office to effect change. It's why they had targeted him, he was certain.

He opened his mouth to comment upon it to Marshall, but suddenly doubted himself. The lecture he had just given, it was the sort of lesson he was happy to give to those under his guidance. Young men, like Jon Bassett, and Devon of York. One still missing and likely to never resurface, the other dead. His protégés had a disturbing tendency to suffer cruel fates, and Guy wondered what percentage of that curse was his. It seemed every time he spoke truth to the world, someone suffered for it.

"Both," Ferrers said, crisply. "It's better to be both ambitious and intelligent."

He smiled to Guy, awkwardly. It was as rousing a compliment as the young man had ever given. And if he continued to follow Guy, he was likely to be murdered by nightfall.

"Thank you, Ferrers." Guy tried to mean it. "Look at you, already so much smarter than your father."

To call Thorney a village would be insulting, like calling a beggar a king. Something of a mockery by association. A small collection of shambling hovels clustered around a barren fire ring, and the nettled woods receded just enough for a few sickly fields of vegetables and grain fighting back stalkrot. Guy and his company kept their distance, but saw no indication that Locksley or his men were anywhere nearby.

"Captain." Marshall pointed two fingers at a solitary figure watching them, alone at the outskirts of the fields. Guy prompted Merciful forward. The thick man was made thicker with mangy hair that poured from every available orifice. He half squinted, his hands dangling uselessly at his sides. No weapons hung from his belt, but the lumps of his ill-fitting clothes might easily conceal a knife. *Hell, so could his beard.*

When they were close enough, Guy shifted so the hilt of his stolen sword could be easily seen. "We're looking for Robin Hood."

"Well, you've found Stutely," the other said, blinking slowly.

"Excellent, just the man we're looking for," Guy lied. "We were told you were the one that could lead us to him."

"I can do pretty much anything I want."

"So you do know how to find him, yes?" Guy climbed down, hoping to appear as non-hostile as possible. He groaned and rubbed his aching thighs.

"It's possible I've been to his camp. It's possible more than a few times." The evasive answer was as good as a yes, and Guy felt his pulse quicken. "But there are a lot of guards looking for him lately, so I don't imagine he'd like me bringing a couple strangers to them, unannounced and such."

"Oh, we're not strangers," Guy laughed, pouring all his focus into appearing casual. He hoped that Marshall and Ferrers could follow suit. They couldn't afford to spook the man, when he was their only lead. "Will Scarlet sent us. He broke out of the Nottingham prison, with our help of course, and he sent us ahead to tell Robin. Robin's been planning to break into the castle to save Scarlet, and he needs to know . . . not to come. Before it's too late."

Guy quietly stepped out of his own skin and slapped himself in the face. He was a terrible liar, but his lips just seemed to keep moving.

Stutely, quite rightfully, stared in stupor. "Why would he do that?" he asked. "Will Scarlet hates Robin Hood."

Guy threw a sharp look to Marshall, who appeared equally confused. He stammered to cover his surprise. "He *does,* he does hate Robin Hood, and that's precisely why Scarlet doesn't want him to go to Nottingham. Wouldn't want Robin to take all the credit."

Damnation. Guy was no actor, and was proving it now. Lying and stealing must come easily for the outlaws, but Guy had only a lifetime of honesty to prepare him for moments such as these.

"I don't know. Why didn't he come himself?"

"He didn't say." Guy feigned an equal confusion. He needed the right answers, and had none. If this went south, the trees would no doubt come alive with this beast's cohorts. Even if he were lucky enough to arrest the man, Guy didn't fancy the odds of leveraging any truth from him. Most folk are just as like to lie to save their skin than anything else, and any diversion on this trip meant failure. *Everything was against them.* Guy shrugged his shoulders and aimed for a non-answer. "I didn't ask why. You know how Will Scarlet is."

"Yeah, that's true." Stutely bobbed his head, having agreed with something that only he could know about. Guy suppressed a sigh of relief. "But you'll have to give me something more than that. Anyone can tell a story, you know? I could tell you I'm the King of England, but it wouldn't make it any more true, now would it? Not that I couldn't be."

All Guy had was the stolen sword, but he had a hunch it wouldn't do. "We don't . . . Will didn't really think it would be an issue."

"What we ought to do," Stutely lit up and ground his hands together, "is think of some sort of secret phrase. Something that only a real member of Robin's men would know. That would do it."

He kept rubbing his fingers and waiting expectantly, convinced he had just invented the greatest breakthrough in the history of military strategy. A library of phrases that would be fitting slogans for the outlaws came to mind. *Strength in Cowardice. Real Men Hide in Trees. Kill All Who Disagree.* But Guy tried to think from their perspective—these men rallied the weak through fear, and they exploited the vulnerable.

"Remember Bernesdale," Guy said.

Stutely's eyes squinted ever so slightly, and he gave a long low nod. *Bernesdale,* where they'd sent a child to be a murderer. They trained young boys to kill, and still arrogantly claimed to be the victims. Guy had lost three men at Bernesdale, counting Bolt. *Remember Bernesdale* should be the cry of the Nottingham Guard. After a few heavy moments, Stutely scratched at his beard. "Yeah, I remember it. What about it?"

"That . . . that should be the pass phrase." Guy couldn't fathom that anyone could be so dense.

"Why would that be the pass phrase?"

"Are you serious?" He had been wasting his worries. This man was no gatekeeper, he was a base idiot.

"What does Bernesdale have to do with anything?"

Guy's patience packed up its belongings and traveled far away. "Are you going to fucking take me to Robin Hood or not?"

"Yeah yeah yeah."

It took all of Guy's focus to climb back atop Merciful, his thoughts consumed with splitting the man's skull open to marvel at its vacancy. "You trust him?" Marshall whispered at the first discreet opportunity.

"Ho God, no." The idea sent spiders down his spine. "But it's as good a sign as any that we're on the right track."

More accurately, it was the only track they had. All his hopes were poured on the back of this dim-witted troglodyte. The worst part was that he was damned lucky to even have gained this much. He was reminded of the empty feeling in his belly when they were tracking Jon Bassett, when the tracks disappeared into rain puddles and they had nothing left to follow but guesses.

Perhaps, like Bassett, they were about to fall off the earth.

STUTELY DIDN'T HAVE A horse, and there wasn't a man alive who would ride double with him. Fortunately the oaf offered to walk on his own, boasting that he could walk as quickly and as far as a horse anyhow. He lumbered ahead, just out of earshot, picking his way down an unrelenting slope covered by an endless bed of fallen brown needles. But Stutely's distance allowed Marshall to ask the most important question. "What do we do when we get there, Captain? There's only three of us, we can't fight them."

"We're not going to fight them," Guy kept his voice low. "I just need to talk to Locksley."

"Talk to them?" Marshall gulped aloud. "You think that'll work?"

"Not all of them," Guy had to laugh. "Just Locksley. Remember what their plan is—Locksley intends on walking them all into a trap. If we threaten to reveal that betrayal, he'll have to bargain with us. Otherwise he'll be at the mercy of his own men, and they have not shown themselves to be a particularly forgiving group."

Marshall murmured an agreement. "What sort of bargain?"

"Anything we can use against Wendenal. In exchange, we keep his secret . . ." he gave the prison guard a wink, ". . . for an extra minute or two." Even if Locksley gave him nothing, turning the thieves upon themselves would spoil Wendenal's plans.

Marshall chuckled as he figured it out. "Alright. What if they don't let you talk to him?"

"They have to," Guy scoffed. "A parlay between enemies is sacred. Only a tyrant would kill a messenger."

Merciful lost her footing to a hidden pit, but recovered.

"Then what if they're tyrants? What if they kill us?"

"Then we'll be dead," Guy considered, "and we won't have to worry about this anymore."

Marshall grunted. "If they try anything, I intend on taking more than a few of them out. They've got their due coming, and I owe it to George to see that they pay."

Guy paused for a moment's deduction, as he hadn't realized the connection. "George Sutton?"

"Cousin. Didn't care for him much, little runt as he was, but he was still family. They killed him for his uniform, a fucking disgrace." Marshall spat at the ground.

Guy didn't know what to say. "Your family must be proud. Two sons in the Guard."

"Like I said, wasn't much about George to be proud of, but that don't make it alright."

"No, it doesn't."

"No, it don't."

They continued their descent in silence.

At length, Stutely led them to a large muddy pool of still water at the foot of a wall of wet boulders. The terrain on either side of the rocks rose up again sharply.

"They've been moving camp a lot lately," Stutely explained, "and this here is one of their favorites. You'll have to leave your horses behind, only way up is to climb." He indicated a crooked vertical ascent of striated limestone, which rose to a lip beyond which they could not see. "We'll need to wait a bit, though. My legs are screaming."

"This can't wait, friend. You can rest here." Guy was happy to be rid of the man. "Ferrers, take the horses."

"Actually," his eyes widened ever so slightly, "I'd prefer to join you."

Guy could hardly blame him. "Stay," he repeated, holding a forced stare. In case it went just as Marshall feared, in case he had miscalculated Locksley's motives, then Ferrers could at least bring word to the others.

A few obvious placements of broken shelves noted the path up the limestone slope. It looked even steeper up close, but was definitely navigable. Guy tried not to think about how sharply it might crack open his skull, were the outlaws to throw him back down from above.

"Captain," Marshall spoke softly as they tested out their first few footholds, "there's something else I've been meaning to speak to you about."

"Can it wait?"

"It can, but I'd think straighter if I didn't."

Guy let him continue.

"It's about Morg, sitting down in my gaol cells. I thought this would blow over, thought the Sheriff would see straight and let him out again. Doesn't seem to be going that way yet."

Guy's hands were abominably tied in this situation. "What about him?"

"The boys and I would sure be interested in getting Morg out of there in any other way."

He was talking about breaking Morg out of their own prisons. "If that were possible, he'd have to leave Nottinghamshire entirely. He couldn't rejoin the Guard after that."

"I know it. But if he stays there, he'll die, that's a fact."

"The prisons aren't under my control anymore," Guy reminded him.

Marshall wiped the sweat from his head and looked up at the climb. "Lud and I know how to get a man out of there. Can't be done by one person, but I wouldn't involve you in the details. All I'd need from you is to be sure nobody is stationed between the Rabbit Cage and the postern door. And your key to the Rabbit."

Guy nodded. Frankly, he didn't know how he felt about the proposal. It was one more step away from doing things lawfully, and closer to doing what was right. It was not a thin line, as he had expected, but a long gentle ramp—certainly one easier to walk than his travel today. Still, at this moment he needed Marshall's head clear above all else. He risked nothing by giving his promise now, when a thousand things could believably keep him from fulfilling it later. Trivial things, such as being dead.

"The Guard is nothing if we don't have each other's backs," he answered. "The Sheriff doesn't understand that. We take care of our own."

Marshall seemed satisfied, and they started bouldering up the wall.

The climb was tricky but not as perilous as it seemed, always offering enough rock to rest upon. Guy watched the lip up above grow closer, where waited the true danger. The ascent gave the foreboding sense of climbing up to some giant's kingdom, up to another world. It was easy to see how the commonfolk had been seduced by the cult of this *Robin Hood* persona. But Robin of Locksley was just a man, a slave to the same desperations of survival as anyone.

You're not going to die here, Guy tried to convince himself.

Not in the middle of the woods. Not forgotten in a hole.

His whole life had been a whetstone, sharpening him for a moment like this.

When Guy made his final scrambles up the slope, his stomach turned.

There was a small flat glade, well-protected by natural walls, an absolutely perfect spot for Robin's men to hide. But it was empty, and the few signs of any campsite were well grown-over with tussock.

Guy turned in panic to look back down below. The tiny shape of Ferrers was on his back, clutching his head with both hands, and beyond him was the last glimpse of Stutely riding off on Merciful, leading the other two horses by their reins.

BETWEEN THEN AND NOW, an eternity of humiliation passed. The world was black and burnt, and those who suffered deserved it. It was past midnight and Guy's body could barely move, but his soul couldn't bear to sit still. He was done with civility, he was done with the cat-and-mouse bullshit that was Robin of Locksley.

There was too much at stake, and not enough time.

Rising from the earth in front of him, the Rabbit Cage was a gravestone. Cold bars for a cold night. Guy dismissed the unfamiliar Derbyman, who retreated back down into the stairs within the cage, leaving only the limp prisoner he had dragged up.

"Sorry to disturb your sleep." Guy ground his teeth. "I could come back at a more convenient time."

Will Scarlet coughed out dirt and slowly roused himself to a seated position, back to Guy, against the bars, but gave no answer.

"You're supposed to be hanged on Sunday morning, you know."

Scarlet's voice was small and dry. "Go to hell."

"There will be an execution for you, yes, an extravagant affair. Too much pomp if you ask me. Sadly, you won't be attending. We'll kill you in the morning instead, just a quick knife to the throat. This is the last time you'll be out of your cell. We probably won't bother feeding you anymore."

Scarlet breathed in, the air rattled from his lungs. "I could eat your heart."

"You could!" Guy laughed. "You could pull those bars apart, rip my body open and eat my heart, right here. By all means, be my guest. It is ever so close." Guy tapped his chest, only a few feet away from the young outlaw, who still refused to face him.

Bitterly, "If you have a heart at all."

"That would be a risk you'd have to take." Guy stared at the back of Scarlet's head. "It's also possible you wouldn't recognize one. Perhaps I'm mistaken, but you're the one in prison for murder."

That did it. With more strength than he'd pretended to have, Scarlet twisted his body around with precision, his head low, eyes locked on Guy.

"You're really going to look me in the eye," his face was half-bruised, "and tell me you're not a murderer?"

Murderer. The word struck too hard. A murderer plans his kill, he intends to do violence upon another. The blood that Guy had spilled was not intentional. But if it made Will Scarlet angry, then Guy would talk about it.

He needed him angry.

"The child."

"His name was Much."

"I know." How many times had Guy replayed that moment, wondering if he could have stopped himself? "I don't suppose you would believe how I regret that."

Will's face quivered. "It didn't look like you had a problem with it at the time."

He swallowed, preparing for what he had to say.

"Let me ask you," he started, shaking his head to stay focused. "Do you blame yourself for what happened? For bringing that boy?"

Will snorted. "No."

"And why not?"

"Because we were trying to do the right thing. We were—"

"I know," Guy raised his hand gently, to quiet him. "Let me say something?"

Will's eyes flickered.

"I had a son, about that boy's age," Guy said, and his eyes instantly watered. "I had *two* sons. Every man should have children. They make you a better person. My sons . . . they both caught sick around the same time. John was always the stronger one, he could . . . he came through it alright." Guy couldn't feel his fingers or his feet now. There was nothing but a muted world and the patch of ground he was staring at, and the memories. "But Henry was smaller. He was only a little thing. You can't do anything to help, you know, when they're sick. When they cough, they don't know what's wrong. Henry fought, but . . . the sickness won."

Henry had been a kind boy with an adventurous spirit, quick to giggle. Watching that joy leak away from him was the most wretched thing Guy had ever lived through. His throat was clenched, he couldn't keep thinking about it.

"There was a moment," he continued, "when Much fell into my arms, that he felt exactly like Henry."

The dark all blended together and in it was the boy's face, Much's face—just as it was the first and only time he had seen it, held aloft by the knife in his own hand. He felt the boy's weight, suspended.

He blinked, freeing the tears to roll down his cheeks, so that he could look Will Scarlet in the eyes. "Do you honestly think I would intentionally kill a child?"

He didn't answer.

"You've been in enough fights before, you know how they work. You saw it happen, it was over before I even realized it was happening. I understand why you hate me, because we have to blame someone. But I didn't mean to kill him. *And you know it.*"

He didn't look away.

"I was the same when Henry died, I had to hate someone. Someone had to be responsible. I hated—" a lump in his throat choked him, he bit his lip against all of it, "I hated my wife. She didn't deserve it, I didn't want to hate her, but I did. She did everything right, too. I should have hated the *sickness,* but I blamed the wrong thing."

Will's eyes were wetter.

"You know I'm not to blame. And you know you're not to blame. And you've probably figured out by now that the Sheriff wasn't to blame, either. Everyone, *every damned one* of us was trying our best. But who wasn't there, Will? Who caused this thing to happen? Who was the sickness?"

During the endless, disgraceful trek after their horses had been stolen, Marshall had cursed about how their entire day was wasted. At first Guy had agreed with him, hot and furious, but the tiresome walk had given him a moment of clarity as well. It had not been entirely wasted, for they had learned two new things. First, they learned they could not simply rely on chancing upon Robin's camp in their remaining few days.

And second, they learned that Will Scarlet hated Robin of Locksley.

"You're blinded by your rage, Will Scarlet. That boy's not on you. But your girl, Elena? You should never have brought her here, *here* of all places. You'll both be dead soon, because you blamed the wrong person. I suggest you start thinking about your actions rather than just . . . *doing* them."

Scarlet shook his head, the muscles around his eyes contracted. "What do you mean?" Finally, he was actually listening, rather than just waiting for his next opportunity to piss and shit.

"You'll get them all killed, Will. In the name of revenge, you've killed all your friends. Was de Lacy really worth it?"

"The people will know I stood up for them."

"That *you* stood up for them?" Guy sighed. "Don't fool yourself. The people think the Sheriff was killed by Robin Hood."

Scarlet kicked and stammered over his words. "Robin—? He's gone! He left! He walked out on us—"

"Well, he's back," Guy sighed, "and he took responsibility for what you did. The people, they think Robin Hood will save them from their troubles. They love him, they flock to him in droves. He's making a peace impossible. He's going to lead an army of innocent people into a bloodbath."

Guy searched Will's face for any recognition of what he needed to do. The boy's eyes darted back and forth, his lips whispered things he didn't voice, until finally he figured it out.

"If he were gone," Will pieced it together slowly, "things could return to normal."

It was a painful way to play chess, but a checkmate is a checkmate.

"I can arrange for you and Elena Gamwell to both escape from here," Guy whispered, now only inches from Will's face. "No one will be stationed between here and the postern door, you can get out of the castle, safely. Out of the city, well that'll be on you. All you have to do is find your way back to the Sherwood. In exchange for your lives, I want Robin's."

Scarlet glanced around the courtyard. Perhaps he remembered there was a world of possibilities open to him beyond the confines of these bars. Perhaps he was only pretending to consider it. But Guy had offered enough men a new chance at life now to recognize the flash of hope.

"If I kill Robin, they'd kill me."

"I can give you a poison." Ferrers was meeting with the visiting Bishop of Hereford even as they spoke, procuring the rare vial. "You mix it into a drink, it only takes a small amount. It takes a few hours, so no one will know it was you."

Scarlet's eyes retracted into slits. "What if I didn't go through with it? You would be setting both of us free, I could simply lie to you and walk out of here."

"You could, I suppose," Guy bluffed, "but my instinct tells me you care about more than just your life. If all you cared about was yourself, you wouldn't be here in the first place."

In reality, it didn't matter at all if Will went through with it. If Scarlet and Elena escaped now, Wendenal would be humiliated—and Locksley's men wouldn't have any excuse to come on Sunday at all. Guy could spoil Wendenal's scheming just by setting the captives free, and if they killed Robin in return then that was simply gravy.

It was curious. Dying was literally the only thing Guy did not want Will Scarlet to do.

"The escape," Will asked. "How will it work?"

It wasn't the lawful path. Disguises and lies, deceptions. Guy had become that which he hated. But under the thumb of such corruption, at the mercy of unprecedented danger, what other tactics were there? What was the value of an honest life if it served no others? By doing nothing, Guy would have doomed those that had no other voice. Once this threat was over, he would live with the weight of his decisions, balanced by the lives that would be saved. That was his sacrifice to make.

He wondered if this was how the outlaws justified their crimes.

For there was one more deed Guy needed to do this night, and it was the darkest one yet. It grew a black pit in his stomach to even think upon. He had strategized with himself in circles, finally resigning on the necessity of this last action. It played to the worst of man's nature, to prey on the vulnerable, and Guy trembled already at the prospect of going through with it. But it had to be done.

Poor, poor Arable.

FIFTY

ARABLE DE BUREL

NOTTINGHAM CASTLE

ARABLE LEANED OVER THE edge of the ramparts, ignoring the wind that took her hair and slapped it against her face. She was at the southernmost bend of the lower bailey wall. Down below, the river Trent sparkled in the sun, pretending life was anything more than a slow compilation of disappointments. Out and away, specks of homesteads hugged the water as it slept away from the city, full of people who were living their lives. Arable could do the same. *She had survived worse than this.* She had forged forward as only barely a young woman, when the rest of her family was dead or exiled. Compared to that, this was nothing.

She was exhausted, she told herself. Nothing more. Though she had grown accustomed to wearing a handmaiden's dress and countenance, she was iron within. William may have forgotten the quality of her character, but that loss was entirely his to bear.

A gasp from her left caused her to turn sharply. A wide ox of a man was reaching for her, his face panicked. She bleated—yes, like a sheep—as his hand found her waist and pulled her weight from the edge. She hadn't even realized how far over she had been leaning, and her head swam as she regained her balance.

"Are you alright?" he asked, his arms forming a protective wall.

"I'm fine," she said, then again, and someway found reason to give it a third go.

"I thought you, perhaps . . . meant yourself some harm." He had the faded blue stitched doublet of the Sheriff's Guard, but his face was only vaguely familiar. A bald head and a bulbous nose gave him a bubbly sort of attitude, though there were scars and scratches in his cheeks, and scabbing about his ears. "I'm Marshall Sutton," he said, as softly as he could with gravel for a voice. "And you're . . . you're Arable de Burel?"

She stared at him, her every nerve flaring at the sound of her own surname. His familiarity boded poorly. She leaned away but hit the crag of wall behind her, causing the Guardsman to move again.

"Do you need anything?" he asked. "Water?"

"No, no," she said, but should have said yes. To be rid of him.

"I am sorry to trouble you, but I think might be it was good I was here."

"I'm fine," she said flatly. She glanced about, but found they were quite alone on the walkway. Even the wind seemed intent to isolate them from the world.

"If you're sure you're alright."

"I am."

"Then, Miss Arable, I beg a word." All of his attention was on her, and his eyes flicked at her every movement. "I would offer to come back at a more favorable time . . . but I'm out of options."

"Is this your post, Guardsman?" she asked harshly, hiding her uncertainty. "Should I report your absence, or can you see yourself back?"

"Please hear me out." His face softened. "You should know that I do not come to you lightly, and I realize what I ask of you is no small thing."

"You haven't told me what that thing is," she laughed, because she did not know how to react to him at all. On another day she might have appreciated his concern. It was rare for a Common Guardsman to speak so gently, when they were normally prone to pawing at her and boasting of things they would like to do to her. *The things they were like to try now, without the protection of either Roger or William.*

Marshall swallowed. "Do you know about what happened to Morg?"

It took a moment for Arable to even wrap herself around the question, it was so far removed from herself. But yes, she had been there in the dining hall that night.

"Morg never meant to kill that boy, but truth be told I'm glad he did," Marshall said. "We're all safer for it."

Arable pursed her lips and nodded, though she didn't necessarily agree. Morg had always been a sweetheart to her. But when a man chooses to show one side of himself to the world, she had learned to be wary of the one he hid.

"He's still in prison." Marshall glanced over his shoulder and lowered his voice. "He can't stay there. He's being held with the same people he arrested. It's not safe. Even if he were wrong to do what he did, he doesn't deserve to die down there."

Arable suddenly wondered if there was a reason nobody else was nearby. "I don't know why you're talking to me. I can't do anything to help you, I'm sorry."

"I've talked to Sheriff Wendenal, but he won't listen to me, and neither will Captain Gisbourne." That caught her attention. *William now shared the same moral compass as Gisbourne.* "They think Morg is safe, but they don't know the prisons as I do. There aren't enough men in there to protect him, and the Derbymen won't let anyone in that's not one of their own. They think we'll try to let him loose."

"But you *are* trying to let him loose?"

"I'm not asking much, I'm not, I swear."

"That's not what you said a moment ago."

"I just need you to get something to him, that's all, it's as simple as that." Marshall twitched, matching her tiniest movements, apparently desperate to keep her here. "Nobody would ever suspect you. You could say you need to scrub the cells or collect laundry, them Derbymen won't know the difference." His hands trembled. "The key to each cell hangs on a ring just outside the block's entrance. All you need to do is get it into his hands. He'll get himself out. Just tell him to meet me at the Rabbit. I'll be there waiting for him, after I get the key from Gisbourne."

Arable's thoughts reeled, trying to find some advantage to this offer. "You're taking an awful risk in telling me this," she said. "What if I were to turn you in?"

"As I said," he gulped, "I'm out of options. Please, I can't risk getting the key from Gisbourne unless I know you're willing to help."

Two more Guardsmen were within eyesight now. She lowered her voice. "I'll think on it." She hoped that would appease him. "Talk to me again in a week."

"It has to be tonight," he whispered, harsher now, his own eyes locked on the approaching men.

"Then my answer is no." She peeled herself away. "I'm sorry."

She bit into the wind and left, pushing past the two Guardsmen without even looking back to see if Marshall was following her. At the end of the walkway a stair led up into the bottom level of the barracks hall, where she risked a glance behind. Marshall had not budged, and his body had a defeated sag to it.

She ascended inside, her eyes numb from the sunlight. Nottingham was too dangerous for her now, with no allies. Marshall and the Guard, they were remnants of her old life, trying to entangle her, to keep her from leaving. She had to look no farther than the scars on her cheeks to witness the dangers this place held for a woman on her own. It was an option, her *last* option, to return to the kitchens and ask humbly for forgiveness. Mistress Roana would understand and take care of her, but Arable couldn't do that. She only became Roger's serving girl as a disguise. If she went back to the kitchens now she would be a servant in heart as well as in title. It was a smothering sort of obscurity—she would disappear into it and never crawl out again.

Fortunately, she didn't need to.

A new life. She steeled herself, ignoring the foreboding weight of those words.

She continued straight through to the top floor of the barracks and out to the battlements on the opposite side. Again the chill wind bit into her cheeks, but it kept her alert, it kept her body feeling. It was a late morning, and Lady Margery d'Oily would still be in the large bedroom of the upper keep.

"DOES IT EVER OVERWHELM you?" Arable asked. Roger de Lacy sat on the thick wooden table he used as a desk, cracked and flawed, both of them. He rocked back and forth, arms cupped around his knees. He looked like a child, despite the grey hair he could try to hide and the responsibilities he couldn't.

"Of course not," he mumbled, his eyes focused on something out the window, far off but moving, a bird crossing the sky. "Nobody has ever been overwhelmed by anything. It's the sort of thing people say that doesn't make any sense. Overwhelmed. What would it take to actually overwhelm a person? How many troubles can a man have before they ooze out of his ears? Would my chest rip open and all my difficulties pour out, onto the ground, for me to simply lace myself up again and go about my day? To be overwhelmed would imply there exists a point that man cannot possibly take any more, and, were he given even the tiniest of troubles further, he would cease to be, or

explode perhaps. Astonishingly, this has never happened. That is our strength—mankind, that is. We can always take more. Even at the edge, when you feel the cliff crumbling beneath your feet, when you think you're falling, you're not. You're floating. You've just never felt it before. We can always take more, Arable. There is no such thing as being overwhelmed."

There were tears in her eyes, and she felt a strange sort of humility.

He turned and winked. "I am, however, absolutely and utterly whelmed."

MARGERY WAS INDEED IN the high keep's master solar, but she was not alone. Her husband, the squirrelly Earl Waleran de Beaumont, was pacing in circles about a tall-back chair whereupon sat their recently arrived son. The younger Waleran was a rugged and charismatic man who would have been attractive if not for his pervasive sense of entitlement. Arable guessed that his moniker, *the Young Bear,* was one of his own devising.

"Where are your manners?" Margery snapped, and only then did Arable realize she had barged into the room without having knocked. She had been enveloped in her thoughts, and flustered to find an apology. But Margery abandoned her with a flick of her wrist and continued in conversation. "I think it's a terrible idea, positioning yourself in the very role with which you do not wish to be associated."

"It will make him look like a hero," the earl said to his fingers.

Margery leveled her eyes on her husband. "It will make him look like a captain."

"I *am* a captain, Mother, and it would serve me well to be the captain who captures this infamous Robin Hood." The Young Bear spoke distinctly and did not fidget like his father, nor did he seem afraid to contradict his mother. "I don't see how anyone would think poorly of me for doing so."

Arable found a discreet position to wait. Whatever mild friendship she shared with Margery in private was nothing she would recognize in front of her family.

"You should be on the balcony with the Sheriff Wendenal," Margery was saying, "so the people will identify you with that level of prestige."

"The *people* don't know who I am," her son countered, reaching out for a glass of wine on the table beside him. He held it by its rim but did not sip, tilting it back and forth as he watched the liquid roll. "If I stand next to Wendenal, nobody will notice me. At least on the gallows they'll see me wield authority, and they'll call out and cheer when we put Robin Hood's men in irons. At a moment such as that, I will have their love more than Wendenal ever will."

Arable's mind fluttered. For some reason, the earl was under the impression his son would be appointed the new sheriff by Prince John. But Arable knew better.

"You're not allowed to be stubborn with me," Margery took the glass from her son and set it down again, "as I was the one who taught you the talent."

"By such reasoning I should not be able to disagree with you, either," he returned, "as you constantly teach me how to be disagreeable."

"That doesn't make any sense. You're just like your father, you like to move words around until they sound like wit, when you frankly have nothing worth saying."

She should help them, Arable realized. Her fate was now entangled with theirs, after all. But the last few weeks had been full of William's politics, and she fumbled to keep track of whose lies were whose. She needed a moment to clear her head, but they kept speaking.

"Consider the alternative, Mother," the Bear was saying. "If I am not the one to arrest the outlaws at the funeral, it will be another. Who? Captain Gisbourne will be with his men, guarding the city entrances, so the honor will fall on some other contingent. The Yorkies, feasibly. How will that look when I take the Sheriff's seat, if we needed York to capture this criminal for us? It makes Nottingham look weak, and it will make *me* look weak."

"You assume too much." Margery scowled, staring at her husband. "You put all your faith in John's empty promises."

"Prince John gave me his word," the earl grumbled from the window, "that he would name my son as Sheriff. He signed the edict. I wish to God he'd simply sent it rather than wait for the funeral to announce it, but it's no matter." Arable had that edict, tucked beneath her straw mattress, the letter that could undo William's claim. *But it did not have the young Waleran's name on it . . .*

"Our son shall be Sheriff, regardless of where in the hell he stands during the funeral."

"A promise Prince John made when de Lacy was still alive," Margery bristled, "but much has changed. Have you met with him yet?"

The earl snorted. "I tried. He's a very busy man."

Arable's silence wasn't helping anything.

"The prince sent the edict," she blurted out, before she could think through the ramifications. "It arrived a month ago, the day that de Lacy was killed."

"What?" Margery startled, as if Arable had suddenly appeared out of a puff of smoke.

"He sent it?" The earl descended on her. "But if my son was appointed as Sheriff, what in the hell is Wendenal doing here?"

"The prince didn't appoint your son," Arable said. "I saw it with my own eyes."

"That letter was from the *prince*?" Margery's face was ever sharper. "Not from the Chancellor? Roger told me . . ." Her eyes closed, an unfamiliar wash of defeat sank into her face. "He told me nothing, he let me assume what I wanted. Damn him and his pride."

"This makes no sense." The earl started twirling his fingers again, closing the shutters as if there were spies listening in.

"You idiot," Margery turned on her husband, her wrists clattering with jewelry as she waved her finger in the air, mocking him. "Prince John had no intention of appointing our son. He sent a letter, and Wendenal was appointed as Sheriff. It's no more complicated than that. William de Wendenal has been the prince's man all along."

The earl sat down. "My God."

"You and your damned conspiracies," Margery seethed. "They blind you to the simple truth! Wendenal is marrying the prince's cousin, for pity's sake, and you think they're not in bed together? You think they didn't plan all of this?"

"Do you suppose, then," the young Waleran looked gravely to both his parents for an answer, "that Prince John was behind the assassination as well?"

It lit a chilling possibility in Arable's mind. *Might the prince have orchestrated de Lacy's death, appointing Gisbourne to replace him?* Her mind raced to shuffle through the logic of it. She fought to keep the panic away. Prince John was only a single story beneath them.

The earl spoke through his teeth. "You're right, son. There is too much coincidence to pretend otherwise. De Lacy's death must have been Prince John's doing."

"Then what was the point of coming here?" the Young Bear fumed. "You told me I would be the Sheriff in Nottingham. I made considerable arrangements to leave my post at Warwick. Am I supposed to simply return and pretend this never happened?"

"Do not use such a tone with us," Margery scolded him, "when you had as little to do with earning this title as you did with your current one."

"What is that supposed to mean?"

"Quiet!" the earl shouted, a paralyzing intensity about him. "Let me think this out! Prince John has betrayed me, that much is certain—"

"He did not *betray* you. You aren't important enough to betray. He simply ignored you, as one does a fly."

"I don't care what you call it, Margery! We made a deal, and he chose to break it. He *chose* that. He knew we would all come here, thinking he would keep his word." He chomped his jaw shut, quickly, then took a half step back. "I don't think we're safe here."

Margery laughed, but it seemed hollow.

"If Prince John wants control of Nottingham for himself, he would do anything to secure it. And he knows my plans are not in line with his. His first step would be to remove any threat to his power here. My God, son, *that's* why he wants you on the gallows the day of the funeral. A few phony accusations, and he may hang you alongside his outlaws as a conspirator!"

The young captain's mouth dropped, he turned to his mother for appeal. Her own jaw had done the same.

He pivoted to his father. "I'll summon my men."

"We must leave as soon as possible, if not sooner."

Both went to action, gathering their belongings, as Margery stood baffled between them. "We can't leave now, we can't leave before the funeral."

"It's not a funeral for de Lacy," the earl warned her, "it's a funeral for us."

"That's ridiculous. We can't leave now."

"Don't question me on this, Margery!" The earl was suddenly invigorated, and whatever strength he lacked before came now with precision. "You have no idea the people we are dealing with, and what they will do to accomplish their goals. I misjudged Prince John. I thought he would be on our side, but he is something else, something else entirely. He has set a trap for me. Look at this place, this grand bedroom! They've been begging us to stay."

Margery wilted, and Arable knew why. She had grown somewhat fond of Nottingham—she'd confided as much in their private talks. The work she had done to revive the markets, the subtle politicking she had done with both de Lacy and William, she was watching it unravel uselessly through her fingers. "We can't leave . . ."

"We can and will," her husband spat.

"We can't leave . . ." she repeated, sharper, "because if you're right, they won't let us leave."

The earl froze midstep, more alarmed than ever. "We must take that chance. Son, make as little noise at this as possible. Discretion is our only ally now. We go one by one, and leave what we can. If anyone hears we are trying to depart, Wendenal may expedite whatever plans he has for us."

"I can help," Arable said, rising to action. She could move about the castle as she wished, and could safely burn whatever few bridges she still had here. "Just tell me what you need."

Margery's eyes flared wide, drilling into her. She said nothing, just continued with that crazed withering stare Arable could not understand. The earl looked and sighed. "God's mercy."

"What is it?" Arable asked.

Margery signaled to her son to do something, but Arable could not tell what. "We cannot let you go, girl, surely you see that."

For a moment, Arable wasn't sure Margery was addressing her at all. She had not called her *girl* since their first meeting. "Let me go? Why would I go? I'm here to help."

"Don't play coy, you're Wendenal's whore."

Arable gasped.

"You've been playing me all along, part of whatever plan this is. You've known about this letter for a month, and said nothing! I offered to take you in. What a fool I was to trust you, but that is a mistake I can correct now."

This wasn't supposed to happen. They had to understand she had nothing to do with this. *Except she had, she had lied to Lady Margery. Lied about the letter.*

"No, that's not true," she stammered. "William and I are over, you have to take me with you. Please, you don't understand."

Lady Margery curled her lips back, showing her teeth. "Don't you cry at me, you insipid little cunt. You appealed to my feminine softness once with that appalling act and I assure you that it will not work again. I think perhaps I'll cut your tongue out. I'm sure its loss will be mourned by half the men in Nottingham."

All of Arable's words rushed away, she choked and keeled down to her knees, gasping for air. Lady Margery knelt, her face suddenly terribly close and wretched.

"Now then, what do you suppose we are to do with you, Miss Burel?"

"We don't have time for this, Mother."

"If we leave, she'll go straight to Wendenal."

"I won't," Arable said, but it bubbled and caught in her throat.

"Just pack your things," the captain took control. "I'll handle the girl."

Lady Margery pursed up, her face sour. At length she squinted at Arable, the crust in her wrinkles flaking. "Aren't you lucky, dear? My son has a soft spot for pretty faces. Be sure that we never see yours again."

Arable searched the man's face for any sign of compassion, but he merely frowned. "Listen to me, then. You're to stay in this room for the rest of the night. By morning they'll surely know we've left anyway, and then you can do as you wish. But I'm leaving one of my men outside the door until then, to tell any visitors my family is quite indisposed. In the morning, he'll catch up with us in Warwick. His name is Kendrick, and he is not a kind man. If you so much as touch these doors, I give him full authority to do anything he wishes to you. For your sake, you should hope he kills you at the end of it. However, stay inside and quiet until morning, and you have nothing to fear. Tell me that you understand."

Arable swallowed, gasping for air. "I understand."

"You're too kind." Lady Margery d'Oily was fixing her hair. The fact that she considered rape and murder a kindness made Arable shiver.

The young Waleran squeezed Arable's shoulder. His face was suddenly kind, and relaxed despite the circumstances. Arable whispered to him, "I didn't do anything wrong."

"I believe you," he whispered back. "But that doesn't really matter now, does it?"

Arable stayed there, in the middle of the floor, and they subsequently forgot about her entirely. They collected their belongings and side-stepped around her as if she were a puddle of mud. Eventually, Arable closed her eyes and sank further down, exactly as important to the world as they made her feel. She wrapped her arms around her knees and tried to think, tried to find whatever it was she was missing. Her options couldn't have run out, she simply had to figure out what was left. Her mind scattered, running down every opportunity left before her, but found only dead ends. She stayed there even as they left, even as the sun crawled across the floor, waiting, desperate, for anything to reveal itself.

Closing her eyes, she wondered what Roger de Lacy would do.

"Give up," de Lacy suggested, rapping his fingers together, and snuffing out the candle on the desk. "What is the point in continuing to live when there is no one alive who wants you to do so?" He walked to the back of his office, pushed open the window and heaved his body out headfirst, his robes ripping as he slid through its opening and out into a plunge to the bailey far below.

She shook away the false memories. There had to be something.

Sometime later, she became aware that the stone floor was grinding into her hip and she repositioned herself. Hours had passed. It was dark, but she had not slept. Despite all the luxuries of the sprawling suite, she curled in a stony crook under a window. There was food about, too, but she didn't see a point yet in eating.

A knock at the door startled her from the grey haze, and she looked about wildly for a place to hide. She hadn't touched the door, but maybe Kendrick wasn't interested in waiting for her to misbehave. The knock repeated and she ran to the bed just to turn away from it again. When the door creaked open, Arable fell to her knees, only to see a pretty face peeking in. A girl's face.

"Oh, I'm sorry!" the stranger gasped and disappeared, leaving the door ajar.

As slowly as her body could move, Arable inched around the edge of the room, far from the gaping door. There was no indication at all that anyone was there guarding her. No Kendrick. Just a scare, to keep her in line. She crept right up to the doorway and dared to flash her head through it, finding the hallway on the other side entirely empty.

The castle felt different when she had no destination. Time slowed around her, pulling at her legs and numbing her senses. *Not William. Not Roger. Not Margery.* She had even flirted with the idea that she might attach herself to Prince John's company, but that was gone now, too. *Not the Guard. Not Roana.* So she pushed. Her heels plied away from the stones that wanted to absorb her. She leaned into the emptiness. Forward, elsewhere, it didn't matter. She couldn't stay here, so there was no point in walking as long as she could still run. If she kept running, something might present itself, it had to. There was something she had missed, some opportunity she had never considered, but would now be a perfect solution.

This was not the most difficult thing she had endured, she reminded herself. She had lost William before. She was, in fact, an expert at losing him. Roger de Lacy had been like a father to her, but she had lost her real father and survived that. And being abandoned by Lady d'Oily was nothing compared to being abandoned by her family. She had fended for herself before, so to think she could not save herself again was a selfish sort of victimism. *But she was tired.* Starting over again now . . . it was almost too much to grasp.

There had to be another chance.

There had to be something she hadn't yet seen.

There simply had to be.

When she came to a stop, she was in front of the guest room William had kept before he took the sheriffcy. He had made promises to her there, just like his promise a lifetime ago that he would return for her. If only she could whisper to herself here and be someway heard in the past, to warn herself. Or to tell her younger self to never fall for the man in the first place. Would that such a thing existed.

"Hello, Arable."

She turned, and her heart froze in midbeat. In a single white moment, all her hopes poured into this one possibility. William had come to find her, to apologize, to take her in his arms and keep her safe. He had been walking the castle in the same milk-sopped daze as she, and found himself here as well.

The man who should have been William crashed forward and shoved her violently into the room, far more careful to shut the door silently behind him.

"I've had a hell of a week," Gisbourne snarled at her, "so it's about time I get something I want."

Her skin curled.

He struck her across the face so hard her entire body went numb. Ears ringing, she landed on the bed. She couldn't see. She scrambled, tearing at its sheets to get over and away from him, to get something, anything, between them.

"You make any noise and God help you," his growl, "you'll wish you hadn't."

Down on the floor, on the other side of the bed. Fingers scratched at the wood, to find something. At the door, his belt clattered to the ground with a riot, his breeches untied.

"Get back on the bed or I'll hurt you."

Air left. Her neck wrought itself. She didn't move, she couldn't.

"What a day, what a hell of a day. Awfully easy for you, isn't it? Just a matter of cleaning and scrubbing and laundry, you don't have the first clue what a man has to deal with, and how could you? Get on. The fucking. Bed."

Arable pushed away from her eyelids and hid at the back of her skull.

But her body, good God, her body slowly crawled on top of the bed.

"I've got these prisoners, these forest outlaws, who think they're better than me. I know they can show me the way to their hideout, but they refuse to talk! Of all the gall, wouldn't you agree?"

Arable bowed her head. If he was talking, it was better than him doing anything else. Her eyes moved but found nothing, nothing, there was an iron lantern on the wrong side of the room.

"Of course you agree, because you can't understand anything I say. You're like a dog. You're exactly like these criminals, you and Will Scarlet and Elena Gamwell, none of you understand what's really going on here." He tugged his breeches free and started unclasping his doublet. "I think I'll probably kill them tomorrow. I can't risk them defying me." From his boot, he pulled a thick knife. "Now take your dress off before I cut it off you."

Her guts were stone. They sank her, they bore down through her and further.

She closed her eyes.

Then, a knock at the door, and he quickly blew out the lantern. In pitch black she moved without thinking, leaping from the bed to where the lantern had been, her fingers screaming for its frame, ready to sling it into the captain's skull. But her fear betrayed her, her legs stumbled from the bed, she smashed into the wall and his hand found the back of her neck. She told herself to fight back, but her body gave up. Muffled, from the other side of the door, "Captain Gisbourne, are you in there? I thought I saw you go in there. I have some rather urgent news."

No movement.

"Captain Gisbourne?" The door moved a breath against its hinges.

"Yes, Marshall," Gisbourne called softly.

Marshall Sutton, the guard who had approached Arable earlier. She would trade him any favor in the world if he would just come inside at this very moment.

Gisbourne pretended to yawn. "Just thought I'd catch a few moments of sleep, could you give me an hour or so?"

"I think you'll want to see this right away, Captain. Sorry, Captain."

Gisbourne sighed. "Wait for me, then, I'll be out in a moment."

Another rustle of buckles and clothing, a jangling violent nonsense with whispered curses behind them. Then the air shifted, he was right on top of her, the heat of his breath on her mouth, "You will come to my quarters tonight, and you will do anything I want, or I swear every Guardsman in the castle will know how you spied on Jon Bassett, how you're to blame for his disappearance. I have had enough of not getting the things I deserve."

Then the air shifted again, the doorframe opened and light from the hallway poured into the room. Gisbourne's shape disappeared, his voice mixing with Marshall's as they marched out and away.

Arable put her hands over her lips and clenched her eyes as tight as she could. Her skin was clammy, and she massaged her swollen jaw. There was blood in her mouth, and her tongue found a sharp cut in her cheek. The pain was better than the numb, though, and she pushed her tongue against it, just to keep feeling something, anything.

She crawled back to the bed, finding comfort in the tiny space between it and the stone. There, with the fear still raging through her body and her limbs quivering, Arable let go. Hot tears poured out, but she did not wail, or lose herself. Instead it all flowed out of her. Whatever had been scratching at her skin flushed out her eyes and onto the floor to disappear, and more than her face felt the warmth of being washed clean. Silently. She didn't whimper or heave. The tears just came, and streamed, and left, and then there was nothing left but Arable, sitting on the floor by a meaningless bed. She had thought there was nothing else for her to do, but she had been wrong. She had thought she was so overwhelmed by it all.

But no. Not *so* overwhelmed.

Not ever overwhelmed.

Never overwhelmed.

Liberated.

Because literally anything she chose to do now would be better than doing nothing.

And there, on the ground, casting a long oval shadow dripping halfway across the room, directly in the middle of the still gaping doorway, was the one opportunity she'd been hoping for. Arable picked her fucking self off the ground, held her head high and walked out of the room, determined, only slowing to swing her hand down and pick up the ring of keys Gisbourne had lost in the darkness.

FIFTY-ONE

JOHN LITTLE

SHERWOOD FOREST, JUST OUTSIDE BERNESDALE

John's boys ran about, each one faster than the last, springing over fallen limbs and back upon themselves. Robin had them playing at chase, claiming it wasn't just a children's game.

"Knowing how to run, how to dodge, how to tire a pursuer, that may save their lives. And besides, it's fun." Robin smiled, on account of him being Robin. And the others enjoyed their time of it, somehow forgetting come morning they would be on the road to Nottingham, to do as dangerous a thing as ever they'd done.

Every now and then one of the boys would look at John, thinking to tag him into the game. He'd be an easy target but they never picked him, choosing to turn and run at another instead. Ten of them here, hand-picked by Robin from those that volunteered. They'd left the bulk of the group behind in one of their camps deeper in the Sherwood, that the ten of them might sneak into the Sheriff's funeral. To rescue Will and Elena from the gallows they'd earned, and Marion against a wedding she hadn't. Ten against too many.

The Delaney brothers had prepared this small camp, just barely away from the village of Bernesdale at the southern spear of the Sherwood. They'd used it as a halfway point to Nottingham, exchanging messages with Prince John, their ticket to getting into the castle safely. If he could be trusted.

Alan-a-Dale tagged David of Doncaster, who tagged Arthur, and so on, in circles around John, but never did they bring him into it.

"Why'd you come south with us?" John asked Friar Tuck, sitting on a log and watching the others. "You don't mean to come to Nottingham tomorrow."

"I try to be where I'm needed." Tuck fidgeted. "I don't always get that part right."

"But supposing your arm were right as your head, you still wouldn't go with us."

The friar kept his lips tight. "That I wouldn't."

"I don't value shame none, Friar, so I don't mind telling you I wish it had been my arm they broke instead of yours."

"That's kind of you."

"It's not. It's not kind. I wish it, so that I might have a reason not to go."

They watched on silently, as Arthur tagged Nicks Delaney, who swatted at Geoffrey and Thomas. These two were young farmhands with thick moustaches from Bernesdale, joined not a week ago. Men John barely knew, who were spry to risk their lives without enough reason. The Delaneys insisted, being so close to Bernesdale, that they could rally another dozen men from the village like it was nothing. But Robin wouldn't have it. They'd labored over the details of the plan too much to change it now.

"You don't have to go," Tuck said.

"I do," John corrected him. "If I didn't go tomorrow, I'd have no business staying none neither. These are my boys, and I don't fancy losing any more of them."

Thomas tagged Gamble Gold, who tagged Peeteys Delaney, who tagged Robin and fancied himself the king of the world for having done it. John's stomach twisted. *Iffing they needed to run tomorrow, there would be no keeping up for him.*

Iffing they couldn't find Will and Elena, or that their faces were recognized in the crowd and a host approached, John knew he couldn't outrun the first of them. It's why he didn't play now, and why they didn't make him. These boys all hoped for success tomorrow, but in failure they also had a chance of escaping again. John, on the other hand, would only be coming back if all went well, every last bit of it.

He could have made an argument against his own participation, to say his size was a hindrance, that he would endanger them all. His was a unique shape, more likely to draw attention than anything else. But there was no pretending John believed it himself. If forced to stand his ground, at least he might be able to give his boys a head start. There was no knowing how many of them he might save by simply being there.

But if he didn't go, and they came back missing a few, he'd never know how many of those lives he'd traded for his own. Nor did he know whether or not it made him coward to wish he could risk it.

Alan hooted out a victory as he tackled Arthur a Bland hipwise, the both of them tumbling over another through the brush. Arthur responded by pulling Alan to the ground and slapping his arms about the lad's face. All playfully, but still. "You're not allowed to tag me back," Alan cried out, laughing.

"I'm not tagging you back," came Arthur as he pinned Alan down. "I'm kicking the shit out of you."

"You can't change the rules," Alan shrieked. "That's why they're called rules."

At length, Arthur relented and disappeared into the late-evening fog to find another victim. John took in the dusk glow, thanking whatever quirk of nature it was that made such a thing possible. A heavy thick white slipped through the trees, turned to a curious blue-green by the moonlight. It might mean rain in the morning, but for tonight it gave them a blanket, and let them burn a campfire without risk.

Alan crawled to John and took the stump Tuck had abandoned in search of some ale.

"You're not wearing your necklace," John scolded him. When they'd left their Oak Camp and said their goodbyes, the young pretty Malory had thrown her arms around Alan and tied a string about his neck with a few trinkets on it. John hadn't seen it since.

"What?" Alan asked, then shook his head. "It was stupid. She said it was for luck. Wearing a necklace isn't going to give me luck."

"You don't wear it for luck. You wear it to make her happy."

Alan made some noises. "She doesn't know I'm not wearing it, so it can't make her not happy. She's silly."

"You're silly, too. She'd be good for you."

"You don't understand," Alan mumbled to himself, always thinking nobody knew who he had his eyes upon. He'd never grow out of such a thing by keeping it a secret, only making it the more precious. John was about to say as much, when Robin appeared suddenly and sliced through them with purpose, his finger to his lips.

"Down!" he whispered fiercely, with more at stake than a game of chase.

Alan dropped quick enough to the dirt while John lowered himself to a knee, keenly aware of how little he was concealed by doing so.

"What is it?" Alan asked, but Robin just pointed out into the mist, whereupon a moment later came the snap of a twig and rustle of leaves. If there was anything to be seen, John's eyes couldn't make it out. But Alan slowly rose, pulling the hood off his head, and spoke at his loudest.

"Holy fuck me."

"Hullo, boys."

Just as casually as if he'd been playing chase with them the last hour, Will Scarlet strolled out of the fog with his arms out wide.

John couldn't but stare, with no words at all, just a shock that took over the whole of his body. It was Will alright, smiling and a little thinner, and unbelievably here. Alan started four or five sentences, but couldn't finish any of them, and settled for grabbing Will violently and slapping his back.

"It's good to see you too, Alan! Hullo, Robin."

Robin stood, so alarmed he might burst. "How did you get here?"

Will crinkled his nose. "We escaped!"

"Escaped! But we were supposed to rescue you!" Alan nearly lost his mind and bent over laughing. "Where's Elena?"

"She's near, I was scouting ahead." He turned and called out for her, while John saw in his face the tale of the last month, written in bruises.

Robin saw it, too, and softened. "Were you followed?"

"No, no. What are you doing this far south? We were aiming to camp outside Bernesdale for the night when Lena noticed the ribbons, followed them here. This a new camp?"

"One of a few. This one we've been using—" Alan started, but Robin interrupted him.

"Don't—let's get everyone here first. I'll rally the others, you can tell us all at once." He shook his head and backed away.

Will waved his hand slowly in front of John. "Hullo, John."

He hadn't even realized he'd been standing there mouth agape, without the first clue what to do or how to go about doing it. Then, as simple as that, the emotion overwhelmed him and he snatched Will up off the ground, his face already stung for smiling too wide and his lungs burned. For reasons he couldn't quite place, John felt guilty for having his doubts about going to Nottingham tomorrow. He might have robbed himself of this feeling, of seeing Will and Elena again, of being reunited with the only thing he still had that felt like family.

"You don't know what you've put us through," Alan said. "We've been leaving fake trails and camps, to keep the Sheriff looking."

"Well, we were lucky to find you, especially in this fog." Will coughed. "We could have passed right by and never even known it."

"We were going to get you tomorrow, you know?" John said. "It's all we've been working at."

Will seemed genuinely touched. "Are you serious? Is that why you're here?"

John gave a solemn nod, and fought the lump in his throat.

"That's insane," Will winced at the thought, "you . . . you shouldn't . . ."

"We had to at least try," John said.

"I can't believe Robin let you do that."

"It was his idea."

Will stopped shy of any response, and chewed it back down. A heavy moment passed before Alan sighed. "You gave us quite the scare. I thought I was going to watch you die tomorrow!" He punched Will hard in the chest, which looked to hurt more than it ought. Will was probably hungry and thirsty, and in desperate need of recovery. A thousand questions came to John's mind, but they'd have to wait.

"You would have been too late." Will put his arm on Alan's shoulder. "They were going to kill us tonight, and hang a couple nobodies tomorrow. They wanted you to come get us."

"I'll be damned," was all Alan could say, and John too felt a wave of relief. Everything they'd been planning, it would have been for nothing.

"It would have been suicide." Will shook his head in frustration. "You say this was Robin's plan?"

"Where's your girl?" John asked, more or less at the same time he heard her voice, scrambling through the brush. John felt his heart clench, his eyes water. Marley had never borne them any children, but if she had, he could only have wanted two such as these to call his own. Alan rushed to Elena first, and near took the wind from her, holding on a bit longer than he ought. When finally John had his turn, he nearly suffocated her. Her head was tiny between his hands, and she sniffed away a tear or two of her own when he bent down to kiss her forehead.

Then commotion overtook them as the others joined, their laughter filling the forest thicker than the fog. Arthur and David tackled Will to the ground, and the Delaney brothers introduced themselves with all politesse. Even the surly Gamble Gold seemed happy. The two boys from Bernesdale kept their distance from the group but were clearly relieved.

Friar Tuck, of course, let out with his usual cackle. "This calls for a celebration! Two friends back, two drinks each!"

Alan tried to tell Will five stories at once, about Much's funeral and the prince's visit, while Tuck busied himself at pouring drinks. Will and Elena rushed to help, on account of Tuck's broken arm.

John moved as well. "You two should be sitting down and resting. Let us tend to you."

"It's no trouble," Will said, and started gathering cups with Elena to pass out. There was only a small cask by the campfire, but a larger one was still on their oxcart, down the hill and concealed just off the road. Arthur and David rushed off with Geoffrey and Thomas to fetch it, and would likely make it a little lighter during the haul. Robin tried to stop them, but they started a drinking song as they ran and his protests went unheard.

"Come on then," Alan whined as they disappeared, "I can't wait to hear how the hell you two got out of there. I'll bet you left a trail of blood all the way!"

"We'd best hope not," Robin warned.

Will patted Alan's cheeks. "All in good time. We got the Sheriff. I assume you heard that?"

This changed the mood sharply, by John's estimation. None seemed eager to answer, which usually meant they were waiting on him. "We did hear that," he answered, letting his voice speak to his disapproval.

But Elena was just as eager as Will. "They know we keep our promises now."

There was no shame to either of them, like dogs looking to be praised for a kill.

"That's something we should have decided as a group," John grumbled. He'd practiced this, in the event he ever saw them again. He knew the words to chastise them for being so impulsive, for neglecting the consequences of their actions. But he didn't have the heart to bear it down upon them now.

"You're right," Will was even apologizing, "but there wasn't time. We had the opportunity, and we took it. In the heat of the moment, we had to make a call."

"The heat of the moment," Robin's words were crisp, he stared down into the cup he hadn't even touched, "is the most important time to think clearly."

Elena took offense. "You weren't even here. You left. What are you complaining about?"

"Alright, alright," soothed Alan, moving between them. "Let's not get into that now. Tonight we celebrate! Hand me another drink!" His enthusiasm was joined by the boys, rallying him to empty his cup.

Robin's hand found his shoulder. "Let's take it easy, Alan."

"Where's the point in that?" he laughed. "I intend on sleeping all day tomorrow!" He made to upend his cup, but Robin stopped him again, more forcefully.

"We're still going to Nottingham tomorrow. This changes nothing."

That was ever an unsettling moment. John was as confused as the others. "What are you talking about?"

"Scarlet and Elena are alive, that's great. But, no offense now, that's not the most important thing. Scarlet just told us they're planning on hanging two other people tomorrow for the murder of the Sheriff."

Will squinted, but he didn't take Robin seriously. "Oh come off it. He's just going to hang a few old prisoners that have been around for years, they'd be dead anyhow."

"That's not the point." Robin shook a hand at him, but didn't meet his eyes. "The people are going to see it, and they won't know the difference. William doesn't care about killing us. He cares about killing our reputation. Our credibility."

Will's smile faded. *"William?"*

"The Sheriff."

"You mean, your friend."

"Hardly," Robin bit back, quick and bitter. "He's trying to take away our support. If he hangs anyone tomorrow, he'll declare it as a victory against us."

"Against us?" Will asked, stepping softly forward, then turned to the others, "or against Robin Hood? Personally, I don't care if the people love us . . . but seems that may be the only thing you do care about."

"Well, you should," Robin sneered. "You think you can accomplish anything without the people on your side? You think you're safe here in the woods without the people keeping your secrets? If William wins them over, they'll turn on you and hang you from the trees just for a break of bread."

"You think that will happen just because the Sheriff hangs a few patsies tomorrow? That's ridiculous."

"If I may, Robin?" Nicks stood up. Robin nodded at him, but seemed distracted. "We risk a terrible lot going to Nottingham tomorrow. Our chances were slim before, and now we hear that it's a trap anyhow. If you want to defend our reputation, then why not do it with the truth? We bring Will and Elena to every town and village and tell their story, about how the new Sheriff put two innocent men on the gallows just for show. That ought to show him for who he really is."

John felt the weight of many eyes floating onto him, and it seemed an unspoken agreement that he ought to decide the matter. It was not a responsibility to be envied. "I'd say he has the ring of it," he sighed. "There's nothing for us in Nottingham tomorrow."

Will laughed smugly at Robin. "Sorry you don't get to be the hero."

"Damn it, Will," Robin flinched. "Stop posturing and listen to me. You were always angry we were doing too little, now you're angry we're doing too much? You want a make a difference? This is how it starts. Tomorrow we have a chance to prove to every noble in twenty leagues that the people are willing to stand up for themselves. If we don't go tomorrow, we'll never have an opportunity like it again. And worse, we'll have disappointed one of our only allies."

Will and Elena exchanged an uneasy look. "Allies?"

"Prince John," Robin said, looking to John for support. "We've been coordinating with his men to gain entry tomorrow. He wants to help. So if we don't go through with it . . . I don't see any reason for him to ever trust us again."

Again, bless their hearts, they left it to John. "Robin," he said, as gently as he could, "that may be for the better. We were putting too much faith in that prince, and his messengers never told us half of what Will just did. I don't think he means to do us right."

Most nodded in agreement, but Robin's eyes grew desperate. "John."

"I'm sorry, Robin, but Will's right."

"Damn it, we have to go tomorrow!" Robin wiped his brow and set his cup down, a defeat sinking into him. "We have to rescue Marion as well."

At this, everyone had their own reaction, though John's was only of pity. They had discussed this, at length, though never to Robin's liking. What was happening to Marion was terrible, but at least she was safe, and alive. They'd tend to her eventually, but the plan for tomorrow was mostly for Will and Elena, seeing as how there had been a heavy deadline on their lives.

"What's happened to Marion?" Elena shouted over the others.

"She's been taken to the castle against her will, to be married to William. I'm not going—" Robin cut himself off, but it was a thing he couldn't unsay. "*We're* not going to let that happen."

"Robin," John tried to whisper it, "that's not for tomorrow."

"She's not going to marry him!"

A silence smothered itself upon them, during which nobody would look at Robin. John was reminded of a snippet of conversation he had shared with Tuck once. *Only the desperate mistake volume for reason.* Robin had already lost his argument, but he alone couldn't see it.

"We have plenty of time for her," John urged him. "We'll plan something new, and we'll have Will and Elena to help, even. But not tomorrow."

Even Will, who would normally pride himself in picking at scabs, treated Robin carefully. "You'd never get to her. It's just not possible. Every gord in four counties is there for the funeral, and they're waiting for you. You'd be massacred."

"You escaped," Robin insisted. "That should have been impossible, too. So you know a way in and out, don't you?"

"It wasn't as easy as that." Will hesitated to say it, sharing an odd look with Elena. "We had help."

Elena bit at her lip, then glanced behind into the woods. "We were hoping to tell you all about it first, but . . ." Something was said between them that John couldn't understand. Then Elena skipped backward and cupped her hands over her mouth. "It's alright, you can come out now!"

The hairs on the back of John's neck, they ever woke up.

"Don't be angry now," Will started.

"You brought him here?" Robin hissed, reaching for a sword that wasn't there.

"No," Elena snapped back. "We brought *her* here."

The fog whipped around the edges of a cloaked figure, moving silently out of the blue-green nothing, and everyone scrambled at the shock of an intruder. John's heart pounded and he strode forward. His first instinct was to move Elena behind himself, but she moved to meet the stranger. The heavy blue weave of the cloak gave way to a delicate woman's frame underneath. Her face had both particular beauty and emptiness. Her head was low, her hands clasped, her face shut. But her presence was a danger.

"You'll be wanting to stay behind me, Lena," John said softly.

"What's wrong?" Elena asked.

"You led an outsider directly to our camp," Robin breathed it. Twice now this night they had been discovered without warning, and whatever safety they once felt in the fog was boiling over into fear.

"There's nothing to worry about," Elena was carefree, "she's the one who set us free." She tried to lead the stranger closer, but John moved his staff to keep them separate. He was the only one with a weapon on him. The others had left them fireside.

"I know exactly who she is," Robin warned. "She's working with William."

"My apologies, gentlemen." The woman's voice shook at its edges, but she spoke with confidence. "I understand your caution. My name is Arable de Burel, and I beg for your hospitality."

"Hospitality?" Robin sounded alarmed.

She tilted her head back, but her voice wavered. "I have nowhere else to go. I'm not safe in the castle anymore. Robin, you struck me as a kind man when I met you. I was hoping that if I helped your friends, as I have, that perhaps you would help me in return."

"She's not with them anymore, and she means well," Will explained. "She's risked a lot."

"She risks less than you do, Will," John scolded him. It would seem his incarceration had taught him nothing of thinking on his actions. "She knows where we are, and what we plan on doing."

Will didn't understand. "She's not going to tell anyone."

John lowered his voice. "They're not going to ask her nicely."

The girl, Arable, had clearly not considered it, either, and started to tremble.

"She's not going back," Elena explained. "She wants to stay with us."

"What she wants is to use us, again," Robin sneered at the intruder. "I've met her before, she brought me a message from William, which I was foolish enough to listen to. I don't know what she's told you, but she is no ally. She can't stay."

Will turned on him. "She *has* to stay, she's in danger there."

"We're all going to Nottingham tomorrow, Will. She can't come with us."

"I thought we decided we weren't going—"

"We didn't decide anything yet!"

"There is no way Elena and I are going back tomorrow," Will said with finality. "So Arable can simply stay with us."

"This is reckless." Robin started pacing. "Even if you believed her, you should have left her in a village, someplace safe. If she truly wants to join us, we could have gotten her. Later. But you've decided it for us, Will. Again. There are things you seem never to consider."

"Such as?" Will asked. He positioned himself between John and Arable.

"Such as the timing." Robin glared. "We're on the eve of something important, and a stranger from the castle is suddenly amongst us. Someone within the enemy's walls offers to set you free, and all you have to do in return is show her where your secret camp lies. You don't find that at all suspicious?"

That wasn't where John's mind had gone, but it was a solid point. As usual, Robin was thinking two steps ahead of the rest of them.

Will's jaw was tight. "That's not how it happened."

"We obviously can't let her go." Robin was thinking aloud. "But without knowing where her loyalty truly lies, she can't roam freely about us, not even for a night. Not this night."

Elena looked as terrified as Arable. "What are you going to do, lock her up?"

"We didn't mean to bring her here, Robin." Will's voice was softer now. "We didn't know you had a new camp down here, not until we saw the ribbons, so we followed them. We were headed north, to the Oak Camp. I'm not the idiot you think I am."

"Well which idiot are you, then?"

"Settle now!" John burst out, fed up with their bickering. They were keen on extremes, the both of them, but the situation called for a bit of understanding. "Let's at least hear her out."

Tuck agreed, and took the opportunity to approach the young woman. She still stood, wrapped in her own cloak, precisely where she had appeared. Her eyes were buried in the ground before her, but Tuck stooped to smile at her. "Arable, is it?" She bobbed her head. "You are either greatly brave to be here, or equally foolish. You'll need to give us a reason to trust you, if it can be done."

She spoke only to him, somewhere between anger and terror. "I brought you two of your friends, out of the prisons, that were to be hanged. Does that count for nothing?"

"Not if you bring back thirty guards here tomorrow," Robin answered.

"Tell them what you told us," Will prompted her.

Arable gathered up her cloak in her fists and tugged at it, trying to find a face in the crowd that offered sympathy. John steeled himself, knowing how easy—and dangerous—it would be to trust the kindness of her face.

"I have no loyalty to Nottingham, I never did," she said. "I was only trying to survive, but everyone I needed has abandoned me. And the Captain, Guy of Gisbourne . . . he was going to hurt me to get at William. I'm not safe there."

"She knows a lot about the castle," Will added. "About the Sheriff, about the Guard and how they operate."

"I'll earn my own keep, I won't be a burden," Arable said. "Even if only for a little while. I understand why you don't trust me, but these two would be dead if I had not done what I did. And believe me, I didn't rescue them for their sakes. I hate what they did. Roger de Lacy was like a father to me." She stole a glare at Will and Elena, and John could swear it was true. There was hatred there, hard, but tempered. "No, I came for you, Robin. William said you were a good man, perhaps the best man he'd ever known. If I can overlook what they did and ask for your help . . . I don't know how else I can prove I'm telling you the truth."

John didn't have it in him to disbelieve her. If she were lying, then never had he seen honesty. "Give us a moment," he said, and motioned for the others to join him aside the dying fire ring. He raised his hand to keep Will and Elena from following. This needed to be decided upon without them.

They sat at the stumps about the ring. "I'm willing to believe her," John said, drinking from his cup. He wished Tuck had made some of his hot cider this night, but the beer still warmed his belly.

Tuck agreed. "She seems genuinely scared."

"That's what troubles me," Robin added, fingering the lip of his own drink. "Assuming this isn't a trap, then she made this decision rashly, emotionally. In a few days when she's no longer afraid, she'll realize how much she's giving up. She hasn't thought this out."

"She certainly doesn't give us much to trust," Nicks said sadly. "She claims she has no loyalty to Nottingham, but she has even less loyalty to us. She betrayed them."

"That doesn't mean she'll betray us," John argued.

"She betrayed her entire life because she was afraid," Robin sighed. "The next time someone threatens her, you think our secrets are safe? No, she can't stay here." He stared into his cup, but his eyes weren't looking at anything. "And she can't go back."

John's mind reeled with what that meant. No one else seemed brave enough to say it aloud. "What exactly is it you're talking about here?"

Robin didn't meet his eyes.

This wasn't a thing they could do. It was too dark to consider. Robin was so hell-bent on going to Nottingham tomorrow he could see no alternative. But in the grave silence, nobody else denounced it.

"Shit." Nicks coughed, so suddenly it made Alan drop his cup.

"Listen," Alan blurted out. "Maybe we're thinking about this the wrong way? We're only thinking of the worst-case scenario." His hands shook as if it were his own life on the line.

"Meaning?" Robin asked, passing his beer to Alan, who drank a gulp and recovered his courage.

"You see her as a possible spy against us," he looked from person to person, "but what if she were a spy *for* us? She knows the inner workings of the castle, she was able to get Will and Elena out with no trouble. She could get us inside, get us to Gisbourne. Or to Lady Marion. I'd trust her over Prince John any day. If she wants to help us, I say let her."

"What does she really know about us, Robin?" John asked. "She knows about this one camp, which we've never even used before. Maybe she can read our markings in the woods. But we can change our ways. That's not worth her life."

"John," Robin was aghast, "I have not suggested that. That is the last thing that I or anyone here wants. But we have to protect ourselves first."

"No," Alan stated, with finality.

"No, what?"

"No, that's not what we *have to do.*" Alan stared into Robin, his eyes wet. "It sounds fine, doesn't it, *protecting* ourselves? But at the cost of someone who needs us. She came here and offered help, and you think she's the enemy? We came to trust you, Robin, when you offered us help, even though you had only come to stop us. None of us would be here if someone hadn't given us a chance. Your father had no reason to trust me, but he took me in. He could have *protected himself,* he could have turned me away. He could have turned all of us away. We can't be afraid of the worst in each other, it only brings out the worst in ourselves. So no, we don't *have* to protect ourselves. What we *have to do,*" his voice strained, his hands shook, "is trust each other."

John might have never been prouder of another man in his life. Alan had just shamed them all, simply by being right. "If we're wrong, then we're wrong." He put his hand on Alan's shoulder. "But at least we'll have done the right thing."

Robin swallowed. "It's a big risk."

"I'd rather die with people who trust, than live with people who don't." Alan stood. "What's the point of any of this if we don't take risks? What's the point in helping people if we don't . . . help people?"

"Frankly," Nicks touched Robin's elbow, "if you still want us to entertain the idea of going tomorrow, then using her help is the only way I feel comfortable going."

Robin shook his head. "It seems too suspicious, too convenient . . ."

"That's because your first instinct has always been to doubt," Tuck said. "But now and then, you ought to try having faith."

"What sort of plan do you think she's a part of?" John laughed. "They return two of our own back to us in exchange for what? This little girl's going to kill us in our sleep?"

"Not kill," Robin said. "But spy. Our only advantage has been that they don't know where to find us. If she knows that . . ."

"Fine!" Alan lurched upward ferociously. "Then we're going to have to kill her!" He turned but lost his footing, caught it again, and barreled toward Arable. John yelled at him to stop, but Alan turned again just as suddenly, and darted back to the campfire. "We have to kill her, don't we? Right? There's no other way!"

He smashed into one of the tents and emerged a moment later with a sword in his hand.

"If she's a spy, we have to kill her. And we don't know if she's not a spy, so we have to treat her like one, so we kill her."

"That's enough, Alan," John warned. The ale had gotten the best of him. He'd drunk too fast. Alan dragged the sword from the fire ring with one hand, steadying himself with the other, his eyes dead set upon the poor girl.

"Please," Arable sobbed, "nobody even knows I'm gone, I won't tell anyone. I'll leave, I won't tell anyone, I won't . . ."

"That's the way it's always been though, right, Will?" Alan swung the blade in front of himself, slow, clumsily, but its tip caught the ground and it tumbled from his hands. "It's fine to put anyone else in danger just so long as you get what you want!"

Will didn't know how to react. "What?"

Alan took another step forward and his knee buckled, then he rose again, tripping forward, pushing himself back up to his feet, stomping the ground until he was next to Elena, and he reached out to touch the side of her face. "Hello, Elena. How are you?"

She brushed his hand away.

He spat blood into his palm.

He dropped.

When Marley passed, she'd been ill for a week, for a month, they had both known it was coming. She went quietly in her bed, made as comfortable as John knew how, though it wasn't halfway enough. When she went, in the whenever moment after she closed her eyes, when he knew she was truly gone, John felt something inside himself break off and fall away. It was tied to every bit of him, it pulled at his face and his eyes and his name. It dragged him with it, heavy, and he was falling, sitting there in the chair beside what-was-her, he fell, a sickening lilting dive that he'd never known before. A terrifying tip into emptiness.

As Alan dropped, John felt it again.

He fell in time with John's gut, but the others flew to action. Will dove to catch Alan, Robin called for water, and for help, and Tuck bolted into the woods, saying there were salts on the oxcart he needed. Alan's legs shot out, his hands slashed around and contorted, his fingers twisting into themselves, seizing. His back nearly broke as he spasmed backward. They tried to hold him down but he spat blood in their faces and broke free. Will cried out his name again and again, until a black gurgling noise came from Alan's throat, and he kicked harder. His hands grasped for something, but found nothing. He stopped moving, only to twitch again, then stop. Then a last burst of blood and snot came out his nose, and he smashed his face into a rock. His body slumped.

John was standing over him now, yelling something, but he couldn't hear himself. Will looked up, his eyes begging, his face flush purple. Behind John, steel scraped stone, and Robin screamed in an inhuman roar.

"On your knees!"

John turned to see Robin take up the dropped sword and aim it at Arable's neck, who had knelt to the ground, cowering in horror.

"What did you do to him?"

"I did nothing, I swear," she gasped, staring at Alan's body.

"We tried to help you," Will bellowed, still clutching Alan's doublet, "and you came here to kill us?"

"I didn't do it, please believe me!"

Elena was doubled over, clutching her stomach. "We trusted you!"

"What did she do?" John asked. He couldn't keep up. He didn't know what was happening. Everybody seemed to know something he didn't.

"She poisoned him." Robin shut his eyes. "It's in the drink. It was in *my* drink. I gave Alan my cup." He tried to raise the sword up, but instead took a step back and let it sink into the ground. "She was trying to kill me."

Arable bawled. "I don't know what happened to him . . ." and her words jumbled together, indistinguishable from each other.

"I knew we shouldn't trust her." Robin was pacing, then turned on Will. "I told you not to bring her here! You brought an assassin into our camp. This is on your head."

"Don't you dare—"

"I say we kill her," Elena straightened, her fury larger than her little body. "Kill her *right now.* We swore it, didn't we? We swore that whoever is responsible for killing one of our own will *pay in kind!*" She lost control of herself by her final words, wailing them out as she keeled over again.

Will stood straight, his face deathly blank. His voice was dry. "She'll be dead before he's cold."

He moved with purpose and took the sword from Robin, who didn't even flinch at its loss. Arable made a noise, not a cry or a scream, but it came from her soul.

John couldn't tell which of them moved first, but he found himself standing in front of her, protecting her. "Wait!" he pleaded as Will circled around him.

"Please listen to me," Arable cried, clutching at John's back. "Think about this. I couldn't have poisoned him. I was standing there the whole time. I never came anywhere near him, please help me!"

"Put it down, Will!" John yelled, but his friend's face was emotionless.

"Get out of the way."

"She's right. She was never near the cups!"

"She was out of sight for a while when we arrived, waiting for us to introduce her," Elena sneered. "Before we even got to the campfire. She must have snuck around and poisoned the beer then."

Will nodded, his eyes passing right through John. "Now get out of my way."

John looked around desperately for help. Robin's mouth was open, but he didn't seem interested in intervening. Nicks and Peeteys were positioning themselves behind John, but he did not know their intent. John had seen this chaos before. The panic. The too many of peoples who didn't know what was happening. It was Locksley Castle, burning.

"Let me think this through!" John yelled.

"Think it through?" Will moaned. "Alan's dead!"

"Wait, just wait!" John didn't have an answer, but he had the questions. "If she poisoned the beer, as Lena said, then we'd all be dead, wouldn't we? Wouldn't we?"

"He drank the most," Nicks answered.

"Good God," Peeteys cut in. "Are we all poisoned?"

"Please somebody kill her," Elena cried.

"We're not all poisoned," Robin's voice was unusually crisp, "we would have felt something by now. And it started directly after he drank from my cup."

"Only Robin's cup had poison," John repeated, slowly. "And Arable was never near it."

Robin squinted. "That's right." He looked back at the cups by the fire, the empty cask on the ground. "She wasn't."

The world held its breath. Every one of them replayed the last few minutes in their heads, from the moment Tuck opened the cask. John couldn't remember, his brain hurt to even try, there had been too much happening at once. Robin, on the other hand, had a queer calm to him now, and he looked up and breathed heavily.

"*She* wasn't."

Step by curious step, all eyes watched Robin as he picked a careful path that circled around them. "You know, Will," he asked, casually but precisely, matching his movements, "when you showed up here, you said hello to me. As if you expected to find me here. But the last you knew, I had left to go back to the war."

He finished the circle, side by side with John, in front of Arable. Then, with sudden violence, "Why weren't you surprised to see me, Will?"

He couldn't be right, John thought. There was another solution. Those Bernesdale boys, Geoffrey and Thomas. They had been there when the beer was poured, and then run off. That was it.

But Will hadn't moved.

Nor had he let go of the sword.

No.

John couldn't believe it, but not because it wasn't true.

He couldn't believe it—he knew—because he simply didn't think like that.

Not like *that.* Not like Will Scarlet.

Will wet his lips, and let his eyelids drag down. Every bit of the fury he had a moment ago seemed to drain from his body. He no longer looked the boy John knew, his face had aged a decade in only a few moments. Quite carefully he knelt, placing the sword on the ground, as if he were afraid to damage the grass that pierced through the gathering frost. When he stood again, there were tears in his eyes.

"Lord Gisbourne came to me in my cell."

No.

They'd chosen to risk everything, even after everything Will had done, to dive into danger to save their tortured little souls, all while Will had been planning *this.*

John didn't want to hear any more, it was too terrible.

Will spoke deliberately, but his voice strained at the effort. "He told me you had returned." Every sentence was an eternity. "He offered me my freedom, both mine and Elena's. If I came back and poisoned you."

John stopped breathing.

Will looked up at John, a desperation within him, then over to Robin. "But I told him no, Robin."

Just as slowly, he turned around, perhaps the hardest thing he'd ever done.

He repeated, "*I* told him no."

And across from him, in the same moment that John realized it himself, came Elena's response, choking on her own tears. "I told him yes."

My Elena.

It shouldn't have been possible, that the world could continue to be, after such a thing. It should either be done with and end, all of it, or let them start anew. Anything would be better than plodding forward from here.

"I didn't mean to kill Alan," she cried still, as useless a thing to say as ever.

"No," Robin huffed. "You meant to kill me."

"You'refuckingrightImeanttokillyou!" She turned savage, eyes blood red, swinging wildly at Robin but stumbling to the ground. "You never drank from your cup, why didn't you just fucking drink it? Why did you give it to Alan?"

Will seemed incredulous. "You're blaming *him?*"

"It wasn't supposed to take effect for hours." She turned back to him, the rage gone, her face pleading for understanding. "I don't know what went wrong."

"Lena, why?" Will tore at himself, his face riven. "Why, Lena?"

"Because he was right." Again she tried to touch him, and again he skipped away, turning and wringing his hands. "Gisbourne was right. He was right that Robin is to blame for all of this! The Sheriff and Robin are the same, they're both using us! He doesn't care about us, about what we're doing out here. He pulled us back, he wanted us to be nothing. He was working with William the whole time! He's the reason Much died. We said the Sheriff deserved to die. Why wouldn't Robin deserve the same? He's brought all this pain upon us, and then we sing songs about him. We should be singing songs about you." Her voice broke, she swallowed against tears. "The people should be singing about Will Scarlet."

"What the hell is wrong with you?" Will growled at her, at the world. "You're working with the man who killed Much! Didn't you see Gisbourne was trying to manipulate us? You've done exactly what he wanted!"

"They were going to hang us," she broke down. "I wasn't going to let you die."

"I do not accept Alan's life as a trade for my own."

"I didn't mean to kill him—"

"I don't accept Robin's life either!" He pounded at his chest, hard enough to bruise. "We made our decision. We knew the consequences. I did, at least. I was willing to die for it, to die for what happened to Much. I should never have let you come."

"You deserve better."

A third time she reached for him, instinctively, and he swatted her away, striking her forearm. "Don't touch me!"

"Don't touch him," John echoed, in instant reaction. He didn't say, *Don't hit her.* He didn't even think it.

Elena clutched her arm in pain, but fought through it, focusing on Will. "You should be leading us, not this stranger! If one of you two had to die, why should it be you?" Elena withered, collapsing down to the ground. "You're better than him."

"That's the thing, Lena." Will hovered over her. "I'm *not.* I'm not better than him. You've been whispering that in my ear ever since he showed up, but it's not true. He's a better leader, he's smarter. He knew something was wrong about this, something I couldn't see even though it was right in front of me. He didn't get us here, Lena. *You* did."

He fought through tears and fury, seemingly driven by a terrible new clarity. "While Robin was teaching Much to defend himself, *you* taught him to sneak up from behind, which is what got him killed. *You* were the one that wanted to use him on the raid in Bernesdale. *You* attacked Gisbourne at Locksley Castle, that was *you,* damn it! Hell, it was even your idea to kill Sheriff de Lacy! I let you convince me, because I loved you—" His voice cracked and he lost himself, but a moment later he overcame it. "I loved you and I trusted you, *I trusted you.* And now you've killed my best friend." He almost looked down at Alan, but didn't. With the last of what he had left in him, as his will collapsed, "What exactly about my life have you not ruined?"

The rest of them stood aghast. Will and Elena both kneeled in the frost, only a few feet from each other but impossibly far apart. Elena's fingers scratched at the ground, as if she could pull him closer to her, but she couldn't reach him, and he gave her nothing in return.

John watched, but felt no pity for her. Deep inside him, whatever it was that comprised a man's soul turned to stone. "You lied to us, Lena."

"What?" She raised her head. "John, no, I never did . . ."

"You're lying to me now." John's blood was cold, it pumped black. "You wanted us to kill Arable, to kill her for what you said she'd done to Alan. You begged us. You begged us to kill her before we found out the truth."

"You were going to kill me to hide your secret?" Arable's voice trembled behind him. "I risked everything to help you. You'd be dead if not for me . . ."

"No," Elena gasped, but had nothing else to say. Anything would have been another lie.

"Alan died trying to defend her, to say we have to trust each other, that we have to help each other."

John felt his skin go cold, an ice that wrapped around him. Maybe Elena moved, or maybe he did, he couldn't tell, but his hand came down upon the back of her neck and she cried out. Her neck fit in his palm. The world was inky blue-green, time didn't move, or it did all at once. "You swore an oath, Elena. You swore that we should pay in kind anyone who does us harm." Her dark hair, the twine in her braid, she might have been a child. "And you've got quite the headcount." *How long had it been since he kissed her forehead? A few minutes? Or forever?*

Someone's voice. *Wait, John.*

"What are we supposed to do with you, girl? You say you're sorry and we all go about our business? Pretend none of this never was? You're working with the enemy. We were thinking about killing that poor girl just for *suspecting* as much."

"John." This one was her voice, she grasped at his arm, she wrenched her head and twisted in his grasp until he could see her face. "John, you can't mean this."

"You betrayed us! You killed Alan!"

Words and tears and lies *and lies.* "I'll go away. You'll never see me again."

Someone. *Gisbourne will find you.*

He can't let you live either, he arranged for your escape.
He didn't arrange it, it was me.
Arable, how did you get the keys to the cells?
He left them behind. My God, he left them behind.
Don't you see? He positioned you into this.
He used you to bring Elena to us.

"John, you know me. You know I'm on your side. I made a mistake."

"I know you did, girl. A big mistake."

"It's me." Her body shook. Or the world shook. Or John shook. "It's me, John, not some stranger! Doesn't that count for anything?"

"I have an idea." The world lost its color. He shoved her face down, down into Alan's body, down so that their faces were inches apart, down the way he would punish a dog, down so she would see what she had done, down, down, the only direction that was left. "Let's have Alan decide!"

"I'm sorry!"

Those were words. She said them. They didn't matter.

"I promise to make it quick," was more kindness than he needed give her, as he plucked her up and put his other hand on her jaw. She didn't fight back.

John, no, please. It's Lena. It's my Lena. Let her go, let her run.
Will, my love—
You don't get to call me that.
Everything I did—
Stop talking!
Please.
John, look at me, please, wait, God, wait, please, look at me—

—look at me, please."

In front of John was Will's face, so close, his eyes bloated and red, his face half-bruised, somehow his hands were on John's lapel, he was pulling. The world was out of focus. Had he done it yet? No, she was crying still. His fingers felt too big to fit on his hands.

"Turn your head, Will. You shouldn't see this."

Elena said something. John couldn't hear her.

"Please." Will again. "Let her go. I'll go with her. I'll leave, too. This is my fault, I brought her here."

"They'll catch her, Will." John recognized this voice as his own. "They'll torture her. You won't be able to live with yourself. It's better if we do it. There's a pity there."

"I would hate you for it, John. I don't want that. I'd rather hate myself."

Every part of John was old. He should have left with Marley.

"I can take it," he lied. "You can't."

John closed his eyes

and

watched himself snap his arms together, to break her neck.

But he couldn't do it. In a gasp of life his anger vanished, his vision was clear, and he wanted it all to go away. Anything for her to still be there, brash little Elena curling her lip like a brat. He let her go and she slipped away.

Behind, someone yelled, "Stop her!"

Let her run, John thought. *Let her run.*

He turned to watch her disappear into the woods, but she wasn't running. She was at the campfire, finishing the last of the cup.

Robin's cup.

"I'm so sorry," she said as she dropped it.

Then there was nothing left to do.

Will moved, he grabbed her, he kissed her, his hands brushed her hair.

"I'm sorry, I didn't mean it," he whispered an inch from her face. "We'll get out of here, together. Let's just go."

"I love you." She said it flatly, calmly. "You know that, right?"

"We'll go back to the road, we can go anywhere you want, like we've always done. This was just a place. We'll go to the next one. Come on."

"You're the best man I've ever met." She pulled his head even closer to her own. "Of course you said no to Gisbourne because you're so good, and I'm not."

"No, no." Will put his hands on her cheeks. "Let's go. Let's go now."

She tugged his hair and smiled. "You did the right thing when nobody else would."

"But it wasn't the right thing, Lena," he said as they both lowered down to the ground, and he cradled her in his arms. "It wasn't the right thing to do."

"I tried," she said, then gasped and rolled her head away and coughed red into her hand. She looked at her own blood. "I tried to do the right thing."

"I know," he said, taking her hand back, not letting her see it.

"I'm sorry."

"Don't think about that."

She started to say something else but it came out in a hack, and before she could recover came another one, worse, and when she bent her head back, John couldn't watch anymore.

The sounds were terrible enough. There was no way to close his ears. She choked for air. Every now and then came a little whimper between her fits, the scratching of her feet and hands clattering through the dirt, and the gentle pattering pecks of Will kissing her as she convulsed. His own breathing was fast and heavy, but he made no other noise except to say *I know* again and again, until they weren't even words at all. Eventually the unbearable sounds of her struggling body faded, bit by bit, and was replaced with a telling quiet that was so very much worse.

There

didn't

seem

any use in opening his eyes, so John didn't.

After she was still, and some time even later after that, Will screamed. It sent a chill down John's spine, a wretched naked noise he would never forget. Will let it out now, all of it, and part of himself, too.

After that he made no noise at all, for so long that John opened his eyes simply to be sure anyone was still there. Will was clutching Elena's body on the ground, his head sunk down into her chest, her lips covered in blood. The others stood unmoving, like John, gravestones in the mist.

Will sobbed while they stood in silence.

When he had no more to cry they stood in silence still.

As the fog grew barely thinner, just enough to reveal a few of the figures in the trees, still they stood.

It

didn't

really matter

when the first of the intruders stepped forward.

FIFTY-TWO

GUY OF GISBOURNE

THIEVES' CAMP

THERE WAS NO WAY to interrupt that wasn't cruel. In the face of such stark humanity, the past didn't matter. No depth of animosity Guy held for Will Scarlet could overcome the crippling display of his grief. And so they stood in utter silence, watching one murderer mourn another. Even the forest itself was not wicked enough to break the stillness. It lasted so long Guy might have doubted he was even visible through the fog, if not for a few meaningful glances he shared with Robin of Locksley. They acknowledged the moment, an understanding of that which would come next, and that it could wait.

So they waited, longer, and longer, as Will Scarlet heaved over his poisoned lover. The world had no pity for her regrettable fate. She had once placed a blade to Guy's throat, but grown to see the greater good over her own selfishness. Hers was the only heart here that had shown a glimpse of redemption, only to end so tragically.

Still longer, they all stood.

Guy had two dozen men from the common ranks with him, as well as the entirety of the Black Guard. They had silently encircled the outlaws, who finally started to twist nervously at their presence. When Guy spoke, he did everything he could to keep his voice quiet, respectful.

"I am genuinely sorry it came to this."

Arable gulped air in shock. "You followed me?"

"As I said," Robin told her, emptily, "you led him right to us."

It was hardly that simple. It was impossible for thirty of them to follow Scarlet's escape unnoticed. Instead they relied on Eric of Felley's tracking skills to keep their trail. Guy had also posted men disguised as peasants in strategic places, anticipating their flight toward the Sherwood, but even still Eric had almost lost his quarry several times. Avoiding nearby Bernesdale had been particularly tricky, and its village full of poorfolk who still blamed the Guard for their troubles. But the gamble had paid off—Guy already held two of the thieves captive, catching them drinking from a cask of ale by the road. There were only ten left to apprehend, none of them visibly armed.

Still they stood. Will Scarlet seethed, but most of the outlaws bore defeat from head to toe, and Guy's men were prepared. Tempers would settle. The horror story of Robin Hood ended here. And, with Locksley as his prisoner instead of dead, Guy could still get what he needed to end Wendenal's reign as well.

But first, he had amends he needed to make.

"Arable, I owe you a profound apology." Guy moved to her, lowering his voice, desperate to rid himself of the torment he'd put her through. "I have treated you beyond unkindly. I took no pleasure in scaring you as I did."

She stammered for words. "You used me?"

Will Scarlet had rejected Guy's proposal in the end, but convincing Elena to return to the Sherwood and poison Robin of Locksley had been surprisingly easy. The hard part had been to orchestrate their escape in a way that left Guy plausibly uninvolved.

"I needed to protect myself, Arable, in case it went poorly," Guy explained, searching her eyes. "You can see that, can't you? I had to compel someone outside the Guard to set them free."

Her mouth opened and closed quickly again. Guy felt genuinely wretched. The way he had threatened her, assaulting her in the bedroom, it was a despicable thing. But he needed to push her far over the edge, to give her no choice, to force her to leave the castle that night. He had arranged for Marshall's interruption, had dropped his keys for her to find. They had given her every hint she needed. The worst part had been playing the role of someone sinister enough to say such heinous things in earnest.

"I thought for certain you saw through my ruse. I'm both relieved and extremely sorry you didn't."

She only stared at him. "How did you know I would go through with it?"

"I didn't," he admitted. "I didn't think Elena Gamwell would go through with it, either. Made a botch of it, obviously, but still." Why the poison had worked so quickly, he did not know. He would have to take that up with the Bishop of Hereford once everything settled.

Arable backed away from him. "You're a monster."

That hurt. He tried to prove otherwise, by ignoring it. "As I say, I apologize. You will not be held accountable for your actions tonight, and are welcome to return with us. Nottingham owes you its thanks."

But she kept backing up. "I'm not going back there."

Guy lowered his head and winced. He had been afraid of this. She was reacting emotionally. Surely if she were calm she would see the folly of leaving the city's safety.

"You *will* be going back," he said sternly, for her own sake. "You can choose the manner. After all, there are two stories I could tell when we return. The first, the truth, is of a loyal handmaiden who played her part in avenging the late Sheriff de Lacy. The second is of an insolent girl who released two murderers and betrayed her country. Which would you prefer?"

"I can't . . ." Arable shook her head. "You . . . I never . . ."

Guy couldn't believe it. He had more important things to do than coddle a servant girl into caring about her own life. "You'll come with us, and someday you'll recognize the kindness I've shown you. Alright, men, let's take them all into custody."

At his command, the circle of Guardsmen constricted. Then froze. Will Scarlet had risen from where he knelt beside Elena's body, the lone discarded sword back in his hands. Whatever was left of him was gravel.

"Come and get us."

Against all sanity, Robin of Locksley walked forward and joined Scarlet, even though he had no weapon to carry. John Little put his hand at Arable's waist and urged her to hurry behind them. Then he stepped forward as well, because nothing was ever easy. "Now's as good a time as any."

Fortunately, and despite recent precedent, Guy was not an idiot.

He laughed, mostly to keep his men calm. Letting these bastards go out fighting was precisely what they wanted, and Guy had no interest in feeding their desire to follow the traitor lord into martyrdom.

"Ooh, I have an excellent idea, actually, let's *not* do this again. We've been here before, you recall, us hacking at each other to nobody's benefit. Last time you shot one of my best men in the chest from the rooftop and then you all escaped. And that's fine, that's one option, but I was thinking another for today. Let's have you come along willingly and we'll save ourselves the nastier bits."

Robin frowned. "Why would we do that?"

Guy flopped his hands out, hoping for levity. "Generosity?" From face to face he found no response. "No? No one? Alright then, perhaps this." His black doublet gave way as he revealed the creased parchment, which he elevated above his head. "This is a signed edict from Lord William de Wendenal, the High Sheriff of Nottinghamshire, Derbyshire, et cetera et cetera—that's his signature and seal right there, if you're doubtful—" he handed the document to Robin for inspection, "—that demands the razing of the Sherwood."

"The most ridiculous ploy I've ever heard," Sheriff Wendenal had said, even as he begrudgingly signed the prop. *"Robin will never fall for this."*

But Guy had bet the opposite, because Robin of Locksley would always believe in the worst in people. Predictably, he gasped and scoured the parchment. "You couldn't . . ."

"Every last tree, burned to the ground," Guy elaborated. "Fire brigades are preparing even as we speak. They'll leave the castle on first light, and start fires throughout the Sherwood, traveling north, burning it from the inside out. The smoke will make an excellent backdrop for Baron de Lacy's funeral." That much was true, even. He'd set the task to his Common Guard, in the hopes that the word would travel. To back up his bluff.

Guy spread his arms wide and bowed theatrically, then let it drop to laugh at his own charade. "Oh, stop your worrying, it's not going to actually happen. If I give the word, I can stop it. This edict only takes effect if you refuse to surrender yourself to me. Or, I suppose, if you kill me. So no, let's not fight."

And it worked. John Little slumped, even Will Scarlet seemed to lose his fire. Guy had made himself unkillable—the survival of the Sherwood was bound to his own.

"All of us?" Robin asked, with a humbling defeat. "Or just me?"

Guy blinked. "All of you. Are you joking? There's no bargaining here. You lost. Lay down, put your hands behind your backs. All of you. I can't believe I have to explain that."

None of them moved.

"You won't burn the forest down," Arable said, thinking herself incredibly brave by standing straighter. "It would kill thousands of people. It would devastate Nottinghamshire. Nobody is that insane."

Guy withered her with his stare. "I absolutely agree. You're not listening. The plan will only be enacted if I fail to stop it. So I'm putting that choice in your hands. As you say, I'm banking that *'nobody is that insane.'* So will you give up, Robin, or will you let it all burn down? Actually," an odd thought struck him, "perhaps you *will* pick the latter. Seems to run in the family."

Robin flinched, and John Little shouted to stop him. "Don't, Robin! It's exactly what he wants."

"What I *want*?" Guy shook his head, incredulous. "I guarantee you there is nothing about this situation I have *wanted*. Because what I *want* is for you all to obey the law! That's it! Is that so unthinkable? Is that what makes me *monstrous*?" He tilted his head toward Arable, recalling her insult. "I didn't want to hike out here in the middle of the night, risking my men's lives. What I *want* is for you to respect your country enough to live fairly, the way the rest of us must. You do remember you're the criminals, don't you? You stole from the King! You assassinated a public official! You're inciting a rebellion while we're at war! And why? Because your taxes are too high? And your life isn't as easy as you wish it were? What I *want* is for you all *to grow up*."

Guy bristled, pacing back and forth in front of them. "And if you refuse, then yes I also want to kill you."

There were other sounds, just underneath his own words, that came from the trees. With his final syllable he recognized what they were, and then it was too late.

The mist moved, in hair-thin horizontal slices, met by grunts and *thunks* and screams. Time was arrested, letting Guy witness it all fall apart—with no way of stopping it. The hair on Guy's neck stood as the Guardsman on his left, a diligent veteran named Curtis who had served for five years without complaint, took three arrows in the chest and fell screaming to his knees. One whisper cut the air so close to Guy's face he felt it across the tip of his nose. The arrow ended its flight by punching a hole through both the hood and the cheek of a tall dark-skinned Guardsman, Sergio, who had been born in Nottingham and now died in the middle of nowhere.

Stop! He screamed, though he didn't. He was still frozen, feeling victory slough through his fingers, clenching every muscle to return to where he was a bare moment ago. But it was gone. *He was sliding backward, back into the hole.*

A wall of raiders crashed through their circle, shattering everything.

Half of Guy's men were taken by surprise, slammed off their feet, overthrown, in an instant. The new combatants were nobodies—a throng of enraged villagers from Bernesdale, no doubt—a damned mob of Robin's followers. They brought weapons, bundles of them, and quickly armed the remaining outlaws while Guy's men still rallied to make sense of what was happening.

"What the hell is wrong with you?" Guy screamed, pulling his longsword from its sheath and making a wide spin, daring anyone to close distance with him. "What the fuck did I just say? Don't you understand what will come of this?"

Of course they did, but they didn't care.

There were fire brigades preparing already, who had no idea the plan was a ruse. If Guy caught an errant arrow, if he were even delayed . . . the forest would burn.

They had to be stopped.

There was no controlling the chaos now. Guy twisted, he needed to pinpoint Locksley in the crowd, but he was no longer where he had been last. The Guard was overwhelmed and ambushed, Guy knew it in the stone of his stomach, he knew each and every one of his men would die here in a straight fight. *But the outlaws would fall apart if Locksley fell.* It was his only chance.

The villagers met his men in fury, steel tore through the night, but Guy stood motionless.

There.

A single glimpse of Locksley on the opposite side of the throng.

But before he could move, his world shrank to the size of the two thieves rushing him. They raised their weapons and howled.

In open combat, the odds favor nobody.

Instinct drew his attention to the attacker on the left. His face was puffy like knotted dough, and he held his sword out as if he meant simply to skewer Guy in one move. Guy cracked his sword down upon the blade, up high by the guard in hopes it would break, but the second attacker did not slow at all to attempt a swing. He simply barreled into Guy at full speed with his shoulder, rolling Guy off balance. He was able to pivot and twist counterclockwise, dragging his longsword behind him and ending its circle with a reckless slash at the doughman. He lucked out, and the end of his blade caught the edge of the man's jaw, slinging purple pulp in its path. But Guy lost his footing, his sword swung out of weight in only his right hand. A spike of dull pain smashed into his back, no doubt a hasty pommel attack from his shoulder-happy friend. The mail beneath his tabard protected him from a laceration, but his spine screamed.

Guy rolled with the attack, rotating and withdrawing his sword back to his hip in a side-plow, and struck forward. The man had raised his sword high, giving Guy exactly the window he needed, driving the tip of his steel up under the man's rib cage and then high, a burst of heavy blood blossoming down the sword's fuller, letting Guy know he hit his mark. He pushed the man's body away, easing his sword out. He could not help but notice a plume of steam that trailed off the blade from the hot blood meeting the crisp night air.

Those men had delayed him too long. Guy looked again for Locksley, but could not find him. The threat of Wendenal's corruption seemed like a trifle now, compared to this madness.

No individual training mattered here. Wars are won with numbers, not finesse. Superior weaponry, superior armor, superior numbers. It doesn't matter if the people are expert fencers or a mob. And Locksley had the numbers.

Guy tried to focus, to keep calm. If he panicked he would die, and his death would make him complicit in the burning of the Sherwood. *He would not die helping Locksley do this.*

All around him, the torture of steel and men clattered through the trees. Either Guy had traveled, or the bulk of the melee had moved away already. Someone ran through the commotion, his head ducked down, and disappeared again. Guy could barely distinguish ally from enemy—there were only shapes and fog. He gave the mist a slice with his sword, to no avail. He was at the disadvantage here with such a long weapon. He needed open space and clear vision.

A cluster of horrific shrieks from somewhere in the mist made Guy think of Will Scarlet, and the damage he could do with his two knives in a riot like this. He could plunge those blades into every shape like a ghost, no doubt careless of which side his victims fought for.

Every interaction was a roll of the dice. Survive one, you get to roll again. Every direction held a new player.

How many stood between him and Locksley, Guy did not know. It didn't matter.

In most small skirmishes, the key was to pick the terrain, that they could be protected. That was how it went at Thieves Den. That was how it went at Bernesdale. Here, there was no wall behind them. No direction to aim their attention.

A man rushed him, his hands behind his back, hiding a weapon. No, his hands were bound, he was one of the raiders they'd already captured at the ale cask. Guy moved quickly, swinging his sword in for the man's belly, but pivoted at the last moment to give the prisoner the pommel of his sword instead of the blade. It was unwise. It strained his wrist to do it, but the man would survive. The crunch of a broken rib was enough to put him down, keep him down.

Death was such a lazy way to end it all.

The sounds shifted, the fight was straying even farther away from him. He moved, as quickly as he could without being careless, back into the melee. To his relief he came first upon Eric of Felley, squared off against an outlaw, both of them holding their weapons out and screaming at the other to surrender.

Guy joined, but his presence spooked the thief into attacking—a swing at Eric's shoulder that was easily deflected. Guy did not hesitate. He curled his longsword high and right, letting its weight fall down into the outlaw's neck, splitting cloth and skin and bone. Nearly a full hands-length it buried down into the man's chest, and Guy had to kick his foot on the dead man's sternum to retrieve his sword again.

"Thanks, Captain," Eric coughed.

"Stay sharp! Where's Locksley?" Guy shouted. He hadn't realized how loud it was until he needed to use his voice.

"That way!" Eric pointed to his left, and *his mouth exploded with blood.*

Guy lit with rage.

A brief flash from behind, a hand pulling the knife out from the base of Eric's neck. It flew into the mist.

Guy grabbed Eric's arms and held him up, but he dragged downward. Whatever bastard had done it was gone, fleeing as cowards do. Guy shifted Eric's weight down to the ground, his mind detaching from the unimaginable grief that would come later.

"Fucking hell was that?" Eric sputtered blood between his missing teeth.

"Don't talk," Guy ordered him, torn between his need to return to the battle and the guilt of leaving Eric alone. Eric's face contorted until Guy could barely recognize him. Screams ripped the air in two. There were others out there Guy might be able to save.

Eric's mouth opened and closed in confusion, a fish gasping for water. His eyes were unfocused and wild, straining to understand how he could die like this. *Like this.*

"I have to go," Guy whispered, more for himself. But Eric grabbed him and pulled him close, shivering, his fingers clutching for companionship in this, the final moments of his life. And Guy could not even give him that. Eric was the last of Guy's old regiment, the only one who still remained from barely two months ago. Guy had lost every last one of his men, to the scourge of Robin Hood.

The world split into sparkles before Guy even realized there were tears in his eyes.

Eric's mouth sputtered out blood.

"I can't . . . I have to go," Guy said, and left his friend to die.

Mercy had no fairness to it. No kindhearted soul was spared. No cruel heart received his due. That was how the outlaws win, because they didn't care who remained when the insanity was over.

Guy wouldn't survive this, either, he knew that now. His men were being butchered around him—there was no knowing how many of the Black Guard still stood. He thought about fleeing, flying back to Nottingham to stop the fire brigades at least, but he knew they would catch him. Guy's fate was writ, there was nothing about tomorrow to regret now.

But before he fell, he would take the devil with him.

Steam pumped through him. His muscles burned afire.

"That way," Eric had said, his final words. There were people in that direction, so Guy cut through them.

His body moved on instinct. He parried a skinny man's lunge and used the momentum to cut through the man's arm below the elbow, then a side step and a drag of his blade through the man's belly. Guy moved as if in a dream. He swept low and took the legs out of one opponent—and left the rest to Silas of York, who came down on the enemy with an overhead smash. As his body fell, Guy had already moved on.

He buried his sword into another villager's head. He didn't even stop moving.

That way.

Locksley.

His path was blocked by a bearded sack of meat who was quick to find steel, and his body tumbled into Guy and spun him around. Guy punched his blade into the meat-man's neck and turned back, but he had lost his bearings. A Guardsman was nearby, Ryon, a thin young man that was a better archer than swordsman, fumbling with his bow to find a target in the mist. Then his bow slipped from his hands, the arrow jumped limply forward, and the young bowman sloughed to the ground.

Another knife in the back.

Guy moved forward but a tree branch tripped him. He looked up just as a shadow disappeared *with a white glove.*

Traitor, Guy cursed. *The White Hand.* One of his new recruits had turned against him. Unless he had been a spy all along.

It didn't matter. He'd already become too distracted. *Locksley first, his allies after.* The sounds of the melee drew him closer, but he tumbled again. It wasn't a branch on the ground that tangled his feet, but a body, a woman's body. He was standing over Elena Gamwell, her face frozen in an open-mouthed scream.

A snap of leaves behind him gave warning, and Guy ducked and twisted at once. Still, he felt a blade glance into his side, a fatal blow if not for the mail beneath his tabard. His ribs took the brunt of the force, and Guy spun to avoid the inevitable second attack. He dove for the ground and let go of his sword. He snapped his boot out and found his attacker's kneecap, rewarded with a harrowing snap as the leg bent at an undesirable angle. The man fell on top of him, screaming, and Guy struck quickly for the man's throat to stun him. But he was now pinned down, his legs trapped beneath the huge man. Guy's hands grasped to find purchase, a heavy stink and horror rose as his vision faded to black. This was his unfortunate end, at the bottom of a mountain of dirty flesh, *and the forest would burn.*

If he died before killing Locksley, it was for nothing. All his men, for nothing.

His fingers scrambled through his assailant's beard and found soft skin beneath. He squeezed, even as his opponent's hands found his own face. Guy angled away, trying to free himself, but the beastman's thumb clawed upward. One smashed down into Guy's left eye, pushing, his vision burst white with stars, something *popped* and a panic surged through him, giving his muscles renewed strength. He clawed at the man's throat. He buried his fingernails in and crushed it. The instant he found any meat thick enough to grasp he tore as hard as he could. The man spasmed, abandoning Guy's eye and rolling away. Guy followed and punched down into the man's throat again, then was back on his feet, blindly, moving without seeing, but he had already retrieved his sword and drove it down into the man's skull, all of his weight pushing, heaving, until there was nothing left but the surging pressure of his eye socket, and exhaustion.

The way that noises distort underwater, such was how the world now appeared. Guy waited, praying for his own breath to catch, his vision black and blurred. He probed his left eye for any vision. For all he knew, his eyeball might have been pierced or dangling from its socket. But the world was there, where he expected it. It was simply milky and unfocused. He leaned on his sword, still piercing his would-be murderer's head, and tried to assess what he could see.

A shape that could only be John Little was grappling with an unknowable Guardsman. Little's staff was around the man's back, held with both hands, trapping the Guardsman between the wood and Little's chest. Little screamed, pulling the staff toward him, and even half-blinded Guy could see as the man's back broke, limply collapsing into nothing. Guy had no idea who had just died, so close to his captain who was unable to help.

To another side, a crowd of blurry bodies was gathering, the way men rallied at the edges of a barfight. But the entire throng seemed to be involved, moving and undulating around something at its center, reacting as one. Through a hole between bodies, Guy caught a glimpse of the carnage. This had to be the assassin Will Scarlet, spinning like a top, a hurricane of death, blades in both hands. The wall of men shifted, blocking Guy's view, spotty as it was. He told himself to move, to go and help, but his legs didn't budge. He released the pressure from his eye and blinked away the pain, trying to focus. Again, the crowd groaned as one in horror. Another splash of Scarlet leapt from one man to another, then nothing. Guy's vision faded black and foggy and back again, then another pop in his head exploded as before, and pain folded him over, a white hot lash.

When it passed, his vision was clearer but everything twinkled. He watched Scarlet slash down at a guard twice his size—Marshall Sutton—who caught both Scarlet's wrists midair. It was like watching an eagle pluck a mouse from the earth. But Scarlet jumped up and kicked into Marshall's stomach, and when his wrists were released he stabbed them both up—*Good God*—up through Marshall's big ox face. Down to the hilt.

Guy's body thundered. He ran in, not caring if it was the last thing his body would ever do.

Scarlet caught another man's sword with one knife, rolled the other in his palm to reverse its grip and stabbed it down into the Guardsman's chest. In the next breath, he twisted away and windmilled his arms through the air as he slapped a sword down with one strike and slashed through its owner's shoulder with the next. *Too many,* Guy swore, finally close enough, unnoticed, and buried his longsword into Scarlet's side.

Incredibly, the man had moved one blade in time to protect his ribs, barely saving himself from being cut in half. But the blow sent Scarlet tumbling off his feet, and Guy followed him as he scrambled away. The ground was littered with dead and wounded. Few were still standing, and Guy would not allow Scarlet to be counted amongst the day's survivors. But as Scarlet collapsed, another shape interceded between them, saying something lost to the din. Though Guy could not recognize the words, he was far too familiar with their author.

The traitor Robin of Locksley's face was bloodied. He held his own sword in the Fool's stance, begging for absolution.

Guy gulped down air. There was still hope. This one slim chance.

He didn't have the strength to stand, but he didn't need to.

Devon and Jon Bassett were there behind him, propping him up. Reginold and Bolt spied the terrain for him. Eric and Marshall helped him raise his sword. Henry and Much, they reminded him he could do it.

For a brief, joyous moment, Guy felt pity for Locksley. Because he was outnumbered.

They did not speak. Their heads bobbed, a silent agreement. It was only appropriate to end in this way. Whatever raiders were still alive stood back, as if to recognize the necessity of this duel. Guy could not tell how many of his own men were left. It wouldn't matter. Even if Guy died here, Locksley would pay for his reign of terror, Wendenal's coup would be over, and Nottingham would be safe. The woods would regrow. Robin Hood would not.

They began properly, a slow circle, watching each other's footwork, shifting their blades between stances. Guy transitioned to the front Plow and Robin appropriately brought his tip high in a Roof. Guy shifted to a right Fool and Robin matched with a left Ox. It was almost welcoming to see a worthy duelist, rather than his mob of drunken brawlers who pounded their swords like clubs. Guy weaved from a crab-walk to a deer's, and Robin met him in a plowman. He was trained well, but he favored his right foot, and some cut on his lip made him infrequently tongue his cheek.

Guy, on the other hand, knew how to hide his own injuries and project others instead. He feigned a limp in his left knee, and waited for Robin to take note of it. That was all Guy needed.

They moved forward, together, fluid, in a dance. Their blades dipped in unison, sweeping in the same lines, returning and rejoining. They only barely even made contact, the two swords but kissing as they breathed through the air. Each man read the other's move as it was made, sliding their feet in exact calculation, using the energy of each swing to feed into the next. They did not dodge each attack so much as slide out of its path, they did not parry an attack but rather suggest it go elsewhere.

Guy made his moves when Robin was slightly off balance or nursing his cheek, and Robin took a desperate lunge that sought to take advantage of Guy's false limp. Guy riposted against Robin's rhythm, and it worked. Robin panicked, the grace of his training wasting away. His swings became harder, born from anger rather than experience. Their swords stopped kissing. They clashed down upon each other, occasionally drawing a spark. At the perfect rare chance, Guy backhanded Robin across the face and came swinging down into him again, and Robin dropped to his knees to block. The strength of the blow was massive, and Robin's sword smashed down and out of his hands.

It was, impossibly, over.

"Is this what you wanted?" Guy shouted, his voice gone, betraying his grief, low and grave. "There was no reason for anyone to die here. What have we done, what have you accomplished with this?"

"Don't act as if you care," Robin said, still at his knees. "You mean to burn down the forest."

"You . . ." Guy stared him down, ". . . mean to burn down the *country.*"

Around him, shapes rose from the earth. Guardsmen. He recognized the faces of a few of his men, weary but mercifully alive. Silas, Quillen Peveril. Even Jacelyn was there. He did not see Simon, and prayed the Scotsman still breathed. He did not waste the same thought on FitzOdo or his men, who were nowhere in sight. The finest men Guy knew held no knighthood, they were those that lay now in the dirt, who had faced down the outlaws in the forest and—

"You don't get to blather on," Robin hissed, and Guy realized he had been speaking aloud, "about what is right. You don't know the first thing about it. All you know is the power you have and the power you want."

"You're the definition of hypocrisy," Guy called out. "Silas, you have anything to bind his hands?"

Silas nodded and limped forward. Robin flinched, but Guy elevated his sword's tip toward his face. "You stay on your knees."

"No argument there," Robin moaned. "You're not the sort of man I'd ever stand up for."

That's what it all came down to for men such as this. Recognition. Wendenals and Locksleys hated the world because it wasn't theirs. Guy shook his head. It was time to lead from a place of unity, not vanity. "I don't need your respect," he sighed. "Everyone else will stand for the man who stopped Robin Hood."

In retrospect, he should have heard her approach.

He should have noticed the gasps on his men's faces the moment before she struck.

Guy felt mail break in his lower back, barely punctured; a single shard of metal link stabbed the flesh in his already bruised ribs. The pain was no worse than the rest of his body, but it jolted Guy forward. Robin rose and plucked the longsword from his hands in that one moment of disadvantage. No amount of skill or valor or decency mattered in the instant of her craven attack from behind.

Arable was just fucking lucky.

"That's a coward that does that," he breathed.

Their positions had quickly reversed. Guy now kneeled before Robin, who clutched Guy's sword in both hands, one on each knee as he buckled over to catch his breath. Arable held her stolen sword out in front of her, her heavy cloak whipping behind her, as though she were the greatest hero that ever walked the earth.

His men scattered. Some ran into the woods. Others were quickly surrounded and disarmed. "Fine then, don't hurt them. You won. But damn you for it. Damn you for *how* you did it. You lied, you cheated." Guy's thoughts fluttered to the White Hand, stabbing Guardsmen in the back. Possibly he'd been the one to rally the villagers from Bernesdale. "You snuck one of your own amongst us. But you could only do that because we're better than you. Because we trust one another. And we saw how your kind treat each other tonight, with suspicion. Poison.

Murder. Remember what your friend said, the one you poisoned. I'd rather die with my people than live with yours."

Robin didn't answer him.

"We didn't come out here to do violence upon your people, Robin, and you know it. We came peacefully, you answered with arrows." Guy felt blood trickle to his lips. "We could have killed Will Scarlet and Elena Gamwell, could have taken our revenge for the men they murdered, but we didn't. Not because we didn't want to, but because it wouldn't have been right. If you were ever once a man of conscience, I wonder what you'd say to that."

"You think it was right to send Elena to poison me?" Robin said at last. "You think your hands are clean, you bastard?"

If it had gone well, it would have been a mercy. Robin couldn't understand that.

"What does it matter, Robin? You can't kill me. If you kill me, the forest burns tomorrow. So what, then? We go our separate ways for now, just to do this again later? And again and again? How many more of my men have to die, how many of yours will you sacrifice before I inevitably catch you?"

Robin's breaths were shallow, his eyes dead set on Guy. He didn't move. He did not so much as blink.

"Just come with me, Robin. Your plans with Wendenal in Nottingham tomorrow are spoiled either way. We'll find a peaceful way to settle this. If we don't, we'll keep on as we have. As animals. Butting our heads. We fought at Locksley Castle. We fought at Bernesdale. We fought here. We'll fight at de Lacy's funeral. We'll fight at Lady Marion's wedding, all for nothing."

A flick of his hand and Robin Hood slid the tip, *just the tip* of his sword through Guy's neck.

PART VIII

TWO RIVERS

FIFTY-THREE

ARABLE DE BUREL

SHERWOOD FOREST

IT SHOULD HAVE FELT good to watch him die.

Admittedly, it *did* feel good. But it should have felt *better.*

Instead, it was unfulfilling. It wasn't that she felt bad for him, his throat cut open in the middle of nowhere, half-crawling through his own gore as his body twitched lifeless, no. It was not pity in her bones, but rage. Rage for the things she would never get to yell at him, rage for the things for which he would never be punished. At the end of his life, Guy of Gisbourne would never know how terrible a person he was. He had used her, he had threatened her, he had made her believe he was going to rape her. And he died thinking that was alright. It wasn't enough that she had stabbed him in the back, because he escaped her now by dying. *The coward.*

She was only dimly aware of what else was happening. Robin Hood had not stopped with Gisbourne. He floated through the trees like a ghost, cutting down the remaining Guardsmen who were not fast enough to flee. One took Robin's sword through the shoulder down to his heart. Another stumbled as he ran and was skewered from behind, Robin's blade pierced his body like a potato. Arable could only watch with half her attention—the rest was memorizing Gisbourne's final disappointing spasms.

It was better than nothing, she conceded. He was dying alone, in the cold, in an unknown place. There was that, at least. There was that.

Arable watched Robin Hood pull his weapon out of a young man in a tattered brown smock. She had seen more blood in the last ten minutes than in her entire life, and already it ceased to horrify her. Robin raised his sword again, this time at John Little. The only one who had defended her, his giant fatherly face was riven in grief. John held his hands out at Robin, cringing, "That's enough, Robin! That's it!"

She'd heard the word *bloodlust* before, but never thought it was real. Robin was gone from the world, like a drunkard. It took all of John Little's efforts to bring him back down. Eventually he dropped his weapon and shuddered in shame—there was nothing of the light-hearted showman she had met a month earlier.

She had bet everything on her hope to find a future with these people. She had begged their hospitality.

John was holding Robin's head, shivering tightly, mourning. Once he could, Robin looked upon what he'd done. Not at Gisbourne's body but the final man he'd killed, the one in the brown smock. Arable didn't understand at first, but eventually it hit her. *That brown smock was no Guardsman's tabard.* Robin had killed an ally, defenseless, in blind rage. Probably one of the villagers from Bernesdale who had rallied to their aid. So many bodies, so many had lost their lives here. During the battle, nobody could be blamed. But this final death . . .

"It's alright," John was whispering to Robin, though it wasn't.

Robin looked up to him, his lips quivered. "I saw red," he whispered. "I saw red."

"I saw red."

John held Robin's face to his chest. "I know. But you're back."

It was a terrible thing, but it was only one more of a hundred terrible things that had happened in the last day. Arable's emotions were closed off. She simply didn't have the ability to care about any new problems. It was too hard to imagine these were real people, with entire lives of their own.

"Is that it?" came an uncertain voice. "Is it over?"

The survivors were regrouping. Already they were gathering the dead, or trying to bandage the wounded. Some had earned grievous injuries. The crowd thinned quickly by necessity, as the healthy helped carry the less fortunate away, hoping to get them to Bernesdale where they might find better assistance. Those who remained were a mix of furious and mortified. They fell instantly upon each other, arguing over what would happen next, and whether William's edict to burn down the forest was anything but an empty threat.

"He won't go through with it," Arable said. Nobody here knew William the way she did. Looking at the parchment, she recognized William's signature at its bottom, but it had to be some ploy. "He's not Gisbourne. He wouldn't."

"He would," Robin countered, his voice strained. "We've done it before. In Sicily, King Richard ordered us to catch a gang of bandits, so we burned them out of a forest. It took a month. War tactics. And William sees this as a war now."

"He's not like that." She struggled to wrap her mind around it.

"Like what?" His voice was soaked in disappointment. "Driven? Dedicated? Single-minded?"

She couldn't say no.

"I think perhaps you've only known him at his best, Arable."

A dull warning rumbled through her. If he could cast her aside as easily as he had, if he could break every promise and authorize something like this, what else might he do to protect his secrets?

Would he come after her?

"Then we have to stop him," Will Scarlet coughed, massaging his ribs. "Not tomorrow. Tonight."

Despite everything, those words terrified her. If they meant to *stop him* the same way they stopped de Lacy . . .

"We're in no shape to do anything," the bald friar scolded, crouching over a dead body. Nearby, the remaining Bernesdale men were scavenging from fallen Guardsmen. Arable absently wondered if she knew any of them, wondered if she'd care.

She noticed John Little catch Robin Hood's eye. *Are you alright?* he mouthed.

No, Robin shook his head.

"We have to do something," said a man nursing a swollen arm. It was no suggestion but a simple fact, and Arable found herself nodding. Whatever William had done to get himself here, he had now gone too far. He had done nothing to protect her, despite his every promise.

He was her past. For the second time. It was time to look forward.

"We only have one option." Robin seemed cornered. "We'll have to trust Prince John. He can get us into the castle."

"What?" Arable interrupted, alarmed by the name. "What sort of deal do you have with Prince John?"

"He's offered to help us," Robin explained.

"Sort of," Little muttered.

"Alright, he offered to *meet* with us," Robin elaborated. "Arthur and I are meeting with him in secret tomorrow morning. He's arranged to sneak us into the castle."

"He thinks it's to talk business," added the man she assumed was Arthur. "But once we're done, Rob an' I get the others in, too."

Arable scoffed before anyone could argue. "I don't know what he's promised you, but you can forget about it. Do you honestly think he doesn't realize the coincidence, that you want to meet on the very day of de Lacy's funeral? He's using you, for his own purposes. This is the man who tried to appoint Gisbourne to Sheriff, who supports William now. He's *not* on your side."

"I said as much," Little sniffed. "That man's only side is his own."

"Let him go," a tall blond man added. "The prince, the sheriff, the king, they were all friends of Robin of Locksley. Let him go, too. Like it or not, you're Robin Hood now."

Robin nodded, long and hard, and locked eyes with Little. Not in sympathy this time, but with certainty.

"Besides, we don't need him to get into the castle." There was a clarity to Will Scarlet's words that made Arable instantly aware they were directed toward her. He walked up, he reached gently for her hands. "Is there any way you can get us back inside?"

"That depends," she said coldly, not looking up. "Are we still thinking of killing me?"

How quickly they had forgotten their rotten treatment of her. She had risked everything by breaking Will and Elena out of the prisons. She had freed Roger de Lacy's murderers, all for a lie. Gisbourne had manipulated her into abandoning the last of her life that still existed, and they had nearly killed her for it.

Will Scarlet didn't contest that. "Please."

In his poor, haunted face, was her own.

Pushed to the edge, having lost everything, he now needed the help of someone who had no reason to do so. He needed the trust of someone who shouldn't even be capable of trusting, not ever again. He was a reflection not only of her desperation, but of her hope that there was still a path up. The hope to climb.

She would always hate Will Scarlet for the role he played in de Lacy's death. But there was more to a person, and to life, than hate. Will had apologized, during their travel from Nottingham, admitting Roger's death solved nothing. These people knew about mistakes, as did Arable. *And they'd asked about her scars.* Robin, when she met him in the woods, and both Will and Elena despite their furious escape from the city. They did not ignore her face as the people in the city did. These people were familiar with pain, and chose not to shy away from it, but to grow from it.

These people were the people she needed.

"Yes, I can get you inside," she answered. "But only tonight. After tonight, word will return to the castle of what happened here, and I would be killed on the spot. But at the moment, nobody knows I'm missing." Her eyes found Gisbourne's face again, his dry eyes staring upward. "At least, nobody still *alive.*"

The crowd murmured. They seemed inspired by the possibility. Will Scarlet knelt beside her, crouching on the balls of his feet, and waited for her to look at him. His features were soft, there were streaks through the dirt on his bruised face where his tears had run rampant.

"Are you sure you want to do this?" he asked gently. "Simply running away is one thing, but getting revenge is another."

"I understand," she answered. "I'll get you inside the castle, but I won't go with you. William is dangerous, and out of control, but I couldn't bear to see him hurt." No one responded to that, and she knew why. She swallowed.

"One more question," Robin asked with some hesitation. "Lady Marion Fitzwalter, she's being held in the prisons. Do you know where?"

"Not in the prisons," Arable answered. "She's in the tower keep."

Robin exchanged a look with his men, as if asking for permission, which they silently gave.

"How many are going?" she asked. "The fewer the better."

"All of us," Robin answered.

"No, she's right." Will dropped his head. "No more than two or three. Any more, and it would have been too difficult for us to get out. The same will be true for getting in. Besides, the rest of us need to see what we can do about stopping those fire brigades. We need to spread the word. We'll need a lot of help, not just from our camp but from every village we can get to. We've got to start right now."

Robin looked at Will in wonder. "You don't want your shot at William?"

"I do," Will said, choking on the words, looking anywhere but at Elena's body. "But we need to do this right. You go to the castle, I'll handle the fire brigades." He raised his voice, "Any of you here who can, your help would be invaluable."

"I have horses in Bernesdale," came a voice from the crowd.

"Thank you." Will turned now to John. "What do you think, John? Is it good?"

"Oh, Will," John sighed. "You don't need me to tell you it is." He hollered at the man who had spoken. "You have a horse big enough for me?"

"Aye."

"Then I'm going with you, Robin."

They both smiled, something humble and genuine.

Robin reached out and clasped Will around the shoulders. "Good luck, Will."

"Good luck, Robin. And thanks. We'll reconvene here in the morning."

They parted with precision, with drive. Robin paused to turn back and offer his hand. "Lady Arable?"

Whatever her trepidations about these people, she could not fault their desire to do what was asked of them. Even broken and scattered, weary from the battle that just happened, not a single one of them complained as Will Scarlet called out his orders, organizing them into groups, laying out the plans of what had to happen in the hours between now and dawn. Arable followed the horseman, along with John Little and Robin Hood, back into the woods to find their way to Bernesdale, and back—one last time—to Nottingham.

It was the last place she wanted to go, but they needed her.

It had been a profoundly long time since Arable de Burel had been on that side of need.

FIFTY-FOUR

MARION FITZWALTER

NOTTINGHAM CASTLE

Marion opened her eyes, not alarmed but instantly awake. There had been a faraway clamor, such that she thought it a creation of her dreams. Even her conscious thoughts strayed too often of late to disturbing fantasies, and when she slept her head swam with the positively bizarre. Regardless, she maneuvered from the bed to have a peek out the clapboard window. It was dark, perhaps a few hours still until dawn. The sky mottled itself with heavy clouds, scattering the moonlight irregularly over the baileys of Nottingham Castle below.

For nearly three weeks she had been here, and the last few days in particular saw the castle churning in preparation. The yards had filled with multi-colored tents and camps, the ever-increasing complement of prestigious guests to tomorrow's funeral. The castle was not continent enough to hold them all, so only the most influential were now housed in its stony keeps. Prince John's detail had claimed all the grounds about the highest keep, leaving other lords' entourages to fend for themselves in the sprawling lower bailey. From her window, Marion had seen their colors go up, banners that sprouted like flowers in spring. A small green tent for Rutland next to the larger red-crossed canopy of Lincolnshire, while the yellows of the Yorkshire host sprawled wall-to-wall across half the yard. It was practically a miniature model of the whole of England, all contained within the castle's footprint.

Each day she strained to search for the white swords of Essex, never certain whether she hoped to find them or not. Her grandfather was earl there, though she doubted his health was reliable enough to travel. She had spied the horn of Huntingdonshire the day before, which filled her with dread. The Earl Robert of Huntingdon had been one of her most lucrative secret supporters. She feared what the present nobility would say if they knew they were sitting beside the man who had purchased all the precious gemstones and necklaces they had lost in the Sherwood Forest.

More prominent than anything else, Marion's room offered a prize view of the gallows that had been erected. Raked seating wrapped the middle bailey's perimeter the way it might for a tournament. The constant clamor of its construction had finally abated, and only silence now surrounded the haunting wood sentinel that promised the next day's "entertainment."

The violence of the hangings would be the reason the commoners came. They were always drawn to the smell of blood. The visiting aristocracy, however, only used the event as an excuse. Most of them had neither met nor dealt with the late Roger de Lacy in life. Their feigned grief was an act, disguising their hope to fill the holes he left behind in death. They, too, then, had come for the blood.

Seeing it all from within, seeing the entire castle from her new perspective, she shuddered to think of Robin's original plans to come tomorrow. It took staggering naiveté to think they would have been successful, but such was her life only a few short weeks ago. If nothing else, she could take solace in the knowledge that she had saved their lives. Sir Amon had carried her message to stay away. All their old futile tactics of pounding their heads against unforgiving stone walls were, appropriately, left behind now.

"Robin."

She said his name aloud, better than to keep all the regret and grief within.

Again, noise from far off, of brief hushed voices and movement, riding the wind. Even if it was only her imagination, there would be no returning to sleep for her. No matter how many hours away daylight waited, she wouldn't spend them staring at the arched stone ceiling again. She settled on the hairbrush, as she often did. At least it was something, anything, to do. William had promised to fetch some of her personal belongings from her residence in Sheffield, but had yet to do so.

William de Wendenal, the man to whom she would be married. That was not yet something to which she had acclimated.

These were not the circumstances by which she hoped to marry, to say the least. But there were things that could be controlled, and others that could not. Her grandfather once told her to never worry herself with the latter. Her father, however, had said the exact opposite. That was something of a habit of men, their need to give advice in succinct little sentences that sound like great worldwide truths. Marion preferred her mother's counsel, which was to treat advice as you would a stranger's soup—taken in small, cautious sips.

She wondered what her family would think of her if they knew everything. About *Marion's Men*. About her upcoming marriage. About every consequence of the things she had done with—and for—power. Her grandfather warned that power is a poison, while her father claimed it is an illusion. She imagined she could say that power is quite like anything at all, and it would sound equally witty. *Power is a sunrise. Power is an old horse. Power is a borrowed hairbrush.*

She had learned the real truth. In a world full of unforgiving stone walls, power was a doorway.

Her quiet was broken by the sudden opening of her room's door, and Marion gasped at the dull face in a leather coif that pushed itself in to stare at her. She scrambled to close her gown as the face apologized and disappeared, only to return a moment later. "Sorry. I didn't know if you were awake."

"You could very well have knocked."

"Well, I didn't know if you were awake," the Guardsman repeated, as if that explained his rudeness. "It's just, well, there may be something going on. We thought we'd check in on you."

"If there's something going on," Marion rolled her eyes at his vagueness, "you ought to investigate. It's certainly not going on in here." Two guards were always posted on the other side of her door. It must have been a coveted position for its sheer eventlessness.

This one took the suggestion as an insult, as well he should have. "We're here for your protection, my lady." Marion knew quite well what they were there for, and it was difficult to pretend otherwise. Her *protector* nodded his head bluntly toward the window shutter. "We should probably keep that closed."

"Are we afraid I'll jump out of it?"

"Just please close the window," he repeated, turning to leave. "There may be something going on."

If he thought that explained anything, he had failed twice. Marion wasn't actually interested in looking out the window again, but she did so anyway just to enjoy the act of willful disobedience. The day promised very little else she could enjoy.

The gallows made a bleak outline, like some great skulking beast looking down into the bailey for something to hunt. She was distinctly aware of how easily she might find herself standing on that platform. Ironically, if it were not for her sudden engagement to William de Wendenal, she would likely be forced to hide in the Sherwood with John Little and the others. There were many who might choose to label her as co-conspirator, and it took little creativity to imagine she was involved in de Lacy's assassination. If the right person were to make the accusation, she might easily share tomorrow's stage with Will Scarlet.

Scarlet. His very name agitated her.

Tomorrow's grim spectacle would at least turn the page on him.

That maddening boy had always found too much enjoyment in their more criminal exploits. She'd been foolish to think a motherless runt from the wharf-scraping gangs would find anything in common with families struggling to feed themselves. But John Little had fought for them, and Marion had allowed it. There was a morbid silver lining that Scarlet and Elena would not be able to hurt anyone else after this. Marion had agreed to Robin's plans to rescue them because of the victory it represented for the people, but not for their sakes. She would have had to punish them once they were back, a conflict she had not looked forward to. This outcome, at the very least, would deter others from following their reckless lead.

Their decision to kill Roger de Lacy had marked the end of Lord Walter's dream.

Mercy on their misguided souls, she realized they were probably dead already. Gisbourne meant to parade their corpses at the funeral, rather than give them the dignity of execution. Marion closed her eyes, willing away the image of Will Scarlet's smug face, thinking himself smarter than the world. He had earned his fate.

She wanted to blame him for all of this, but he was not the only one at fault. Marion carried her share, as well as Robin. Even de Lacy, even Lord Walter. Perhaps they all should hang tomorrow, everyone who had ever braved an opinion and the strength to act on it. England would be a safer—if less interesting—place for the few survivors.

A clatter broke again outside, and the door opened abruptly a second time. Marion reeled at the guard. "What have I asked you about knocking?"

"Sorry, mum," the voice replied, but it was not the same Guardsman. This one was much larger and wore no tabard. He slammed the door behind him, barricading it with a rather familiar heavy quarterstaff.

"Oh my God!" Marion screamed.

"Oh my God!" John Little screamed back, and nearly fell over in shock.

"John! What on earth?"

"Lady Marion! Well that works out—" He caught himself and hushed his voice, sheepishly avoiding the door. "Well that works out nicely!"

"What are you doing here?" she asked, because it was the only thing she could possibly say, second only to "How did you get here?" which she asked as well, not waiting for an answer to the first. She was at once thrilled and horrified at his presence. He was red-faced and sweaty, with one eye fully bloodshot.

"No worrying about that now, it wasn't anything difficult." He grabbed at her hand, missing once and then slipping off a second time, breathing heavily. A dried patch of blood covered his arm at the shoulder. He waved clumsily for her to join him, which hardly counted as good counsel.

"Come on then, we'll be off." From the corridor outside, muffled voices and a commotion of bodies rampaged closer. John pushed his weight against the door and braced the staff with both hands. "Best we stay here for a bit, actually, if it's all the same."

Against reason, Marion planted her hands against the rough wood of the door as well, barely able to reach it around John's body. The door had a keylock but his chest blocked her from using it. Fortunately, the Guardsmen rumbled past her door without stopping, and Marion relaxed her grip as their clamor receded.

"You are going to get yourself killed, John!"

"Me? No, no." He shook his head again, wiping the sweat from around his eyes. "I'm safe, see? Robin might, though."

His name struck her cold. "Robin might what?"

"Get himself killed."

"He's here, too?" She flung herself from the door to dress, but stopped just as suddenly. "What's going on?"

"Well it was going fine for a while, it's not as though we botched the *whole* thing," John burst out, defensive, barely remembering to keep his voice down. "We got through the city and the castle, too, and nobody saw us. And then somebody saw us. I don't remember how many. And then there was a lot of running. I don't like running. Robin . . ." he whistled, ". . . he's fast. And he knows what he's doing with a sword, he ever proved that. But I couldn't necessarily tell you where he is just now. We got separated."

Marion's imagination lurched, to wonder what danger they had put themselves in. This was the last place Robin should be. "John, catch your breath." She poured him a glass of water from the decanter on her bedside. "Slow down and talk to me. Let me see your wounds."

"Get on." He swatted her away.

"Why are you here?"

He reached for the glass but gave up, letting himself slide against the wall to an armless chair by her vanity. His face bulged red and he wheezed when he breathed, he managed to answer without even a trace of irony, "We're here to rescue you."

Whatever sickness it was that made men confuse idiocy for chivalry, Marion was glad it was not contagious. "You're here to rescue me. Who's *we*?"

"Robin and I?" He seemed to fear his answer was incorrect.

"You came alone?"

"No!" he protested. "There was a girl that came as well."

There were no words, so Marion simply stared at him.

"Admittedly, it made more sense earlier."

"Here's the tricky part, John." She waited for his eyes to focus on her, blinking away his distractions. "What are you rescuing me *from*?"

"From the Sheriff," he answered proudly. "From his . . ." and he paused, looking about the room for the first time since he'd entered. She could imagine his surprise at the full-canopied bed, the ornate French wardrobe and writing desk, a platter of fruit, bottle of modest wine, the open window. She could read it on John's face. This was no prison cell. ". . . from his clutches."

"His clutches." Marion checked herself, but remained as thoroughly unclutched as ever. "It isn't that I don't appreciate the gesture, but when have you known me to be incapable of taking care of myself?"

He snorted, still stubborn. "Well we're not only here for you, don't get a head about it. We've come to stop the Sheriff."

"Stop him from doing what?"

"He's going to burn down the Sherwood, Marion." John said it as if he were serious. She laughed, but it only fueled him. "He signed an edict, and if we don't stop him by morning then he'll burn it down at first light."

"What? That's ridiculous. He's not going to burn down the forest."

"He is."

"He is not!" She could barely contain herself, every statement John made was more ludicrous than the last. "Do you have even the slightest idea of how much work that would take? It couldn't be done in a month, much less a morning. Much less *this* morning. Besides, I wouldn't let him."

"You wouldn't let him?" John rubbed his eyebrows and calmed himself, finally taking in a slow steady mouth of air. "What's going on here?"

"You first, John. What do you think is going on here?"

"We thought the Sheriff captured you, and was forcing you to marry him."

Marion blinked.

"Is that not true?"

"I am going to marry him."

"We have to stop that."

She knew it would break his heart. "No, you don't."

There was noise outside from the window, more shouts, but neither of them paid it mind. It was Robin, she knew it, out there somewhere. But her world had grown so very far from his now. The clatter moved from one side of the yard to the other until finally it disappeared again beneath a riot of dogs barking. John's lips trembled and his face winced. "You care to fill me in on the why?"

If ever there was someone that should have understood, it had to be him. "What have we been doing, John? All this time, what have we been trying to do? The new taxes cut a division in Nottinghamshire that has become worse and worse. Lord Walter tried to take care of the people that were left behind. After him, we tried to find our own way in the woods. But it didn't work, and ever since it's been all we can do just to keep the pieces near each other."

She had genuinely believed they were building something, but the previous weeks had proven that her efforts were more akin to applying bandages.

"What did we think would happen, living in the woods and stealing from nobility?" It was a question as much for him as it was for a younger version of herself. "This wasn't ever what we wanted. I know some of the boys think they're accomplishing great things by pissing on the Sheriff's boots, but we were wrong."

"Were we?" His face frowned. "Were we wrong to help people?"

"We were doing it the wrong way, John. I wanted a place where people could make decisions for themselves, where they didn't have to fear the head of a household. And we successfully took away the power and the fear the master had, but we gave every bit of it to the servant. What Will and Elena did, they did it because we convinced them they had a right to do it. We swung too far, don't you see? There needs to be a balance. And for the balance to work, there need to be rules."

John shook his head, but out of confusion, not refusal.

"We were trying to effect change from the bottom, pushing up, John. But by marrying William, I can do it from the top, pushing down. That's where the power is."

His brow was full of questions.

"Wendenal wants peace. He does." William was a sharp man, and not so enamored with politics yet as to behave like a politician. "He has a better chance of putting Nottinghamshire back together than anyone else who would claim the title. But he has no backing. His father is notable, yes, but his influence ends at Derbyshire's borders. Lord Gisbourne challenges William's authority daily, and has the ear of powerful men who don't care whether there is enough grain to feed the needy. We cannot suffer anyone but William to hold the Sheriff's seat. I've promised him I would do everything in my ability to help him."

John's bloodshot eye glistened. "By marrying him?"

"By marrying into my family, yes. My father is the castellan of London, my grandfather a baron and the Earl of Essex. And of course my cousins John and Richard, but they're only royalty."

John Little smiled at that. His will had at last softened.

"He needed allies, and I am valuable at that. A bit controversial, I've come to realize, but valuable nonetheless. Our betrothal will stay the hand of those that would seek to destroy him before he begins. It will give him the chance to strengthen his position, to make himself unrootable."

"So then," John struggled, "it's just for show?"

"A bit. But I *will* marry him."

"But why?"

"John, this helps me, too!" Marion flinched, trying to unfold his confusion. He only knew her through Locksley, through their time in the Sherwood. None of them ever truly understood the other half of her life, her struggles for agency in London's courts. This marriage was no punishment, it was opportunity. "I'll be able to actually make a difference. With more powerful connections, I can influence policy. I can protect you all much better from here than anywhere else. The answer was never to get rid of the Sheriff, the answer is to *work with him*. And that's what I'll be doing."

"Work with him?" John asked. Whatever hideous image he had built in his mind that defined William, he could not seem to let go of it. That was precisely the type of thinking that led Will Scarlet to kill de Lacy. "You don't honestly think he'll listen to you?"

Marion sighed. "He *does* listen to me. He already has. He came to me in Sheffield, John, for advice in this. William knew he couldn't keep his position for long. He assumed he might only have power for a week, two if he were lucky. So he asked me for advice on what he could accomplish in that time."

It had been such a bittersweet visit. The new Sheriff of Nottingham had personally asked her what he should do to help its people, which was as close to a miracle as Marion could ever have hoped for. But she told William the truth, which was that he could not accomplish anything at all that could not be undone just as swiftly. True reform takes time. But time was precisely what she was able to offer him.

It had meant changing everything. Leaving the community she had grown to love, leaving Robin. But those sacrifices were nothing compared to what she could accomplish, the lasting effects that would benefit them all. Not just for now, but potentially for generations.

"I was the one to convince him he should stay, that he could keep the power if he was able to properly support his leadership. Marriage was my idea, John."

He looked both shamed and proud, a father who had underestimated his own daughter. He neither protested nor pouted, despite the enormous effort he had made to come find her. Instead he opened his hands and laughed. "Well, what in the hell am I doing here?"

Marion felt a weight lift from her, and she touched her hands to his cheeks.

He smiled and patted her softly. "Why didn't you tell us?"

The question was alarming. "I thought you knew," she said. "Sir Amon told me he brought you the news."

"He did," John nodded slowly, "but now for the life of me I can't recall how he phrased it. He certainly didn't give the impression it was your idea. But he didn't stay long."

Marion's heart clenched. To think they had been worrying about her all this time. They had organized to *rescue* her, of all ungodly things. "I asked Amon to tell you to stay away from this, to not come after me. Did he not say that?"

"He did. But we thought you were just trying to protect us. Thought you were being selfless."

"It was an *order,* John. I gave it for a reason."

"We didn't know."

Marion cursed under her breath, that a misunderstanding could carry such consequences. "I'm so sorry," was all she could say, "I thought he made it clear."

John shook his head, sadly, but his pout pursed into a smile that let out his familiar laugh. "Well, damned if we didn't have the whole thing wrong! We thought he locked you up in some tower and meant to marry you by force."

"How on earth would that help him?" She joined him in laughter. "Who would respect a union made that way? It's the stupidest thing I've ever heard."

"I don't know." He shook his head. "I don't suppose we thought much about it." John shrugged his shoulders as he put it all together.

"I wanted to send more messages, but I was hardly at liberty." She pointed at the door.

John followed her with a curious face. "That'd be my next question. If you're not a prisoner, why is there a guard outside your door?"

"There are normally two guards outside my door."

"There was only one," he said guiltily. "I may have clobbered him."

"Oh dear."

"Why are they guarding you if you're here on your own?"

"They're not guarding me." She could be proud of this one. "They're afraid of me. The Captain of the Guard thinks I may be a spy, so he has them watch me day and night. If it weren't so annoying it would be quite flattering. But if I sent Sir Amon again, they would have known. And then they would have found you."

John humphed. Finally he took the glass of water and stood, stretching his back and slapping his arms. She noticed a wet dark circle at his side. "You're bleeding."

"Probably."

"Let me see that," she reached out, but he twisted away.

"It's nothing." He stretched his body around to prove it. "But I'm too old for this. Maybe ten years ago, but I'm not as strong as I remember myself."

Marion tugged at his lapel, straightening it out. "Don't sell yourself short."

He sighed and patted her leg, leaning back and taking in the room again. "So he's not so bad then, this William de Wendenal?"

"Not at all." Marion thought on it. In the admittedly short time she had known him, William had shown a degree of responsibility and temperance she had rarely seen. "He reminds me quite a bit of Robin."

John didn't respond, but held her gaze. He always had that way of looking into someone's eyes, deeper, as if he were reading a person's soul. "But you don't love William."

She had to look away. "There is that distinction."

"Marion—"

"It's fine."

In many ways, William was a better man than Robin. But circumstance had given William an opportunity to use his talents for good, while Robin had always struggled with his place in life. Still, John was right. Love had little regard for logic.

"You were lucky, John. You and Marley shared so much together. Not everyone has the luxury of marrying someone they love. It's a silly thing. William is a loyal and decent man. And he's pretty, I like pretty things." She tried to get John to laugh, but he no longer seemed interested. "In his own way, at least. I could certainly end up with a lot worse."

"I think that may be why Robin wants to rescue you."

"Why?"

"He probably loves you."

"He probably does."

There wasn't anything else to say about it. Letting her thoughts linger on Robin, that was better not done. Their entire lives had been like two boats on a river, side by side for a moment but then drifting away from each other, only to come back and away again, endlessly. For so long, she had seen her own boat as constant while his went weaving. He would always try too hard, try to be just slightly more man than he was. And when he failed, his emotions flared and he pushed himself away in the current. All she ever wanted was for him to accept himself, and what had happened. But he bore his brother's act as if it were his own, always overcompensating. Always trying to impress her enough to make it go away, to make up for things that could never be undone. It had taken him years to return to her, to finally claim ownership of his misgivings, and seize responsibility for those he taught. When they kissed under the eaves of the Oak Camp, she thought their boats were finally side by side, as she had long hoped.

And then she'd suddenly keeled her own boat toward the farthest bank.

"So that's it?" John asked.

"As I said," she stood, with finality, "I don't get that luxury. What I can accomplish here is far more important." She forced herself to forget about Robin. To forget he was here, that he was here for her. "You should go find him. I don't know that I can protect you if they find you in here with me."

"Well," John said, slapping his knees and standing, "that certainly isn't how I thought this would go."

He opened his arms for her and she went right to him, letting him wrap around her, squeezing. She buried her forehead into his chest, ignoring the rank of his sweat. She couldn't help but wonder when next she would be able to embrace him.

"You're a good man, John Little."

"You know what, Lady Marion?" He raised an eyebrow and looked down at her. "You're a better man than I am."

She laughed and had to dab at her eyes to dry them. "Oh, am I?"

"That you are." He let her go, and turned to unwedge his staff from the door. But as soon as he touched it, he froze. "Oh hell, you don't know."

"Don't know what?"

His face lost all the love that made it so gentle a moment ago. "Elena. She took her own life, Marion."

He might as well have punched her in the chest.

"She broke out of the prison with Will, but things went bad. Alan's dead, too, and Lord Gisbourne, and more than a few others. Some men from Bernesdale that got involved."

The floor of the room dove down—it spun sickeningly away and her legs were a hundred stories tall. Marion bent over in shock.

"Stop it, John!" she yelled.

"It was such a fury, everyone's tempers were up, I don't know—"

"*Stop it!* What are you doing? What the hell are you all doing out there? Don't you see you're making it worse?" She wanted to grab him and shake him, to shake all of them, to go and put them in a box where they couldn't do themselves any more damage. "I'm trying to save you, that's why I'm here! I'm trying to save all of you, but I can't do it if you keep running around killing each other!"

"I'm sorry." He looked devastated, as he should. "We were just doing what you told us to do."

"Did I tell you to come here? Or did I specifically tell you not to? Did I tell you to kill Gisbourne?"

"We thought you were captive, Marion . . . we didn't know . . ."

"What have you done?" Her thoughts threw to the gallows outside, and the hanging tomorrow. Gisbourne's death, Scarlet's escape, it meant immediate danger for William, for his hold on the sheriffcy, and by extension her own safety. "What is wrong with you? *Lord Gisbourne?*"

Little bobbed his head. "Robin."

Her mind staggered at the consequences, racing down cruel paths that had no end. "Dear God. And then you two came here? You killed the Captain and came here afterward? Have any of you, *have any one of you* ever stopped to think about what you do? I can't help you now, don't you see that? If they catch Robin they'll put him on the gallows tomorrow. Why in the hell would you do that?"

"We didn't know."

What a worthless bunch of words. "*You should have known better!*"

"You didn't tell us what you were doing."

"Get out of here!" She pointed at the door so harshly it could have cracked. "Before somebody sees you, get Robin, get out of Nottingham, right now! Let me make my instructions unmistakably clear this time. I command you to get Robin back to the others, and just . . . just *do nothing.* For God's sake, for once, just do nothing. Don't rescue anyone, don't kill anyone. Get drunk, sleep for a week, and let me handle this!" Her face burned, her hands clenched into fists, she wanted to rip the walls down. She didn't mean to take it out on him, but he could take it. "We are on the verge of bringing things back to some kind of order here, we are on the edge, the very edge of succeeding—for once!—but you all just keep stirring things up!"

John put his hands up. "Alright, alright. I'm sorry. I'll go."

"Good God, find Robin before he does anything stupid." A dozen more nightmares went through Marion's mind, all of increasingly idiotic acts that Robin might think were justified, all to prove himself to her. He was still trying to save her.

John said what Marion was thinking. "I don't think he'll leave without you."

"Tell him I'm not here. Tell him I'm somewhere else."

"He won't believe that."

"Then tell him you found me and I'm already gone." The words came out as quickly as she thought them, overlapping his excuses. "That I left the castle first and will meet you at the camp, and you two ought to hurry and catch up with me. Tell him he'll see me tomorrow."

John's mouth twisted into a knot. "He won't appreciate being lied to."

She had to get him out of the castle, before it was too late. "Please, do this one thing for me, get him out of Nottingham. Tomorrow you can tell him the truth, and you can tell him I ordered you to lie about it."

"He'll come back for you."

"Then tell him I love William!"

John knew she didn't mean it. "I couldn't."

"Fine! Tell him I love him! What does it matter?" It wouldn't matter if he knew, it wouldn't matter if she said it, not like this. They had driven everything to the edge, the terrible lip beyond which nothing mattered at all. "I don't care what you tell him, just don't let him come back here. That goes for you, too, you cannot ever come back here. Ever, do you understand me? Some day in the future, a month, a year, I will call for you. Until then, my instructions stand. *Do nothing.*"

Poor John Little, he had meant so well. His mouth opened and closed, his eyes watered and he held his breath.

"Robin is here," he tried, "and he's fighting for the people."

"No he's not," Marion sighed, the truth of it crushing her. "He's fighting for the dream I sold him, and I was *wrong,* John. I was wrong." Her eyes welled up, her throat closed. "Don't mistake me, I was happier than anyone that he came back to help, but it wasn't because he believed in helping us. He's just fighting because he doesn't want to disappoint me, again. If he genuinely had the people in mind, he wouldn't have led you here, *here.* It makes no sense to come here, except that he can't stand the guilt of leaving me."

John hesitated.

"That's always been the way with him," she continued. "With Much, with his brother, with me. He's always fighting because of the things he *didn't* do. He's never fighting *for* something. He doesn't care about what comes with success, he's just afraid of what comes with failure. You think he *cared* about the Crusade? You think he *cared* about his father, or us?"

"I think he cares about you."

It was her turn to falter.

"So he fights because of his mistakes, so what?" John asked. "He's fighting now because he doesn't want to make another one. Because he knows what happens when he does nothing—he loses someone he loves. And you're next on that list."

She bit her lip. It didn't matter if he was right. "I'm sorry, John."

When finally he let it go, it came as a rolling groan, and a great melancholy seemed to overtake him. He turned his back to her and let the door drift a few inches open. "We were just trying to do right by our own."

"I know," she cried, just for a moment, and regained herself. "We all are."

He nodded, respectfully, and put his fist to his chest. "M'lady."

He opened the door wide and left. She thought about stopping him. She could summon Sir Amon, to help find Robin get them out safely. Even as John's shape lumbered away, even as she watched him heave to a run down the corridor. Until it was no longer an option. How easily she might have helped, but she didn't. She couldn't. There would be consequences, cruel consequences, and there was more at stake here than yesteryear's memories of lost love.

Everything, *everything* she'd been working toward in Nottingham had led to this. More than a few times she had worried about the risks, about the selfishness she feared within herself. There was no pretending she did not envy the power she was finally so close to claiming, and she knew its cost. But if Robin ruined this, if Marion ended up in the woods running from the law, every life lost was an unconscionable waste. Here, at the head of the city, she could finally make right on the wake of pain that had brought her here. It was a bittersweet victory, but the only kind she could ever expect.

Well after John was gone, she realized she was staring at the gallows again, imagining what Robin's neck would look like with a rope around it. She pictured him looking out in the crowd, finding her, whispering her name just before he dropped. She ran back to the door and locked it, as if shutting out the world could make it smaller and less important. She went to the mirror and her hairbrush and told herself that Robin would escape, and that he'd understand.

They would have to say goodbye to whatever selfish fantasies they may have once had. Those dreams belonged to young Marion Fitzwalter, but not to Lady Marion de Wendenal. Both of them had to recognize it, that their boats would never again drift together, because they were no longer going to the same harbor. They had come to a fork. Two different boats. Two rivers. She tried to convince herself. She brushed her hair so hard she bled.

FIFTY-FIVE

ROBIN OF LOCKSLEY

NOTTINGHAM CASTLE

ROBIN SMASHED HIS WEIGHT into the door. Its answer came in the form of a sharp crack, but it did not open. His shoulder swore at him, but he had no time to waste. Instead he leveraged his weight against the opposite wall of the narrow stone hallway and kicked at the door's handle, satisfied with its splintering response. He burst upon a room too tiny to be burst upon, containing little aside from a crude oak desk and a man who had once been his closest friend, clambering to the far side.

"How did I know you'd be hiding in here?" Robin growled.

The highest room of Nottingham's highest tower was the only place pompous enough for what William had become. Robin should have started his search here. He could have avoided all the troubles that were, at this moment, shortly behind him. He could only hope the makeshift barricade he created at the base of the staircase would slow them down, almost as much as he hoped for some clever means of escape to reveal itself before then.

Between the inevitability of those two moments, there was just him and William.

"Hello, Robin," William said.

And the squire.

"Sheriff Wendenal!" Gisbourne's squire burst into the room as well. He pinched his little weasel face into a little weasel scowl, and held his bent braquemar up as if he knew which end was the dangerous one. "The outlaws are inside the castle walls, they are—"

"Here, yes, they're right here!" William interrupted. "Look, he's in this very room! Watch out for the outlaw!"

Despite the ridiculous dimension of their room, Robin found a position to triangulate between them, his bastard sword held at a readiness that might take him toward either one. William appeared unarmed, but he also appeared too dressed for the late hour, and Robin did not intend on being caught by surprise again.

Robin had failed to anticipate that any of Gisbourne's crew might follow them to Nottingham so swiftly—the squire had been quick to rally the castle's host to action only minutes after Arable snuck them through the postern gate. Robin had been separated from John Little after a brawl in a dining hall, and could not reliably account for much of what had passed since then.

"Robin, will you sit down, please?" William gestured to one of two chairs in the room. "You look exhausted. Let me get you something to drink."

Robin flinched toward him, staying him from whatever weapon he meant to find. "You're not going anywhere."

"That's true," William said with minor annoyance. "You are both in my way. Very well. Ferrers, could you get us some drinks please?"

Ferrers. Robin swiveled to scrutinize the squire's face. A son, no doubt, of the earl who died in Acre. Stabbed by the young foreign boy—Stabhappy—that Robin had shown mercy. The world was entirely too small.

Ferrers postured nervously. "Get you *what*?"

"Some drinks!" William repeated, almost celebratory. "For Christ's sake, why must everything be so difficult? Is anyone capable of simply talking to each other anymore?"

Though his muscles seized, Robin returned his sword in line with William's chest. "The time for talking is over."

William puffed out his cheeks. "Well, that was dramatic, thank you." A lone fingertip slowly moved the tip of Robin's blade with curiosity. William noticed the wound on the back of Robin's hand. "You're bleeding."

"He'll do more than that." Ferrers made a sound exactly as threatening as a weasel choking. If he had any sort of competence with a sword Robin might worry, as the half reach of his braquemar was far better suited for the small room than Robin's own full-length—

"Get out of here!" William admonished the squire. "Get us some drinks—and some *gauze*—and tell everyone else to settle down."

His mouth fluttered about, searching for a response. "They snuck in through the servants' gate," Ferrers explained. "There's another one—"

"Ferrers!" William shouted again, using it as both the name and the insult. He pointed out the door, as if it were not obvious that Ferrers was unwelcome. Robin did not mind the pause. He took the opportunity to catch his breath, to steady his nerves, to prepare for what had to follow. Ferrers eventually left, the door floating shut of its own accord, the broken plank keeping it slightly ajar.

"I'm sorry about that," William chuckled, as if they had nothing to deal with other than idle banter. "You could have told me you were coming, you know? Would you put that away? This room is tiny, what do you suppose you're going to do with it?"

William batted at Robin's sword again, but Robin did not let his casual swagger sway him. Of course he would try to downplay everything. He knew he was in the wrong, so he was appealing toward Robin's sympathies.

The words rose from a place of fury in Robin's gut. "You're a traitor to the King, William."

"What? Who have you been talking to?" William sat on his side of the table, kicking beneath it at the other chair. "Have a seat."

The chair slid across the cobbled floor, caught a stone, and tumbled over, which was perfectly fine. Robin had neither the time nor the desire to sit.

"I've been talking to your dog, Lord Gisbourne. He brought me this." Robin withdrew the edict, stamped equally now in both wax and blood. He threw it onto the table for William to deny. "Are you going to tell me that's not your signature?"

There was only a low, selfish sort of laughter from William, as he poked the paper with two fingers. "Do you think I'm insane? I'm not going to burn down a forest. This was just a ruse, it was Gisbourne's idea, he insisted upon it. He thought it might lure you out into the open." He chuckled a bit more, tapping the table in delight. "Apparently it worked!"

"It bears your signature!"

"If I thought you'd actually fall for it, I wouldn't have signed it. Robin, this is a delicate position, I think you could appreciate that. Anything I could do to keep Gisbourne off my back was worth it. I'm barely keeping things from unraveling here." He traced his fingers through the papers on his desk, as if his menial administrative tasks could in any way compare to what Robin's men had experienced. "What about you, how are things going on your end?"

"How are they going?" There was a pile of bodies in the forest outside Bernesdale that answered the question. Many of them were good men who had come to defend Robin in the middle of the night. One of them died by Robin's own hand, his mind lost to the bloodlust. Once this was over he would deal with those ramifications, but for now he forced it to a corner of his mind. And William wanted to know *how things were going.* He answered. "You're killing people!"

"Robin, where are you?" William clapped his hands. "You're not talking to an enemy, this is me, your friend, you remember that, don't you? I know we had . . . heated words when last we saw each other, but that doesn't change who we are. I know where your heart lies, I know you wanted to protect those people. But you're not safe here. You come in here, waving a sword around . . . don't you think you've taken this too far?"

The casual razing of a forest, the destruction of thousands of people's homes, and William thought that trying to save lives was *taking it too far.* Robin could barely recognize his old friend. "I'm not the one who declared myself Sheriff."

"I didn't declare myself Sheriff."

"That's not what Arable says."

"Arable—*what*?" William's calm demeanor instantly gave way to a shocked panic. "What did she say to you?"

"Well, that got your attention. She told me all about the letter from Prince John. Maybe you remember it? The one stating Roger de Lacy was to be replaced by Lord Gisbourne? The one you told her to burn, while you forged documents to claim the seat for your own?" She had explained every step of William's coup.

He responded without a hint of his previous levity. "There's no proof."

At that, Robin could laugh. "Arable didn't burn it, William. She gave it to me."

"She *what*? Arable, goddamn it, what have you done?" That affected him. William stood, hands out but with nothing to do. The trap was closing. He would have to give up, there was no other choice.

Robin pushed harder. "You are acting in direct opposition to an order from the prince, and you have disregarded the commands of King Richard himself.

You have practically staged a rebellion by illegally taking control of Nottingham Castle!"

"Now wait just a moment. Robin—"

"Then you order the murder of my men on no grounds, you abduct Lady Marion and force a marriage upon her . . ."

"What?"

". . . all in the name of order? In the name of peace?" Robin's words came out faster than he could think them. "You sign an edict to raze the forest, to scare hundreds of people from their homes, as a joke? Families are fleeing in the middle of the night, this is safety to you? This is why you deserted the war, to seize power and terrorize the innocent?"

"Robin, slow down. Let me explain myself."

But the door opened to his left and Robin startled, wielding his sword around. For a dreadful heartbeat he thought he had dallied too long, that the rest of the Nottingham Guard had found him. But it was just Ferrers. A silver platter of wine rested in his hands and a stretch of widow-lace gauze lay over his right forearm. His sword, at least, was left behind.

"Ah, thank you." William cleared a space on the desk for the wine glasses. "Right here, please. Would you do me the favor of dressing the wound on Robin's hand?"

"I gave that to him," Ferrers stated, his face assuming something he would probably call pride.

"All the more reason!" William snapped. But Ferrers seemed uninterested in debasing himself that far. He gently tossed the gauze, allowing it to float down onto the table, and proceeded to set the bottle and each glass down. One glass in front of William and the other by Robin, positioned as close as possible while staring at the blade in Robin's hands. Robin was aware of the ache in his muscles. His sword's tip drooped, he had been holding it aloft for too long.

William pointed to the glass. "Here, Robin, drink."

"Why," Robin sneered, "so you can poison me as well?"

William paused, he seemed genuinely hurt. With a slow gesture, he reached across the table to pluck up Robin's glass, brought it to his lips and pulled. He rolled the wine in his mouth, swallowed as loudly as he could, wiped his face with his forearm and smacked his lips with condescending spectacle. After not dying, he returned the glass to the edge of the table for Robin.

For the first time since entering the castle, Robin's conviction wavered.

"I'm not trying to kill you, Robin. If that was my design, I could have done it by now. I'm not staging a rebellion. I'm not deserting a war. I'm not chasing people out of their homes. And I'm certainly not forcing anyone into a marriage. You, on the other hand," he angled forward forcefully, leaning his elbows on the table, "have taken control of a band of mercenaries. You're calling the people to revolt during wartime. Your men have been responsible for the assassination of a High Sheriff . . . what else? The least of your offenses, stealing from the King's resources, is—if I may remind you—what we came back to

England in the first place to stop! So you tell me, which one of us is more likely a traitor to the King?"

A mote of dust floated down and up again, carried by the heat of the room's candles. Robin squinted, softly shaking his head. "You were never appointed Sheriff. You're sitting on a throne you *stole,* and you call me a traitor?"

It took a moment of decision, but William ground his jaw and accepted the answer. "Saying I stole it is a bit theatrical," he said. "I'm finishing de Lacy's legacy. Would you honestly prefer Lord Gisbourne as Sheriff? A man who would rather kill all those who oppose him, who steals from the poor and gives to the rich? Ask this man, his assistant. Tell me honestly," he asked Ferrers, "how would your captain fare as Sheriff?"

"Deplorably," Ferrers answered without hesitation.

"That's what I'm up against."

William brushed his hair from his face, shifting his feet in rapid little circles. "Do you think the people would be safer under his command? I'm trying to protect them, same as you. Damn it, Robin, you would have done the same thing. If we had changed places, if our roles had been reversed. When we were attacked in the woods, if your leg hadn't been injured, if you had run and I stayed instead. You would have done this the same as I. Every step along the way."

"I say *deplorably,*" Ferrers continued, "largely because he is dead. Robin cut his throat out in the Sherwood."

The image was burned in Robin's mind, bathed in red. He had always thought it was a metaphor, but the world had lost all definition, turned the color of blood. His reactions had been instinctive, but he could not pretend they were not his.

William's jaw dropped to his chest. "You can't . . . this . . ." He slumped back down into the chair. "You can't just go around killing public officials whenever it suits you!"

"And you can't just slap on a warcrown every time you think you know better!" Robin returned, regaining his composure. It startled William, as if he thought Robin might forget his history in seizing power. "*Step down.* If you took the Sheriff's office to prevent Gisbourne from doing so, as you claim, then prove it. He's no longer a threat, not to you, not to anyone. Step down, and release Marion."

"Marion," William snatched the name, plucking it from the air with his hand. "Is that why you're here? Is that all it comes down to?"

It was not a subject for him to broach. Robin repeated his question, "Will you step down?"

"Why, because you fancy her? Because you're jealous? You can't see beyond that?"

Don't let him twist this. "You know you won't, because you like the power." Robin raised his sword again, perfectly horizontal over the table, his muscles fighting back. "You don't care about peace, or about protecting the people, those are just your excuses. All you really care about is yourself. King William!"

"Myself? What have I gained from this?" He slammed his fist on the table, rattling its contents. "I am surrounded by strangers and enemies, all of which seek my destruction! I still try to find a peace for people that hate me, while you call yourself noble for surrounding yourself with admirers. The great Robin Hood, the savior of the people! *You* accuse *me* for thinking too much of myself? You teach the people songs defiling me and calling me a villain, and they believe the tripe about you. A thousand people saying you're right doesn't make it true. Look beyond yourself!"

"And yet when a thousand people say you're wrong," Robin rolled his head, "you take it as proof you're right."

Out the window behind William, a slight blue warmth caught Robin's attention, the first sign of the coming dawn in the sky beyond the city. A blur in his vision spoke to how many hours he had been awake, and active. He had to settle this soon.

"I can make a difference, Robin." William was stammering. "With Marion by my side, I can restore a peace here—"

"I will denounce you," Robin closed his eyes, refusing to let him speak of her. His sword wavered. "I will show everyone that letter from Prince John."

"Prince John supports me!" William threw his hands out wide. "He's here! He's . . . two floors down! Shall we go ask him together?"

"Then I'll take it to the Chancellor," Robin answered. "I'll send a message to Richard himself and detail every step of your treason. What, then, will be the point of marrying Marion? Step down, William!"

"*And then what?*" William erupted, his face flush. "Who will take my place? If not Gisbourne, then who? You and I should know better than anyone. It doesn't matter who wears the crown, the orders are the same. If you kill the king, there's another one behind him. What did killing Roger de Lacy get you? Me. What would denouncing me get you? Hm? This man, perhaps." He flung his hand at Ferrers. "William de Ferrers, why not? His father is the Earl of Derbyshire, so let's make him Sheriff. So, what would you do if you were Sheriff, Ferrers?"

Again, the lad's answer was immediate. "I'd raze the forest."

"You see?" William snapped his teeth together, turning his back to Robin. "I can make this better! I can enforce peace over revenge! This isn't a war. You don't win by killing the most people! There are those who would sit here and do just that. We should be working together—I need your *help* Robin, but all you offer me are threats."

"You call it peace," Robin sighed, "but you're building it on lies. Peace needs to be built with trust, William. It will all come crumbling down when your corruption is exposed, and you'll do far more damage in the long run. You're not creating anything. All you're doing is destroying."

William struggled for words, because they couldn't support him. His voice was strained, he was begging, because it was all he could do. "I am Nottingham's only hope."

"What you are," Robin's lips tightened, "is a tyrant."

They both gasped for air, eyes red, almost at tears. William opened his arms wide, every word slick with emotion. "How long have you known me?"

He took a half step forward until his chest met the point of Robin's sword. *And he leaned.* He pushed his weight onto its tip, forcing Robin to pull back a hair. William grabbed the sword with both hands and centered it on his chest. Once more he pushed forward, he winced briefly in pain but Robin instinctively pulled the sword away. He saw the blood, he saw the faces of the men he'd already killed this night, and suddenly his composure cracked to realize who he was threatening.

His sword dropped to his side. Robin's entire body sagged with exhaustion, and the two stared at each other, utterly barren.

"I won't kill you." Robin had nothing of his own to call a voice. "But I won't back down on this."

William nodded, as if he expected the answer. Quietly, "Can you even tell me why? What are you even fighting for?"

"I'm fighting for the people."

"No, you're not. You're fighting because you think it's the noble thing to do. It's the thing *Robin Hood* would do. You're just trying to live up to some fantasy, so you can spew out worthless phrases such as *'I'm fighting for the people.'*"

The damned thing about William was that he was always right, he had perfected the art. "But that doesn't make me wrong," Robin said.

Maybe earlier, but not now. Now he was fighting for his father, he was fighting for Alan-a-Dale, he was fighting for Much. For Stabhappy. For his brother Edmond. He fought for Marion, for her sister. For Robin Hood, whoever the hell that was.

FIFTY-SIX

WILLIAM DE WENDENAL

NOTTINGHAM CASTLE

THE TWO MEN STARED at each other, both knowing their words had long failed them. If there was any solution left, it lay in the sword by Robin's side. He would have to use it or give up, there was no middle ground. One of them would have to break, and there was too much at stake for it to be William. Of course it was tempting, to walk away from all this madness. He longed to travel with his old friend Robin again at the king's side, where right and wrong were neatly delineated by the war's front line.

But that was the very reason he was needed here, because he could think in terms of grey, surrounded by people who had never heard of it. Robin couldn't see his proverbial forest from his trees. He had to back down.

They breathed each other's air, one inhaling as the other exhaled, two halves of a pump that kept the room alive. Their eyes were locked and William searched desperately for any sign of understanding. The moment lasted a few seconds, then longer, ten, twenty. It was a comically long time for nobody to speak, but it told William what he needed to know.

Eventually, instead of a flash of violence, William ended the silence with a long slow sigh. He dropped his head and brushed his hair from his face. It was objectively ridiculous, the two of them, squared off in de Lacy's office, the whole world rallied around their shoulders. He slid into his chair, which creaked stubbornly to take him. Robin's grim demeanor now seemed forced and out of place, and William couldn't keep himself from smiling.

"Well, this is stupid."

Robin's face relaxed. He slumped back against the wall, he looked too weak to keep standing. Then his face turned quizzical, he raised one hand limply and pointed at the wall behind William's back.

"Hm?" William twisted around. Robin had noticed the metal wreath William had salvaged from Locksley Castle. It had been cleaned now of its ash, its red and bronze colors brilliantly capturing the room's candlelight.

"Sorry, Robin, I didn't think you'd ever see that. I hope you don't mind." He reached up and plucked it from the nail where it hung, careful of its crooked pointed leaves pricking out at odd angles. "You left without it. I didn't want it to get destroyed."

"It's fine," Robin replied softly. "I don't think I would have gone back for it."

"I liked what you said about it." William held it up with two fingers, slowly rotating its frame, watching the light worm around its edges. "Something about the mistakes that we make, and that we keep making."

Again they caught each other's eyes, and finally Robin smiled, albeit sadly. It had been some time since he had seen Robin's smile, which was a lot to say.

William returned the wreath to the wall, watching the warped reflection of the room behind him. He suddenly realized his back was exposed to a man who was carrying a sword, and he burst out laughing.

"What?" Robin asked.

"You pointed behind me, and I looked!" William was nearly hysterical. "Master tactician here!"

Robin eased as he understood, and chuckled at the absurdity.

"Didn't think it could be that easy, did you?" William could barely speak through his laughter. "*What's that over there?* Stab."

"I honestly didn't think about it," Robin answered, but his smile broke wide.

"Neither did I," William sighed. That there, that was everything about them. It was a thousand shared memories of unflinching trust, a comfort in one another that spanned years and years, in any language, in any war. And *God,* how William had missed it. "I would have been so shocked. I would have made the same face you made when you were shot with that arrow."

"Ah." Robin chuckled as well. "Did I make a face?"

"You made a face."

"Well, in my defense, I had just been shot with an arrow."

"Oh no," William put his hands up, "you were amazing. You didn't scream at all. The arrow went right through your leg and into the horse, and you still had every wit about you, calling out, *'Hold, hold!'* to the men. It was a sight, let me tell you. An army enraged, all halted in midstep." He shook his head. "I doubt I could have done that."

Robin's chest shook up and down silently, then he rolled from a private little laugh to a full one. "I wasn't calling out *'Hold!'* to the men. I was talking to my horse!"

William couldn't believe it. "You're fucking kidding me."

"No, I didn't want him to run away, we were pinned together!"

"You—" William slapped the table in shock, replaying the event in his mind. *Robin, his sword held high, commanding his men to hold . . .* "I thought you were the bravest man I'd ever seen that day."

"Nope," Robin could barely contain himself, "I was talking to my horse."

He was talking to his horse.

It was so damned easy to misread a situation, even amongst the closest of friends. William slapped the table again, overwhelmed with the ridiculousness of it all. When their laughter subsided, William reached out carefully and tapped the table by Robin's untouched glass. He still had not taken any drink, parched as he must be, despite William's assurances. What seeds of mistrust had been sown in him during his time away, it was abhorrent. Robin's smile faded, but still he couldn't trust in something as simple as a glass of wine. William stood and picked up the glass, stretching his arm out until Robin was forced to accept it.

"Thank you," he said, sipping from its top, and all the tension between them was gone. William offered the gauze as well, but Robin waved his hand, ignoring the minor wound. "If I remember correctly," he grinned whimsically, "I wasn't even supposed to be in the crown that day."

"That's right!" William snapped his fingers. "It was my day. But you . . ." He thought on it, but couldn't quite recall what had happened. "You had lost a bet the night before?"

"No, I didn't lose a bet." Robin picked up the wooden chair. "You tricked me."

"That sounds like the sort of thing I would do," he joked, though he couldn't remember the details. "Well, you shouldn't have made the bet if you knew I was up to something."

"That's true." Robin smiled. "That's true. But I didn't care."

"You were talking to your fucking horse," William repeated it, bringing tears to his eyes. He moved from behind the desk and picked up Locksley's sword, placing it on the desk as if it were not a weapon at all. Just some *thing* he didn't want his friend to forget about. Robin didn't even react that the sword had changed hands. "You know, the face you made notwithstanding, my first instinct was to laugh when you got hit with that arrow."

"Oh." Robin bobbed his head. "How nice of you!"

"But you didn't scream. You can say you were talking to your horse, Robin, but that doesn't change the fact that you didn't scream." He moved to his chair, sipping from his own glass. "What went through your head?"

Robin leaned back, trying to recall the moment, and his answer was slow and tender. "I remember that. I remember feeling it, and I looked down, and I thought, *The King shouldn't scream.* So I didn't."

He looked sideways now, and William knew what he was thinking. Richard would have respected him, to take an arrow like a king, to still stand as a beacon even with his life in danger.

"Then I remember being proud that it worked. I was actually proud they attacked me, and Richard was safe. Until then, we never really knew if we were any real use, if posing as the king was a good strategy or not. Richard said it gave him time to think, but there had never been any attempts on his life. At times, it even seemed cowardly. But when the arrow hit . . . I knew we were doing the right thing."

He would do anything, absolutely anything, for what he believed was right.

William let the moment linger. "Do you know what I was thinking?"

"What's that?"

He grinned wide. "I remember being glad it wasn't me."

"Hm." Robin sighed.

William reached over and held his glass out. "Cheers, old friend."

With a hollow tink, Robin touched the two together. "Cheers."

William took his drink in one large gulp, wincing at its bitter taste, and set it down on the table. Robin only looked into the liquid for a moment, his thoughts somewhere else entirely. When he drank it was slow, measured, but he continued to the last drop, tipping his head all the way back to finish.

As simply as snuffing a candle, William speared the small knife from his boot through the meat of his friend's neck, and instantly wept.

"I'm sorry, Robin," he cried, words so painful his throat squeezed at them to keep them in. He grabbed Robin's forehead with one hand and tore the knife downward with the other, opening the front half of Robin's throat in a torrent of blood and wine. To end it sooner, to put him from misery.

"I'm sorry," he cried, "I'm sorry. I'm so sorry."

Robin flailed, trying to claw at his own neck, but William forced his head back, letting the blood pour sickeningly forth. Robin's legs spasmed, his hands lunged for the sword on the table but William kicked it away, scattering the table's contents to the floor. Both their bodies crashed to the ground, William on top, his hands over Robin's face. "I'm sorry, Robin, please, I'm sorry, just let it go, don't fight it, let it go, let it go, I'm sorry, God, I'm sorry." Robin's body convulsed and thrashed a few more times, but eventually flickered down to mere twitches until slowly relaxing into a lump of nothing.

"I'm sorry," William kept saying, his hands and arms soaked in blood, his face pressed against his friend's. He could feel Robin's warmth fading already. "We swore an oath to the King, an oath of fidelity, an oath to protect our country from all dangers. All dangers, even from within itself, even from ourselves, even from those we love. You broke that oath, not I. All you've done is endanger the people. I couldn't let you stop this peace, you have to see that! Why wouldn't you back down? All you had to do is let this go, but you wouldn't back down!"

He then stood, ferociously, wheeling upon Ferrers, who had borne witness to all of it and stood uselessly, an exacting symbol of the people William was trying to protect. He screamed, because he had to. "There will be peace in Nottingham!"

His legs were weak and he had to lean against the wall, but still he directed all his fury and grief at Ferrers. "There will be peace, and I will be its architect. I will do it, even if I have to drag everyone along *like a child,* even if I have to kill every man who would stand in my way, I will see it done. And there isn't a friend, or a father, or a lover that is worth more than that! And if I am the only one willing to sacrifice for it, then—"

He coughed, his throat too tight to continue, he tried to speak again, but there was bile now. He hacked violently and nearly vomited. He choked and spat into his own hands, bracing himself to recover. He opened his eyes and forced himself to focus on a single spot, to pull himself back. It was the wreath he stared at, but it would not stay still, it rotated around its center, slowly, its leaves sharpening, growing.

William looked down into his hands, covered in blood, changing shape. He smeared them on his shirt and coughed again, fresh blood spattering his palm.

Not Robin's blood, not bile. His own blood.

His attention was sliding away, but his eyes made the long dangerous journey from his hands, to the wine glass on the floor, and finally, rightfully, to Ferrers.

"The Bishop of Hereford gave me the poison," Ferrers said, unmoving, leaning against the door frame that curved unnaturally taller. "Gisbourne wanted it for the assassins. He wanted a poison that would take days to work, which I did not agree with. I asked the bishop for one with more immediate results. It made our journey into the forest more interesting, for certain."

William's legs slid away from him, or he was already on the ground, he could not track which happened first. He was on his back now, though he was standing upright. The wall had become the floor and his feet only found air.

"I'll always wonder," Ferrers's voice said, "if you would have killed him without being poisoned. It's supposed to amplify your emotions, so the bishop said. Something like being drunk, I understand. I'm sad I'll never know."

The world shrank and constricted, only to balloon outward again with no warning, William rolled onto his belly to crawl. He had to get to Ferrers, he could not let this go unpunished. He could fight this, he could survive it.

"What *would* I do if I were Sheriff?" Ferrers continued, walking closer, but William could not convince his hands to work together. Ferrers swept his hand down to peel a slip of paper from the floor. William lunged for his legs but fell tragically short. Robin's sword was nearby, melting into the cobbles. William heaved his body to claim it but it vanished, floating into the sky, replaced by a weightless piece of fabric, the gauze that Ferrers had brought. "Here you are," Ferrers said, dropping the gauze into the blood, soaking up the surrounding gore. "My father isn't actually the Earl of Derbyshire anymore. He was killed in the Crusade, in Acre, you know. I don't say that casually. You knew my father was killed, and you never told me. I was only just informed a little over a week ago. That makes me the new Earl of Derbyshire, and Chancellor Longchamp assures me I have his support in leading Nottingham as well."

No, William couldn't allow it, but his body was no longer his to command. The world ceased its new fluid form and changed now into daggers. His arms and legs seized, he twisted onto his back as his muscles fought back—a thousand pains coursed through his body as his bones quivered. He could do nothing, he could say nothing. All his effort was worthless, all his life was worthless.

You could marry the King himself, and you'd still be worthless.

She was right.

His eyes alone still worked, and Ferrers leaned over him to speak.

"As per this edict, the last official act of Sheriff de Wendenal before he was slain by Robin Hood, the Sherwood Forest will be razed to the ground. Commencing tomorrow morning. To end this rebellion once and for all."

William sputtered, red mist flying into the air. The ceiling cracked and rent, the walls stabbed down into him. He was dimly aware of Ferrers, tipping the portrait of Roger de Lacy off its mount to fall into the blood. He almost did the same with the metal wreath, but instead tucked it under his arm and turned to leave. His last act was to pour a glass of wine down onto William's face. The world at last calmed, William could feel the wine splash and pool in his eye sockets. He could not blink, the world was red.

EPILOGUE

KYLE MORGAN

SHERWOOD FOREST
MONDAY, 2ND DAY OF DECEMBER 1191

KYLE HATED THAT HE was awake.

He didn't so much mind the traveling, even though he had never been comfortable on a horse nor had a horse ever been comfortable having him. He also didn't mind that they were entering the Sherwood so recently after what happened just two days earlier. Kyle tended not to mind most things. He liked that he was out of the prisons, but honestly the prisons had not been so bad. Aside from the fear they'd hang him, his cell had been a nice break from the madness of the job, which he definitely didn't care for. When it came down to it, if Kyle had to be awake, he didn't really care what it was he spent his time doing, since it was all equally miserable compared to being asleep.

He had slept all yesterday and could have slept a week longer and not been half done with it. They'd released him from his cell in the morning, which was supposed to be a kindness in that he'd get to watch the funeral and the hanging. Instead, Kyle went to sleep. A few times he had stirred when the noises of the crowd outside swelled, but he wasn't interested in whatever they made their moanings about. He was told the funeral was a sight not to be missed, but he had missed it just fine and was only the better for it. They said Robin Hood had been hanged, but some said it wasn't the real Robin Hood anyhow. They said fights broke out in the baileys, and Kyle didn't care who was involved. They said Prince John spoke for a while and that seemed pretty neat, but still not worth waking up for.

If it had been a funeral for Captain Gisbourne, Kyle might have felt the need to go. But he hadn't really known Sheriff de Lacy well, nor did he understand who the new Sheriff was before Robin Hood killed that one, too. But Kyle was proud of Ferrers for becoming the newest Sheriff. He thought that must be interesting, but probably dangerous, too, on account of so many of them dying lately. If they had asked Kyle to be Sheriff, he probably would have said no. So good for Ferrers.

"Morg! That's far enough, isn't it?" Quillen Peveril called from the horsecart. Kyle turned around slowly and grunted a response, the cask still in his arms. It wasn't as far from the road as Kyle would have liked, but he didn't care enough to argue. He set the little barrel down on the ground, though it hurt his back to bend over. The ground was a little soft from the rains the night before, and the weather was cold and seemed like to start snowing. One less reason to be awake at all.

Not so far off, Jacelyn de Lacy was placing a cask of her own against the base of a tree. "What's in these things, by the way?"

"I don't know," Kyle answered, "but they'll burn for a good long time."

"We'll put one more a bit farther in, shall we," Quill commanded from the horsecart, even though he'd just said they had placed them far enough. "Then we'll light them from the road. Morg!" He called again, gesturing to a new cask.

Kyle grunted and returned to the cart. Why Quill couldn't carry one himself, Kyle didn't know. Even Jacelyn could carry them, and she was a woman. But it wasn't worth griping about. It didn't matter to Kyle none as long as the work got done. He bent his knees to tilt another cask into his arms. Twenty more or so were on the cart bed, which they would plant at regular stops on the way back to Nottingham Castle. They'd traveled halfway to Tickhill before stopping to ready their first fire, and Kyle was eager to get it lit. Even though the trip back would take longer than the ride out, at least they'd be moving closer to home and closer to beds.

"I can't believe we're burning down the whole forest," Jacelyn said, wiping the dirt from her hands.

"It won't burn the whole forest," Peveril tisked. "But it will clear the trees away from the road. Make it harder for them to sneak up on anyone."

"Good luck with that," Jacelyn scoffed. "But I wasn't complaining. All the better if it burns them right out of the forest and into our hands."

Kyle hauled his cask off, waddling, shuffling well past where he had lain the first one.

"I don't get it," he called back to them. "We killed Robin Hood, so why bother?"

"It sends a message," Quill answered, "about keeping our promises. We cannot suffer the people to see us as weak."

Jacelyn argued something against this, but Kyle wasn't interested enough to keep listening. He kept ambling off until he seemed a good enough distance away from the previous cask to tie his lines together and they could be on their way.

The cask suddenly jumped in his arms, pushing against his chest with a sharp snap that made Kyle shout in surprise. He dropped it to the ground, scared it might light afire in his hands and roast him like a pig. But as it rolled over he noticed an arrow sticking out of its side that clearly hadn't been there earlier, its head buried in the wood not a few fingerwidths from where Kyle's right hand had been. Then there was noise all around, footsteps in the sloggy earth and the rustling of bodies, and Kyle looked up at a man holding a longbow loosely in one hand, his face completely covered by a dark brown hood.

"Another present from the Sheriff!" the stranger shouted. All around him, bodies revealed themselves from the trees, and Kyle had to admit it would have been much nicer if they hadn't. The bowman led Kyle back to the wagon, which the outlaws had circled and were claiming as their own, casks and all. Kyle half recognized a good number of their faces. There was the bald friar whose arm he had broken in Bernesdale, and the giant man who fought with the quarterstaff. A bearded villager, who had once promised to bring them information. Poor Arable was there, who he'd miss seeing around the castle, and the one they called

Lady Marion. All of them had weapons out, even Arable had a bow in her hand. Further off, Quill and Jacelyn were on their knees, their hands on their heads. A few other men behind them drove the horsecart away. *Another long walk back.* Kyle could feel his legs hurt already.

"Thank you for the delivery, gentlemen," the hooded figure bowed gracefully.

"What's wrong with you?" Kyle scolded the man. "Shooting an arrow at this?"

"Oh, you're fine," the stranger laughed. "Besides, I need you alive, to send a message to the new Sheriff."

"A message?" Kyle groaned. Seemed messages were all anyone cared about anymore. "What message?"

"You let him know this isn't over," the man said in an angry whisper. "Not by a long shot. We tried to be civil, to only take back as much as we'd lost. We tried to play *fair,* to help the people, and in return you hunted us down and named us outlaws. A funny thing, when the people running Nottingham are the filthiest thieves of them all. But that's fine. You want to make us criminals, then we're only happy to oblige. You tell your new Sheriff this—you're not ready for my brand of outlaw."

Kyle stammered to remember it all. "What are you talking about? Who . . . who are you?"

The hooded figure sprang up close and pulled his cowl back, his young face smiling, disheveled blond hair sticking to his forehead. It was the boy with the knives, the one who killed Sheriff de Lacy, the one they released from the prisons.

"God's teeth, man." The blond winked. *"I'm fucking Robin Hood."*

AUTHOR'S NOTE

This is a work of fiction, inspired in equal parts by history and folklore.

It is faithful to neither.

There's no historical consensus on whether "Robin Hood" was even a real person, much less who that person was. Even in the earliest versions of the constantly evolving legend, many acknowledged anachronisms abound. While this book explores the tale in a realistic context, many elements subscribe more to our modern romanticized version of medieval England. I have made many efforts to respect historical accounts of dates, figures, world events, even chronologically accurate phases of the moon—but I am not a historian. I have knowingly deviated from record with a few historical figures, shortened certain timelines, and omitted other elements entirely. Moreover, the sensibilities and vocabulary of many of the characters are decidedly modern—let's face it, today's curse words just pack a better punch.

So why does this book exist? As some people might ask, did we "really need" another Robin Hood story? Haven't we had enough of them already?

Well, if you want the *full* version of how and why this particular novel came to be—evolving from its first incarnation as a stage play in 2011—please visit my website, nathanmakaryk.com.

But here's the short version: I think every telling of Robin Hood so far has missed the mark in the same way. And if you've read this far, it's hopefully pretty obvious what exactly it was I hated about most Robin Hood stories. Suffice it to say that I wanted a version that explores the real dynamics at play rather than polarized ideologies. I wanted to do away with good vs. evil, and find out what happens when you pit good vs. good vs. good.

And in order to best explore that theme, I actually *needed* a story the reader would already recognize. Robin Hood has been rebooted and retold so many times that the characters have become part of our cultural knowledge. Everyone can picture a Robin Hood and a Little John in their heads, and I wanted you to bring those merry preconceptions along for the ride. I wanted you to show me what you expected from a Robin Hood story, so I could hold your hand as we tore it to pieces—and decided which parts are still worth respecting, which parts needed a deeper explanation, and which parts deserved outright mockery. I hope you enjoyed it! If not, well then I'm just one more guy who had his hand at these characters. But if you *did*, there's much more to come in the next book. . . .

ACKNOWLEDGMENTS

Unquantifiable thanks . . .

To my wife, *Cassie,* (who also belongs in several of the categories below) who kept believing this book would be published, even after years and years of that seeming painfully unlikely. For every hour I spent working on this, she sacrificed her own time to take on the lion's share of keeping the baby alive, so that I could focus on writing. She's the unsung hero that made every word in this book possible.

To my agent, the incomparable *Jim McCarthy,* who first took the chance on this book and never gave up. His patience and tenacity are solely responsible for its existence as anything other than an abandoned dream.

To my editor and tireless champion, *Bess Cozby,* whose passion and excitement made the editing process one of the best parts of this journey. She's an expert at asking the perfect questions that pushed the book to grow in the right directions, and I couldn't possibly hope for a more insightful or enthusiastic ambassador to represent the book.

To every member of the Tor/Forge publishing team who had a hand along the way, some whose names I'll never know, but am nonetheless indebted to.

To those wonderful humans who gave me valuable feedback on the early drafts:
Melanie Boudreau, Megan Heyn, Veronica Tioicha, Alexandra Wesevich

To those other humans who said they'd give me feedback and never did:
You know who you are

To the esteemed authors who gave great advice on the world of publishing to a novice who had no idea what he was getting into:
James Blaylock, Victor Koman, Kathryn Rose

To those unfortunate few with whom I could openly chat about the process:
Amy Teegan Hann, Patrick Heyn, Scott Keister

The first version of this story was a stage play I wrote, produced, and directed in 2012. Many thanks go to its spectacular cast and crew:
Frank Tryon, Michael Keeney, Andrea Dennison-Laufer, Elisa Richter, Scott Keister, Sabrina Ianacone, Larry Creagan, Jaycob Hunter, Glenn Freeze,

Jeremy Krasovic, Gabriel Robins, David Chorley, Bryce Wieth, Ryan Young, Evan Green, Kyle Hawkins, Rob Downs, Lauren Shoemaker, Brian Newell, Heidi Newell, Sara Haase, Amber Robins, Amanda Zukle, and anyone else who I forgot

I know most people won't read that previous list, which is why I inserted one random character from *Game of Thrones* into the mix, just to see if anyone noticed.

Actually, I didn't do that. But hopefully you went back to look more carefully, and now you've acknowledged all the fantastic people who first brought this story to life. It's been my privilege to carry their performances forward every day I've worked on this.

And finally to my high school creative writing teacher, *Mr. Ty Devoe*, who first taught me twenty-plus years ago the value of working all night on something you're passionate about.

Turn the page for a sneak peek at Nathan Makaryk's

LIONHEARTS

Available now from Forge Books

PROLOGUE

SARRA BILLINSGATE

THE FRENCH WARD

"God's teeth!" Little Hugh tried—and failed—to wink. "I'm fucking Robin Hood!"

"Mind your tongue!" Sarra snatched his earlobe with a mother's precision and twisted it. Her son's joy vanished as he writhed between her fingertips. "I don't ever want to hear such language from you again, understand? Now go find your father, he's waiting on you!"

She slapped his bottom—always too hard but never hard enough—and his legs *flik-flacked* away down the alley slop. Sarra's shoulders slumped. *I don't remember ever having that much energy.* She was exhausted just watching him, and jealous of the simplicity that came with being a child.

Mindful of her bruises, Sarra tugged her roughspun shawl closer at the neck and winced. Above, the sky spat in little pockets and rolled grey behind the silhouette of Nottingham Castle, looming furiously over them. Thin waves of black coursed over its frame as the wind and water fought across the battlements. It gave the illusion of a castle with hair—long, uncontrollable wisps whipping out, vanishing, then lashing out again elsewhere.

"We're going to starve either way," her husband, Rog, had explained, *"but it will be better in the city. You'll see."*

You'll see.

It sounded like wisdom then, as hope always does to the desperate. And Rog had always held a clever sort of patience, knowing when to ignore an easy lure. It broke Sarra's heart to remember how Rog once kept their spirits high, singing at night for Hugh when they had nothing to eat, even just a few months ago. She'd always loved that toothy smile of his, especially when she could see it in their son. But now, Sarra's husband could hardly bear to look her in the eyes. There was no predicting each day if it would be rage or humiliation that made him keep his distance.

"Gack," some noise snapped for attention at her right—a dirty, bony thing reaching out from a hole in the alley's stone wall, a too-skinny old man covered in dried mud or excrement. Eyeballs shining but shrouded in dark. Panic froze her for only a moment, but long enough for him to grin black gums. "I'll trade you a dry place for a wet one." Clacking his few remaining teeth, he uncurled one finger out toward Sarra's legs. She busied herself away, to outrun her disgust.

Sarra wondered, again, if anyone else from Thorney had survived. Most fled after the fields had burnt, but some stayed behind. Rog's only brother, Hanry, swore he'd join them in Nottingham, but winter was halfway through with no sign of him.

She pushed away from the alley, and through the unwelcome clamor of the French Ward.

This place was an infected sore in the city's armpit. The French Ward had grown out of sheer spite to the north of the castle's hill, wedged between the foot of its craggy cliffs and the slope of the western Derby Road. The finest parts of the French Ward were an overrun lot of ramshackle wooden buildings and filth. The worst parts were appropriately worse.

"It's the only place we can go," Rog had explained, *"but it's better than nothing. You'll see."*

You'll see.

What she *didn't* see was *him,* not anymore. A year ago she would've gladly left Thorney for any place he suggested, so long as they were all together. But here in the city, he was always working—or *hoping* to work by waiting in lines, which rarely paid off—and they merely traded Hugh off between them, sometimes with barely a word. That wasn't *together.*

At the makeshift stairs up to Park Row, a commotion seized her attention. Splashing carelessly off the uneven cobbles and into another muddy alley, a pack of young street boys—just barely older than Hugh—chased at each other. Their faces were smiles and they laughed the way Hugh laughed, until one turned and swung the heft of his knapsack into the face of the boy behind him, who spun and fell into the muck. The rest pummeled the fallen boy with their sacks and fists and feet, then turned heel and sprinted right past Sarra. The last one barked in her face and laughed as she startled.

Ten paces away, the poor boy in the mud didn't move, his face down.

Get up, she thought at him, because she didn't want to know what she'd do if he didn't. At the very edge of her mind, her guilt replaced this boy with Hugh. Sarra tilted her face up to the rain and refused to think on her son being beaten so. *Or worse,* it came before she could stop it, *what if he becomes one of the boys who delivers the beating?*

The image of the barking boy's greasy, pock-ridden cheeks burnt in her mind.

Get up.

She suddenly regretted letting Hugh run to Rog on his own when she could've easily accompanied him. It didn't matter that Rog and his shovel were waiting with the other hopeful dayhands only a few buildings away. She could've held Hugh's hand and told him something important and true about making good choices. Something about character. Something that would stay with him. *Next time,* she promised herself. Again.

Get up.

The street boy didn't move.

She couldn't be late, she had a *gentleman* waiting. Well, they were rarely *gentle,* but she had no other word for them. *They have a word for you, though.* She hadn't said that word to herself yet, nor had Rog. At least, not out loud. His eyes screamed it, but they both knew their marriage would only last until its first utterance. So he stayed his pride and didn't ask how she came about the occasional coin that kept the three of them alive. When they spoke, it was only of Hugh, and of how to protect him from the city's grime.

Get up.

With a gasp, the fallen boy jerked and pushed up to his hands and knees. Sarra exhaled, hot tears mixing with the rain down her cheeks. She lingered to watch the boy shake himself off and limp away, when something smashed into her side.

She yelped as she turned, but the little familiar something wrapped its arms around her legs, and Sarra tugged her son's hair.

"You gave me a start!" she said—reminding herself of her own mother—and wrapped her fingers into his sopping mop. "Where's your cap, now?"

"He's here, Mum, you have to come!"

"Where's your cap, young sir?" she repeated, twisting him to see his face, cheeks pinpricked red from running. He pulled the thing from a pocket and tugged it over his head, along with a grumble of protest. Sarra grumbled right back at him and readjusted the cap over the tips of his ears. "Who is this, now? Who's here?"

Hugh pulled at her. "Come on then, and hurry!"

"*Who's* here?"

"I can't say."

"Well you'll have to," she chided him, glancing down the alley where the imprint of the street boy's body had already turned into a puddle of dirty rainwater.

Hugh's entire face squirmed. "I can't. You told me to never use such language again."

An anxious crowd gathered outside the Pity Stables—which, despite its name, hadn't housed any horses for years. The Pities had only a few upright wooden walls, but provided relative shelter for those with the greatest need. Today its open frame was packed shoulder to shoulder with soggy onlookers, but Hugh weaseled himself forward and dragged Sarra along until they were under its roof.

She'd heard over and again that Robin Hood had been making appearances inside the city of late, though she'd tried not to let that build up her hope. If this really was Robin Hood, and if he was giving coin out as he had last year, there was no knowing how many warm meals that might put in Hugh's stomach. *Or boots!* Or more realistically, to grease the right palm that might pick Rog's name for day work. Robin Hood's presence was a lucky turn, for certain . . . but it came with a price. Hugh was at an impressionable age, and it might not do for him to see how easily a thief could bring in coin when his father's honest work could not.

Inside, the musk of wet men was palpable. A few hands pawed at her as she squeezed in, grunting their objections to her slipping by, but Hugh found handholds in the exposed beams of the back wall and climbed until his head was above the crowd. Sarra found a foothold beside him and eased herself up for a better view.

"Quietly, all!" An unfamiliar man hushed them from the center of the Pities, and silence rippled outward. "I have a story I think you'll find most interesting." He pulled back a slick hood from his head and raked his fingers through blond hair, matted dark from the rain. One finger flicked water off his pointed nose as he sized up his audience. Young for a man, and dangerously handsome, but there seemed to be an age about his eyes. *Not Robin Hood,* Sarra knew, but probably one of his closest men. Here to rile everyone's spirits before the real man arrived.

Sarra spotted Rog's head bobbing up and down near the front of the crowd, but was quickly tisked when she called his name. So she wrapped an arm around Hugh's waist to watch with the others.

"I found some men on the road to the north," the handsome man drawled out, stretching the tips of his mouth wide and squinting his eyes, smiling with both. Behind them, the light rain turned heavier, as if to veil them from the outside world. "Well, not really *men,* I suppose. That's not what they'd call themselves, at the least. They'd prefer the word *looords.*" He treated the title like an insult, and received a collective groan of agreement. "These *looords* had everything a man could want. Why, I'd never seen finer clothing. Excepting yours, of course, love." A wink at a young woman whose dress was the definition of threadbare. Still, she blushed and patted herself down as a few others whistled. "These *looords* had not a speck of dirt on their breeches, white as their asses!"

That made Hugh snort, which Sarra hated. The last thing she needed was for Hugh to idolize a rebellious man with a thirst for danger.

"Found more than a bit of gold on them, too, didn't we?" the man asked, and at his side two larger men gave a *hurrah.* One stout and bald, the other with the long careful face of a greyhound, they both positioned themselves to create a respectful distance between the speaker and the crowd.

"So I reach out with my hand," he continued, "this one right here, and I pluck the ring from his finger and whisper, *'Is there anyone who might need this more than you?'"*

"Aye!" answered one timid voice in the throng, then another.

"Aye, sir!" was Rog's intellectual contribution, craning his skinny neck and grinning stupidly. Sarra was at once relieved to see his smile, and pained that it had been so long since he'd shown it.

"I wonder, Friar, is there anyone else who needs any gold?"

The bald man shrugged theatrically, while the crowd called out once again, louder.

"I said, is there anyone here who could use a shilling or two?"

And the answer bellowed back, packing the room with noise and anticipation.

The showman backed up in affected shock, as if their voices had thrown him off his feet.

"Not so loud, friends!" he laughed. "We wouldn't want our voices to travel all the way up to the Sheriff, now would we?" Laughter, now, all around.

"I thought you killed the Sheriff!" shouted a young girl not much older than Hugh.

"I did, my lady," he responded. "And the Sheriff before him, too."

"Then what's taking you so long with this one?" came a deep man's voice, and the crowd erupted in agreement.

"All in good time, friends," and his smirk was all charm. "For you are my friends, are you not? Who here considers themself a friend of Robin Hood?"

Every hand in the building went up, every man and woman and child shouted out their love for the man, even as Hugh turned to Sarra and whispered, "*That's not Robin Hood.*"

"*I know,*" she whispered back, surprised he remembered.

They'd met the real Robin Hood once, when he visited Thorney. Back when he was only a rumor, back when Thorney was a place to call home and not a patch of ash. Before the winter, before the raids and the fire brigades, before hunger and the French Ward. But that Robin Hood had a soft face and a curious sort of humility. It was hard to believe the stories that he killed the Sheriff, and had been hanged for it.

But Robin Hood or not, this new fellow had the people's love. They stretched their hands to the air and called out, "*Friends, friends!*" Even Rog seemed happy to call this stranger Robin Hood, so long as there was a promise of coin.

"Then never let it be said," the-man-who-was-definitely-not-Robin-Hood knelt down to the floor, whipping a wet cloak up to reveal a small wooden chest, "that Robin Hood has ever neglected his friends!"

His toe kicked the lid open, one hand reached in and then flicked a few coins out, one by one by one, each touching the air gently before falling into the crowd. Sarra instinctively pushed herself against the wall as the room churned inside out, grasping and pushing and tumbling over itself. Despite her best effort to hold him, Hugh slipped right out of her arms and dropped to the ground to disappear into the mash of arms and legs.

Sarra steadied herself on a post, frantic for any sign of her son. The boy in the mud invaded her thoughts again, freezing her with the same empty sense of indecision. But the crowd calmed as winners claimed their prizes, and Sarra pushed the image of a trampled Hugh to the back of her mind. *He knows to come back.*

"Don't worry, there's more for all of you," Robin called out, quieting the room. "But I have to ask for a little help first. Do you suppose you can help me out?"

"Aye, we can!" came the reply. Expectant faces and open palms waited upon Robin's every movement.

"Those of you who received a coin, could you come forward, please? Let them through, make way now!"

He gestured them closer, and a few lucky bodies held their coins up proudly and formed a row before him. Five in total, though Sarra only recognized one—a curly-headed friend of Rog's by the name of Dane, a dockworker who'd shown them rare kindness.

Robin smiled at the winners. "My friends, I am happy to help you. After all, who else out there is going to help you out?"

"No one!" Dane answered, instantly earning Robin's attention.

"No one!" Robin snapped his fingers. "Why not the King, why doesn't he help?"

"He's in Austria!" came one answer.

"He's in prison!" came another. Both were true. Somewhere on the other side of the world, King Richard the Lionheart had been captured. But those still at home were the ones suffering for it.

"Why not the Sheriff, then?" Robin continued. "Why doesn't he help?"

"He's too busy taking our money!" was a gruff answer, followed by laughter.

"You have the right of it, friend." Robin smiled. "One quarter of everything, to pay for Richard's ransom! You have to be careful these days. I have two hands and two feet, and the Sheriff's like to take one as my payment!" The grumble that followed had only an empty mirth. The collections for the king's ransom was no mere tax. For many, surrendering a quarter of all their worth was the brutal snap of a branch long bent to its breaking point.

"Well I wish I could give these coins to you and ask for nothing in return," Robin continued, "but even Robin Hood needs help sometimes. You understand that, don't you?"

"Whatever you need," Dane answered for them. "Just name it."

"It's very simple, it's nothing really." Robin paused. "I need that coin back."

Dane chuckled, as did the crowd, but Robin held his hand out as the laughter faded into embarrassment.

"This coin?" Dane asked cautiously. "The ones you just gave us?"

"The very one."

His next laugh was smaller, dumber. "Is this a trick?"

"A trick, no. Call it a curiosity!" Robin clicked his tongue. "Right now that shilling is yours, and you may do with it anything you like."

"It's a crown, sir."

"A crown?" Robin's eyes widened in disbelief. "My, but I'm more generous than I thought! But it's yours, I won't take it from you. You've had it all of a minute but I'm sure you've already thought well on how you'll spend it, no? What will you do with it?"

Dane looked to the other four coin-bearers, but the question was clearly for him alone. When he spoke, there was doubt in his voice. "Food. Boots, maybe."

"Boots, maybe, that's good. That's good," Robin looked down, kicking his own dark leather boots against the chest. "Would you like *my* boots?"

"No, sir."

"Don't call me sir, I'm not a knight."

"No, sir. Er, no . . . m'lord."

"Even worse."

"Sorry . . . sorry."

"Hm."

Sarra wished very much that Hugh would find his way back to her.

Robin leveled his eyes on Dane, who buried his attention into the ground. "Food, you say? Nottingham has a Common Hall, does it not? Why aren't you there?"

Someone in the crowd answered angrily, "You have to be on the lists!"

"And they won't put certain types of people on those lists, will they?" Robin prompted them. "Deserters, gang members, . . . *tax evaders,* yes?"

An unsettling murmur rumbled in assent, while a few other titles were called out—other types of people who could be refused the charity of the Common Hall. Sarra hated that she flinched when the word *whore* was shouted.

"And with this damned ransom, everyone's a tax evader, aren't we?" Robin Hood smiled. "A crown's a fine amount, I'll bet you could pay your way onto that list for a crown. Is that what you meant when you said you'd spend it on food?"

"I hadn't thought about it."

"I'm aware of that." Robin suddenly raced through his words with precision. "So think about it now. You have a choice! You can give that coin to Nottingham, and to the Sheriff, and pay your way and feed yourself and be considered a lawful man. Or you can give it to me, as I ask for it, and show that you can be as generous as I am. If you are my friend, as you claim to be, why would you refuse to do for me that which I gladly did for you?"

Dane opened his mouth to answer, but Robin silenced him with one finger.

"But if you *do* give it back to me, know that you're choosing my side. Know that you would be considered an outlaw, as I am. An enemy of Nottingham. I will not *take* the coin from you, friend, it is yours. I simply want to know what you'll do with it, when I ask for it back."

Robin's hand extended again, just as before, and the room was ever silent. Even the steady patter of rain outside had somehow faded beyond Sarra's ability to hear it.

Dane resolved himself, the muscles at his jawline flexed. "I don't think I will, no."

"You don't think you will, what?"

"I don't think I'll give it back to you."

Robin Hood's smile. "And why not?"

"Because when you gave it to me, it was a gift." Dane swallowed, trying his best to look tall and proud. "I didn't ask for it. It was your choice to give it. But if you ask it of me, that's different. You always say that nobody should be able to take anything from us."

"Is that what I always say?"

Dane pursed his lips.

The greyhound man's fist smashed bloody across Dane's face and brought him to the floor.

Sarra lost her footing, her heart pounded furiously, and she gasped for air as the crowd reeled in horror. They had all gone blurry—*no, there were tears in her eyes*—and she blinked them away. Looking twice, she realized the attacker had not used his fist. He was holding a short bludgeon. He flipped the tiny club about in his hand as he heaved Dane back to his knees and pried the gold crown from his fingers.

"Who else received a coin?" Robin barked out, and the other four cowered. "I ask for it back. Do you give it to me?"

In unison they dropped and held out their hands, desperate to be rid of their incriminating prize. The man with the bludgeon gently reclaimed the crowns from two more coin-bearers, then turned with horrifying speed to crash his weapon onto the tops of both their skulls. Sarra screamed, but threw her hand over her mouth to keep from drawing any undue attention her way.

Hugh. She searched desperately for him, but couldn't avoid watching what was next.

One man and one woman remained, quivering, on their knees. The others cradled their heads, rolling in pain.

"I ask for that coin," Robin's ferocity was naked now, "will you give it to me?"

"I don't . . . I don't know," the next man whimpered. He pounded the coin onto the ground and turned to scramble away, but the greyhound man bounded over him and twirled the bludgeon by a short rope at its handle, slinging it upward into the man's chin. His teeth cracked loud enough to silence the room. Robin seemed startled by something, then wiped the fine spray of blood from his face.

There was still no sign of Hugh.

"I ask for that coin," Robin growled at his final victim, a thin woman with ratted black hair. "Will you give it to me?" By now, the friar had brandished a thick knife that kept anyone in the crowd from pretending to be a hero.

The woman stayed at her knees but straightened upright and bore herself into Robin's eyes. "Don't pretend to give me a choice!" she bellowed back at him, her volume masking her fear. "You'll hit me either way. You'll hit me if I give it to you. You'll hit me if I don't. You'll hit me if I do nothing. So hit me. Because you're going to. You're going to hit me because you're a bully." She clenched her neck. "You're going to hit me because you're a coward."

"No." Robin held his hand up, staying the greyhound. He crouched down on the balls of his feet to bring his face next to hers. "You've got it all wrong, love. You *did* have a choice. But you already made it."

He stood.

"I'm going to hit you because you took my money in the first place."

The bludgeon came up but Sarra closed her eyes before it fell, the sound was enough. The crowd panicked at long last—they'd been frozen in disbelief but now fell prey to hysteria. A few fled into the rain, but the rest were halted by Robin's voice.

"Quiet!" he shouted. "We are not done here! Nobody leaves."

Eventually the entire room buckled down, curling into balls, to be as small and unnoticeable as possible.

Sarra slipped down from her post and hid as well, then burst with relief when Hugh splashed out of the crowd and flung himself around her. His face was white, and she engulfed him in her arms that he might see nothing more. She closed her eyes as the tears ran hot down her cheeks and into her son's hair. But she could not close her ears.

"These five of you took coin from me, and have been punished." A moment or two of silence, save for the moans of those five. "But I threw six coins."

The room shifted, Sarra peeked out. Robin picked his way with care through the huddled bodies, a wolf stalking in the bushes. The greyhound signaled—just a nod of his head, really—but it led Robin Hood to stop directly in front of Sarra's husband.

"Show me your hands."

"I didn't get one, none."

Robin turned back for confirmation. "He does," the greyhound stated. "I watched him pick it up."

Back to Rog, Robin's face was all smiles. "Are you calling my friend a liar? We know you have it."

Sarra didn't have enough hands to stop Hugh from watching and also to muffle the whine that rose in her throat.

Rog kept his face stubbornly down, away, his fists behind his back, his mouth tight. He didn't respond when Robin Hood repeated the demand. Nor when the friar grabbed his shoulders and wrestled him to the ground. Rog simply stayed where he landed, unmoving, as if he could ignore himself out of the room.

"It'll be better here, you'll see."

You'll see.

The friar handed his knife to the greyhound, then revealed an iron hatchet from beneath his cloak.

"I'm not going to pry your fingers open like a child," Robin said. "You either give me the coin, or we'll take a king's ransom from you. One in four. You hear me, friend? We'll take your hand."

Rog made noises, they weren't quite words.

"Try that again, friend. Use a language this time."

"I-don't-have-anything."

"It's either in your fucking hand or you gave it to someone else, and I don't think it's the latter. Open your fist, then."

"I don't . . . I didn't . . ."

"God's cock, man. Give me the coin."

Someone braver than Sarra shouted, "He doesn't have it!"

Robin looked sideways at the greyhound a third time, who nodded again. Small, but with an absolute and grim certainty. Sarra wasn't the only one who knew Rog was lying.

Robin hesitated, but his voice was strong. "Alright, Tuck. Do it."

White funneled in from all sides as Sarra's vision closed tight on her husband. She felt somehow twenty feet tall, her hands impossibly large and numb, her stomach churned as her balance span, but somehow she kept watching, noiselessly, breathlessly, as they held Rog's arm across the wooden chest, a strap of leather went around his wrist, the greyhound pulled it tight and stepped on it, Rog's mouth was open, in pain, maybe, but his hand still a fist, and the friar knelt on him, one knee on his chest, and nobody helped *and nobody helped andnobodyhelped* and the hatchet split flesh and bone but it didn't cut the hand off, no, it was left dangling by a strip of slick bloody meat and the friar nearly toppled as Rog screamed, the greyhound went down and kicked Rog in the ribs, they fought and kicked him again until his arm was braced back across the chest a second time and the hatchet chopped down once more, just missing the wrist as he squirmed, gouging deep in his forearm, a well of dark red pouring out, it wasn't until the third try that the hand came off and Sarra stared at her husband's blood, it was so much blood, and nobody helped and *he didn't even have a coin* and it was so very much blood and *Hugh was choking.*

Her son was gagging at her breast, struggling to be free, she'd been holding him too tight. She let him loose but held onto his cheeks—always too hard and never hard enough—preventing him from seeing his father's mutilated arm. Hugh coughed a mouthful of spit into his hands and gasped for air, then buried himself into her chest again.

Friar Tuck was hammering an iron spike through the palm of Rog's severed hand, nailing it high on the back wall of the Pity Stables.

Robin Hood, his face white, thrust a finger at it. "That's *mine* now! And it stays there. I'm starting a collection. If anyone tries to take it down . . ." He may have picked anyone at random to focus on, but it was Sarra's eyes he found. "Well, you've seen how I deal with people who take what's mine."

She could only barely feel its tiny uneven ridge through the shawl at her neck, slimy but firmly held in her son's little hands, but Sarra knew well enough that Hugh had coughed out a gold crown.